SENTENCED TO TROLL COMPENDIUM

BOOKS 1-3

S.L. ROWLAND

AETHERVALE PUBLISHING

ALSO BY S.L. ROWLAND

Tales of Aedrea

Cursed Cocktails

Sword & Thistle

The Halfling's Harvest

There Be Dragons Here

Pangea Online

Pangea Online: Death and Axes

Pangea Online 2: Magic and Mayhem

Pangea Online 3: Vials and Tribulations

Sentenced to Troll 1-6

Path to Villainy: An NPC Kobold's Tale

Collected Editions

Pangea Online: The Complete Trilogy

Sentenced to Troll Compendium: Books 1-3

Sentenced to Troll Compendium 2: Books 4-6

SENTENCED TO TROLL

PROLOGUE

"Died to the trolls again, did you, Glenn?" asked Randy. The dark skinned man emerged from the shadowy corner of The Dancing Donkey, his boiled leather armor and long black cape making him almost invisible in the dimly lit inn. His sword hung from his waist opposite a dagger the length of his forearm. Glenn wondered if he could grab the dagger and shove the pointy end through Randy's eye before anyone noticed.

Maybe later, thought Glenn.

"They're tougher than they look." Glenn patted Randy on the shoulder and forced a smile. "They nearly destroyed this world once. They could do it again."

"Most of these people have never even seen a troll." Randy laughed, pushing his thumbs against his belt. "From what I've heard, they're on the verge of extinction. I don't know how you keep convincing so many NPCs to follow you to your death, but you can have your trolls, Glenn. I'll stick to the dungeons and keep all the good loot for myself."

Glenn found a table in the corner of the room, taking in the other players who were settling in for the night. To them, this was a game, but to Glenn, this was everything he had ever dreamed of—an island where he could be anything he wanted to be and do anything he wanted to do. Sure, it was prison, but it was also paradise.

Glenn didn't care about dungeons. They were only useful in replenishing the gear he had lost each time he died to the trolls, along with a hard-earned level. He was interested in survival. If he wanted to become anything in this world, he needed to make sure the trolls wouldn't hold him back. He could influence people, bend them to his will even. He knew his Charisma was higher than most players and more than that, he knew how to use it to get things done. It didn't work on trolls, though. Somehow, they resisted his charm. In the end, it didn't matter. With every death, he took more trolls with him. And they didn't respawn.

He'd read the stories of old and talked to the townspeople. If there was anyone that would inhibit his rise to power, it would be the trolls.

The trolls were the problem, and they had to be destroyed.

CHAPTER ONE
SENTENCED TO TROLL

My heart races. I sit behind the table. Its dark cherry wood is polished and pristine, unlike my reputation. To my right, my lawyer shuffles papers in a bored manner. He doesn't give two shits about this case. I'm sure he's ready to be out of here so he can meet his cronies for a beer or a game of golf. The swish of the paper is like a thousand papercuts to my eardrums. This must be how teachers feel when the whir of zippers crashes through their lecture like a tidal wave and there are still five minutes left in class. Except this is much worse. This is my future on the line.

I shouldn't be here. I should be at home logged into my computer, slaying orcs, trolls, and every other manner of foul creature.

The clock ticks by slowly on the wall. Tick. Tick. Tick. Who knew a second could be so long?

Sitting back in my chair, I straighten my tie. My hands shake slightly as I align it with the buttons on my shirt. It always seems to go askew, no matter how many times I fix it. The action doesn't waste nearly as much time as I want it to.

Any minute now, the judge should be coming out to announce my sentence.

I know I'm toast. I screwed up big time. Being a professional streamer, I'm supposed to set the example. Set the culture. I'm known for my clever taunting and never-say-die attitude; it's the main reason people follow me. I'm not a phenomenal gamer. If I were, I'd be a pro gamer and not just a glorified commentator. I screwed up, and I lost my temper. If it had been the first time, I probably wouldn't be here, but I'm a repeat offender. The sad thing is that I learned my lesson. Finally. I regretted what I said as soon as the match was over.

When they cuffed me and brought me into the station, that's when I knew that I had really screwed the pooch. The city wants to make an example out of me. If one of the top streamers in *League of Mythos* can be punished, it'll set a precedent for those below me. They hope to stamp this behavior out of esports entirely. Honestly,

I don't blame them. I've dealt with my fair share of bullying and name-calling. I get trolls every time I stream. A lot of people would say I brought it on myself. The way the system works, it's almost like you're set up to fail. An entire community that hides behind a keyboard or an avatar. Some would call me a troll, but that's not true. Not really. I'm a rager. Not that it's any better. At least by punishing me, they'll finally show the world that no one is safe.

Sweat runs down the back of my shirt. I don't know what they have planned. The maximum sentence for online griefing is one year in prison, though I don't know anyone who has ever served that much time. Even though it's a crime, it's often ignored. Much like jaywalking. Those that are brought to trial, they get community service, a fine, and a slap on the wrist, but ever since the mayor's son offed himself because of online bullying by a rival guild, the city has been on a witch hunt.

I just happen to be the unlucky son of a bitch who lost his cool on a nationally-televised event. I had been invited to participate in a 'celebrity match' with other popular streamers before the championship.

Apparently, telling your teammates they are worthless cockroaches who only have one brain cell between them and that they probably have to pass it back and forth in the middle of the fight is frowned upon. If I had stopped there, I'd probably be fine. But I didn't stop there. I definitely should not have told Jordan to go kill herself for healing our DPS instead of the tank. Multiple times. I yelled at her so much that she had a mental breakdown right in the middle of the match. That was a dick move. I realize that now. And yes, using racial slurs is never a good idea. I had been breathing fire by the end of that match.

I lost my temper, plain and simple, and now I'm about to pay for it.

Just please don't send me to prison. I'm too pretty and too skinny to survive the ogres that are in there for real crimes, like murder and assault. I am not made for that type of environment.

The click of the doorknob announces the judge's return. Her face is stern, giving nothing away. The black robe she wears swishes when she walks, like some wizard of doom. The long black sleeves conceal a small envelope in her hand. I imagine that is the sentence she will be giving me. It's almost like winning an award, except for the part where it's not. There will be no afterparty once she reads its contents.

Anything but prison. I repeat the mantra in my mind like it will make a difference.

She takes a seat and bangs her gavel, bringing the courtroom to order. My lawyer sets down the papers he has been torturously shuffling and smiles. I want to punch him. Of course I was guilty, but he never even seemed interested in fighting for me or letting the judge know that I was remorseful. I bet the sorry sack of shit already has one foot out the door.

She clears her throat before reading the sentence that may change my life forever.

"In the case of New York vs Chadwick Bryan Johnson, based on video and audio evidence presented in court, I find the defendant guilty of online griefing." She sets the envelope down and looks at me directly. "Mister Johnson, this is not your first time being accused of griefing. Hell, this isn't even your fifth. You are widely known as a toxic player throughout your community, and I'm surprised it has taken this long for charges to be brought against you. Telling someone to kill themselves, hate speech, those are things that are no longer tolerated in League of Mythos or anywhere in society."

The entire time she is talking, the only thing I can think is 'please not prison.' I repeat it over and over. Anything but prison. Anything but prison.

"Is there anything you would like to say before I sentence you, Mister Johnson?" she asks.

I had a speech planned before we came in today, but now that the moment is here, all I can think of is the mantra running through my mind. My throat is suddenly parched. I open my mouth to speak but only a croak comes out.

"Mister Johnson?" she asks again.

"I-I'm sorry," is all I'm able to get out. This was my moment to at least show some remorse and maybe convince the judge to give me a lighter sentence, and all I can do is croak like a frog.

"Very well. The law states that one year in prison is the maximum allowed for offenses such as yours. Prison may very well be where you end up if you don't change your ways, but in your case, I feel it may do more harm than good."

I let out a sigh of relief. I'm not going to prison. I have to fight to keep the smile that dances at the edge of my lips from taking over entirely.

"It is not my goal to punish you, Mister Johnson, but to make you better understand the seriousness of your actions. Yes, they may just be words in an online game, but let me assure you, words do have power. If Miss Jordan had indeed acted on your words, you would be being sentenced for far more than online griefing right now. Let that sink in for a minute." She pauses and looks back down at the envelope. I'm on the edge of my seat, wondering what is in store for me. Prison is off the table, but I can tell by the look in her eyes that she has something bigger planned than community service. "Mister Johnson, you have been, for lack of a better word, a troll. A bully. Miss Jordan, the victim of your tirade, doesn't wish to hurt you or your ability to play online games. She wishes that you treat her and other players with respect, both your teammates and players on the other team. To help you learn what it feels like to be constantly attacked and berated, I think it is only fitting that you become the very thing you already are. You have therefore been sentenced to one month of full-immersion rehabilitation in Mythos Games' newest development, *Isle of Mythos.* You will be forced to play as a troll, the most hated faction on the island. For the next month, you will experience the same degree of verbal assault and backlash you have dealt out on so many occasions. I hope you are able to learn from this experience."

I let out a breath I didn't know I was holding. That's it? My punishment is to play a game for a month? Piece of cake. If I'd known that was an option, I wouldn't have been so worried.

"Guards, please take Mister Johnson to his holding cell while he awaits transport to Mythos Games Headquarters."

The guards grab me by the arms, and my lawyer is already out of the courtroom before they even have my hands cuffed.

As they walk me out the back of the courtroom, I scan the room, hoping to see my mother or father. They were in Japan on business. Business that was more important than seeing their only child before he was potentially shipped off to prison. That's the story of my life, though. Their business was always their favorite baby. I honestly don't even know why they had a child. Maybe it saved their marriage by giving them something to ignore together.

"You got this!" a voice shouts. I turn to see Taryn, with his giant billowing afro, giving me a thumbs up. He's the only person I consider a true friend, as well as my queue partner in most games. The one person I can count on to have my back when things go south.

The guards lead me to the holding cell where a man in a black suit waits inside. He looks like some kind of special agent with the way the suit fits him perfectly at every angle. You can tell he's well-built underneath and could probably kick my ass in a hundred different ways. I wonder if he's here to make sure I don't escape. Not that I could.

I step inside and take a seat on one of the metal benches. It's cold and hard against my backside, a far cry from the ergonomic gaming chair I use when playing games.

"Feeling sorry yet, kid?" he asks. His voice is deep and gravelly. There's more manliness in those four words than I have in my entire body.

I nod. Now that I'm out of the courtroom, I wonder what kind of game I'm about to be logged into. I know full immersion has existed for a few years now, but it's so expensive to produce that it hasn't been marketed on a mass level yet. With Mythos Games being the biggest name in virtual reality gaming, it only makes sense that they would have something running on the down low.

Thirty days of full immersion. How is that even possible? It can't be healthy for a human to be still for so long.

We sit in silence. Mr. Secret Agent is content to let me sit and brood with my own thoughts. A few minutes later, his cell phone rings. He answers it, but doesn't say a word. When the call ends, he taps on the bar of the jail cell and a guard comes over to unlock the door.

"Our ride is here. Don't try anything stupid, and I won't have to hurt you," he says. He nods to the guards as we exit through a door into an alley where a black SUV waits with one door open.

My hands are still cuffed, so Mr. Secret Agent guides me into the SUV and takes a seat next to me. Two other men, both dressed in similar black suits, sit up front. As soon as the door shuts, we're on the move.

All of this makes me feel more important than I am.

"Where are we going?" I ask.

"Mythos Games Headquarters." Mr. Secret Agent pulls out his phone and sends a quick message to someone. "They take their security very seriously."

"What, do you think I'm going to escape?" I ask.

"Don't flatter yourself. This isn't for you. We're here to make sure you aren't followed. There are a lot of people who would love to get their hands on the technology you are about to experience."

Consider me intrigued. Mr. Secret Agent reaches into his jacket pocket and pulls out a fabric bag.

"This is for you, though." He puts the bag over my head and everything goes black.

The driver takes turn after turn, jostling me against the door, and I wonder if it's necessary or if it's all an attempt to lose anyone who might be trailing us. I don't understand what the big deal is. Everyone knows where Mythos Games Headquarters is. It's the biggest building downtown, dwarfing all the others. The architecture makes the building look like a giant wizard's tower and at night, it glows and smoke billows out the top. I've done several press events there with my team.

The SUV makes a sharp turn, slamming me into the wall. Mr. Secret Agent removes my blindfold and I see we are in an underground parking garage. A metal gate closes behind us and we go down three levels before stopping in front of another gate. The driver rolls down his window and scans his badge. The gate opens, and we speed through. This far down, all the levels are empty. We descend three more levels before coming to a stop in a parking space far against the back wall in a dimly-lit parking deck. There are only a handful of cars parked here, along with a few more black vans. We're so far down that this is practically a dungeon.

I can see an elevator tucked into the wall near where we park.

Mr. Secret Agent opens his door, and I attempt to do the same. It doesn't budge. They child-proofed me.

"This way," he orders.

Surrounded by the three men, I feel like someone important, a president or a celebrity. For a moment, I'm not a criminal.

They guide me towards the elevator, but when I stop in front of it, Mr. Secret Agent nudges me in the back to keep walking. There is nothing ahead of us but a brick wall and a flickering light attached to it.

A thought runs across my mind, and I stiffen. Are they going to kill me?

Mr. Secret Agent must sense my nervousness, because he says, "Relax, kid. Nobody is going to kill you today. Now get moving."

For whatever reason, I believe him.

I do as I'm told, and we walk to the corner of the parking deck. One of the other men faces the brick wall, searching for something. I try to see what he is staring at but can't see anything other than brick and mortar.

His fingers run along the bricks before abruptly stopping. He presses against a single brick and it slides deeper into the wall.

A secret entrance!

The brick recedes and a door seems to form in the wall, opening into another dimly-lit cavern. The hidden entrance closes behind us as we step through.

Old Edison bulbs dangle from the ceiling, their light bathing the tunnel in an eerie glow. I follow the two men in suits through a labyrinth of brick tunnels for what seems like forever. We could be anywhere under the city by now. Eventually, the dungeon-like atmosphere morphs into something more industrial. The concrete floors smooth out, the old bulbs are replaced by white neon lights, and the aged brick walls become painted cinder blocks. At the end of the hall, a metal staircase winds upwards next to an elevator.

The two men stop in front of it. It looks like we might actually be able to use this one. One of the men flashes his ID card in front of a proximity reader next to the elevator and the doors whoosh open.

What could possibly be so important that we have to go through this much secrecy?

The doors close rapidly after we step into the elevator. There are no floor numbers for the men to press, but the elevator begins to move all the same. My legs give way slightly as we ascend at a rapid pace, and then just as suddenly, we stop moving.

The doors open, and I find myself looking into a pristine laboratory, whiteness engulfing the room. The floors, the lighting, and even the walls are white. The four of us are like specks of pepper in a salty landscape.

Men and women in white lab-coats shuffle about the room. They carry digital pads, making notes and checking figures. One lady bends down, inspecting one of several pods in the center of the lab.

I suddenly notice that there are people inside the pods.

Full immersion.

Ignoring the three men who brought me here, I step further into the lab. They don't say anything or try to stop me. There must be two dozen pods, each one occupied. Those inside are completely submerged in a blue liquid. They look peaceful, asleep almost. Video feeds display their movements in the game.

"Mister Johnson," says a silky-smooth female voice. A brunette woman in a tight high-necked blue dress appears to my right. It's modest, but clings so tightly to her body that it leaves nothing to the imagination. She can't be older than thirty. Much too young to be running an operation like this. "Welcome to Mythos Games, the part we don't show the public." She looks oddly familiar, but I can't quite place where I've seen her. She winks at me, then turns to the men who brought me here. "Adams, Franklin, Roosevelt, I think I can handle it from here."

The men nod and leave. I wonder which one is Mr. Secret Agent.

"What is this place?" I ask.

She flashes me a smile. I'm sure her pearly-white teeth have been the downfall of many men.

"This is R and D." She waves her hand through the air, putting the laboratory on display. "Research and Development. The next wave of Mythos Games."

"And why exactly am I here?" It doesn't make sense why I am in some highly secret technohub for a crime that would land me a year in prison max. There has to be more to it.

"Follow me," she instructs, taking me across the lab to a white desk near the wall. It's oddly neat for a research department, with only a computer and keyboard. "Have a seat."

I take a seat, and she sits across from me.

"You're here because you were a bad boy." The way she says it has me feeling like she is toying with me. She bites her lip, and I feel blood rushing to my face. "And because your parents happen to know some very influential people."

So my parents can call in a favor, but they don't have the decency to call me. Typical. I could have spent a lot less time over the toilet if I knew this was an option.

"And them?" I point to the other pods in the center of the lab.

"They're even worse than you."

"Worse than me?" Who is this woman?

She leans forward, her dark brown eyes gazing into me. "Each of those men, all twenty-four of them, are in prison for violent crimes. We have an agreement with the state of New York that allows us to use prisoners to test out the effects of reha-bilitative gameplay while in full immersion. Each of them volunteered to play *Isle of Mythos* as a hero to see if it would cure their violent tendencies."

"Has it?" Nobody mentioned anything about other prisoners. I mean, it's not like they could actually hurt me, could they?

Her smirk has me on edge.

"It looks like you're about to find out."

CHAPTER TWO

INTO THE POD

"Why me?" I lean against the hard back of the chair. Even if my parents did manage to call in a favor to someone, this is next-level technology. There are twenty-four pods, maybe a few more I haven't seen. How am I being punished but also lucky enough to be able to test out the next wave of gaming at the same time? There have to be people who would volunteer, no questions asked, for this type of experience.

"The simple answer is that we wanted a gamer in the mix," says the beautiful brunette who still hasn't told me her name. "Someone to test the boundaries of our creation. We knew from the get-go that your case would be found guilty. Not that many gamers wind up in prison."

"So, what, am I not actually being rehabilitated?" I mean, I'm perfectly fine playing a game for a month with no consequences. What I really want to know, though, is why prisoners?

She leans forward and flashes me a dangerous smile.

"Oh, everything the judge said is true. You will most certainly experience what it feels like to be attacked, to be bullied, to be persecuted for simply being what you are. We have embedded a deep history in *Isle of Mythos*, and trolls are hated like no other. In time, you will find out why. But that is not to say you won't have any fun. This is a game after all. There will be quests and crafting and all the adventure of a traditional RPG, but it will be more real than you have ever experienced. You will feel pain, but you will also smell, taste, and experience everything as if you were actually there."

"Pain?" I interrupt. How in the hell is it legal to put criminals in a simulation where they can be hurt? Isn't that torture?

"Absolutely. That is one of the things that separates full immersion from traditional VR. If you get stabbed, you feel it. Luckily for you, trolls have a thick hide and a higher tolerance for pain. Plus, we set the pain settings at fifty percent to make things more bearable."

"What if I don't want to do it?" I challenge. Maybe being an outcast that everyone hates isn't something I want to partake in.

"You go to prison," she says matter-of-factly, as if that solves everything. "Now, unless you wish to go to prison, I suggest we get started."

I don't want to go to prison. She stares at me, waiting for a response. Her smile never falters, and her vibrant white teeth mesmerize me. They are almost too white. Unnatural. What other choice do I have? I know people who would pay good money to be in this testing phase, pain included.

"What's your name?"

"Valery Barrett. Anything else?"

I shake my head. All that's left is to see what this is actually about.

"Now if you don't mind, please follow me. The next several hours will be spent gathering your vitals and running tests to make sure your body can handle thirty days of immersion. You look like a healthy kid, so I don't foresee any problems." She leads me through a door at the other end of the room, down a hallway, and into a waiting room. It's really no different than one I might see at a doctor's office, minus the posters for erectile dysfunction and heart disease. The walls here are white and bare. Just like everything else in the lab.

Barrett. That's the last name of the owner of Mythos Games. I suddenly remember where I have seen her before. It was at a ceremony after the last season of *League of Mythos*. She was sitting next to John Barrett at the head table. Is she his daughter? Niece?

Valery disappears, and over the next several hours, I have my vitals taken. They draw blood, take my temperature, and stick me with an assortment of cold medical instruments in places I wouldn't let my mother touch me. I run on a treadmill, sit quietly, look at ink splotches on a piece of paper. It all makes me feel more like a lab rat than a prisoner.

I'm pretty healthy, except for asthma and acne. Part of me wonders if I would still be approved even if they found something that disqualified me? It's like she said, though, gamers aren't just lining up to go to prison. Maybe if they knew this was the punishment, they would. Even if I'm not a professional gamer, I still make my living playing games, so I'm probably a hell of a lot more useful than some of the players they have now.

It definitely makes me wonder why only convicted criminals are in this stage of the testing. Maybe because they know we won't be able to talk about it?

After my visit with the doctor, Valery shows up and takes me back to the lab. "Are you excited to see what you're going to be getting into?"

I nod.

"Well, first, we need you to sign the non-disclosure agreement. Once you get out, we can't have you talking about everything you've seen in here."

I flick through the legal jargon on the tablet and sign my name before being led back to the pods.

There's a new pod added to the end of one line, except it is black and the others are all white. It's sleek and beautiful, looking more like a spaceship than a gaming machine. The glassy surface reflects a distorted picture of my face back at me. My greasy black hair and obnoxiously large nose seem comical. In my peripheral, Valery's curves are only more emphasized in the glass. I still can't comprehend why she is here. Maybe she has some expertise, but at that age, it seems unlikely. She presses a button on the side, and there's a hiss as the pressure equalizes and the lid to the pod slowly rises.

"We've added a few updates to the newest model," she says.

Inside, a translucent blue liquid fills the pod.

"What's in the liquid?" I ask. There's an almost radioactive glow to the substance.

"That is what makes all of this possible. There are millions of tiny nanites that report feedback from every inch of your body, inside and out. This will be the most realistic gaming you will ever experience. They will clean you, feed you, and caress you ever-so-gently. They'll take better care of you than your mom or girlfriend ever could. Go ahead, touch it." She motions to the liquid.

I'm hesitant, but I do it anyway. Reaching my hand into the pod, I expect the liquid to part around my fingers like water, but when I submerge my fingers, it's like it molds to my skin, changing density in an instant. Then suddenly, it's like I'm touching nothing at all. The temperature of the liquid has mirrored my own perfectly. I pull my hand back and the nanites release as if they have no viscosity whatsoever.

"Pretty amazing, huh?" She gives me those seductive eyes. Dark brown and full of mystery. "The nanites are like a second layer of skin. They form to your body, mimicking the resistance you feel in the game. They can contract and expand in a fraction of a second. They will allow you to taste, to smell, to feel. Essentially, they will replicate the gameworld around your body. The difference between the game and reality will be indistinguishable."

"And what if I have to go to the bathroom?" It's a silly question, but I don't want to be swimming in my own filth for a month.

"There is a state-of-the-art filtration system. As soon as the nanites detect a change in their habitat, they attack the invader and flush it out of the system. Sweat, dead skin cells—" She pauses. "—other forms of waste. It's all filtered out immediately. The environment in the nanite gel is a thousand times cleaner than most hospitals. They will also be responsible for your breathing and nutrient intake while immersed."

"So, what now?" I ask.

She closes the lid to the pod and it locks into place. "Now, we get you in the game."

One of the technicians brings her a package and she hands it to me.

"I'll need you to change into this," she says, handing me the package.

I open it and find a pair of silky white underwear inside. They remind me of the tighty-whities I wore as a child. I guess she senses my consternation at stripping down to my underwear, because she comments on them.

"Apparently, no one likes getting naked in front of so many people, so we had these made. They are constructed from a special material that doesn't interfere with the nanites. There's a bathroom over there where you can change. Leave your clothes by the sink and we will have them put away and waiting for you when your immersion is over."

"Don't I get to look through the game manual or anything?" I ask.

"Where's the fun in that? You'll find out everything you need to know as you play the game."

In the bathroom, I take off my gray suit jacket and lay it delicately on the counter. So much has happened today that I've hardly had a chance to process it. As I take off each article of clothing, it almost feels as if I am shedding my old skin. The skin of a streamer who lost his cool one too many times. For a moment, I just stare at myself in the mirror. In real life, I'm a skinny nobody, but online, I've always been a giant among men. With quicker reflexes and a better understanding of game mechanics than most, I never had a problem excelling at whatever games I played. I take a deep breath. This will be no different. Prisoners or not, this is my element. I've always enjoyed playing the characters no one else touches—the ones labeled weak and ineffective—and using them to wipe the floor with my opponents. It doesn't matter what they throw at me, I'll be just fine.

I put on the tighty-whities. My new skin. I have no idea what my new skin will become in the aftermath of my sentencing. It's much too soon to tell, but I have a feeling the next thirty days will be the basis.

If I want to continue to play games at a professional level, then I have to be able to control my emotions, even under stress. If what they say is true about *Isle of Mythos*, then this'll be a very real test.

I leave my clothes on the marble counter and meet Valery back out in the lab. The chill of the room nips at me and goosebumps prickle along my body.

Truth be told, I'm nervous. Who wouldn't be at least a little nervous knowing they are about to be trapped inside a game for thirty days with felons convicted of violent crimes? Yes, the whole purpose of the game is to let them play the hero in the hopes of rehabilitating them, but when I'm their sworn enemy...I don't know what to expect.

"Ready?" Valery asks, her voice as seductive as ever.

It's time to quit stalling and either nut up or shut up.

"Let's do it."

As the technicians prep the pod, I get into my normal pre-game routine. I tune out the outside world and drift inside my head. I can see them working, but I'm not watching them, not really. Heavy metal blares inside my head. A montage of some of my greatest battles plays out before me. I sling fireballs as a wizard at an oncoming goblin mage. Our spells collide in a maelstrom of ethereal energy. As a stealthy rogue, I teleport behind an elven archer and slit her throat. One of my personal favorites was when I played as a damage-based support and cast an ultimate healing spell on a vampire, exploding him into red mist.

A peacefulness washes over me as the chaos replays in my mind. The only thing I'm missing is an energy drink and a bag of chips.

"Mister Johnson." Valery motions toward my home for the next thirty days. "Please step into the pod."

Some of my confidence has returned and I wink at her as I slide into the nanite gel.

"Please, call me Chad."

She laughs. I don't know if it's because of my sudden boldness or the absurdity of it, but it doesn't faze me. I submerge into the blue liquid. It's only cold for a split-second before the nanites mimic my body temperature. The door to the pod closes with a hiss, and more nanites begin to flood in. I can see Valery leaning over the pod, her features clouded by a blue haze as the nanite gel covers my face.

When I can no longer hold my breath, I give in and the nanite gel flows into my lungs. I'm not sure what I expect, choking maybe, but it's not this. The nanites coat my lungs and it's like I'm breathing on a misty day where the rain is so thick that you can't help but take it in with every breath.

Valery waves at me, and suddenly everything goes black.

I don't know how long I sit in the blackness, seconds or minutes, I'm not sure. My heart beats in my eardrums and the rasp of my own breathing are all that I know.

Gradually, the blackness fades. A tiny dot appears far away in my vision and begins to grow. It grows and grows until I realize it's a planet. A planet with blue oceans and green continents. Not that different from Earth except that the land-masses are all the wrong shapes. I zoom through the atmosphere and the green continents develop different hues. There are sandy deserts, snowcapped mountains, lush dense forests. My vision focuses on a particular continent floating all alone.

It's longer than it is wide, and a rocky mountain range separates the continent in two. The camera halts and the words *Isle of Mythos* appear atop the continent in letters carved from stone.

CHAPTER THREE

CHARACTER CREATION

The logo fades away and is replaced by something I know all too well. A character creation screen. Epic instrumental music has me ready to click randomize and hit the ground running. Except there is no randomize button. I'm also not playing this entirely for fun. The judge wants me to play to better myself. Valery and Mythos Games have their own unknown reasons. Personally, I don't want to be tortured by a bunch of murder hobos just because someone told them they should hate me. I'm going to make the strongest character I can right from the start.

A forest green, lumbering troll rotates in the center of my vision. A flat face with two gigantic tusks jutting upwards stares back at me. Blue freckles adorn its wide nose. Pointy ears protrude from both sides of his head, where two long, black braids dangle down each side and drape over his massive shoulders. Each shoulder is covered in patches of rough walnut skin, almost rock-like in appearance. He holds a wooden club in one giant hand tipped with razor-sharp black claws that it occasionally lifts, sending ripples through its thick, bulging muscles. A loincloth is the only clothing he wears.

These aren't the fat lovable trolls from children's TV shows. These are beasts. Warriors.

Awesome!

Enter Name.

"Chad," I say.

Chod pops up above the troll's head.

"No. Chad," I say again.

The name doesn't change.

"CH-AD," I do my best to enunciate my single syllable name.

Nothing.

According to Valery, all of my in-game icons will be activated simply by focusing on them, so I try to mentally click on the name to see if I can change it, but it doesn't work. Nothing I do changes the name.

It seems I'm already being trolled by the game. Great. At least it didn't call me Chode. I'll take that as a win.

Choose Race.

I cycle through several races, but they are all grayed out and unavailable. There seems to be a wide variety for players to choose from in the future. Or maybe if you're not being punished by a court of law. There are dwarves, elves, humans, gnomes, halflings, minotaurs, wereraces, and many more. There are even a few shadows that must be for special races they aren't showing yet.

Troll. *Trolls are barbaric creatures, gifted with physical prowess but not much else. Very rarely are trolls able to learn magic, and those that do are not of much renown. Most of their lives are spent trying to fill their insatiable appetite. Trolls have the ability to blend in with their surroundings when not moving.*

Bonus Abilities: Night Vision, Increased Regeneration, Thick Skin, Camouflage, Savage.

I focus on troll and a new category appears.

Choose Subspecies.

Several subspecies of trolls now appear before me with their stats displayed to the side—mountain, desert, and forest. Arctic and seaside are grayed out for some reason. Each one is uniquely different from the others.

The forest troll is my current selection.

Forest Troll. *Forest trolls dwell in the depths of the forest. They can usually be found in a wide clearing, having uprooted the surrounding trees in boredom. Forest trolls are big and strong, but they are also the fastest of the subspecies of trolls.*

Strength: 18
Dexterity: 15
Constitution: 19
Intelligence: 7
Wisdom: 10
Charisma: 6

Next, I cycle to the mountain troll. His light plum-colored skin is dotted with speckles of gray. A short gray mohawk runs down the center of his head. A hawk nose nearly touches his lips, and the tusks are shorter but more girthy. He is stockier than the forest troll, built for strength and not speed. A large fur shawl is tossed over his shoulders.

Mountain Troll. *Mountain trolls are most commonly found tucked away in the depths of caves. The strongest of all trolls, they find entertainment in tossing boulders from great heights and watching them tumble into the depths below.*

Strength: 20
Dexterity: 12
Constitution: 20
Intelligence: 7
Wisdom: 10

Charisma: 6

The final option available to me is the desert troll. Its skin is a dull tan with patches of hazelnut and toffee around the shoulders. Shaggy orange hair is pulled into a ponytail that falls down his back. He is less muscular than the other two, but far wider.

Desert Troll. *The largest of the troll subspecies, the desert troll can survive for days at a time without food or water due to extra fatty tissue stored in their backs and midsection.*

Strength: 18

Dexterity: 13

Constitution: 21

Intelligence: 7

Wisdom: 10

Charisma: 6

The last two subspecies of troll are grayed out to me. I can't see their stats or descriptions, but the arctic troll has black skin and is covered with long white fur everywhere except for its belly. The seaside troll, with baby blue skin, is the smallest of them all, and it appears to have webbed fingers and toes.

I take a moment to look over the three available subspecies, weighing the pros and cons of each. I quickly disregard the desert troll. While the higher Constitution and the ability to travel without food and water is nice, I want to be more than just a walking tank. Especially considering I might be going at this alone.

That leaves the mountain and forest trolls. The mountain troll definitely looks the coolest with his purple skin and bulging muscles, but the trade-off of Dexterity for Strength just isn't worth it for me. I want to be able to move quickly and hit hard.

I guess I'm going to be a forest troll.

I select him, and a new category appears.

Select a Class.

Only four classes are available to me, most likely based on my low Intelligence, Wisdom, and Charisma. They are barbarian, fighter, ranger, and rogue.

It would be cool to be a wizard or paladin troll, maybe even a bard. Had the choices actually been there, I might have even taken one just to stick it to the man. But then I remember the pain settings and the other players. If I'm going to do this, I'm going to play to my strengths.

Ranger. *Masters of both close-combat and ranged weapons, rangers are in tune with nature and use natural magic in conjunction with physical attacks to tackle quests across the realm.*

Ranger is a no-go. Trolls aren't really known for their ranged attacks and my low Intelligence means I would have a hard time mastering any of the magic usually associated with the class.

Rogue. *Known for their seedy antics and untrustworthiness, rogues are masters of stealth and trickery. Experts in bladed weapons and poisons, these scoundrels thrive in their nighttime escapades.*

Rogue is also not a good choice. While my Dexterity is on the higher side, I'm too large to be sneaky. My night vision would be an asset, but I'd essentially be wasting my Strength and Constitution on sneak attacks and subterfuge. Plus, I doubt I would be a very good poison-maker with my Intelligence. My Charisma is basically nonexistent, and who has ever met a rogue that wasn't a quick talker? Like I need another reason for society to hate me.

Fighter. *Masters of a multitude of weapons and fighting styles, fighters are able to learn to use any weapon or martial art with ease.*

Barbarian. *Savage warriors capable of using basic weapons and entering into a berserker rage.*

So, it looks like I'm either a fighter or a barbarian. Being a fighter would be easy with the ability to master weapons and fighting techniques. Being a troll, though, I think I should rely on my natural abilities. Brutal strength with basic weapons. Barbarians are capable of going into berserker rages, which considering why I'm here to begin with, seems fitting.

I select barbarian and my character locks into place.

Chod, the Barbarian Forest Troll appears above my avatar.

I'm not going to lie, I look like a badass. I'd like to see somebody take a swing at me.

The next thing I know, the screen fades to black and I open my eyes in the middle of a forest.

CHAPTER FOUR

THEY SEE ME TROLLING

The smell of cedar washes over me. I stand in a clearing, a beam of light breaking through the canopy and bathing me in warm sunshine. A brook murmurs somewhere nearby and I can hear the scuffle of insects and birds chirping all around. This is by far the most peaceful place I have ever been. Maybe I'll just chill here for the next thirty days.

I take a step forward, my legs stumble, and I fall straight on my face. My chin slams against a rock and even though my tough troll skin keeps me from feeling more than a bump, stars dance in my vision.

Attempting to rise to my feet, I stumble and sway back and forth. My body slams into a tree, causing a flock of birds to take flight and several exotic fruits to fall to the ground. I wrap my hands around the tree to stop the world from spinning and dig my sharp black nails into the bark. It holds me steady.

It takes me several minutes to acclimate to my new troll body. Being eight feet tall, I didn't take into account that it might be like a toddler trying to walk for the first time as I stumble through the forest.

Eventually, I adjust to my new body and feel its power coursing through me. Once I get the hang of it, this is going to be fun. I must weigh several hundred pounds, because every step I take leaves deep impressions in the earth.

Slowly, I begin to jog and then run. Each step rumbles the nearby earth, sending anything foolish enough to be in my path scurrying into the forest's depths. I move faster than I thought possible, faster than any human.

Now that I know my speed, I want to test my strength. I grab a nearby tree and its bark crumples beneath my grip. With a heave, I uproot it almost effortlessly. I lift it over my shoulder and toss the tree like a javelin. It soars through the air and lands with a violent crash.

"This is awesome!" I yell. My voice is deep and cavernous. Terrifying, really; it sounds more like the roar of a lion than anything.

Wanting to test my strength some more, I cock my fist and unload into a nearby pine. Wood splinters at the impact and sawdust rains down all around me like the fallout from an atomic bomb.

"Chod smash!" I hit the tree again and another large chunk of timber explodes into sawdust and splinters. It takes five more hits before I hear a loud crack and the pine falls. It crashes through the canopy, clearing a wide path before smacking against the earth and disheveling everything that isn't rooted in place. Pine needles fall like confetti on New Year's Eve.

I am one powerful motherfucker.

But there is always a bigger beast.

Something rumbles in the depths of the forest. Whatever it is causes the remaining birds to take flight. Several deer run by me, escaping what is coming from the other direction. I stand tall, awaiting my challenger. The crunch of trees announces its arrival and a moment later, I am face to face with my first opponent.

Ogre. *Level 5. Big, strong, and ugly. Ogres are quick-tempered, powerful brawlers.*

Standing a good two feet taller than me, the ogre has pasty yellow skin and crooked brown teeth, all dull except for the row of jagged, sharp teeth at the front of his lower jaw. He's draped in an assortment of furs with a bone necklace dangling from his neck. In one hand, he holds a wooden club, crudely fashioned from a broken tree, and in the other, the bloody remains of a deer. I guess I interrupted his dinner.

Large, bloodshot eyes stare at me with fury. The top of his head ends above his eyebrows, showcasing what little brains he has. Ogres have never really been known for their smarts. He tosses the carcass of the deer to the ground and unleashes a deafening roar. Spittle flies from his mouth and hot breath permeates the air in my direction.

He yells something at me, but I don't speak fucking ogre, so I just stand there and wait for the showdown that is inevitably about to happen. Yeah, he's big and ugly, but so am I.

The ogre obviously takes offense to me not responding, because he swings his club at me. Luckily, I am expecting it and dodge the attack. While he recovers his balance from the swing, I jab him in the ribs and his HP drops by ten percent.

I really should have taken a moment to look through my abilities before I got in a fight, but here we are and there is no time like the present. The ogre swings again, and I step back and to the side. His club collides with a tree and cleaves it in two.

I finally take stock of the icons floating in the edge of my vision. They're translucent except for when I focus on them. One looks like a notebook. That should be where my abilities are listed.

The ogre swings again, and I sidestep, dodging the attack as he falls past me. I kick him in the back, and he stumbles forward. I use the momentary distraction to check my abilities.

The book opens across my vision, obscuring my sight completely. I'm looking through, searching for my skill list, when a sharp pain erupts in the side of my head. My vision goes dark around the edges and the words become unreadable as my vision wavers. I try to close the notebook and focus on the fight at hand, but I can't do anything until my head stops spinning.

The spinning stops, and I close the notebook just in time to catch another club to the side of my face. Again, my head spins and I notice I'm down to a third of my health. No wonder. He's level five and I'm still level one.

The world moves back and forth like a crashing wave. My head is throbbing, and I want to throw up. I blindly throw a punch, hoping against hope I connect with something. The action throws me off balance and I feel two large, powerful arms grasp me around the neck. Hot breath and heavy breathing assault my ears. The ogre says something, but it only sounds like grunts to me. A moment later, my neck goes tight, I hear my vertebrae crunch, and everything goes black.

CHAPTER FIVE

LET'S TRY THIS AGAIN

Alert! You have died. All items on your person have been lost. Items can be retrieved at the site of death in the event they have not been looted. One level and any stat points associated with it have been removed.

I respawn in the same clearing as before, fuming. Man, that was so stupid of me. The middle of a fight is not the time to study up on my abilities. I know better. I've been playing games for years, for crying out loud. Just because this feels like I am actually here, it doesn't mean I can just forget everything I know about gaming. I uproot a tree, breaking it in half in my frustration and tossing the remains deep into the forest. Not to mention taking on an ogre five levels higher than me. Of course he could kill me in three hits. If I wasn't a level one scrub, I would have lost everything I had on me, including a level.

If I want to be the best, then I need to play smarter. I need to know what I'm working with here.

I pull up the notebook and look at my abilities.

Abilities: You have three starter ability points to use. A new ability point is unlocked at every odd level. New abilities may be learned from completing quests, equipping new items, and various achievements.

Bite. Using your massive tusks and powerful jaw, you take a bite out of an opponent, dealing immense damage. Cost: 10 rage. Level 2. **Massive Bite.** *Deals double damage. Cost: 20 rage.*

Claw. You attack with sharp claws, swiping at an opponent and dealing extra damage. Cost: 5 rage. Level 2. **Claws.** *Swipe at an opponent with both hands, dealing extra damage. Cost: 10 rage.*

Multi-Attack. Bite and Claw at the same time. Cost: 20 rage.

Iron Will. Immune to slows and stuns for 15 seconds. Cost: 50 rage. Cooldown: 180 seconds.

Intimidation. You let out a roar at your opponent, freezing them in place so that they are unable to attack for two seconds. Cost: 10 rage.

Berserker Rage. (Ultimate. Available at level 5.) Attacks and physical damage build your rage meter. 5 rage per attack. Rage meter deteriorates over time when out of combat at a rate of 5 rage per second. When Berserker Rage is activated, for 30 seconds, rage meter is full, deal increased damage, increased attack speed, health regenerates at 5x the normal rate, cannot be stunned, slowed or otherwise affected. Cooldown: 60 minutes.

I'm Always Angry. (Available at level 10). Once rage meter is at 50%, it will not deteriorate below 50% when out of combat.

Beneath those, there also five bonus abilities for picking troll as my race.

Increased Regeneration. (Passive) Regenerate health at a faster rate. Level 2. **Rapid Regeneration.** *(Passive) When below 10% health, regeneration is doubled.*

Night Vision. (Passive) Increased vision in darkness and low light.

Thick Skin. (Passive) Take 10% less damage from physical attacks.

Camouflage. (Passive) When out of combat and not moving for 20 seconds, trolls blend in with their surroundings.

Savage. (Passive) Ability to eat uncooked meat without consequences.

Not a bad list of starter abilities. The five racial abilities are already unlocked, so I'll need to pick three more from the list above them. The low cost on Claw will boost my basic attacks significantly. The fact that they all rely on rage instead of mana is nice, because I can always replenish it by simply attacking. Bite and Claw are easy choices, because they play off my already high Strength. Multi-Attack seems like a luxury at my current level, so the choice for my final ability is between Iron Will and Intimidation. I elect to go with Intimidation because of the low rage cost and its ability to be used for offense and defense.

In the top right corner of my vision, an avatar of my character's face looks down at me. Beside it, there are bars detailing my Health, Mana, Rage, and Experience Points.

Chod, Level 1 Barbarian Forest Troll
HP: 475/475
Mana: 0/0
Rage: 0/100
XP: 0/300

It's interesting that I don't have any mana, but seeing as how all of my abilities feed off of rage, it makes sense. The creation screen did say that trolls were not known for their magical aptitude. I wonder if it means I can't learn magic or if I just need to find a way to unlock it. At least I won't have to waste my money on mana potions until I know for sure.

In the bottom right corner of my vision, there is a map. I focus on it and it enlarges, displaying the *Isle of Mythos*. I am currently smack dab in the middle of a giant forest on the southern half of the island. An enormous mountain range separates the northern ynd southern halves of the island near the center. Several towns are marked on the map with question marks. The map will probably fill itself in as I travel.

Above the map, there is an icon of a backpack. I focus on it and it opens my inventory. Between my Strength and Constitution, I bet I can carry a massive amount of loot. The only item I have right now is the ragged loincloth that drapes over my trollberries. I pick up one half of the broken tree and it shows in my inventory as a wooden club.

Item. *Wooden Club. +1 Strength.*

I'd like to replace it with something made of stone or metal once I have the chance, but first I'll need to earn gold or find something worthy of a trade.

First things first, though. I need to find a town and see what this game really has to offer. Looking at the map, the closest town is on the outskirts of the forest to the west. That's where I'll go and maybe find out a little more about what makes this world tick. If I'm lucky, I might even run into another player.

On the way, I can farm and test out my abilities.

The first animal I come across is a tiny bunny. One smash of my club kills the poor creature. It drops a rabbit pelt, and my XP goes up by five. I tuck the rabbit pelt into the strap of my loincloth. I need to find some better monsters. At the current rate, it'll take sixty rabbits for me to get to level two.

Remembering my Camouflage passive, I stop moving. When the twenty seconds is up, I don't notice any difference in my appearance, but nature explodes to life around me. Birds tweet from the trees above, insects rattle and buzz in a violent cacophony. It's like I completely vanished from the forest. Then I notice an icon flashing next to my avatar. It's a small picture of a more animated version of me hiding between two large bushes. It pulses slowly. I move and the icon disappears. The forest goes quiet once again.

That'll be useful.

I freeze my movements again. When the timer is up and the icon appears, the forest roars back to life. I sit and wait, letting the animals grow comfortable. Several more bunnies appear around me, hopping and frolicking as if all is good in the world. They're not even worth my time at this point. I'm way too strong to be wasting my time killing bunnies and rats. I need bigger game.

So I sit. Patience is a virtue for a reason. Five minutes later, my patience is rewarded by several fox-looking creatures walking in my direction.

Jackal. *Level 2. Ranging in size from as small as foxes to as large as wolves, jackals are known for being sly and for their high perception.*

They are about ten feet away when one of them senses something isn't right. It lifts its nose in the air, smelling my scent.

Not wanting the creatures to run away, I end Camouflage and leap towards the small pack of canines. I smash one with my club, dropping its health by a third and claw at another. The three jackals turn to face me, teeth bared and ready to fight.

With my ten rage, I use Bite and attack the first jackal again. The bonus damage is enough to kill the creature in one attack. The biggest of the remaining two lunges at me, taking a bite out of my leg. A dull pain runs up my leg, and I smack the jackal to the side. I kick the other before it has a chance to attack. Using the newly acquired rage, I activate Intimidation and let out a roar that freezes both jackals in fear, unable to attack for two seconds.

By the time the effect wears off, I've killed another jackal and use Bite to finish off the third.

Congratulations! You have reached level 2. +1 stat point to distribute. +1 Strength and Constitution racial bonus.

Not bad at all. I elect to save my stat point until I have more and can decide the best way to allocate them. Without an in-depth tutorial, I'm kind of learning this as I go and don't want to do anything I might regret so early in the game.

I gather the jackal pelts and tuck them in my loincloth, setting off toward the town marked on the map. I really need to find a satchel of some sort to carry my items in. My little loincloth is only going to be able to carry so much.

For a moment, I contemplate going in search of the ogre. To prove to him and myself that I'm not really as big of a chump as I was in that first fight. I think better of it and realize that maybe that's why I raged so much online. Because as long as I've been playing, I've had a chip on my shoulder. Something to prove. Deep down, I wanted to be a professional gamer. If I could somehow show the world what I'm capable of, then maybe my parents might actually notice me. The fact that the mistakes of other people kept that from happening was the trigger that set me off each time.

I flip a calloused green middle finger into the air and wonder if Valery and her team are watching me as I contemplate my life's work while walking as a monster through a lush forest in a video game.

Along the way, I cross paths with a wild boar, which gets me almost to level three. Not wanting to let a good opportunity go to waste, I kill a few more bunnies and go the distance. I use my new ability point to unlock Iron Will.

Between the tusks from the boar and all the pelts, I've run out of places to store items unless I want to carry everything in my hands. That just won't do.

The boar hide is the largest, so I lay it flat on the ground and then fold it in half. Using my razor-sharp claws, I poke several holes along each side of the hide and a couple along the top. I search a nearby tree and find exactly what I'm looking for: thin, green vines. I pull several down and strip the leaves from them. Next, I run the vines through the holes on each side of the boar hide, creating a makeshift satchel. It's not the best work, but it should last me until I make it to town and can either buy some string or purchase an actual bag.

Now that I have the bag made, I loop the remaining vines through the holes I poked in the top to make a strap. I intertwine the vines together to make it sturdier and then tie off the loose ends on the other side.

I stuff the remaining pelts and the two boar tusks in the satchel and admire my work. Not bad. Not bad at all.

Congratulations! You have unlocked the skill 'Leatherworking.' You are now a level 1 Leatherworker (Novice). Increase your skill and learn advanced techniques for working leather by finding an advanced leatherworker (Apprentice or above). Crafting Ranks: Novice, Apprentice, Journeyman, Expert, Artisan, Master, Grandmaster.

Sweet! That means I'll be able to learn to make leather armor and as my skill goes up, the quality should increase. Since none of the animals have dropped gold, I'm guessing this is the type of game where you make gold from completing quests and selling the items you make. That's good. It means I won't spend all of my time fighting monsters. Not that that isn't fun, but it's nice to spice things up. I wonder what other types of crafting I can learn?

I toss the satchel over my shoulder and set off towards town. It's peaceful walking through the forest. New York City was never this calm. Walking down the street, even at three in the morning, car horns blared, lights flashed, and a thousand voices blended together in a raucous buzz as people talked on cell phones and ignored everyone else around them. Even at Central Park, it was hard to find a moment's quiet.

I take in a deep breath and just enjoy the sound of nature around me. Sure, I'm here because I screwed up, but this is a once in a lifetime experience. I'm going to make the most of it.

CLINK.

My communing with nature is interrupted by a sound I know all too well.

A swordfight.

CHAPTER SIX

RANGER DANGER

I follow the sound of clashing swords. As quietly as my troll body will allow, I do my best to find the source of the noise without being detected. There is something about the ringing of metal on metal that makes my blood pump. Probably the thousands of hours I've poured into games over the years. Magic is flashy, but nothing beats a good swordfight.

The clinking gets louder, and I'm finally able to see the source. Two men, both wearing brown leather armor and green cloaks, attack and parry on the bank of a gurgling stream.

Forest Ranger. Level 4.

The men are almost identical, except one has a brown beard and the other's is blond. The blond man attacks with a fierce slash, knocking his opponent off balance. He then follows up with another swift swing, but the one with the brown beard is able to deflect the blow, sending his attacker stumbling past him.

He turns to charge his opponent, but the blond man slips in the sand and falls to one knee, losing his sword. The brown beard raises his weapon overhead and swings, stopping an inch from the man's neck.

He says something I can't quite make out and they both laugh, then he extends his arm and helps the man to his feet.

That's when I notice their belongings piled neatly against a tree. Several bags, two bows, quivers full of arrows. They're traveling companions enjoying an afternoon spar. But are they players or are they NPCs?

If I had to put money on it, I would say the latter. As far as I know, there are only twenty-four actual players in *Isle of Mythos* right now. With this being a pretty large continent, not to mention the size of the planet, I would say that the majority of inhabitants are non-player characters. But which ones? And how do I tell?

It can't hurt to ask. Even if they are real players, convicts, they're supposed to be playing the hero. What do I have to lose?

"Hey," I shout, waving and poking my head over the embankment.

The two men immediately rise to their feet, swords drawn and pointed in my direction. They scowl at me as I approach.

"Whoa, no need for that." I toss my club to the ground and put my hands up in defense, showing them I mean no harm, but it does nothing to calm the men. They slowly back away towards their belongings. "I'm not going to hurt you. I'm on my way to town to get set up and maybe learn a few things."

Their faces are completely void of recognition to anything I am saying, their eyes wide in terror. I know Valery said trolls were hated, but this seems like an over-reaction. They must not see too many trolls around these parts.

Brown-beard says something to Blondie, but once again, I can't make it out. Blondie sheathes his sword and grabs his bow. With shaky hands, he nocks an arrow and points it at me.

"Hey, man. What the actual fuck?" I stop my advance to give the little asshole an opportunity to calm down. His arm shakes as he holds the arrow pulled back against his neck.

Brown-beard says something else. Why in the hell can I not understand what they are saying? It all sounds like gibberish. Blondie shakes his head. What is this little twerp planning?

Sweat beads on his forehead and he starts speaking fast. I have no idea what he's saying, but it's coming out his mouth a mile a minute and he's shaking worse than ever. The man is having a full-on panic attack.

"Okay, guys. I'm just gonna leave you be. I'll find my own way to town."

I turn to leave and the next thing I know, I feel a dull pinch in my left shoulder. Reaching up to see what bit me, I find the shaft of an arrow sticking out of my forest green skin. Dark blue blood trickles down my back.

Not cool, little man. Not cool at all.

I pull the arrow out and toss it to the ground.

The two men are now yelling at each other while Blondie attempts to nock another arrow. His hands shake so badly that he misses the string each time and the arrow falls from his grip.

He finally puts one in place and lets it fly. I swat it from the air like a fly and his eyes go wide. Brown-beard has obviously had enough, because he grabs his belongings and hightails it out of there. Blondie is not so smart.

I run at him full force while he tries to nock another arrow. When I'm a few steps away, he tosses his bow to the ground and draws his sword. He swings at me, but I step back and the blade whistles through the air, inches from my midsection.

Activating Claw, I attack his exposed side and rip through his leather armor with ease. He yells out in pain and slashes at me again, connecting with my shoulder. The blade cuts me, but not as deep as I expect. The wound is not much more than an inconvenient sting. Between the arrow and the cut, Blondie has only managed to drain ten percent of my health. Due to my increased regeneration, it's already recovering.

He, on the other hand, lost twenty percent from my single attack with the Claw bonus.

We stare at each other for a moment, sizing one another up. I'm stronger, faster, and tougher than this guy, and judging by the panicked expression on his face, he knows it. If his friend had stayed, I might have had a worthy match, but even though he is a level higher than me, I'm a warrior. He's a ranger. His strengths are in his quickness, and now that I've gashed his ribs, he's not going anywhere.

He attacks me again and I dodge his blow. I have just enough rage to activate Bite. Before Blondie can react, I bypass his guard and sink my tusks into his shoulder. The taste of blood surprises me and I let go. I didn't expect it to be so lifelike. Silky smooth iron coats my mouth and I attempt to spit it out. This is way too realistic for my taste.

Ow!

A sharp pain flares from my side and I look down to see a large gash running along my ribs. It's not deep, but it hurts a hell of a lot more than the other two attacks.

I've had just about enough of this guy.

"You picked the wrong day, asshole."

I uproot a nearby tree and swing it at Blondie with all my might. It crushes into him and I hear the crack of broken ribs and branches. He falls to the ground, stunned. It takes him a moment to come to, but when he does, the only thing I see in his eyes is fear.

Taking the tree, I break off the end to where it is the size of a club and walk over to Blondie.

"There's a saying where I come from," I say, but there isn't a hint of recognition on his face. "About picking on someone your own size. It's usually for when people pick on those smaller than them, but I think it works for you and me too. You should have left with your buddy."

Blondie doesn't understand me, but he knows he's about to die. He lets out a defeated sigh and drops his head. I send him swiftly into the next life.

Warning! *You have killed a human NPC. If word of this reaches a human settlement, your reputation among humans will be decreased by 100. Stop the ranger from reaching town before it is too late. Current reputation with humans: -1000. (-1000 Racial Penalty)*

You have got to be kidding me.

I quickly loot the belongings of the ranger. His pack is smaller than the satchel I created, but it is well made. I throw it in my satchel, along with the bow, arrows, and sword so that I can examine it better later and see what it holds inside.

Right now, I have a ranger to catch.

CHAPTER SEVEN

NO GOOD DEED GOES UNPUNISHED

After looting the body of anything useful and stuffing it in my satchel, I set off in search of the brown-bearded ranger. Due to my increased regeneration, my wounds are already healing at a rapid rate. The sting of the cuts were uncomfortable. I can only imagine what an injury might feel like on someone without my defenses and tough skin.

I scour the area behind the tree where their belongings were. The ranger is light on his feet and there are no traces of which direction he went.

Of course, it had to be a fucking ranger. Why couldn't it be a lumbering warrior and not this nimble-footed nutsucker? If his stupid friend had just kept his shaky fingers on the damn arrow, I'd be strolling through the forest now instead of worrying about further damaging my reputation with humans. I was expecting a little bit of racism, maybe paying more for goods and not being allowed into certain establishments, but I wasn't expecting to be attacked on sight for saying a friendly hello.

Really, though, can eleven hundred really be that much worse than one thousand when you're hated that much?

I'd rather not find out. If there is a chance I can stop him, I need to at least try.

Opening my map while I walk, the most logical location is the town on the edge of the forest. It's far closer than any of the others, and if he is looking to rat me out, that'll be his best bet. If I'm going to stop him, I don't have to track him, I just have to get there before he does.

Apparently, this is a big fucking forest, because, for the next two hours, I only move halfway towards the town. With my high starting stats in Strength, Constitution, and Dexterity, I don't need to stop for breaks often, but the rumble in my stomach tells me I am getting hungry.

Using Camouflage, I take a moment to blend into the surroundings. As soon as I disappear, the forest comes alive. It finally answers the age-old question, if a tree falls and no one is around to hear it, does it make a sound. The forest is full of sounds even when it assumes no one is around.

A rabbit hops out from a burrow beneath an old tree stump and nibbles on a nearby plant. A swift swing of my club and dinner is ready. I use my sharp claws to remove its fur.

What I have left is slimy, bloody, and not the least bit appetizing. Putting away my human inhibitions, I embrace the troll I am and take a bite. It's not as off-putting as the ranger's blood that had filled my mouth. Maybe it's my new taste buds, but it actually doesn't taste that bad. It's more chewy than cooked meat and the tiny bones give it crunch every so often. Almost like eating a pretzel. Thanks to the passive from Savage, I don't have to worry about getting sick and it looks like I won't even need to invest in a cooking skill!

My hunger abates, and I feel like I have the energy to keep going for a while. With my stamina replenished, I take off through the forest at full speed.

It is truly amazing how fast and powerful I am. In real life, I was never that great of an athlete. The whole reason I got into esports was because I finally found something I was good at. I joined my school esports league and won the championship the first year I entered. After that, I joined the school team and we traveled for tournaments, playing whatever games were popular that year. It didn't matter what the games were, I could adapt. I had a natural affinity that most others didn't, and for once, I felt good about myself. Whatever the challenge was, I could master it. It turns out that the big leagues of esports are a lot different than being the best on your high school team. I tried out for a couple of pro teams, even got an interview, but never made it past that. I met Taryn at one of the tryouts. He was shy and quiet, but he was a damn good player. When he didn't make the team, I was shocked and asked him to join me as a streaming partner. We've been best friends ever since.

Even if I'm not a pro gamer, I'm still a gamer and that means I have a leg up on my competition.

I have to do a double-take when I see something swinging through the trees in the edge of my vision.

There is no way in hell I am this lucky. The ranger I've been chasing dangles from a rope tied to a large pine. His dark silhouette swings back and forth several feet off the ground as he struggles to free himself.

I walk towards him and incoherent babbling flows from his mouth like a waterfall.

"I can't understand you," I say. I don't know if he understands the words or not, but he quits talking. He's a lot smarter than his partner.

Underneath him, I spot the wooden stake that was attached to the noose that is now cinched tightly around his boots. The ranger must not have been paying attention, because he somehow got himself snared. The ultimate irony would be if he'd laid the trap himself. But seeing as I can't speak anything but fucking troll, I'll never know how he got into this predicament.

His bow and sword both lay scattered on the ground next to his pack and a few other items. The cloak he wears dangles past his head, nearly touching the ground.

The ranger continuously tries to bend up and grab his feet, but time and again, he fails. Blood rushes to his head, making him look like a tomato.

I step closer and he stops struggling. There's fear in his eyes, but not the uncontrollable fear of Blondie. No, this is a fear built out of respect for what I can do. This ranger doesn't fear trolls simply because they are trolls. He fears us because we are predators. Because he is at my mercy.

Killing him would be so easy right now. He's practically served on a platter, dangling in front of me completely defenseless. One hit and my reputation remains the same.

Yet something stays my hand. I have a negative one thousand reputation. With the way things are, I'll never have a chance to better it. Trolls are hated and any humans I run into will try to kill me on sight. This could be an opportunity to change that.

I pick the ranger's sword up off the ground. It's light in my hand, almost like holding a paper sword. The ranger doesn't flinch, but his eyes follow my every movement. He knows I hold all the power in this situation.

Reaching up, I take the rope in my hand just above his boots. Using his sword, I make a swift slash and the ranger's full weight pulls against my hand. I gently let him to the ground and step back. He looks at me with wide eyes, like he doesn't understand what just happened. I point at his feet and he begins frantically untying the rope.

When he stands up, I don't move. I want him to know that I mean him no harm. He begins gathering his belongings, but never takes his eyes off me for more than a second. His hands shake as he gathers his bow, evidence that he doesn't truly believe I will let him live.

He tosses his satchel over his shoulder and stares at me for a moment. I imagine he is questioning if he is allowed to leave. I point a calloused green finger in the direction of the nearest town. He nods at me and turns to go.

"Wait," I say.

The ranger freezes in place and turns his head over his shoulder.

"You might need this." I take the blade of the sword in my hand and offer the hilt to the ranger. He doesn't have to speak my language to understand the gesture. He takes the sword and says something in return.

Then, he is gone.

Alert! *You have spared the life of a human NPC. The ranger knows you acted in self-defense and will no longer report you to the authorities. Instead, he will sing your praises for releasing him from a snare trap without harm. However, no one will believe him. Your reputation has increased by 1. Current reputation with humans: -999. (-1000 Racial Penalty)*

My jaw hangs open once I finish reading the prompt. Are you kidding me? I spare the guy's life and get one measly point of reputation. Why would I ever want to be a good guy if that's the reward? I should have just killed him and taken his weapons.

I'm about ready to punch something when I hear movement behind me. I turn and see a giant green head towering over me. Two yellowed tusks jut into the air, one broken at the tip. A metal nose-ring gleams in the sun, and two dark black eyes bore into me. It opens its mouth and a deep, cavernous roar assaults my face.

"What have you done?" it asks.

THE WELL RUNS DRY

The troll standing before me has skin darker and more scarred than my own, but there is no doubt he is a forest troll. He's at least a foot taller than I am with thick corded muscle running down his entire body. When I focus on him, the gamertag tells me he is level ten. Several furs are sewn into a vest and the tails of the dead creatures swish in the breeze against his massive tree trunk legs.

"What did you do?" he asks again.

His deep voice reverberates in my chest. His eyes don't blink as he waits for me to respond.

He's level ten, so I know better than to antagonize him.

"Uhm, I set him free."

The troll rubs his massive fingers over his eyes and lets out a sigh.

"You know the rules forbidding contact with humans, and the punishment for humans who wander into our tribal grounds. Come with me and the chief will decide your punishment. Try to resist, and I will take you by force." The nose ring that hangs from his septum moves with each word. I know better than to try and escape, so I follow the troll through the forest.

It seems that the fuck-up fairy has visited me once again.

This guy is no-nonsense as he leads me through the woods. He marches with purpose, intent on delivering me to some troll chief where I will undoubtedly be punished for breaking a rule I didn't know exists.

"What's your name, big guy?" I ask. I am thankful to actually speak to someone and have them understand what I am saying, even if he is a bit of an asshole.

"I am Gord, son of Guilda."

"Nice to meet you, Gord. What is it that you do out here? Besides bringing guys like me to the chief." Maybe a little sweetness will unsour his disposition.

"I am a guardian. One of many who watch the boundaries of our tribe and keep the humans away."

"So you placed the snare that caught the ranger?"

He grunts and nods in affirmation.

"Humans know the rules. The heart of the forest belongs to us. It is all we have and the penalty for trespassing is death."

Shit. I am so going to be in trouble. All for one sliver of reputation.

"Why do the humans hate us so much?" I ask.

Valery said that trolls were hated like no other and that in time, I would find out why. Maybe now is the time.

"Hmpf." Gord snorts. "Why does the sun rise in the east and set in the west? It is the way of life."

Really helpful. The first person I meet who speaks my language, and he talks like Confucius. What have I gotten myself into?

"What will my punishment be?" Maybe I can at least squeeze that much information out of him.

"That is for the chief to decide."

"Good talk." It's clear Gord isn't much of a talker. Hopefully, the chief will cut me some slack since I am new here and maybe I can be on my way to adventuring and not getting attacked by humans every time I turn my back.

I almost don't notice when we enter the troll village. It's rustic and earthy in a way that I have never seen. Almost elemental. It's like the village was formed out of the forest itself. Surrounding a large firepit are several wooden huts made out of living trees that seem almost like they were bent into the shape of the structures. The roofs of the huts are covered in vines and tree leaves still growing from the oddly-shaped trees. A large female troll sits on a throne constructed in the same way. A young troll nestles in her lap, no more than two feet tall, suckling at her teat. A half-dozen other female trolls sit in lesser chairs to her left and right. They seem to be discussing something and stop abruptly at our approach.

The woman on the throne is the same forest green as the other trolls I have seen, but her body type is starkly different from myself and Gord. Her arms are more lithe, less bulky, but still defined. A long, dark braid runs down her left shoulder. Where Gord and I have massive tusks, hers are smaller. Her chin is more pointed while ours are broad and square. Despite her slender physique, I am certain she is far more powerful than the rangers I met earlier. All of the female trolls that surround her are built in the same way. It's very sexy, in a barbaric sort of way.

Gord steps in front of the throne and bends a knee. The woman on the throne stares at him for a moment, and then her eyes fall upon me. They widen for a split-second before she resumes her stoic pose.

"Gord, what brings you into the tribal center?" she asks, her eyes still piercing into me.

"I found this one in the forest. He is not a member of our tribe. I witnessed him letting a human escape our lands. He helped him, even."

The child finishes feeding and unlatches. I find it hard to look away as the woman hides her breast beneath the fur shawl that covers her shoulders and chest. Those are some giant troll titties. Like watermelons. I don't mean it in a sexual way, just, wow.

"Is this true?" she asks.

"Technically, yes. But to be fair, I didn't know any better." It's not like I was dropped in the forest with a book of tribal laws at my disposal.

"Where do you come from?" She looks at me quizzically. "We are the last tribe of forest trolls on the island, and I know all who come and go within our land. You are not a member of our tribe, but there is no doubt that you are one of us." All eyes are upon me, except for Gord, who still kneels before her.

"I'm new to the area." That sounds better than saying, "I was sent here because I am a criminal."

"I see." She leans over and whispers something to the woman sitting next to her. The woman is much older, but the only things that give away her age are the gray braid she wears draped over her shoulder and the crow's feet around her eyes. She nods and then their eyes are on me once again.

"There are stories, ancient stories, of those sent here from other realms. They look and talk like us, but they are not us. Sometimes they have special powers, often they are gifted in some way, and when they die, they do not pass on like the rest of us. There is word that these beings have begun appearing in the human settlements. Many of our guardians claim they have killed the same man on several occasions and that he continues to reappear. It seems the trolls may finally have found our own hero."

"I'm no hero, miss. I'm just trying to find my way."

There is a sudden gasp by the other women, and I know immediately I have violated some custom.

The troll on the far end stands and extends a long pointy finger in my direction. Her red braid seems to almost hiss at me when she shouts.

"Show respect when addressing the chief!"

"Easy, Tormara," says the chief. "It is clear he does not know our ways. Do not reprimand him for his ignorance, instead, educate him." Tormara is fuming, steam practically flowing out of her nostrils. "Now, you, what is your name?" she asks me.

"I am Chod." The eyes of all the women but the chief bore into me, telling me without words that I am not welcome here.

"Now, Chod, it is custom in our village to address those in power by their title. I am Chief Rizza. This is my council, and together we decide the fate of the forest trolls. We were discussing urgent business just as you arrived. However, it can wait, because if you truly are a hero, then we have great need of your assistance."

Whatever they need help with must be pretty bad if they're turning to me, someone who violated their customs and they know absolutely nothing about. Since I'm here to go on quests and hopefully better myself, I guess I owe it to them to help if I can. Judging by Gord, though, it looks like they have warriors much stronger than me already.

"What is it you would have me do?" I'm game for anything as long as it gets me the hell out of here.

"Gord, you are dismissed. Thank you for your service. We will handle it from here." Her eyes flicker to Gord before returning to me.

This feels like I'm in court all over again.

"Yes, Chief." Gord cuts his eyes at me as he disappears into the forest.

"Before I tell you of our needs, first you must understand the predicament that our people, *your people,* are in." The troll child has fallen asleep in her lap and snores softly. He's kind of cute to be so ugly. "Forest trolls are fading from this world. We have been for some time now. We do not have the luxury of inaccessible mountain passes like the mountain trolls or harsh environments like our desert or arctic sisters to keep our enemies at bay. Or the ocean's depths like the seaside trolls.

"We have the forest. It is a source of life, accessible to everyone, and the only protection it offers are its depths and our own fortifications." Her eyes don't break from mine while she speaks. I'm certain she is taking in my reaction to every word she says. "For thousands of years, we have been able to craft the magic that enters this forest and mold it to offer us protection. We have used it to hide our presence within its depths. To live our lives unmolested by the humans that spread out through the world like a parasite. For several years now, the magic that feeds the forest has been failing. Little by little, our presence had been discovered, the magic that hid us no longer working.

"To fight this, we reduced our borders, we made the magic cover less ground, we split into smaller tribes, but still it faltered." She turns to her council with a look of defeat. "Humans discovered us, they hunted us, until now we barely remain. The well that fed magic into the forest has been obstructed. We are no longer hidden from prying eyes. The guardians, like Gord, are the only defenses between us and the outside world that would have us dead."

"I'm sorry, Chief, but I thought trolls were unable to use magic." That's what the creation screen told me.

"For most, that is true. Very few of us have actual magical ability, only one in our village, but all trolls are gifted with the ability to craft magic if it is already there. Raw magic is powerful enough to burn most races if they touch it, but our tough skin allows us to craft it as we will. That is why we need your help, young Chod. Our well is dry."

"Why entrust this to me, though? Why haven't you tried to fix it already?" From what I've seen so far, I'm the runt of the litter.

"The journey is far and dangerous. We do not have the bodies to spare as it is. If we send our men away and they do not return, it will certainly spell our doom. It is no coincidence that you arrived when you did."

Great. I'm just an expendable piece of meat to these people.

"And why should I help you...Chief?" I add the last part when I see Tormara's nails digging into the bark of her chair. "What's in it for me?"

She smiles at me. It takes me by surprise how beautiful she looks when her face isn't stern and chiefly. Just as quickly, the smile is gone.

"As chief, it is my responsibility to look out for my people. My council guides me, they provide me with insight to help me make the tough choices, but at the end of the day, the decision is mine. Something must be done or my people will not survive. We need the magic returned to the forest. Take a day or two and explore our village, explore our tribal lands. If you bring magic back to the forest, you may have whichever reward you wish."

For the second time since I've been here, the women all gasp. They chatter in a dull roar at the chief. Tormara stands to her feet again and extends a hand in my direction.

"How could you? What if he would have your throne? You have offered too much, sister."

Chief Rizza responds calmly. "If my throne is the price of saving our people, then he shall have it. Nothing more will be said on the matter. Chod, do you accept my offer?"

Quest Alert. *You have been offered the quest 'Restore the Magical Well.' Something has blocked the magical stream that feeds into the forest. Find a way to clear the obstruction and return magic to the forest and tribal lands.*

Reward: Variable

It doesn't take me long to decide to help them. The fact that I can pick my own reward is amazing, and I'll make sure to do my due diligence before heading out. Becoming a troll chief right out of the gate wouldn't be such a bad thing. I need to complete the quest, but first, I want to know what I'm fighting for.

CHAPTER NINE
PARTY HARD

Chief Rizza instructs me to walk around the village while they finish up their council meeting. Honestly, there's not that much going on. Though the architecture is some of the most beautiful I have ever seen, their village doesn't offer much more than the most basic necessities. This is indeed a tribal village, not a town or city. Was it always this way or were they forced to live like this once their magic ran out? Most of the huts appear to be living quarters.

I pass a pergola where a woman boils leather and has an assortment of hides hanging from several branches. Underneath another one, a giant stew boils and several wild hogs roast over an open flame. A female troll slices meat off the roasting hogs with her sharp claws and stores it on a bed of waxy leaves in a wicker basket. She watches me warily as I pass.

I do my best to smile, but it comes off as a snarl.

The smell of the meat has my mouth watering. Based on my own experience with the rabbit, I would have expected a slew of uncooked red meat. Apparently just because we can eat raw meat doesn't mean that all trolls do.

Behind the huts, a troll sits fishing on the bank of a small lake. A line of large purple fish is displayed beside her.

One thing I notice as I walk the paths through their village is that aside from children, there are no male trolls around.

In the heart of the village, there is some kind of temple. It is constructed in the same way as the huts, with living trees forming the walls and roof, but smoke seeps out of a hole in the roof. A strong whiff of incense hits me as I come closer. The musky aroma reminds me of the cologne Taryn would wear anytime I saw him. I've told him a million times that it's not a good smell. And yet he wonders why girls don't sit near him. Next time I see him, I'll be sure to let him know it's reminiscent of a troll village.

I peek through the open door and spot a troll covered in furs sitting on the floor. He wears a mask that covers his eyes and a bright array of feathers stick out from it, making him look like some demonic bird. Dark dreadlocks with white tips hang across his back and shoulders. Both hands rest on his knees. He's smaller than I am, leaner, with painted white stripes running down his arms. He chants softly, and I swear there is a faint blue aura around him. When I focus on him, all it tells me is that he is level twelve.

A hand grasps my shoulder and I turn to see Chief Rizza. I was so focused I didn't even notice her approaching.

"Do not disturb the shaman while he is meditating," she says. Her eyes are like a golden wheat field.

"A shaman? What is he doing?" I ask.

He must be the only troll here with magic.

"Communing with his totem. The phoenix grants him great power and wisdom. Like I said, it is very rare for a troll to have natural magic. May we go for a walk?"

"Lead the way."

I follow the chief through the village, passing several other huts and a clearing where a half-dozen young trolls are training with wooden clubs. One of the children takes a club to the head and starts crying, throwing his own club to the ground and running to the instructor for comfort. The instructor gives the boy a stern talking to and sends him back out to battle.

There is no coddling around here.

"You have a very cute child," I say, remembering the baby that suckled at her breast earlier.

"He is not mine. Tormara is his mother, but we raise the children together here. If one is hungry, I will feed it like it is my own."

"That's...interesting." I can't imagine anyone whipping out a tit and just giving it to another child back in the real world. Maybe in some cultures but definitely not the US.

"We are raised to care for one another. That is the only way we will survive. When the rest of the world wants to destroy us, we only have one another to rely on."

"Do you have any children yourself?"

She smiles. "Not yet. In a way, the entire village is my child. While we are fighting for our very survival, I must focus on the task at hand."

The fact that she can feed the child, despite not having any of her own, is pretty incredible. The chief leads me through a dense patch of bushes to a bubbling stream and motions for me to take a seat on a large boulder on the bank.

"My grandmother used to tell me stories of the great heroes of the past. Long before our time, they would appear throughout the lands. They would go on quests, battle great monsters, and defeat powerful threats." Chief Rizza tugs at the tip of her braid and stares down into the stream. Minnows dart back and forth beneath the water. For a moment, she doesn't look like the stoic chief, but a young girl dwelling on old memories.

"I know that those times are returning. I can feel it in my bones. Great battles will come. Portals will reopen making it possible to travel to other continents in minutes, not days. Kingdoms will rise and fall with great heroes on all sides. It is my job to make sure that the forest trolls are still around when that time comes. To do that, we need your help."

She looks at me, all hints of the childhood stories gone. Rizza is a good leader. The leader I never have been on my own teams. She would do anything for her people.

"What makes you think I am the one who can help you do that? Gord is stronger than me. I mean, you have a shaman, for fuck's sake. I'm probably the least qualified person to take this mission." We sit in silence for a moment. The only sounds are the bubbling stream and the birds in the trees. Day one in *Isle of Mythos* and I'm already offered a grand quest. I just wanted to be able to stretch my legs for a bit before I took on the hard stuff. Just to make sure I don't screw anything up.

This is a once in a lifetime opportunity, though. I'd be a fool to turn down this chance.

Deep down, I know that I'm the man for the job. Solving problems is something I'm pretty good at. With the penalty trolls take just for being themselves, I know not many new players will choose that race even after the beta phase has ended. I may very well be the only shot they have at survival.

"I'll do it."

Chief Rizza wraps her arms around me in a firm embrace. She smells of spice, nothing like what I would imagine her to. I get the feeling that it is not very chiefly for her to hug me, but I don't fight it. She squeezes tight. I don't know if I have ever been hugged so hard in my life. Growing up, I was never hugged. Mom and Dad provided for me, they gave me everything I could possibly want, but were hesitant with affection. Whenever the newest video game system came out, I always had it first. When there were games that sold out day one, they could get me a copy. I drowned myself in my games, because the better I did in them, the more people followed me. They would comment on my streams, logging in simply for the entertainment of watching me. And the more trash I talked, the more they loved me.

When Taryn joined my stream, he didn't talk much, but damn was he good. It was a nice dynamic we had. He was the embodiment of the strong, silent type. No one would ever mistake him for a gamer, yet he was. And a damned good one. My viewers soared because not only did we entertain, we also won. His family didn't have a lot of money, so I always made sure I had an extra copy of any new game coming out.

"You will leave at dawn. Anything that we can provide for you on your journey, do not hesitate to ask. Tonight, we will celebrate finding our first hero in many generations!"

I'm not gonna lie, the prospect of a troll party has me excited.

"How will I know where to go?"

She raises her hand and places it against my temple. A tiny spark of energy flutters near my head and the next thing I know, the map in the corner of my vision has another layer over it. It looks like tiny cracks running along the map.

"What is that?"

"Those are magical currents. Ley lines. They travel underground. At certain locations, there are magical springs where raw magic filters into the air. These are usually the sites for temples and other magical buildings."

Looking at the ley lines around where my own location is marked, it's almost like looking at the central nervous system of the human body. Hundreds of veins branch out and break off, splitting from the main line that runs through the forest. I search the map and nowhere else on the island has such a concentration of ley lines. This place must have been something when they were active.

"Can I ask you something, Chief?"

"Of course."

"Why are there no male trolls inside the village?" It's been bothering me since I entered their lands.

"When our magic failed, we had to find ways to protect our way of life. The troll women have always held positions of power in our culture. We do not possess the ability to go into a rage like our male counterparts. We were blessed with something else, though: insight. For thousands of years, women would stay and raise the children and pass laws while the men were at war or off hunting. We each play to our strengths. For as long as our magical barriers have been down, our men have stood sentry at the perimeter, only coming back when it is absolutely necessary."

"That sounds terrible." I can't imagine being forced to guard a place indefinitely.

"We have all had to sacrifice, but tonight, we will toast to a new era. Perhaps even some of our brethren will join us."

I'm not quite prepared for what happens at the troll party. Before it begins, I spend most of the day roaming the forest and fighting what monsters I can find. The male trolls don't bother me this time. I guess word got out that I would be staying the night. They sit still as I pass by, statuesque guardians of the forest. When they are using Camouflage, I can still see them, perhaps because I am a troll as well, but they take on a translucent tone. Almost like looking at a ghost. When they move, their coloring returns. It's pretty wild to watch.

Slaying jackals and the occasional warthog, I manage to squeeze out a level before dusk hits and I have to return to the village center. My muscles seem to increase slightly due to the bonus points to Strength and Constitution I get each level for being a troll. I wonder if I will look like Gord by the time I reach level ten?

Only one more level until I am level five and can unlock Berserker Rage. I'd like to grind it out tonight, but I am so looking forward to watching these trolls get down. I've never been to a real party, only press events and launch parties, unless you count a Saturday with energy drinks and snack food with Taryn a party, which I'm sure most people don't.

I pass Gord on the way back to the village and he watches me out of the corner of his eye. I don't know what his problem is, but I don't stay to find out.

The village is lively by the time I return. I am greeted with a wooden mug filled with a frothy liquid. The gray-haired troll from the council smiles as she hands me the drink.

"I am Guilda. My son is the one who brought you here. He and his brother have been great protectors of our people for a long time. You are also our protector now. You have the support of the council, even Tormara, though she may not admit it."

I don't know what to say so I chug the frothy liquid. It is sweet, yet it also burns like the fires of hell. The burning sensation starts at my throat and creeps along my body all the way to my hands and feet. My extremities tingle, like tiny strikes of lightning igniting inside my body.

"Wow!" is all I can say.

"Sweetwater. It's a gift of the gods." She clinks her mug against mine and disappears into the crowd.

The female trolls dance and drink, while giant drums echo through the air, reverberating against my chest. Children play amongst the chaos, chasing small horned animals that I assume are pets. The wary glances I experienced earlier are gone, replaced by welcoming smiles. Just like that, these people have embraced me as their own. Now that I have their support, I can't let them down.

Chief Rizza spots me and comes over.

"Aren't you worried about people hearing you?" I ask.

"Humans do not travel into the forest at night. Without night vision, they are fearful of what hides in its depths. Make yourself at home and enjoy yourself, there is no doubt your journey will be fraught with peril." She touches her mug to mine and we both take a drink. The sweetness washes over me, followed by the burn and tingling, but this time, it burns a little less. My head buzzes slightly, and I can't seem to fight the smile that tugs at my face.

I've never drank alcohol before, but I love the taste of sweetwater. The burn isn't so bad, either.

The chief returns to the crowd, dancing and singing and taking drink after drink. Trolls definitely know how to hold their alcohol. Even Guilda is chugging it down like a frat boy on Saturday night. I make my way through the crowd and can't help but let the rhythm flow through me. The beating drums remind me of a ceremonial performance we once watched in school about Native American tribes.

Darkness descends, and several pyres are set up throughout the village center. The flames flicker and dance, making the festivities seem even more alive. Massive bugs the size of birds flutter through the air, their abdomens glowing and flashing like Christmas lights.

I find the shaman sitting on the steps of the same building where I saw him earlier. He watches the tribe intently, but doesn't seem to be having too much fun himself.

"Hi, I'm Chod. I saw you earlier, but you were meditating."

He looks up and our eyes meet. His pupils are a vibrant red and it's very unsettling to stare at them for long.

"I'm Jira. You witnessed me communing with my totem." He looks out into the crowd, watching their dancing bodies flutter through the night. "The closer I am to my totem, the more of its power I can channel."

"Why don't you go and restore the magic line then?" I ask.

He shrugs, his white-tipped dreads shuffling as he does. "What good would a ley line be if my people perished while I was away? Besides, magic does not clear an obstruction. Only brute force can do that."

"Then why not send Gord or any of the other male trolls?"

"Because we simply do not have the resources to spare. Our lives are hanging on by a thread as it is."

A young troll is running through the village and bumps into me, colliding with my leg and knocking herself to the ground. She giggles at me before standing up and running off into the night.

"Go and enjoy yourself, for I am old and need my rest."

He disappears into the hut, leaving me alone with my thoughts.

Several of the male trolls have returned from scouting. The women clear a space in the center and five of the males gather in a circle, Gord the largest among them. They let out a roar and the drum beats stop. Gord beats on his chest and a moment later, the other four do the same. They fall in line behind him, one beside the other. They bend their knees, slowly descending into a half-squat, their massive thighs displayed in all their glory. What happens next is a sight I will never forget.

In perfect unison, they all smack their legs at once, the sound echoing through the village. Then they smack the other leg, followed by a thunderous stomp and a deafening roar. They repeat this movement over and over, changing the sequence of stomps and slaps and roars. They roar like lions, and I see admiration in all who watch. The rhythm continues, musical madness composed of flesh and bone. It reminds me of a haka, the traditional war dance of the Maori people. I remember seeing it before a rugby game once on the television. But those players didn't have the same power as these trolls. As they dance, something in me resonates with it, wanting to join in.

With a final roar, the dance is over and there is clapping and cheering all around. The men are rewarded with sweetwater and slabs of warthog ribs.

Everyone is so excited by the performance that no one takes notice of the troll who stumbles through the crowd, blood dripping down his neck and shoulders, and collapses on the ground. He's covered in gashes and several arrows stick out of his back. One of his arms is charred up to the elbow.

I push through the crowd, making my way to the injured troll. Several others finally notice him and bend down to help him up. Somehow, I'm the one he makes eye contact with. My head buzzes as I try to process his words.

"We're under attack," he says, as a flaming arrow soars across the reflection in his eyes.

CHAPTER TEN

BLOOD AND STONE

A barrage of flaming arrows filters through the trees and shrubbery, igniting the night. The revelry is extinguished almost as quickly as it began, and nothing but sober faces surround me now. The panicked yells of women and children intermingle with the war cries of the few male trolls. Trees snap as trolls arm themselves with whatever weapons they can find.

In the depths of night, I hear the crack of branches and trees and wonder what chaos awaits.

"This is your fault," Gord roars at me. Caked earth falls from the tree trunk he holds.

"It can't be," argues Chief Rizza. Her eyes are wide with shock, taking in everything around us. "There is no way the ranger could have made it back in time for this to happen. This had to have already been planned. Regardless, there is no time to argue about it now. We must defend our homes. Guilda, gather the children. Everyone else, prepare for battle."

"Come on then, hero. Make yourself useful," Gord goads me.

I seriously don't understand what his problem is, but now is not the time.

I uproot a tree and take off into the battle behind him. Away from the pyres and burning huts, my night vision kicks into gear. In the depths of the forest, everything has a green hue to it. The occasional flaming arrow bursts through in a white blur. One hits me in the shoulder, and it burns like hell. Either it's coated with poison or I take extra damage from fire, because it hurts way more than the arrow that hit me earlier. I yank the arrow from my arm and toss it to the ground, leaving a wound which continues to sting long afterwards.

Battle rages all around me. Screams and grunts, along with the crunch of blunt force attacks, fill the air. I'm used to the clang of metal, not this. This is somehow worse. More brutal.

Whoever these men are, they came to wreak havoc. Most of them wear boiled leather armor, studded about the shoulders and chest. They carry bronze weapons, and most use wooden shields. Clearly, they are an organized militia, but more likely from a small town rather than a large keep. Dozens of torches glitter in the distance as they make their way forward. Many of the arrows have lodged high in the canopy of the surrounding trees, setting them ablaze and filling the night with the scent and crackling of the burning waxy leaves.

Gord rushes into the fight, not waiting a second to analyze the situation or formulate a game plan.

I survey the battlefield, seeing where I can be most useful. Dozens of mini skirmishes unfold all around me, one troll for every three or four humans. However you want to slice it, we're outnumbered. The trolls seem to be doing a good job of holding their own, even against such unfavorable odds.

The archers are peppering them with damage, though. There is the constant thwip of arrows sailing by and the occasional grunt when they make impact. Without shields, we only have our own tough skins for protection. Against normal arrows, we would be fine, but the fiery arrows are inflicting actual damage.

I need to find a way to get past the warriors and into the back lines. If I can somehow take out the archers, we might actually have a shot at saving the village.

I look for an opening to either side, but there's no way I can manage to sneak around with things as chaotic as they are. The rogue class is looking awfully good right about now.

Several men armed with spears and torches surround a troll to my right. An arrow shaft sticks out of his left bicep and he swings a club savagely at the spears closing in on him, brushing them aside. The spears offer the men a safe distance from the long reach of the troll. They scream words I can't understand and jab blazing torches more for effect than actual damage. Another arrow lodges in the troll's chest, and he shouts in pain. One of the spearmen jabs low, piercing the troll's calf and causing him to buckle at the knees. He tries to stand but can't put any weight on the leg.

I have to get in there and help him.

I take off running. At full speed, I collide with the offending spearman, knocking him to the ground and smashing the end of my club into his face. Notifications pop across my vision, but I ignore them and they fade into the background, barely noticeable.

The wounded troll is unable to stand, but scoots against a tree so that his back is protected. I toss him the dead man's spear and we make eye contact briefly. Anger burns in his eyes. At least with the spear, he can fight from the ground if he has to.

I'll do my best to make sure they pay. A spear jabs at my throat, but I smack it out of the way and unleash a powerful kick, sending my attacker to the ground. He gasps for air and I turn to face the final spearman, but he has already retreated. Turning back to the man on the ground, I don't listen to his cries for mercy as I stomp his head into the earth.

"Can you hold your own?" I kneel before the wounded troll.

"I will be fine. Help the others."

A sharp pain flares in my back and I turn to see a bloody sword about to pierce me again. I dodge at the last moment, leaving my opponent swiping at air.

"Big mistake."

He attacks again with a quick slash and the blade lodges against my club. I jerk hard and his weak human arms are unable to keep a grip on his weapon. A flick of my wrist and the sword comes free, sailing into the night.

He holds up his shield in defense and it splinters under the blow of my club, shattering the bones in his forearm. His arm hangs limp, unable to let go of the rickety shield still strapped to it.

I'm up to twenty rage, but I don't need to use it. Not yet.

The man screams like a child, and then he screams no more.

So much of the forest is ablaze that I am worried the village may burn to the ground if we do not stop this carnage soon.

I spot Tormara in the distance, her red braid swishing through the air, almost alive. The female trolls fight much differently than the males. They attack with speed and grace, not power. She holds a stone dagger in each hand and sparks fly as it clashes, pieces of stone flaking off against the metal sword. She parries the sword to the side and slides the other dagger into the man's neck.

The chief must be somewhere among the madness, but I don't have time to search for her. I still need to stop the archers.

Ahead of me, a dozen men with swords and shields surround one of the trolls I saw earlier on my walk. He's level six and not much bigger than me. He keeps the warriors at bay by swinging a large club, but they are closing in.

Gord comes out of nowhere, his body covered in red blood. Human blood. He rushes to his comrade's defense, knocking two men to the ground with a single blow. The other troll takes action and the two are able to hold their ground, backs to back. The swordsmen move in, five on each side, but are unable to press any further.

The two sides are at a stalemate. The men are wary to move any closer, and the trolls are afraid to give up their position of strength. Their hand is forced when a volley of flaming arrows rain down upon the two trolls.

Gord and his partner cry out in pain, and the humans use the opportunity to attack. They land several blows before Gord swings out blindly, connecting his club with one man's head and dropping him instantly.

I can't just sit by. I need to help.

Using Intimidation, I release my battle cry and join the fray. The men look confused and sway back and forth for a moment, unable to attack. With our foes momentarily dazed, I help Gord and the other troll pull the arrows from their bodies just in time for our opponents to regain their senses.

"Keep our backs together," I say.

"I will give the orders here!" shouts Gord. He cracks his knuckles. "Keep our backs together."

I suppress the smile that I know will turn into laughter if I let it escape.

Three more men join and once again, twelve surround us. They range from level four to ten, but I can't really pick and choose who I want to fight. I'll take whoever attacks first.

"We need to end this before they attack with more arrows," I say.

"Arrows do not frighten me," Gord says, but I can tell he is favoring the side where I just removed six arrows.

"We can't stand here all day!"

"Fine, give me your club."

I don't know what he has planned, but I do as he says, mostly because I'd like to be fighting together and not with each other and the humans.

He takes it and hurls it like a boomerang at the men closest to him. It collides with two of them, knocking them unconscious.

"Attack!" yells Gord.

The men are so surprised that we actually get in a few good hits before they react. I use Claw and rip out the throat of the man closest to me. He collapses while his heart continues to pump several streams of blood onto his fellow soldiers.

A sharp blade pierces my side and I kick out in that direction, feeling the crunch of bones beneath my foot. I don't have time to plan my attacks, so I flail and claw and kick anyone unlucky enough to step in my direction. It's not pretty, but it gets the job done. A moment later, it's only the three of us still standing.

"We need to get the archers," I try to tell Gord, but his eyes are fixed on something in the distance.

"Him." He points. "He brought this on us."

A man marches forward from the line of archers. There is nothing remarkable about him, but I can tell that he is a cut above the rest of the soldiers. For starters, he wears chainmail and carries a sword made of steel. A silver helm with a ruby set in the brow catches the light from the fires that rage around us. His armor is a hodgepodge, with no two pieces belonging together. Two separate bracers shield his forearms, one silver and one black. He carries a golden shield engraved with a raven.

Didn't anyone ever tell this clown you don't wear silver and gold together?

"Who is this guy?" I ask.

"He is the one they call a hero. Many times, he has come into our lands and many times, he has been slain." Gord growls. "Today will be no exception."

He shouts something as he walks, but it is all gibberish to me. There is no doubt in my mind that this man is a real player. No one else would ever dare to look so stupid on the battlefield.

I focus on him and his stats appear.

Glenn Orickson

Level 14

Warrior

Human

What's left of his men have retreated behind the archers. Many are injured, with only the archers coming through unscathed. At level fourteen, he is the highest level of anyone in the battle and would undoubtedly kick my ass. Gord seems anxious to have a go at him.

A large level nine troll charges at Glenn, stone club in hand. Glenn takes a battle stance and a yellow aura surrounds his body. The sword connects with the club and a violent arc of lightning lashes out, striking the troll and stunning him in place. The gasp from those surrounding me sounds like a thousand hissing snakes.

Glenn lets out a cruel laugh. It needs no translation. Then he pushes his sword into the troll's throat.

"Ramu!" cries Gord, mourning his fallen brother. "He has never attacked like that. The undying one has grown stronger since our last battle. I must avenge Ramu."

I grab him by the arm. As big of a dick as Gord has been, if he goes out there, Glenn will kill him.

"Unhand me!" He shakes his arm free.

"If you go out there, he will kill you."

"If I don't go, he will kill us all."

Gord is one of the strongest trolls I've met. The village needs him. I can't let him die.

"Let me go. If I die, I will return. You won't."

A fierce struggle rages behind Gord's eyes as he wrestles with his intelligence and his pride.

"Then I will die." He picks up a fallen club and sets out in search of Glenn, a loud roar erupting and setting his challenge in stone.

A smile flits across Glenn's face. There is history between these two.

The remaining skirmishes have all but dissolved and both sides now watch intently at the match before us. Several trolls lie dead, but far more humans. With the troll population shrinking as it is, this battle could prove to be catastrophic. I don't know how Gord can win this. If he dies, I fear his people die with him. I may very well be the last forest troll by the end of the night.

If only there was something I could do. I'm a hero, but I'm outclassed by the NPCs all around me.

Gord is almost to where Ramu died when Glenn takes a defensive stance. He sheathes his sword and holds firm behind his shield. What in the hell is he doing?

A silver sheen runs across the shield and when Gord attacks, there is an explosion like fireworks. It tosses Gord back nearly ten feet, sparks raining down around him.

All around us, the forest continues to burn.

Glenn pulls his sword and his laughter rings through the forest. It's almost maniacal. He's walking towards Gord, a yellow aura surrounding his sword, when I hear a flutter of wings pass by me.

Crimson wings, almost black in places, glide through the underbelly of the forest. As fast as it appeared, there is a puff of feathers and the giant bird morphs into Jira, the shaman.

Glenn takes notice and halts his approach towards Gord.

Jira stands proud, his white-tipped dreadlocks swaying around his shoulders.

Glenn raises his sword and charges Jira. I sure hope he knows what he is doing.

Jira stretches his arms wide and the forest goes silent. Even the crackle of fire disappears. His hands connect with a thunderous clap and flames spark from inside. The fiery tips of the archer's arrows and the flames that dance in the trees disappear, causing red streams of light to streak across the battlefield towards Jira. A flaming bird rushes out of the shaman's chest, screeching. It dives for Glenn, pecking and clawing and scorching. He screams in agony, the fiery phoenix burning him alive.

The archers abandon ranks and run.

"After them!" Chief Rizza's voice cuts through the chaos.

Gord is on his feet, club in hand, running at Glenn. I take off after the fleeing archers and leave him and Jira to their vengeance.

CHAPTER ELEVEN
PEACEMAKER

There's no trace of the fires that raged through the forest only moments before. Whatever magic Jira used sucked every flame from the surrounding forest. I still can't believe the power of that attack. The fiery phoenix attacked Glenn like a bat out of hell. It makes me wish that magic among trolls wasn't so rare.

Speaking of Glenn, I return to find his gear stacked next to a larger pile of weapons and armor stripped from the humans. His body is nowhere to be found. The bodies of the fallen soldiers are being piled atop one another. Not a single human survived. Our night vision made the task of tracking them through the woods child's play.

Four trolls lay side by side on the scorched earth. Jira stands over their bodies, whispering silently.

Chief Rizza rubs ash across each of their foreheads, some ritual I have no knowledge of.

"The undying one will return. He grows stronger each time, but this is the first we have heard of him using magic," she says.

It won't be the last. I don't say it aloud, but I think they know it, too. There is no doubt that Glenn has been questing. His assortment of armor, his abilities, I'm going to need to hit the ground running if I'm going to have a chance at defending this village. He's already eleven levels ahead of me. Well, ten after his death. How can I be a hero if I can't even fight my own battles?

Jira finishes his chant and turns to the chief. There is a heaviness about his crimson eyes. A heaviness I'm sure the trolls have experienced far too often.

"I'm sorry I failed you," he says to the lifeless trolls. "I was deep in sleep when I heard the chaos. Old age has its pitfalls, but I never thought sleeping would lead to the death of my brothers and sisters."

"It is not your fault, brother," says Chief Rizza. "We were attacked unaware. We will have time before the undying one tries our village again, but it is all the more reason magic must be restored soon. The night benefited us this time. It may not be so kind again."

I look over the bodies, but I don't see Glenn's anywhere.

"Where is his body?" I ask.

"The only thing heroes leave behind when they die are their belongings." She tosses a bracer among the pile of looted armor. "We will add these to the stock from previous attacks. Perhaps we will have enough to work into weapons of our own."

"What now?"

Chief Rizza looks at the pile of bodies. "We will burn the dead enemies, and then we will mourn our own. You will leave first thing in the morning. Help where you can. I have business to attend to." With a flip of her braid, she is gone.

I suddenly remember all of the notifications I dismissed during the battle. I focus on recalling them and they appear in the left of my vision.

Congratulations! You have reached level 5. +1 stat point to distribute. +1 Strength and Constitution racial bonus. +1 ability point to distribute.

Congratulations! You have reached level 6. +1 stat point to distribute. +1 Strength and Constitution racial bonus.

Warning! *You have killed a human NPC. If word of this reaches a human settlement, your reputation among humans will be decreased by 100. Stop your enemies from reaching town before it is too late. Current reputation with humans: -999. (-1000 Racial Penalty)*

Warning! *You have killed a human NPC. If word of this reaches a human settlement, your reputation among humans will be decreased by 100. Stop your enemies from reaching town before it is too late. Current reputation with humans: -999. (-1000 Racial Penalty)*

Warning! *You have killed a human NPC. If word of this reaches a human settlement, your reputation among humans will be decreased by 100. Stop your enemies from reaching town before it is too late. Current reputation with humans: -999. (-1000 Racial Penalty)*

Warning! *You have killed a human NPC. If word of this reaches a human settlement, your reputation among humans will be decreased by 100. Stop your enemies from reaching town before it is too late. Current reputation with humans: -999. (-1000 Racial Penalty)*

Alert! *You have failed to stop your enemies from reaching town. Your reputation has decreased by 400. Current reputation with humans: -1399. (-1000 Racial Penalty)*

What the hell!? We killed all of the soldiers. Not a single one escaped. There is no way I should have lost that reputation. Then, I remember.

Glenn.

Fucking Glenn has become a serious thorn in my side. One that I'm not likely to get rid of any time soon.

I pull up my stats and look them over.

Strength: 23

Dexterity: 15

Constitution: 24

Intelligence: 7

Wisdom: 10

Charisma: 6

My Strength and Constitution are really improving thanks to my racial bonus every level. I feel much stronger and healthier than I did earlier in the day. My loin-cloth even seems to fit a little tighter around my waist.

I now have five stat points to distribute, but I'm still unsure if I should put any into non-physical stats, so I hold off for now. What I'm really excited about is my new ability point. I don't even hesitate to use it on Berserker Rage.

Berserker Rage. *(Ultimate.) Attacks and physical damage build your rage meter. 5 rage per attack. Rage meter deteriorates over time when out of combat at a rate of 5 rage per second. Once the meter is full, Berserker Rage becomes available. For 30 seconds, rage meter is full, deal increased damage, health regenerates at 5x the normal rate, cannot be stunned, slowed or otherwise affected.*

I can't wait to test out this bad boy in battle.

"Make yourself useful," says Gord. He scowls at me as he tosses a body onto the pile.

"What's your problem, asshole?" I challenge. He really makes me wish I had more than two middle fingers to point in his direction. I've had enough of this guy thinking he can boss me around. "You've been nothing but a giant dick to me since I got here. What gives?"

He's in my face quicker than I expect, saliva raining down on me as he yells, hot breath assaulting my face.

His voice is a growl when he speaks. "You come here and think just because you have green skin that it makes you one of us? You are no more one of us than the men who attacked. Ramu and I grew up together. We hunted and battled together. We have fought off countless attacks like today. Just because you can't die, do you think that makes you special? That I should respect you because the chief gives you a special mission?" He puts his finger against my chest and I feel his heated tempera-ture radiating through it. "You are nothing."

"That's enough, Gord." Jira's raspy voice comes between us. "Leave the boy be. Chod, come with me."

I follow Jira back towards the village. Thoughts of pushing Gord off a high ledge run through my mind. He has the charm and charisma of a burning orphanage.

"You have to forgive Gord, he has always been spirited. He lost his father at a young age to an attack and has been distrusting of outsiders ever since."

That makes a lot of sense, but it still doesn't excuse his dickish behavior.

"I would think he would be grateful for any help he could get." I don't owe anything to these people. I'm agreeing to help because they got a shitty lot, and if I don't help, no one else will. A little gratitude would be nice.

"Give it time. Chief Rizza knows we are lucky to have you. I do as well. Gord doesn't yet know the power of heroes. Besides, I think he may feel a bit threatened by you."

"By me? Gord is, like, ten times stronger than I am. Why would he possibly feel threatened by me?"

"Think about it. You come into our lands, commit a crime anyone else would be punished for, and end up receiving a quest and falling into the chief's good graces."

Damn. I hadn't even thought of it that way. Nobody likes a person who has everything handed to them. He doesn't know that I'm here as a punishment, that the very reason I am here is because I didn't have Mom and Dad bail me out. Or did I? I could be in prison right now, but instead, I'm playing a game for thirty days because of a favor they called in.

Back in the village, Guilda reunites the children with their parents. I'd like to think that something like that would frighten the young ones, but judging by the looks on their faces, they don't seem too upset. Is it their natural troll resilience or the fact that they have seen this type of thing way too often?

Many of the huts are charred in places, but for the most part, they are okay. The fact that they are living homes means that it wasn't just dried timber that caught fire. Living things are harder to burn.

"That's enough excitement for one night, children. Everyone to bed." Guilda says it kindly, escorting children to and fro. She's like the nurturing grandmother who can bench press a truck.

I don't really know that there is too much more for me to help with. The funeral pyre has already begun for our attackers, and I'm not sure what will be done with the fallen trolls. I have a long day ahead of me tomorrow, so it's probably best if I rest for the night.

"You can stay in Ramu's hut for the night until we find you someplace more permanent," Guilda offers.

"Are you sure?" Something feels wrong about staying in the hut of a dead troll. I'm positive Gord will have something to say about it, but it's not like I can really argue. Guilda is on the council after all.

Stepping into the hut is a bit unsettling, like when people die in real life and they still leave behind their social media profiles. They're just there, forever, like nothing ever happened. Their pictures still smile, and the funny cat video still plays when you scroll over it. This room makes me feel like that.

A small wooden toy sits on a bedside table. I pick it up and notice it's a carving of a troll, very intricate and detailed. Heavier than I would have thought. The contours of its muscles and the loincloth are textured. He holds a tiny club in his hand. Whoever did this had skill.

A leather blanket covers a wooden pallet used as a bed. It's a step down from my pillowtop mattress, but I have a feeling that with my new body, I could sleep on a rock and not really notice. The room is all very rudimentary, but kind of endearing in a way.

I try not to think about Ramu, about what kind of troll he was. If he carved the troll or if it was a gift. Who he was giving it to or who had given it to him. I'll think of him as a video game character who died in a battle, not as someone who lived a life long before I ever got here.

Laying down on the pallet, I realize this is my first night sleeping in *Isle of Mythos*. My first night of full immersion. Somewhere out there, tiny nanites are cleaning my body and making me experience all of this like I'm really here. Whenever this game is ready to launch, it's going to be a worldwide hit. There's no doubt about it.

I don't recall falling asleep, but I wake up to the beating of drums. When I step outside, the bodies of the four dead trolls each have their own funeral pyre in the middle of the village.

The bodies are about three feet off the ground, covered in an assortment of brightly-colored flowers. Their fragrant aroma fills the air along with the musk of incense. Nobody says anything as Chief Rizza circles the pyres holding a torch.

"Ramu, son of Redma. Uhmi, daughter of Ezra. Hethe, son of Teja. Yavo, son of Zalma. You gave your lives for our village. For our people. We will see you in the next life."

There is a loud stomp that echoes from everyone, and they smack their fists against their hearts. I'm the only one who doesn't do it. Part of what Gord says rings true—I am an outsider. A foreigner to my own people. Chief Rizza ignites the kindling around the feet of each pyre and the bodies are engulfed in flame.

We all stand in silence as the fires crackle and burn, incinerating the bodies of the four trolls. They burn hot and bright, disguising what happens beneath the flames. When the fires begin to die, trolls disperse to their everyday jobs. Gord cuts his eyes at me as he makes his way into the forest.

"I have a few parting gifts to help you with your journey before you go," says Chief Rizza.

She leads me into the temple where I first saw Jira. The smell of incense is as strong as ever and several wooden bowls send off blue and purple smoke that rises to the ceiling. Jira stands over a chest covered in furs.

"It has been too long since we have been able to craft with magic, but we still have a few items from the old days. I pray that they will help you on your quest." He moves the furs aside, revealing a dark chest complete with gold latches and studded with precious stones.

It's the most non-troll thing I've seen since I came here. Rizza pulls a key from her pocket and hands it to Jira. He opens the chest and the lid falls back with a thud.

He pulls out a dark crimson feather. It's almost black near the center and gradually fades into red tips. I focus on it and its stats display in the edge of my vision.

Item. Phoenix Feather. 10% resistance to fire-based attacks. *A very rare item, phoenix feathers can only be gathered if they are willingly given by the host. Feathers plucked from unwilling birds turn to ash.*

"As you know, trolls are very resilient, but we take more damage from fire than most races. I don't know what you will face on your journey, but this should prove helpful if you come across any humans. They have a strange fascination with fire." Jira hands the feather to Chief Rizza, and she ties it into the bottom of my braid.

Next, he pulls out a necklace. It is basically a long leather strap with a polished stone attached to it. The stone is a rusty brown with streaks of gold going through it.

Item. Tiger's Eye Pendant. Removes one debuff. Cooldown: 10 minutes. *A rare stone believed to ward off evil and bring balance to life.*

Chief Rizza takes the necklace and ties it around my neck.

"Trolls are not known as great metalworkers or weaponsmiths. Mostly, we use our own powerful bodies and sharp claws and they serve us well, but the time may come when you need a weapon. This one has been passed down for many generations." Jira reaches in the box and pulls out a glittering double-edged battle-axe. The handle has several engravings that run along its edges and three empty sockets where stones once sat. "Long ago, before the trolls were so despised, this axe was given to the great troll warrior, Gohma, by the dwarven weaponsmith, Kerrus Silverhammer. It has several sockets that can be set with enchanted stones to make the weapon stronger. It is a weapon fit for a hero. Its name is Peacemaker."

Item. Peacemaker. An enchanted battle-axe capable of taking on the properties of up to 3 attached stones. +3 Strength. A relic from another age given as a symbol of peace and fortune among allies.

From the bottom of the chest, Jira pulls out several green and red vials and places them in a small leather pouch.

"These should help if you fall into trouble."

Item. Health Potion. Restores 100 HP over 10 seconds. X5

Item. Potion of Greater Stamina. Increases stamina for 5 minutes. X3

Item. Potion of Greater Resilience. Increases total HP by 10% for 5 minutes. X3

He closes the lid and covers the chest. I have the feeling there are more items inside that I couldn't see.

"Oh, and one more thing." He hands me a large satchel. It's filled with pouches and compartments and has an actual leather strap for carrying. "The bag you were carrying looked like it was made by a child. Your leather skills definitely need some work. Perhaps when you return, Ahso can take you under her wing. Unfortunately, this is all we can offer you for now. Anything else you need you must find along the way."

"Now, come," says the chief. "I will walk you to our borders and see you off."

I'm not sure exactly where the village border ends or how to tell, but Chief Rizza comes to a stop and I know this is where we say our good-byes. In such a short time, I feel like I've already grown attached to the place and to the people. All except for Gord, he can sit on a pointy stick for all I care. It's going to be an adventure, but at least I feel like I have something worth fighting for.

"Good luck, Chod. You are our hero now. The fate of the village depends on you. Once you reach the obstruction and clear it, return here at once." With a quick turn, her braid whips through the air and I'm left watching as she walks away.

I thought she was supposed to be watching me go.

"Chief Rizza," I call out and she turns her head. "How will I know how to clear the obstruction?"

"I cannot answer that. We don't know what has stopped the flow of magic, but I have no doubt you will figure it out."

Looking at my map, my destination feels far away.

CHAPTER TWELVE

MUCK IT UP

Peacemaker is a massive axe, even by troll standards. So big that I can't imagine a human being able to lift it. It cuts through branches and vines with ease as I noisily make my way through the forest. Even after all these years, the blade has remained sharp.

The three sockets that run down the side of the handle are what really interest me. The item description says that it takes on the properties of whatever magical stones are inserted in them. The power of this axe is only limited by the enchanted stones I am able to find. My mind runs wild with possibilities of an axe that deals fire damage or increases my movement speed even further, making me a giant fucking ninja troll.

I need to find out where the stones are.

Unfortunately, I don't know anything about enchanted stones or how to find them, and neither Jira nor the chief seemed too concerned about telling me. There could be a million different ways of getting them. Dungeons, quests, special monsters. If only I wasn't bound by my bad reputation and the ability to speak only one language, then I could ask one of the more magically inclined races.

As it is, I'm on my own.

I'm minding my own business, walking through the forest, when something hits me in the side of the face with a splat. My health drops by a tick and a cool gooey substance slowly slides down my face and falls to the ground. The mud-like substance moves across the forest floor like some sentient mud pie and disappears into an even larger pool of goo.

Sludge. *Level 8. Though not the smartest of creatures, sludges are hard to kill and even harder to get your hands on. They can only be destroyed by killing the core, which can move to any part of its body. Some are even known to hide poisonous stingers beneath their slimy exterior.*

"Can't a guy just walk in peace?" I ask the sludge, but there is no response, just a dull gurgle from inside.

Instead, a ghost-like pile of sludge rises from the pool and tosses another mud pie at me.

"Alright, you walking pile of diarrhea, let's go!" I take off after the sludge, but immediately notice I'm moving slower. My normal troll movements that I've grown accustomed to feel almost...human. I pull up the notifications from the background to see what is going on.

Alert! *You have been slowed. Movement and attack speed reduced by 50%.*

Well, that's annoying. Another mud pie comes whizzing by. I attempt to dodge it, but the debuff makes it impossible for me to move out of the way and it hits me in the chest, turning my green skin a murky brown.

Remembering the Tiger's Eye Pendant that Jira gave to me, I mentally activate its ability, removing the slow, and immediately move faster. The sludge tosses another mud pie, but this time, it sails over my shoulder as I shift to the side. I can't get hit again because the cooldown on the pendant is ten minutes.

I cover the distance between me and the sludge in a few quick steps and bring down my axe with a mighty swing. It cuts through the sludge but does no damage at all. Instead, the sludge seems to move around the blade, almost as if it's cutting through water.

"You have got to be kidding me. How am I supposed to kill something I can't hit?"

A long, scorpion-like tail rises from behind the sludge and strikes at me like a cobra. I jump to the side and it whirs through the air where I had just stood. Something hard and metallic protrudes from the end of the tail.

A stinger!

It strikes again, and I swipe at it with my axe, severing the tail. The stinger falls to the ground and crawls back to the host.

I have no idea how I am supposed to kill this thing when it can separate at will.

The damage I've taken has given me enough rage to use Intimidation. I let out a roar, expecting to confuse the sludge, but nothing happens. It rises as tall as me and six tentacles sprout out, assaulting me with mud balls. Unable to dodge them all, several of them hit me, slowing me and dropping my health down to seventy percent. Little by little, they are wearing me down. I might just have to say screw it and bail.

While I am still slowed, the sludge shrinks back down, retracting its multiple arms. Its stinger rises in the air and hovers like a snake about to strike.

Pain runs through my chest as the stinger penetrates my skin. Ten percent of my health vanishes instantly. My HP continues to drop as a throbbing pain traces from the wound and down my right arm.

Poison.

If only I hadn't wasted my pendant's ability, I could cleanse the poison. I grab one of the health potions from my bag and down it in one gulp. It battles with the poison as my health drops and rises, drops and rises, caught in a tide of life and death.

Another barrage of mud flies into me, dropping my health by a chunk. I take the other two health potions and my health begins to recover faster than the poison can drain me.

Moving at a snail's pace, I'm still unable to dodge the incoming stinger and pain flares through my left shoulder.

I'm about to die to a soggy turd alone in the forest. If I had invested points into Iron Will, then I could at least null the effects of the slow for long enough to run away. As it is, I'm pretty sure the sludge could chase me down if I tried to run.

Then I remember. *Berserker Rage.*

I activate the ability, and immediately the slow disappears and the poison vanishes from my system. My health ticks up and my muscles seem to pulse with power.

I hack at the sludge with violent enthusiasm. The edge of my vision glows red, which I assume is a side effect of full rage. I hack and slash at the amorphous blob, separating it into delicious-looking nougats that flutter around the forest floor. The stinger rises again, but I cut it down before it can attack and punt it deep into the forest. I continue to chop like a lumberjack on cocaine, but somehow, I'm unable to locate the sludge's core. With no way to beat the creature, I take off running into the woods before my rage wears off.

Sometimes you just have to know when to bail. As much as I would have loved to spend all day cutting chocolate, I have a quest to complete.

I wasted all three health potions for no reward, but at least I'm still alive.

I make it a few miles before I hear a rustle in the bushes and a lone wolf steps out into my path. Finally, something I can actually kill, hopefully quickly, and be on my way.

Forest Wolf. *Level 7. Quick and powerful, a wolf is not to be trifled with.*

The beast snarls, revealing a set of sharp teeth intent on seeing just how tough my troll skin is.

"Let's dance," I goad the wolf, but as soon as the words leave my mouth, two more wolves emerge from the bush.

Just my luck.

I don't wait for the pack to surround me. I attack with a mighty slash that gashes the first wolf on the shoulder. He yelps in pain and the other two wolves bite at my ankles. My health dips and dark blue blood streaks down my feet and stains the forest floor.

Before I know what is happening, a fourth wolf pounces me from behind and a sharp pain flares through my shoulder as it sinks its teeth in.

Without thinking, I grab the beast by its neck and throw it into a nearby tree. It collapses to the ground and sways back and forth as it tries to regain its footing.

At four against one, the odds are not in my favor. Not that they ever will be in this game. I've lost twenty percent of my health from the three attacks, but it's already regenerating.

I swing my axe back and forth in an arc in front of me, keeping the wolves at bay while I attempt to come up with a plan. I only have twenty rage at the moment, but that is enough to use Intimidation. I roar, and the wolves' eyes roll in opposite directions, confused.

With a sweeping strike, I manage to hit all three wolves in one blow, gaining me fifteen rage off one attack. I use Bite and Claw at once, sinking my teeth into the middle wolf's neck while simultaneously raking my claws across its chest. When I toss it aside, it doesn't get up.

The confusion wears off, and the other two wolves attack just as the dazed wolf that bit my shoulder regains its footing. My axe catches one wolf as he lunges and scores a critical hit to his head, but the other manages to bite me in the side. It lets go and retreats just as I reach for it.

My body stings all over from the attacks and I find it hard to focus.

Shaking my head, I push the pain to the back of my mind. If I die, I'll probably lose all the items that they gave me. What kind of hero would I be if that happened?

Taking a step back, I try to assess the situation. Just because I can take the damage they are dishing out, it doesn't mean I have to. The wolves come forward and begin circling around me. If I let them, they'll attack from my blind side and try to weaken me that way.

I take a stamina and strength potion, close my eyes, and listen. Their heavy breathing is the closest thing to me, so I try to pinpoint it. There's an intake of air behind me just before I feel a stabbing pain in my calf. I open my eyes and kick out, but the wolf has already returned to circling. Another wolf digs into my other leg as I turn away and it retreats just as quickly.

Hot blood trickles down my leg, no doubt increasing the fervor of the wolves. I push it away and close my eyes again, listening to their breathing. My heart pounds in response to the two potions.

The intake of breath gives away the attack and I turn, slashing my axe through the air like a pro golfer. It connects with the wolf's jaw, splitting it in two. I'm not quick enough to stop the counter-attack on my rear, but I'm down to two wolves and fifty percent HP.

I repeat the process until only the final wolf remains. We square off in front of each other, the final showdown.

I'll give it to the guy, he has some major balls staying around after watching three of his pack sliced to pieces.

I make the first move this time, attacking with an overhead swing. The wolf is surprisingly fast and darts out of the way. He lunges and takes a bite of my arm before I can regain my balance. His teeth sink into me as he shakes his head back and forth. It hurts like a bitch, but I use Claw against his snout and he sets me free.

The wolf licks his muzzle, tasting both my blood and his that has caked into its silver fur, and lets out a huff. He eyes me intently and begins circling once again.

"I've had about enough of your shit," I say.

I feint a swing of my axe and the wolf moves to the side, but I'm already prepared for his movement and spin to the other side, bringing the axe down in a beautiful arc that connects with his side, ripping the remaining life out of him.

Congratulations! You have reached level 7. +1 stat point to distribute. +1 Strength and Constitution racial bonus. +1 ability point to distribute.

I notice that when I look at my abilities now, there is a new tab for melee weapons. It must be because I have Peacemaker equipped.

Sweeping Slash. *Form a sweeping arc in front of you, dealing damage and knocking your opponent off balance. Cost: 5 rage.*

Cleave. *Your next attack causes bleed damage, dealing 1% of opponent's health per second for 5 seconds. Cost: 10 rage.*

Battle Cry. *You let out a ferocious roar, increasing Rage by 20. No Cost. Cooldown: 60 seconds.*

Thinking back on my fight with the wolves, I elect to put my new ability point into Sweeping Slash. Battle Cry is a nice way to get the upper hand early, but due to my natural tankiness, I can increase my rage simply by taking damage. Having an ability that knocks opponents back is a great defensive maneuver and may come in handy if I find myself surrounded again.

I'm feeling pretty good about myself after taking on four wolves and the lowest they got me to was half-health. By the time this quest is over, I should be leveled up nicely.

After looting pelts from the wolves, I pull up my map and find the location Chief Rizza marked for me. Focusing on the overlay, I'm able to see the ley lines that run beneath the surface. She did say she wasn't exactly sure where the obstruction was, but at least was able to pinpoint the source of the ley line that leads into the forest. The cause of the obstruction could be anywhere between here and there. I just hope it's something visible so I don't walk past it.

By the looks of it, it will take me several days to get to my destination. Two human settlements stand in my way, and unless I want to divert my course and go around them, I will have to thread the needle and hope I don't get caught. Since I don't know the exact location, I can't really afford to take any detours.

I am Dorothy and the ley lines are my yellow brick road. Let's just hope the flying monkeys stay away.

CHAPTER THIRTEEN

WALKING, WALKING, AND MORE WALKING

The first settlement isn't anything special. It's a typical medieval town complete with spiked wooden palisade and several soldiers standing around the entrance. What lies inside is a mystery because I don't feel like dying, and with a negative thirteen hundred and ninety-nine reputation, I will be attacked on sight. Still, I watch them, wondering what could have been if I were a less hated race.

People come and go. There is a road system where farmers and other traders travel on horses and in wagons. A man wearing full plate armor and a plumed helmet sits in a wagon with some reptilian horned creature tied to the back of it. The creature doesn't appear to be moving.

Could that be another real player? He doesn't look as stupid as Glenn in his mismatched armor, but it's a damned knight riding in a wagon. I have to assume anything as ridiculous as this is the product of player ingenuity.

I try to focus on him to see his stats, but he's too far away.

Something cracks behind me, but when I turn to see the source of the noise, nothing is there. It's enough to remind me that I shouldn't be so close to human settlements. I grab my bag and my axe and set off away from the town. If I go at least a mile, I should be far enough away that no one will see me.

A beautiful sunny day waits for me outside of the tree line, but I'm nervous to leave the forest. It's the only area I've been a part of since logging in to *Isle of Mythos*. As silly as it seems, it feels like home. Out there, in the open, I'll have a massive target on my back. An even more massive target on my back. And in here, I won't have Taryn to watch my back.

I stall for a moment, slaughtering a few rabbits and filling my belly while I still have the cover of the trees. After eating the roasted boar at the celebration, the rabbits don't taste as delicious as before. They are still serviceable, and it's nice to not have to worry about learning a cooking skill.

When I step out into the open, I feel naked, and not just because the crisp morning air is brushing against my undercarriage. In spite of my tough skin and hulking physique, I feel as vulnerable as I did at school when I had to walk up on stage once to accept an award for placing in a gaming tournament. All eyes were on me, but I kept mine focused on the floor, so worried I might trip and make a fool of myself. I didn't realize until later that my fly had been open the entire time and pictures of my exposed boxers were doing the rounds on social media. I need to get my head in the game. There are more painful things than being called 'Ballsy McChadwick' out here.

I take a deep breath and set out towards my destination. A golden field stretches before me, dotted with wild animals running through it. If I had the time and desire, I could level up nicely out here. An assortment of deer and bison roam freely, but I don't want to spend any more time in the open than I have to. It's too close to the humans for my liking. I cross the dirt road that splits the field in a hurry a half-second after a wagon approaches on the horizon.

At full speed, I rush through the field until I can no longer see the road or the town.

The other settlement is still a few miles from my location so if I stay on my current route, I should be able to avoid it entirely. Once I make it through the field, there is another stretch of woods that leads to the base of the mountain where the ley line begins.

Magic. I can't wait to see what happens to the troll village once magic returns. So far, the only magic I've seen has been from Jira and Glenn. Glenn's was brutal, up-close, and personal, while Jira's was simply amazing to watch. I'll never really get to experience it, but at least I have Peacemaker and with a little luck, I might be able to find some magical stones.

The sun is starting to fade across the horizon, turning the blue sky to shades of lilac and tangerine. With my night vision, I will be able to travel well by night and plan to cut out a day's travel, making it to the obstruction by tomorrow evening.

Eventually, the sun falls off the horizon and my nightvision takes over. New animals and monsters appear all around me. I avoid them as best I can, but one time, a lone gnoll attacks me when I step too close to his den. The humanoid hyena's primitive wooden spear is no match for Peacemaker. I see the glowing eyes of several other gnolls in the darkness, but they leave me be after that.

Several hours into the night, a notification flashes across my vision.

Warning! *Your body needs rest. If you do not sleep within the next two hours, your stamina, strength, and health regeneration will be greatly reduced. Recommended sleep: 6 hours.*

Well, that blows. I thought I was going to be able to travel all night. I wonder if the sleep requirement is because of the full immersion. Maybe my mind still needs a rest in order to function properly.

I travel for another hour before finding a place to camp for the night. A river that runs down from the mountain rushes before me. Several trees line the banks, and rapids form around the rocky underbelly. There's not a bridge as far as I can see, so I elect to cross through the frigid water. The current is swift, but I find a location where I can still see the bottom and cross over. My massive frame weighs me down and even though the water pounds me, my feet remain secure.

Once on the other side, there is a thicket of bushes where I set up camp for the night. I tuck my belongings underneath the bush and not long after, Camouflage sets in.

Owls hoot in the distance and frogs croak amongst the reeds that adorn the river's edge. Somewhere far off, beasts howl into the night. With the nighttime melody, it doesn't take long for me to fall asleep.

I awake with a start as two bulging yellow eyes struggle in front of me while tiny hands vigorously try to remove the pendant from around my neck.

CHAPTER FOURTEEN

TINKER TIME

The creature pulls at my pendant again, its bloodshot yellow eyes manic with desperation.

"Hey, let go!" I yell, startling the creature.

"Ahh!" it screams and flutters back for a second before swarming to my pendant again.

It tries another heaving pull, and I swat it to the side. The buggish creature falls to the ground with a splat. Now that it's out of my face, I'm able to see it more clearly. Long, spindly limbs and a forked tail. Dull reddish skin. Bat-like wings and a hooked nose.

Imp. Level 8. Small, angsty creatures, imps often align themselves with beings on the more chaotic side of nature.

The imp rises to its feet, a little woozy from the impact, and sways back and forth. It points a long finger at me.

"Give it." It stomps its foot against the ground.

"What do you mean, 'Give it'?" I ask. "It's mine. Wait—how do you speak troll?"

"Limery speaks many languages. Mother taughts him well. Now, gives us the magic." He extends his hand, waiting for me to hand him my pendant.

"I'm sorry, Limery, is it? But this was a gift. I need it for a quest I am on."

The small imp drops to his knees.

"Oh, please," he wheezes. "We needs it. We really needs it." He clasps his hands together, pleading. Tears stream down his demonic face.

I almost feel sorry for the guy.

"Hey now, no need to cry." I try to calm him. "This thing is almost as big as you are. Can't you find something more to your size?"

He stops crying long enough to answer. "We don't wants to wear it. We needs its magic."

I know I should just kill the bugger and be on my way, but there is something about his bulbous eyes and childlike mannerisms that stays my hand. I'm curious as to what he has to say.

"Why do you need its magic?"

Limery stands up, straight as an arrow, as if he is giving a very important speech.

"The magics is gone. Makes life hard. Limery tries to make life easier for Mommy, but needs more magics. Now, please, gives it to us." He extends his hand again.

It sounds like he might be affected by the same lack of magic that the trolls are. Maybe I can kill two birds with one stone. Still, I'm not exactly sure how the lack of magic is affecting Limery.

"I'm not giving you my pendant, *I* need it, but I may be able to help you. Can you tell me a little more about your magic? What it does, how you use it."

His eyes light up at my words. "Oh, yes, Limery can do this. We builds things. Most times, magic makes them work. We takes the magic and puts it in the machines. But now, no magics. So we takes the items and they gives us the magics." He stands there, arms held neatly behind his back, smiling his sharp-tooth demonic smile.

"So are you able to touch magic too? Like trolls?"

He shakes his head violently. "Oh noes. Magics is too strong for imps to touch, but we can calls it. When it's there." He jumps into the air and his wings spread, keeping him aloft at eye level. "Comes with us. We shows you."

"Limery, I can't. I have a—"

"It's okay. Not far at all. Follow Limery, he shows you the way."

What have I gotten myself into?

Limery takes off with gusto, and I follow him to a rock formation about a half-mile from the river. When I get there, I realize it is actually an underground cave. He lands at the entrance and motions for me to follow him. The cave is plenty big for the small imp, but I don't know if I will fit.

"Limery, I might be too big." The last thing I need is to get stuck in a cave where someone can kill me while I'm helpless. I'm not even one hundred percent sure this isn't a trap.

"It's okay. You fits. You fits." He grabs my leg and pulls until I start walking.

I have to duck my head, but I'm just able to fit inside. The cave is dark, but a faint glow emanates from down the tunnel. We turn a corner to see a female imp stirring a pot over an open flame. She looks the same as Limery, except for a patch of hair that runs across her chest. Her wings are tucked in, and she doesn't look up as we enter.

The inside of the cave has a cozy vibe to it. There are cabinets carved into the cave walls, several tables and chairs, clearly homemade, but they look to be sturdy. Small furs and tapestries line the walls.

"Mommy!" shouts Limery and she turns to embrace her child. "I broughts a friend. He is going to fix the magics."

She looks up and eyes me warily. "Is that so?" I get the feeling this isn't the first time Limery has brought home an unwelcome guest.

"I hope so," I say.

She laughs shrilly. "And how does a troll plan to fix magic when he can't even use it?"

"I'm not sure yet, but I'm going to give it my best shot."

She rolls her eyes. "Son, why did you bring him here?"

"To show him the magics. To show him what we builds."

"You know we can't do that. We have very little magic to use as it is. If we waste it on a demonstration, then what will we do when we need it?"

"Please, Mommy. We will find more magics. We must shows him. We musts." Limery gives her his best pouty face.

She lets out an exasperated sigh. "Fine, follow me. Don't knock over my mole soup with your giant legs, Mister Troll."

"My name is Chod, if you'd rather call me that."

"I'd rather be left in peace. Things are hard enough without someone meddling in our business. Limery should have known better."

Limery's mother conjures a fireball in her hand and shoots it across the cave. It hits a torch, bringing the cavern to life. The end of the cave is filled with a multitude of machines, each one made out of an assortment of parts and materials that clearly do not go together.

"What is all this?"

"We builds it," says Limery. He runs over to the pile and pulls out a contraption.

There's a small colored box with several rods that extend upwards, which then connect to another set of rods and curve around like a hook. A funnel empties into the box at the bottom. Limery picks the whole thing up and carries it past me to the soup. He pulls the ladle from the soup and attaches it to the end of the extendable arm so that the machine holds the ladle.

He runs past me again to a chest in the far corner, opening it and pulling out a ring.

Item. *Ring of Stealth. +2 sneak.*

Limery tosses the ring into the funnel and a moment later, conjures a fireball and drops it into the funnel as well. There is a moment of sizzling, and then the arm that holds the ladle begins to spin.

"See? So easy." He gives me his toothy grin.

He just melted a magical ring to make a magical mixer.

"Wow! That's really cool. How does it work exactly?" I inspect the contraption as it moves of its own accord.

Limery's mother is the one who answers. "When a magical object is destroyed, its magical essence returns to the earth. We are able to harness that power to run our machines. This cave used to be a fountain of magical activity. Our machines could run simply off the magical current in the air. Unfortunately, due to the disappearance of magic in this area, we've had to resort to more primitive ways of doing things."

The ladle continues to stir, and chunks of meat and vegetables rise and fall in the pot.

"How long will that ring power the machine for? And what do you do if you want it to stop?"

She walks over to the mixer. "A ring of that size should last for a day or more. If we want to stop it, we simply remove the container." She reaches down and pulls the box from the bottom of the machine. The ladle quits spinning. "Some magic is lost while it sits, but we are lucky enough to have come across some precious stones which better insulate the magical barrier." She puts the box back under the machine and the ladle resumes stirring.

"This is all really fascinating. I have so many questions. I mean, why don't you just move to another magical site? And what do you do with the machines? Couldn't you sell them?"

"Limmy, where did you find this troll?" She looks at me with wonder. "I've never met one who asks so many questions."

Limery is in the back of the cave searching through various machines.

"To answer your questions, though, this is our home. We've been here for many years. Why would we leave? One day, the magic will return, but until that time, we will live as we must. We sell what we can, but due to our size, there are not an awful lot of buyers in the area. Our creations are viewed more as novelties than anything. In other parts of the world, we could sell to dwarves or halflings or gnomes, but the humans have little need of our inventions. They despise anything they didn't create themselves."

Limery comes back with a machine that has a basin filled with some liquid and three ringlets attached to rods that connect to a motor underneath. He pulls the container from beneath the ladle machine and inserts it in a similar receptacle underneath the new one. Immediately, the machine comes to life and the three ringlets dip into the liquid. They come out of the water and a tube that exits from the motor blows air against the ringlets. A spray of glowing bubbles flutter across the cave and Limery chases after them, popping them with his tiny claws and letting out little demonic giggles. I look over and see his mother has an adoring smile on her face.

"Limmy is the youngest, but he has more aptitude for tinkering than the others combined. It's a shame he can't put his talents to maximum use."

Footsteps approach from the mouth of the cave and I turn to see an imp entering, carrying a small sack stuffed with items. He's slightly bigger than Limery, with a patch of black hair between his ears that resembles a mohawk.

He drops his sack upon seeing me and fireballs materialize in both palms.

"What's going on here?" asks the one with the mohawk. "Mom?"

"It's okay, Leo. Put your fire away. He's friends with Limmy."

Leo does as his mother commands, but he looks at me with distrusting eyes as he walks past.

"Let me guess, you send Limmy out to find magical items and he comes back with a troll. Just like him. Useless." Leo dumps the contents of his bag out on the ground.

"Don't talk about your brother like that, Leo," his mother scolds.

"Well, it's true."

I scan the items on the floor. There's an assortment of things, some magical, some not.

Item. *Buckler Shield. +1 Constitution.*

Item. *Pearls of Wisdom. +2 Wisdom.*

There are also several bracelets and a necklace, none of which seem to be magical, as well as a broken sword. I wonder where he found all this stuff. If it was anything like what I experienced, then there are several people feeling pretty angry right now.

"What do you do with the non-magical stuff?" I ask.

"We will melt it down and use it for materials." She turns to Leo. "Good job, son. Now go place these with the others."

Leo does as his mother commands.

"Can I ask you one more thing?" I ask.

"This is the last question I'm answering, so you better make it good." Her patience must be wearing thin at my game of twenty questions.

"How is it we are able to understand each other? Every other race I've come into contact with sounds like grunts or nonsense."

Limery continues popping bubbles as they float through the air. His mother stirs the soup before answering.

"For a long time, imps were the preferred means of message delivery. If you needed anything sent anywhere in a timely manner and wanted to make sure it was delivered, the Imp Messaging Service was the best there was. Due to this, imps needed a way to be able to communicate with many different species all at once, without the hassle of learning every language and the risk of having meanings lost in translation.

"The solution was communication stones." She touches a tiny pendant that hangs from her neck. "They have the ability to translate any language in real time, and accurately, but they are very expensive. They can't be stolen, only given away willfully. Any imp who enlisted in the IMS was given one for free in exchange for ten years of service. Then it turned out that it was all a ploy by the wizard who created them to form a contractually-obligated demon army. There was a huge war, and the continents severed ties with one another."

"How does one get one of these communication stones nowadays?"

"I thought I said no more questions." She smirks and goes back to her soup. "You said you have a plan to restore magic to our lands, right? Well, do that, and I may just have one for you."

"Mom, are you serious?" interjects Leo. "That stone belonged to dad. You can't give it away."

"Your father is not here, Leo. The stone is mine to do with as I wish."

"But you could sell it, you could trade it, you could—"

"Enough!" Her shrill voice cuts through the cave and heat rises off her small body.

Even though she is small, I have a feeling she has a lot of power inside her.

"That is my offer for you, Mister Troll. Take it or leave it."

Quest Alert. *You have been offered the quest 'Restore the Magical Well—Part 2.' Something has blocked the magical stream that feeds into the imp cave. Find a way to clear the obstruction and return magic to the imp cave.*

Reward: Communication Stone.

CHAPTER FIFTEEN

DUNGEONS AND DRAGONS

With a clay pot filled with mole soup in hand, I leave Limery and his family in the imp cave. The promise of a communication stone has me excited and ready to be on my way. It was nice to be able to just speak and be heard, even if Limery did talk like he has spent hundreds of years eating fish inside of a mountain cave system.

I plug the stopper tight into the clay pot, ensuring my mole soup doesn't spill. Despite its name, the soup offers some pretty good buffs.

Item. *Mole Soup. +3 Constitution, +3 Charisma for one hour.*

I'm not sure where the Charisma comes from. I wouldn't be too keen on believing anyone who was offering me mole soup. I'm pretty sure there was fur still attached to a few pieces of meat floating inside.

Most of the day is spent walking. I'm far enough out from the two towns that I don't risk randomly running into someone unless they are out on a quest. Studying the map Chief Rizza gave me while I walk, I find the ley lines interesting, the way they seem to clump in certain areas and are very sparse in others. They almost seem to miss the human settlements entirely. I wonder if the humans even know they're there?

There is actually a very dense clump of magical veins not too far from where I am. I can spare a few minutes to go check it out and actually see what I am up against.

When I come to the spot on the map where the ley lines converge, nothing looks out of the ordinary. There is a large copse of trees and bushes, but nothing special or magical. Maybe once I unclog the line, things will change.

I step into the copse and look around. In the middle, there's a large rock formation surrounded by giant herbs and mushrooms. One of the rocks has some sort of smudge on it, so I go to take a closer look. Once I get closer, I realize there are engravings under a thick layer of dust and dirt. It's in some language I can't read, but it's writing nonetheless. I wipe away the smudge of dirt to try and better decipher the engraving. When I do, a notification flashes across my vision.

Faerie Dungeon. *Would you like to enter?*

"Hell yes," I say without thinking. There is no way in hell I'm leaving a dungeon unexplored. There could be all kinds of loot inside. I know the magic lines need to be restored, but I just found my first dungeon! I can't pass this opportunity up.

The rocks shake, but nothing else happens. No door or cave or anything opens. Then another prompt appears.

Faerie Dungeon is currently unavailable.

Dammit! I bet it has something to do with the magic lines that are affecting the rest of these parts. I mark this spot on my map. When I complete my quest, this will be the first place I stop.

As evening approaches, the long windswept fields finally come to an end and I'm face to face with the forest that forms around the base of the mountain. It's very different from the forest I came from. This one is more evergreen. Pine, spruce, and cedar trees spread out for as far as I can see, running up the mountains like thousands of troll hands crossed in prayer.

When I step into the forest, everything is muffled. The millions of pine needles offer a soundproof insulation. There is still the occasional birdcall or scuttle on the forest floor, but it's so much quieter than the troll's forest.

It's beginning to get dark again, and I know I need to rest soon. Judging by the map, there are maybe twenty miles or so between where I am and the beginning of the magical vein. Tomorrow, I should be able to make it by late afternoon at the latest.

I tuck my belongings underneath me and prepare to Camouflage when I hear a leathery flap of wings at the edge of the tree line.

You've got to be kidding me. A red blur moves through the tree branches.

"Limery, what the hell are you doing here?" The red imp with bulging yellow eyes plops on a tree branch in front of me.

"Mom saids Limmy can come. Limmy likes Chods, wants to helps him." He gives me his best smile, but his razor-sharp teeth are not the most welcoming.

Imp moms must be really lax caretakers. Not that my mom was any different. I got to do pretty much whatever I wanted as long as I stayed out of her hair and didn't get into too much trouble. I'm not going to turn him away, though. I have a feeling I'll need all the help I can get.

"How long have you been following me?" I ask.

"Just a bits." He leans back and lets the momentum take him as his knees curl around the branch until he is hanging upside down like a bat.

"Okay, you can come, but I'm about to camp for the night. Do you want to keep watch?"

"Oh yes! Limmy will watch all the things. Night night!"

I lean back against a tree, the aroma of pine a welcoming smell that almost seems to cleanse my lungs. As darkness creeps in, Limery's bat-like ears are the last thing I see before drifting off to sleep.

I'm awoken in the middle of the night by something nuzzling against my chest. I look down to find Limery cuddled against my arm, his wings wrapped around him like a blanket. I almost wake him, but then he starts snoring, cute little bubbly snores, and I can't help but let him stay.

When I finally wake a few hours later, Limery is no longer in my lap, but once again standing watch on the tree branch in front of me.

"How'd you sleep?" I ask.

He gives me a toothy grin. "Limmy slept good."

I share my mole soup with him and we start our day. When the buff hits me, I get the usual increase of heartiness that comes with Constitution, but there is something else. I feel more confident, like I could walk up to anyone and start a conversation. Is this what Charisma feels like? It feels so good that I almost unload all of my remaining attribute points into Charisma just to chase that high. I stop myself before I complete the action, but damn, that feeling is something else.

I try to shake my head and focus on the task at hand. The obstruction. With my Charisma bonus, I know I won't have a problem fixing things. Hell, it'll be a piece of cake. When I get back to the troll village, I'll take my crown and before long, the whole island will be mine.

Over the next hour, I continue to contemplate how good of a ruler I will become. Limery jumps from branch to branch, flying in between. When the buffs finally wear off, it's like a moment of clarity.

Holy hell, Charisma is powerful stuff! Is that what it feels like to be a celebrity or a politician? I felt damn near invincible for a moment there. I make a note to be very careful with Charisma buffs in the future. There's no telling what they could make me do.

My foot suddenly sinks into the earth and I'm buried up to my knee. Grabbing hold of a nearby tree, I pull myself out. There's a faint glow beneath the surface where I fell through. Looking at my map, we're right on top of the ley line.

I bend down and look into the hole. It's a tunnel about three feet deep and two feet wide. A blue, jelly-like substance clings to the walls in places. Then I notice that there are dozens of holes spread throughout the nearby forest. My first thought is that maybe this is what caused the obstruction. My next thought is what kind of creature could do such a thing?

"What could make these holes?" I ask.

Limery jumps down from his tree branch and takes a look at the hole. He reaches in, touching the blue goo, then screams in pain and shakes it off his finger.

"Limmy doesn't know." He sucks on his thumb, eyes watering in pain.

That's weird, it didn't burn me when my foot fell through. I take my finger and rub it against the same spot where Limery just touched. The gel is warm to the touch, but it doesn't burn. I remember Chief Rizza mentioning that trolls were one of the few races that can handle raw magic. Is this raw magic or something else entirely?

"Are you okay to keep going?" I ask Limery.

He nods, and we continue onward.

The farther we go, the bigger and more spread out the holes seem to be, like whatever made them has been growing. The same blue gel covers the inside of every new hole we see.

Limery has taken a seat on my shoulder, his tiny claws digging into me with each step. Whatever caused these holes has soured his normally playful disposition. I hold Peacemaker at the ready for whatever may come, carefully watching each step I take.

We come to a spot where the holes are so wide that full-grown trees have fallen through them, their tops sticking above the earth like bushes. Twenty-foot wide tunnels weave through the forest, the blue gel now appearing in globs as big as Limery.

Then I see it: the source of all the trolls' problems. The reason for the magical drought. There is a huge cavern where the earth has collapsed in on itself. Dozens of large glowing blue eggs, each one nearly as big as me, radiate magical energy. So much energy that the air is distorted around them.

The earth quakes and debris falls into many of the holes around us. Something slithers underground. It moves so fast through one of the tunnel openings that all I see is a trail of blue.

Limery clings even tighter to me when, suddenly, the ground erupts and a massive blue creature towers over us.

Wyrm (Mana-infused). *Unique Monster. Level 20. These legless, wingless dragons burrow deep underground, producing a natural toxic slime that allows them to glide through rough tunnels unimpeded. With magic-resistant scales, strong jaws, and powerful elemental magic, wyrms are some of the most powerful creatures in all of Mythos.*

The wyrm glows, and a neon blue, toxic gel runs down its body, dripping onto the ground. It hunches over us like a gargantuan cobra, ready to strike.

Limery takes off from my shoulder, flying into the canopy above and leaving me face to face with my doom.

The good news is that I found what is obstructing the ley line. The bad news is that it is about to kick my ass.

CHAPTER SIXTEEN

BIG BAD BOSS

Blue slime oozes from the wyrm's scaly body. Its massive dragon head strikes at me, and I jump to the side, barely dodging the attack as it burrows underground. Its hooked snout rips through the earth like a spade as it disappears beneath the surface.

"Limery, destroy the eggs. I'll handle the monster."

"Whatever yous says." The imp darts off through the canopy, a fireball blazing in each hand.

My head turns like a sprinkler, searching for sight of the dragon snake, but it's nowhere to be found. The ground rumbles beneath me and I'm knocked skyward as the wyrm breaks through the surface. I somersault through the air and land on my feet, covered in dirt and dust.

Thank god for my troll reflexes. Reaching into my bag, I down my last potions. My stamina and HP both receive a boost, and I do my best to set my resolve for what is about to happen. This wyrm is so far out of my league that my only chance of winning is to outsmart it. But how can I outsmart something I can't even see when it goes underground?

The wyrm rears back and lets out a fiery attack of blue flames that singe the trees and set the forest ablaze. A stream of fire hits me in the shoulder and it sears with pain. The wyrm dives for me again and this time, I swing Peacemaker with all of my might into the side of its dragon head. It leaves a gash but barely does any damage. The beast knocks me aside and burrows underground once more.

In the distance, Limery tosses fireball after fireball at the mountain of eggs. I can't tell if it is doing any damage, but he zooms through the air, his bulging eyes focused on his mission.

I'm knocked into the air again before I have time to react, but this time, I'm not so quick on my feet and tumble into a nearby pine, snapping it in half. My back throbs from the blow, but I get to my feet.

The wyrm towers over me, blue smoke rising from its nostrils as its head weaves back and forth. I roar, using Intimidation, but nothing happens. Whether it is because of its magic-resistant scales or because it's too far out of my level, the confusion doesn't work. Instead, I'm scorched by another flame barrage. This time, it doesn't just graze me, but full-on roasts me. Every pain receptor in my body is on fire, even with my phoenix feather negating ten percent of the damage. My health drops by half from the attack, and my skin turns a darker shade of green.

A massive tail smashes into my side faster than I can react, dropping my health by another quarter. With the way things are going, one more direct hit and I'm dead. I don't know if I can beat this monster, but I have an idea that might just keep me alive long enough to try. If I screw this up, I will most certainly be dead. I'll lose my items and will respawn somewhere in the middle of the troll forest.

The wyrm dives at me, and I jump to the side. Its scaly body brushes past me as it burrows underground.

I have about ten seconds to put my plan into action.

"Limery! Over here, now!" I yell at the top of my lungs. The small imp flies in my direction, still holding a fireball.

"What does you needs?" he asks.

"Hit me with a fireball. I don't have time for questions. Just do it now." I pull the phoenix feather from my hair and place it on the ground. I don't need to block any of the damage.

Concern radiates from his enormous eyes, but he does as I tell him. The fireball collides with my chest, dropping my health down to fifteen percent.

"One more," I say with gritted teeth.

The second fireball hits me, and I drop to five percent health.

Just as I expect, my health regeneration kicks into overdrive. When I am under ten percent health, my regen is doubled. Now, it's time to abuse the system.

I order Limery back to the eggs and activate Berserker Rage, turning my vision red at the edges. Quickly, I re-attach my phoenix feather while my health bar climbs rapidly. Normally, Berserker Rage increases my health regen by five times, but since my regen is already doubled due to being so low, it's regenerating at ten times the normal rate.

By the time the wyrm smashes into me from underneath, my health bar is full. The damage from the impact disappears almost as quickly as it happens.

Getting up, my rage meter is full and my blood pumps with righteous fury.

I have thirty seconds of near invincibility. Please don't let me screw this up.

I throw myself at the wyrm just as it releases a jet of flame. The flames graze me, but aside from the burning pain, it's almost like I was never attacked. I use Sweeping Slash. It doesn't knock the wyrm off balance, but it does do a sliver of damage. Then I use Claw with my free hand and cast Bite, sinking my teeth into its scaly flesh. A tail-smack knocks me down, but just as quickly, I am on my feet and attacking once again. I hack, slash, bite, and claw, all while taking a massive beating that could have killed me ten times over. Every inch of my body is burned and regenerated, but still, I fight. A final tail-whip knocks me through a tree, its burning branches igniting the pine needles that cover the forest floor when it collapses.

The wyrm burrows underground just as my Berserker Rage fades away. I'm able to catch a glimpse of its health as its tail sneaks below the surface.

Ninety percent.

It still has ninety percent health. I hit it with everything I had and barely did any damage.

Fire rages all around me. Without my increased regeneration, I'm as good as dead. Not knowing what else to do, I jump in the tunnel the wyrm left behind. At least I won't burn to death down there.

The sides of the tunnel walls are slick with the wyrm's toxic sludge and I have to focus to hold my footing. It's only a matter of time before it attacks, and I have about zero ideas for how to get rid of the rest of its health. My best bet might be to run away and regroup. Maybe I can think of a plan while I level up in the surrounding areas.

I don't know if the trolls have that kind of time, though. Glenn has already had three days to regroup. How long will it be before he manages to gather forces for another attack?

I have to find a way to end this now.

Isle of Mythos isn't like any other game, where everything runs on a script. It is based on action and reactions. Every action sets a new course of events for the game. If I want to beat this monster, I can. I just have to figure out how.

The ground rumbles nearby and I know the wyrm has just resurfaced. A shrieking roar tells me just how close it is. Everything that has happened in the battle crosses my mind as I try to piece it together in a way that might help me. The crackle of fire lets me know the wyrm has just attacked. In about five seconds, it is going to burrow.

I jump out of the tunnel and pinpoint the monster. It has just sprung forward, and I think I know the spot it is aiming for. I take position right in front of it.

Instead of clamping its mouth shut and using its pointed snout to burrow underground, the wyrm reacts to my presence and opens its jaw, expecting to take a bite out of me. I've got other plans.

"Eat me," I say, lunging at the monster and targeting its throat. I don't aim for its exterior throat, the part on the scaly underbelly. No, I aim for its actual throat, the part behind its enormous and extremely sharp teeth. The part that spews fire.

I land on its sandpapery tongue as its mouth closes and claw my way down its throat. Everything is warm and dark and clenching all around me. I imagine this must be what it feels like to be born. Inch by inch, I claw myself deeper into the wyrm, biting and clawing and jabbing with my axe. Notifications of critical attacks fill my vision. The wyrm continues to thrash and heave, but with my claws stuck deep, I refuse to leave. I'm stuck in its throat like the sharp edges of a broken tortilla chip it just can't swallow.

Minutes pass as I attack the monster from the inside. Slowly, its fight begins to fade, until finally, it moves no more.

Notifications flood my vision, but I push them aside. Right now, I need to get out and find Limery. We need to destroy those eggs ASAP. I've seen enough horror movies to know what can go wrong if those things are allowed to hatch.

Unable to cut my way out, I have to climb out the same way I came in, but it's a whole lot harder going feet first down a slimy tube. Eventually, my feet hit against something hard and I know I'm in the creature's mouth.

With a heave, I lift its mouth open and flop my slime-covered body on the ground.

There's an explosion next to me and I look up to see Limery hurling fireballs at the dead wyrm. Tears stream down his face.

"You killeds our friend. You killeds Chods." He runs up to the wyrm and claws and punches the dead monster. His desperate cries fill the air. He pounds his fist until he falls into a crying heap on the ground.

I had no idea he was so attached to me.

"Limery..." I say, but he doesn't look up.

"Limery, it's okay. I'm fine."

He looks up and recognition dawns on his face.

"Is okay?" He stands up. "Chods is okay!"

He leaps onto my body and gives me the biggest hug his small arms can muster. I hug him back. This might be the first time in my life someone has cried over me. Mom and Dad never have. Not even when they found out about my sentence. As I hug the small creature, I can't fight back the tears that creep into my own eyes. Perhaps for the first time in my life, I feel loved. And it's by a creature that doesn't really exist.

"It's okay," I whisper. "It's okay."

When we end our embrace, I clear my eyes and focus on the remainder of our quest. The eggs.

"Did you destroy the eggs?" I ask.

"We dids not. Eggs too strong, they only crack."

That's when I notice the cracks forming along the edges of several of the eggshells. They look almost like they're moving. Vibrating. A piece of shell cracks and breaks off, and I realized that it's because they are. A massive black snout pokes through the hole and a tongue licks at the air.

"Limery, we have to destroy those eggs now!"

I'm off and running before I even finish the sentence. I leap down into the cavernous nest just as the first wyrm hatches. It slithers by me and into one of the tunnels before I have a chance to kill it. Another one hatches, but this time, I'm able to lop its head off before it escapes. Limery tosses fireballs all around me, but it only increases the rate at which the eggs crack. The fire must be forcing them to hatch.

There's no way I can get them all. I need to attack the eggs themselves and crush them if I have too.

I use a Sweeping Slash and shatter the eggs closest to me. Bloody wyrm babies spill out and onto the ground. It's gruesome, but I have to do it. I prepare for another Sweeping Slash when the entire pile of eggs explodes, and I'm engulfed in a ray of bright blue energy.

For a moment, it's all I see. The energy washes over me. Through me. Nothing exists except for the purity that surrounds me. Then everything fades black.

CHAPTER SEVENTEEN
SUMMONER

Blue skies. That's all I see for such a long time.

The blue skies fade, and I feel two tiny hands push at my shoulder. My ears ring, and I try to remember what just happened. There was the wyrm, the eggs, an explosion. Then everything went blue. Did I pass out? If I died, I wouldn't be here right now.

I open my eyes, but there are no blue skies. Just charred branches and smoke. The fires no longer rage, but the damage has been done. Two pointy red ears cross my vision followed by bulging yellow eyes. Limery's mouth is moving, but the ringing in my ears blocks out everything he says.

I turn my head and the ringing fades a little.

"Chods, is you okay?" His words come in and out of focus. "Is you okay, Chods?"

The concern on his face forces me to smile.

"Yeah, I'm good." The truth is that I do feel good. It's like all my wounds from fighting the wyrm just disappeared. Aside from the ringing in my ears, everything feels fine.

"You dids it!" He jumps in the air. "You fixed the magics!"

I sit up and go to wipe my brow when I notice something strange. My skin is blue. Well, bluish-green. It's almost like there is an aqua-blue aura surrounding me. Not just my hand, but my entire body. Did the raw magic cause this?

"What the—What happened?" I stand up to get a better view of the canyon where the eggs were nesting. A stream of blue energy flows through the canyon. There's no trace of the eggs or the wyrms.

So that's what magic looks like. It's just flowing through the ground like an underwater river. The wyrm must have burrowed in it somehow, causing it to become mana-infused. Those eggs, though, I wonder what happened to all the babies. There is no way we destroyed them all.

"What happened?" I ask again.

"You smashes eggs, they goes boom." Limery mimics an explosion with his fingers.

"And what about me? How did I get up here? How long was I out?"

"Explosion knocks you up here. You sleeps for long time. Limmy wanted to help, but you was too hot. Magic burns Limmy's hands."

I guess I'm lucky to be alive. If I were any race other than troll, that blast probably would have killed me. I look at my hands, they almost glow. Could it be a buff of some sort?

I pull up my notifications to find out and am surprised to see there is a wall of text waiting for me.

You have defeated a unique monster. *Wyrm (Mana-infused)*.

Item. *Mana stone. 50% increased mana regeneration. Taken from the heart of a mana-infused monster.*

Congratulations! You have reached level 8. +1 stat point to distribute. +1 Strength and Constitution racial bonus.

Congratulations! You have reached level 9. +1 stat point to distribute. +1 Strength and Constitution racial bonus. +1 ability point to distribute.

Congratulations! You have reached level 10. +1 stat point to distribute. +1 Strength and Constitution racial bonus.

Quest Alert. *You have completed the quest 'Restore the Magical Well.' Reward: Variable. Return to Chief Rizza to claim your reward.*

Quest Alert. *You have completed the quest 'Restore the Magical Well-Part 2.' Reward: Communication Stone. Return to the Imp Cave to claim your reward.*

Alert! *You have been infused with mana. New class option available.*

Regional Event Alert! *Mana-infused wyrms have descended upon Isle of Mythos. They will gravitate towards areas of magical affinity to lay eggs. Locate the wyrms and wipe them out before they infest the island. 20/20 remaining. Rewards: Each wyrm contains one mana stone. Failure: If wyrms are not eliminated, they will lay eggs and spread out from magical sources, devastating crops and towns. 20 days remaining.*

There's so much there that I don't know how to process it all at once. I'm infused with mana. The raw magic that the trolls described, that must be the same thing as mana. Does that mean I can cast spells now? Will I be powerful like Jira? There are new class options available. I can't wait to see what's available to me now. Maybe I can be a badass troll wizard or a paladin. I'll also need to get back and claim my quest rewards as quickly as possible. Where do I even start?

Then there is the regional event. No doubt every player on the island received that notification. Twenty wyrms escaped and we have to eliminate them before they spawn across the island. I have no idea what the life cycle of a wyrm is, but if they manage to lay as many eggs as the one we just killed, this entire island could be taken over in no time if we fail. It worries me that others might not be able to kill them. I would try to warn them, but it's no use, even after I claim my communication stone. Everyone hates trolls so much that my only hope is to get a group together from the village and travel to the most magical areas on my map.

I'll just have to deal with that once I make it back to the village. Right now, I want to check out my new class options, so I pull up my character screen and take a look at my stats.

Chod, Level 10 Barbarian Forest Troll
   HP: 1960/1960
   Mana: 5000/5000
   Rage: 0/100
   XP: 64,153/85,000

Strength: 27 (+3)
   Dexterity: 15
   Constitution: 28
   Intelligence: 7
   Wisdom: 10
   Charisma: 6

Five thousand mana? Wow. That must have been some seriously potent magic to do that when I had no mana at all to begin with. I have nine stat points as well as the one new ability point, but I'll wait to see what my class options are before I spend it.

Below my stats, a blinking box says, 'New Class Available.'

That doesn't make sense? Five thousand mana and only one new class option? Could it be because of my Wisdom and Intelligence stats? I focus on the box and the new class description pops up.

Class:
   Summoner. *Magic users capable of summoning magical beings to fight on their behalf.*

Sub-Class:
   Elemental. *Summon golems created from the elements.*
   Brood. *Summon insects that evolve.*
   Horror. *Summon monstrous creatures. Requires 20+ Strength and Constitution.*
   Techno. *Summon robotic beings. Requires 20+ Intelligence.*
   Undead. *Summon undead creatures from nearby bones.*
   Champion. *Summon one powerful creature at a time.*

. . .

I only have one new class, but damn if it isn't awesome! There are so many intriguing possibilities for where this new class can take me. I can actually use magic and won't be forced to just slug it out. Techno is out of the question because I don't have the Intelligence requirement. I quickly disregard champion as well. With as much mana as I have, my power is going to come from summoning multiple monsters at once, not just one strong monster. Undead is too restricting based on the need for nearby bones. Plus, I'm already hated enough and could do without the stigma associated with necromancers. So, it comes down to elemental, brood and horror.

It's a big choice, and I'm not sure which one is right. I don't have a lot of ability power, so whatever I end up summoning is going to need to be able to crowd control my opponents while I still physically beat them down. With my low Intelligence and Wisdom, it won't matter if I can summon a hundred beings if they can't do any actual damage. I wish there was a way to see what abilities each sub-class has before I choose. There is something about the Horror class that calls to me. And the fact that there is a requirement of Strength and Constitution makes me wonder if the beings it summons feed off those stats as well.

To hell with it, my gut hasn't let me down yet. I select Horror and a new set of abilities pop up.

Summon Horror (Passive). *Ability to summon a horror. Each horror grants a unique ability. For every horror active, gain 1% increased damage and health points. Horrors decay 10% every minute outside of combat.*

Horror of Power. *Summon a horror with 20% of your Strength. Cost: 100 mana. Cooldown: 30 seconds. Bonus: Your next attack deals double damage.*

Horror of Vitality. *Summon a horror with 20% of your health points. Cost: 100 mana. Cooldown: 30 seconds. Bonus: Opponents near Horror of Vitality are slowed by 20%.*

Horror of Finesse. *Summon a horror with 20% of your attack speed. Cost: 100 mana. Cooldown: 30 seconds. Bonus: Your next attack heals you for damage dealt.*

I definitely made the right choice. All three of these abilities play off my strengths and two of them benefit from my racial bonuses. I can't wait to start summoning monsters, but first I need to decide which one to spend my ability point on. They all look so appealing that it is hard to decide. With five thousand mana, I could essentially summon fifty horrors if I were in a long, drawn-out battle. Especially considering my physical abilities rely on rage. I can pretty much summon my own army to take down the wyrms.

Even though I'm a big tanky troll, I was constantly running low on health in that last fight. If I were part of a team complete with healers and ranged attacks, I could probably take the power or vitality horror, but with it just being me and Limery right now, the Horror of Finesse makes the most sense. If it heals for damage dealt, then it is basically a one-hit potion.

After selecting the Horror of Finesse, I immediately cast it. A blue, gangly creature not much bigger than Limery materializes with a puff of gray smoke. It has long, pointy fingers, huge bat-like ears, and a dog snout. Basically a blue imp without wings.

Limery screams when he sees it and conjures two fireballs, hurling them with ferocity at my new pet.

"Whoa, whoa, whoa," I say. "It's okay, Limery, it's mine. It's not going to hurt us."

Limery holds another fireball in his hand, unsure of whether or not to trust me.

"Friends?" he asks, eyes full of suspicion.

"Friends." The two fireballs took out nearly half of the horror's health, making me wonder if it has the same weakness to fire that I do. It also makes me keenly aware of how fragile they will be in battle until I have the other two horrors unlocked. One horror is nice, but an army will be unstoppable.

Limery cancels his fireball and it disappears in a blur. He walks up to the horror and tries to talk to it.

"It's not much of a talker. It's here to fight and make sure we don't die," I say. That seems to be enough for Limery to leave the horror alone.

After the first minute passes, ten percent of the horror's health disappears. My chances of keeping a standing army are low because they deteriorate outside of combat. I'll worry about that when the time comes.

With my new class sorted, I elect to put all of my stat points into Dexterity to help benefit Horror of Finesse even more, bringing it up to twenty-four.

Looking at my stats, even though my mana pool is massive, my mana regeneration isn't very high, probably due to my low Wisdom. Luckily, I have just the fix. I pull out the mana stone left behind by the wyrm. It glows with the same vibrancy as raw magic, only crystallized.

Mana Stone. Would you like to equip mana stone to Peacemaker? 0/3 slots filled.

When I agree, the stone fits perfectly into the socket on the axe's side. I cast another Horror of Finesse and this time, my mana almost doubles its regeneration rate. I couldn't be happier with the results of beating the giant wyrm.

To my surprise, I look over and see Limery tossing a rock with the first horror I summoned. Though it doesn't speak, it seems to be enjoying the playtime with the imp. It makes me appreciate all the more how advanced this game is. Each horror acts of its own accord, not some preassigned robotic set of movements and commands.

"Are you ready to get going?" I ask Limery.

"Where's we going?" Limery stops the game of toss and the horror turns away, on guard duty once more.

I need to retrieve my quest rewards, but there is somewhere I want to go first. It seems like the perfect place for a mana-hungry wyrm to go.

The faerie dungeon.

CHAPTER EIGHTEEN

DUNGEON DIVING

We travel to the faerie dungeon without event. I use the time to practice casting Horror of Finesse. Every thirty seconds, I summon a horror. Since we are not in combat, they begin decaying after the first minute. It takes ten minutes for one horror to lose all HP and die, so I am able to summon twenty of them. The horrors of finesse have ten percent of my HP, giving them one hundred and ninety-six health upon casting. Due to the bonus increase in my own HP and Strength for having horrors summoned, I gain three hundred and ninety-two HP with all twenty horrors active. By the time they start dying off, the weakest of the bunch have twenty-four HP, hardly a threat to anyone.

For now.

I'm glad I put my stat points into Dexterity to bring it up to par with my other stats and increase my overall attack speed, but I'm thinking it might be more bene-ficial in the long run to invest in Constitution. The longer they can last, the stronger I become, and in turn, the stronger they become. Once I have the other two horrors unlocked, I'll be able to summon a maximum of sixty horrors when I'm not in combat.

The days of trolls hiding away in the forest may be nearing their end.

Limery perches on the rock in the center of the copse where I first found the faerie dungeon. The mushrooms and herbs that surround the rock formation have changed slightly. The mushrooms all have an aura around them—it's faint, but I can definitely see it. A small blue furry creature with large round eyes sits atop one of the mushrooms, watching me intently. When I move forward with my small army of horrors, it scurries away.

I approach the carved runes and the same prompt hits me as before.

Faerie Dungeon. *Would you like to enter?*

This time, when I accept, the ground trembles beneath me. The rock Limery sits on rises higher into the air, causing him to jump off in surprise and revealing a cavernous archway that leads underground. Stone steps descend into darkness. Limery hovers in the air above my shoulder.

"We goes inside?"

"That's the plan."

I cast another horror and instruct them to lead the way into the dungeon. They respond to my thoughts just as quickly as my commands. It's dark underground, but my night vision allows me to see unimpeded. Limery must be able to as well, because he doesn't complain.

Rubble and dirt crunch underneath my feet with each step. It must have been a while since the last time someone was in here. Spiderwebs hang from the ceiling and small feet scurry away from our approach. A door closes somewhere beneath us with a thud. I continually cast Horror of Finesse, keeping my rotation at twenty. Whatever comes next, I want to be prepared.

Somewhere in the depths, the trickle of water echoes, but I can't pinpoint the source.

Light shines in from the foot of the stairwell. My horrors move into a large room where dozens of yellow wisps float through the air.

Wisp. *Level 10. Harmless unless touched, these ethereal creatures are light incarnate.*

The wisps range from level ten to fifteen. At the other end of the room is a door. Whatever scurried away must have gone through there. Limery could probably make it through without touching the wisps, but I'm way too big.

While I'm in the process of formulating a plan, one of my horrors bumps into a wisp. Electric bolts shoot out from the floating ball of energy, killing the horror in one shot. The oldest horrors are always at the front so that they can disarm traps or take lethal blows without risking the HP of the stronger ones.

The next thing I know, the rest of the wisps come swarming towards us.

"Oh noes!" Limery shouts and tosses a fireball, sending one of the wisps up in smoke.

The wisps swarm my horrors, electricity filling the air as bolts zap out like an electrical storm. The horrors attack, but their blows seem to be missing entirely and I've already lost a quarter of those with low HP.

I activate Sweeping Slash and swing for a nearby cluster of wisps, hitting them square on, but my blade passes straight through, doing zero damage. Several arcs of lightning strike the axe and travel down the handle, stunning me in place and taking out a chunk of my health.

Limery seems to be the only one having success as he fires fireball after fireball at the incorporeal damage dealers.

"We need to get to that door!" I shout.

With my horrors falling by the wayside, the wisps have turned in my direction now. Limery zooms through the air, too quick for their lightning strikes. Several bolts hit me even as I try to dodge and make my way across the room. With so many of them, all of the damage is beginning to add up. None of my physical attacks are working, not even Intimidation, and without anything to land a blow on, my healing from casting Horror of Finesse isn't working either.

Every third lightning strike stuns me in place. If I don't find a way out of here soon, I'll be swarmed and unable to move at all as I'm hit with bolt after bolt.

I'm stunned once more when a group of wisps pin me against the wall. Limery tosses a fireball at the cluster of wisps and it sets off a chain reaction, exploding four at once. There's still a minefield of wisps on the other end of the room that haven't moved. As it is, there's no way I'll make it without being hit unless I waste Berserker Rage in the first room. I wish I had a giant bubble of protection around me to just barrel through them.

That's it! I call what horrors I have left to me and instruct them to climb on my body. I don one of them over my head like a helmet along with one on each shoulder, two on my back, and several more on my legs and arms. Their health begins to drop as the wisps converge on us.

I take off running like a bat out of hell, the crack of lightning raging all around me. The horrors' HP drop in droves as we cannonball across the room. I lose the imp-like monsters clinging to my arms first and take a shock to the shoulder. The one on my head goes and I dive through the open door just as two final strikes kill the horrors on my back.

The door closes behind me and the wisps disperse back into their original positions like we were never there.

"Holy shit." I let out a sigh.

Dungeon diving is not for the faint of heart. I probably should have put together a team before attempting something like this, but there's no turning back now.

I send one of my horrors down the hall, and a dozen poisoned darts shoot out from the walls, killing it.

Better him than me.

"Chods okay?" asks Limery.

"Yeah, I'm good. Thanks for your help back there. I didn't know those things only responded to magic attacks."

"Nasty little balls. Limmy doesn't like." He shakes his head in disgust.

Hopefully, the next level will treat us better. I wait for my health to regenerate as we sit in the corridor that leads to the next level. There is another wooden door at the end of the hall. Limery peeks through the slat in the door we just came through. The wisps managed to kill all but three of my horrors, pinpointing my weakness against anything that isn't flesh and blood. Maybe Jira will have answers for how to deal with monsters like that once I get back. All of this mana has to open more opportunities than just summoning.

As I heal, I continue to cast horrors, hoping this next batch fares better than the last. Ten minutes later, I have twenty ready to go. At the door, something scuttles on the other side. It's almost a clacking sound, like horse hooves on pavement. There is no slat to look through on this door, so once it opens, it's game on.

"Ready?" I ask Limery.

He nods.

With a quick heave, I open the door, and my horrors spill into the room. A chittering sound rings out and the clattering intensifies. Torches line the walls of this room, casting eerie shadows from large columns that stand throughout. I immediately spot the source of the noise. Large beetles, the size of a golden retriever, rush towards us, their shells a shimmering iridescent rainbow. Pincers hinge open and close with each step. Wingless faeries sit astride the large beetles while faeries with dragonfly wings zoom through the air firing arrows.

The fairies are bigger than Limery, but not by much. They have ivory skin, colorful hair, and daggers for teeth.

"Stay behind me and target them with your fireballs. Me and my horrors will push the attack."

The first row of horrors collide with the beetles and are immediately mowed down. The wingless faeries shoot bolts of magic from their hands while those airborne fire imbued arrows across the room. One hits me in the chest and I get a notification that I have been poisoned. I have my Tiger's Eye Pendant to clear the poison, but I want to save that until we clear the room. For now, I'll use my healing bonus to keep the poison at bay.

I cast Horror of Finesse and the icon telling me my next attack will heal flashes in the top left corner of my vision. I jump the line and bring my axe down with a powerful strike that tops off my health. Luckily for me, most of the faeries are attacking the horrors that rush to them like ants on a fallen ice cream cone and leave me be.

Behind me, Limery hurls his fireballs all the while yelling "take that" and "stupid faeries." His attacks are pretty accurate, incinerating the wings of many airborne fairies and forcing them to fight on foot.

I kick and claw as I continue to summon more horrors as time allows. One faerie comes running at me, hands glowing, and I stomp him into the stone floor with a crunch.

My horrors attack like rabid animals, moving from one beetle warrior to another. The pincers rip at their flesh, but they remain undeterred, sinking their claws and prying the shells apart with sheer numbers. I continue to raise more as soon as the cooldown allows, using each opportunity to fill my health with a basic attack, countering the poison that continuously damages me.

Though I lose more than half of my horrors, it doesn't take us long to overwhelm the faeries. With my Tiger's Eye Pendant, I clear the poison that runs through my veins.

The door out of the room opens and we enter another corridor.

So far, this dungeon hasn't been so hard. I don't know if I'm overqualified with my new class or it's really just a beginner dungeon. Careful not to become skewered by darts or some other contraption, I send one of my horrors out first. It trips a tile and the floor collapses underneath it, sending it falling into darkness that not even my night vision can penetrate. I hear a splash and then can no longer feel the horror's presence.

I toss the rest of my horrors across the pit, and when they make it to the door unmolested, I follow.

We exit the corridor into a wide room with a large fountain at its center. Glowing blue water illuminates the room, eliminating the need for torches even if we didn't have night vision. The water reminds me of the nanites in the pod where my body is.

The room itself is similar to a Roman bathhouse with the way water drips down from the ceiling and spills out from an obelisk in the fountain's center. The fountain overflows into a large pool with channels that carry the water into drains. It explains the dripping I heard when entering the dungeon. I remember passing a stream not far from the dungeon's entrance, and I bet it runs underground and into the dungeon as well.

Aside from the fountain, the room is empty.

This has to be where we fight the boss.

As we wait for something to happen, I continue to raise horrors, making sure I am continually topped off. After several minutes of nothing happening, I approach the obelisk in the center of the room.

At the room's center, the stone floor quakes, sending out ripples through the pool where the obelisk rises. There's movement in the water and something moves beneath its depths. I take a defensive position with my axe, ready for whatever vile monster is about to emerge.

I'm surprised when a humanoid creature with beautiful eyes and hair rises to the surface.

Water Nymph. *Level 17. Guardians of the world's most beautiful places, nymphs are wild and spirited, embodying the elements of the locations they protect. They are naturally charismatic towards all manner of creatures.*

Her skin is light blue and only a few thin pieces of cloth cover her curvaceous body. Blue eyes stare out at me and she speaks, but I can't understand her.

"What is she saying?" I ask Limery, wishing I already had my communication stone. I keep my eyes on the nymph but turn my head towards Limery.

His yellow eyes bulge even larger than normal. "She says, 'Prepare to meets your doom.'"

There's a splash from behind us and I turn just in time to see two wyrms slither through the drainage pipes and into the room. They rise up like cobras, ready to strike, their scales glistening with the toxic slime that seeps from their skin.

Wyrm (Mana-infused). *Level 12. These mana-infused wyrms have been mesmer-ized by a water nymph, answering her beck and call.*

CHAPTER NINETEEN

FIRE AND WATER

The twin wyrms sway back and forth, their hooked snouts hissing like snakes. They aren't as big as the wyrm I faced in the woods, but they are still massive. At least seven feet tall. Plenty long enough to wrap me up in a tight embrace, and not the warm and fuzzy kind.

The nymph continues to talk, even though I can't understand a word she says.

"Limery, I'm going to need you to translate everything she says until we make it out of here. Got it?"

"Yes! Limmy can do it! She says, 'You is not welcomes here. This dungeon is hers. Prepare to die.'"

"Alright, Limmy. I hope you're ready for a fight."

I hear the familiar crackle of fireballs igniting in his palms and know I can trust the imp to have my back.

Without waiting for my opponents to get the fight started, I send my horrors on the offensive. They split and claw at the towering wyrms, dropping slivers of health with each raking scratch.

Blue flames erupt in a cone from the wyrms, setting the horrors on fire and destroying the front line. I cast another horror and a blast of water from the nymph knocks me off my feet, taking five percent of my health. There's a dull ache from the blow, but it's nice to put my actual tanking to use against something that isn't breathing fire at me.

I rise to my feet just as the wyrms slither across the stone floor, knocking the horrors aside. Evidently, the wyrms aren't strong enough to burrow through solid stone.

Not yet, at least.

Limery tosses fireballs at the wyrms, but they do very little damage against those magically-resistant scales.

"Focus on the nymph," I say, not knowing if he will fare any better against her.

I swing at one of the wyrms as it passes by to join its master, connecting with its side and healing myself just as a massive tail smashes into my ribs from the other side and knocks the breath out of me.

Horrors rush to my aid, blocking a wall of flame meant for me. Several of them die to the blast. I cast another and land a claw in the side of one wyrm as they retreat behind the nymph in the fountain.

Every fireball that Limery throws her way is negated by a water bubble that shoots out from the pool, intercepting the blast in a puff of steam.

We are truly fucked.

A wave of luminous water rises from the pool and rushes across the stone floor. It collides with my horrors, scattering them around the room like bugs in a rainstorm. I stand my ground, unable to move against the rushing torrent as the toxic water slowly burns me. The toxic slime from the wyrms has contaminated the water and it damages both me and the horrors with every touch. When the water recedes into the drain, I call my horrors to me and lead a charge toward the fountain. Flames target me and I barely dodge to the side as puddles of water sizzle on the floor, causing a curtain of steam to rise into the air.

I'm hit in the face by a giant water bubble that surrounds my head, cutting off my air and obstructing my vision. I try to pop the bubble, but my axe and claws just cut through the water like jelly.

My lungs start to burn, and I don't know how much longer I can hold my breath, when the bubble dissipates and hot steamy air coats my lungs.

Limery zooms through the air as streams of water and fire chase him across the lair. The effect of both elements intertwining causes a huge layer of steam to rise. If this continues, we won't be able to see anything soon.

Maybe that's the key to winning this.

I cast another horror and instruct them to spread out. I have twelve still alive at the moment and since we are in battle, they no longer decay over time. If only I had a way to heal them, then I would be unstoppable.

They take their positions around the edge of the room. I don't want any of them to be hit in a cluster. A dozen orbs of water rise from the pool and hover in the air. My horrors have attack speed but no agility, so when the orbs come soaring across the room, only one manages to dodge the attack. Luckily, the water negates some of the fire damage by simply boiling their skin instead of burning them. It's not ideal, but the damage is a little less. Steam rises with each attack, until I can barely see the horrors on the other side.

We're still screwed, but I'm hoping an opening will appear at some point. As of right now, the wyrms still have ninety percent of their health and the nymph has all of hers. Limery and I are topped off, but my horrors won't last forever.

I'm far enough away from the nymph to dodge the next drowning glob she sends my way, but when she uses tidal wave again, the horrors are tossed aside like spiders in a shower. I lose two more horrors to the flames that follow before I am able to cast another.

The steam is thicker than ever, and I can only see the horrors closest to me. However, I can still sense the others as they retake their positions. If only there was a way to stop the inflow of water, then the wyrms might actually evaporate it all, leaving the nymph powerless.

Even if we could stop the inflow, their positioning makes the fountain inaccessible.

Limery flies too close to the nymph and a beam of water hits him in the chest, knocking him to the floor. I'm quick to his rescue, narrowly dodging a stream of flame, but the little guy is dazed.

I hide him in a corner and instruct one of my horrors to make sure he isn't carried away by a wave. It puts me a body down on the battlefield, but I can't lose Limery. He's become a friend, and he's part of the reason I'm even here right now. There's no way I'm letting anything happen to him.

If I don't figure out how to deal some actual damage, then my horrors will die and we'll have no shot at defeating this dungeon.

It's time to go all-in.

I take off towards the fountain, casting another horror along the way while calling all of the others towards it as well. We're almost there when a wave comes roaring, knocking us down and scattering my horrors once again. The water stings against my skin, but as quick as I can, I'm on my feet and rushing the fountain once more. I can see another wave forming, so I use Berserker Rage. This time, the wave has no effect on me other than slight damage and I carry on, hopping the ledge of the pool and diving into the abyss. I feel an intense heat near my feet, telling me that the wyrms are trying to roast me in the water, while the toxic water burns my eyes.

Hacking at anything near me, my axe connects with flesh and then a tail collides with my side, knocking me against the pool wall. My vision goes dark at the edges, but I do my best to gain a sense of direction. The pool is deep, and I wonder how the wyrms are floating on its surface. It must have something to do with the nymph's water magic. My head breaches the surface and I gasp for air before swimming below again. The water grows hotter as another set of flames boil the area where I just was.

With all the focus on me, my horrors have managed to climb into the pool and now join me in its steadily heating waters. I send them after the nymph, content to keep her distracted, even if it means sacrificing my horrors. The hot toxic water drains my HP, but the increased healing from Berserker Rage is keeping it steady. For now.

Another flame attack and the water grows hotter still. I can sense the horrors dropping like flies. I come up for air and the steam is so thick, it's almost like breathing in water. Flames bear down on me again and it feels like the water is melting off my skin. Berserker Rage wears off and my HP starts dropping rapidly. Bubbles rise all around me. The water is actually boiling from all the heat. Cooking me alive.

This is it. All or nothing.

I activate Sweeping Slash right before my last horror expires, doing my best to focus on anything but the burning pain that engulfs my body. The blow connects with the nymph, and the knockback sends her out of the fountain.

Notifications flash across my vision, but I push them from my mind. Right now, all that matters is her.

She lays on the ground unmoving as I crawl out of the fountain and fall over the edge with a splat. I'm tired and in pain, every pain receptor on my body screams at me, but my rage meter is full.

She says something, but I use Intimidation before she can finish, sending her into confusion for two seconds. Using Claw and Bite, I take out her remaining health before collapsing on the ground beside her.

For the longest time, I just lay there. The fact that I haven't been roasted alive means the wyrms are dead.

"We dids it!" I hear Limery's voice somewhere above me.

The steam is starting to fade, but it still takes up the majority of the room.

"We did, didn't we?" I sit up and take in the chaos around me.

There's not a single horror left. My skin is covered in boils, even though my increased regeneration is doing its best to heal me. Rising to my feet, I walk over to the fountain, where the two wyrms float lifelessly on the surface.

Limery perches on the ledge of the fountain and mumbles something about "filthy wyrms."

I never really believed the story people told me about frogs. That if you slowly heat up a pot with a frog inside, it'll boil to death before it realizes what's happening. In the chaos of the battle, the nymph had no idea her new pets were actually boiling her alive. Not until it was too late. They even managed to kill themselves while they were at it. If not for Berserker Rage, I'd no doubt be joining them.

Then I notice the obelisk in the middle of the fountain. There's a crack running along the edge of it. Not a crack like it was broken, but an opening with something glowing beneath it.

"Hey, Limery. See if you can open that?" I say, pointing at the obelisk.

He flies over and presses his tiny fingers in the crack and slowly pulls up. It flips open like a clamshell and a bright yellow glow emanates from within.

Item. *Elemental Stone. Boosts the power of elemental attacks by 20%.*

Item. *Water Potion x2. Allows user to breathe underwater for 10 minutes.*

Item. *Aquatic Boots. Allows user to walk on water.*

Not a bad haul. Along with what's in the chest, the two wyrms drop Lesser Mana Stones, which increase mana regeneration by ten percent.

I don't really have much use for the elemental stone, since I have no elemental attacks. I bet Jira would make good use of it if I took it back with me, but he wasn't here to help me win it. Instead, I give it to Limery.

"For me?" His eyes glisten with tears as I hand him the stone.

"I couldn't have done it without you."

"Oh, Chods." He wraps me in his tiny arms as his tears run down my shoulder.

"Give me a second to look over my notifications."

Limery releases me and immediately starts testing out his new item. He casts a fireball and it seems to burn brighter than before.

I pull up my notifications.

You have defeated Faerie Dungeon. *Claim dungeon prize.*

Congratulations! You have reached level 11. +1 stat point to distribute. +1 Strength and Constitution racial bonus. +1 ability point to distribute.

Congratulations! You have reached level 12. +1 stat point to distribute. +1 Strength and Constitution racial bonus.

Regional Event Alert! *Two mana-infused wyrms have been slain. 18/20 remaining. 19 days remaining.*

"Come on, Limery. Time to get the hell out of here."

Once we exit the dungeon, the rock formation falls back into place, making the entrance no longer accessible. I swipe my hands across the runes.

Faerie Dungeon. *Would you like to enter?*

I focus on yes, just to see what happens, but I'm not surprised at the response.

Faerie Dungeon is not currently available. 7 days until respawn.

CHAPTER TWENTY

RULE THE WORLD

At level twelve, I'm one of the strongest trolls from the village now. If that doesn't get Gord to respect me, then I don't know what will. I'm actually looking forward to rubbing my new summoner class in his smug face. Gah, he was such a dick. But that will have to wait, our first stop is the imp cave to collect my communication stone.

I also need to assign my new ability point. There are still a few abilities I haven't unlocked in my barbarian class as well as the melee weapon abilities I unlocked after acquiring my axe, but with the way I plan to level from here on out, upgrading my horrors makes the most sense. I want to be unkillable, a true brute capable of taking pain and dishing it out.

Summon Horror (Passive). Ability to summon a horror. Each horror grants a unique ability. For every horror active, gain 1% increased damage and health points. Horrors decay 10% every minute outside of combat.

Horror of Power. Summon a horror with 20% of your Strength. Cost: 100 mana. Cooldown: 30 seconds. Bonus: Your next attack deals double damage.

Horror of Vitality. Summon a horror with 20% of your health points. Cost: 100 mana. Cooldown: 30 seconds. Bonus: Opponents near Horror of Vitality are slowed by 20%.

It's a tough call. More power or more life? The slow that Horror of Vitality offers is a game-changer, though. I'll finally have my own crowd control abilities. And the twenty percent HP that these new horrors will have is essentially double what my current horrors have. I do the math in my head. At level twelve, I have two thousand and four hundred HP. If I gain one percent health for each horror and I'm able to summon forty now that I have two classes, that's a nine-hundred and sixty HP bonus. Holy shit! At full power, my horrors of Vitality will have almost seven hundred health.

I add my attribute point to Horror of Vitality and summon my first new horror since leaving the dungeon.

There's a puff of smoke and then a rotund, furry monster with orange and blue stripes appears. Its head is orange and the stripes run horizontally across the rest of its body. It has two black ram's horns that protrude from its head and curl around its fuzzy orange ears. It has the same round and bulbous eyes as the other horrors, but its body-type is completely different. Sharp tusks stick out from its jaws not that much different than my own.

It reminds me of a stuffed animal, if a stuffed animal could eat your face off.

A bison roams through the golden field not too far ahead, the perfect victim for a test run. I motion for Limery to stand back and instruct my horror to do the same as I approach as quietly as possible. Crouching through the tall grass, I move like a lion on the prowl until I am only a few feet from the grazing animal.

I attack it from the rear, drawing a critical strike and when it turns to charge, I summon a Horror of Vitality. It pops into existence and the bison slows noticeably, allowing me to sidestep its charge like a matador. It doesn't take me long to kill the bison without taking a single point of damage.

The next day, we arrive at the mouth of the imp cave and something feels different. The rattle of machinery echoes out of the cave's mouth.

"Mommy!" Limery yells as we enter the cave. "We dids it! We kills the wyrms and the baby wyrms and then we goes to the dungeon and Chods gives me magics stones!" He's speaking a mile a minute as he recounts our adventure and finishes by pulling out the elemental stone and showing it to his mother.

She laughs at her son, embracing him against her furry chest. "It seems I may have underestimated you, Mister Troll. I'll be honest, I didn't think you had it in you." Her eyes run up and down my body, taking in my new look. "Blue looks good on you, by the way."

I don't pay much attention to the comment as my eyes wander around the cave. It's almost nothing like the primitive cave I left a few days ago. All of the machinery that was piled in the back of the room is whirring with life. There are contraptions weaving blankets, sweeping the floor, turning a rotisserie over an open flame. A giant pot of stew is continuously stirred, and there are several others that I can't even begin to grasp their purpose. One is shaped like a giant mixer and pops little blue cubes out of the bottom. There's even a line of glass tubes that cast light from the ceiling. They have magical electricity!

"Magic does all of this?" I ask.

"When it's around. The machines pull it from the very air. It's hard to make them much bigger than this and have them work effectively, but considering this isn't a fountain of magical activity, it works pretty well. We also have a battery maker. It takes the magic from the air and stores it in common stones that last up to a day."

This has me even more excited to see what is happening at the troll village. The magical veins that run underneath it are massive compared to here.

"If I remember correctly, I promised you a reward if you brought magic back to our cave. Let me go and grab it right quick."

She disappears in the back of the cave, and Limery pulls strips of meat off the rotisserie. His mother pops his hand when she returns and hands me a small circular stone with a hole in its middle.

"Most people wear them around their necks, since they only work when they are on your person. May it help you in the days ahead."

I pull a strip of leather from my bag and run it through the communication stone. There's nothing special about the stone, nothing to signify that it may be one of the most useful tools in this entire game. Communication will be the key to me leading the trolls out of the forest and into better times.

"I hope you will stay for dinner before heading out." She flashes me razor-sharp smile. "We're having roasted deer. I also have more mole soup you can take with you on your journey. You are more than welcome to rest here for the night if you desire."

Thoughts of the last time I had mole soup cross my mind. The last thing I need is another Charisma high.

"Dinner sounds lovely."

I'm anxious to get moving, but after receiving the communication stone, I feel I owe it to Limery's mother to stay for dinner. Besides, twilight is approaching and I'll need to rest for the evening anyway.

We fix our dinner and take it outside to eat, just as the sun begins to set over the horizon, casting the sky with streaks of watercolor.

There is a delicious smoky and spicy flavor to the deer meat. It reminds me of Indian food. For a second, my mind drifts back to the real world, to the many nights I called in takeout from the Indian restaurant on Sixth Street because neither Mom nor Dad were going to be home in time for dinner. I wonder if they even know I'm here? If they even care? Do they know I feel real pain when I'm hurt here or that there are violent criminals who want nothing more than to kill me on sight just because of my in-game race?

Suddenly, I'm not so hungry anymore.

"Where's Leo at?" I ask, trying to take my mind somewhere else. I hadn't seen Limery's brother since we came back.

"He's off on his own. Since magic returned, we no longer need the constant influx of magical items, so he's taking a well-deserved break. He received news of the regional event and is going to form a party to try and defeat one of the wyrms." She laughs. "If he knew Limmy had managed to help defeat three already, I'd never hear the end of it."

In the distance, I watch Limery as he zooms through the air, blasting glowing bugs out of the sky with tiny fireballs.

"He's a good kid. Smart, talented, heck of an aim."

"You best take care of him," she says, her face suddenly serious.

"What do you mean?" I thought Limery would be staying here once we returned.

"He's taken a liking to you. I can see it in his eyes, Chod. He'll follow you to the ends of the world."

That's the first time she has called me by my name since I've known her. It must be something intimately cultural about referring to someone by their name for the imps. I still don't know hers.

"Then I will do my best to protect him."

We sit in silence after that. The sun sets and the only light comes from the stars above and the occasional fireball in the distance. My entire life, I've been an outsider. My fans who watched me stream were only there for the entertainment. Maybe part of the reason I've been a loner is because I always push people away, afraid of getting hurt. I've never really let anyone other than Taryn get to close to me, never really had anyone who wanted to.

I wonder what Taryn is up to right now. What I would do to be able to tell him about my adventures so far. He'd love this place.

I don't know what the future holds, what will happen when my time in *Isle of Mythos* is over. All I know is that right now, this two foot tall, energetic, insane, loving, demonic spawn wants to be a part of whatever adventure I'm on now, and I'll be damned if I let him down.

I officially have a party. And before this is over, we're going to rule the world.

"Can I ask you something?"

"You are a curious troll. What is it this time?"

"You mentioned that all the continents used to be accessible to one another before the great war with the wizard. What happened?"

"Come inside and I'll tell you about it." She cleans up the leftovers from dinner and I follow her inside. The gentle whir of magically-powered machines hum and purr. There's a machine against the wall where Limery's mother places our plates. It lifts the plates, scrubs them, then dips them in water to rinse them off.

She pulls a bottle of amber liquid off a shelf and grabs two clay cups, motioning for me to take a seat against the cave wall. Due to our size differences, none of their furniture is large enough for me, but she does offer me a leather hide to sit on.

She pours the bottle, nearly filling the cup, and I pray it doesn't have a Charisma buff.

Item. *Imp Mead. -3 Intelligence for 1 hour. Useless, but it feels so good.*

We tap our glasses together and the sweet flavor of honey coats my throat. Then an uncontrollable smile comes, and everything seems to be just a little bit funnier than usual.

"It's terrible for you, but damn if it doesn't take the edge off." She laughs, but then her tone grows more serious. "The world used to be such a wonderful place. People traveled to different continents, all the various races traded together, and the world was a better place for it. There was less hate back then. After the war, the wizard that started it all retreated to his homeland and sealed off the magical transport portals. Now, the only way to travel to other continents is by ship. And there are things that lurk in the oceans that have the power to devour them whole."

"Do you think the portals will ever reopen?"

"I have no doubt it will happen. No spell lasts forever, no matter how powerful. My worry is what the wizard has been up to during all this time. Most of the imps were able to escape through the portals before they closed, but some races were not so lucky." She gives me a half-smile.

"Which races?" My chest feels tight as I ask the question.

"There was a large number of giants and goblins, no doubt the wizard made promises to coerce them to his cause. They don't often engage in large-scale warfare. The real threat were the dark elves, though. It was said that some could raise the dead to fight on their behalf."

That's not what I was expecting. I thought maybe I had found the reason the trolls were hated so much. Will I ever find out the true reason?

"It's nothing to worry about now," she laughs. "For now, your focus should be the wyrms or else there won't be an island left."

CHAPTER TWENTY-ONE
WELCOME HOME

When we set off the next morning, it is a tearful good-bye. As much as she encourages his adventure, I can tell his mom will miss him dearly. I mean, who wouldn't miss a clown like Limery. He's like the little brother and the pet I never had all rolled into one.

His mother even gives me a hug around the knee.

"I am glad to have met you, Chod. You are more curious than the average troll. Take care of my boy."

"I will."

"Lillith, you may call me Lillith. Now, get going before I regret telling you my name." She releases her embrace, and Limery and I set off towards the forest.

It's a beautiful day and excitement fills the air. Two days from now, I'll be back at the troll village claiming my reward. I still don't know what I will ask for. Chief Rizza offered me literally anything I wanted. Tormara seemed to think I would want the village, but truthfully, I have no interest in ruling a small village. I want adventure. The thrill of fighting the wyrm, of exploring the dungeon, that's what I'm truly after. Not council meetings and planning how to stay hidden from the outside world.

I want to make trolls respected so that we don't have to stay hidden. If I can't make them respect us, then I will at least make them fear us. Enough power and people like Glenn will think twice about attacking the village.

When we come across the river, I pull out the Aquatic Boots I won at the faerie dungeon. They're made out of green leather with pearls sewn into the upper half. They must have some enchantment that sizes them to the wearer, because they manage to fit my giant troll feet, claws and all.

I step into the rushing river and it's like I'm walking on sand. The water gives a small amount, but then it's firm. Rapids form around my feet with each step until I am safely on the other side. Limery flies beside my shoulder.

Pretty cool.

Limery and I chat the day away as we travel. He tells me about some of his favorite games he likes to play with his brother. One of them is similar to tag, but they throw fireballs at one another.

"We meets you family soon, Chods?" he asks.

"I— I don't have a family here." I don't know why I say it, but I start talking to him about my life outside of the game. "I have a mom and a dad where I'm from, but we're not really close. I'm their only child, and we're not close. How sad is that? I honestly can't remember the last time Mom gave me a hug or Dad took an interest in any of my school activities. You're lucky, Limery. Your mother loves you."

"You mother loves you, Chods. You good son." His tiny hand pats me on the shoulder.

"I don't know about that. Maybe it's not them. Maybe it's me. Maybe I'm not the son they wanted." I never had an interest in business, especially when it was always more important than I was. How many tournaments did I have to win for them to notice me? Not enough, apparently.

"Don't says that, Chods. Don'ts. If they don't likes you, then you comes and stays with me."

I don't know what I did to deserve his love, but I'm glad to have it. If only I had a Limery in the real world.

"It's not all bad. I have a friend named Taryn and he's about the closest thing I have to a brother." He's been there for me more times than I can count. He's not much of a talker, but whenever I just needed some company, anything to break up the loneliness, we'd sit and play games for hours in silence. There's a lot to be said for that. "We're going to go see my people, though. They're like me, but they aren't my family. You'll like them."

I hadn't really thought about whether or not the trolls would be welcoming to Limery. They live in a closed society, so they may not be accepting of outsiders, even if they're non-human. He's a big part of the reason they even have magic at all.

We're making our way across the golden field when a notification pops into my vision.

Regional Event Alert! *Jason Montoya and Lester Hobbes have slain a mana-infused wyrm. 17/20 remaining. 17 days remaining.*

Maybe I underestimated the other players. Three days in and they've slain their first wyrm.

Out of the corner of my eye, I notice a black splotch moving across the golden fields in the distance. Straight in our direction.

I contemplate running for a moment, but then my mind clears and I realize I don't have to. I have natural abilities to conceal me. If I simply quit moving, Camouflage will take effect.

"Limery, come here. We need to hide, nestle against my arms."

I take a seat and Limery climbs against my chest. I cover his body with my arms until he can't be seen, his skin is warm against my own.

The black splotches continue to grow in size until I can clearly tell they are two humans on horseback. The clop of horse hooves is all I hear as they trot towards us.

A dark-skinned man in boiled black leather armor wears a black cape that flows in the wind. He rides next to a man in a ruby red robe holding a scepter made of a dark wood that's fitted with a piece of obsidian on the end. Several runes are engraved down its side. A gray beard falls to his chest and blows in the wind. The man in black wears a sword to one side of his hip, but I can see several daggers strapped along his leg. He must be some kind of rogue.

They pull the reins of their horses and come to a halt a few dozen yards away from me. They both wear the same emblem, a white skull with a sword and staff crossed together in the background.

"This is where I saw it," says the rogue.

"I don't care what you say. Doesn't look like there is anything here," says the wizard.

They both scan the area and I focus on them, displaying their stats in my vision.

Randy Billson
 Level 17
 Rogue
 Human

Don Othello
 Level 16
 Mage
 Human

"Fuck off, Don. I know what I saw. There was something big and blue moving over here right next to that giant rock." He points to me as he says it. "I have advanced eyesight. It was a monster, I tell you. A big, ugly monster. Could have been one of those wyrms."

"Well, like I said, whatever it was, or wasn't, it ain't here now. Regardless, we need to be getting back to town. Word is that Glenn attacked the damn trolls again." Don rolls his eyes.

"Fucking Glenn. I don't know what his fascination is with those things. There are much better options for leveling up that don't rip your face to shreds. Trolls are so stupid that the best loot you're gonna get is a stone club. Like we could even lift the thing to use it. He's lost all of his items, what, three, four times now? No, I'll stick to dungeons and finding actual loot. Glenn can have his trolls." Randy laughs.

"Still, the mayor wants us back at town by sundown in case the trolls try to exact revenge."

Randy pulls a dagger from his leg and spins the blade around his fingers with precision. "I'd like to see them try. Besides, if they were going to attack, they would have done it by now."

With a quick pull of their reins, both men are off towards the other town.

That was a close call. I didn't take into account that other players might have enhanced senses as well. I'm lucky it wasn't a ranger or someone capable of tracking my footprints. I wait for another ten minutes before removing my camouflage and setting off again.

One day with my communication stone and it's already paying dividends. I can't stop thinking about what Randy said as I walk. Apparently, not everyone is out to destroy the trolls. Yes, they hate us, but they're more content exploring dungeons.

Still, if Glenn is continually out to get us, then he needs to be stopped. Soon.

We do our best to stay away from the two human settlements that stand between us and the forest as we camp for the night. I refrain from casting horrors just in case we need to hide. If what Don said is true, and the mayor of one of those towns is recalling his people, then we need to stay as far away from them as possible.

The next day, we make it past the towns without trouble. I'm so excited to get back to the village that I don't even spy on the humans this time. There's plenty of opportunities to level up, but the priority is to make it back in one piece without drawing any extra attention.

When we cross into the forest, it feels like I'm back home. The vines, birdcalls, and the musty smell of the forest floor calm my spirit for the first time since I stepped out into the larger world.

I cast a Horror of Finesse and Vitality, thankful to be under the safety of the canopy and away from prying eyes. As soon as the cooldown is up, I cast another, until I'm trampling through the forest with my own personal army of forty horrors. They're loud as they walk, gnashing their teeth and grunting as we move along. Limery zooms in and out of them, occasionally landing on one of the Horror of Vitality's heads and holding on to their horns.

With such a large force, I draw the aggro of several woodland creatures as we walk and my army tears through them like it's nothing. I know I've only scratched the surface of my power and that if I keep leveling, there could be even more summoner abilities for me to unlock. I'd like to see Glenn try and attack us now.

As we make our way to the village, nothing really seems all that different with the ley lines returned. There are a few exotic animals roaming the forest, and I'm pretty sure I spot a centaur at one point, but by and large things are the same.

I'm surprised when I come upon the boundary of the village that there are no trolls on guard. When I left, I saw several in Camouflage around the village's edges.

Behind my army of minions, we cross the line into troll lands.

A barbaric grunt stops me in my tracks, and it's like a veil is removed from my eyes. The empty forest I was looking at disappears and I see the translucent shapes of several trolls on guard. The troll closest to us abandons Camouflage and charges into my horrors with a club, obliterating several of them and tossing others aside.

Fire crackles next to me as Limery readies his fireballs for battle.

"Wait!" I yell as several more trolls come from the nearby area. "Wait! It's me, Chod! I'm back."

The troll is about to take another swing at my horrors when I hear a deep voice bellowing to my right.

"Trogden, halt!" I'd know that voice anywhere. Gord steps into view from behind a massive oak, his metal nose ring reflecting the fire in Limery's hand.

He looks me up and down with disgust, then over my minions, and finally to Limmy.

"Blue skin. You finally decide to reveal your true colors? You are welcome, but outsiders are not permitted on troll grounds."

I know I shouldn't take his bait, but he really pisses me off with his smug attitude.

"Are you fucking kidding me? I look this way because of you. I risked my life for this village and actually succeeded, and now you're telling me I can't bring my partner on troll grounds."

"Partner," he scoffs. "More like vermin." The other trolls chuckle at his joke. "Rules are rules, even for you."

"I'm not going anywhere without him."

"Then stay and rot." He turns to leave.

"I'm not as weak as I was when I left." When I check his stats, I see we are now the same level.

"Is that a challenge?" he roars.

I call my horrors by my side and they hiss and snarl in a violent mob. I still have over thirty left and hear the crackle of Limery's fireballs behind me. The other trolls take a defensive position and I see more approaching. This isn't exactly what I imagined my return to look like, but if I have to fight my way in, then so be it.

I twirl Peacemaker in my hand. "If you want to dance, then let's dance."

Gord's lip curls above his broken tusk and he jumps through the air, club raised to attack.

A fireball hits him in the chest and then all hell breaks loose.

"You no hurts Chods!" screams Limery.

Three trolls rush me, but I send out my horde, stopping their push with the horror's AoE slow and overwhelming them with sheer numbers. The trolls fight against the horrors, slinging them off with ease, but with every horror they remove, another takes its place as I continue to cast every chance I can.

A loud screeching caw cuts through the chaos and Jira appears on the battlefield.

"That is enough!" he yells. His dreads seem to rise from his body, an unearthly heat emanating from him.

I call off my horrors and the trolls cease to fight.

"Now, what is the meaning of this?" he asks.

"This fool is attempting to bring outsiders on tribal lands," spits Gord.

Jira recognizes me for the first time. "Chod, is this true?"

"We completed the quest together and I want him there when I choose my reward. As for the others—." I motion to the horrors. "—they are mine."

Jira gives me a curious look. "What do you mean they are yours?"

I cast a Horror of Vitality in front of him. With a puff of smoke, the rotund orange creature appears at his feet. As strong and as powerful as the other trolls are, they still gasp at the showing.

"I see. As village shaman, I grant access to the imp. Everyone, back to your posts."

Gord cuts his eyes at me as he walks away, but I take pride in the scorch marks that stain his chest.

The walk to the village center is long and quiet. There's no parade of thanks or even any real acknowledgment for what I've done. Is it because I have blue skin or is there more at play than I know? Now that I'm not being attacked, I notice that everything since crossing into the troll lands is different from when I left. Evening has come upon the forest, but there are glowing flower bulbs, like light posts, lighting our way. They light up before us and when we are out of range, they shroud the forest in darkness once more. Is that the power of troll magic?

"Jira, what happened back there? I couldn't see anything and then suddenly trolls were everywhere."

"There is a reason that trolls have survived in the forest for so long. Using the power of the magical well, we are able to conceal our location among the trees. Think of it as a barrier of sorts, reflecting the world outside our lands back to those who pass by. Those who aren't trolls will even have a desire to travel in other directions. Unless they cross the boundary, they will never know we are here. Even sound stays within our grounds."

"How is that even possible?"

"All in good time. I apologize for Gord. He's not quick to trust an outsider, and many of the other trolls look up to him. We are grateful for the journey you made, and I look forward to hearing all about it. As well as why you are now blue."

Whispers and pointed fingers greet me as we walk into the village. All of my horrors have expired, but Limery sits on my shoulder. The village has changed too. I can't quite explain it, but it feels more alive, like there is power running through the very trees. In the short time I was gone, the village seems to have healed itself. There are no traces of the fire to be found.

Jira leads me to the council area. The chairs carved from nature itself have blossomed and flowers adorn them, framing the council members in lilies and roses. Shocked faces gaze upon me and Limery as we kneel before the council. Even Tormara's scowl has disappeared for the moment.

Chief Rizza tells me to stand, and I feel Limery poking at my side. The chief and I stare at each other for a moment but the imp continues to poke me until I acknowledge him.

"What is it?" I ask.

He points at the foot of Chief Rizza's throne. I'm not sure what he is showing me until something slithers and two bright blue eyes stare back at me.

CHAPTER TWENTY-TWO

MAGIC AND MAYHEM

"Welcome back, Chod," says Chief Rizza.

I should respond but the only thing I can think of is, "Why in the hell is there a wyrm wrapped around the foot of your throne?" The wyrm raises its head, licks the air, and lays down once again.

"As you can see, your efforts were successful and the trolls are once again hidden away from the prying eyes of men." She smiles, her small tusks framing her face. "I believe the undying one will trouble us no longer."

My hand grips a little tighter on the axe handle as I force myself to look away from the creature. They had to have received the same notification that I did about the wyrms. They must know that unless they are killed, they will infest the island. These aren't ordinary wyrms that burrow in a small area, these are mana-infused, and they will grow into the size of a barn if left unchecked.

"We are all interested in what led to the obstruction. If you don't mind, please recount the events of your adventure."

For the next half-hour, I have their full attention. Chief Rizza, Tormara, Guilda, and two others hang on to my every word. One of the council seats is empty, but I don't recall who sat there. Jira stands behind me, but I know he is following every word as well.

I tell them about the wyrm, the eggs, my new abilities, the regional event, the dungeon, and my communication stone. When I am finished, it is Guilda who speaks first. Her gray braid marks her as the oldest of the bunch.

"It has been many years since we last had two magical trolls in the village. I believe this is a warning of grave things to come."

"Hardly," scoffs Tormara. "It was a freak accident, not some divine intervention. Now that magic is restored to the forest, I think it is time to focus on rebuilding what we lost, on building up our tribe."

"There are no accidents, Tormara. Everything prepares us for what is to come next. That is the way it has always been."

"Heroes are not influenced by the wills of the gods, Guilda. You know that as well as anyone. They are pure chaos and I would have them on their way before any more damage is done."

Limmy stands quiet beside me, the quietest I have ever seen him. Even at such a young age, he knows more about troll customs than I do.

Chief Rizza raises her hand, and the debate ceases.

"Before you left, I promised to reward you with anything within my power if you completed the quest. You have succeeded. Now it is time to claim your reward."

The wyrm adjusts itself beneath the throne. How in the hell am I supposed to kill it without making the chief irate?

"Chod?" she asks again.

"You know you have to kill the wyrm, right?"

"I have to do no such thing. It will one day be a great and powerful protector of our village." She reaches out her hand and the wyrm uncoils, rising to rub its head against her palm.

"It's what blocked the ley lines. It's the reason there is a regional event. The thing is infused with mana and attracted to magical energy. That's probably why it came to the forest. If you allow it to live, then it will breed and sooner or later, this will all happen again." They can't really be so obtuse to think that keeping a violent monster as a pet is a good idea, can they? "Jira, back me up here."

I turn to face the shaman, thinking he may at least be thinking rationally.

"I'm sorry, Chod, but I stand with the chief. For too long, we have been hated and oppressed, forced to hide away from the men that would do us harm for nothing more than the color of our skin and the tusks on our faces. Let the humans destroy the rest, but this one, it is ours, and it may one day be the difference in our survival or extinction."

"And what if it cuts off your magic again? What if it rises up and kills you?"

"How is it you know so little of troll ways?" asks Tormara. "Were you raised on an island?"

"Enough, Tormara. There is no need to worry about the wyrm." Chief Rizza stands and the wyrm rises next to her, equaling her height. "We are bound and the wyrm will do as I command. Now, Chod, tell me what you would have of me."

I don't know. I could ask her to kill the wyrm. Would she honor that? It seems like such a waste if there was actually a way for me to convince her on my own. Would she really hand over the village to me if I said that's what I wanted? I really have no desire to rule, but I've done too much to just stand by and watch them destroy themselves. And what did she mean about me not knowing troll ways? What am I missing here?

"Can I have more time?" It's the only rational solution to make sure I get this right.

"Very well. You may have one day. If you do not request your reward within the

MAGIC AND MAYHEM

"Welcome back, Chod," says Chief Rizza.

I should respond but the only thing I can think of is, "Why in the hell is there a wyrm wrapped around the foot of your throne?" The wyrm raises its head, licks the air, and lays down once again.

"As you can see, your efforts were successful and the trolls are once again hidden away from the prying eyes of men." She smiles, her small tusks framing her face. "I believe the undying one will trouble us no longer."

My hand grips a little tighter on the axe handle as I force myself to look away from the creature. They had to have received the same notification that I did about the wyrms. They must know that unless they are killed, they will infest the island. These aren't ordinary wyrms that burrow in a small area, these are mana-infused, and they will grow into the size of a barn if left unchecked.

"We are all interested in what led to the obstruction. If you don't mind, please recount the events of your adventure."

For the next half-hour, I have their full attention. Chief Rizza, Tormara, Guilda, and two others hang on to my every word. One of the council seats is empty, but I don't recall who sat there. Jira stands behind me, but I know he is following every word as well.

I tell them about the wyrm, the eggs, my new abilities, the regional event, the dungeon, and my communication stone. When I am finished, it is Guilda who speaks first. Her gray braid marks her as the oldest of the bunch.

"It has been many years since we last had two magical trolls in the village. I believe this is a warning of grave things to come."

"Hardly," scoffs Tormara. "It was a freak accident, not some divine intervention. Now that magic is restored to the forest, I think it is time to focus on rebuilding what we lost, on building up our tribe."

"There are no accidents, Tormara. Everything prepares us for what is to come next. That is the way it has always been."

"Heroes are not influenced by the wills of the gods, Guilda. You know that as well as anyone. They are pure chaos and I would have them on their way before any more damage is done."

Limmy stands quiet beside me, the quietest I have ever seen him. Even at such a young age, he knows more about troll customs than I do.

Chief Rizza raises her hand, and the debate ceases.

"Before you left, I promised to reward you with anything within my power if you completed the quest. You have succeeded. Now it is time to claim your reward."

The wyrm adjusts itself beneath the throne. How in the hell am I supposed to kill it without making the chief irate?

"Chod?" she asks again.

"You know you have to kill the wyrm, right?"

"I have to do no such thing. It will one day be a great and powerful protector of our village." She reaches out her hand and the wyrm uncoils, rising to rub its head against her palm.

"It's what blocked the ley lines. It's the reason there is a regional event. The thing is infused with mana and attracted to magical energy. That's probably why it came to the forest. If you allow it to live, then it will breed and sooner or later, this will all happen again." They can't really be so obtuse to think that keeping a violent monster as a pet is a good idea, can they? "Jira, back me up here."

I turn to face the shaman, thinking he may at least be thinking rationally.

"I'm sorry, Chod, but I stand with the chief. For too long, we have been hated and oppressed, forced to hide away from the men that would do us harm for nothing more than the color of our skin and the tusks on our faces. Let the humans destroy the rest, but this one, it is ours, and it may one day be the difference in our survival or extinction."

"And what if it cuts off your magic again? What if it rises up and kills you?"

"How is it you know so little of troll ways?" asks Tormara. "Were you raised on an island?"

"Enough, Tormara. There is no need to worry about the wyrm." Chief Rizza stands and the wyrm rises next to her, equaling her height. "We are bound and the wyrm will do as I command. Now, Chod, tell me what you would have of me."

I don't know. I could ask her to kill the wyrm. Would she honor that? It seems like such a waste if there was actually a way for me to convince her on my own. Would she really hand over the village to me if I said that's what I wanted? I really have no desire to rule, but I've done too much to just stand by and watch them destroy themselves. And what did she mean about me not knowing troll ways? What am I missing here?

"Can I have more time?" It's the only rational solution to make sure I get this right.

"Very well. You may have one day. If you do not request your reward within the

CHAPTER TWENTY-TWO

MAGIC AND MAYHEM

"Welcome back, Chod," says Chief Rizza.

I should respond but the only thing I can think of is, "Why in the hell is there a wyrm wrapped around the foot of your throne?" The wyrm raises its head, licks the air, and lays down once again.

"As you can see, your efforts were successful and the trolls are once again hidden away from the prying eyes of men." She smiles, her small tusks framing her face. "I believe the undying one will trouble us no longer."

My hand grips a little tighter on the axe handle as I force myself to look away from the creature. They had to have received the same notification that I did about the wyrms. They must know that unless they are killed, they will infest the island. These aren't ordinary wyrms that burrow in a small area, these are mana-infused, and they will grow into the size of a barn if left unchecked.

"We are all interested in what led to the obstruction. If you don't mind, please recount the events of your adventure."

For the next half-hour, I have their full attention. Chief Rizza, Tormara, Guilda, and two others hang on to my every word. One of the council seats is empty, but I don't recall who sat there. Jira stands behind me, but I know he is following every word as well.

I tell them about the wyrm, the eggs, my new abilities, the regional event, the dungeon, and my communication stone. When I am finished, it is Guilda who speaks first. Her gray braid marks her as the oldest of the bunch.

"It has been many years since we last had two magical trolls in the village. I believe this is a warning of grave things to come."

"Hardly," scoffs Tormara. "It was a freak accident, not some divine intervention. Now that magic is restored to the forest, I think it is time to focus on rebuilding what we lost, on building up our tribe."

"There are no accidents, Tormara. Everything prepares us for what is to come next. That is the way it has always been."

"Heroes are not influenced by the wills of the gods, Guilda. You know that as well as anyone. They are pure chaos and I would have them on their way before any more damage is done."

Limmy stands quiet beside me, the quietest I have ever seen him. Even at such a young age, he knows more about troll customs than I do.

Chief Rizza raises her hand, and the debate ceases.

"Before you left, I promised to reward you with anything within my power if you completed the quest. You have succeeded. Now it is time to claim your reward."

The wyrm adjusts itself beneath the throne. How in the hell am I supposed to kill it without making the chief irate?

"Chod?" she asks again.

"You know you have to kill the wyrm, right?"

"I have to do no such thing. It will one day be a great and powerful protector of our village." She reaches out her hand and the wyrm uncoils, rising to rub its head against her palm.

"It's what blocked the ley lines. It's the reason there is a regional event. The thing is infused with mana and attracted to magical energy. That's probably why it came to the forest. If you allow it to live, then it will breed and sooner or later, this will all happen again." They can't really be so obtuse to think that keeping a violent monster as a pet is a good idea, can they? "Jira, back me up here."

I turn to face the shaman, thinking he may at least be thinking rationally.

"I'm sorry, Chod, but I stand with the chief. For too long, we have been hated and oppressed, forced to hide away from the men that would do us harm for nothing more than the color of our skin and the tusks on our faces. Let the humans destroy the rest, but this one, it is ours, and it may one day be the difference in our survival or extinction."

"And what if it cuts off your magic again? What if it rises up and kills you?"

"How is it you know so little of troll ways?" asks Tormara. "Were you raised on an island?"

"Enough, Tormara. There is no need to worry about the wyrm." Chief Rizza stands and the wyrm rises next to her, equaling her height. "We are bound and the wyrm will do as I command. Now, Chod, tell me what you would have of me."

I don't know. I could ask her to kill the wyrm. Would she honor that? It seems like such a waste if there was actually a way for me to convince her on my own. Would she really hand over the village to me if I said that's what I wanted? I really have no desire to rule, but I've done too much to just stand by and watch them destroy themselves. And what did she mean about me not knowing troll ways? What am I missing here?

"Can I have more time?" It's the only rational solution to make sure I get this right.

"Very well. You may have one day. If you do not request your reward within the

next twenty-four hours, then it is forfeit. Jira, show him to his quarters for the night."

I don't get it. She was so welcoming last time I was here. It was like I was the savior of the village that they had all been waiting for, but now it feels like I'm the outsider Gord claimed on day one. Is the magic having this effect on them or had they lost so much hope that an outsider was all they had to believe in?

Jira leads Limery and me away from the council area and back to the village. The glowing flower bulbs make the village feel alive as we walk.

"You will be staying here tonight." He stops in front of a small hut.

"What am I missing about the wyrm? Why is no one else worried about it destroying the village?"

He raises an eyebrow at me, but then motions into the hut. "Step inside."

The inside of the hut is warm and welcoming. Vines adorned with tiny glowing berries run along the ceiling like Christmas lights. Branches form a bed layered with living leaves that looks incredibly comfortable. There is a small table against an open window that has shutters that open and close, all made out of living foliage. A small bush grows from the wall, ripe with berries. Limery picks one off and tosses it in his mouth, mumbling something about how good it is. This all has to be crafted with magic somehow. If not, it would take years to bend each individual piece into the correct shape. And to do that for every hut, the manpower it would take would leave time for nothing else. I for certain want to learn how it is done, but first I want to understand what the chief meant.

We take a seat, and Jira pulls the shutters closed.

"She's right, you know," says Jira, his red eyes boring into my own.

"Who?"

"Tormara. You know so very little about our culture, yet it is undeniable that you are one of us. Well, it was." He looks down at my arms and hands, my blue skin so different from his own. "You know the seaside trolls are the only ones with blue skin, but they don't glow quite like you do. They're much smaller, too. If you were raised a troll, or rather, raised by female trolls, you would know of their inborn ability to bind with creatures that most other societies view as monsters. Once they bond, they bond for life, until one or the other dies. A mental connection forms between them, one that remains no matter how far they are separated."

"Then why don't all of the women bond?" I ask.

"It is not always an easy task. The creature must first be subdued. Once that happens, a bonding of blood must take place. All of this while not dying to the creature. Chief Rizza is lucky to have found a newborn."

Newborn...yeah, seven feet tall and loves to snuggle. I can see why it's not worth the risk for most.

"And the men, it's not possible?"

"No, most were blessed with great strength only and the ability to go into a powerful rage. It's the women who have the high intellect. I'd be lying if I said I trust the temperament of most males to control a bond."

I agree with that. The last thing we need is Gord running around with a fully-grown wyrm at his beck and call.

"If women have higher intellect, does that mean that if they went through the same process that I did, that they would have stronger powers?"

"Perhaps, but they do not have the constitution that you have. That much raw magic would surely rip them apart."

There's always a catch. The ones who could use this power best are not strong enough to survive getting it.

"You know we cannot complete the regional quest while the wyrm still lives, right?"

"Indeed, but that does not mean you can't save the island. Chief Rizza's wyrm will not breed, it is one of the consequences of the bond. If not for this, the trolls would never have been forced into hiding to begin with."

"How do I save the island then?"

He stands and smiles. "I will leave that for you to figure out."

As he walks to the door, I call out one last time. "Jira, one last thing. Will you show me how trolls control the magic?"

"Tomorrow." He half-smiles before leaving.

I think about Jira's words long after he leaves. Limery curls up at the foot of the bed and goes to sleep. Soft snores fill the hut as I'm left to ponder my future.

How can I save the island without completing the quest? The other players are already out hunting the wyrms, what will they do if they reach the last one and find out that it is here?

I already know the answer to that. By allowing the wyrm to live, the trolls are dooming themselves.

No, ourselves. I am one of them. It doesn't matter if my skin is green or blue, I went on the quest because I believed in these people. They might not be perfect. Hell, they suffer from many of the same flaws that humans do—pride, arrogance, anger—but that doesn't make them monsters.

Or maybe I'm looking at it all wrong. Who gets to decide that being a monster is a bad thing?

I know what I want for my reward.

I'm awakened the next morning to the clatter of wooden clubs. The troll children run through the village, beating each other as they duck, roll, and otherwise tumble around learning the ways of battle.

Limery flies out into the chaos, juggling fireballs above their heads. The children laugh at his antics until the instructor comes over.

"Excuse me, Chod," she says. Even though she is female, she is seasoned from battle. Scars run down her dark green arms, making her look like a tiger in places, and one stretches across the entirety of her face. Her hair is pulled into two ox-horn buns on the side of her head. I'm sure I'm about to be reprimanded for Limery's behavior.

"Yes?"

"My name is Ismora. I train the children during the day, but I have also fought many battles for our village. I have heard that you are a great warrior yourself, that you raise demons from thin air. I just wanted to say thank you for bringing magic back to our village. For protecting the little ones."

"Uh, you're welcome."

"Thank you to your little one as well. I can tell he has the heart of a warrior."

Limery continues tossing his fireballs as the children watch, then he catches one in each hand and slams them into the third, making an even bigger fireball that vanishes into the air. The children laugh with delight.

"I see you are providing entertainment now," Chief Rizza says from over my shoulder.

I turn to see her with the wyrm following close beside her. She's smiling, at least. The wyrm licks at the air and watches me with its icy blue eyes.

"I have decided on my reward," I say.

Ismora nods to the chief and leaves to rejoin her students.

"Let it wait for now. There is something I want to show you first. There is no doubt you have taken in some of the changes to the village since your return, but I want to show you why it was so important to clear the obstruction. What it really means to our people."

Limery joins me and we follow her to the village center, where several of the other council members, along with Jira, stand around what looks like a well. To one side, pigs roast over an open flame in one hut and a woman tans leather in another. When we arrive, Jira removes the lid that covers the well and a dull blue glow can be seen coming from inside.

"This is the fountain of our village. It is one of very few wells on the entire island that tap into the ley lines directly. They were formed long ago, long before the trolls were hated. When we all simply roamed the lands. A new well has not been created in many years. Most of the humans do not understand their true power, because they are not able to touch or control raw magic. It has the power to rip through their very flesh. There are those, the imps being one of them, who have managed to pull a fraction of the magic's power from the air around magical areas and harness it, but even they cannot do this."

A chain goes down into the well. Jira turns a crank and it slowly pulls up, the glow growing brighter as it does. When the crank will turn no more, a bucket filled with bright blue energy, the same energy that passed through the ground when I fought the wyrm, sways back and forth.

Chief Rizza reaches into the bucket and cups some of the energy in her hands. It jiggles like slime but doesn't spill. She walks over to a tree and gently forces the energy into its bark. When it's gone, she presses her hands to the tree and closes her eyes.

The tree shakes momentarily, its roots rumbling the earth and its leaves swishing far above. As quickly as it started, the tree moves no more.

"What happened?" I ask.

"Tell your friend to throw a fireball at the tree. The biggest one he can make."

"Is okay, Chods?" Limery's eyes radiate concern.

"Give it your best shot," I say.

Limery flies from my shoulder to the ground about twenty yards from the tree. He looks back at me as he takes his position, and I nod for him to go ahead. He gives a small bow to the chief, then turns towards the tree.

A small fireball erupts in his hand. He pushes both hands together and the fireball grows between them, doubling and then tripling in size. He raises his hands over his head and the fireball grows even larger, until it is bigger than he is. The air around the fire is distorted to the point that I don't know how Limery is even controlling it.

With a flick of his wrist, the fireball erupts from his hands and soars toward the tree. It sends nearby leaves up in smoke before colliding with the tree in an explosion of fire and smoke.

The smoke dissipates and I expect the tree to be charred, thinking that the magic might help it heal faster, but the tree isn't damaged at all. The grass and leaves beneath the fireball's path are singed, but the tree itself is undamaged.

"How?"

"Magic." She smiles.

That fireball probably could have dropped me for half my health, maybe even more, and yet the tree looks like nothing happened.

"We have the power to infuse mana into living objects. If the object accepts our will, then it may continue to pull magic from the ground itself until no more magic remains. We can't infuse weapons or non-living items; only certain mages may do that. Animals are tough because they very rarely accept our will and can only use the magic we infuse in them, unable to replenish it from the earth, but plants, they love anything that will make them stronger."

"How do you do it, though?"

"Come, let me show you."

She leads me to the well and dips her hands in the bucket of swirling energy.

"Hold your hands out," she orders.

I cup my hands and she pours the energy into mine. It's hot, but it doesn't burn. Hot like a bath that's not quite ready. The kind you can put your feet in for two or three seconds but then it starts to hurt. Except this doesn't hurt. It's like being constantly on the edge of hurting, definitely not a pleasant feeling.

"Now, pick a tree."

Looking around, I try to find a tree that suits me. I settle on a small but sturdy maple, not much bigger than I am.

"Now, try to focus your mind and pour the magic into the tree."

I do as she says, and the tree absorbs the magic like a sponge.

"Good, now place your hands on the tree, close your eyes and feel the tree within your hands. When you do, impart your will upon the tree. It will let you know if what you wish is possible."

When I close my eyes, I feel something reach out to me. Another presence, but entirely inhuman. It's like I can feel the tree's energy in the blackness. There's nothing there, but at the same time, something very special. I try to do what Chief Rizza says, focusing my intention on the tree before me. I go crazy at first, willing it to uproot itself and walk, but I'm met with a forcefield of resistance in the darkness.

Something simpler, then. A shield perhaps. I focus on the tree using its branches and leaves as a shield, protecting it from anything that might harm it. This time, there is no resistance and the tree accepts my offer.

Congratulations! You have unlocked the skill 'Magical Infusion.' You are now a level 1 Infuser (Novice). Increase your skill and learn advanced techniques for working magical infusion by finding an advanced infuser (Apprentice or above). Crafting Ranks: Novice, Apprentice, Journeyman, Expert, Artisan, Master, Grandmaster.

I open my eyes and look to the chief for confirmation.

"Well?" she says.

"Well, what?"

"See if it worked."

I feel stupid doing it, but I pick up a rock and toss it at the tree. I don't use my axe just in case it doesn't work and I kill the tree. Just as the rock is about to hit the tree, several of the tree's branches move with blazing speed and block the projectile. It's almost like the branch has an invisible forcefield around it, because the branches aren't even damaged.

"Wow. This is amazing."

"It truly is. And we have you to thank for it. Now, tell me, Chod. What is your reward?"

As I lay in bed last night, I kept thinking about Jira's words and about the trolls. Even though I've helped them the best I could, I haven't really embraced their culture, embraced my new culture. I've treated this game like every other, content to fight and level, assuming that humans are the main race and that nothing could be done to counter that.

It doesn't have to be that way. I've been given an opportunity to make the trolls relevant, to make them powerful.

"I want two things. One, I want to become a citizen of the village, with a seat on the council to have my voice heard in all council decisions."

Tormara and the other women shake their heads and whisper among themselves.

"And secondly?"

"I want to take a party of women to hunt down the remaining wyrms."

"What makes you think that I would allow that?" She crosses her arms, but behind her, I can see Jira's eyes light up.

"Because I want them to bond together so that if the humans attack again, we can wipe them from the map."

CHAPTER TWENTY-THREE

BEGGARS CAN'T BE CHOOSERS

Tormara stares at me from across the council area. Her red hair blazes vibrantly against the white flowers that bloom from the headrest of her chair. I don't know if she is angry or intrigued by my request to form a party in an attempt to bond the remaining wyrms to the women of the troll village.

"The humans have already killed one mana-infused wyrm. Limery and I slew two others. Taking away the one Chief Rizza has already bonded with, that leaves sixteen. We don't know where they went, all we know is that they are attracted to magical areas. We'll be racing against time to find them before the humans as it is, so I think we should get a group together as soon as possible."

"How many trolls do you require on your adventure?" asks Chief Rizza. Her wyrm lies coiled beneath her feet. "It is not often we send our people outside of the forest, but the cause is worthy of the risk. I have no false hope that we will bond with all of the wyrms, but even one can turn the tides of battle when fully grown."

If it were up to me, we'd take sixteen women in the hope of bonding every wyrm, but I know the chief will not allow it. We still have our reputation to consider. If we are met out in the open by humans, they will attack us on sight. The village can't afford to risk that many lives, no matter how good the reward may be.

"I think at least five should come with me. That will give us the trollpower to tackle any challenge that comes our way and if we succeed in bonding all five, then we will come back and journey out again. I want Jira to come as well."

The council sits in silence, letting my words sink in.

"It's too much," says Guilda. "The village cannot afford to be without Jira. To lose one magic user is enough, but both will leave us in grave risk even with our protections."

"I agree with Guilda," says Kina, one of the other councilwomen. She has bluish-black hair and is the only one who doesn't have it braided or in a bun of some sort.

"I'm sorry, Chod, but Jira must remain here. I'm sure you understand," says Chief Rizza.

I nod. I do understand. Taking Jira was a long shot, but I had to at least ask. Limery and I will be the only magic users in our party.

"I cannot offer you five women either. Many of these magical sources are located within dungeons. You will have to defeat each dungeon just to be able to see if the wyrms are inside. With luck, they may be, but us trolls are not known for our brilliant luck. Every troll I send with you risks death. If they die, they will not come back like you heroes do. For us, death is the end of this world and the beginning of another. Therefore, I will offer you three. If you succeed in bonding all three, then we will send more upon your return."

A party of five to clear a dungeon. Pretty standard. I was hoping for more, but we will have to make it work.

"Do I get to choose who comes?"

"Since anyone who joins you risks death, I will not force them to go against their will. We will have a village gathering where you will ask for volunteers and may take your pick from them."

The council doesn't take long to gather up the villagers. We meet in the village square and for once, I'm able to see the entirety of forest troll society. I now see why they are so worried about leaving the forest. Even with all the male trolls and children present, there can't be much more than a hundred trolls here.

Are the other troll sub-species this depleted as well? If so, why not gather together? There is safety in numbers.

Chief Rizza steps up onto a small pulpit constructed out of living trees. I know for a fact it wasn't there last time that I was here. It's definitely mana-infused. There's still so much I don't know about that aspect of my power, like how to remove the buff or if it's even possible. Could I press my hands against the podium and return it to its natural shape? There's so much I don't know about trolls and about this game in general.

She lifts her hand, and everyone falls silent. "As you know, Chod is now a member of our village. He has also been granted a seat on our council."

There are many nods of affirmation, but the grumbles among some of the trolls are not lost on me. There are those who think I have risen too quickly within the tribe.

"The recent event with the mana-infused wyrms has granted us an opportunity if we are bold enough to take on the challenge. These wyrms, while already strong and powerful, are ripe for bonding if we manage to locate them and subdue them to our will. You all know the power of a full-grown wyrm. Imagine if we had several to protect our village.

"Chod and his companion have volunteered to lead a party out into the world to search for these wyrms so that we may bond them to our cause. I have authorized three females to go. It will be dangerous and there is the very real possibility you may not return, but it is a cause that I find worthy. Now, who among you will join Chod on this quest?"

Silence.

Not a single person volunteers. Whether it is because of how dangerous it is for a troll to leave the forest or because it's me who is leading the expedition, I don't know, but I had at least hoped for three volunteers.

The silence hangs in the air for far too long until Limery pokes me in the back.

"What?" I ask.

He points to the pulpit. "Talks to them. Makes them believe in Chods."

Whispers begin to snake through the crowd. If I can't convince three of them to follow me, then what the hell am I doing here? I might as well be out there alone, being the loner I always have been. If only I had some mole soup right about now. I've never had a problem tearing people down with words, but now, I need to lift them up.

Chief Rizza moves to the side, allowing me to take center stage on the pulpit. Hundreds of eyes, some angry and others ambivalent look back at me. Most of them are probably content to stay in the village and live their lives. With the ley line restored, what do they have to lose by staying?

I've never been one for public speaking, avoiding it at all cost. Streaming was different—no matter how big the audience, it was always just me. Every person watching was nothing more than a number on a screen. I take a deep breath, searching deep inside for something to help me convince these living and breathing pieces of data that I'm worth following into possible death.

"I know you don't know me that well. To many of you, I'm just an outsider who has come into your village and stirred up trouble. To others, I'm nothing more than a tool to help accomplish your objectives, someone who can be sent on foolhardy missions because death doesn't come for me as it does for you. The truth, though, is that I am one of you. I may not have been born here and my skin might not be as green as it once was, but I've been on the outside looking in for my entire life. All I ever wanted was for someone to notice me. I've hidden away for most of my life, just like you. Now, we have that chance to change that. We have the opportunity to make sure the entire island remembers the trolls. If we capture these wyrms and bond them to our cause, we can forge a path for greatness and annihilate anyone who stands in our way. I say the days of hiding away and hoping no one stumbles upon the village are over. We aren't just another monster to be beaten. We are trolls, and we are mighty!"

Congratulations! You have unlocked the skill 'Public Speaking.' You are now a level 1 Orator (Novice). Increase your skill and learn advanced techniques for public speaking by finding an advanced orator (Apprentice or above). Ranks: Novice, Apprentice, Journeyman, Expert, Artisan, Master, Grandmaster.

By the time I finish my speech, I'm ready to tear down the whole fucking forest and siege our way across the island, taking town after town until it's the Isle of Trolls. My blood is pumping, and I'm ready to rumble, but when I look out over the crowd, I see I didn't have the same effect on them. No one is cheering. There's no pounding of chests or thumping fists in the air, only silence.

Long bouts of silence.

If no one volunteers, the mission is off.

There's movement in the crowd and Ismora, the scarred female who trains the children, steps to the front.

"I'll go. I've been aching for a good fight."

Tormara joins by her side, her red braid falling down one shoulder. I've already witnessed the damage she can inflict on a battlefield.

"What the hell, the kid has spunk. I'm in." She actually flashes me a smile for once. "Screw this up, and I'll kill you myself."

For a long moment, no one else volunteers, until Tormara shouts at the crowd.

"Come on! I thought you were braver than this. I remember stories of when the trolls were feared above all others on the island. When we adventured and roamed and battled man and beast alike. Chod is offering us our lives back. A chance to be the warrior tribe that our ancestors were. Will no one answer the call?"

Whispers turn to mumbles until eventually the entire crowd is talking. Women step forward, and the men cheer them on. The ground begins to quake as feet stomp, chests pound, and a roaring chant fills the air.

Damn, Tormara is good.

I practically have my pick of anyone in the village to take with me, but since Ismora and Tormara volunteered when no one else would, they are my first choice.

"Who else should we take?" I ask.

My two new companions look out over the crowd. Ismora whispers something in Tormara's ear and she nods.

"Yashi."

I have no idea who that is.

"Yashi," I yell above the chaos and the roar dulls.

The crowd parts along the middle and I search for Yashi. It's not until she reaches the front that I am able to fully see her. She's small for a troll, even by female standards, and can't be taller than five feet. Her body is composed of nothing but lean muscle, like a young gymnast. Her black hair is split into two braids that flow over each shoulder and two tusks frame an almost innocent-looking face.

"She's not the biggest, but she is sneaky and fast," says Tormara. "We may need her skills."

"Very well. Welcome to the team, Yashi."

She nods and takes her place beside the others.

Chief Rizza steps up beside me and once again the crowd quiets. The respect they have for her is astounding. It makes me wonder how she was able to come into such a position of power.

"There you have it. The future of our tribe rests in the fate of these five individu-als. I pray that—"

"Wait!" a booming voice cuts through Chief Rizza's speech. "Wait!" A giant green body pushes people aside as he makes his way to the front, his giant metal nose ring bobbing with each step.

"I want to go," demands Gord, his broken yellow tusk accentuating his snarl. "The others can keep watch without me."

The chief doesn't speak for a moment. "I'm sorry, Gord, but that is not my decision to make."

He stares into my eyes, but he doesn't speak. I've never noticed that his eyes were so green, like a moss-covered tree.

Gord's an asshole, there is no denying that, but he loves this village like no one else, save the chief. Letting him join us could either be a great advantage or a total mistake.

Fuck it, at least it'll be interesting.

"Let him come."

CHAPTER TWENTY-FOUR

EMPTY THE CHEST

My merry band of trolls and I meet inside of Jira's hut along with the chief to gather our supplies before setting off in search of adventure. Chief Rizza's wyrm waits outside, a blue-eyed sentry. The smell of incense inside is once again overwhelming. Limery sits quietly on my shoulder and Gord broods silently in the corner while Tomara, Ismora, and Yashi talk in excited voices about what's to come. They've been to the edge of the forest and looked out into the world, but none of them have ever set foot outside of the forest since they were born.

Time is of the essence, so we need to grab our supplies and get a move on as soon as possible.

"As far as weapons go, we need to play to our strengths, but we also need to build a decent team composition," I say.

"Meaning what exactly?" asks Ismora. She's a great fighter, but I don't feel that the trolls have ever been one for tactics.

"Meaning all of you shouldn't be swinging clubs. We need some ranged attack. Variation means that one obstacle doesn't shut us all down. Since Gord and I have the most Constitution, we'll be the frontline."

Gord snorts at my suggestion. He doesn't like the idea of me telling him what to do, but it was part of the agreement allowing him to go, so he better get used to it. This is my party and what I say goes.

"Daggers are my specialty, but I'm also decent with throwing knives." Tormara takes a stone dagger from her belt and spins it around her finger.

"I can use a bow." Yashi pulls at one of her black braids and runs her sharp fingernail through the tip. "We have taken several from the humans over the years. They're too small for most trolls, but they're just my size."

"Perfect. What about you, Ismora? What weapons can you use?" Being the one who teaches the trolls to fight, I'm interested in what she brings to the table.

"As you can see..." She displays her scarred arms. "I'm not one to shy away from battle. I am skilled with most melee weapons, but my greatest strength is hand-to-hand combat."

I think we can make this work. "What about other skills?"

"I am quite adept at gathering and potion-making." Yashi still twiddles her braid. "My mother taught me when I was young."

"And I'm a high-level mana-infuser, though I am not sure how useful it will be once we leave the forest," says Tormara.

Neither Gord nor Ismora respond, so it looks like that is what we are working with for the moment.

Jira opens the chest from where he pulled Peacemaker before my journey to the wyrm.

"Chod, your time with Peacemaker has come to an end. It served you well on your quest, but there is another who is worthy now. Remove your magic stone please."

I take out the mana stone and hand the axe to Jira. I knew I wouldn't have it forever, but I was really getting used to having it by my side. I guess it is back to swinging a club until I find something better.

The double-edged battle axe glitters in his hand. Through all the muck and battles, not once did it ever lose its luster. Perhaps one day, I will find some dwarven-made weapons once again.

"Gord." Chief Rizza takes the axe from Jira. "You have been a watchful guardian of the forest for many years. Your loyalty has never been questioned, and therefore, I believe there is no one better to carry our most revered relic of days past. I present you with Peacemaker. May it serve you well."

There's a glitter in Gord's eyes that I have never seen before. He clears his throat and stands taller than before. "Thank you." His voice thunders.

"But that is not all." She moves closer to the chest. "There are a handful of weapons that have been passed down through our people for many years. We have not dared to bring them into the open, for fear of them being lost in battle when so few still remain. However, I feel now is the time to empty our troves and bet everything on ourselves. Jira, if you will."

He reaches into the polished trunk and pulls out a wondrous shield. The trunk must be enchanted, because there is no way that shield should have fit inside. It's made of black steel with a ram's head engraved in the front.

Item. Shield of the Ram. +5 Constitution. Capable of blocking one attack and reflecting damage back to attacker. Cooldown: 60 seconds. *Forged in high altitudes by the Mountain Dwarves, this shield is lightweight, yet unyielding.*

Gord takes the shield and straps it to his arm. It protects the majority of his body and looks like it would weigh several hundred pounds.

Next, Jira pulls out a folded leather pouch and places it on the ground. Untying the leather belt that secures it, he unfolds it, displaying five glittery silver daggers.

Item. Daggers of Light. +3 Dexterity. +3 Strength. Double damage against

dark-aligned monsters. Bonus: Cleanse. Removes all debuffs. Cooldown: 5 minutes.

He lifts a dagger and places it in Tormara's hand. She spins it around her finger, feeling its weight before nodding in approval. Those daggers will be much more durable than the stone ones she currently uses.

Over the next few minutes, we are gifted with an array of weapons, clothing, and jewelry meant to make our journey easier.

Yashi receives Arrows of Truth, increasing her Dexterity and accuracy with the bow, as well as a Blighted Quiver, which infects each arrow with poison.

Ismora is gifted with Boots of Swiftness and Warrior Gauntlets, increasing both her movement speed and strength.

Several small rings go to Limery, boosting his Intellect and Wisdom and no doubt making him even more deadly.

Everything we are gifted goes to my companions. They are the ones who risk true death, so I'll do my best to keep them alive by taking as little as possible.

It hits me hard when I realize how easy all of this would be if we had the opportunity to walk into town and buy weapons or armor from a smith. Instead, everything the trolls have was either taken in battle or passed down from ages ago. No one would ever pick to play a troll after finding that out, no matter how great the physical benefits. The difficulty in competing against other players who have access to everything from the start, I wouldn't be surprised if they came into this world with a small amount of gold already in their pockets.

"We have one final gift," says Chief Rizza. "Chod, you have proven yourself an asset to the village in the short time you have been here. For so long, Jira has been the only magic wielder in our village. I was not sure if we would ever find someone worthy of this next item. Now, it is yours."

Jira pulls a rust-colored staff from the chest and then closes the lid with a thud. The staff looks like a gnarled branch, but it gleams like polished stone. Three sockets run down its side, the same as Peacemaker.

Item. Petrified Staff. An enchanted staff capable of taking on the properties of up to 3 attached stones. +3 Intelligence. +3 Wisdom. Bonus: While holding Petrified Staff, the user can cast ranged physical attacks once every 10 seconds.

I take the staff and it feels natural in my hand. The gnarled head will be strong enough for blunt attacks and the ability to cast a ranged attack every ten seconds means I can stand back while raising horrors and still do damage.

These new items have me feeling better about our chances already. That is until a notification flashes before my eyes.

Regional Event Alert! Percy McDonnell has slain a mana-infused wyrm. 16/20 remaining. 15 days remaining.

CHAPTER TWENTY-FIVE

KNOWLEDGE IS POWER

After receiving the notification of another slain wyrm, it feels like we're racing against the clock. Fifteen wyrms remain in the wild, and there are at least twenty-four other players after them, not to mention NPCs. The entire reason these criminals are in here is to play the hero, to vanquish monsters and claim loot using their violent tendencies for good. We just happen to be the ones they consider monsters.

Our work is definitely cut out for us, but we have something they don't.

The map of ley lines.

I superimpose the magical map the chief gave me over the map of towns and landmarks and it paints a pretty good picture of where we need to look.

There are a total of thirteen human settlements across the island as well as two castles, one on the southern tip and one on the northern tip. A mountain pass separates the island in the middle. Curiously enough, the ley lines bypass every single settlement on the map, aside from the northern castle. It's like the humans have no idea that there is a hotbed of magical activity underneath the surface.

This is good for us because it means we can stay away from humans as much as possible while we try to complete our goal.

The dungeons are hidden from the main map, but based on the way the magical veins converge in certain areas, I think we have a good shot at finding them. The faerie dungeon was right on top of a cluster of ley lines. Limery's cave was over a small vein. He is the only one who might be of any help in locating the dungeons since he alone has knowledge of the world outside the forest.

It's time to follow the map and see what comes of it.

We go south this time around. The original location of the eggs was northwest in the forest, and I don't think it's likely the wyrms went north into the mountain because of where we found the first two. Chief Rizza's managed to find the forest rather quickly as well. There are more magical spots closer together in the south, so it should be easier to hit those first if we go south. If we manage to bind three wyrms, then we can save time by regrouping at the village on our way north.

It takes a little longer for us to reach the southernmost part of the forest and by the time we do, it is already dusk.

"Let us go ahead and camp under the safety of the forest tonight and we can leave first thing in the morning," I say.

No one complains, not even Gord. They must all be incredibly anxious, whether or not they want to admit it. They might be seven feet tall and full of rippled muscle and destruction, but right now, they're kids about to go to their first day of kindergarten.

I'm lost in thought when Yashi approaches.

"Would you like to accompany me to gather herbs? There are certain varieties that only bloom at night and they may aid me in potions for our journey. I would be glad to teach you." There's a twinkle in the small troll's eye when she says it.

"Yeah, that sounds good." I'd like to add more skills to my repertoire anyways and herb-gathering could be particularly useful.

I tell the others we'll be gone for a bit and follow Yashi to the edge of the forest. The sun dips below the horizon and the edge of the forest takes on a silver hue, bathed in moonlight. The hoot of owls is calming and somewhere deep within the forest, howls sing across the night.

Yashi bends down next to a large oak and runs her green fingers along its mossy bark. The moss shimmers under the moonlight.

"Snowy moss," she says, using her claw-like nail to cut the moss from the bark. Even in the moonlight, I can see how it gets its name. The moss has snow-white tips. "It's used in perception potions. They will allow us to boost our Wisdom and see things we might normally miss. Now, you try."

I extend my finger and run my claw underneath the moss. It peels it away from the bark like a sticker on a glass bottle.

Congratulations! You have unlocked the skill 'Herbalism.' You are now a level 1 Herbalist (Novice). Increase your skill and learn advanced techniques for herbalism by finding an advanced herbalist (Apprentice or above). Ranks: Novice, Apprentice, Journeyman, Expert, Artisan, Master, Grandmaster.

Suddenly, I'm able to spot snowy moss all along the forest's edge. A faint green outline appears around it, almost like a notification. Yashi notices my reaction.

"The more herbs you learn, your ability to locate them will improve. Now, gather as much as you can so we may return to the others."

We spend the next twenty minutes cutting moss from the trees until we have a sizable amount and return to our camp, where Gord is roasting some sort of meat over an open flame.

"Do you think it is safe to have a fire blazing at night?" I ask.

"No humans for miles." He turns his back on me, returning to his roast.

"He's right." Tormara leans against a tree, sharpening her new daggers. "We should be safe."

I don't argue, but instead join Yashi as she pulls several clay pots from her bag and places them on the ground next to a mortar and pestle. Some of the pots are filled with a red liquid that looks like blood.

"Your snowy moss, please."

I take it from my satchel and hand it to her. She rips a piece off and places it in the mortar, using the pestle to grind it to a fine pulp. Once the moss is ground up, she pours in some of the red liquid and continues until it forms a dark pink paste. Then she adds more, this time stirring until it becomes a milky-pink liquid and I can finally analyze it.

Item. Perception Potion. *+2 Wisdom. This potion heightens awareness of details and that which might normally go unnoticed. Duration: 2 hours.*

Yashi empties the contents into an empty pot and passes the mortar and pestle to me.

"Now, you."

The moss rips easily in my hands as I take a small amount and place it in the mortar. I follow Yashi's steps exactly until it is time to add the liquid.

"What is this?" I ask, carefully pouring it into the bowl.

"Jackal's blood."

That's when I remember the jackal that spotted me on my first day in the game. It had known I was there even though I used Camouflage. It makes me wonder what other potions are possible in this world. What could we make using the toxic slime from the wyrms?

After mixing in the blood, I'm greeted with notifications.

You have created Perception Potion. Item. +2 Wisdom. This potion heightens aware-ness of details and that which might normally go unnoticed. Duration: 2 hours.

Congratulations! You have unlocked the skill 'Potion-Making.' You are now a level 1 Apothecary (Novice). Increase your skill and learn advanced techniques for potion-making by finding an advanced Apothecary (Apprentice or above). Ranks: Novice, Apprentice, Journeyman, Expert, Artisan, Master, Grandmaster.

Sweet, if I keep hanging out with Yashi, there's no telling how much I'll learn by the end of this trip.

Once we mix the entirety of our snowy moss, we all join around the fire to eat. The meat is juicy and fatty as we devour it with gusto. Limery's sharp teeth rip through the meat like an imp possessed.

After dinner, we all lay down for the night. Limery curls up against my arms, using my Camouflage to conceal him from whatever may pass by in the night.

I'm awakened by Limery's tiny hands shaking me and two pointy red ears bouncing in and out of my vision, an event I've grown accustomed to.

"Get up, Chods. It's times to goes." He's like a needy younger brother waking up his sibling for Saturday morning cartoons. His bulbous yellow eyes radiate excitement.

Everyone else is already packed by the time I wipe the sleep from my eyes, even though the sun is just now breaking the horizon. They must be anxious to get off to an early start. I am, too. Once we find our first dungeon, I'm sure everyone will relax a little, but for now, the anticipation is like another member of our party.

"Morning," I say.

Tormara cleans underneath her claws with her new daggers as she leans against an oak. Gord faces the rising sun with his massive shield strapped across his back. The eyes of the engraved ram's head seem to stare at me ominously.

Yashi and Ismora talk quietly together, but when they notice I am up, Yashi runs over to me.

"We're excited to get started." She looks up at me. "I've been thinking, in order to save our perception potions, we should only take them when we are close to where we suspect a dungeon to be. That way we don't waste it out in the open."

"That's a good idea." If snowy moss is uncommon outside of the forest, then it might be a while before we find any more.

Ismora walks up beside her. "I would like to scout ahead if possible. My Boots of Swiftness will allow me to travel faster, and I can spot any trouble that may threaten our passage."

They all have the same map that the chief gave me, so there's no worry of her not knowing where we are going. It would be so much easier if we had party chat and she could just tell us what was ahead. Instead, we'll have to do it the old-fashioned way.

"Go ahead. If you see any danger, return to us at once." Ismora is a seasoned warrior and I trust her judgment.

Ismora is almost to the forest's edge when Limery calls out to her.

"Waits!"

She stops and turns to the imp with a curious expression. He flies over to where she is and scrounges through his small pack, pulling out a small sphere made of clay. A short piece of string hangs from it.

"Limery, is that a bomb?" I ask.

"Noes. If they's is trouble, lights this and we finds you." He hands the item to Ismora and she looks it over.

Item. Signal Flare. *10 seconds after activating, a beam of light will explode into the sky.*

"Sorry, little one, but we do not carry fire like you." She attempts to hand the flare back to Limery, but he has his fingers to his chin, deep in thought.

"It's okay. Don't needs fire. Just pulls the string and throws it." He flashes a toothy grin and flutters through the air to Ismora's shoulder. "I goes with you. It's okays, right, Chods?"

"Okay, buddy, you lead the way."

Ismora and Limery take off ahead of us, the troll in a dead sprint and the imp flying close behind her. The boots give her noticeable movement speed, but I wonder if my natural boosts to Strength and Dexterity put me at much of a disadvantage. Either way, we will conserve our stamina for our first dungeon.

"Do you really think you'll be able to control the wyrms when they are fully grown?" I ask Tormara as we walk.

It's something that has concerned me since we left. The wyrm seemed well-behaved in the village, but what happens when it's digging tunnels big enough for us to walk through?

Gord rolls his eyes, but he says nothing.

"You don't understand, do you?" She spins a dagger around her finger, its glittery metal sparkling in the sun. "When we bond with a creature, our wishes and desires merge. The bonded creature becomes part of the tribe and would never do anything to hurt us."

Never say never. "I guess that after seeing the mother wyrm in the forest, I have a hard time believing that. I mean, it was so big and powerful that I don't see how anyone could control it."

"One day, you will see."

As we journey south, we pass through wooded areas populated sparsely with trees and bushes. Yashi identifies several new plants for me, such as demon tea leaf, brown creeper, witch's mint, and bloodfennel, and before long, my herbalism skill is at level two. At level five, I will graduate from novice to apprentice.

Midday comes and goes until we aren't more than a few miles from a large batch of congested magical veins. Ismora and Limery return, informing us that the terrain is about to change, and we all down our perception potions. Immediately, I notice a difference, particularly with my herbalism skill. The outline of the plants I can identify glow from further away, even some that are hidden between other plants where only a fraction of it is visible.

The area where the veins converge is full of rolling hills and scattered boulders. Gnarly trees reach out with branches that grasp like fingers at the sky.

We spread out and scan the area, searching for anything out of the ordinary. I cast my horrors, instructing them to move out and scour the area. Before long, our group looks like a search party combing the woods in a horror movie. My HP and Strength are boosted by the forty horrors that roam the hills like ants.

"Over here," Gord's deep voice rumbles.

I find him standing next to a stone entrance carved into one of the hills. The door is closed, and two gnarled trees extend from the top of the hill, their branches blocking the entrance.

Underground Dungeon. *Would you like to enter?*

I accept and wait for the branches to move out of the way.

Underground Dungeon is not currently available. Occupied.

CHAPTER TWENTY-SIX
TALES OF OLD

"Occupied? Someone is inside?" asks Tormara.

Gord tries to smash the gnarled branches that block the entrance to the dungeon with his axe, but they don't give. The magic that powers the dungeon must be protecting them.

"Looks that way." I hadn't expected to encounter other players so soon. Thinking on it now, they have been here for an entire month before me, why wouldn't they have spread out to explore the island? With so many human settlements, it was stupid of me to think they were all in the two nearest the forest.

"What do we do?" asks Ismora. Her warrior gauntlets clink together when she touches them.

"Well, either we stay and wait, hoping they fail the dungeon and it opens up for us, or we try to get a head start to the next magical area."

Two of my horrors die off in a puff of smoke and I cast two more to take their place. The blue impish horror and the fat furry orange one join their siblings on a nearby hill.

Regional Event Alert! Jude Duggan and Michael Didato have slain a mana-infused wyrm. 15/20 remaining. 14 days remaining.

"You have got to be kidding me," I mumble under my breath, knowing everyone else just received the same notification. Whoever is in that dungeon just killed a wyrm. "Everyone, take positions behind the hills. We don't have time for anything else."

We scatter to both sides of the narrow valley that leads into the dungeon. Yashi and Limery join me on one side, and Gord, Ismora, and Tormara take the other. For a long moment, all that can be heard are the soft grumbles of my horrors as they huddle together.

There's a twist of a knob and the door to the dungeon opens. A group of four exits. They are laughing and cajoling one another even though they are covered in blood and gore. The branches rise, allowing the group to pass, then cross together once more.

Two of the men are the players who killed the dragon. Their stats display in my vision.

Jude Duggan
   Level 14
   Fighter
   Human

Michael Didato
   Level 14
   Paladin
   Human

Jude is broad shouldered with an unkempt beard and shaggy brown hair. He wears a brown boiled leather vest while carrying a small round shield and a shortsword. Several knives hang from his belt and a couple of glittering rings adorn his fingers, but there doesn't appear to be anything remarkable about him. Michael, on the other hand, is clad in massive blue and silver armor with a billowing cape that flows to the ground. The armor swallows him whole and might actually fit me if I put it on. He carries a broadsword at least four feet long. His shield is nearly as big as Gord's and is emblazoned with a white raven on a blue background. He screams heavenly power as his golden hair blows in the breeze, and somehow, he is the only one not drenched in blood. He must have the holy dry clean service on speed dial. The other two are level ten foot soldiers wearing the same blue and silver as the paladin, small white ravens adorning their chest pieces. One carries a spear and shield and the other wields a crossbow.

"Sorry about your friend," says Michael the Paladin. He places his hand on the spearman's shoulder. "He fought valiantly and will be reveled in the next life."

"Price of doing business," says Jude the Fighter.

The two soldiers nod.

"Glad to be of service," one says.

"The king will be glad to know Timothy died for the cause," says the other.

Gord's head rises from behind the hill across from us and I suddenly remember they don't understand what these men are saying. Limery and I are the only two with the communication stones.

A wild fury burns in Gord's eyes when we make eye contact, but I shake my head. We're not that far out-leveled by these guys, but we don't need to rush into a fight if we don't have to. Let's just stay put for the moment.

"Where to now?" asks Jude.

"Do you think we should head back to the castle and try to round up a few more men for the next one? I hear that the Paltras Ruins are tougher than this dungeon. We might need the extra manpower. It would be smart to deposit these items as well."

Several more of my horrors have vanished while we hide, but I don't want to risk giving away our location, so I don't cast anymore.

"Paltras Ruins? Is that the old castle by the sea? The one they say is haunted?" asks Jude.

"Good luck finding men to follow you there," says one of the soldiers. "That place is cursed. They say the dead still roam the halls of the castle."

"Ha." Jude smacks the soldier on the back, knocking him forward. "The dead don't bother us. Michael here is a paladin, for fuck's sake. What do we have to worry about?"

"Paladin or not, not many men will risk their lives for Paltras. Not after what happened," the other soldier chimes in.

"What happened?" asks Michael.

They all stop and listen to the soldier while he recounts his story.

"Trolls. It was many ages ago, back when there were four kingdoms on the island. The humans divided the south between Paltras and Vanaria, up north, the dwarves presided over Seascape, and the trolls ruled over all the forest, mountain, and desert between the humans and dwarves."

"The entire thing? I thought there were barely any trolls left?" asked Jude, suddenly serious.

"Now, yes, but back then, trolls were the most populous race on the island. They had access to magic the others did not. While only some of the humans and dwarves possessed the power to use magic, the trolls were able to control it directly, as long as they had access to its source."

"So what happened?" Michael moves in closer.

"What always happens. The trolls got greedy. They wanted more and they attacked Paltras. It's said that they rode in on the backs of giant wyrms and drag-ons, burning the city alive and tearing down its walls. The male trolls went into violent rages, their skins so hot that swords melted when they touched them. It was a massacre."

"That's insane. How were they defeated?"

"Once word of Paltras's fall reached the other two kingdoms, they formed an alliance out of fear that what was happening to Paltras would happen to them. No kingdom alone could stand against the trolls, but perhaps together, they would have a chance. Before the trolls knew what was happening, the women and children that had been left behind in the forest were slain and put on display around its edges as a message. When the troll army returned home, many of the trolls went mad upon seeing them. It's said that the troll king surrendered his army that day, his desire to fight completely gone. They had nothing left to fight for with their offspring dead. You see, they care more about family than most of us in their own twisted way. Take away what they fight for and they crumble like dirt. With no clear direction, the troll kingdom fell apart into what it is today."

"Haha," Jude bellows. "Ghost stories...that's all it is. I'm not gonna say no to fortune and fame because of a few old wives' tales. Not when I've got my man Michael here. When we get back, tell your friends that they have nothing to worry about, okay?"

The two soldiers respond with nervous laughter before following the men away from the small valley between our two hills.

When they are far enough away, I stand and motion for the others.

They gather around me, but I can't stop thinking about the story the soldier told. I finally find out why the trolls are so hated, and it's for a reason that's intrinsically human. Greed. In my time with the trolls, I never would have thought them a greedy race, but yet they wanted to expand their empire just like everyone else. They paid the price for it. A price the trolls are still paying to this day.

"What did they say?" Gord thunders as he looks in the direction the men left in. I can tell he is aching for a fight.

"They were talking about the battle at Paltras," I say. "Is it true?"

Tormara responds, her red braid whipping through the air like a snake. "That they murdered our children and women in cold blood while our ancestors fought to save the princess who had been kidnapped? Yes, it is true," she snaps.

"Wait, what? They said that the troll kingdom was expanding, that they tried to take over the castle out of greed."

All four trolls roar at the same time, snarls on their faces. The roar of frustration is so intense that I can't make any sense of what they are saying.

"One at a time!" I cut them off, and they stare at me in silence. "Will one of you please tell me what happened?"

"I will." Tormara takes a deep breath, letting some of the anger subside. "In ancient times, the troll kingdom was the strongest on the island. Our queen governed and our king led our warriors in battle and adventure. We had the respect of the dwarves in the north and the humans in the south. As we grew more powerful, resentment began to build among the humans. The dwarves were not worried, content to build and mine in their mountainous fortress, but the minds of men are weak and grow troubled when they are not in control. On many envoys, they asked how we were able to control magic simply by touching it, for they had tried and many had died. When we told them that it was simply our way, they refused to believe, certain that we were hiding a powerful secret from them.

"One day, they sent spies into the troll kingdom and stole away the king and queen's daughter, believing that the princess had answers that could be coaxed out of her. And if not her, then certainly the royal family would tell all they knew to get their daughter back. When the queen found out, she ordered the king to gather all of our forces and march on Paltras. He was ordered to tear their kingdom to the ground if the princess was not returned. When the king arrived at their gates, Paltras refused to return the princess. Their human king had gone mad and no rational argument could be made to convince him to let her go. He said that if we would not give him our secrets, then he would kill the princess.

"Our king tried to talk to him, but there was no reasoning to be had. When we had no secrets to give, the princess was burned alive." Fires burn in the eyes the other trolls, angry for a crime none of them were alive to witness. "In a fit of rage, our king attacked the castle, killing everyone inside. When he returned to the forest, the bodies of children and women lined its edges, his queen among them. Many trolls killed themselves in that moment, certain that our race was doomed and unwilling to live a life without their loved ones. On that day, the troll kingdom crumbled. With the majority of our women dead, our population grew smaller and smaller each year, until we split off into the tribes you know today. We were once a mighty and proud kingdom, but now we hide in the shadows."

A solemn anger radiates from the four trolls before me, and even Limery seems on edge by the story. The truth is that I am, too. I know it's a game, but the situations, the history, it's all so reminiscent of real life. And when I look at my party standing before me, the hurt and the hatred feel real, too.

The trolls have had one shitty hand right after another. Even when they were the most powerful kingdom on the island, a lack of understanding caused them to be hated and feared for no other reason than the fact that they were different.

Tormara was right. The minds of men are weak.

The creators at Mythos Games think it's okay to put prisoners in a game and use their violent tendencies against a misunderstood people because it will make them seem righteous and good.

Let's see how they feel about it when we fight back.

CHAPTER TWENTY-SEVEN

HEAVEN AND HELL

My heart pounds in my ears as we run through the hills. With each lumbering step, the power that flows through my body makes itself known. Trolls are something special, and I'll be damned if I'm just going to sit back and watch while their society slowly erodes and their people, no, my people, fade away. For once, Gord and I are on the same page. We hunger for reckoning. Our plan is to ambush the group that just left the dungeon, take their items, and make it to Paltras Ruins before they have time to replace their armor and supplies. They'll also lose a level upon dying, setting them even further behind. After that, I'll talk with the council and we'll make a plan for what comes next.

If they want to make us the villains, then it's high time we acted the role.

Ismora runs ahead of us, her Boots of Swiftness proving useful as she scouts for the group. She comes to a stop and raises a fist, letting us know she found them.

"Does everyone know their roles?" I ask when we all gather. Less than a hundred yards away, the group walks, oblivious to our impending attack.

They nod in affirmation and then we break into our positions. The terrain is jagged and rocky, rolling hills splotched with bushes, and small trees offer just enough concealment for us to attempt an ambush. Gord, Tormara, Ismora, and I, along with my army of horrors, descend upon the group from behind while Yashi and Limery flank them from the sides. Their objective is to cause as much chaos as possible so that we can attack them without being noticed.

As we approach, our footsteps sound like a herd of buffalo. If Yashi and Limery don't draw their attention soon, then there is no way they won't hear us coming.

The flick of a bowstring lets me know the battle is on. Yashi's poisoned arrow soars through the air, penetrating the neck of the footsoldier carrying the spear. He staggers back and forth for a moment before pulling the arrow from his neck. Blood sprays from the wound in an arc. She scored a critical hit! That'll be one less opponent to worry about. Each spurt of blood grows weaker and I'm certain the soldier is about to die, until a stream of holy light shines upon him and the wound closes.

Yashi fires off another arrow, but this time, the men are prepared. The paladin rushes forward, blocking the arrow with his shield. He yells something and then a white aura surrounds all four men.

A fireball soars across the battlefield, striking the fighter in the back. He falls forward, losing a sizable chunk of health, the back of his boiled leather armor scorched black. The two foot soldiers make to escape, but a fiery wall erupts in front of them as Limery zooms overhead. He taunts them, calling the men 'filthy humanses and dirty scoundrelses,' all the while peppering them with fireballs the size of softballs. A crossbow clanks and a bolt narrowly misses his giant head, forcing him to retreat further into the air.

In that moment, the fighter rises to his feet and sees us coming. The look he gives us is one of pure hatred. As he raises his sword to attack, a wicked grin creeps across his face. This is a man who loves to fight.

"Gather up," he shouts to the two soldiers and they prepare for our onslaught. "Cedric, take out the bitch up on the hill. The rest of you, follow me. Michael, cast an aura of protection overhead to ward off the fireballs for now."

The paladin raises his sword and a silverish barrier, almost like glass, appears overhead, repelling Limery's fireballs as if they were nothing.

We charge at the three men, the soldier with the crossbow having fallen back to target Yashi.

"Gord, take the lead. I'll be right behind you. Ismora and Tormara, if you see an opening, then make them bleed."

Gord runs straight ahead, using his shield as a battering ram. He collides with the paladin, knocking him aside and into the spearman. The fighter jumps to the side and does a barrel roll, springing back to his feet. He raises his sword to attack Gord's blind side, but I use Petrified Staff's bonus ability to fire a stream of physical energy that hits him square in the chest, knocking him off balance and causing him to miss.

A wave of ten horrors scurries on the group, slowing them and attacking with their razor-sharp claws and teeth. The paladin raises his sword in the air and a beam of holy light tears through the horrors, sending them up in a puff of smoke.

The foot soldier hacks and slashes against the horrors, giving as good as he gets, but his health depletes with each hit he takes until the paladin washes him with holy light, replenishing lost health. Out of the edge of my eye, the soldier with the crossbow makes his way towards the hill where Yashi continuously fires on the larger party.

Gord and the fighter square off in the rear as my staff cracks against the paladin's shield.

"Trolls! The blight of the earth!" he shouts as his imbued strike slashes through an entire row of horrors. Half of them die, but I immediately cast two more in their place.

Tormara and Ismora pick at the foot soldier who desperately tries to free himself from the horrors surrounding him. The movement speed debuff of Horror of Vitality thwarts his efforts, and the two trolls make short work of the man.

That leaves us five on two while Yashi and the crossbowman play their game of cat and mouse in the distance.

"Ismora, go help Yashi. Tormara, assist Gord. Leave this asshole to me."

The paladin looks up in surprise at the fact he can understand me, momentarily forgetting about the horrors that surround him. It's like he just now looked at my stats for the first time.

"You're a hero? But how?"

"Just lucky, I guess." I shoot him in the chest with a ranged attack from my staff. I cast another horror and use Claw, but he blocks my attack with his shield. My claws grate against the shield, shrieking through the battle.

"No matter, you will die just the same."

Limery continues his attacks from above and eventually, a crack forms in the heavenly barrier overhead as the fighter and paladin move back to back.

With at least twenty horrors still alive, my HP and damage are pretty high. I attempt to move in to use Bite, but a blast of light knocks me back, taking out a chunk of health. I cast Horror of Finesse and my next attack heals me even though the paladin blocks it. He's tough, a great defensive tactician, but our sheer numbers will overwhelm them in the end.

A powerful swing of his sword connects with my ribs and pain flares through my side. I look down to see a massive gash where blood spills down my side.

I retreat as my regeneration takes effect, letting my horrors have the frontline. I need to get back in the fight to use heal, but all I can think about right now is the stinging pain in my side.

A deep yell from beyond the paladin draws my attention and for the first time, I realize the true difference between a hero and NPCs.

Blood streams down Gord's body. His shield drags against the ground. Something is wrong with his arm, keeping him from lifting it. Tormara looks no better, a gash runs along her face and her clothing is drenched red around her midsection. They both look on the verge of exhaustion.

In a blur, the fighter moves from Gord to Tormara, his blade moving quicker than I can see it. The only evidence he attacked at all is the fresh wounds on both of my party members. He pulls a dagger from his waist and throws it at Gord, lodging it in his ribs.

Gord keels over in pain before removing the dagger and tossing it to the ground. He takes another step towards the fighter when a new pain takes over.

"Poison..." He stumbles and almost falls to the ground.

The fighter twists the pommel of his sword in his hand for show. Tormara attacks with a dagger of her own, but the fighter sidesteps it with amazing speed, leaving a shadow in his place. The shadow explodes and the dagger clatters to the ground. A fireball comes hurling towards his head, but he raises his shield at the last moment, absorbing the attack. The shield glows red, but he takes no damage.

He takes a lunging step and a wave of energy erupts from his sword, knocking both Gord and Tormara to the ground. If I don't do something soon, they will both die. A death neither one can come back from.

I leave the paladin to my horrors for now, even though his holy attacks seem to be having a greater effect on them.

At full speed, I slam into the fighter from behind, using Bite and sinking my teeth into his neck for a critical attack. I follow up with Claw and rake his side. There's a grunt of pain just before something stabs into my stomach. I roll to the side and spot a dagger held in a reverse grip in the fighter's hand. He stumbles to his feet, facing me.

"So you're the big bad champion of the trolls? Chod, is it? We were all wondering who it was that managed to start a regional event. Looks like the higher-ups have a few tricks up their sleeves." He lets out a cold laugh. "I bet Glenn would love to have a crack at you. Too bad I'll be the one popping the cherry."

Tormara slings another dagger and once again, the fighter moves in a blur, leaving a shadowy trail in his wake.

"I've about had enough of you," he says. With a flick of his wrist, another dagger strikes Tormara just above the heart. She grimaces in pain and grasps at her wound, her health nearly depleted.

I feel my bonus HP dropping as the paladin continues his holy war against my horrors. If I don't do something now, I'll lose any advantage I might have.

"Limery, cut him off," I yell, and a wall of flame erupts between the fighter and the trolls.

I use Berserker Rage and my vision reddens at the edge as power and chaos take control of my body. Quickly, I summon two more horrors and feel my HP grow even more. Without wasting any time, I charge the fighter. I feint a swing of my staff, but instead, fire a bolt of physical damage, taking him off guard. He counters with a quick slash of his sword, but my increased health regeneration barely drops from the attack.

"After I kill you, tell your friends that the trolls are done hiding. You can either make room for us in the world, or we will make it ourselves."

He wipes away a drop of blood from his lip and spits blood to the ground.

"You have no idea what you're doing." He smirks. "You have no idea what we're capable of."

I summon a Horror of Vitality right next to him, slowing his movement speed. Limery's fireball engulfs him from behind.

The paladin raises his sword to perhaps cast a heal, but his spell is interrupted by an arrow finding the soft spot in his armor. He falls forward as my horrors dogpile on his body.

I use the moment to cast Intimidation, and the fighter's eyes glaze over for a moment. My staff connects with the side of his head, dropping his health to twenty percent, and I follow up with Bite and Claw. Limery casts a giant fireball that swallows the man whole like a hungry sun. By the time the fireball dissipates, all that remains is the man's armor and weapons.

With the fighter down, I focus my attention back on the paladin. Only glimpses of his armor can be seen beneath the pile of blue and orange miscreants. Gord tries to join me, but I can see the anguish in his face and motion for him to sit. Yashi, Ismora, and I will finish this.

Above the grumbling, gnashing teeth, and claws that grate against the paladin's armor, I hear the sound of singing. It reminds me of the choirs I heard on the few times my family attended church, usually on a holiday. A gentle, warm hum pervades through the chaos and death.

And then, an explosion of light. My health depletes in an instant as every last horror vanishes in the light, taking my entire bonus HP and Strength along with it.

The paladin takes to his feet, still at half-health. He must have just blown his ultimate ability. It reminds me of every cheesy action movie where the hero rises from the ashes. Cue corny dialogue.

"Is that all you've got?" he roars, his blond hair blowing in a breeze only he seems to be standing in.

"Hardly."

Limery lands on my shoulder, and Yashi and Ismora approach from the paladin's rear. Tormara stumbles over, clutching her chest and grimacing.

I quickly cast one of each horror and my health and Strength rise a small amount.

"Why don't we show this asshole what hell feels like?" I say, and in that moment, I know I'm finally one of them.

Everyone, even Tormara, manages to smile.

"Yous funny, Chods," says Limery, a fireball crackling in his palm.

An aura of white light surrounds the paladin and his HP slowly replenishes.

"Now!" I take off into battle as fireballs, arrows, and daggers find their mark. They do little damage against the paladin's stout defenses, but his defenses won't last forever. I'm several yards away from the paladin when I use my staff to pole vault over his body, leaving him swiping at air as I land behind him. Ismora arrives beside me just as I land. She punches him with one of her gauntlets, leaving a dent in his armor at the same time as I kick him like I'm breaking down a door.

His legs curl under as his body flies forward. Yashi's poisoned arrows stack their damage and deplete his health faster than he can regenerate. A holy beam descends from the sky, burning my skin, killing my horrors, and dropping my health by ten percent.

The paladin rises to his feet, his sword and shield bathed in divine enchantments. He tosses his shield aside and runs at me, sword held over his shoulder with both hands.

A massive force smashes into him from the side. Steam rises off Gord's emerald skin, his wounds healing before my eyes. Berserker Rage. Gord hacks at the paladin with otherworldly force, and I'm taken aback by the beauty in the destruction. The paladin raises his hand as if to say something, but with one final chop, Gord separates head from shoulders.

Notifications fill my vision, but I push them away. Ismora and Gord are already gathering weapons and armor and placing them in a pile. The paladin's body has already vanished, but the two foot soldiers remain. They drag the bodies over, and I notice the one with the crossbow has an arrow lodged in his eye.

"You all fought bravely. It was a good fight, but our teamwork could use a little work. It's nothing that fighting side by side won't fix. Yashi, next time you get singled off like that, I want you to retreat to the group. You're more useful fighting alongside us than pulling away a single opponent." She nods. "Gord, what took you so long to go into a rage?"

He tosses the fighter's shield on top of the pile. "For us, we do not choose when the rage happens. It is in our blood," he thunders, but for once, his answer isn't contemptuous.

Once we strip the men of their armor, we have a pretty sizable pile of loot. I pass the rings from the fighter off to Ismora and Tormara. They are an assortment of Strength and Dexterity buffs. I offer Gord the paladin's armor, but he refuses, saying that his skin is the only armor he needs. It's a bit foolish, but movement speed is key for his battle style. Ismora takes the crossbow, and Tormara adds a few more daggers to her collection.

When we have what we want, we wrap the rest of the items up in the looted clothing, forming makeshift bags. If we happen to come across a boar, then maybe I can fashion another leather satchel to help carry the extra items. The paladin's shield is too massive of a burden, so we leave it behind, even though I'm sure it would fetch a good amount if we ever had the opportunity to sell it.

With everything sorted, I pull open my notifications.

Congratulations! You have reached level 13. +1 stat point to distribute. +1 Strength and Constitution racial bonus. +1 ability point to distribute.

Warning! You have killed a human NPC. If word of this reaches a human settlement, your reputation among humans will be decreased by 100. Stop your enemies from reaching town before it is too late. Current reputation with humans: -1399. (-1000 Racial Penalty)

Warning! You have killed a human NPC. If word of this reaches a human settlement, your reputation among humans will be decreased by 100. Stop your enemies from reaching town before it is too late. Current reputation with humans: -1399. (-1000 Racial Penalty)

Warning! You have killed another player. Your reputation among humans has been decreased by 100. Current reputation with humans: -1499. (-1000 Racial Penalty)

Warning! You have killed another player. Your reputation among humans has been decreased by 100. Current reputation with humans: -1599. (-1000 Racial Penalty)

Alert! You have failed to stop your enemies from reaching town. Your reputation has decreased by 200. Current reputation with humans: -1799. (-1000 Racial Penalty)

Not that I expected anything less. As soon as the players respawned, our reputation was bound to take a hit. It might as well be negative one million at this point. But the good news is that I have another ability point and I can finally unlock my final summoner ability.

Horror of Power. Summon a horror with 20% of your Strength. Cost: 100 mana. Cooldown: 30 seconds. Bonus: Your next attack deals double damage.

I summon my new horror and it appears in a puff of smoke. It looks completely different than the other two. While Horror of Finesse is lean and quick, and Horror of Vitality is fuzzy and tanky, Horror of Power is solid muscle. It walks on all fours, wide-stanced like a pit bull with a massive head, sharp teeth, angry red eyes, and tusks that shoot out of its jaw like a warthog. Its fur is golden with a black mane around its head. A barbed tail with four spikes swishes through the air like a mace.

It paces like a lion on the prowl, ready to battle whatever comes its way.

Everyone stares at the horror in admiration. I'm pretty sure I see a fleeting smile cross Gord's face. Our army just got a hell of a lot stronger. As I look around, I notice everyone else leveled up from the battle as well.

I still have three stat points to use from the last few times I leveled up. I elect to put them in Intelligence in the off chance that it helps me with my casting and am surprised when I receive another notification.

New Class Ability (Summoner). Each ability requires one ability point.

Sacrifice. *Sacrifice X amount of horrors to receive a temporary buff. Horror of Power: +1 Strength. Horror of Vitality: +1 Constitution. Horror of Finesse: +1 Dexterity*

Kamikaze. *Sacrifice a horror to deal a burst of damage.*

Holy shit! I don't know why I just assumed that there were only three abilities for being a summoner. It's a magical class, so of course, there are perks to increasing my Intelligence. Probably some for increasing Wisdom too. I can't wait for another ability point so that I can unlock one of these new abilities. All the more reason for us to get a move on.

"Is everyone ready? We are officially in a race to Paltras Ruins."

CHAPTER TWENTY-EIGHT
NO ONE SAID THERE WOULD BE SO MUCH WALKING

Congratulations! You are now a level 2 Leatherworker (Novice).

I finish the last stitch using the technique Gord taught me and neatly place the clothing and weapons we looted inside, along with the mana stone the wyrm dropped. Maybe Jira will be able to use it once we return. Mine is much more powerful so there is no need to equip it to my staff.

We have made great progress throughout the day, managing to go the entire day without seeing any humans, so now we can finally settle down for the evening and enjoy the great boar that Ismora shot with her new crossbow. It's twice the size of a normal boar, plenty big enough to feed all six of us.

Gord roasts several giant slabs of meat over a spit that Limery built, his natural aptitude for building machines benefiting us all. Yashi is off picking herbs for potions. After the battle today, it's more important than ever that we manufacture our own health potions.

"How are you feeling?" I ask Tormara, who is leaning against a tree and sharpening her daggers.

She moves aside her red braid and rubs at a sage-colored scar just above her chest, the only remnant of the brutal wound she suffered earlier.

"I'll be fine. A little sore. My pride was hurt more than anything."

I know that's not true. The fighter would have killed them both if not for my intervention. She and I both know it. The fact that heroes have these special abilities makes such a big difference in battle. The NPCs with magical abilities are the only ones in the same ballpark. It's like taking a knife to a gun-fight for most of them. Sheer numbers can do a lot, but one on one, there's no comparing. Which is all the more reason we need to make it to Paltras Ruins before Jude and Michael have a chance to regroup. If we manage to bond with these wyrms, they will even the playing field for our side more than anything. Well, those and my horrors.

The whole thing seems a little unfair, how I and the other heroes come into this world and level up in days what it takes these people years to do. We unlock abilities most of them can only dream of. I can't imagine what it would be like to witness something like that in the real world.

Real world, ha.

Aside from the mythical creatures and magic, this honestly doesn't feel that different.

By the time Yashi returns, the rest of us have already finished our portions of the boar. The gamey texture of wild meat is something I've grown accustomed to. She carries an armful of thorny brambles and sets them down in front of me.

"Tonight, you are going to learn one of our most ancient potions. It's hell tracking down this particular ingredient, because it grows high in trees and is not often visible from the ground. But with the perception potion we made yesterday combined with my high herbalism skill, I was able to find some. While we are natural healers compared to most, I'd rather not leave our fortune to chance if we find ourselves in a grave battle once again."

"What is this?" I pick up the plant to inspect it.

It resembles a brier, with a long, thick stem covered in thorns. Pink berries the size of grapes blossom from its fuzzy leaves. Each stem is about a foot long.

"It's Horned Thimbleberry. Both the stem and berries have properties that aid in healing. We are going to mix it with the bloodfennel and powdered crow's feet for an even more potent product. When we add the final ingredient, we'll have a rapid healing potion that might just save your life one day."

Or yours, more likely.

Her knowledge of herbalism is astounding. "Yashi, what did you do back in the village? With all the excitement, I never thought to ask." I already know about the others. Ismora trains the children in combat, Tormara holds a seat on the council, and Gord is a guardian, but Yashi is a mystery.

She gives me a smile. "You couldn't guess? I make potions. Not that we have a particular need for them, but every now and then, someone has need of my skills. In the old days, it was said that our potions were widely regarded among both men and dwarves, but times have changed. I know potions to help with sleep, to heighten senses, even to conceal one's scent from animals. It's best to have someone knowledgeable in the art of potion-making and not need them than to be lacking when the time comes. Now, grab your mortar and pestle and get to work."

I do as she says, taking the horned thimbleberry and mashing it until it forms a paste before adding in the bloodfennel, a bright red stalk, and doing the same. Once they are mashed, Yashi pours a little of the powdered crow's feet into the mix. Out of the corner of my eye, I spot Limery and Gord having a conversation. Did today's battle actually soften his hard exterior?

"What's the final ingredient?" I ask.

Tormara pulls one of her daggers from her belt and tosses it towards me, the blade landing in the earth.

"Blood," says Yashi.

"Wait, what?" Nobody said anything about blood magic.

"Blood activates the bloodfennel, which combined with the horned thimbleberry and crow's feet will form the health potion."

"Does every race use blood in their health potions?" I know it's always been red for health potions and blue for mana, but have gamers secretly been drinking blood all these years?

"No, there are other ways, but we are lucky that our blood has such power. It cuts out a lot of ingredients, and the horned thimbleberry is the only one difficult to find. Now, if you are done being squeamish, I'd like to finish these up before the sun rises."

To be so small, Yashi has a lot of sass. She takes the knife and pricks my finger, squeezing several drops of blood into the mortar. The paste steams and bubbles for a moment before turning into a semitransparent liquid.

You have created Health Potion. Restores 10% health over the course of 20 seconds.

That's not bad at all. Then a thought dawns on me.

"Whoa, wait a minute. Whose blood was in the potions I took with me to fight the wyrm?" I ask, but Yashi just rolls her eyes at me.

I level up my potion-making skill as we fill up several clay jars with the potion.

"Why do you keep pricking my fingers?" I ask. "There's five of us. Couldn't someone else help out?" Even with my tough skin and regeneration, the force it takes to draw blood stings just like a real doctor would.

"Because you're the student," she laughs, revealing her small tusks.

When I wake the next morning, a notification crosses my vision.

Regional Event Alert! *Kevin Harris has slain a mana-infused wyrm. 14/20 remaining. 13 days remaining.*

Someone had a late night. Not counting the chief's wyrm, that means thirteen wyrms still remain out in the wild. I'm feeling less confident about finding three wyrms by the day and it's becoming even more important that we reach Paltras Ruins before anyone else. There are plenty of options for leveling up in the countryside, but I aim to reach the ruins by nightfall.

Tormara falls in line beside me as we walk. Far ahead, Ismora is but a small dot on the landscape as she scouts for anything out of the ordinary. Gord pulls up the rear, and Limery flies high overhead.

"What is it that you hope to accomplish with all of this?" she asks.

"What do you mean?" I thought my intentions have been pretty clear.

"Once we have the wyrms, once we are back in the village. What then? What happens to our people?" Her face radiates concern. I've only ever seen Tormara as strong and powerful, spitting fire and challenging others with an iron tongue, but deep down, she cares for her people above all, just like Gord. These trolls are just as complex as any real person.

"Honestly, I don't know. I've only been here a short while, but you all have accepted me as one of your own. Some of you took longer than others. I feel a great connection with this community, and I don't like the way you're constantly shit on by the other races. If everyone wants to stay in the forest and hide out, then that's fine, I won't push the issue. But I'm sure you feel the same as I do, that there is something in our blood that begs for greatness. The greatness the trolls once had."

She gives me a half-smile. "Many will die to attain greatness and our numbers are already low. You know there will be retribution for our attack on the undying ones, right?"

"Yes, but if we get a wyrm before it is killed, then I believe it will be worth it. Once we have them, we can lay low until they are grown."

"They will come looking for us," she counters.

"Will the magic from the forest not keep us hidden?" I ask.

"From most, but you have already seen the power of potions. Those who know where to look can always find us."

"Then we will just have to make sure we are ready."

We carry on in silence for a while. Yashi identifies several new plants as we walk and eventually, my herbalism skill increases again, allowing me to spot the plants I have identified from further away.

At one point, I hear a loud caw and look up to see a falcon diving for Limery. A shimmer appears around his pointy little fingers and there is a sizzle before the bird falls with a thunk to the ground. Gord picks it up and bites off the head.

"What?" he asks as the bones crunch in his mouth.

By late evening, Ismora comes to a stop, and we catch up to her on the top of a high hill. From atop the hill, the coastline is visible and near its edge, Paltras Ruins.

The castle is indeed in ruins, the exterior walls are crumbling in places and vines and other plants have overtaken the castle. Moss covers the stone walls, and trees grow above them in places, evidence no one has been there in years. Several large black birds perch along the parapet. The castle hugs the coastline, only walled on three sides, the keep sitting far back against the rocky cliffside that serves as its own form of defense.

It is still several miles from where we are, but with a little luck, we will make it by nightfall.

"Let's speed it up, team. We can rest once we make it."

By the time darkness falls and the moon casts its silver glow over the ocean, we are within a mile of the castle. The salty air of the coast fills our lungs. Limery perches on my shoulder, and there is a look I haven't seen before in his bulbous yellow eyes.

"This place no goods, Chods. Limmy no likes it one bit."

My eyes fall on the castle and I know what he means. There is something unsettling about the abandoned structure. Deep within its walls, I swear there is a green glow coming from the keep.

"I agree with the little one," Gord thunders. "Something is very wrong with this place."

I'm reminded of our encounter yesterday. The human soldiers were adamant about this place being haunted. Looking at the map, this location is a hotbed for magical activity. Maybe it's more than the average dungeon.

Sounds of the night come alive as we approach. Crickets chirp, owls hoot, and something a little more haunting seems to linger in the chilly air. The hairs on my neck rise the closer we get until finally, we arrive at the entrance to the castle. The portcullis that once kept out intruders lies rusted and broken.

When we step beneath the gateway, we are greeted with a notification.

Paltras Ruins. *Would you like to enter?*

I accept and we walk through the gateway. Limery's claws dig a little deeper into my skin.

There's a loud clank, and I turn to see the portcullis moving of its own accord. It rises from the ground and flies into the gateway, hinging itself in place and blocking our exit.

CHAPTER TWENTY-NINE
PALTRAS RUINS

The portcullis secures itself in the outer gateway, blocking our escape. Our only way out is to go forward. Before us stands a second wall with another gatehouse that bars our way to the courtyard. Everyone holds their weapons at the ready, and Limery clings ever tighter to my shoulder. High above, clouds frame the moon, lighting the sky with eerie shadows.

"Somethings is here, Chods," Limery whispers.

I peer around the decaying castle. Everything is empty and desolate, except for the faint green light that glows from behind the furthest windows of the keep.

"That's where we need to go." I point to the keep.

We step into the gatehouse, where murder holes remain from long ago, though they are now mossed over. I'm sure that this castle was magnificent once, full of life and bustling activity, but now it is nothing more than a skeleton. And more than that, a graveyard. Along the battlements, several of the stone walls are still scorched from the battle long ago. I can only imagine the force it must have taken to wipe this place off the map.

The other trolls seem somewhat in awe as they take the castle in. Sure, they have had battles, but they've never experienced anything like this. To be able to tear down one of the greatest human structures on the island on a whim is not the same as winning a battle in the forest. I'm sure it just reminds them of how far the trolls have fallen.

"Let's find the wyrm and then leave," says Tormara.

Suddenly, there's a flash of silver behind the murder holes and I swear for a moment an arrow is pointed in our direction. As quick as it appears, it is gone.

"Did anyone else see that?" I look deeper into the murder hole, but nothing is there.

"See what?" Ismora faces me, always the first one on alert.

They all look around, but whatever I saw has disappeared. Goosebumps erupt along my arms, and the hair on the back of my neck reaches for the stars. This place is really giving me the creeps.

"Nothing, let's just get through here." Before this turns into a horror movie and we all die.

A cloud passes in front of the moon, and I'm struck with a shooting pain in my shoulder. Yells of anguish ring out around me, and I turn to see a shimmering ethereal arrow protruding from my right shoulder. An angry silver face shouts at me from behind a slat in the wall.

Ghost. *Level 12. The haunting remains of those unable to pass into the next world.*

Limery slings a fireball at the ghost but before it connects, the silver man vanishes once more. I reach to pull out the arrow, but it is no longer there either, only the bloody wound where it had entered.

"They were right. This place is haunted." Blood continues to stream down my arm.

Gord, Tormara, and Ismora all have blood streaming from various spectral injuries.

That's when I notice the courtyard is bathed in the light of the moon once more. It doesn't take a genius to see the connection.

"It's the moonlight. Whenever it disappears, that's when the ghosts come out. Let's get out of this gatehouse before they return and we're sitting ducks."

"Sitting what?" asks Ismora, not understanding the reference.

"Nothing. Before we're dead."

As soon as we are out of the gatehouse, I find the moon. It's a cloudy night and they shuffle across the sky, able to blot out the moon at any point. There's no way to know if there are ghosts everywhere or just outside the castle until we make our way inside.

"Get moving before the clouds come out. We need to make it to the keep."

Before we are even halfway across the courtyard, an army of silver foot soldiers erupts before us. One rushes at me, sword raised, and I use my staff to block its attack, but the blade passes through my weapon and cuts into my skin. I cast a Horror of Finesse and attempt to use heal, but my attack goes straight through his translucent body. The horror wanders around, unable to attack until the ghosts bludgeon it to death.

The strained cries of my teammates surround me as archers fire a volley of spectral arrows down upon us, dropping our health in droves.

"We can't attack. We can't defend," yells Gord. "What the hell are we supposed to do?"

"Take thats!" screams Limery, tossing a fireball at a nearby soldier. When the fireball hits him, the ghost goes up in a puff of smoke. He follows up with another fireball just as I'm hit in the chest with an arrow. I reach to pull the arrow out, but my hands pass through it and then suddenly, it vanishes.

Everyone breathes heavily as they try to patch their wounds as best they can. I continue to cast my horrors. Even if they can't attack, the bonus health might just save my life.

"Yashi, the potions. Pass them out." Her small frame has left her unscathed so far. "Magical attacks are all that work against the ghosts. Limery, we're going to make a run for the keep. If the ghosts appear again, I want you to cast a wall of fire on both sides of our group. It's the only way to keep the ghosts off of us. Can you do that?"

He nods and flies in the air. "Limmy is ons it!"

The rest of the group downs health potions and we take off running towards the keep. The clouds blot out the moon, and once again the courtyard becomes a battle-field. I can't even count how many soldiers surround us before flaming walls rise on both sides of me. The heat is uncomfortable, but it beats the alternative. Arrows sizzle into nothingness as they enter Limery's wall of flame and several ghosts vanish trying to rush through it. Yashi and Ismora race ahead of me, and the entrance to the castle keep comes into view.

The door is closed when we arrive, but with our strength combined, Gord and I are able to force the rusted hinges.

The door shuts with a thud and we all take a moment to gather ourselves.

"That…was intense," says Ismora. Her normally neat ox-horn buns are messy, with strands falling over her pointed ears. Our entire team looks like they just went through hell.

Then I notice a hulking black figure cloaked in darkness on the other side of the room. Several more figures spread out along the first floor of the keep, none of them moving. I rise to my feet, ready to fight, but the cloaked figures stand pat.

Wraith. Level 13. Although unable to attack while being looked upon, wraiths are deadly to those who pass by unaware. They shroud their victims in darkness, draining the life from them.

The creature wears a black hood of tattered fabric, obscuring the face that lies underneath in total darkness that even my night vision can't see through. For most races, the inside of the castle would prove foreboding, the lack of light allowing the wraiths to swoop down upon their enemies before they were ever spotted.

We're not that unfortunate.

"We need to get to the glowing door," I say, pointing across the hallway. "Keep your eyes out for wraiths and make sure we are always focused on them. If you turn your back, they will move forward and attack, but if we stay aware, we should be able to pass through without incident. There is rubble all along the floor, so be careful where you step."

A set of staircases on each side of the entrance spiral up to what I imagine are the living quarters and a long, wide hallway extends forward to a set of massive doors where green light emits from underneath. I'm certain it is the throne room and that is where we need to be.

I take the lead, keeping my eyes focused on the wraiths before us. They hover in the air ominously, but aside from the swish of their cloaks, they don't move. Foot-steps tell me my party is behind me, but I can't look to confirm.

"Is someone watching the rear?" I ask.

"I am," Gord replies.

"Limery, if any of the wraiths start moving, I want you to let us know."

"Limmy can do it."

We pass by a wraith that towers above us, hovering a dozen feet off the ground. Its tattered clothing sways ominously as we pass, and its cold raspy breath chills me to the bone.

We're a few yards from the door when a firm body plows into my back, knocking me to the floor.

"Oh no, I slipped!" says Tormara as we scramble back to our feet.

I turn my head and a wraith comes to an abrupt halt a foot from my face. Its arms are spread wide, opening the cloak and displaying the infernal darkness that resides within. The emptiness inside threatens to swallow me whole if I will only give in. It's mesmerizing, almost welcoming.

Peace surrounds me as I let the pull take over.

"Chod!" Ismora's hand grasps me on the shoulder, bringing me back to the world. "We're at the door."

I'm lost for a moment as I reacclimate.

"Okay, keep your eyes on the wraith, and when I give the order, we all rush inside."

The handle of the door is ice cold with a small streak of green light escaping through the keyhole. Whatever is on the other side, I pray there is a wyrm with it. My fingers wrap around the cold bronze handle and I pull. The door opens with ease, and we are all bathed in green light.

CHAPTER THIRTY

GHOST STORIES

We hurry into the room, and the door slams behind us. Immediately, I feel my HP begin to drain. We're all bathed in a neon glow from the other side of the room, and I look up to see a decrepit man sitting on a rusted throne. His body radiates spectral energy, every part of him an opaque neon green. A crown sits lopsided on his head, displaying a wide gash that cuts from ear to nose. The other side of his face is covered in burn marks. An old robe lays curled around his feet.

To his side, three knights, all the same greenish hue, stand watch with their swords displayed in front of them, point down while their hands rest on the hilts. They're not quite ghosts, but also not quite living, caught somewhere in the middle.

King Bartholemy. Specter. *Level 16. A specter is a ghost gone mad. Their very presence depletes the life of anyone around them.*

What Tormara said appears to be true. The king did go mad. He is level sixteen, and the three knights are each level fourteen. He leans one arm against the side of his throne, oblivious or uncaring to our presence.

My HP drops to ninety percent and I notice that everyone else's is doing the same.

"Yashi, we need the health potions. Just being in this room is draining our life!"

"What do we do?" asks Tormara, eyes wide.

"We fight!" Gord thrusts his axe forward, "Instead of standing around and dying."

The king lifts his head, his pupil-less eyes finally noticing us.

"You will all die soon enough." He leans back against the throne. "They always die."

The robe around his feet moves and I realize that it is not a robe at all. Two blue eyes stare at me before falling back to the floor. This wyrm looks nothing like the others. It's deflated and shriveled, like it had the life sucked out of it.

Because it has.

The specter's ability must be constantly draining the wyrms HP while the mana source is enough to keep it barely alive at the king's feet.

"The wyrm," I say. "It's the priority. How do we bond it to one of you?"

Limery's claws dig into my shoulder just before he falls from it. I'm quick enough to catch him before he hits the ground, but his HP is nearly gone.

"Quick, health potions, now!" I shout, and Yashi places one in my hand. I pour it in the tiny imp's mouth and his bulbous eyes open, though he still looks a little dazed. All of the female trolls' health bars are dropping dramatically faster than mine and Gord's. It must be a flat decay and not a percentage. "Keep the potions for you all. Gord and I have higher regen."

I just hope we figure out what to do before we all die. I pass Limery to Yashi and she continues to nurture him back to health.

"There's no point in fighting it." The king stares forward blankly. "You will all die eventually."

He stands up from the throne, leaving the wyrm wrapped around its base, and steps forward. His knights lift their swords and follow him. There is something sinister about the way they walk, like they are puppets on a string.

"If we can keep them distracted, can you bond with the wyrm? He's already at low health."

Tormara and Ismora nod before rushing off to the wyrm.

"Alright, Gord, are you ready to fuck some shit up?"

He gives me a wicked snarl and lets out a roar so powerful it echoes off the walls.

The king unsheathes his own sword, the blade the same spectral green as his body, as we race across the throne room. My horrors follow me, nearly twenty in total, but they seem lost on what to attack. Our health is already over a quarter gone when we reach our opponents.

I fire one of my ranged attacks and it shoots straight through the specter king.

Gord charges two knights with his shield like a battering ram, but he passes through their armored bodies just the same. They turn to slash through him, drawing blood and taking a chunk of Gord's health.

The king slashes at me and I jump to the side, barely avoiding the attack. There's no way for us to fight them as my horrors run back and forth, unable to attack yet dying to the attacks of the king and knights.

"I's better now, Chods." Limery hovers next to me, his leathery wings flapping like sails, holding a fireball in one hand and a potion in the other. He tosses the fireball at the king and it explodes against his disfigured face, dropping his health for the first time. How in the hell are we supposed to defeat them without magic?

"You're the only one who can hurt them," I say. "Gord and I will distract them, but you need to deal the damage."

He takes a sip of his potion and slings another fireball.

I check my own health and realize it has dropped below fifty percent. "Gord, I'm going to need you to get real angry real soon or you are going to die."

The ladies need the health potions, and I'm certain we will run out before all of this is over. For Gord and myself, our only hope is to use Berserker Rage and counteract the decay so that we can bond the wyrm and leave.

I dodge a swing from the knight who isn't chasing Gord. His greatsword moves with ease and he follows up with another swing as if the weapon weighs nothing. Which, apparently, it doesn't. The blade connects with my chest, ripping flesh and spilling blood.

"You no hurts Chods!" screams Limery as he tosses another fireball that bursts against the knight.

Gord's health is down to thirty percent, but at least Tormara, Ismora, and Yashi have managed to get to the wyrm. They lean over it, Ismora and Yashi holding it down, belly-up, while Tormara cuts it open with her dagger.

Limery's attacks are not doing nearly enough damage, and Gord and I continue to lose health at a rapid rate. I cast horrors to try and counteract the effect, but they die quicker than I would like. With every bit of health we lose, the specters grow more powerful, replenishing their lost health with our own.

As our health continues to deplete, I don't see any way we make it out of this. Even if we bond with the wyrm, we're still locked in here.

Gord's health drops below ten percent. By the throne, the wyrm thrashes as it fights against its bonds even in its decrepit state.

Gord is going to die if he takes much more damage, so I do the only thing I can think of: I sacrifice myself. Running in front of Gord, I take the brunt of the attacks that were meant for him until my own health drops below ten percent. Using the same trick that saved my life with the first wyrm I encountered, I trigger Berserker Rage and use my rapid regeneration in conjunction with my bonus healing. My health spikes like it took a shot of adrenaline to the chest. Beside us, Limery continues his assault, but it's evident he can't do much against these creatures.

There's a violent roar behind me and I turn to see Gord's health increasing just like mine, steam radiating from his green skin.

Thank God.

The king's health has already replenished. The damage Limery deals is simply not enough and the horrors that I cast to raise my own health feed the specters just the same as we do. It feels like we are caught in a riptide, being pulled out to sea, and no matter what we do, we are destined to be pulled under.

A stream of flame sprays across the throne room and I turn to Limery to see what the hell just happened. He's just as shocked as I am.

Tormara steps down from the throne, the wyrm at her side. It's no longer shriveled and weak, but rises up proud and strong like a cobra, several feet taller than Tormara. It tilts it head back and a shrieking roar cuts through the room. The specters bend over as if in pain. The shriek actually deals a small amount of damage.

While they are distracted, the wyrm lets out another spout of flame, dropping their health even further.

Limery doesn't waste any time getting in on the action, peppering the specters in a blast of miniature fireballs. The specters seem panicked for once and slash out at anything and everything around them. I let my horrors fall and cast no more. It means I have less health, but I'll no longer be replenishing the HP of our enemies.

"Limery, box them in with a flame wall," I shout.

Two walls of fire form to one side of the specters, forming an 'L' shape and preventing them from escaping the wyrm. Another blast of fire pushes the specters back into the fiery corner and their health drops even further as they are assaulted on both sides.

Right now, I'm feeling about as useful as nipples on a breastplate as I bark orders, unable to actually fight.

"Okayy, Limery, it's time for the big guns."

The wyrm shrieks, momentarily immobilizing the specters while Limery lifts his hands over his head and a swirling ball of flame grows ever larger.

The specters recover from the shriek and the last thing I hear is the king's colorful curses as the mega-fireball swallows him whole. There is a clank as his crown falls to the floor, no longer a spectral image. Another fire blast from the wyrm finishes off the knights, and the green glow fades from the room. I push the notifications to the side to check on my party members.

Everyone's health begins to tick up with the specters gone. Tormara, Yashi, and Ismora's health bars are below twenty percent.

"Do we have any potions left?" I ask.

"That was the last of them, I'm afraid," says Yashi. "And not a minute too soon."

Tormara runs her fingers down the back of the wyrm, the toxic sludge it creates just beginning to seep through its scales.

"That was some good timing. How did you manage to get its health up enough for battle?" The last I saw of the wyrm, it was still shriveled up as they tried to bond with it.

"That's where the rest of the potions went." Tormara strokes the snout of her new pet. "I didn't see any other way, so I made a tough decision. Either heal the wyrm and maybe die or save ourselves for a bit longer and definitely die."

She made the right choice. Even at such a young age, the wyrm has already proved invaluable. I approach it with caution and when I extend my hand, it nuzzles its hardened snout against me.

"I wish there had been more than one, but I will count this as a serious win. I say we camp here tonight. No one can get inside the castle while we are still here and then we can set out for our next stop early tomorrow."

Limery steps up beside me and pushes the king's crown towards me. It's silver and sleek, encrusted with sapphires.

Item. *Kingly Crown. +10 Charisma.*

I still remember the bonus Charisma I received from eating mole soup. It only gave three Charisma for one hour and I felt like I was losing myself. I don't think I can handle ten Charisma even if I wanted to. It's just not me, even if it does make me a smooth-talking son of a gun. Maybe one day I'll have use for it, so I place it in my satchel.

Everyone takes their spot on the stone floor. It is well past midnight and we will need our rest for tomorrow. As I settle in with Limery tucked against my chest, I use the opportunity to sort through the notifications from before.

Congratulations! You have reached level 14. +1 stat point to distribute. +1 Strength and Constitution racial bonus.

I'm a little bummed I only got one level since I was really looking forward to unlocking that next ability, but considering we didn't actually defeat any wraiths and only a few ghosts, the fact that I leveled up at all is a blessing. Maybe I can farm on the way to our next magical area.

Something else bothers me, though. It's kind of strange that I only got the level up notification. When we defeated the faerie dungeon, there was a chest filled with loot and a notification that I had defeated the dungeon. Is there more to these ruins than just defeating the king?

Either way, we got what we came for. The endgame was never loot. Wyrms are more valuable than anything we could possibly find in these ruins. The fate of the entire troll race rests on the scaly backs of these two bonded creatures.

CHAPTER THIRTY-ONE
LICHES BE CRAZY

Sunlight spills through the high windows of the throne room, urging me to wake. Daylight is a welcome sight since it means we won't have to worry about the ghosts in the courtyard. But that doesn't mean there won't be new challenges on our way out. Limery stirs as I sit up, his bulbous eyes groggy with sleep.

I cast my horrors as the others wake and gather their belongings. Tormara's wyrm curls in a ball by her side while she sleeps, a watchful guardian.

We are all out of potions, so whatever happens next, we need to be careful until we have a chance to replenish them.

Our goal is to get out of the castle without any problems. We have what we came for and I'd like to get as far away from this place as possible, regardless of what loot may be hidden on its grounds.

"Is everyone ready?" They all nod in affirmation. "Same routine as before, eyes on the wraiths at all times. I'll keep my horrors out front in case there are any surprises. Tormara, I want that wyrm by your side at all times, Chief Rizza would kill me if something happened to it before we made it back. Gord, pick up the rear."

The door opens with a groan and we are greeted by a troop of wraiths drifting aimlessly. Their dark presence watches over us, but we keep them in our vision, freezing them in place. This time, we make it to the door without incident and exit into a warm, breezy day by the coast.

My horrors are organized in line formations. Two rows of horrors of vitality lead the way, with their curling ram horns and furry orange and blue bodies ready to tank anything that comes near. Next, there are two rows of the horrors of power. They are the most vicious-looking of the bunch, pure muscle and elegance rolled into one. Muscles ripple beneath their golden fur as they prowl the hall, barbed tail swishing back and forth. They wear the black mane that surrounds their heads like a crown. Finally, the horrors of finesse bring up the rear, their gangly bodies swaying side to side as they walk. They may look goofy, but their claws are deadly.

The presence of the wraiths keep the horrors from decaying and by the time we exit the hall, I have over seventy horrors at my disposal. Due to their added buffs, I feel stronger and more powerful than I ever have. As we make our way down the steps from the keep and away from the aggro of the wraiths, the decay resumes, but I quickly cast another horror for each one lost.

We're walking across the courtyard when something rumbles in the tower along the wall near the cliff.

All eyes turn to the tower as its scorched walls shake, stone and dirt falling from the tower's base, then winding upwards as if whatever is causing the ruckus is moving up its spiral staircase.

There's a moment of silence and then a crack forms in the top-most section of the tower. A battle rages on the other side.

It doesn't make any sense. No one else is supposed to be able to enter the dungeon while we are in here.

The tower wall explodes and pieces of stone and dust rain down as a wyrm and half a dozen bodies tumble to the ground. The wyrm lands hard and slithers away. The bodies rise in pursuit as if nothing happened, though I'm one hundred percent positive one of their necks broke from the fall and hangs sideways.

That's when I see someone standing in the exposed section of the tower. Dark hair drapes down over a black robe, the shadows concealing the face beneath. Grey, deathly hands hold a scepter, its end glowing an eerie green.

Duchess Ravana. *Lich. Level 16. Once a powerful necromancer and sister to the king, it is rumored that her dealings with the dark arts led to the king's eventual madness. Unwilling to leave the mortal world, Duchess Ravana made sure she would never have to.*

The wyrm burrows underground and the trailing undead follow with outstretched hands and rotting flesh.

Duchess Ravana leaps from the tower, a fall that would seriously injure most, and lands silently, her feet hovering several inches off the ground. The robe she wears reveals her decayed chest, speckled with death, and pasty skin that has not known life in a very long time.

For the moment, she seems more focused on the wyrm than the rest of us.

"It must be our lucky day," I tell the group. "We get a chance to clear the dungeon and get the wyrm. If we hold off the lich, do you think you can bond the wyrm?"

"Leave it to us," says Tormara. She, Yashi and Ismora fall back to where the ground rumbles.

My army of horrors approaches the lich. She stops moving.

"Do not stand in the way of what is mine," she bellows, her voice shrill and cutting.

"Sorry, lady, but that wyrm is ours."

"Then prepare to meet your doom!" She lifts her scepter into the air and with a flourish, the ground beneath her rips apart. Hands reach out, grasping and covered in dirt. They pull themselves from the ground until heads break through the surface and dozens of fallen warriors with exposed bones and ribcages rise, ready for battle. The warriors carry rusted weapons, while some use the bones of their fallen comrades.

Gord and I make brief eye contact.

"At least it's something we can hit," I say.

The sunlight catches his nose-ring and a smirk crosses his face. "At least there is that," he rumbles.

There's another explosion of earth behind us as the wyrm breaks through the surface. The three female trolls chase after it, along with Tormara's new pet. I trust that they can handle the wyrm on their own. They have proven themselves.

The undead horde marches toward us, but I'm not worried. I have an army of my own.

Keeping them in formation, my horrors march toward the undead madness.

They collide in the open courtyard, the wave of horrors of vitality slowing the movement of the undead. The demonic lions that are my horrors of power launch themselves off the backs of the horrors of vitality, catapulting themselves into the fray. Their powerful barbed tails swing back and forth, cracking bone and knocking the dead to the ground.

They've nearly demolished the undead when a new crop springs up to the left and then another to the right. Suddenly, my summons are surrounded on three sides.

"I think it's time we help out," I say to Gord and Limery.

Limery takes flight and fireballs dart through the air. They hit the skeletal warriors, but do little more than burn off the clothing, way less effective than the attacks on the ghosts.

Gord charges the horde nearest him, plowing through them with ease. The clatter of bones rings out as he slashes Peacemaker in powerful arcs. Horrors of finesse fall in behind him, watching his blind side as he wreaks havoc.

All the while, I continue to raise more horrors between attacks. I blast roaming dead with my ranged physical attacks and smash the skulls of any who stray too far from the chaos.

No matter how many we defeat, there seems to be a fresh batch of undead for the duchess to beckon to her call. How many died here so long ago?

My horrors swarm the dead, overwhelming them with power and numbers, while the duchess continues to raise more. She stops for a moment and raises her scepter overhead.

A buzz spreads over the battlefield and a darkness surrounds the undead. It moves about their feet, turning the earth as black as night and slowly rising into the air. I feel the life of my horrors start to dampen. Whatever she has cast, it is draining the health of everything around the undead, including myself.

The duchess laughs. It's cold and deadly.

"Death always wins. It's the one thing you can never kill, only postpone. You will all make great additions to my army. And when I take the wyrms, I will bring death upon any who oppose me. I will—"

A fireball to the face cuts off her evil speech and her robe goes up in flames.

She swats at the flames and I dive into the moshpit of horrors and undead, allowing my inner beast to take control. Bite, Claw, Summon Horror, Summon Horror, Bite, Claw, ranged attack, Summon Horror. Rinse and repeat. Gord does his own thing off to the side and the growls of rage he emits let me know he's okay. In a strange way, they spur me on.

My health drains from her area of effect spell, but before it gets worrisome, I use Berserker Rage and tear through the undead like a troll possessed. I never worry about dying, not like last night. No, this is actually fun. This is the reason people will do anything to play this game once it launches.

My horrors of finesse have armed themselves with the bones of their fallen enemies and have now added blunt force trauma to their attacks. The duchess raises her hordes, but we destroy them all the same.

When the last of her undead falls, she simply stands there, mana depleted and useless. Gord does the honor of separating her head from shoulders, and several notifications fill my vision.

On the far end of the courtyard, our companions gather around two wyrms coiled together. We run over to find that Tormara's wyrm has overpowered the wild wyrm and holds it in a death grip. Arrows and daggers stick out of the wild wyrm's legless body while Yashi leans over it, dagger in hand.

She presses the blade between a slit in the scales and peels it back. A trickle of blood runs down the wyrm's side. Yashi then cuts her own finger and presses it into the wound. There is a sizzle, and the wyrm writhes as if in pain, then the wound heals and the wyrm quits fighting. Tormara's wyrm loosens its grip, and the newly bonded wyrm coils around Yashi's feet, its wounds healing miraculously fast. Its tongue licks at the air and Yashi gently pets it on the back of its head.

She flashes me a smile. "We did it."

"That we did. Now let's get the hell out of here. Actually, give me a second."

I pull up the notifications from the battle with the Lich.

You have defeated Paltras Ruins. *Claim dungeon prize.*

Congratulations! You have reached level 15. +1 stat point to distribute. +1 Strength and Constitution racial bonus. +1 ability point to distribute.

Awesome! I can finally unlock a new ability, but first, we should claim our rewards.

We walk back over to where the tattered remains of the lich lie spread across the ground. Her obsidian scepter catches the sun and I reach down to pick it up.

Item. Forlorn Scepter. *Increases the range of summoned creatures by 50%. +5 Intelligence.*

Item. Cloak of Ruin. *Allows wearer to walk in the shadows undetected. +5 Dexterity.*

So that's how she was raising the dead from so far away. Those are some pretty good stats on the cloak as well. I know just who to give it to.

"Ismora, you didn't get a wyrm out of this dungeon, but I have no doubt your time is coming. For now, I think this belongs to you. It will make you unnoticeable at evening, night, and anytime we find ourselves in shadowy places."

She wraps the cloak over her shoulders. Even with the sun out, the shadows inside its creases seem to go on forever.

"I am here to serve the village. Yashi and Tormara have earned their wyrms. If it is seen fit that I earn one as well, then so be it, and if not, then I will carry on as I always have. The wyrms are not trophies, but members of our tribe."

Holding the Forlorn Scepter in my hand, it seems like a natural fit for my class, but the ranged attack of Petrified Staff has been invaluable so far. For now, I put the scepter in my bag.

"Chods, looks at this." Limery has his fingers buried in the dirt, pulling at a bone-white handle of what is obviously a chest. Gord reaches down to help him and the chest comes free.

The dark wood of the chest is speckled with dirt and the hinges are carved of bone.

It opens with a click. Inside, it is filled with bones, but when I look closer, I notice it is actually a set of magical armor.

Item. Bone Cuirass. +3 Constitution. When all four pieces of bone armor are equipped, wearer takes 50% reduced damage from fire attacks.

Item. Bone Greaves. +3 Constitution. When all four pieces of bone armor are equipped, wearer takes 50% reduced damage from fire attacks.

Item. Skull Helm. +3 Constitution. When all four pieces of bone armor are equipped, wearer takes 50% reduced damage from fire attacks.

Item. Bone Vambraces. +3 Constitution. When all four pieces of bone armor are equipped, wearer takes 50% reduced damage from fire attacks.

That's one hell of a set of armor, not to mention how intimidating it will look to go into battle against someone clad in bones. The bonus fire resistance will almost even out the weakness that trolls have to fire.

"Gord, this has your name written all over it. It's loose enough to not dampen your mobility."

He scowls at the armor as he takes out each individual piece. I know he doesn't like the idea of wearing armor, but the stats are too good to pass up. Twelve Constitution is insane. No wonder defeating this ruin was so difficult.

Gord carefully puts on the armor, each piece magically fitting to his giant body. When it is all equipped, he looks like a demonic warlord. The skull helm has an actual skull that covers the top half of his face, only revealing his nose-ring and massive tusks, one broken and shorter than the other. His emerald eyes are piercing through the mask. The giant ribcage wraps around his chest, while still allowing his mossy green skin to show through. The greaves and vambraces cover his forearms and shins in an assortment of welded bones.

Between the wyrms and assorted clothing and armor, we're starting to actually look like a formidable group.

While the others admire both Gord and Ismora's new looks, I take the time to sort through my ability and stat points. I have two stat points that I'm currently holding on to, but there's no point in waiting to use an ability point. I pull up both options for my summoning abilities. They are the only ones I have any real interest in at the moment.

Sacrifice. Sacrifice X amount of horrors to receive a temporary buff. Horror of Power: +1 Strength. Horror of Vitality: +1 Constitution. Horror of Finesse: +1 Dexterity

Kamikaze. Sacrifice a horror to deal a burst of damage.

Both are tempting. Sacrifice would make me a one-man wrecking crew if I happened to have a full army of horrors to sacrifice all at once. Plus, with a twenty Strength, Constitution, and Dexterity bonus all at once, I'd be godlike. Thinking back on the fights with the ghost and the specters, though, we need more than just Limery's magic damage. The wyrms are an added bonus, but right now, we need to keep them safe more than anything. I need to be able to deal magical damage myself.

I select Kamikaze and summon a Horror of Vitality. The plump orange and blue monster looks around, unaware of what is about to happen, staring at me with its big round eyes.

I use Kamikaze and the horror explodes in a burst of orange light. There's no blood or gore, only the explosion, so I don't feel quite as bad about sacrificing it.

With no cooldown, the thought of an entire army exploding at once sets my hairs on end.

CHAPTER THIRTY-TWO
SEASIDE STROLLS

Does it make me a sadist to have my horrors jump off the cliff and explode their bodies right as they hit the water just to see how big of a splash they can make?

I hope not, because even Gord is laughing as three horrors of vitality explode simultaneously, creating the biggest splash yet.

The two wyrms slither side by side between Yashi and Tormara. Far ahead, Ismora is but a blip along the cliff. Occasionally, a tree casts a shadow and she vanishes completely within it. Is it possible that she is truly as selfless as she proclaims, not caring whether she is bonded with a wyrm or not? In the short time I've known her, she has seemed pretty genuine to me. They all have. Sure, Gord and I were sworn enemies at first, but he has definitely dialed down his asshole antics, and I feel confident that he will have my back in every fight.

It makes me miss Taryn. With his personality, he would fit in well with the trolls. He's quiet and puts in the work, never complaining if he has to play support or fill in any roles that the rest of the team doesn't want to play. He's the embodiment of a good sport. I don't know how he put up with my antics for so long without punching me in the face. Hell, if he were in my position, he'd probably have handled things so much better. When he gets in the zone and his mind starts ticking, it's something to watch.

I lengthen my stride and fall in line with Tormara. She always has her eyes peeled, looking for anything out of the normal.

"Do you think you'll be able to ride them one day?" I ask.

The wyrms are as tall as me, but not yet sturdy enough to support the weight of a troll.

"I believe one day. The stories of old say that the trolls used to ride all manner of beasts. Wyrms, dragons, bears that could topple trees, but it has been a long while since our leatherworker has had occasion to make saddles. Perhaps the time is nearing." A few wisps of red hair that escape her braid twirl in the coastal breeze. I wonder if her temper will be more controlled by bonding with the wyrm or if her own tenacity will bleed into her bond? "You've done a great thing, Chod, securing the wyrms for our people. We will be forever in your debt."

I didn't do it for their gratitude. I did it because I felt they deserved more than they have been given. They are good people, regardless of what the outside world thinks. One day, the rest of the world will see them as I do, but I fear there will be bloodshed before that happens. I remember from my history classes that revolutions rarely happen without violence.

There are two smaller magical sources between us and the forest, though neither one as promising as Paltras Ruins. However, there's really no way of knowing until we actually get there. One lies by the coast and the other several miles inland. We will hit the coast first and then work our way back inland toward the forest.

My herbalism skill increases again as I learn new plants associated with the coastal climate. We pick sea ivy and bay juniper, then strip the bark from the sunburst palm.

"There are also very powerful plants that live underwater," says Yashi, pointing to the ocean. "If we find an area where the cliffs fade off and are able to make it to the beach, I will show you." Now that we have secured two wyrms, we can also focus on stocking the village with rarer potion ingredients.

"How is it you know so much about the plants outside of the forest if you've never left it?"

"My mother made potions, and her mother before her. And her mother before that. The knowledge has been passed down for many generations. Trolls may not be known as great scribes, but we do preserve what is important to us."

Most of the day is spent traveling. Seagulls and other large birds patrol the coastline, filling the air with squawks while the salty air pervades every breath we take. Eventually, the rocky hillside fades off into a ravine, exposing the sandy white beaches below. As we descend, I am startled when Ismora emerges from the shadows.

"Wow, that cloak really does work. We would have walked right past you."

She just smiles as we walk past, her black cloak billowing in the breeze.

Waves crash against the shore, filling the air with salt spray. A variety of different sized crabs scatter along the beach. Limery hits the larger ones with fireballs while Gord gathers them up. The two wyrms lay straight as arrows against the sand, sunbathing.

Several hundred yards out at sea, there are many small islands with lush vegetation. No doubt it will be a great place to increase my herbalism skill even further. But first, Yashi mentions that there are certain plants we can find under water.

"Looks like Yashi and I are going for a dip. The rest of you can rest or explore."

The warm water is welcoming as Yashi and I dip our taloned toes. The water is a brilliant blue, not that different from my own skin. Tiny fish nibble at my toes and farther out, I can see through to the ocean floor as brilliantly-colored rays soar across the sandy bottom.

Yashi takes a breath of air and submerges underwater. Her stroke is elegant, perhaps from swimming in the lake near the village, and she darts through the water like a giant frog. The sandy bottom stirs and she comes up with a handful of green seaweed.

"Dragon seaweed." She hands the slimy plant to me and I understand why it has that name. The leafy structure looks like it is covered in scales. "It can be used in potions that temporarily raise Constitution. Now, grab as much as you can while I go catch us some fish for dinner."

Crab and fish. It'll be a nice change of pace.

I spend the next half-hour, delving deeper into the ocean as I pick seaweed and stuff it in my belt. It doesn't take long for me to look like I am wearing a hula skirt. Before I realize it, I'm all the way out towards the islands, so I decide to take a moment to rest on the shore.

The feeling of the sun on my shoulders is something I could get used to. Maybe one day, I'll journey back here just to take it easy for a few days. Almost like a real vacation.

The trees shake overhead as birds fly through the canopy, escaping something inside the forest.

My time in the sun is over when I feel a pointy object poking me in the back.

"Who are you and what business do you have on our islands?" The voice is raspy, like someone who has spent their entire life screaming at the sea.

A short but stout baby blue troll stares me down from the other end of the spear. He's no taller than Yashi, but his muscular proportions are no different than my own. Gray speckles cover his shoulders, tattooed from years spent on sunny beaches. A dense but short white beard covers his face and two thick tusks rise to the length of his nose. His braided white hair is adorned with seashells that clatter when he moves.

He holds the spear with purpose, webbed fingers wrapped around the tan wood.

"I mean you no harm. My party and I are just passing through. We stopped to gather herbs for the village."

He doesn't speak, but the spear tip lessens its pressure against my back.

"You have blue skin, but it is not the skin of a seaside troll. Explain."

"I'm from the forest. There was an accident. Too much magic turned me this way."

"You are from the forest? Then you should have known better than to step on our lands." He shoves the spear harder into my back. "Follow me and you will meet your judgment."

Great, Gord 2.0 has entered the fight. I stand up and the momentary widening of his eyes doesn't slip past me. He's but a dwarf compared to me. Even though he's level sixteen, I'm certain I could defeat him one on one. Regardless, these are my people and I don't want to start out on the wrong foot, so I take the lead and allow him to steer me by carefully-placed jabs in my backside. Is there a hidden rule that the first male troll I meet has to be an asshole to me?

"What's your name?" I try to be as friendly as possible.

"I am Imoko, son of Molma."

"You know my friends are going to come looking for me, right?"

"Do not worry, they will be handled."

I can't help but smile at the thought of someone telling Gord what to do. Or Tormara for that matter, especially with our new slithering companions.

Imoko leads me down a forest trail with dense vegetation. Brightly-colored birds chirp from high in the trees. There are no male trolls on guard in this forest. Why would there be? I bet they are all swimming in the ocean, hunting for fish or whatever else it is that these trolls do.

We travel all the way across the island and I don't see anything even remotely resembling a village. I want to ask where they live, but I keep my mouth shut and let the web-footed blue hobbit poke me forward.

My jaw drops when we exit the far side of the forest and step onto the beach. A floating village spreads out across the water with dozens of huts with green fronds covering the roofs. It's not as big as the troll village, but it is a sight to behold. A raft-like structure runs between the huts all the way from the beach to farther out in the ocean where I see many trolls standing on rafts, pushing themselves along with giant poles. One dives off a raft and comes up with a fish impaled on the end of his spear.

Children play in the water while the females watch them.

As soon as Imoko and I step onto the beach, several more seaside trolls rush to his aid, spears pointed at my throat.

"Imoko, what is the meaning of this?" one asks. He's younger and less weathered than Imoko, with many long brown dreads pulled together and tied with a leather thong at the top of his head.

"I found him on our lands. He says there are more across the channel. Take some of the others and see that they are brought here. I will take this one to the chief."

The others exchange glances before disappearing into the forest. They have no idea what they are in for.

A poke in the back tells me to go forward. Several pergolas are scattered along the beach where female trolls tend to various tasks. Fish roast over an open fire in one. The cooked fish hang along a rope that stretches from one support to another. Next to it, a bamboo shoot sticks out of the earth, spouting what I assume is clean drinking water into a massive clamshell the size of a bathtub. In another, spears are being dipped in a glowing purple substance. Several jellyfish-like creatures sit in baskets beside the table. Poison-tipped spears, maybe?

Another stab forces me to abandon my view and step forward onto the structure that floats in the ocean. The roots of whatever plant is being used disappear into the sand. This entire structure was created by mana-infusion, I'm certain.

When I bring up the map the chief gave me, I see that a small magical vein runs out to the island. Nothing major, but big enough to support this.

The pathway is surprisingly stable, even for my big size. I'm guided down the dock, past the huts to the open deck at the far end. The village is remarkably well hidden, not visible at all from the cliffside. When the female trolls notice me, they all stand in a defensive posture, backs towards their children. One of them steps forward. She has navy dreads that look fierce against her baby blue skin. Loose fabrics adorned with shells clatter as she approaches. A blade wrapped in leather hangs from her side. A shell necklace dangles around her neck, and eyes as blue as the sea give me a questioning look.

"Imoko, explain yourself."

"He crossed into our lands." Imoko looks at his feet.

Evidently, he is sensing something in the situation that I am not, but what? It's clear her tone is not what he was expecting.

"And this is how you think to treat him? Can you not see that he is our kin? You bring him here with a spear in his back. Do you know how long it has been since a land troll has stepped on our grounds? Too many years." She sighs and looks to me. "I am sorry for the inconvenience. We are a peaceful tribe. We do our best to stay away from the eyes of men and do not go looking for fights we cannot win. Now, tell me—"

"Chod." I fill in the blank.

"Now, tell me, Chod. How did you find yourself on our little island?"

"Well, it's a bi—"

Before I have an opportunity to explain, there's a loud crack of branches from the forest, causing many of the other trolls to gasp in horror. I turn to see the seaside trolls that were sent to find the others kneeling in the sand weaponless. Gord stands behind them, clad in his skeleton armor, roaring with defiance. The two wyrms flank his sides and the rest of the party emerges behind him.

CHAPTER THIRTY-THREE

DINNER AND A SHOW

Imoko thrusts the tip of his spear against my throat. I don't blame him. Right now, I'm the only insurance policy that he has against my companions.

"Release our brother!" Gord shouts from the tree line, his deep voice carrying across the waves. I find it kind of sweet that he called me brother. I guess I'm growing on him.

"Imoko, drop your weapon," scolds the chief.

"Chief Lida, they have our brothers," Imoko protests.

"And we have theirs. Release him now so that we can move forward from this nonsense. Chod, I trust that you will make peace with your brothers and explain that this was all a misunderstanding. We are not fighters. We want no quarrels but the fight for our own survival."

Imoko removes the spear from my throat and I raise a hand towards the shore to let them know I am okay.

"Allow me to go talk to them. And then perhaps we can all speak together."

She nods, and I take off down the dock.

The seaside trolls that kneel in the sand look apprehensive when I approach.

"Gather your weapons and go. You have nothing to fear from us." Ismora tosses their spears in the sand and the trolls gather them, joining their chief at the end of the dock.

Limery flies up to my shoulder and takes his perch. "Chods, don't you disappears like that again."

"Yeah, he was about ready to kill every last one of them," says Yashi. "Gord, too. What the hell happened to you, anyways? I leave you alone for five seconds and you get captured." She rolls her eyes at me.

"It's okay. I'm actually glad we found them. Imoko is a little trigger-happy. Not that different from someone we know." I nod at Gord. "But their chief seems to have a pretty good head on her shoulders. At least as far as I can tell."

"They are so small." Tormara gawks at the seaside trolls. "I've heard stories, but I've never actually met a seaside troll myself. It's hard to believe we're the same species."

"I would like to sit down with the chief to talk. Maybe they will be valuable allies in the future."

The chief waits at the end of the dock. Several more trolls have returned from their rafts and stand beside her. The warriors Gord and company defeated stand by her side, the ends of their spears buried in the sand. Every face has the same look of wonder as we approach. Perhaps from seeing the wyrms that stick close like well-trained pets or maybe it's our very presence that awes them.

"Chief Lida, allow me to introduce my companions." I go through the line, acknowledging each in turn, telling their skills and talents.

She smiles when I finish. "It reminds me of the tales of old, back when the trolls used to travel the world in search of adventure. Nowadays, we are lucky to simply endure. I'm sure you are famished from your travels. Would you care to join us for dinner where we can talk more freely?"

"That would be nice."

We stand to the side of the dock as everyone prepares for dinner. Several of the female trolls go back to the massive platform at the other end of the dock and place their hands on its surface. Channeling the mana that runs through the living floor, they raise up many long tables. Others carry fish and pails of water from the pergolas. Once they are finished, the tables are filled with platters of roasted fish of half a dozen varieties, roasted crab, and even bowls of fish eggs and what looks like snails.

We all take a seat at the newformed tables, sitting on the bare floor of the dock. Our table consists of our party as well as the chief and several other female trolls.

The fish is delicious, much better than any seafood I've eaten in real life. Limery eats like an imp possessed, shredding the small fish he holds in his tiny hands. He scoops handfuls of fish eggs up at a time and swallows the snails whole. Everyone seems to be enjoying their meal, but Tormara looks at the snails with a questioning eye.

"It's not that bad," I tell her. "Don't chew it, just swallow."

"So, tell me, how is it you find yourself so far from the forest?" The chief bites into a massive roasted fish the size of my hand and its bones crunch in her mouth.

I go on to tell her about the attacks on the village, and after witnessing Chief Rizza bonding with her own wyrm, I had the idea to try and track down the others. "We need to show them that attacking the village will have consequences."

"It is a noble pursuit. We do our best to stay far away from the troubles of men. We are lucky to be so well hidden. It has been many years since unwanted eyes have stumbled upon us. Once again, I hope you will forgive Imoko's overzealous approach. He was only trying to preserve what little we have."

Looking over their tribe, it's evident just how close to obliteration they are. They have less than half the population of the forest trolls. One false step could erase them from history.

"What if you didn't have to hide away?" The other females at the table cut their eyes at me, but the chief looks on with a blossoming curiosity. "What if you could have more than just this little set of islands?' I may have overstepped my bounds on that last one, because I hear whispers, not just at my table but at those that surround us as well.

"What exactly are you saying, Chod?" she asks, no longer touching her food.

"I want you to join us. Side by side, we can stand up for ourselves. Wouldn't you like to be able to travel freely, to trade and expand, to adventure like the days of old? We could make a place for the trolls in this world again. I know you feel it, all of you, that burning desire inside of you to face greatness and grab it by the horns."

She stares at me for a long moment while her people murmur.

"The trolls have a place in this world, Chod, and it is right here. We are still a great and powerful tribe. In the water, our fighting is unequaled, but on land, we are not great warriors. I don't know how you do things in the forest, but I will not risk the lives of my people just because you happen to have a few wyrms and wear armor."

The sea splashes against the dock, the only sound in the otherwise silence. No one argues with the chief's words, not even me. How could I expect someone I barely know to send her people away for a cause they know nothing about? The seaside trolls live a good life here, even if it's not the one I would have for them.

"We don't just have the wyrms," Yashi interrupts. "We have magic. The imp can cast fire, our shaman has the phoenix as his totem, and Chod here, well, he's practically a one-troll army. Go on, Chod, show her."

"Magic, hah. Magic will not save you." She stands up and walks over to the edge of the dock, gazing into the clear blue water. Her navy braids sway in the breeze.

After a moment, she turns back towards us and spreads her arms wide. A fish jumps out of the water and wiggles through the air before splashing back into the sea. Then another does the same thing. After a few seconds, dozens of fish are diving out of the water in a beautiful arc.

"Tell me, girl, what good will this magic do on the battlefield? If we are attacked, then the seaside trolls will defend themselves, but we will not go marching to our doom. I will hear no more of it."

"But he's a hero. Chod, just show her your power. Once she see—"

"I said enough!" roars Chief Lida, and for the first time, I see the power that dwells within her. The power that makes her chief. Then and there, I know that the seaside trolls will have no part in whatever comes our way. "I have heard enough. When you are finished eating, take your belongings and be on your way. If you remain on our lands past nightfall, it will not be Imoko who comes for you this time."

CHAPTER THIRTY-FOUR

BLOOD SPILLS

"Why were you so adamant about convincing the chief to join our cause?" I ask Yashi as we walk along the coastline once more.

There was something about the way she pleaded with the chief that I just can't shake. I've never seen her look so desperate.

The small troll twists the end of her black braid as we walk, her bow strapped across her back. Her wyrm stays close by, sensing her unrest. I am amazed at the change that they go through after bonding. There's no training period or acclimation, almost like they can read each other's thoughts. Maybe they can.

"I can see what is coming." She stops walking, and so do I. "Everyone can see what is coming. Blood will be spilled before we are left in peace. If more of the undying ones come, how can we possibly stand a chance?"

I don't know what to say. Am I going about this all wrong? Even though everything here feels real, I've still been treating this like a game in a lot of ways. Death doesn't come for me the way it does for them. The trolls are so powerful, so strong, that I didn't think for a minute that they might be afraid of dying. Maybe death isn't what they are afraid of, but losing everything, their way of life. Chief Lida didn't hesitate to protect her people. I could be leading them all to certain death, for all I know. If only there were another way, but with our reputations, there will be no option for peace unless we take it by force.

The only way to attain peace is by bloodshed. The irony isn't lost on me.

"I'm sorry, Yashi. I know it's unfair. At the end of the day, it's you and the others who will pay the steepest price if this all goes south. I wish I could guarantee that everything will work out, that when the time comes, we will crush whoever opposes us and things will be far better than they were when I met you all, but I can't do that. All I can promise is that I will do my best to make sure that no lives are needlessly lost. I'll die a hundred times over if it means I can spare one troll."

"That is more than enough," says Gord.

Limery rides on his shoulder, conjuring tiny fireballs and flicking them into the air until they dissipate. Clad in his skeletal armor with the small red imp on his shoulder, Gord truly looks like a being from hell. "When you first came to the forest, on that night we were attacked, you offered to risk your own life in exchange for mine against the undying one. In that moment, I was too proud to accept your help. You were an outsider, and I had no reason to trust you. But now, I will gladly let you die for me." Gord places his powerful hand on my shoulder.

Did he just crack an incredibly dry joke? There may be hope for him yet.

"I'm sorry, Chod." Yashi straightens her back and puts her chin up. "I know we are doing what needs to be done, for the good of our future tribe, but we have not known a real war in a long time. Not in any of our lifetimes. Small battles, yes, but not the horrors of war."

I pray it doesn't come to that, but if it does, we must be ready.

__Regional Event Alert!__ Richard Hummel, Ethan French, and Otis Wiggins have slain a mana-infused wyrm. 13/20 remaining. 11 days remaining.

That's the first time three people have teamed up together. I don't know if that means they are starting to work together more or if it is just coincidence. No doubt every one of them wants their shot at the regional event and the loot it provides. Even though the notification says thirteen, in reality, there are only ten wyrms still left in the wild. If the humans found out we had three wyrms, nothing would stop them from attacking the village.

We make camp for the night among a copse of trees. Right now, remaining hidden is the most important thing. While us trolls have Camouflage, the wyrms do not, so I have Tormara and Yashi order their pets to burrow underground for the night just in case anyone happens to stumble upon us. Ismora disappears in the shadows of night underneath her cloak, invisible to even our heightened senses.

I wake to another notification.

__Regional Event Alert!__ Pressley Allen has slain a mana-infused wyrm. 12/20 remaining. 10 days remaining.

No one speaks a word when we wake up. Two more wyrms have been slain in the course of about eight hours, and I can't help but think of how many adventuring parties must be out there. Eight have been slain by other heroes and not a single name has been repeated. Some of them must be traveling around with a group of NPCs like myself, but there is evidence that others have begun forming alliances. All the more reason to get to the next dungeon faster.

Even Limery can sense the unrest between us, because for once, he flies in silence overhead. The slain wyrms, combined with Yashi's worries and the interaction with the seaside trolls, have put a heavy cloud over our party. I hope that clearing a dungeon may put it to rest.

By midday, we are near the next cluster of magical veins. If we find a wyrm here, then we can head back to the village without checking the last magical area.

The mountainous coastline morphs into more docile and friendly beaches that stretch on for miles. Crashing waves are replaced by a gentle purr. A mixture of palm trees and oaks with swooping branches line the forest where brightly-colored birds flutter through the canopy. Long strands of moss hang from the trees like cobwebs.

We make our way through the wooded area until a hand appears out of nowhere and Ismora emerges from the shadows, telling us to stop.

"Someone is here," she whispers. "The dungeon must be close because I heard talking and then it just vanished."

"How many people?" I ask.

"I don't know. At least two, maybe more."

"Okay, spread out. We need to find the entrance before they emerge."

Ismora disappears into the shadows, Limery goes with Gord, and Tormara and Yashi stay together with their wyrms. I cast several horrors as quick as I can and set out in search of the entrance.

The forest is alive with sound, which is good for concealing our movement. Bugs chirp and birds caw. Nearby, something slithers through the tall thicket of grass. I wish we had a few more perception potions, but we haven't resupplied since leaving Paltras Ruins.

As I do my best to sneak through the humid underbelly, there's nothing that even remotely resembles a dungeon. Only trees, bushes, and more trees. Could Ismora have been wrong? It wouldn't be the first time the forest has played tricks on the ears. I continue to cast horrors regardless, and soon, I have a small army at my disposal. I'm thankful for the cacophony of sound to muffle their murmuring. Far away, I can see the blue glistening skin of one of the wyrms as they search as well. If Ismora did hear voices, then the entrance has to be close.

A shrill shriek cuts through the forest, silencing the wildlife, and a bright beam of light explodes beneath the shady canopy. It takes me a moment before I realize it is Limery's flare! Ismora must be in trouble. The blinding light burns white hot as I rush to see what the commotion is. Branches and limbs break off against my trampling body. I run with reckless abandon, panic throbbing with each powerful beat within my chest.

The flare fades and I find Ismora surrounded by a group of men, a dagger held to her throat. I count six well-armed men. Two of them clearly heroes by their garb. I focus on them and the names Jason Montoya and Lester Hobbes display. A wizard and a ranger, both level eighteen.

The names sound familiar. Pulling up my notification history, I see that they were the first group to slay a wyrm before Limery and I returned to the forest. They've been busy.

Ismora shouts as the men hold her captive, telling the rest of us to stay back, that we should take the wyrms and flee.

One of the foot soldiers has his dagger pressed to her throat. The blade of the dagger is black as night and a small skull adorns the pommel. Ismora towers over his body, causing him to have to reach up to apply pressure.

"Hey!" shouts the wizard. "If you don't shut up, Raymond here is going to stick his knife all the way through your throat."

Jason, the wizard, is clad in light green cloth armor with a red hood pulled over his head. Next to him, the ranger, Lester, wears similarly-colored attire. His armor is heavier, consisting of silver greaves and bracers, both shimmer with a green hue, and a studded leather vest. A cowl covers most of his face. He holds his bow at the ready, an arrow pointed out into the forest.

Beside the two heroes, there are three other soldiers, two clad in heavy armor holding shields, and another with light chainmail much like the one holding a knife to Ismora's neck.

"She doesn't understand what you are saying." I try to remain as calm as I can as I say it. One, to hopefully keep them from doing anything stupid, and two, to keep any of my party members from escalating an already volatile situation.

The wizard licks his lips. "We've heard about you, Mister Troll. Yes, we have. A troll that can speak the common tongue is a rare find indeed. Even rarer, a hero troll. You've made quite the name for yourself with your regional events and murder and whatnot. Hasn't he, Lester?"

"Oh, he definitely has, Jason. Definitely has. And now we find out that he not only started this whole thing, but he's also collecting the wyrms for his own private collection. If we would have known it was possible, we wouldn't have killed the first one." He changes the position of his arrow toward where the others are standing, and fiery red tendrils extend down his fingers and wrap around the arrow. "Don't be scared, honey. We see you. You and your little blue wyrms can come right on out. We've been watching you approach all day long, so no surprises."

They must have some sort of buff or potion that is allowing them to see us in the forest.

"What is it you want?" I ask, casting another horror behind me so that they can't see it.

"Experience, gold, women..." The wizard smirks at his comment and both men laugh. "Give us the wyrms, and we'll let you go in peace."

"We can't do that. The wyrms are bonded." Not that I trust a word they are saying.

"I don't care if they're bloody brother and sister. You give us the wyrms or the troll dies. And then you all die."

My blood boils at their audacity. Ismora's eyes are locked on me.

"They want us to give up the wyrms," I know that the men can't understand me when I talk to the other trolls. "Tormara and Yashi, they know you're there. I don't know what kind of abilities these men have, but they are higher level than us and they won't hesitate to kill."

"Take them and go!" roars Ismora. "For the good of our people. The wyrms are our tribe's only hope."

"There is no way we are leaving without you," I counter, but I can see on her face that she has already given in. She doesn't believe she will make it out of here alive.

"Enough of that gobbledygook," says the wizard, licking his lips again. "Tell them to bring the wyrms."

"They won't obey you. They are bonded."

"Let me handle that." The way the ranger says it makes me feel like he has something up his sleeve. In other games, rangers sometimes have the ability to make pets or control low-intellect animals. Wyrms aren't common forest creatures, though. "And while you're at it, tell Mister Big Scary Skeleton and the others to drop their weapons."

"They want you to drop your weapons," I tell them. A few seconds later, I hear the sound of their weapons falling to the ground.

"You too, Mister Big Shot. Weapon on the ground."

I drop my staff. Luckily, I don't need it to cast. I have nearly fifty horrors tucked in tight behind me, each new horror crouching lower than the last in an effort to not be seen. The mental connection we share is invaluable right now. Even if they have been watching us all day, they don't know how many horrors I am capable of casting. Still, I have no idea how we get out of this with everyone in one piece.

"Now, the wyrms. I won't ask again."

"Send the wyrms." The look on Tormara's face is one of absolute betrayal. Nevertheless, she does as I say and both wyrms slowly slither towards the group of men.

Their eyes light up with greed as the wyrms approach and the ranger lowers his bow, the red tendrils of energy retracting into his hand.

"Kill her!" the ranger orders his soldier and I'm drowned in the roars of my party as the blade digs into Ismora's skin, spilling her blood. She collapses to the ground and all hell breaks loose.

Blue energy sparks out from wizard's hands, wrapping the wyrms in arcane chains from head to tail. The ranger bends down over one of the wyrms, his hands glowing a vibrant emerald as he passes them across the body of one of the bound wyrms.

I don't know what he's doing, but I have to stop it. Grabbing a Horror of Vitality by the horn, I toss it with all the force I can muster straight at the ranger, exploding it right as it hits his body. It knocks the ranger off balance, disrupting whatever spell he is casting.

Chaos unfolds all around me as we gather our weapons and rush towards the evil bastards that murdered our sister.

Absolute terror paints the faces of the NPC soldiers as we descend on them. The wizard conjures a cube of energy around him and the ranger as they continue their ritual against the chained wyrms, leaving their companions to die.

We take care of the foot soldiers first. With my horrors and the furious rage of my party, they don't stand a chance.

With the foot soldiers dead, Gord swings Peacemaker with all his might at the cube shield to no avail. Limery pelts it with fireballs, but still nothing. The wizard must be charging a hell of a lot of energy to keep it in place.

"We need to break it!" shouts Tormara. The ranger presses his hand to the wyrm's body and Tormara seizes in pain. She bends over, screaming, barely able to move as emerald energy penetrates the wyrms scales.

The wizard has his arms extended, reinforcing the magical energy of his shield. I have a suspicion that the ranger is trying to make the wyrm his own pet, and it looks like the process will kill Tormara if he succeeds.

We've already lost one member of our party. I can't let them take another.

"Everybody, step back."

Gord lifts Tormara and carries her a dozen or so yards from the shield.

My horrors surround the cube, standing one on top of another until every side of the box is blocked from view.

"Yashi, ready your arrows."

I cast Kamikaze and every horror explodes simultaneously. The shield shatters and the wizard falls to the ground, knocked out from the backlash of energy. An arrow zips across the forest, hitting the ranger in the shoulder. He stumbles and the energy connection breaks for a moment. Without looking up, he presses his hand against the wyrm, focused on his task. Another arrow rips through the side of his neck and blood sprays in a sickening stream onto the wyrm. He grimaces in pain but keeps his hand pressed. He must know he'll never escape. His only hope is in bonding the wyrm and using it to defend himself. A third arrow connects with the side of his head and he falls to the ground.

The chains that bind the wyrms are still active as the wizard groggily comes to. I ready my staff to finish him off, but Tormara stops me.

"This one is mine." She bends down over the blood-covered wizard and their eyes lock as he finally recalls where he is. She buries the blade of her dagger in his throat and rips it out with enough force to sever his throat down to his spine. The chains vanish from the wyrms' bodies, and they rush to their masters.

I receive a notification telling me I've hit level sixteen, as well as a -2399 reputation, but I brush it away. There's no celebration to be had in the victory. Instead, we all sit in stunned silence.

I'm the first to break the quiet. "I don't understand how she got caught. She had her Cloak of Ruin. It should have kept her hidden."

"Rangers have higher perception than most." Yashi wipes a tear from her eye.

I stand and walk over to Ismora's body, her chest covered in dirt and blood. Her scarred arms spill out from her cloak and I can't help but think that after so many battles, I am the reason for her most fatal wound. Did I make a mistake bringing them down here?

Bending down, I take her hands in mine. They're still warm to the touch.

"I'm sorry." As I wipe a stray hair from her brow, there's a slight gurgle in her throat.

CHAPTER THIRTY-FIVE
DEATH MARCH

"She's not dead," I say it but no one comes. The words linger in the air for what feels like an eternity. Ismora's hands are too warm for there to be so much blood. I've never seen this much blood in my life.

As I watch the blood trickle out of her open wound, my mind drifts for a moment. Back to the day when I knew for certain that I would have to take care of myself in life. At eight years old, home alone, I was hungry. Mom and Dad had left the credit card for me to order takeout, but I wanted to cook for myself, to show them that I was a big boy. I sliced my finger opening a can of ravioli and blood went everywhere. It covered my clothes, the marble counter, the hardwood floors. Thinking back on it now, I don't know why I didn't panic. Maybe because I knew there was no one to help. I soaked an entire towel mopping up the blood and when Mom and Dad finally made it home, the kitchen looked as if it never happened. There had been so much blood, but not like this.

How could we be so careless not to check her body? "She's not dead!" I repeat, louder this time. I hold Ismora's hand in mine, but I'm not sure what else to do. She's still alive for now, but that could change at any moment. Should I lift her head or will that just make her bleed out more? I don't know how she survived and frankly, I don't care, but we need to figure out how to get her help fast.

Our group surrounds me. I'm so focused on Ismora that I didn't even notice them approaching. "Yashi, can you make us more potions?"

"I don't have the ingredients." Urgency coats her voice.

"Can you not find them?" I say it as more of an accusation than I mean to.

Yashi flinches at the harshness of my words.

"Maybe, but I could also spend all day searching and not find anything. I don't know this area. We need to get her back to the village. If we can stop the bleeding, then her natural healing will take over enough for us to travel."

I hope that's true. She's lost so much blood already that it pools around my knees.

I use Ismora's cloak to try and stop the bloodflow, but it does little more than soak it up. It looks like the knife missed its intended target. Her throat is intact, but a gash runs down the side of her neck. That will mean little if she bleeds out.

"Limery, I need you to cauterize the wound. Can you do that?"

"What's that means?" he asks me with wide eyes.

"Burn her skin until it closes the gash. It's the only way to stop the bleeding."

He nods at me apprehensively and moves in close. A tiny fireball crackles in his palm and he molds it until it is a thin layer of flat, radiating heat that fits him like a glove.

Limery presses his hand to her neck and the blood sizzles. The smell of cooked meat fills the air and something primal in me causes my mouth to salivate uncontrollably. Ismora thrashes for a moment before falling still once again. When Limery removes his hand, a white handprint is burned into Ismora's skin. If she makes it through this, she will carry Limery's mark for the rest of her life.

"Reach in my bag, there should be a strip of leather. I need you to hand it to me."

The satchel on my back shuffles and then a strip of leather dangles in front of me. Tormara takes hold of Ismora's hand. I rip off a piece of her cloak and fold it. Placing the cloth against her wound, I tie it securely around her neck.

She lays there unmoving.

"What now?" I ask.

"I think it is time we cut our journey short, Chod." Tormara's face is strained. "The undying ones know we have bonded with the wyrms. They will be coming for us. We must warn the village and do what we can to prepare. We still have two more wyrms than we started with and if we save Ismora, I will count us as truly blessed."

She's right. I know she's right.

"Okay. Gord, chop us some wood. I'm going to build a stretcher to carry Ismora on."

A few minutes later, Gord returns with two branches about eight feet long. Using some of the leftover leather, I strap it across the two pieces of wood. With my nails, I poke several holes and run small strips of leather to secure it in place. When it's finished, we have a primitive stretcher. Lightweight, but strong enough to hold her body.

Congratulations! You have unlocked the skill 'Inventor.' You are now a level 1 Inventor (Novice). Increase your skill and learn techniques for advanced inventions by finding an advanced inventor (Apprentice or above). Ranks: Novice, Apprentice, Journeyman, Expert, Artisan, Master, Grandmaster.

I focus the notification away. The last thing I care about right now is leveling up my skills.

"Help me move her onto here." Gord grabs Ismora by her feet and I take her underneath her armpits and we lift her from the blood-soaked earth and onto the stretcher. "Now, let's get moving."

It's already evening as we set out towards the village. Judging by the map, it will take us nearly two days to get there. I fear Ismora doesn't have that much time. She's still unconscious and her health has not started to replenish at all. Could the weapon she was attacked with have been poisoned? I would give her my Tiger's Eye Pendant to remove any potential poison she may have, but she has to be awake to use it. Right now, our only hope is to get her back to the village so that she can be healed.

We walk with purpose, constantly on alert. Without Ismora to scout ahead, Yashi keeps her bow strung with an arrow and Tormara has a dagger in both hands. Gord and I march as fast as we can without jostling Ismora, until eventually, night descends upon the land.

Our night vision kicks in, allowing us to see for miles under the starry sky. No one mentions taking a break and we continue well past dusk.

Eventually, I'm hit with a notification telling me it's time to rest.

Warning! *Your body needs rest. If you do not sleep within the next two hours, your stamina, strength, and health regeneration will be greatly reduced. Recommended sleep: 6 hours.*

Two hours comes and goes.

Warning! *Your body needs rest. Your stamina, strength, and health regeneration have been reduced until you sleep. The longer you go without rest, the more depleted you will become.*

My Strength and Constitution reduce by nearly a quarter and I have to stop for a moment to catch my breath. I just lost the equivalent of four levels of stats and I feel it in my bones. I can tell Gord is experiencing the same thing by the way he readjusts his grip on the stretcher's handles. It seems heavier and my body feels weaker.

"We must push through." No one argues.

I shrug off the fatigue and we continue. Each step comes with increased effort and I can't help but notice the heavy breathing of everyone as we walk. Everyone except for Limery and the wyrms. I have a feeling the imp could go all night without sleep and not miss a beat.

By morning, my stats have decreased by fifty percent. Every step is a slog as the sun rises. We stop briefly to eat, but it does nothing to raise our stats. Not until we sleep.

I lose myself again in my own thoughts, robotically putting one foot in front of another. It's the only thing that keeps me going as I wonder how I got myself into this situation. A few weeks ago, I didn't really care about anyone. My parents were practically non-existent, and the only joy I got was from belittling strangers on the internet. Now, here I am, voluntarily going through hell to try to save someone I barely know.

It's interesting... I viewed my sentence to play this game as a bit of a joke at first. Just another challenge to overcome or castle to beat. The judge said it wasn't a punishment though, but a new form of behavioral therapy. Looking back on my actions, I'm beginning to wonder if that's true. Has this game influenced my actions or has this always been the person I am when I have people depending on me?

Kind of a chicken or the egg scenario since I've never had anyone depending on me.

Before I know it, we cross into the forest. Only a few more hours until we arrive at the village. Ismora hasn't stirred in a while, but each time Tormara presses the back of her hand against Ismora's forehead, it's still warm.

Our stats continue to drop, forcing Gord to leave his shield and the rest of us to strip down to our bare essentials. I leave a mark on the map so that we can return to claim our items at another time.

With nothing but pure determination, we push forward, nearing exhaustion. Some of the creatures sense our weakness and try to attack. Limery and the two wyrms defend us from what would be certain death multiple times over.

"It's okays, Chods. We's almost there." He offers encouragement and once again, I'm thankful for the little guy. I'm thankful for all of this.

We burst through the magical barrier of the village, and I've never been so happy to see the translucent bodies of guardian trolls in the distance. They rush to our aid, sounding roars of alarm throughout the forest.

"Ismora needs healing," I manage to say before collapsing.

CHAPTER THIRTY-SIX

THE CALM BEFORE THE STORM

Incense fills my lungs when I wake. Somewhere nearby, birds chirp, welcoming in the morning. I open my eyes and the familiar living roof of the troll hut calms me. Good to know they didn't just leave me lying in the forest. I sit up, fully expecting the fatigue from the journey to hit me like a ton of bricks, but I feel fine. My stats have returned to normal, and I am none the worse for the wear.

The hut I'm in is mostly empty but for a few pieces of furniture and a bowl of smoking incense. I'm pretty sure it's the same hut I stayed in on the first night, all traces of the previous inhabitant gone. A couple of notifications beg for my attention.

Regional Event Alert! *Tommy Sullivan has slain a mana-infused wyrm. 11/20 remaining. 8 days remaining.*

Regional Event Alert! *Troy Malloy has slain a mana-infused wyrm. 10/20 remaining. 7 days remaining.*

Seven days remaining? How long was I out?

I step out into the courtyard and receive several warm smiles as trolls move to and fro on their morning routines. Several children hit a stone ball with a club across the ground. The action stirs some laden thought inside of me.

Ismora!

"Excuse me." I pull one of the children aside and his eyes go as wide as saucers. "Have you seen Ismora? Where have they taken her?" I'll search out the others later, but for now, I need to find her first. She has to be alive.

"She is with Jira and Chief Rizza." The small troll points at another hut on the other side of the courtyard, and I spot Chief Rizza's wyrm coiled up around the entrance.

The wyrm allows me to pass without incident and I find Jira sitting on the floor, legs crossed, as he chants and waves a burning piece of brush over Ismora's face. Ismora's forehead and cheeks are covered in ash.

"What is he doing?" I ask.

Chief Rizza signals for me to be quiet and motions me over.

"Ismora was injured with a cursed blade," she whispers, her face grave. "You were right to bring her here. She would not have survived for much longer had you not."

I can't quite place the look on her face. Is it worry or something else entirely?

"What kind of curse is it? Will she be okay?"

"Jira is doing all he can to remove the curse, but it is not so simple. Every bit of health she regenerates is being absorbed by the curse." Jira's white-tipped dreads sway back and forth as smoke rises from the burning herb.

"Is there anything I can do to help?"

"For now, all we can do is wait. I would like to have a council meeting once the others return. Bring Gord with you this time, I think he has earned it." She smiles.

"What do you mean return? Where's Limery and the others?" I would have thought he would be right by my side when I woke.

"The imp left, something about his mother. He seemed to be in a frenzy. I'm sorry, I wish I knew more. As for the others, they woke yesterday and mentioned something about gathering gear."

"Yesterday? Wait, exactly how long was I out for?" It must have been some time if Limery left and the others went back for our weapons. The little guy has stuck by my side like glue since I met him.

"This is the second day." Two entire days of sleep for depleting my stamina. Is it possible the game forced me unconscious after going so long without rest or was that the punishment for completely depleting my stamina? If it was the second, then why were the others not affected the same way? "We will talk more when the others return." Her dismissal is firm. There's not much that I can do here anyway.

What the hell am I supposed to do while I wait for the others to come back? And why could Limery possibly need to see his mother at a time like this? Maybe I'll go for a swim in the lake or take a walk in the forest. On second thought, I think I've walked enough.

The cold water of the lake is calming. It's a strange feeling, being able to actually relax for once. I don't think I have truly taken a moment just to breathe since entering this world. It all started with an angry ogre, then an angry troll, then an even angrier wyrm and her demon-spawned babies. Sprinkle in a couple human interactions and attempted kidnapping by tiny blue trolls and it has been quite the adventure. More excitement than I've had playing a game in my entire life. I'm kind of sad to know it is all going to come to an end. I just hope I can really help the trolls before my time comes.

After a dip in the lake, I make my way around the village and attempt to learn more about the people who actually live there. I meet Kea, who always has a pot of soup boiling, and then Makali, who boils the leather and uses it to make clothing and whatever else the village needs. Bunu and Tayo nurse the youngest trolls today, but all females help raise them, or even feed them if need be. Zelia has filled in for Ismora while she has been away, teaching the children in the ways of combat. Jojin, Watu, and Malak guard the southern side of the village.

There are so many more that I don't have the opportunity to talk with. Each with their own lives, their own personalities. I burn their names into my chest as I try to envision what's next. War is coming to the village. To the other heroes, we aren't people. We're monsters, and they are doing the righteous thing by destroying us. For all I know, they think that we are bonding with the wyrms to try and sabotage the rest of the island.

When I meet with the council, I need to have some sort of plan. Honestly, I don't know what to do other than wait. We can reinforce the boundaries, setting up spikes and defensive measures, but we can't go on the offensive. We don't have the numbers, and marching away from the village leaves it at risk for attack.

Maybe the others will have better ideas at the council meeting.

I'm talking with some of the villagers, telling them of how we battled our way through Paltras Ruins, when I hear a cavernous voice calling to me.

"About time he woke up."

"Don't pretend you weren't worried about him, Gord," teases Tormara. She hands me my satchel and staff. "We weren't sure when you would wake so we went out for our items. Gord couldn't bear to go another day without Peacemaker."

"Thank you. Really, thank you all. There's no way we could have saved Ismora unless we all pushed through. And both of you, too." I reach out and pet the top of both wyrms' heads and they nuzzle against me.

"We're not quite out of the woods yet." Yashi twists her braid between her fingers. "The weapon that cut Ismora was cursed."

"I know, I've already spoken with the chief. Jira is doing the best he can, and she wants to have a council meeting this evening, Gord included." I can't help but smile at the look of surprise and then pride that crosses his face. "How much does she know about what happened?"

"We've filled her in on just about everything," says Tormara.

A half an hour later, we gather at the council area. Chief Rizza, Tormara, Guilda, Kina, Sonji, and I take our seats while Yashi and Gord stand before us. With the three wyrms coiled up at the feet of half of our council, the area is beginning to feel a little crowded.

"Jira will not be joining us this evening. His talents are needed elsewhere." She pauses and her wyrm lifts up to touch her fingertips. "I have called this meeting to discuss our future. Based on your reports and interactions with the humans, I fear an attack is imminent. We do not yet know if all of the undying ones are working together. There could be one massive attack or several small ones, but we need to be prepared. I welcome advice on how we should proceed. Those of you who have dealt with them have an advantage over the rest of us, which is why you are here as well." She motions to Gord and Yashi before sitting back against her throne and giving us the floor.

I don't know what I expect from them, but silence is not it. Every council meeting I have been to so far has been hot-tempered and full of action. Even Tormara keeps her vipered tongue at bay.

Gord clears his throat. "These men are like none we have faced previously. The undying one we faced before may be the weakest among them. I fear we cannot win against them in open combat."

"I think we should start by increasing our defenses." Their eyes fall on me as I offer what little help I can. I'm a fighter, decent in small battles, but I'm not a commander. I say the simplest things that come to mind. "Spikes, thorns, vines that choke. Make use of your mana-infusion before they ever get close to the village. We know they will come with fire, so we'll need to infuse the trees. I'd also send our scouts out further. We want time to gather our forces before they are beating on the door."

"And what of the wyrms?" asks the chief.

I don't know. I've never planned an actual battle before. I don't know the first thing about battle formations or how to win against a superior foe. All I know how to do is play video games. I've skated by this far, but if they keep following me, I'm going to get them all killed.

I can't focus. They're bringing clubs and tough skin against magical abilities. They're all scared, afraid of what will happen if they fight fair.

"Chod?" She must sense my consternation.

Maybe that's the thing, though. We're the bad guys...We don't have to fight fair. A movie scene flashes across my mind where a small village is under attack by invading forces. They're coming onto our lands. That's something we can use against them.

"If we are camouflaged, how close do they have to be to see us with a perception potion or anything that modifies their awareness?"

"I was asking about the—"

"How close?" I cut the chief off. "Yashi?"

"It would depend on their skill?" She glances at the chief and then back to me. "Perception potions only increase awareness for what you are looking for, they don't point it out for you."

"Then I think I might have a plan."

***

The rest of the evening is spent infusing the areas at the magical barrier with as much defensive power as possible. Every troll is put to use, carrying raw mana from the well to the edge of the forest. It's slow, laborious work, but it might just make the difference between life and death. For anyone who attacks us, I want it to be a hell of a lot of work just to get past the barriers. There will be more work to be done tomorrow, but once night falls, I do my best to explain my plan to everyone who is available and then have the others tell the plan to the guardians.

By evening, Jira still hasn't left his hut. I pray that he has a breakthrough soon, because we're going to need his power if we hope to have a shot.

"I don't know if there is anything more nerve-wracking than waiting for an attack that you know is coming." Chief Rizza steps beside me. The toxic ooze from her wyrm catches the moonlight in a beautiful way. It already seems bigger than when I first saw it. "I never had the chance to properly say thank you. We'd fight tooth and nail until there were none of us left if it came to it, but with everything you have done, I feel like we are finally embracing who we are again."

Proud warriors fighting for their lives.

"I don't know if I made a mistake going after the wyrms. I was so angry at everything happening here, at the lack of respect. I just wanted you to have something, and I don't know that I ever really thought about what could happen if we were caught. Or what my actions might bring upon the village." This is the first time I've been truly honest with myself about it. Part of me was channeling my own insecurities through the trolls. I thought that if I could save them, then maybe I could save a small part of myself too.

She pats me on the shoulder. "Don't beat yourself up about it. We were dying out long before you showed up. More likely than not, we would have faded out with a blip. Now, if nothing else, we'll go out with a bang. Hell, we might just have a shot at winning. Now get some sleep. Tomorrow I'm sending scouts to the edge of the forest."

CHAPTER THIRTY-SEVEN
HEALERS ARE OVERRATED

My mana-infusion increases another level as I focus on the vine in front of me. The goal is for the vine to wrap around the foot of any human that steps on it, lifting them high into the air. When the plant accepts the mana, I give the vine a tug. It feels strong. At worse, it trips the person, and at best, they'll be dangling in the air, ready for Yashi or another archer to take them out.

We're making steady progress on the barrier, but it is slow going.

"Someone is approaching," one of the guardians calls out.

My body immediately tenses as I reach for my staff. Two small, red humanoid figures flutter through the air towards us.

"Limery? Where the hell have you been?" My heart feels a million times lighter now that he is back.

"I had to goes home. Gets Mommy to helps fix Ismora." He wraps his tiny arms around my neck, giving me a hug.

Right behind Limery, his mother hovers, carrying a bag of what looks like junk parts.

"Limery tells me you had quite the adventure and that one of your party members has been cursed."

"Yeah, but what are you doing here? And what's in the bag?"

Limery flashes me a big toothy grin, his eyes bulging even bigger than normal with...excitement?

"I makes it, Mommy helped. Long time ago. Now lets goes. Lets goes." He pulls me by the arm and I take the bag from his mother as we walk back towards the village.

"You want to fill me in on what's happening?"

"And ruin the surprise? Never." She smirks and bats her long eyelashes at me, making her look all the more devilish.

Chief Rizza and Jira are already in the hut when we arrive. She stands next to Ismora, protesting our entrance.

"What is the meaning of this? Jira needs peace to work his magic."

"We's here to helps," offers Limery.

Chief Rizza looks at me questioningly and I nod for her to let them proceed. Limery hasn't led me wrong yet.

Jira opens his eyes, and they are as red as the heart of a rose. He sets the burning herbs aside and allows Limery to take his place. Limery pulls piece after piece from the bag and carefully begins assembling them together.

"Long times ago, Leo was very sick. He tooks an item from a mans. An items he shouldn't haves. It was cursed. For three whole days, Leo doesn't moves. Mommy thinks he's going to die. Daddy thinks so, too. They pays all our moneys for healer to come see Leo. Healer says Leo needs clean bloods. Healer says needs more moneys to helps Leo. Daddy sells himself to the healer for moneys but the healer doesn't help Leo. The healer says Leo can die."

As Limery fits his pieces together, I wonder how I never knew about Limery's father. Out of all the words he spoke, he never once talked about him. I wonder if he's still alive or where he might be.

"Mommy gets real sads when Daddy is gone. Says soon Leo will be gone too. But Limmy doesn't want to lets that happens, so he builds this."

Limery stands up, proudly displaying the finished product. I honestly have no idea what I'm looking at. It's all a mess of tubing and coils, a couple of bellows, and a container on the bottom. Two of the coils have needles attached at the ends of them.

"Wait. Is that a blood transfusor?" I ask.

"Limmy doesn't know what that is. This makes the bloods clean. I just needs the magics. Will you gets some, Chods?"

Limery hands me a small metal cup and I take it to the well and fill it with raw mana. The substance glows brilliantly and I'm careful not to spill any as I walk. When I return, I hand the cup to Limery, and he places it into the container. Limery's mother takes one of the needles and inserts it into Ismora's arm. She stretches the second tube out and does the same thing in her other arm. When Limery shuts the door to the container, the machine whirs to life. The bellows start pumping, forming pressure inside the device. The tubes are not transparent, so it is hard to see what is happening, but I can hear suction and blood dripping into one of the beakers. When it sounds like it is filling up, Limery places his hands on the beaker and I can see the heat radiating from its edges. He's literally boiling the blood to recycle it back through Ismora.

For a second, I'm reminded of Berserker Rage. When its active, our skin grows hot and steam rises from our bodies. Maybe that's why we can't be slowed or poisoned or cursed while its active.

"How long does this take?" I ask Limery's mom.

"A few hours. She has a lot of blood within her. It will all need to pass through."

"I'll leave you to it. There is still work to be done."

On the eastern barrier of the forest, I'm forming a fence of thornbushes when trampling feet catch my attention. Several of the scouts Chief Rizza sent out run towards me. When they arrive, they're out of breath and panting like dogs.

"They're coming. The undying one has returned."

"Are there others with him? Other undying ones?"

"Not that we saw. They'll be here within the hour."

"Warn the chief. Then I want everyone who can fight out here as soon as possible."

I cast my first horror and it appears in a puff of smoke. I hope like hell this works.

Within minutes, trolls flock to my location. It's the most trolls I have seen since the party before I left to clear the mana obstruction. Each face tells a different story. Some, like Gord, are angry. Others are worried, apprehensive, or downright afraid. Not of dying, but of losing everything. Then there are those who simply love the art of battle. Ismora would have been one of those.

Chief Rizza takes center stage, her wyrm rising to full height beside her. Its tongue licks at the air and it sways back and forth like a snake ready to strike.

"A great deal has changed in these past few weeks. Magic has returned to the forest. We have been blessed with three new protectors." At this, her wyrm spits fire into the air. "And a hero. For the first time in a very long time, it feels like we are on the path to greatness once again." Several trolls beat their chests at those words. "But there are still those who want nothing more than to destroy everything we have built. The undying one has marched on us many times. Each time, we have defeated him and pushed him back. We have lost many troll lives in the process. Today, we have a chance to defeat him once and for all, and to show the rest of the island that trolls are not to be trifled with. Even now, other armies march on us from the south, aiming not only to take your lives, but the very essence of the forest trolls. Tonight, we will show the world of men that the biggest mistake they ever made was entering this forest!"

Chief Rizza smashes her fist to her chest and every other troll repeats the gesture. A deep, thunderous pound resonates in the air. "Take your positions."

I stand alone in the forest, an eerie silence stretching on forever, almost like it knows what's coming. It's true what Chief Rizza said before: there is nothing worse than waiting for an attack you know is coming. I'd much rather be on the offensive than waiting. The end of the Forlorn Scepter glows green as I cast another horror. I need its increased cast range for what comes next. As each horror fades away, its health depleted, I summon another in its place. Once Glenn crosses into our lands, I will be able to summon a greater number, but for now, they are capped at sixty before one completely decays.

The fiery tips of our enemies' torches blink into existence like fireflies. With each step forward, the dots grow bigger. My heart pounds in my chest, a mixture of excitement and nerves.

Glenn has upgraded his armor since I last saw him. The hodgepodge of armor he lost in the first battle has been replaced with golden plate. A yellow aura surrounds him and the men closest to him as he marches. He even has a fancy red cape that billows behind him. Not to mention he's now level eighteen.

His army is much larger than last time too. I don't know how he managed to find soldiers, especially after his repeated attempts ended in failure, but nevertheless, here we are.

Several rows of foot soldiers armed with swords and spears follow behind Glenn. They lack the plate armor of their leader, but many are clad in chainmail or boiled leather. Further back, rows of archers follow.

They cross the barrier into the forest and several men are stuck by thorns and sharpened limbs before their eyes adjust to their new surroundings. Many more are tripped or trapped and hang in the air from vines. Glenn's golden armor leaves him unscathed.

The second row of men quickly assess the situation and chop the wild plants down, but not before we draw first blood.

Glenn's eyes light up when he sees me from a hundred yards away.

"You." He smiles. "I've been looking forward to you." He continues to talk as his men regroup and march forward. "You plan to stop me and my army all by yourself?" He laughs a cold, calculating laugh. "They say you're strong, but I don't think you're that strong."

He's a talker, but for once, I have nothing to say.

"Where are the others? Are they afraid to fight their own battles?" He pauses. "Never mind it. I'll kill you, and then I'll kill the rest of them for good this time. We can hang your head in the town square."

Glenn's army comes to a halt and I can sense the internal struggle going on in his mind as I stand here alone. I just hope he takes the bait.

"What do you say we do this old school, just you and me?" I try to goad him, though I know it won't work. He's here for blood, not glory.

"As fun as that sounds, I think I'll just take the village."

"Don't say I didn't give you the chance."

"Kill him!" Glenn orders. He unsheathes his sword and it glows with lightning that arcs down the blade.

Before he has a chance to attack, I raise my fist high into the air, signaling the camouflaged guardian trolls in the trees high above the archers to attack. They fall from the canopy like meteors, smashing archers and ripping them to pieces before they even have time to nock their arrows.

With the momentary distraction, I cast Kamikaze, exploding the wyrm tunnels filled with horrors beneath Glenn and his army, creating a crater big enough for a small pond. Soldiers are buried in the rubble and many die from the explosion. Glenn stares up at me, his face contorted with rage.

"You will pay for this!" he shouts.

"No, it is you who will finally pay for all you've done."

The wyrms emerge from their tunnels on the outer edge and blue flames ignite the battlefield. Chief Rizza and the rest of the female trolls rush from their hiding places to join the wyrms on the rocky terrain. Their job is to handle the soldiers. Jira's punches land with the power of the phoenix, and Limery soars through the air, raining fireballs from above.

Glenn struggles to his feet, his heavy armor making it hard for him to move. I can't risk anyone else dying to him, and I made sure everyone knew that before the battle began. His reign of terror ends with me.

I cast Berserker Rage as he climbs up from the rubble. I attack with Claw, my nails scratching against his golden chest and shrieking across the battle. He counters with a slash to my arm that's fueled by lightning. The electricity flows through me, but it does nothing to calm my rage. I pry back his pauldron, snapping the leather that holds it in place and exposing his shoulder. My tusks sink into his skin and warm blood floods my mouth. He screams in pain, but I don't release. Instead, I cast a Horror of Power with my free hand and the lion-like demon rips off Glenn's armor, prying it from his body with razor-sharp talons. I cast two more horrors, and they help me pin him to the ground. With his helmet removed, my claws rake across his face until he looks more demon than man.

He tries to say something, but it comes out a broken mumble. With my horrors pinning him to the ground, I stand up and let their explosion send him to his next life.

All around me, the trolls finish up the battle. Tormara stands over a man pinned in the rubble, dagger raised, when I call to her.

"Wait! I need to ask him something."

The man's jaw shakes violently as I approach.

"If you tell me where he will be reborn, then I will show you mercy."

"L—lynchton," the man stutters. "Now, p—please, help me out of here."

"Make it a clean death," I tell Tormara. That is the only mercy he deserves.

"No, wait! You said you would show merc—" His words trail off as I search out the chief.

I find her back by the fallen archers as they pull armor and weapons from the bodies. She smiles at me as I approach.

"We did it. Without losing a single troll. We did it!" She embraces me in a firm hug, her excitement palpable.

"It's not over yet. We need to finish this once and for all."

My reputation has plummeted even further since the battle, almost doubling, but I did gain a new level, putting me at seventeen and giving me another ability point. I spend it on Sacrifice.

Sacrifice. *Sacrifice X amount of horrors to receive a temporary buff. Horror of Power: +1 Strength. Horror of Vitality: +1 Constitution. Horror of Finesse: +1 Dexterity.*

"Limery, stay behind and burn the dead. The rest of you, we're going to Lynchton."

CHAPTER THIRTY-EIGHT

POLITICS OF WAR

From the forest's edge, Lynchton looks almost peaceful. A soft glow radiates from the lanterns that light the gate and just by looking at it, you would never know that they just marched on a troll village intent on exterminating an entire race. I'm hesitant for the precedent I'm setting, but what comes next must be done for not only the good of the village, but for trolls everywhere.

The half-asleep soldier on gate duty almost shits himself when an army of over one hundred trolls, sixty horrors, an imp, and three wyrms casually strolls up.

"You have two options. Either you open this gate and allow us to find the man we are looking for, or we tear the whole thing to the ground."

"Fuck me," he mutters before unlatching the gate. "I knew I should have called in sick today."

The gate swings open, revealing the first town I've seen since entering the game. Even at night, it's everything I love about fantasy worlds. Several buildings line the road as soon as we enter the town. There's a blacksmith, a tailor, and an apothecary all on one side. On the other are the stables, an inn, and a market. Several other buildings line the street farther down that sell everything from pottery to spices. In the center of town is the church, its steeple rising high into the sky. All of the houses are on the other side of the town.

"Where is Glenn?" I set my mind on what must be done next.

We need to end this as quickly as possible.

"He stays at The Dancing Donkey." The guard points to the inn down the street. "Please, don't kill us. I have a family."

"Give us what we want and no one will be hurt. Now follow me, you're going to convince Glenn to join us outside."

The streets are mostly empty, but the vagabonds and night owls that roam at this hour quickly scurry away from our approach. The guard tells them that everything is okay, that there is no need to worry. I'm certain he is scared out of his mind right now, but people will go to great lengths to protect the ones they love.

We come to a stop in front of the inn. A donkey wearing a dress and standing on its hindquarters is carved overhead of the entrance.

"What's your name?" I ask the guard.

"Jameson."

"Well, Jameson, it's your time to shine."

He wipes the sweat from his head and opens the door to the inn.

"Are you sure we can trust him?" asks Chief Rizza.

"I trust that he wants to protect his family," I tell her. This man has a life he wants to protect, and I'm sure he wants us out of town as soon as possible.

Gord and Malak, another guardian troll, wait beside the door as Jameson leads Glenn outside. Glenn wears nothing but a gray tunic and socks when he emerges.

"Now, what's this you said about a talking donkey?" asks Glenn just before Gord and Malak grab him by the arms.

"You!" He struggles against their grip. When he realizes they aren't letting go, he spits in my direction. "And you, guard, you'll pay for this too. I promise you that."

Jameson looks fearful of Glenn's threats as he backs away.

"Don't worry about him, Jameson. I need one more thing of you and then you are free. Ring the town bells. I want everyone here for what happens next." The only way for them to know the truth is for them to witness it with their own eyes.

He disappears from sight and several minutes later, the church bells ring out. There are gasps of horror as people spill out of the inn and from their homes. Some run back in for weapons, but return too afraid to use them. I'm sure many of these people have never seen actual trolls before, having only heard of them from stories. The rogue and the wizard heroes that I recognize from my encounter in the field exit the inn, ready to fight, but when they see so many trolls standing before them, they simply watch from the porch. Jameson does his best to calm people as they enter the town center, where Glenn is forced to his knees.

A man in frilly pajamas and wearing slippers rushes through the crowd. "Jameson, what is the meaning of this?!" His face is beet red as his head twists between us and Jameson like a sprinkler.

"They don't want us. They want him." Jameson points at Glenn.

"This is an outrage!" the man shouts. "There will be consequences!" He puffs out his chest and points an old wrinkled finger in my direction.

"You are sure this is the spot?" I ask Jameson.

"We have witnessed it several times," he confirms.

By the time people quit filing into the courtyard, several hundred wide eyes search for answers. I wonder how many of Glenn's army came from this very town. It's as big of a shock for the trolls to see how the other half lives as it is for the humans to wake to the stuff of their nightmares. Whispers snake through the crowd on both sides.

"I'm sure you are surprised to find us here." Many faces wince at the roar of my trollish voice. "If there was another way, we would not be here. You all have been taught to fear the trolls, told that we are nothing more than murderous monsters dead set on destroying everything you know and love. I am here to tell you that is a lie. We live, have families, grow old, and die, just like you. The heroes of old have returned to this world, many of them human, but I am also a hero and I have set it upon myself to right the wrongs against my people. The man standing before us is a murderer. He has led raid after raid on my village, killing my people and terrorizing their way of life." I pause to let that sink in. "Long ago, the trolls were a mighty race. They traded and adventured beside man and dwarf alike. I hope that one day, they do so again.

"As with man and troll alike, there are those who do good and those who do evil. The same is true for heroes. The man before you is not a true hero. He takes pleasure in the pain of others. Therefore, it is my duty to make sure he hurts no one again. Tamora."

She hands me a dagger.

"You will pay for this, you son of a—" The dagger slices through Glenn's throat, draining his HP and decreasing my reputation yet again.

He vanishes from existence, leaving Gord grasping at nothing before reappearing a few feet away, this time level sixteen.

"Someone help me!" he shouts just before I rip through his throat a second time. The crowd stirs, but no one moves to his aid.

This time when he respawns, his eyes are full of madness. "Help me or I'll kill you all!" he rages at the crowd. I kill him again, but this time, my reputation only decreases by half.

"I'll burn this whole town to the ground!" At level fourteen, my reputation stays the same. It seems they are finally seeing him for the monster he is.

"...your children, your children's children, for as long as I live!" Level thirteen.

By level five, Glenn has broken down to tears. When he hits level one, he drools at the mouth and just mumbles to himself.

"This is a dangerous man. If I were you, I would lock him up before he has a chance to hurt someone you care about."

"What now?" asks someone from the crowd.

"Now, we will go back to our village. We wish you no harm, but if we are attacked, we will respond in kind. My people do not speak the common tongue, so it will be hard for them to communicate with you for now. We will leave you in peace and pray that you will do the same for us." I turn to the trolls. "It is time to return home."

Glenn crawls on all fours as we walk away, mumbling to himself with drool dripping down his chin and madness raging in his eyes. I know this isn't the end of him. In a world where heroes never die, how could it be? I just hope the townspeople keep him locked up long enough for me to finish the final stages of my plan.

Ismora waits for us next to Limery's mother when we return. Aside from a new scar in the shape of Limery's hand, she looks back to normal.

"How did it go?" she asks.

"Time will tell, but I think I may have changed some minds. If nothing else, it will be a while before Glenn troubles you again."

"What do you mean 'you'," asks Chief Rizza. "Are you leaving us?"

"My time here is nearly up. While I will do my best to try and come back, I don't know how long I will be away or if I will even be able to return. I want to do everything that I can in what little time I have left to make sure that I set you up for success after I am gone. I think we have gained the respect of one town, but the island is large and there are many others who will attack simply for the wyrms."

"And how exactly do you plan to stop that from happening?" she asks.

"By going straight to the source. Lillith, may I speak to you in private for a moment?"

Limery's mother smirks. "Why, Chod, I thought you'd never ask."

She sits on the table in my hut and I take a seat on the bed.

"What's on your mind, big blue?" she asks.

"I need to get a message to the king."

She sits in silence for a moment. "The king? As in—"

"Yes, *the* king. It's life and death important. Can you do it?"

"Chod, imps aren't the preferred messenger of the crown anymore. Not since everything happened with the wizard."

"Just tell me, can you do it or not?"

She runs the tips of her talons over her bottom teeth. "I may have a few favors I'm still owed from the old days."

"Good. How fast can you get there?"

"If I don't stop to rest, I can have it there by tomorrow."

"Then we have no time to waste."

Lillith reaches in a small pouch and pulls out a quill and some paper. "What? Some habits die hard. Now, what should your message say?"

"Hold on." I find my own satchel and pull out the crown I looted from Paltras Ruins.

Item. *Kingly Crown. +10 Charisma.*

I put the crown on and my head spins for a moment. Confidence rushes through my body, and I feel like I could run the world if I wanted to. Why don't I? I'd make a pretty good king.

"Chod?" Lillith vies for my attention. What is it we were doing?

"Right, the message." I remember my goal and let the increased Charisma guide my every word as I tell her what I want to say to the king. The words flow out of my mouth so easily that I wonder why I never went into politics. I'd be a great king. The thought crosses my mind again. I just need a bigger army and I could conquer this entire island. Why didn't I wear the crown when I spoke to the seaside trolls? If I had, they certainly would have joined our cause.

Lillith pulls the crown from my head and it feels like a weight has been lifted. My mind clears and I'm glad to be returned to my lowly six Charisma.

"Would you like me to read the message back to you?" she asks.

"No, just make sure it finds the king." I trust that the Charisma did its job. "Thank you, Lillith. For everything."

With a wink, she disappears out the door.

CHAPTER THIRTY-NINE
GAME OVER

The blue haze distorts Valery's face as she leans over the pod. The nanite level decreases and the door to the pod opens, allowing me to sit up. I cough up some of the nanite gel and my lungs take in a breath of air they haven't experienced in a month. My body feels fine, better than fine, actually. Like I could run a marathon if I wanted.

I lay there for a minute. It's not easy knowing that I might never see my friends again. Limery loved me more than any real person. Gord became like a brother to me before it was all said and done. Tormara, Chief Rizza, Yashi, and all the others hold a special place in my heart as well. To me, they'll always be more than video game characters, even if I never see them again.

The blue gel filled with nanites rolls off my arms and back as I sit up in the pod. The other twenty-four white pods are closed, their occupants still logged in the game. Video feeds are mounted over their pods, displaying their in-game actions in third person view. Monitors surround each pod with their vitals and in-game stats side by side.

I'm shocked when I see several dozen new pods against the far wall. Black pods like mine. They're empty, but for how long?

"Well, what did you think?" asks Valery. She wears a red dress that hugs her body just like I remember. It's still perplexing to me how someone that looks like that works in a place like this.

"It was amazing. It actually felt like I was a troll. After my body adjusted to the difference in size, it was like I was a six-hundred-pound beast of pure muscle. And the NPCs, they were indistinguishable from you and me."

"That's weird." One of the technicians goes over to the monitor displaying lines of code.

"What's weird?" Valery asks.

"Thompson, come over here," the tech calls another. "You see this?"

"Yeah, that's...strange."

"Will you two nerds tell me what the hell it is you're rambling about?" Valery scolds them.

The first technician runs his fingers through his balding hair. "Something is up with the AI. It's behaving...abnormally."

"Yeah," Thompson echoes. "It's behaving sporadically, almost like it's missing something. You see this?" He points to the screen, showing Valery something I can't see. "This line of code keeps repeating itself. It's like it's searching for something that isn't there."

"What does that mean exactly?" she asks.

"I'm not sure. It's interrupting certain processes. Spawn timers are off for animals, for starters. There are gaps in the mana flow, too."

"What has changed that would explain the sudden chaos?"

"Nothing. We haven't changed anything. We logged Chad out, but he's not a part of the system."

"Okay, well, keep an eye on it and let me know if anything else comes up."

The technicians take a seat and begin typing commands into their tablets. I hope everything is fine for those still in the game.

"Mister Johnson, we have your clothes ready if you would like to change into something less revealing." Valery winks.

In the bathroom, my clothes are neatly pressed and folded on the counter. I slip out of the spandex-style underwear I wore for the last thirty days and quickly dress. I thought I would feel like I needed a shower, but the nanites kept me so well groomed that I feel cleaner than I ever have.

When I exit the bathroom, Valery is waiting for me, tablet in hand.

"We have an exit interview for you to complete. Once you're finished with that, you'll be free to leave."

"Just like that?"

"Just like that. You served your time, now you are ready to become a productive, and hopefully less trollish, member of society. You did a lot of good things while you were in *Isle of Mythos*, Mister Johnson. Imagine if you had that kind of resolve outside the game. You could really make something of yourself."

I've heard those words a million times from my parents. "If you only applied yourself, you could do anything." As if playing games for a living isn't exactly what I wanted to be doing with my life.

"Do you know if my parents are coming to pick me up?"

"We haven't heard anything. We'll be happy to drop you off at your home if you need."

They missed my trial. They missed my sentencing. Thirty days locked away in a game and they haven't made the effort to secure me arrangements. What could be more important than their own child?

She hands me the tablet and I start answering the questionnaire. Questions about my in-game experiences such as "How were the taste and smell receptors?"

"Were there moments where you were keenly aware that you were in a game?" It's nearly a hundred questions asking for my input on ways to improve specific instances in-game.

"Can I ask you something?"

"Shoot."

"Glenn, what's his deal?"

"He's a special case. You know, most criminals are still just normal people. Even for those who commit violent crimes, it usually happens in a fit of rage. They're triggered by something and have a reaction. Not to say they are all nice, because many of them are not, but they are just people. Glenn may be the only true psychopath of the bunch. The things we have watched him do... He's more charismatic than you would believe. No one else besides you and him were able to gather a force of hundreds of NPCs to fight for them. He did it multiple times, even after suffering defeat. You may have knocked him down a peg with the shenanigans you pulled, but I have no doubt he'll be back."

"Don't you think it's dangerous, having someone like that in a game where he can actually hurt people?"

"Until you, he was only ever hurting NPCs. He actually seemed to be functioning better for a while there, so we let it continue. The name of the game is rehabilitative therapy after all. If he can take out his aggression and psychopathic tendencies in-game and live a normal life out of it, I'd call that a win."

I don't know if I buy that. Especially in a game this realistic.

I hand Valery the tablet when I'm done, and she escorts me into a waiting room.

"We'll come find you when your ride is ready."

It feels like hours have passed when Valery burst into the room. "Come with me." She practically pulls me out of the chair. She talks as we speed-walk down the hallway. "Our guys have been going over the coding for hours now, trying to figure out what could be causing the malfunction in the AI. It's grasping for something that's not there. It took a while, but we finally narrowed it down."

"What is it?"

Her dark brown eyes stare into my own. "You."

"Me?" How is that even possible?

"Yes, we don't know how, but the AI thinks that you are part of the system. Something must have happened when you started a regional event, or either all your influence on the game caused the AI to think you were part of the system. We don't really know. All we know is that unless you get back in the game, it is going to crash."

My sentence is up, though. It's finally time for me to go home.

"Can't you just restart it?"

"You don't understand. If the game crashes, it doesn't get rebuilt. It would start over as something new. There's no backup for NPCs when they behave like real people. Players would be booted, and every town, city, and NPC that is currently in the game would cease to exist. Forever."

I want to go home, order some pizza, and team up with Taryn for a good smash-fest. I haven't talked to him in a month.

But then, Limery's face flashes through my mind along with every other member of the troll village. They trusted me with their lives. If I leave, they would all be gone in the blink of an eye as if they never existed. Everything I did would be for nothing.

"What do you need me to do?"

"Log back in. Give us a chance to fix this."

"And if you can't?"

"Then you get to decide when it all comes crashing down."

"I'll do it on one condition."

A smile spreads across Valery's face. "What is it?"

"My friend Taryn, I want him to join me in-game. If I'm doing this of my own free will, then I want my partner in crime for whatever comes next."

I strip down into the nanite receptive underwear and take my position in the pod. I thought I would be going home today. Back to an unfulfilling life of talking down to other gamers on the internet. For the past thirty days, I never really missed my old life. I missed Taryn occasionally, but everything else didn't seem to matter much. The minute I logged out of this game, I missed the people I met there. That tells me all I need to know.

Thirty days ago, I was sentenced to troll.

If Valery's people can't fix the problem, if me being in the game is the only way for my people to keep living, then I'll take a life sentence.

SENTENCED TO TROLL 2

PROLOGUE

"I'm going to kill him." Jude sat in the corner of the Green Giant Inn. He wore boiled brown leather armor and cleaned his fingernails with a dagger. Funny how he was in a game, yet dirt and blood still crept underneath his nails just like in real life. This was some next-level shit, and it certainly beat prison.

"You're starting to sound like Glenn." Michael had no need to clean his nails. As a paladin, the holy light seemed to follow him everywhere he went. Just one of the benefits of his chosen class. "And you know what happened to him. I'd leave this troll alone if I were you."

"I don't get how you're just cool with it. He attacked us without provocation." Jude stabbed the dagger into the wooden table. "And yes, I know the meaning of word. It's what happened. We cleared the dungeon and were walking back home when him and his little troll buddies ambushed us. They took our items, our levels, and killed two NPCS. And no punishment." He leaned back against his chair, crossing his arms. "And now they want peace? I'll give him a piece of something."

"You've got to know when to pick your fights," Michael tried to reason. "We let our guard down, and we paid for it. This game is not that different from prison. Someone new comes in and they either fall in line or do what needs to be done to take a spot at the top. He made you his bitch."

"And what about you?" Jude picked up the dagger and twirled it around his hand.

"I'm not the one sulking."

Jude stared at his reflection in the blade. *Jude Duggan is nobody's bitch.*

CHAPTER ONE

VANARIA

Two sharp claws grip my tough blue skin as Limery perches on my shoulder. The small red imp looks at me with his bulbous yellow eyes. "Is we there yet, Chods?"

Is this what having a kid is like?

"For the thirtieth time, no, we are not there yet. I know you have a map like the rest of us. Pull it up and look for yourself."

Gord erupts in violent laughter, his gleaming nosering swaying back and forth. Limery takes flight from my shoulder, his leathery wings flapping like sails as he flutters toward the massive green troll.

"Did you put him up to this?" I ask. For someone who hated me when I first showed up at the village, Gord has gotten pretty good at pressing my buttons for his own amusement.

Ismora places a hand on my arm. "Let them have their fun. It has been a long time since we have had reason to joke."

I flash her a smile, knowing all too well what she says is true. It wasn't that long ago that she lay on the floor of Jira's hut, the wound from a cursed blade nearly taking her life. A life she wouldn't respawn from like me. She still bears the scarred handprint on her throat from where Limery cauterized the wound with his fiery hands. The handprint is just one of many scars displayed against her hunter green skin, so new that it has not yet lost its luster.

Between Ismora's fighting skills, Gord's brute strength, and Limery's fire magic, we've got a pretty good party. Not to mention the horrors I can summon. The only thing we're lacking is a healer, which is surprisingly hard to come by in this world. At least we have a fair supply of health potions that I helped brew before we left the village. Potion-making is one skill I have been able to build up nicely in the short time I've been here.

We make our way across the sprawling golden plains to the south of *Isle of Mythos*, and I can't help but think about the circumstances that led me here.

Before I logged out from my thirty-day sentence, I sent the human king a letter on behalf of the forest trolls. At the time, I didn't know if or when I'd be coming back to *Isle of Mythos*. With my sentence served, I was a free man. Yet here I am, because the system started crashing the moment I logged out. Something about me led the AI to think I was part of the system and it couldn't function without me.

If I log out, the system resets. Everyone I've met since coming here dies. How could I possibly sentence them to death when I have nothing waiting for me on the other side? Each and every one of them has a history, a personality, quirks that make them unique. They are more than just lines of code.

This doesn't feel like a game anymore. So, I chose to come back and save the lives of these characters instead of living my own life. They don't know that, though, and I'll be damned if I ever tell them.

They call us heroes because we don't truly die. Really, we're just fully-immersed in this game world. We get respawns. They don't. As far as they know, I'm on an adventure from another world, sent to protect and guide my fellow trolls.

That's fine by me. The friends and adventures I've had here over the course of the month beat anything I ever experienced in real life. The only person I missed was Taryn. My best friend.

Valery said she would find a way to get Taryn into the game. That was my only condition for staying immersed and saving the system they have poured years of time and effort into. She was willing to make the deal, because if I log out before they track down the source of this problem, the system will reboot. That means everything is wiped to square one.

A week has passed, and I still haven't heard anything. Considering it's a top-secret rehabilitation project designed to reform violent felons, and created by the biggest name in esport gaming, I'm sure there's tons of red tape for them to wade through. Without a way for me to contact them or log out on my own, I'm just waiting. Well, waiting and adventuring.

What the hell did I write in that note?

I still can't recall. I remember putting on the Kingly Crown that I won defeating the specter king at Paltras Ruins. The +10 Charisma gave me that familiar high that always accompanies increased Charisma, telling me that anything was possible while simultaneously encouraging me to make bold and reckless decisions. And then I started writing. Before I knew it, the letter was finished, and when I took the crown off, I had a hard time recalling what I had written.

Whatever it was, it worked, because the king responded, asking for a meeting with me, Chod, now known to most humans on the island as 'Hero of the Forest Trolls.'

Chief Rizza sent me—along with Gord, Ismora, and Limery—south to the castle at Vanaria. It'll be their first time visiting anything more than a small town. Their first time in an actual human city. With Gord's abrasive personality and hulking physique, I can only imagine the looks we'll get. Not that I look much different aside from my blue skin, but at least I can act civilized. Plus, I don't have a nose ring. Old people hate nose rings. I hope he's on his best behavior for once.

Our destination is Vanaria, the mighty castle where the human king rules over the southern half of the island. Geographically, it's about as far away from Seascape, the dwarven kingdom in the north, as possible. Midway between the two is a giant mountain pass, the Greystone Mountains, and just below that, the forest where the trolls call home.

Where I call home.

I have no idea what to expect when we meet the king. Peace, hopefully. A truce to let us live our lives in peace. The trolls have earned it. Centuries of hatred have left their mark on the forest trolls. For too long, we have been viewed as monsters. It's high time we be reinstated in the world as equals.

The king would be a fool to provoke the trolls. If he wants us at the castle, he most certainly wants peace.

There's no doubt he'll want to talk about Lynchton. Not that I did anything worthy of reprimand. I simply did what needed to be done, storming the town and spawn-camping Glenn, another player, another Hero, all the way to level one without hurting a single NPC. Just because Glenn holds the title of hero, it doesn't mean he acts the part. He had it coming after everything he did to the trolls since he logged in. The man is a psychopath, and I'm glad I put him in his place before he could hurt anyone else.

By the time we were finished, the entire town had seen him for what he truly was. A monster. I wonder what the townspeople did with him after witnessing his vitriolic madness. Locked him away, if they were smart.

We still need to be vigilant as we come upon the castle. Even though we were invited, we still have a negative reputation amongst humans. Anyone who doesn't know our business with the king could attack us on sight, and the last thing I want to do is kill someone because of a misunderstanding. I may be a barbarian, but I'm not a savage. I take no joy in killing innocents.

Moving the needle from hated to untrusted with one town has done little to change our reputation on the large scale. Maybe the king can change that. His word is law after all, among humans, at least.

A herd of bison stampedes across the prairie, leaving a trail of dust in their wake. Stopping to fight them would be some nice experience, but I'm anxious to meet the king and would rather make as few detours as possible.

The crackle of fire draws my attention, and I turn just in time to see a fireball soaring across the sky towards the bison. It sizzles as it hits one of the slower creatures, leaving a scorch mark on its backside.

Limery leans back and cackles.

"Just make sure you catch up to us when you're done," I shout at Limery as he takes off in search of his prey.

"I'll follow him." Ismora turns in his direction, the fading sun gleaming off her black hair that's pulled into two ox-horn buns. "If he manages to defeat the beast,

I'll bring back the meat for dinner. My Boots of Swiftness will allow me to catch back up with ease."

Gord and I continue our march in silence as the sun draws closer to the horizon.

"Do you think this king can be trusted?" His thunderous voice finally breaks the quiet.

"I don't know, but I feel it is our best option. If we spurn him, it only proves us to be the unreasonable savages they already despise us as."

I grip my staff a little tighter. Every time I think about the meeting with the king, my chest tightens. There is a lot riding on this meeting.

Gord adjusts the massive black shield that hangs over his shoulder. The shield is engraved with a ram's head, complete with massive curling horns. "And the chief, she has authorized you to negotiate with the king?" His eyes question me. Even though we have grown closer since our first meeting, he still has his doubts.

"Within reason. I have a seat on the council and have been granted special privileges for our mission." I can negotiate for peace as long as it benefits the village.

"I still don't understand why the chief didn't come herself," he booms.

That's the real issue. The chief is the leader of the village, someone Gord greatly admires. He believes she should be squaring off with the king.

"Because if something goes wrong, if this proves to be a trap, then I'm the only one who will not truly die." The words say what I don't. If this is indeed a trap, then Gord, Ismora, and Limery aren't going home.

I can't allow that to happen. I didn't come back here just to let them die. This has to be a peaceful mission.

As we carry on, the plains transform into rolling hills scattered with billowy trees covered in pink and white flowers. The wind wages war against the trees, speckling the landscape in a fantastical array of petals while simultaneously covering us in fragrant confetti.

My jaw drops when we reach the crest of the hill and Vanaria comes into view. Beside me, Gord can't hide his wonder. Even from so far away, the city is magnificent. The keep in the center shimmers with a pearlescent sheen, with towers that rise high into the sky and disappear among the clouds. Whatever material it is constructed from gleams even in the fading daylight. Even after growing up in New York City, where skyscrapers are a way of life, the magnitude of the castle astounds me. Hundreds, if not thousands, of homes and buildings are packed between the curtain wall and inner walls. I wouldn't be surprised if half the island's population resides here.

Obsidian walls protect the city, gleaming with a dark fervor that dares anyone to challenge their protective power. Fires from the guard towers posted every few hundred feet reflect off its surface, and soldiers clad in white and blue patrol the parapets in between.

So this is how the other half lives.

The flap of Limery's wings bring me back from my astonishment just in time to hear Ismora's own gasp of admiration.

"It's beautiful," she gawks, but I can also see the uncertainty in her eyes.

I can only imagine what it must be like for them. A month ago, they had never left the forest, and now they are looking at a castle that's more like a work of art than a fortress. Just like all the small-town actors who came to New York to make it big, only to be swallowed by the city and eaten alive.

"Let's camp for the night and we will enter the city first thing in the morning."

We find a wooded area to make camp, having a dinner of roasted bison. Even though our passive ability Savage allows us to eat raw meat, it tastes so much better cooked over an open flame.

Limery tucks himself beneath my arms and Camouflage kicks in, concealing us from prying eyes while we sleep.

As I slowly drift to sleep, I can't help but think of what kind of king could live in a castle so opulent. How could someone like that ever understand the plight of the trolls?

Did I make a mistake by coming here? There are five tribes of trolls. I should have at least tried to band them together first. The seaside trolls turned me down, but that didn't mean the others would. If I'd known that this was Vanaria, I would have tried.

I led the forest trolls against an attacking town, against a psychopath, not this. We aren't prepared for this.

CHAPTER TWO

ALL THE KING'S MEN

The eyes of the guards bore into us as we approach the gate. High above the obsidian wall, arrows and crossbows point in our direction. None of them have fired, which tells me that they are expecting us at the very least. I take a deep breath and soldier on.

"Just keep calm." I try to sound confident, but the truth is that I'm just as nervous as they are. My guts rumble in that familiar way that would always come before class presentations. I never showed how nervous I was, but on the inside, it was turmoil.

Regardless of the invite, this is hostile territory. Men and trolls have been at war for thousands of years.

Gord adjusts his massive shield, and Ismora straightens her back. Nervous movements. Limery silently holds tight to my shoulder. I wait for him to say something, anything to relieve the tension, but it doesn't come. He's more worldly than any of us, and his silence only makes my heart race faster.

The portcullis is open and a handful of armed guards wearing blue capes stand beneath the entrance to the city, checking passers as they enter. Carts loaded with wood, produce, and other necessary items for a big city grind against the cobblestone road. None of the humans have spoken to us as we walk, but I hear whispers, and they've all given us a wide berth.

"Trolls, in the city—"

"Stand back, son. We don't know what they are capable of."

"Why are the guards not attacking?"

"I never thought they'd be so big, and that blue one—"

For this being a meeting for peace, I am strangely on edge. I feel for the mana that runs through my body and it comforts me a little knowing I can summon my horrors at a moment's notice if something goes down. These people have no idea what we are truly capable of.

A farmer checking in a wagon loaded with produce tries to speed up his inspection when we get too close for his liking. The guards watch us with suspicion, always one hand on their weapons.

One guard steps forward. He has a blue plume sticking out of his silver helmet that the others do not. His armor glitters in the morning light, and his cloak is spotless. Whoever he is, he lives well.

Captain of the City Watch. *Level 25.*

Twenty-five levels on an NPC is no joke. Gord had ten when I first met him, and he could have ripped me apart. This man could probably kill any one of us if he felt threatened. Perhaps all of us. Most of the soldiers surrounding him range from level ten to fifteen. These must be the best fighters in the land.

"Who are you and what is your business in Vanaria?" The man's voice cuts like ice, and Limery's claws dig a little deeper into my tough skin. The captain stands tall, but there are bags under his eyes. How long has he been waiting for us?

"I am Chod, councilmember and hero of the forest trolls. King Favian has requested a meeting." Certainly, he must know all of this already. Why else would he allow us to stroll right up to the gate unimpeded?

"Very well. Hand over your weapons, and I will escort you to the king."

I translate to Gord and Ismora, and they reluctantly relinquish their weapons. The cloak Ismora wears conceals more weaponry than any of us thought possible. Some of the guards murmur between themselves when she finally finishes emptying it.

I hand over my staff. I don't need it to summon my horrors, but these guys don't need to know that.

The captain whistles, and several dozen men march around the corner and appear in two columns adjacent both sides of the gate.

"All this for us?"

"It's for safety." He points toward the line for us to get moving.

Ours or his, I wonder.

From inside the city, the castle seems even taller than before. Several of the keep's ivory towers are visible, but most of it disappears above the clouds. No matter where someone is in the city, the keep towers above it all, a constant reminder of who is in charge.

Ismora sticks next to me, while Gord grunts at guards who step too close to him. I swear one of them flinches at the sound of his deep voice.

"I do not like this at all," he rumbles.

Nor do I, but it's the cost to play ball. If the trolls are going to finally be able to travel the island trading, adventuring, and exploring without risking certain death, this is the only way. Well, maybe not the only way, but we could never win an all-out war against an enemy like this.

It makes my decision to invade Lynchton feel all the more foolish. The king could want retributio—

Brown liquid splatters on the street before us, and I look up to see a woman emptying a bucket from the second-floor window of a dilapidated building. The smell of human waste assaults my nose as we enter the first line of streets. Disgusting.

A guard mumbles "absolute filth" as we step through it.

"This is the outer bailey. Most people call it Rat Row." The captain finally decides to show some hospitality. "Home of the peasants and other filth who dwell within the city. I'm sure trolls at least have the decency not to shit where they eat." He steps over a pile of what might be mud or excrement.

These are nothing more than well-guarded slums.

We pass through several rows of the same rundown buildings before we come to another obsidian wall. The soldiers guarding the entrance move aside as we approach.

On the other side of the wall, the buildings and streets are much cleaner and less ragged.

"This is the inner bailey. Those with a trade or some valuable skill live inside this wall, as well as soldiers and members of the guard."

"Why doesn't it stink on this side?" I ask.

"There is plumbing to carry waste away to the river."

"Why doesn't the outer bailey have it?"

He scoffs at me before answering. "What's the point? They live, die, and breed in filth. That's about all they are good for." A couple soldiers laugh at his words. "But even if that wasn't the case, the plumbing was installed before the outer bailey was populated. The castle was crafted by magic thousands of years ago, back when crafting was handled by the nimble of mind instead of body. Those ways are lost to us now."

The inner bailey bustles with activity, alive with excitement like every fantasy RPG I've ever played. There are stalls filled with fruits and vegetables where people hunt and haggle for the best produce. A blacksmith bangs against his anvil, and smoke plumes into the air from his forge. I spot shops selling fabrics, spices, medicine, and many more that stretch around the corner.

This is the reason people will play *Isle of Mythos*! This is the experience I have been missing. I can't wait to—

A figure clad in black exits the apothecary and looks in our direction. I recognize him as one of the men we killed after they left the underground dungeon.

Jude Duggan
 Level 14
 Fighter
 Human

He has gained back the level we took from him.

"You!" he snarls before running at us.

Gord lets out a roar that startles some of the soldiers and townspeople alike.

The guardsmen take a defensive stance, spears pointed toward Jude.

Wait, what? Why are they protecting us?

The captain steps forward, his hand on the hilt of his sword and a scowl on his face. "You will turn back now, or else I will send you to your next life before you form another breath."

Jude stops, but his eyes still cut at us. "They killed me. Me, Michael, and two soldiers. What the hell are they doing here?"

"Their appearance is none of your concern. I will not warn you to be on your way again."

"This isn't over," spits Jude.

Just as he turns to leave, Michael the paladin exits the blacksmith, a massive warhammer tossed over his shoulder. He looks at us, but Jude pulls him around the corner.

I feel this isn't the last we'll see of those two.

"Thanks for that," I tell the captain.

"I didn't do it for you." He releases his grip on his sword, and the other guardsmen fall into line.

Well, screw you too, buddy. We could have handled him on our own.

We're making our way through the business district when I notice a wheelbarrow loaded with kegs being pulled by a short, but rather stout man. A braided red beard hangs down his chest, and he wears an apron with the sigil of a beer mug over two crossed warhammers.

"Is that a dwarf?" I ask. Since I've been in *Isle of Mythos*, I've only seen humans and trolls. I know dwarves exist because they have a kingdom in the far north, but I've yet to see one.

"Indeed." The captain looks fondly at the dwarf, the first break I've seen in his icy exterior. "He is here on a trade exchange with the dwarven kingdom. They brew us beer and we send several of our vintners north to help them produce wine. The coastal climate in the north is surprisingly well-suited for a variety of grapes."

The dwarf slows his pace as he comes closer. Several jeweled metal clasps adorn his beard and clink together as he walks. "I'll be looking for ye after yer shift, Captain. The new lager be ready for tasting."

The captain only nods, and we continue our march towards the keep. Gord looks like an owl as he twists his head to watch the dwarf pass by.

"Are there more? Dwarves, I mean." I look down the streets and alleys, but there doesn't appear to be any other races.

I still remember the many races to choose from when I created my character. They were all blocked out to me, but that means they have to exist somewhere. If not on the island, maybe another continent.

"There are some. Most prefer their homeland. They are not great adventurers, the dwarves. They much prefer to toil for the good of their kingdom. Something those in the outer bailey could use a good dose of."

"Chods, look!" Limery seems more like himself as he points to a band of street performers juggling and walking on stilts. A crowd has gathered around them. They toss coins to a small monkey wearing a vest and hat. "Can we watch, Chods? Please," he pleads, hands clutched together.

"Do you mind?" I ask the captain.

He looks around—for what, I'm not sure. "Five minutes."

His men fall into position around us, leaving room in front for us to watch the performance even though we are several feet taller than the guards and have no problem seeing. When some of the townspeople notice us, they step aside, eyes wide and clearing a path. The performers continue their show as if nothing is happening. A man in purple and yellow clothing with a painted face tosses bowling pins into the air. Limery's bulbous eyes are alight with wonder.

He flies from my shoulder and hovers in the air next to the juggler. His palms crackle and a fireball appears in each hand. The crowd gasps and takes a step back. With a flick of his wrist, the fireballs jolt into the air, the hot flames distorting the air around them but remaining intact. Quickly, he conjures another fireball and adds it to the mix, mimicking the juggler's routine. The crowd looks on in a mixture of fear and wonder.

They must not see a lot of imps around here. Or is it magic they're afraid of?

When the juggler finishes, the man on stilts walks through the crowd to 'oohs' and 'ahs' as he fakes losing his balance. He makes eye contact with me and winks, his eyeball disappearing beneath the painted eyelid.

"Time to go," orders the captain.

As we turn to leave, the juggler calls out to us. "Hey, troll!"

The guardsmen block his way as he approaches. Something gleams in his hand, and with a flick of his thumb, it flies through the air, over the guards, and I catch it.

It's a golden coin with the head of a lion engraved on one side.

"Thanks for the show." The juggler winks and places a finger over his mouth, signaling me to keep quiet, before returning to his group.

I analyze the coin and can't believe what I see.

Item. Underground Circus Coin. *An enchanted coin used by the secret society. It will allow you access into areas otherwise unattainable.*

"What is that?" asks the captain, eyeing the coin.

I don't know why, but I get the feeling I shouldn't tell him.

"A coin. I guess he was happy with Limery's performance." I stuff the coin in one of the pouches on my belt before he can inspect it. I'll look into it further when there aren't so many prying eyes.

He looks at me suspiciously but doesn't press the issue.

We make our way through the inner bailey, past much nicer houses and buildings. The closer we come to the keep, the more opulent the homes become. Many are made of stone and are draped in banners emblazoned with their house sigils. Above them all, the shimmering keep towers over everything. Those that walk the streets wear clothing made of the finest threads and materials. Most of them do not carry weapons.

Finally, we come to the stairway that leads into the mighty keep. Beautiful white marble gleams in the sunlight, giving the keep a heavenly radiance. Eleven guards in silver and blue plate armor wait at the base of the stairs, blocking all entry. They stand stoically, unmoving sentinels. Their armor is intricately designed, with small engravings carved throughout. On each of their chests is a silver griffin with a blue jewel for the eye. This isn't the plain armor of a warrior. No, this armor is a symbol. I focus on one of the guards and his stats appear.

Kingsguard. *Level 22.*

Not quite as experienced as the captain of the city watch, but eleven of them could fight off almost any threat to the king. The captain walks to the kingsguard in the center and says something. That's when I notice that particular kingsguard wears a blue cape draped over his armor.

Captain of the Kingsguard. *Level 30.*

Wow! He's eleven levels higher than me. The amount of work it must have taken for an NPC to gain that many levels, I can't even begin to imagine.

The captain of the kingsguard instructs his men to make way, and my three companions and I ascend the stairs. The captain of the city watch takes his men and disappears back into the city.

It's like we're a baton being passed from one captain to the next.

"Follow me," he instructs. His voice is smooth and strangely youthful. I would expect a warrior of his stature to be gruffer, to be older.

Two other kingsguards flank us on both sides. There's no small talk as we ascend the stairs. Why would there be? This man has one job, and that's to protect the king with his life.

At the top of the stairs, two magnificent silver doors engraved with twin griffins facing one another bar our way. Sapphires the size of my fist dot their eyes and an array of diamonds add glitter to their wings.

"Pretty," mumbles Limery, his eyes greedy, reminding me of the first time we met when he tried to steal my pendant from around my neck.

Please don't steal anything while we are here.

With a groan, the doors open and a gray-bearded man in blue robes waits on the other side.

CHAPTER THREE

BLOOD PUDDING

"Welcome to Vanaria." The wizened man sweeps his arms to the sides, inviting us into the castle. Silver tassels hang from his robe, cinched tightly around a belly rivaling that of an expectant mother. The tassels match the color of his long, flowing beard. "The king is indisposed at the moment, but I will be entertaining you until he returns." The edges of his mustache rise slightly, hiding a smile underneath.

He looks like a lovable grandpa, but I keep my mana on edge just in case.

"Returns?" The captain of the kingsguard lets out an exasperated sigh.

"Not now, Warwick. You've made your feelings known, but he is the king. You know as well as I that we can't tell him anything unless he wants to hear it. Now, you lot, come." He motions to our party. "I'm sure you are famished from your travels." He starts walking before abruptly stopping and pressing a ring-covered hand to his face. "I'm sorry. Where are my manners? I am Lord Kassidy, advisor to the king. You must be Chod. Word has spread fast about a giant blue forest troll who can speak the common tongue and summon monstrous creatures. You should be proud of your notoriety. I'm looking forward to learning more about you. And that would make you Limery." He extends a finger for Limery to shake. "I had the pleasure of meeting your mother. A wonderful imp and extraordinary conversationalist."

"Pleased to meets you." Limery flashes his sharp teeth. His small hands linger on the old man's rings a little too long as they shake.

"As for you two, I'm not sure I am acquainted."

I turn to translate, but Gord is already answering. Lord Kassidy must have a communication stone.

"I am Gord, son of Guilda, guardian of the forest trolls."

"And I am Ismora, master of weapons for the forest trolls."

"Pleased to meet you. Now, if you don't mind, let us carry this conversation forward in the dining hall."

What a strange man. He appears more concerned with eating than the three trolls and imp standing before him. Not the least bit worried or hesitant that we are here. He is actually...friendly. His jovial nature is a bit infectious, causing me to let my guard down slightly, but I'm not entirely sure it's warranted. Who the hell is this guy? When I try to focus on his level, all I see are question marks.

Servants scurry through the castle as Lord Kassidy leads us to the dining hall. The table in the center overflows with food displayed on silver platters. Cornucopias spill fruits across the blue silk tablecloth next to roasted fowl, bread, vegetables, and an assortment of pies and puddings. A giant roasted pig dominates the centerpiece. There's enough food to feed a small army.

"Have a seat." Lord Kassidy pulls out a chair for Ismora before seating himself.

All of us, except for the kingsguard, take a seat around the table. The extravagance of the dining hall reminds me of some of the parties my mother and father would bring me to when I was young. Fancy tablecloths, silver spoons, and foods so rich that my stomach would hurt for hours. It wouldn't be complete without giant paintings of old men on the walls. They were always such boring affairs, too. Men in black ties holding martinis and talking about business. I was left alone with the other kids to entertain ourselves for hours.

The guards stand watch outside the entrances to the dining hall. We all sit there, waiting for instruction, when Lord Kassidy bursts out, "Oh, don't be shy. Dig in," before scooping himself a massive helping of pudding.

I reach for a grape and toss it in my mouth, expecting the deliciously tart and sweet flavor I love. Instead, I'm greeted by juices so bitter that I almost spit it out.

"Something wrong, Chod?" asks Kassidy.

"Uh, no, nothing at all." I pull off a leg of roasted goose and bite into it. Delicious and savory. Next, I take a small portion of green beans, but they have the same bitter taste as the grape. Is it possible my taste buds have changed since entering the game? It's not entirely out of the realm of possibility. It did take me some time to adjust to the size of my new body, why wouldn't I develop the palate of a forest troll?

I check on the others. Gord, Ismora, and even Limery have piled nothing but meat on their plates.

"This is a beautiful city." I try to make polite small-talk since we are their guests.

"Truly a work of art." Globs of mashed potatoes coat Lord Kassidy's beard. "You know, Vanaria was formed on the remains of a dormant volcano. Long ago, earth mages pulled obsidian from the earth to form the walls of our great city. The ivory towers were taken from the heart of the volcano itself. Blessed with divine power by a powerful cleric, the towers prevent necromantic activities within our city walls even to this day."

That's surprising. One of my options when I chose my summoner class was necromancy. If this is true, then I definitely made the right choice. "Is that a problem? Necromantic activities?"

"Not here, no. But I'm sure you are familiar with the great wizard that closed the fast-travel portals between continents. Well, let's just say he would have a hard time laying siege to our castle."

Interesting. "So, he was a necromancer?" I don't remember Limery's mom mentioning that.

"He was many things. Powerful in several branches of magic, but that was long ago. Losing access to fast-travel was a small price to pay to be rid of a threat so dire."

"He's still out there, though, isn't he? A powerful wizard like that doesn't just disappear to go die."

Kassidy looks up from his food, and there's a wildness in his eyes. Storms rage behind their gray surface. "I pray to the gods that we never find out." Just as quickly as it went, his jovial nature returns. "Let us enjoy dessert and then we can go up to wait for the king in the viewing chamber."

Remembering the grape, I try to object. "Us trolls aren't really one for sweets." And I'd hate to vomit on this nice tablecloth.

"Nonsense, I had our chef look through some of our ancient books for recipes of old. I quite think you will enjoy this one." He snaps his fingers, and the food on the table vanishes.

Gord scoots back in his chair, a roar of alarm sounding in his chest. Ismora rises to her feet, and Limery flutters into the air with a screech. The kingsguard rush into the room, swords drawn. I'm the only one who seems unphased by the action.

"Oh, sorry. I didn't mean to frighten you." Another snap and a black pudding appears in a bowl in front of each of us. It's going to take more than a nice meal to get these three off-edge. "No need to worry. I only use my powers for good."

"You're a wizard?" I ask.

Gord slowly readjusts himself at the table. Aside from Jira, I haven't seen any other magic users that weren't players.

"Indeed. Teleportation is my specialty. It has so many uses, but that's neither here nor there. What's important is the dish in front of you. I've been told it is a troll delicacy."

Blood pudding. *+3 Strength and Constitution for one hour.*

I pick up the spoon and dip it into the black glob. Gord and Ismora are unsure of how to use the cutlery, holding the spoon facing downward like they're about to plant a stake in the earth. I dip my spoon and take a bite, then they follow my lead. The thick pudding coats my mouth, and I anticipate the bitterness of sweets, but it's actually delicious. Like a cool meaty treat. A small jolt of power flows through my body and my muscles pump gently, the bonus Strength and Constitution taking effect.

"Wow, this is good," I say between bites.

Ismora echoes my enthusiasm.

"Oh yes, Limmy likes. Limmy likes." The imp runs his tongue against his blood-covered teeth.

"The blood was freshly drained this morning," Kassidy laughs. "I'm glad you like it. Now, what do you say we find the king?"

Lord Kassidy leads us to a wide spiral staircase that ascends into what I believe is one of the giant towers. Warwick, captain of the kingsguard, and his two men follow closely behind us.

The wizard sucks in air with each step as we ascend, and I wonder if he needs help. He could be attempting to look weak so that we underestimate him. With his level being hidden from us, there is no way to know how powerful he truly is.

Still, he's a teleportation mage. Couldn't he just teleport himself to the room we are going to? Maybe that's why he is so out of shape.

A lazy wizard. I can't help but smile at the thought.

As we climb the stairs, we pass different levels with doors leading to various rooms and hallways. Occasionally, there is a window that looks down onto the kingdom below.

Our party halts as the wizard comes to a stop, keeling over to gasp for air.

"This man advises the king?" Gord leans in so that he isn't overheard, but his booming voice carries nonetheless. Gord's remark goes unnoticed by the wizard sucking at air, but one of the kingsguard snickers.

"It certainly seems so."

"How can a man who cannot care for and strengthen his body expect to care for a kingdom?"

For a dumb brute, Gord has a good point. The wizard does seem a bit simple-minded.

"Is we there yet?" Limery asks, fluttering down next to the wizard.

Kassidy resigns to his defeat at climbing the stairs. "Hardly. Warwick, lead them the rest of the way." With a snap, the wizard disappears.

"Typical," scoffs Warwick. "I take it you are all in good shape, so let's pick up the pace. I'd have this over with sooner than later."

We move up the tower at a near jog, the metal plates of the three kingsguards clanking with each step. By the time we reach the top, my muscles burn and sweat beads down my shoulder blades. Limery is the only one who's not sucking for air. The endurance of imps still amazes me.

The top of the tower empties into an open-air room above the clouds. Kassidy sits on a large sofa eating strawberries with his feet propped on a pillow.

"I'm glad you are comfortable," quips Warwick. The other two guards take position outside the entrance, not that I think anyone else is making the journey up those stairs ready to fight.

I'm certain we climbed over a hundred flights of stairs to be this high.

Warwick removes his helm, revealing a youthful face and black hair drenched in sweat. His eyes are as dark as coals. He can't be older than his early twenties. And already level thirty. He sits the helm on a stone bench and walks over to the ledge, gazing at the clouds. We're so high that they conceal the ground below.

"Oh, have a seat, will you?" Kassidy bites another strawberry and the juices run through his beard. "The king will be back when he is back. Staring off into the abyss won't bring him any sooner."

"This is foolish." Warwick doesn't turn around.

Something is definitely up between these two. And why are we up so high waiting for the king? What could he possibly be doing?

"The king can handle his own, you know this."

"Then why have a kingsguard at all?" Warwick turns, his face set in stone. "These heroes can't be trusted! All they need is one stroke of luck and the king is gone forever. If I am not around and something happens to him..." He lets the words drift off.

"You worry too much. These heroes are no danger to the king."

Knowing what I know, I wouldn't be so certain about that. I keep my opinion to myself, though.

"You lot." Kassidy points a strawberry in our direction. "Join me and relax your legs. I'm sure the climb up was terrible."

We take a seat on a sofa across from Kassidy. Sitting there, it's the first time I've been aware of the comforts of the real world that the trolls are missing. Not that we need them. Our tough hides and Constitution allow us to sit or sleep almost anywhere in comfort.

"There are a lot of ways to get the king's attention." Kassidy ponders eating another strawberry and then places it back in the bowl. "But taking over a town and then sending an imp-delivered letter straight to the top of the tower, that's a bold move. Probably the only reason you are here now and not six-feet under."

I had no idea Limery's mother delivered the letter all the way up here. I'll have to give her something extra for that.

"I only did it be—"

A monstrous screech cuts me off as a giant winged creature with the head of an eagle and the body of a lion flies into the room. It lands with a grating slide as its claws dig into the stone. Warwick dives out of the way, his armor scraping against the stone floor. The creature squawks at us, revealing its sharp beak and razor-like talons. Its dark gray wings flap in agitation.

Griffin. *Unique monster. Level: ??? Known as the 'King of Beasts,' the griffin is one of the oldest and wisest monsters. Both proud and intelligent, they will only fight with their masters, not for them.*

Upon its back sits a man wearing simple boiled leather.

Kassidy sits up, casually eating another berry. "Welcome home, Your Highness."

CHAPTER FOUR

PEACE OFFERINGS

The leathers that the king wears is simple and rustic. Aside from the griffin branded on his chest, nothing hints at the nobility of the man beneath it. A pair of goggles obscure his face, and short, brown, windswept hair gives him an air of adventure.

Warwick crawls to his feet. "Do you have to do that every time?" The exasperation in his voice tells me this isn't the first time he's been knocked on his ass.

The king laughs off the comment as he dismounts from the massive griffin. With a huff, the griffin stalks to the corner of the room and lays down. I try to analyze the king, but I get nothing.

King Favian. *Level: ???*

"So you're the troll who has the entire kingdom in an uproar?" He approaches with a confidence that tells me his level isn't visible most likely because it is too high for me to comprehend. There's a gentleness about him, but underneath it all, I can sense a raw power. He could kill me before I ever lifted a finger.

Gord and Ismora rise as he approaches. They have no weapons, but I know that if anything happened right now, they would die for me. For their tribe. It's my job to make sure that doesn't happen.

"That was never my intention." I stand beside them, and Limery's body feels strangely hot against my shoulder. After Lynchton, I felt invincible. Defeating Glenn and storming the town without losing a single troll, I was a big fish in a small pond. How little I knew of the world and the other powerful beings that dwelled within it.

"Don't let it trouble you too much. They hate that which they do not understand, and it has been far too long since trolls and humans have understood one another."

I let out a sigh of relief, and Gord unclenches his fist. For now, at least, it seems we will talk.

"Why did you ask me here?" There's no point in beating around the bush.

He smiles at me for a long moment, as if sizing me up. "Partly to see the troll that said he would tear this entire kingdom to the ground if his people weren't left in peace." Gord and Ismora both let out an audible groan of disapproval. "But mostly to meet the hero that would do that for his people. You see, I've met the so-called heroes of my people. Some are noble, some are...not so. Warwick thinks I do not recognize them for what they are, but the truth is that I see all too well. They will do my bidding for gold coin or valuable items, but I do not think any of them would risk themselves out of sheer selflessness for my people, for those who do not come back from death."

The king certainly is no fool. Still, what is his motivation for bringing me here?

"You want peace?" He lifts his goggles and piercing blue eyes stare at me.

"That is all we want. The ability to live our lives like any other race. Freedom to travel outside of the forest to trade or adventure without risking certain death."

"Then let us cut right to the chase. Kassidy, Warwick, will you accompany Chod's party out of the room? I'd like to speak to the hero troll alone." His lip curls up around the edge in a mischievous way, and my chest tightens. What is he up to?

Kassidy and Warwick make for the door, but Gord and Ismora remain.

"Come," orders Warwick.

A fierce growl rumbles in Gord's chest. "I will not leave my brother alone."

"It's okay, Gord. I'll be fine." At least, I hope so.

His eyes flitter between the king and I, untrusting.

"Are you sure?" asks Ismora.

"Yes, I will find you when we are done." It's not like I have a choice in the matter. It's either talk to the king or fight our way out.

"Be safe, Chods." Limery hugs me before jumping from my shoulder to Gord's.

A few moments later, it's just the king, his griffin, and me alone in the room. King Favian takes a seat on the sofa and folds his hands together. I still can't get a read on the man.

He lets out a long sigh before leaning back.

"It's not easy being king, you know. There's so much responsibility. As a child, I thought it was all hunting trips and lavish parties, but more often than not, its council rooms and closed meetings. I take to the air every chance I get. It's the one thing that allows me to clear my mind." He sighs. "My father was lucky he didn't have to deal with heroes. Hundreds of years pass after the great war and then suddenly, immortals show up out of nowhere." He leans forward and looks me square in the eye. "Part of me thinks I should kill them all. Round them up before they are too powerful and kill them. Much like you did in Lynchton. I know they get weaker when they die. That's their one vulnerability. I could kill them and lock them all away and they'd never be a problem."

My body tenses at those words. Maybe he brought me here for just that reason, to lock me up before I become a real problem. Could I make it to the ledge before he stopped me? One long drop and I'd respawn in the forest. But I can't leave my party. They trusted me, and I'm not that big of a dick.

He still seems rather calm, so I abandon the thought of suicide for the moment. "Why don't you?"

He runs his fingers through his hair. "I'm no fool. They will all have their part to play before all is said and done. If heroes are here, it is for a reason. Something is brewing. If not on the island, then somewhere in the world. What, I'm not sure of yet. Mythos has a way of balancing itself out, at least historically. So I find myself in a chess match, where I am forced to guide the heroes to power while at the same time protecting my people. Only I don't know the end goal. Do you?"

"Do I what?"

"Know the end goal?" He rubs his eyes. "Of course you don't."

"Why did you bring me here?" I ask again.

He sits in silence for a moment, as if questioning if he should really tell me. "Because I want to wage war on the dwarves."

That is about the last thing I expected him to say. They're trading partners, so what could he possibly have against them? "The dwarves? Why?"

"Their kingdom sits on one of the largest ley lines on the island. It's so powerful that it influences the metal they mine with magical properties. We have the fewest number of enchanters in the kingdom since I was born, making it difficult to forge many rare and powerful items. The dwarves make them every day. I want what they have, and you are going to help me acquire it. Once the dwarven kingdom is mine, you and your trolls shall have your freedom."

He can't seriously be asking this. It's suicide. The forest trolls are a small tribe as it is, and war would push us to extinction. Perhaps that is his goal—to take over the dwarven empire and rid the forest trolls in the process. There is no way the chief would agree to this.

Anger boils inside, and my mana rages at my fingertips. Would summoning a Horror of Vitality slow him enough that I could tackle him off the ledge? Would the fall be enough to kill him?

I hold my hand for the moment, hoping I can talk my way out of this. "Why do you need the trolls for this? Can't you fight your own battles, reward the heroes to fight for you?"

He smirks before answering. "As far as I know, the dwarves have yet to receive a hero. I find that very strange. Two dozen human heroes and one troll, but no dwarves. It's almost as if fate is tipping the scales in my favor. With enough rewards, every human hero will fight for my cause. Add in your army of trolls, and don't think I forgot about the wyrms you've been training, and I'd lose less than a tenth of the men I would in open combat. I have no misconceptions about how the strength of a troll compares to a human. One troll is worth at least four men, and that's not counting your precious little monsters." He seems to be relishing the victory before the battle has even started. "With the dwarven kingdom under my rule, the entire island would be mine. You and your trolls would be greatly rewarded for your role. Refuse my offer, and the trolls will forever regret the day they attacked my village."

He's not leaving any gray area. Greatly rewarded! Ha! If any of the trolls survived.

We sit in a long silence. The king watches my face intently, and I wonder if he can see the internal struggle raging underneath.

There has to be another way! I can't agree to making my people slaves for a would-be conqueror. Gord, Ismora, and Limery will likely die if I run, but I have to make it out of this castle. The one thing I can't do is allow myself to be captured. I have to alert the chief. If I can manage to warn some of the other troll tribes, hell, maybe I can even warn the dwarves, then we might have a chance at stopping this tyrant.

"I'm sorry, but no." I say it clearly and calmly, though my stomach is in knots. I know nothing about this man other than that he is more powerful than me. Even so, I have to try to escape.

"No?" he asks, and the mischievous grin returns.

As worried as I am for what happens next, I stand my ground. "I came here for peace, not to become pawns in a war we have no part in. If you force us to fight, then we shall, but it will not be on your terms."

He opens his mouth to respond, but before he does, I cast Horror of Vitality and the small monster summons in a puff of smoke. The rotund, furry monster with orange and blue stripes charges the king at the same time as I bolt for the ledge. The sofa I'm sitting on flips backward with the force of my lunge. The black ram's horns of my horror lower as it charges, and I pray that its sharp tusks inflict at least some damage to the king as I leap into the abyss.

Gravity quickly takes hold and the rush of air beats against my skin. Clouded sky is all I see as I plummet towards death. The thought of breaking every bone in my body scares me more than I would like to admit. Even with my tough skin and Constitution, it may be the worst pain I've ever felt in my life. The only consolation is that at least I will respawn in the forest.

My thoughts are with Limery and the others as I fall. Will they be killed for my transgressions or will the king hold them hostage? They are the very reason I came back into this game. I wanted to save them, but I failed.

I fall through a voluminous cloud, everything white as I'm engulfed in its misty embrace. Then suddenly, there's a strange presence around me, like I've been wrapped in a shield. The clouds disappear, and I collide with a hard surface, knocking the air from my lungs.

Stars dance across my vision as I gasp for air. My surroundings come in and out of focus, and I can barely make out two brown boots standing before me. My mouth tastes of blood. I try to push the stars from my vision so I can stand, but as I try to rise, I lose my balance and stumble to the ground once more.

I roll onto my back and look up to see the king. He holds my horror by one of its horns as its arms and feet claw at the air.

CHAPTER FIVE
DIRTY DANCING

So, the fuck-up fairy decides to make another appearance.

What have I gotten myself into?

My head clears and I realize I'm on the floor of the room I just jumped from. The stone is cool against my back, matching the icy dread in my chest. How did I manage to fuck up killing myself? One job. I had one job, and I screwed it up. Who is going to warn the chief about the king's plans now?

Some hero I turned out to be.

The king still holds my Horror of Vitality by the horn as it thrashes against his grip. I could explode the creature, but I doubt it would do more than scratch the king. He's staring at me with a look of what…amusement?

I want to smash that look off his face.

"What happened?" Kassidy's voice comes from behind me. Had he been in here the entire time without me realizing it? He must have teleported me back as I was falling.

"He tried to jump. Turned down my offer and then jumped off the ledge." He looks down at the horror as if he's not sure what to do with it. The creature continues to snarl.

"What offer?" Kassidy frowns. The way he says the words makes it sound like he doesn't know the king's plans.

"Oh, you know. To invade the dwarven kingdom." A half-smile creeps across his face.

"You didn't?" gasps Kassidy. "These aren't nobles in your kingdom that you can just toy with for amusement." He sounds serious, the first time he's acted like an actual advisor. "For all you know, this could be considered an act of war."

"I doubt that. This troll has more honor than most of the men on my council, yourself included." Kassidy lets out a harrumph at that. The king finally looks at me, still holding the horror. "Can you call this thing off now?"

I have no idea what the hell is happening. "What's going on? Are you not attacking the dwarves?"

He waves the horror at me, and I call off its attack. It quits thrashing, and King Favian drops it to the floor.

"I have no plans to attack the dwarves. I simply wanted to understand what kind of troll you were, what your intentions were, and what you would do for power if it was offered to you."

"And what kind of troll do you think I am?" There's a bite to my voice that I don't try to restrain. He toyed with me, and it's not something I'll soon forget.

"The kind who would not put his people at risk for something he did not believe in." The king extends his arm to help me to my feet. "Bring the others in."

Kassidy makes a motion with his hand, and a few moments later, I hear the clank of Warwick's armor before everyone enters the room.

The horror puffs out of existence, his life force depleted, and I catch looks of befuddlement from my party as they join me.

Once we have all gathered in the center of the room, the king clears his throat. "I was surprised today. Surprised that a troll, a race most of my population would consider a monster, showed me what it truly means to make a tough decision. He displayed the true meaning of the word hero. It is my hope that you become not only a hero of the trolls, but a hero for Vanaria and all of Mythos. I pray that you do not hold my methods against me. You want peace, Chod? Then you shall have it."

Regional Alert! *King Favian has struck terms for peace with the forest trolls. Any unwarranted attack upon a forest troll by a Vanarian will be treated as an attack against a fellow citizen.*

Peace. It actually worked. I set out to do something and I actually did it. This will affect the lives of every troll in the forest. I catch sideways glances from the rest of my party. A demonic smile graces Limery's face. We actually did it.

"This won't solve all your problems." He takes the time to look and acknowledge each member of my party and for the first time since meeting him, I see him as a king. As youthful as he may look, he has that undeniable presence that says he is no mere man. "The hate and distrust will not vanish overnight, and there is very little I can do to change the hearts of my people, but I hope that in time, they will see you as equals. My advice is to travel north and make peace with the dwarves, then together, we can work toward a brighter future and prepare for what is coming."

The turn of events has my head spinning. I accomplished what I set out to. We have peace. I should be happy for that. But I just went through a mental obstacle course. I mean, I thought I was sacrificing my friends, for fuck's sake!

"You're an asshole!" I blurt it out without thinking, and the room goes silent.

The king stares at me for a long moment, and I'm suddenly conscious of every sound in the room. Gord's heavy, barbarian breathing. The gentle shuffle of the griffin's feathers as it settles itself in the corner. My own racing heart.

I'm an idiot. The king offers me peace, and I insult him in the next breath.

"I'm—" I start to apologize, but the king's laughter cuts me off.

"Asshole," he chuckles. After a moment, Kassidy joins in. Soon the whole room is laughing, Limery's shrill laugh carrying above it all. Even Warwick has a smirk on his face. "Asshole. I like that. I'll have to use it the next time I'm forced to entertain Lord Reynolds." He comes closer and stands directly in front of me. "I'm sorry if my methods were a bit unconventional, but I feel we will have a great relationship between our people. If I recall correctly, there are more than one tribe of trolls?"

"You are correct." I take a deep breath, trying to release some of my anger as I list them off in my mind. Mountain, seaside, desert, arctic. I've met the seaside trolls, but I have no idea what to expect from the others.

"Do you think they would be interested in peace? I am willing to come to terms with the other tribes so that our races may trade together. I am certain they have products we need, and I am willing to bet that a little bartering would go a long way with easing the hearts of my people."

I would hope so. Even the seaside trolls, who want nothing but to be left alone, might reconsider if it meant peace. "I can't speak for them, but when I return, I will let the chief know. We will do what we can to reach out to the other tribes."

"Very good. Then I think that is enough politics for one day." He tosses his goggles on a marble table. "We can negotiate the final terms of peace tomorrow. Tonight, I would like to host an evening of revelry in honor of the forest trolls. But first, Kassidy, did you save me any dinner?"

Warwick escorts my party and I to our quarters for the evening. We each have a separate room in one of the smaller towers of the keep. The giant center tower that touches the clouds is only for the royal family. A lot of tower for one family, if you ask me.

We have a few hours to kill before the party, so Gord, Ismora, and Limery all gather in my room while I recount the events with the king.

"You were going to leave us to die?" Gord's nose ring reflects the candlelight of the stone room as he scowls at me. "I take back every nice thing I ever said about you."

"When have you ever said anything nice about me?" I point a taloned blue finger at him. "You would have done the same thing. It was the only option. I had to warn the village."

"We know, Chods." Limery hugs me. "I's glad yous didn't die."

"You did the right thing," echoes Ismora. "I will be glad to be back in the forest. Trolls were not meant to be caged away in stone fortresses. There is no life when the ground is made of stone."

"If all goes well, we will be back on the road tomorrow." The quicker we can be back in the forest, the better. We may have peace, but the work has only just begun.

Limery flies up to the candlelit chandelier and latches on with his feet, hanging upside-down. "Limmy likes the city. Lots of peoples for him to watch."

"If by watch, you mean pickpocket, then sure." Sometimes, he's like a child in the candy aisle, in constant need of supervision. All those years stealing magical items to power their home has made thieving second nature to him. "You know, with the magic returned to the forest, you don't have to steal magical items anymore, right?"

He bats the lids of his bulbous eyes at me sheepishly. "Limmy knows."

"Then how about you keep your hands to yourself."

They each return to their rooms to 'clean up' and look 'presentable,' as Kassidy calls it. I don't know how the man can judge us when he always has something in his beard. Nevertheless, I scrub away the dirt and debris of our journey, and the new leather clothing they provide fits surprisingly well. In lieu of my normal loincloth, I wear a leather vest and kilt. It offers no bonuses, but the deep brown leather looks remarkable against my blue skin.

I sit on the bed, waiting for the others to finish. A large tapestry depicting a man riding a griffin and battling a dragon catches my eye. There are so many details in the threading that I could lose myself in it for hours. While the man rides his griffin through the sky, his army battles against a force of armed skeletons on the ground.

A knock on the door interrupts my focus. It's time to party.

A trumpet blares, announcing our arrival to the great hall, and the dull chatter of guests comes to an abrupt halt as we enter. The room is packed with hundreds of people, all wearing fine garments. The bright colors look like a rainbow vomited all over them.

"How do they move in such things?" Ismora stares at a woman in a ruffled gown that billows out twice as wide as she is.

In her slim-fitting gray tunic and pants, Ismora is nothing like the frilly women that surround us.

There are several gasps and whispers as Kassidy leads us to the head table where the king stands surrounded by several members of his guard. To his left sits a beautiful brunette and two young children. I can feel the eyes of the nobles on us as we walk, eyes filled with fear, wonder, and a million other emotions these people must be feeling.

This might not have been such a great idea.

The king has changed out of his riding clothes and now wears a royal blue tunic embroidered with silver thread. It has the same griffin on the chest I have become accustomed to seeing. An ornate design of silver vines runs down both arms. Upon his head, a jeweled crown glitters in the candlelight.

We step up to the head table and the king raises a hand, bringing silence to the hall.

"By now, all of you have received the notification detailing our kingdom's peace with the forest trolls." There are grumbles at this, but the king continues. "It is a peace that I believe will benefit both of our races for many years to come. As the nobility of this fine kingdom, you hold sway over the opinions of the common people. I implore you to see that the trolls are not that different from us. I present to you: Chod, Gord, Ismora, and Limery the Imp, our honored guests. Eat, drink, be merry. Celebrate peace, and when the time comes, make our guests feel welcome."

The king extends a hand to me. "Georgia, Maximus, Delania, meet Chod of the forest trolls." All three stand and bow.

"Nice to meet you." My deep voice causes the young girl to jump.

"Give it time." The king places a hand on my shoulder. "Now, let us celebrate."

We take our seats as food is brought out by the servants. Mountains of meat are set before us. Roasted deer, boar, and many types of fowl, the king spares no expense. I notice that the vegetables and fruits stay clear from our area of the table this time.

While we eat, minstrels play music, and entertainment is brought into the center of the hall. I recognize the juggler from the town center as he tosses balls into the air to the delight of many. I had almost forgotten about the coin he gave me. It's still tucked in one of the pouches I left in my quarters. Limery has an inkling to go down and join the entertainment, but I convince him to stay put this time.

After the food is cleared, people take to the dance floor. Gord and Ismora firmly refuse when I invite them to go down.

"That is not dancing." Gord looks at the crowd in disgust. "That is a mating call."

Remembering the tribal dance I saw on my first day in the forest, I can see why they have the misconception. This is fluid and elegant, with one movement blending into the next. The tribal dance was full of stomping, beating chests, and roaring. It was primal in a way this could never be.

"Fine, suit yourselves." I make my way down to the dance floor, and the flap of Limery's wings lets me know he's following.

I'm not sure what the dance is called, but it seems pretty easy to do. A few steps as they spin clockwise around the floor. I'm not that great of a dancer, but as a member of the council, I feel it's my duty to act stately as best I can.

I glance back at the table and find Gord and Ismora engaged in conversation with Kassidy. At least they aren't sitting alone giving mean looks to the other guests.

The song ends and another begins. I wait for an opening to join in, but one never appears. The dancers seem glued to their partners all of a sudden, unable or unwilling to switch off. I ask several ladies for a dance but receive excuses of sore feet and full stomachs.

King Favian said it would take time, but I didn't think I'd be shunned at a party thrown in our honor.

"It's okay, Chods. Limmy will dance with you." The small imp flutters in front of me, arms outstretched. I'm sure he's experienced his own share of dislike for being an imp.

"Mind if I cut in?" Queen Georgia appears beside us, extending a hand to me. "And I have a partner for you too, Mr. Imp." She smiles. Princess Delania mimics her mother's motion to Limery.

"I'd be honored." I take her dainty hand in my own, swallowing it in my grasp.

We take to the dance floor, and I try to ignore the daggers being stared in our direction, instead focusing on every step so I don't crush the queen's feet with my own. The queen is dancing with a troll. I can't imagine the thoughts running through their ignorant minds.

The queen is miniature compared to me. My massive hand wraps around her side as we waltz, and she has to stare straight up to make eye contact.

"My husband told me about what happened. I hope you won't hold it against him. He has always had an odd sense of humor."

Our eyes meet, and when she looks at me, it's not with hatred or disgust but wonder, almost childlike. Her blue eyes match the hue of her dress.

"I will do my best."

We spin around the dance floor and little by little, I forget that the other people are in the hall. I never went to any of my school dances. They seemed stupid. Or maybe I just didn't have the confidence to ask any of the girls out. But here I am now, my first dance ever, and it's with a queen.

"When I was a child," she begins, and I have to lean down closer to hear her. "My mother would always read me stories about princesses, but every now and then, when father wasn't busy with travel or business, he would read to me. He read me ancient stories about the heroes of old. About Timofy Stillblade, whose sword was so fast it appeared not to be moving at all. About Davos the Wrathful, the dwarven berserker who mined an entire mountain by himself. Even Brod the Vanquisher, the famous troll who cleared the great forest of werespiders."

The song comes to an end and we stop dancing. She looks up at me. "I am not afraid of trolls nor heroes, Chod. I believe we all have our parts to play in this world, you and yours included. I am just sorry it has taken so long for us to correct mistakes of old."

After meeting the royal family, it's a relief to know that these two rule Vanaria. Perhaps things will turn out okay after al—

A sharp pain shoots through my shoulder, and screams ring out all around me. I grasp at the source of the pain and find a dagger lodged in my back. Just as I pull it out, another dagger connects with my ribs. The site of the wounds goes hot and begins spreading through my veins. Poison.

Who would attack me here? Did the king betray me?

I'll kill him!

My head spins, and I can hear Gord's battle-cry and the crackle of Limery's flames in the distance. Who would attack me? Here of all places? I grasp my Tiger's-Eye Pendant and the burning liquid vanishes from my blood, allowing me to think clearly again.

I look up just in time to see Jude the Fighter move between guests in a blur, leaving a shadowy trail behind him. Something glitters in his hands, and I step in front of the queen, determined not to let anything happen to her.

Calling my mana, I cast one of each horror back to back, sending the crowd into even more of a panic. The horrors charge at the cloaked man.

Jude raises his arms in a flash, throwing the three glowing daggers in my direction. As they soar through the air, a trail of darkness follows each blade. I raise my arm and brace for impact.

The daggers vanish from sight. Jude screams in pain and falls forward, shaking violently as he collapses to the ground. Three daggers stick out of his back. My horrors rush to him, but before they make it, he vanishes, respawning only God knows where. All that remains are the daggers and his black clothing.

"Chods! Is yous okay?" Limery hovers before me, eyes full of concern. Gord and Ismora race to the spot where Jude died, only to find he is gone.

Warwick calls out above the frantic crowd, "Everyone out! Clear the great hall!"

Several kingsguards surround the king as he rushes toward his queen, while others usher the guests out of the hall.

Kassidy leans over Jude's remains, holding one of the daggers that killed Jude. "Dammit! I shouldn't have killed him. He could be reborn anywhere." He looks at me. "Chod, do you know this man?"

"Yes, he's another hero, Jude Duggan. We ran into him on our way into the city. He and I have a bit of a history."

"Warwick," Kassidy orders. "Put out a call to the city watch. Jude Duggan is to be apprehended on sight."

"Are you okay?" King Favian holds his wife and daughter tight, combing their hair with his fingers. "That man will pay for this! To attack an honored guest, in my great hall of all places. It cannot be allowed!" He releases his family and joins Kassidy. "How could he have made it past the guards without an invitation?"

"Heroes have their ways. Chod, let us get your wounds tended." Kassidy takes me by the arm.

"He will pay for this," the king reaffirms. "After Chod's wounds are treated, I want him and his party taken to their rooms. Post a guard outside of every door. We will talk tomorrow after we know more."

Of all the ways I imagined this night ending, attempted assassination was at the bottom of my list.

CHAPTER SIX
SNEAKY SNEAKS

The guards escort me and my party to our separate rooms for the evening. Gord, Ismora, and Limery are all on edge, and I don't blame them. I'm just glad Jude attacked me and not one of them. With the bonus critical damage from Kassidy's teleportation sneak attack, the hit was deadly enough to kill Jude with his own weapons. I'd rather not think about how it all could have went down. We can rest easy knowing that it wasn't some elaborate assassination attempt, just an asshole hero with a score to settle.

There's also comfort in knowing he has a bounty on his head. No human city will welcome him until he's been captured, and then he'll be dealt whatever punishment the king sees fit.

I still can't believe he attacked me in the king's castle. With so many people and guards around, he had to know he wasn't making it out of there alive. Maybe the thought of killing me was worth the risk. That's probably the thought process that landed him in prison in the first place. Was it worth enough to risk a hard-earned level?

The more I think about it the less sense it makes. The only logical explanation, aside from him hating me so much that he would do anything to see me dead, is that he was hoping to start a war. If I died at the king's party and had no idea who was responsible, were they hoping I might think it was the king?

This is a fantasy game, but somehow, it's all politics. There's always someone in a dark alley pulling strings. Whatever happened to dungeon diving and monster slaying? Once I get back to the forest, I'm going to take some much-needed time for rest and relaxation.

I sit on the edge of the bed and find myself staring at the tapestry again. The griffin, the dragon, the army of the dead. Is it from history or a fairy tale?

There's a noise from the other side of the stone wall that startles me. It comes from behind the large chest-of-drawers that sits just below the tapestry. A grating, scratching noise that's muffled through the thick stone.

Not wanting to take any chances, I summon one of each horror and wait for the cooldown to cast more. If someone is trying to sneak into my room to murder me, one, they are doing a terrible job of sneaking, and two, they have another thing coming. I will not be attacked unaware twice in one day.

My horrors scurry towards the wall, sensing something on the other side. The Horror of Power takes the lead. It walks on all fours, wide-stanced like a pit bull with a massive head, sharp teeth, angry red eyes, and tusks that shoot out of its jaw like a warthog. Its fur is golden with a black mane that surrounds its head. A barbed tail with four spikes swishes through the air like a mace. It is my primary damage dealer, with each Horror of Power having twenty percent of my Strength. My hands glow faintly after the summon, the bonus from casting it granting my next attack double damage.

Behind the Horror of Power, the Horror of Vitality creeps forward. The twenty percent of my health it receives makes it perfect for tanking. There's also the bonus Area of Effect it has that slows anything in its vicinity. Whatever is on the other side of that wall isn't going anywhere fast if we meet it. The black ram's horns and protruding tusks give a menacing quality to its otherwise cuddly orange and blue fluff.

The Horror of Finesse brings up the rear. The smallest of the three, its strength is in its speed. The blue, gangly creature is not much bigger than Limery. It has long pointy fingers, huge bat-like ears, and a dog snout. Basically, a blue imp without wings. With twenty percent of my attack speed, its sharp claws are deadly. The bonus heal it gives on my next attack isn't too shabby, either.

With three horrors active, I gain a three-percent bonus to Strength and Constitution. The bonus stats feel like a shot of adrenaline. I'd like to see Jude challenge me with a full army of horrors at my disposal.

My minions move closer to the wall, where the scratching continues, growing louder. Something has to be trying to get in.

A crack forms in the stone wall so thin it is almost imperceptible. It goes straight up and then cuts horizontally, like a door. Then, the stone pushes outward and bangs against the chest-of-drawers. Someone mumbles something from the other side.

It's been so long since I have been in battle that I don't have enough rage to use any of my barbarian abilities. When my horrors attack, it'll give me the rage I need to cast Bite or Claw or whatever else I need to seriously fuck up whoever is on the other side.

I pull back the chest-of-drawers and it screeches against the stone floor. The hidden entrance springs forward, pulling down the tapestry, and two bodies tumble to the ground covered in the fabric artwork.

My horrors descend on the bodies, biting and clawing and goring them with their tusks.

"Stop! Oh god, please stop!" a voice squeals, and I temporarily call off the horrors.

"Who the hell are you and why are you sneaking into my room?" I add a little extra roar to my voice for effect.

"Please don't kill us, Mr. Troll. We didn't mean any harm, honest." The bodies squirm underneath the tapestry like a dog caught in a sheet. "Hawkin sent us. He said you had a Circus Coin and that we was to lead you to the circus."

"Is everything okay in there?" a guard yells from outside my room. The door jostles as he attempts to enter, but the wooden beam that runs across the door frame keeps him out.

"Yeah, everything is fine. I fell off the bed." The mention of the Circus Coin has me intrigued, at least for the time being. One wrong move, and I'll explode my horrors on these two dingbats.

After a moment of silence, the guard's footsteps announce his return to his post.

"Who is Hawkin?" I return my attention to the intruders.

There's movement underneath the tapestry, and a freckled-face boy with red hair pops out from underneath. Several scratches run along his cheek. Dressed in tattered clothing, the boy can't be more than ten or twelve years old. Why the hell are they sneaking through the castle walls?

"He's the one who gave you the coin." The boy pulls the tapestry off his companion, an almost identical boy, only with jet black hair and a smudge of dirt on his cheek.

"The juggler?"

"Oh, Hawkin is much more than a juggler, isn't he, Brock?" The two exchange a knowing look.

The black-haired boy, Brock, responds with enthusiasm, "Truly. Now, come with us and we'll show you the way. Make sure you bring the coin, Mr. Troll. You'll need it to get in."

This seems like a terrible idea, but I want to know more about the so-called Underground Circus and why these children are crawling through hidden passages in the castle.

Throwing caution to the wind, I follow them into the secret entrance. "If this is a trap, I'll kill you both."

The boys' eyes go wide before they turn and exit into the tunnel.

Inside the passageway, it's a tight fit. My shoulders are so broad they scrape the walls and I have to hunch to avoid hitting my head. Whoever's idea it was to install these in the castle, they were most assuredly not a troll.

Brock carries a torch to light the way, but with my night vision, I don't need it. The tunnel twists and turns, winding through the underbelly of the castle, occasionally criss-crossing with other hidden passages. We go up and down stairs, and at several points, candlelight flickers through the thin cracks in the stone.

With so many secret entrances, how is it possible the king is unaware?

Eventually, we enter the drainage pipes far beneath the castle. Water drips from the ceiling and trickles down the stone walls. Rats and other creatures scurry away from our presence, their eyes glowing ominously from the torchlight.

At the end of the tunnel, moonlight glows from beyond, casting a silver ring around the entrance. The tunnel empties onto a rocky cliff overlooking a wide stream. It's at least a twenty-foot fall from the tunnel to the stream.

The two boys grip the edge of the tunnel and exit, attempting to scale the cliff.

"Don't fall in the water, Mr. Troll. It's full of jabberfish," the red-haired boy warns before disappearing out of view.

"What's a jabberfish?" I dig my claws into the rock and slowly follow their lead.

"Oh, you know. The big, ugly fish with two mouths full of sharp teeth. My cousin got bit by one once; he lost three toes." He curls up his lip in disgust.

Sounds lovely.

When I'm out of the tunnel, the entrance disappears, blending into the rocky terrain.

"Is it some kind of enchantment?" I ask.

"Very old magic," says Brock. He climbs the hillside like a monkey, jumping and swinging along the steep cliff.

I release my grip on the tunnel and fully commit to my first-ever attempt at mountain climbing. Dirt and debris fall into the stream with each step, and I wish for the first time since coming here that I didn't weigh hundreds of pounds. I keep my eyes on the boys and try not to think about the demonic piranhas waiting in the depths below.

Before I know it, we've scaled the cliffside and find ourselves in the outer bailey, far away from the castle. I'd know it was the outer bailey even if my eyes were closed because of the stench. The center tower looms over us, its pearlescent exterior catching the glow of the moonlight.

No wonder no one knows about the hidden passages. Considering you can only get to it via the outer bailey and it has an enchantment over the entrance, there's not much chance of discovery. It can't be that often that people go scaling cliffs around here. But how does the king not know? Was the entrance lost to history?

The streets of the outer bailey are mostly empty at night. They have a sinister vibe to them, the way everything is covered in shadow. Cats prowl along the rooftops and every so often, a hooded figure disappears into a dark alley. We stay to the shadows to avoid the searching eyes of the city watch as they patrol the walls above.

The two boys take off and motion for me to keep up. They walk stealthily, like little ninja versions of Oliver Twist.

"Where are we going?" I follow close on their heels, but they both shush me.

They come to a halt at the end of the street where it connects with the main road.

Brock turns to me. "When we tell you, run to the other side, but not until we say."

He peeks around the edge of the house, up towards the gated entrance to the inner bailey. Of course, a blue troll walking through the outer bailey would surely alert the guards, and more likely, the king.

Brock reaches into his satchel and pulls out a large rock. He tosses it with a heave towards the guards. "Run!"

We take off across the road and I look up to see the guards all facing the other way. Classic misdirection, no magic necessary.

They take me down several small streets filled with houses that look like a strong wind might tear them apart, and we stop at one with a red lion painted on the door. The paint is faded and scratched, barely visible in the dim light of night.

The red-haired boy opens the creaky door and waits for me to enter. Inside, the house is empty. A small lopsided bed sits in one corner and a frayed rug covers the dirty floor. Aside from that, nothing. Brock moves the rug out of the way, revealing a cellar door.

He knocks three times and the door opens from beneath. Loud music and bright lights flood the small room we're in.

Did I just wander into a fantasy speakeasy?

"Mr. Troll, time to use your coin." Brock flashes me a wicked smile.

CHAPTER SEVEN

THE UNDERGROUND CIRCUS

A large man wearing a black tunic emblazoned with a red lion's head blocks entry into the next room. His eyes are mismatched colors, with one eye brown and the other sky blue. It's almost mesmerizing to look at him. He extends a gloved hand. "Coin, please." A thick black beard twitches when he talks.

Brock and the red-haired boy place a golden coin in the man's hand, and I follow suit. The doorman moves aside, and we enter a world full of swaying candlelight and whimsy.

Dozens of people shuffle through the room, holding large mugs filled with frothy liquids. Some of them bubble, others smoke, but the people drink them down with smiles on their faces.

There's something strange about the lot. Something...off. A woman with a long, hooked nose covered in boils shuffles past me. She passes by a man with splotched skin—the ivory tone is dark brown around his eyes, giving the appearance of a mask. A black man with bright red dreads dances about, his hair swaying like the flames of the candles. Next to him, a woman drinks a bright blue liquid and then bubbles spout from her mouth and waft through the air.

"Mr. Troll!" A voice enthusiastically shouts for me and I turn to see the juggler, Hawkin, flashing me a wide grin. "I was hoping you would make it. Such a crazy turn of events at dinner tonight. I'm glad to see you are okay."

He leads me across the room to the bar, and my two traveling partners vanish into the hustle around me. Hawkin holds up two fingers, and in a flash, a mighty mug filled with amber liquid appears before each of us.

Item. Underground Tonic. *-3 Intelligence for one hour. Useless, but it feels good.*

The stats remind me of the imp mead that Limery's mother served me at her cave.

"What is this place?" I ask. How is it possible that something so lively is going on just below the surface, yet none of it can be heard from above?

"First, we drink." We lift our mugs and they clink as Hawkin taps his against mine. I still don't know why he wanted me to come here, but so far, I'm not feeling any danger. "To the Underground Circus, may she never fade."

Hawkin takes the first sip, and when I'm sure it's not poison, I take a swig of my own. The warm amber liquid is surprisingly creamy and malty. It goes down easy, even with my new troll palette. Bubbles fill my chest and a warm happy feeling winds its way through my veins.

"That's the spirit." Hawkin takes another long gulp. "Welcome to the Underground Circus. The most secret guild in all of Vanaria."

"Guild?" This doesn't look like any guild I've ever seen.

"Yes, guild. Otherwise known as a collective of individuals indebted to one another for the advancement of a common goal." He winks at me and takes another drink.

"I know what a guild is," I laugh. "I was more wondering, how is this one? It looks like a party room to me."

"Who says the two have to be exclusive?" He raises an eyebrow.

I'll give him that. "What common goal are you trying to advance?"

A woman steps up between us and orders a drink, stopping our conversation. "Lion's Roar Elixir, please."

The barkeep pours her a small mug filled with fiery red liquid. She takes a sip and then turns toward the room and lets out a roar that would rival my own. The crowd cheers at her performance, and she downs the rest before returning.

"Acceptance," says Hawkin. He points at the crowd of people dancing and drinking. "We all have our struggles, something about us that the outside world would call freakish. They praise us when we perform, because then it's okay. Then, it's entertainment. But let them catch us on the street in their part of town at a late hour and who knows what may come. Many of our brothers and sisters have scars, both inward and outward, from our run-ins with society." He takes out a gold coin and flips it in the air. "I thought a troll might know a thing or two about that. Perhaps I was mistaken."

"You weren't." I take another drink. He's right. More than he knows. It's the entire reason why I made this journey, why I'm fighting for my people. Acceptance.

"Thanks for the coin, by the way. Does everyone here have one?"

"Members of the guild have one, senior officers may also give out coins to nonmembers for one-time visits. Each coin is enchanted. The red lion on the door, no one can move past it unless they have a circus coin."

"Are you all performers?" I recognize some of them from the party tonight, and others from the street performance yesterday.

"Not all, no. Some are lucky in that their abnormalities are easy to conceal, but I'll not out them. If you are truly interested, you may discover yourself." He drains the rest of his drink and sets the mug on the counter. "I must disappear for a few moments, Mr. Troll, but please, enjoy yourself."

"Before you go, I need to ask you something." It's been on my mind every time I've thought about the coin.

"Yes?" Hawkins raises an eyebrow.

"Why me? You gave me the coin without knowing anything about me. I could have given it away to the guards. If the secrecy of your guild is so important, then why risk it on someone you don't know? Trolls are supposed to be evil monsters, you know?"

He smiles so wide it makes his eyes squint. "Why, indeed?" he laughs. "Enjoy yourself, Mr. Troll."

As he leaves, I analyze him for the first time. Seeing him juggling in the street, I never gave him a second thought, but now, I feel he may be more than a simple performer.

Hawkin. *Level: ???*

What? That can't be right. There's no way a juggler can be in the same league as Kassidy and the King, is there?

I scan the room, analyzing the crowd, and sure enough, one in every four has the same question marks as Hawkin. Are they all that powerful, or is there something I am missing?

"You look confused." It's the roaring woman from before. I examine her more closely this time. Pale features, dirty blonde hair that drapes down her shoulders like a lion's mane. Her level unreadable.

"I am a bit. How is it that many of these people are able to hide their level?"

She looks me over, as if taking me in. "Some of us value our privacy more than others. It's more of a risk to pick a fight with someone if you don't know their level, don't you think?"

I grunt in approval, remembering the first time I met Kassidy and the King. But how do they do it?

"Some say it's not worth it. Guards can see through the Conceal of anyone who is inside the kingdom, but we don't do it for the guards." She taps a finger to the barkeep, and he fills her glass again.

An ability that hides your level from those around you. That could be invaluable. "How do I learn it?"

"It requires fifteen points in Wisdom." She leans in closer. "Most people would rather spend their points on something more practical, but when you make your living on the streets, what is more practical than Wisdom?"

Charisma maybe, but I'm not going down that road ever again if I can help it.

"I see your point. By the way, what's your name?"

"Leona." She smiles. The lion, how fitting. She takes a swig of her new drink and lets out a vibrant roar. "You're turn—?"

"Chod."

"Your turn, Chod." She nods toward the crowd.

I hesitate for a moment, afraid that unleashing my roar might cause a panic, but then I remember where I am. We're all outsiders here.

I roar. It silences the crowd and the music, my ferocity echoing off the walls, deafening. I haven't roared like that since the forest, since Glenn. Tension flows out of my body. The silence that follows makes it all the more powerful. Somewhere in the back, a glass drops and shatters.

Then, applause. Hoots and hollers and laughter. The music resumes and people dance. For the life of me, I can't force away the smile.

"Well done." She pats me on the shoulder. "What I would do for the ability to do that." She looks at me with admiration, like I'm some prized jewel. I can't help but think that maybe peace with the humans might work after all. "It was nice meeting you, Chod."

"Likewise."

With a flourish of her dress, she disappears back into the crowd.

Fifteen Wisdom to learn Conceal. It's been a while since I allocated my stats points, maybe I have enough. I pull up my stats page to take a look.

Chod, Level 19 Barbarian/Summoner Forest Troll
HP: 4255/4255
Mana: 5000/5000
Rage: 0/100
XP: 308,249/355,000

Strength: 36
Dexterity: 24
Constitution: 37
Intelligence: 10 (-3)
Wisdom: 10
Charisma: 6

6 stat points.

1 ability points.

The Petrified Staff offers a bonus of +3 Intelligence and +3 Wisdom, but I don't have any of my weapons since entering the city. My Intelligence has really taken a hit from the Underground Tonic, too. Luckily, Leona said I only needed Wisdom to learn Conceal. I have six stat points, but since I don't have the staff equipped, I'll have to use five of them to learn the ability.

Whatever. It's not like I have any better plans, and hiding my level might make Jude and the rest think twice about attacking me next time. I put all five ability points into Wisdom, bringing it up to fifteen.

Two new abilities appear amid the slew of old abilities I haven't unlocked.

Conceal (Passive). *Hides level from anyone who is not a guard on city grounds.*

Perception. *For 10 minutes, gain increased awareness of your surroundings. Spot hidden objects, as well as unusual sounds, odors, and tastes. Cooldown: 6 hours.*

Oh. No wonder most people don't conceal their levels. If given the choice between hiding a level and increased perception for ten minutes, who wouldn't want to understand the world around them better? Especially for a hero, using Perception after a boss fight might show hidden doors or missed treasure, or lead to escape when lost in a dungeon. For me, though, the ability to conceal my level could have a major impact going forward. I can always invest in Perception later.

I select Conceal. Nothing happens. No glowing light, weird sensations, or anything telling me it worked.

"Ah, thinking smarter already." Hawkin returns, carrying a fiddle in one hand and a bow in the other. "I knew you were a smart one."

"Did it work? Is my level concealed?" How am I supposed to tell if it is active?

"It's as gone as the daylight. Now, come, it's my turn to play." He puts the fiddle to his neck and pulls the bow across the strings.

Dull light emanates from the fiddle, pulsating with each pull of the bow. The notes ring out across the room, overpowering the rest of the music. They carry over conversations until everyone stops what they are doing. The light of each note flows out from the fiddle in visible soundwaves, and when they touch the guests, each note infuses their bodies.

A note hits me in the chest. There's very little resistance as the purple sound-wave disperses into my being. When it does, I feel healthier, more alive. I pull up my stats and sure enough, I have a bonus point in Constitution as well as a notification.

You have been targeted with Aura of Vigor. +1 Constitution for 2 hours. All debuffs have been cleared.

The negative bonus from the Underground Tonic has disappeared as well.

The red-haired boy's words come back to me. "Hawkin is more than a juggler."

He's a bard!

The melody bathes the room in a watercolor fog. Hawkin plays as he walks, the folksy notes of the fiddle winding through the crowd, carefully selecting their targets. It's relaxing, calming. For several minutes, he walks and plays. Some people sit on the ground, others embrace one another and sway with the rhythm. I half-expect someone to start clapping and singing Kumbaya. When the song ends, he spreads his arms and takes a bow to the applause of the crowd.

When his spotlight is over, I catch up with him. "You're a bard. Why do you perform in the streets when you could be out adventuring?" With a talent like that, I'm sure plenty of heroes would want him in their parties.

He leads me over to the bar, where he orders another drink. "I imagine the same reason why you are in Vanaria instead of out exploring some dungeon." He sighs. "The world's not always safe for people like us. And even more so for people like them. These are my people. I do what I can for them."

"You should leave then. Take your circus on the road. There are enough small towns that I'm sure would want a break from their boring lives. You could even stop by the forest. It would be a great gesture for peace." If what he says is true, if it's really that hard for people here, then they should go somewhere else. Let the city see what life is like without entertainment.

Hawkin puts his fingers to his chin, as if pondering the idea for the first time. "Perhaps, but I don't know if the small towns and villages have the coin to pay."

"They will pay. Trust me. And if they can't pay, they will at least feed you." My mind races with history lessons about traveling caravans from the middle ages, of the circuses of the 1900s, of fairs and carnivals. People want entertainment.

"Thank you, Mr. Troll. You have given me a great deal to think about." The crowd begins to gather their belongings. Hawkin's Aura of Vigor must have been the finale to clear the alcohol and other elixirs from everyone's systems. "I hope you have enjoyed yourself. Brock and Neville will escort you back to the castle. I'm certain our paths will cross again someday." He extends his hand and we shake.

The boys lead me out of the house, bypassing the guards with another act of subterfuge before we arrive at the cliffside of the outer bailey.

I'm about to scale the cliff when a message flashes along the side of my vision.

Incoming Message (Admin): Chad, I'm sorry it has taken so long for me to respond. There was a great deal of red tape for entering a player into the game without a court order. Fortunately, that is all behind us now, and your friend Taryn will be entering Isle of Mythos soon. We have also drafted a payment arrangement for you as well. You can find it in your inventory. Read it over and if the terms are agreeable, we will begin drafting money into your account. I will update you when we have more information regarding Taryn's arrival. We have also added in a protocol for you to message the admins. Focus on the icon of parchment next to your stats and it will transcribe your message. Remember, the world is in your hands. -Valery

Holy cow! Taryn's logging in! I can't believe it. My best friend is going to join me in the coolest game on the planet. It's going to be awesome!

The excitement doesn't wear off for some time. Not until I've made it back to the castle and lie in bed. I can't wait to share what I know with Taryn. We'll adventure and explore, and I can help him level up. Now that I've negotiated peace for the trolls, maybe I can finally have some fun.

CHAPTER EIGHT

THE GOD OF CHAOS

I'm still asleep when Gord's giant fist booms against my door. After my adventure with the Underground Circus, I was pretty late getting in.

Wiping the sleep from my eyes, I stumble to the door and remove the board that locks it. I usher him, along with Ismora and Limery, into my room and close the door behind them. I quickly abandon all thoughts of sleep. "You'll never guess what happened to me last night."

The only part I leave out is the message from Valery and the expected arrival of Taryn. By the time I'm finished with my story, they are all three scowling at me.

"You left the castle with someone you didn't know?" Ismora clenches her fist and I get the impression she wants to punch me. "After the attack at dinner? They could have taken you hostage, tortured you, killed you. How foolish are you?"

"Yeah, Chods. You is not smart. What if they takes you away?" Limery pleads with me, his bulbous eyes full of concern.

Gord snorts. "Why they put you in charge, I have no idea."

This is definitely not the reception I was expecting. "Don't you see the bigger picture here? We have allies. There are those who don't hate the trolls."

"The king doesn't hate the trolls. We have peace. Who cares if a few puny humans want us dead?" Gord stands up and walks over to the tapestry, searching the wall for the hidden entrance. He runs his fingers along the stone, but it doesn't open, only accessible from the inside. "We are the only allies we need. Even if they hate us, they have to follow the law or suffer the consequences."

"It's not that simple." I find myself getting annoyed by his brutish behavior. Why make the world our enemy if we don't have to? "Is it not time for breakfast?" I just had an amazing evening and they want to shit all over it. Nothing bad happened, so I don't know why they are so worried. It's not like I can't take care of myself anyway.

There's another knock on the door, and I open it to find Kassidy. His mouth is full of some berry pastry as he attempts to speak. "Breakfast," he mumbles between chews, "is ready in the dining hall." He takes a final bite of the pastry, and before he has fully swallowed, another one teleports into his hand.

All that power and he chooses to be a glorified fast food worker.

Warwick and several other guards stand outside the dining hall. Inside, King Favian and his family wait for us at the table. The king and his son both wear silver tunics embroidered with a blue griffin. The ladies wear silver gowns with blue ornamentation down the sleeves. They all stand as we enter. There are several empty seats along the king's left-hand side, and his family sits to his right.

"Good morning. Please, have a seat." He motions for us to sit. "Chod, if you would," he says sternly. His hand stops at the seat next to him.

I take my seat in front of the glorious plates of food. Eggs, bacon, and sausage cover our half of the table. The king stares at me as I fix my plate, his blue eyes gazing deep into my soul. Is it possible he knows I left the castle last night? Certainly not. If he knew, then why wouldn't he try to stop me? Still, I get the feeling that something isn't right.

My companions stuff their faces like they have been starved. Limery grunts with each bite.

"Once again, I can't begin to apologize for last night." The king's face softens a bit. "An honored guest, attacked in my own home. You have no idea the shame I feel."

"Don't worry about it. It was another hero. I hardly blame you for the anger of someone else." Though I appreciate his worry, my real concern is Jude. "Is there any word on his whereabouts?"

"My men combed the streets, but there is little to go on. He was staying at the Green Giant Inn, but apparently moved his belongings elsewhere yesterday before the attack." The king stares off into the distance. "There is a warrant out for his arrest, and he will not be welcome in Vanaria or any town under my rule until he has answered for his crimes."

Sucks for him. "What will you do if you capture him?"

"When, not if," he corrects me. "When he is captured, he will be shown the error of his ways. Fortunately for him, you did not die, but I will make sure he knows what is and is not permissible under my rule. Hero or not, I am the king. It is my hope that I may be able to correct his behavior and put him on the path to right-eousness. As I told you before, I believe the heroes will have a part to play before all is said and done."

Sounds like a slap on the wrist to me. Let me catch Jude out on the road and he will rue the day he ever tried to stab me in the back. I have no intention of losing any more levels, and once Taryn is in-game, I'll finally have another hero to watch my back. It doesn't matter if it's Jude or Glenn or someone else, if they mess with me or my people, then they will pay.

Over breakfast, we discuss plans for our two sides now that we have negotiated peace. We are free to trade with any of the towns or villages that have need of our supplies or services.

"I don't know how willing they will be at the start, but if you play your cards right, then you may very well find some nice propositions. It'll take time for prices to settle as you each gather the value of the other side." He takes a bite of a strawberry and seems lost in thought. "The forest belongs to the trolls. If I were you, I would set up a station along its boundary and sell permits to local hunters for starters."

That's not a bad idea. We could make money to buy goods simply by opening our borders. We could probably even sell back the weapons we've looted from all the soldiers who have attacked over the years. If we could transport the mana, we could even offer mana-infusion services. "I'm sure we'll think of something."

"If any of your people wish to train in Vanaria, let me know and I will have our masters work out an exchange program. I would very much value an ambassador of my kingdom to go and learn more of troll customs as well." He leans forward and looks down the table at my partners. "That goes for all of you. The trolls are entering this world and for my part, I will do what I can to make sure you do not fall behind."

Gord, Ismora, and Limery all issue their thanks.

"What about our children?" asks Ismora. "I think it would do well for some of them to learn the ways of the world."

"Send them and it shall be done."

"We are grateful for everything you are offering." This trip truly couldn't have gone any better. "Aside from your so-called test..." At that, he laughs. "This has been the start of something good between our nations."

"What are your plans from here, Chod?" the queen finally speaks. "We would love to show you more of the city if you have time. There is so much more than this castle to Vanaria."

"It will have to wait for another time, I'm afraid. This trip is strictly business. Though she has already received word of the truce, I need to inform the chief of the details. The beginning stages will be the most important for ensuring that this peace lasts." I finish off the last bit of sausage from my plate. "But once that is taken care of, I would greatly enjoy a chance to adventure once again."

"I bet you would." She laughs. "Take care of yourself out there. And, Limery, you keep an eye on him."

"Yes, ma'ams. Limmy is on it!" He gives her his trademark demonic smile.

The rest of the meal is spent in polite small talk as we tell the royal family about life in the village. For once, Gord and Ismora do the majority of the talking, and I'm able to sit back and listen. Gord is a proud troll and boasts of the accomplishments of the village and the other guardian trolls. Ismora talks of her training with the young trolls and her position as weapons master.

As they talk, my mind wanders for a bit and I find myself watching Kassidy as he shoves even more food into his mouth. He eats enough for two full-grown trolls. Honestly, I don't know how he doesn't weigh five hundred pounds. I focus on him and his level appears, still unreadable. I wonder if he or the king have noticed my newest ability or if they are able to see through Conceal just like the guards.

Is it possible that the king and Kassidy are not as powerful as I originally thought? Of course they are powerful, but just how powerful? Warwick is level thirty and is responsible for protecting the king. It wouldn't be too farfetched to think that the king's level isn't too far off. If that's the case, he has more to fear from the heroes than I originally thought.

"Are you sure you don't want the guards to escort you out of the city?" The queen has her arm entwined with the king's. The two children stand beside them at the top of the staircase. They look resplendent in their matching silver attire as they look down over their kingdom.

"If it's okay with you, we'd like to enjoy the view out of the city without armed security. To see what it's really like when people aren't being watched."

"Very well." The king nods. "Take care of yourself and your people, Chod. I look forward to our paths crossing again."

The morning sun warms my skin from above, and the pearlescent tower reflects onto the city streets below. It's kind of freeing, walking through the city alone. Especially after my adventures last night. I do wish we could stay longer, but it's important to get back and talk things over with the council.

The streets are alive with the early morning bustle. Workers race to their jobs while the wealthy stroll along the cobblestone, making idle chatter. We're given a wide berth everywhere we go and catch glances from far away. Some people are even bold enough to point. A grunt from Gord is enough to put a stop to it more often than not.

The occasional child we pass is what puts it all into perspective. Not yet old enough to hate, they stare at us with wonder until they are popped on the wrist and told to look away.

"I am ready to be home," rumbles Gord. "Two days in the city is more than enough. The stench of these people..." He fakes a cough.

"Oh, come on. You've got to admit that there is a certain elegance to this place. Maybe not the outer bailey, but up here, the castle. Just think of all the work that went into constructing that."

He scoffs. "If this is elegance, then I do not care for it."

We pass a street vendor selling meat on a stick. Whatever the mystery meat is, it smells divine.

"Can we haves some, Chods?" Limery salivates.

The old man stares at us with wide eyes, but he holds up a meat skewer. "That'll be three bronze."

Shit. I don't have any coins. We've been so used to providing for ourselves that we've never had the need for money. "I'm sorry. I just realized we don't have any money."

The man's wide eyes turn into slits. "Well, this ain't a soup kitchen. We're not giving away food for free. Go on, now. Get!"

Even though Gord can't understand what the man is saying, he can sense his reaction and steps forward with a growl. The old man jumps back, dropping the skewer to the ground.

"It's okay, Gord. We're supposed to pay for things in the city. We'll have to wait until we get back to the village to trade for coin." I can't believe we didn't bring any coins with us since we knew we were going into the city. With all the humans that have died in the forest over the years, I'm sure there are coins tucked away in a chest somewhere.

We turn to leave, and I can hear the man mumbling something about 'stupid trolls' and 'if this is the way things are going to be.' I try my best to tune him out.

"I'm sorry, Limery. We'll hunt for food once we are outside the city gates." He gives me his puppy dog eyes. "I'm sorry, but there is nothing I can do until we trade for coin."

"But Limmy has moneys." He reaches in his small pouch and pulls out a handful of gold coins.

"Where in the hell did you get those?" I know for a fact he didn't have any gold when we came into the city.

He bats his eyes at me sheepishly. "Limmy finds them. Can we eats now?"

I bury my head in my hand for a moment, contemplating who he managed to steal a sack of gold coins from. Certainly, someone from the party had their pouch a little lighter by the time the evening was over.

"You're going to be the death of me. Go get your food."

He flutters off toward the food cart. The man is about to tell him to get lost when he spots the gold coin in Limery's hand. Then his eyes bulge with greed and he licks his lips as he listens patiently to Limery's order. After a few minutes of talking, Limery returns, struggling to carry a large platter of meat. The man waves him off with a smile. Is there anything that a little money can't fix?

Limery bobs and weaves through the air, the food throwing off his sense of balance.

"You bought the entire cart?" We just ate breakfast not even an hour ago. How hungry could he be?

Gord takes the platter from him, and Limery shoves a skewer in his mouth. "Limmy hungry."

The imp has been hanging around Kassidy too much. I'm sure the gold coin he paid for all this food was more than the man typically makes in an entire day, maybe longer.

Not one to look a gift horse in the mouth, I partake in the grilled meats as we stroll through the inner bailey. With food in hand, it almost feels like I'm watching a show as the people around us carry on with their lives. The anvil of the blacksmith and the clop of horse hooves echoes through the streets.

I come to a halt when I see a large brown building with green shutters. For it to be in a nice part of town, it has a downtrodden look about it. Dark, heavy curtains cover the windows. The logo on the door has a tall green man holding a sign that reads, "Green Giant Inn."

The inn where Jude stayed before attempting to assassinate me.

"I want to go check it out." They look at me like I'm crazy.

"I thought you wanted to hurry back to the village?" Ismora plants her hands on her hips. "The king will deal with Jude."

She's probably right, but I can't let this opportunity pass me by. "Just give me a few minutes. I'll be in and out before you know it."

Inside, the curtains block out the sun and the room looks no different than it would at night. Candle chandeliers offer the only source of light, illuminating the room, but not enough to reveal anyone who might be sitting in the shadows. It's the perfect place for lowlifes and criminals to congregate. My night vision has no problem spotting the faces of the men with their cloaks pulled over their heads.

A balding man with a belly stands behind the bar on the far side. A few people sit at tables, eating plates filled with sausages and bread. A heavy-set woman with curly blonde hair carries two mugs of ale to a group of men huddled together in the corner.

Seems a little early for drinks, but it's none of my business.

"Can I help you?" the man behind the bar barks at me.

As I make my way over, the silence in the room tells me that the others are all watching me. Not a single fork scratches a plate. News has probably spread that a group of trolls are in the city, but I doubt any of them expected me to show up here.

"I'm looking for a man—"

"He ain't here." The bartender cuts me off.

"I know that, but—"

"He ain't here." He cuts me off again, and places both hands on the bar. He looks remarkably like a bulldog as he stares me down, one of the few humans not intimidated by my size and presence.

"Sir, if you would just give me a—"

"He. Ain't. Here. I ain't gonna say it again. The king's men come here, scaring my patrons. And now you. He ain't here. Now order a room or be off with you."

My blood boils at the man's response, and I have a mind to smash my fist through his bar. But instead, I turn and stomp across the room. Ismora was right, I shouldn't have come here. I reach for the door handle when I hear a "psst" from a cloaked man in the corner.

I focus on him and his stats appear before me.

Richard Hummel
   Level 17
   Cleric
   Human

. . .

Another criminal. And also a cleric. This seems like an awfully sketchy place for a man of faith to hang out. He motions for me to come over, and I take a seat on the bench next to him. The bartender is engaged in conversation with the barmaid and doesn't notice me when I slip to the side.

The cleric wears dark red robes, and a black chain hangs from his neck. He keeps his cloak pulled over his face, concealing all but his mouth. "You the one Jude tried to kill?" he whispers.

I nod. "Do you know where he is?"

"What's it worth to you?"

"Are you seriously trying to hustle me for information? You're a cleric, for gods' sake."

His lips curl into a devious smile. "I serve the God of Chaos. Now, what's it gonna be?"

CHAPTER NINE

THE ROAD LESS TRAVELED

The cleric's lips curl up as he waits for my answer. What is it worth for me to know where Jude is? I don't know. Will he stop coming for me unless I shut him down? I don't know if I should try to handle him myself or wait for the king's justice.

"I don't have any gold." Limery has the pouch he stole, but I'm not using it to pay for this. There has to be another way.

"Items then?" He stares across the room towards the bar.

I take out my items and let him examine them. "My weapons are with the guards. This is all I have on me."

Item. Phoenix Feather. 10% resistance to fire-based attacks. *A very rare item, phoenix feathers can only be gathered if they are willingly given by the host. Feathers plucked from unwilling birds turn to ash.*

Item. Tiger's Eye Pendant. Removes one debuff. Cooldown: 10 minutes. *A rare stone believed to ward off evil and bring balance to life.*

Item. Aquatic Boots. *Allows user to walk on water.*

There are also a few health potions and perception potions I crafted on the journey from the forest to Vanaria. Luckily, my Kingly Crown is stored safely in the forest. I wouldn't want that falling into the wrong hands. I don't have much, but maybe it's enough to get me a little information.

He eyes the items unappreciatively before settling on one. "I'll take the Tiger's Eye Pendant. In addition, you will owe me one favor, usable at the time of my choosing. You are an honorable troll, yes?"

"I am." And yet here I am making a deal so I can track down a man and punish him. "But I will not do anything that harms the troll population or brings shame upon my people."

He licks his lips. "We can work with that." He extends his hand, waiting for the pendant.

It dangles from my hand, but I can't seem to let it go. Chief Rizza gave me that pendant. Back when she barely knew me, when the entire hopes of the forest trolls rested on the adventure I was about to begin. Would she approve of this?

I wrestle with the thoughts as the pendant dangles precariously from my muscled blue fingers. With Glenn, I had no choice. I either had to make a stand or continue eating shit for the rest of our lives. I did what had to be done and it paid off. But this...this feels wrong. What do I have to gain from this? "I'm sorry. I can't."

"Very well. One thing I know about chaos is that it's always around. And it seems to favor you." He leans back into the darkened corner and I take my leave.

"Did you find answers?" Ismora narrows her eyes at me.

"No. You were right. Let's get back to the forest." I need to do a better job of listening to my companions. I've got a hot head and it has gotten me in trouble more times than I would like to admit. If the cleric hadn't asked for an item the chief had given me, I might have gone through with the deal.

The market square bustles as usual. In the center, I spot a giant archway on a raised platform. It has runes engraved around its edge, and the center of the arch is blocked with stone. No one goes near it, and I can't seem to make out what it is for, so I ask one of the merchants.

"That's the fast-travel portal. Hasn't been active in ages." The merchant pushes a few of his items closer to me, hoping I'll take a look.

As we walk away, I can't help but think how nice it would be to have fast-travel. I could be at the forest in a minute instead of days. People could come from all over to buy items from the capital. I imagine there would be a lot more diversity if the different kingdoms were all connected, not to mention what's out there in the rest of the world.

By the time we pass from the inner to outer bailey, we've polished off the last of the meat skewers. Just in time for the stench of Rat Row to turn our stomachs. I wonder if every exit in the outer bailey is so run-down, or if we just happened to pick the shittiest one. A few hundred yards from the city exit, a group of vagrants loiters next to a dilapidated shanty. They wear tattered clothes and toss dice in the street. They're scruffy, scraggly, and I can smell them from a mile away.

"Aye, lookit this, boys. We got us a couple-a monsters in our city streets." One of the dirty men taunts us. "We best go get our swords and axes."

The others laugh, displaying rotting teeth and wicked smiles.

I can feel trouble brewing, but since Gord and Ismora can't understand them, I elect not to translate. Only a few hundred yards stands between us and the open plains. There's no need to lure Gord into a fight. Not after all we have accomplished.

"Just ignore them," I tell Limery. He clings tighter to my shoulder, and I can feel his feet radiating heat, calling to the power that dwells within him.

"What is it?" asks Gord.

"Nothing. We're almost out of the city. No need to start trouble now."

The vagrants are low level, every one of them a one or two. Even if they attacked, they wouldn't cause much damage. The disrespect for me and my companions is what gets me. No matter how much I want to cave their skulls in, we are on peaceful terms with all of Vanaria.

"Oh no!" one of them screams as we approach. "Call the city watch!" The others burst out laughing.

As we pass them, something small and lightweight hits me in the back of the head.

I turn around and see a stale piece of bread lying on the ground. Every cell in my body wants to summon a horror on top of their ignorant heads.

"What? It wasn't me," one of them says, lifting his hands to his shoulders.

"Me neither."

"Wasn't me."

Gord cracks his knuckles menacingly. He doesn't have to understand their words to know their intentions.

"Let's go." I usher them towards the gate.

Laughter echoes behind us as we walk.

The guards hand us our weapons without incident, and just like that, our adventure in Vanaria is over.

We cross the bridge that leads to the city and come to a crossroads. Ahead lies the hills and plains that we traveled through to get here. To the left and right is, the Mythroad, the road that connects all of *Isle of Mythos*. Travelers pass us by as we stand there.

"Are you ready?" I ask.

"For what?" Gord searches our surroundings for impending attack, holding his axe at the ready.

"For what comes next." I take the road to the right and my party follows. "That's one small step for troll, one giant leap for trollkind."

They all just look at me like I'm stupid.

For the first time since entering the game, we're able to walk along the main roads without risking certain death. The days of hiding as we travel through the countryside, hoping against hope that we don't run into any other travelers, are over. We are a part of this world now.

But this is where the real test begins. Now, we face people who aren't under the vigilant eyes of the city watch. People who only face punishment if we make it back alive. We'll have to be alert.

The first few miles of the Mythroad are fairly busy, not by New York City standards, but it's busy compared to empty stretches of grassland, or the roads outside of Lynchton.

Those on horseback increase their pace to a gallop to pass us. In one instance, a man with a wagon full of lumber takes it off-road to avoid us, nearly spilling his load. I hope these sorts of actions change in time, but for right now, I need to get used to them.

"You think they believe we'll eat them?" A smile curls on the edge of Gord's lips. He is the only one who seems amused by everyone's fear.

"I don't know what they believe." I sigh. "They think we're all savages and monsters."

"We are monsters." Ismora shrugs. She says it so matter-of-factly that it catches me off guard. "We're not human. Why should we act like it? We are one with nature and the monsters that dwell within it. We live and die just like they do. Our village is one with the earth. Humans are the only ones that wish to tame the world. We only want to live in it."

It's the first time since being here that I really see it that way. They are monsters. Their customs and their behaviors have been so tribal that I've always compared it to my knowledge of tribes in the real world. But the truth is that they aren't human at all, only I am. I need to be more aware that every decision I make for the village is tainted because I am human underneath this giant mound of blue muscle. I want to help them, but I don't need to change them.

Maybe it's time for me to step down from the council. They have peace, so why not allow the chief to decide how to enforce it?

I'll settle that another time. For now, I'll enjoy the journey back.

Up ahead, Limery flutters through the air, flipping one of his stolen coins. I still can't believe he pickpocketed at a royal event. For the guards or Kassidy not to notice, he must be pretty good.

The road runs beside a stream that bubbles with small rapids. It's beautiful. Water so clear that the rocks and fish below the surface are completely visible.

The way the stream gently bubbles, it reminds me of a water fountain, bringing back distant memories.

"You know, Limery, where I come from, it's good luck to toss coins into water sources."

They all stop in their tracks as I say this. Maybe it's because I never talk about the real world.

"Really?" His eyes dart between his precious coin and the flowing stream.

"Yeah, you make a wish and then if you toss in the coin, it's supposed to come true. You can't tell anyone what the wish is, though."

His eyes light up and he flies over to the edge of the stream.

I remember going to the mall as a young boy. We were shopping for new clothes for school, so I had to be there. That was one of the few times Mom had taken me with her. To make sure I looked presentable. There was a giant fountain in the middle of the mall, and I saw other children tossing in pennies. I asked what they were doing, and Mom told me that they were making wishes. She said that if you paid off the gods, that it was supposed to make it come true. She gave me a penny and I tossed it in, wishing for more trips with her to the mall.

I guess the gods must have been busy that day.

Limery closes his eyes and I can see the force with which he is making his wish. He flicks the gold coin and it enters the stream with a splash. As soon as it enters, something rushes up and grabs it before disappearing in a silver blur.

CHAPTER TEN
KEEP YOUR SECRETS

We search for the gold coin, but it seems to have disappeared. The clear water offers no trace of its whereabouts. Whatever took the coin vanished in a flash, not even disturbing the silty bottom of the stream as it zipped away. The irony of the pickpocketed coin being stolen isn't lost on me.

Limery frowns at the tranquil water. Hopefully, his wish wasn't stolen along with his coin.

As we are leaving, a splash of water soaks the back of my head. A moment later, Limery, Gord, and Ismora are doused as well.

We turn to see an amorphous blob rising from the stream like a water ghost. Its watery exterior ripples in the breeze, sending a spray of mist in our direction. The gold coin shimmers in the center of the blob like a heart of gold.

Water Elemental. *Level 12. One of the four major elements, the water elemental is difficult to destroy, especially in an open water source. Being bodiless, the only way to defeat a water elemental is to completely destroy the element itself.*

Great. A water elemental in a flowing stream. The smart thing would be to just let it be. Even at level twelve, there's little we can do to fight it.

The water blob morphs its body, mimicking the shape of a troll. It rises taller and flexes its watery muscles.

"Is this thing taunting us?" Of all the things I thought would mock me, a stream was at the bottom of the list.

In answer to my question, another ball of water hits me in the face, and the elemental morphs into a tiny imp.

Limery cackles at the creature. "Look, Chods. It's Limmy!" A watery fastball hits Limery in the head, silencing his laughter. "Hey! You no hit Limmy. That's not nice." Fire crackles in his palms, and he offers his own brand of justice, slinging a fireball at the elemental.

The fireball heads straight for the watery imp, but at the last moment, the elemental disperses, forming a hole in the center where the fireball passes straight through.

Gord roars with laughter at Limery's frustration.

"Not funny!" Limery tosses another fireball and the elemental dodges it again, this time countering with a barrage of water projectiles that soak Limery and Gord both.

Unable to do anything, they both stand there fuming.

I summon a Horror of Power and send the demonic lion toward the elemental. The elemental morphs around the horror, letting it pass through, but right as it is surrounded by the elemental, I cast Kamikaze and the horror explodes, sending a spray of water as the elemental bursts into mist.

"Surprise!" I shout, content to have actually damaged the thing.

The elemental rises from the stream as a ghostly blob again, the gold coin floating on the end of one of its appendages. It flips the coin in the air with one appendage and flicks me an obscene gesture with the other before vanishing into the depths of the water.

We all exchange surprised looks before bursting into laughter. This world never ceases to amaze me.

Incoming Message (Admin): *We are in the final stages of bringing Taryn into* Isle of Mythos. *You should be hearing from him within a couple of days. -Valery*

I focus the message away. Two days have passed since I received it, and I still haven't heard anything from Taryn. Could there have been some kind of holdup, an issue keeping him from logging in? I hope not, because I can't wait to hang out with him again. We used to have so much fun staying up late and pigging out on pizza and energy drinks until our eyes were bloodshot and our hands shook from the caffeine. On nights like that, we never left a quest unsettled until it was completed or we died. With our teamwork, very rarely did we die.

Looking at my map, we're still about three days from the forest's center. I don't know why I didn't ask the king for a wagon or something to make the trip easier. Traveling by foot isn't that bad when you're adventuring and making stops to gather herbs or fight monsters, but when you're on official business, it's a real drag.

I could never be a businessman like my father. All he does is travel and go to board meetings. Where's the fun in that? Maybe I'll stay in *Isle of Mythos* forever, shirking all my responsibilities in the real world. It's not like Mom or Dad would miss me. It might be a few years before they even realize I didn't come home.

We do our best to pass the time as we travel. I taught Limery how to play "I Spy," and we've been playing for a few hours now. When it's Gord's turn, he always picks the closest bush or tree. I'm not sure if he truly grasps the point of the game or if he just picks the thing closest to him. Or maybe he's trolling me. Either way, he's pretty terrible.

"It's a good thing you're strong," I tease, and he makes a very trollish gesture.

As the sun begins to set, we stake out a place to camp for the night. The area we are traveling through is pretty wooded on both sides, offering plenty of cover from passersby. Not that we need it with our Camouflage. A few miles ahead, there's a small town called Dundee, but I'm hesitant to stop there. It looks to be about the size of Lynchton. I'm sure it has an inn, but we don't have any money, aside from what's left of Limery's criminal enterprise, and I don't want to encourage his behavior by spending his gold.

The smart choice is to make camp away from the road again tonight and avoid the other settlements for now. Let them see us from a distance and get used to the idea of trolls in public. The way I see it, our best bet will be to start trading with Lynchton first since we have something of a relationship. Start small and then branch out from there. We don't have to engage the entire island all at once.

When I wake the next morning, I find that I have a new message.

Incoming Message (Taryn): *Dude! This is so cool! I can't believe you had to go to prison to get in here. I know a few guys who would commit a crime just to be able to experience a game like this. Thanks so much for hooking me up with the job, too. The money they are paying me to be here is going to help out the family so much. It still seems surreal. Getting paid to play a game. Wow!*

Sorry it took me so long to reach out after getting in-game, I started my tutorial as soon as character creation was over, and it wouldn't let me message until I completed it. I'm free to travel now, though. Picked up a couple of quests in the city until I hear back from you. Hit me up and let me know where to find you.

Hell yeah! He's finally here. I don't waste any time responding. I focus on the message interface and it appears translucent over my vision. As I think the words, they appear in the message.

Message (Chod): *Taryn, that's awesome! What character did you pick? And what city are you in? I'm on my way from Vanaria back to the forest; we should be there in two to three days. I can't wait to meet up and tell you everything I know about Isle of Mythos. It's unlike anything I've ever experienced. Also, how did you get a tutorial? I was dropped in the middle of the forest.*

. . .

We gather our belongings and set out toward the village. I read over his message several times, trying to garner any information I can about his whereabouts. What city could he be in? There are only two major cities on the island, Vanaria and Seascape. Is it possible that he was in Vanaria at the same time as us? And how the hell did he get a tutorial? My tutorial was being smacked in the head by an ogre.

It sounds like he is off to a good start, though. He already has a few quests. That's one thing that I'm looking forward to about adventuring. There are surprisingly few quests in the troll village.

"What has you so happy?" roars Gord.

I guess I must have been smiling without realizing it. "Oh, nothing. Just looking forward to being back in the village."

He slaps me on the back. "Me too, brother."

A faint ding lets me know I have a new message and I focus on the glowing icon of parchment.

Incoming Message (Taryn): You probably didn't get a tutorial because you are a deviant. Valery filled me in on your character and what's happened in-game so far. Sounds like you have the potential to be pretty OP. And you know I'm totally calling you Chode, right? It'll take me a little while to reach the forest, but I'll message you when I do. I can't believe there's no fast-travel in this game. Somebody should really try to reopen those portals.

Anyways, I've got a quest to finish and then I'll be on my way. I'm going to try and level some along the way so you aren't carrying my noob ass. Don't try to ask for details about my character, I'm not saying a word.

Message (Chod): Alright, scrub, keep your secrets. I'll make sure to rest up for a bit since I know my back will be hurting from carrying your weak self. Seriously, though, hurry up. I've missed you, bud.

Even though I know we'll make it to the forest before him, the excitement of seeing my best friend has me walking a little faster. There's a lot to take care of once I return. I don't want to rush through it, because it's setting up the future for the troll race, but the quicker it's taken care of, the quicker I can meet up with Taryn.

The others are ready to be back home, too, so they keep to my pace, only stopping for food and bathroom breaks.

After we enter the boundary of the forest, I send Limery ahead to find his mother and ask her to come to the village. I have an idea that just might be able to help both the imps and trolls.

Tension seems to melt off my body when we finally return to the border of the troll village. The massive mana-infused flowers drape the village in a fragrant aroma. I didn't realize how tense I had been out on the open road. Luckily, we didn't have any issues once we made it out of the city. Integration might go more smoothly than I had originally thought.

Most of the village is waiting for us when we return. Chief Rizza stands in front of the others, with Jira and Tormara by her side.

There's a loud crash against a nearby tree, and two mana-infused wyrms tumble through a bush, coiled together. The legless dragons break apart and both rise, taunting one another like cobras before slithering back into the forests depths.

They've grown bigger in the time I've been gone. The three wyrms the village has are the only survivors of the regional event I unlocked after defeating the mana-infused wyrm that was blocking the ley lines. The other heroes managed to kill the rest, but the event was still a failure. The penalty for failure was that the remaining wyrms would lay eggs, starting an infestation that would destroy crops and towns across the island. But since these wyrms are all bonded, there's no threat of them laying eggs. Bonding with a troll means they lose their ability to mate.

The chief's golden eyes radiate pride as she pulls me in for an embrace. "You did it, Chod. Once again, you accomplish the impossible." Her green skin is warm against my own. She releases me and I make my way through the crowd, exchanging pleasantries with each troll in turn.

Jira grasps me on the shoulder, his white-tipped dreadlocks swaying with the movement. "This is a new day for trollkind. One day, we will look back and remember this as the beginning of something truly great. Well done."

Tormara holds a young troll against one hip, its hair the same bright red as her own. I expect one of the snarky comments I've grown accustomed to, but instead, she simply nods. "Good job."

Gord boasts of our adventure to his mother, the gray-haired Guilda. Though she is old and wizened, only her hair betrays her age.

Ismora embraces Yashi, the smallest of the trolls, for a long moment, and I wonder if there might be something going on there I wasn't aware of.

Several of the guardian trolls—Jojin, Watu, and Malak—offer me congratulations and speak of their excitement to adventure beyond the forest.

For everyone here, peace will change so much of their lives.

I gather the chief and the other council members. "Can we convene a council meeting? There is much to discuss."

The other council members agree, and we schedule a meeting after dinner. Before returning to the village, I instruct the guardians to watch for Limery's return and to send him and his mother to me when they arrive, even if we are in a meeting.

For dinner, I have some of Kea's famous stew. It boils twenty-four-seven, and Kea constantly adds new ingredients as the old are depleted. I also grab a leg of roasted boar and take a seat against a tree to devour my food.

Gord sits next to me. He turns his bowl up and slurps the stew like a savage.

When he finishes it, broth runs down his chin beneath both massive tusks. One tusk is broken off at the end, and I realize I never asked him how it happened.

"How did you break your tusk?"

He rips off a chunk of roasted boar and responds with a full mouth. "I was very young," he mutters. "There was an attack on the village. Father rushed into battle, and being young, I did not yet understand the dangers of combat. A human must have thought I was an easy target, for it isn't often that humans meet trolls other than our guardians on the fields of battle." He cracks the bone in half and sucks at the marrow. "His sword caught me in the tusk and lodged there. If not for my tusk, he probably would have taken my head off. After the battle, when the sword was removed, the rest of the tusk cracked and broke."

"Well, I think it gives you character." I tap my roasted boar in his direction, mimicking a cheers. "Whatever happened to your father?"

"He died several years later. He was a mighty troll. He fell in battle against a horde of ogres, killing five of them by himself. If not for him, they would have caused great damage to the village." He talks of his father with great reverence. As the son of a great warrior, now I know why Gord carries such a chip on his shoulder. He has a lot to live up to.

"Sounds like one hell of a troll. I'm sure he'd be proud of the troll you've become."

There's a glisten in Gord's eyes for a moment and just as quickly, it fades away. He stands up and tosses his bones into the forest. "It has been an honor to travel by your side, brother, but it is now time for me to guard our boundaries once more."

With a final glance in my direction, Gord disappears amongst the trees.

CHAPTER ELEVEN

THE FINAL COUNCIL

Twilight grasps the forests in its dark embrace. The fire that crackles in the center of the council area gives off an unholy vibe as light darts across our faces, momentarily keeping the shadow at bay. We look more primed for war than peace.

In the distance, the light of the mana-infused flowers twinkles on and off as someone walks through the forest.

Chief Rizza stares at the fire, her dark braid winding down her neck and chest like a serpent. Her long, lithe arms rest against her thighs. She is the epitome of a strong leader. Her mana-infused wyrm curls around the base of her living throne, now big enough to fully encircle it. The mana-infused ooze that coats its scales glows a dull blue in the dim light, and its electric blue eyes search the forest.

Across from me, Tormara strokes the hardened snout of her own wyrm. It licks at the air and leans into Tormara's hand. The only wyrm not present is Yashi's, who is not on the council. The three wyrms have grown a great deal in the weeks I've been gone. In a few months' time, I imagine they will rival the size of the adult wyrm that was obstructing the ley line before I defeated it.

Before long, the legless, wingless dragons will be the greatest defense the village has. With three of them bonded to female trolls, I'm less worried about leaving, knowing that such strong protectors will remain.

Guilda is the last one to arrive, taking her seat to Chief Rizza's right. Next to me sits Kina, the only female troll that doesn't wear her hair in a braid or bun. Women back home would kill for her voluminous blueish-black locks. In the chair beside Tormara, Sonji twiddles her thumbs. Jira stands opposite Chief Rizza. Though he is not a council member, he attends every meeting and offers his advice when needed. As the only magic-wielder in the village beside myself, his shamanistic abilities are viewed with reverence.

"Let us begin," says the chief, bringing one hand to her heart. "We know that peace has been granted, but do not yet know the details. Chod, if you would, please fill us in on your journey."

For the next little while, I tell them of our trip to Vanaria. About my meeting with the king, jumping out of the tower, and even the attack on my life at the feast. They all sit in silence, hanging on every word as I describe the Underground Circus and the suggestion I made to Hawkin about taking his act on the road. I try to impart the way the humans looked at us, leaving no misconception that true equality will take time.

Once I've caught them up, I sit back and wait for their comments.

"Do you trust him?" asks Chief Rizza. "The king?" Her gaze is penetrating. Everything she has helped to build in this community is at stake, and it's my word she's trusting.

"I do. He seems like a genuine man, with a longing for adventure and an easy disposition. He doesn't strike me as one who desires war."

She sits in silence for a moment, her mind elsewhere.

"Then I believe the best thing for the trolls is not to take peace and hide away in the forest, but to make ourselves a part of the world once again."

The council erupts at her words.

"They can't be trusted." Tormara's words cut like daggers.

"It is not wise." Guilda's words are lost amongst the madness.

"I think it is for the best," says Kina.

Sonji sits quietly, tapping her fingers against her chair.

"Enough!" roars Chief Rizza. The council falls silent. "We have all lost loved ones to the humans. Over what? Ancient history. A war between humans and trolls that cost too many lives and left us isolated while our kingdom slowly crumbled. I will not doom our children to the same fate because I was afraid to work for progress." Her eyes fall on each one of us in turn. "If you do not agree, that is your choice, but trollkind will move forward with or without you."

Jira steps forward, requesting permission to speak.

"Go on." The chief nods.

Jira takes in a deep breath. The feathers that hang from his neck swish in the evening breeze. "I agree with the chief. It may not be easy, but the time has come for the trolls to embrace the future, or we will surely perish. Tough times may be ahead, but it will lead to a brighter future."

Tormara clears her throat. "I do not agree. Our place is in the forest, where we may grow stronger, not spread so thin so that we may fall apart. I have said my piece, but you are the chief. If this is your decision, then I will support it. I pray it does not come back to bite us." She slinks back into her chair. Tormara is spirited, but she has great respect for the chief.

"Very well. It is settled."

Night comes, and we spend the next several hours outlaying a plan for the future. Several of the young trolls will be sent to Vanaria to learn the ways of humans in order to better understand one another's culture. Tormara agrees to join as chaperon. I'm glad to not be a part of that debacle. I can't imagine her listening to anyone who is not a troll. We decide to open the edge of the forest to human hunters. They will be granted a permit to allow them to hunt, but the troll village is to remain off-limits.

Our remaining stockpile of human weapons and armor will be traded to Lynchton and then we will begin bartering with them for supplies we may need.

"I do not know how I feel about offering mana-infusion—" Chief Rizza is cut off by approaching footsteps.

Gord appears from the darkness. Limery sits on Gord's shoulder, with Lillith, his mother, fluttering behind them.

"What is the meaning of this, Gord?" asks Chief Rizza.

"It's my fault." I stand, acknowledging our new guests. "I requested they bring Limery and Lillith here the moment they arrived. I have a proposition that may help both imp and troll in this new endeavor. I would like the council to hear me out."

She gives me a questioning look. "Alright then, out with it."

I really hope this idea is as good as I have imagined. "I believe that the biggest struggle for our two sides will be the ability to communicate. Not very many humans outside of large cities have communication stones, nor do the trolls. I am proposing that we reinstate the IMS, Imp Messaging Service. They can serve as translators at the market, in exchange for a small fee. They can also deliver messages between you and the king, keeping a line of communication open. It will serve to make the transition easier, at least until some of the trolls learn the common tongue." I look to both Chief Rizza and Lillith. "What do you think?"

Lillith is the first to speak. "There aren't many imps left on the island. Many were trapped on other continents or went into hiding when the portals closed. I can reach out to those that I know of and see if they are interested, but know that many of them have suffered a similar wrath as the trolls over the years. They may not be willing. As for me and my family, we will help in any way we can."

Chief Rizza smiles. "I am grateful. For this and everything you and your brood have done for us so far. Limery has played no small part in where we find ourselves. Please, reach out to your people. We will be grateful for any who take up the cause."

Lillith bows to the chief. "Then I will take my leave and return when I have answers. Limery, let's go."

"Actually," I interrupt before they leave. "I would like it if Limery could come with me." He flashes me those demonic teeth in response.

"You have a communication stone," says Lillith. "I'm sure he could be of greater use elsewhere."

"I'm sure you're right, but there's something else I want to talk to the chief about." I turn to her and she seems to have a knowing look on her face. She had to know this moment would come eventually. "I don't really know the best way to say this, so I'm just going to come right out and say it. Trollkind is at the beginning of something beautiful. A new day is approaching, and I look forward to watching it all unfold. You are an amazing leader, one that the forest can be proud of." I take a deep breath before continuing. "It is your time to lead. I brought magic to the village. I met with the king for peace. I am a hero, and it is now my time to do what heroes do. I need to leave the forest in search of adventure. The council is more than capable of handling the politics without me. I will always be a hero for the trolls, but it is time for you to lead them into a new age. Therefore, I will be vacating my seat on the council so that someone who has lived and breathed this village for far longer than I can help you going forward."

They sit in stunned silence. Tormara raises a hand, but then it falls to her lap.

Chief Rizza nods several times. "I knew this day would come. I just didn't think it would be so soon." She intertwines her fingers, as if searching for the right words. "Chod, you will always be welcome in the forest. You are a member of this village now and that is not something that I nor anyone else can take away. I pray that your adventures lie elsewhere, and that though you are more than capable, this is the last we need of your services." She pauses. "When do you plan to leave?"

"Tomorrow. If I may, I would like to offer a recommendation to replace my seat on the council."

"Very well. Share your thoughts." She wears a half-grin, and I can't quite tell if she is amused.

"In my short time here, I have witnessed the importance of this council. They weigh in on every decision you make, offering varied points of view, giving you insight you might not normally have. Only sometimes losing their temper." I nod to Tormara, and I swear she blushes. "When my predecessor fell in the battle with Glenn, I was given the opportunity to offer my own advice. In the coming years, it will be important to have someone with experience, but also who isn't afraid to speak their mind. Someone who loves this village more than anything in the world. Someone like Gord."

Everyone except the chief bursts into chatter. Gord's eyes are as wide as I have ever seen them and his jaw hangs slack. I hope I didn't break him. I raise my hand for them to let me finish.

"I know I was the first male to ever sit on the council. It would not have happened if I hadn't completed the quest to clear the ley line. But be that as it may, you are entering a new age. Why not have a council that speaks for all trolls, and for all points of view?" I stand up from my council seat. "Think about it. He's not as dumb as he looks."

CHAPTER TWELVE

FAREWELL

When I wake up, I'm not nearly as well-rested as I would like. Thoughts of whether or not I made the right decision kept creeping through my dreams all night. In the dreams, the village was bombarded with secret attacks and the sky rained fiery arrows. I stood there, watching it all unfold but unable to help. In the end, the bodies of everyone I cared for in this game lay scattered over the forest floor, and I sat all alone in the burnt aftermath.

I sit up and rub my eyes. It's not like I've been at the village every second since I've been here anyway.

They're just dreams, nothing more. A manifestation of my worries. I know the village will be fine without me. Chief Rizza and the others are more than capable, and for the first time in ages, they have peace. Besides, I didn't come back into this game to sit around and babysit them. I need to continue leveling up, because if there ever comes a time when they do need me, I want to be the baddest mother-fucker on this island.

A light knock interrupts my thoughts. Limery hovers at eye level when I open the door.

"Morning, Chods." He beams at me, holding a roasted leg of some small animal in one hand.

"Good morning. Want to come in?"

"I thought we was leaving?" He tilts his head like a confused dog.

"Soon. There are a few things I need to wrap up before we go. After that, it's all adventure. You excited?"

"Limmy can't wait to see the world with Chods." He rips the last of the meat from the bone and contemplates throwing it on the floor.

"Don't you dare." I scold him.

He gives me a sheepish grin before stuffing the bone in a small pouch.

I pack what few items I have into my satchel and prepare to say my good-byes. "I need to go see the chief before we leave. If you want, you can go say good-bye to the others and I'll come find you when I'm done." I know for a fact that he and Gord grew pretty close over our adventures together. He's really grown on the rest of the village, too.

Once I'm finished with the chief, I plan to say my farewells to Gord, Ismora, Yashi, and Tormara.

One of the troll children runs through the village center, a small wooden club tossed over his shoulder. I stop him, and he points me in the direction of the chief.

The spicy smell of incense greets me long before I enter Jira's hut. Smoke wafts out of the chimney. He must be meditating extra hard today.

The chief's wyrm guards the entrance to Jira's hut but moves aside to let me pass. Inside, I find Jira and the chief leaning over a golden chest. The same chest where they plucked items for me and my party before our journey to Paltras Ruins.

I clear my throat and they both turn around.

"Chod." Chief Rizza nods at me. For a moment, we just look into one another's eyes. I hope she doesn't view this as me abandoning the village. I want to spout off all the reasons why I can't stay, anything and everything to justify why I must go. Why must I feel so guilty for doing what needs to be done? Our gaze breaks and she looks past me. "Morning has come too soon. It seems like just yesterday you came to us, and now it is time for you to leave."

"I will always be around if you need anything. All you have to do is offer me a quest, and I will know to return right away. But before I go, I just wanted to say thank you. For taking a chance on me when I was just finding my way in this world. This village has made me into who I am."

She smiles. It's a smile of both happiness and sadness. "Before you go, we have a final gift for you."

Jira pulls out a small pouch and it jingles as he hands it to me.

Currency: *10 gold.*

"You've got better things to do than trade leather. Plus, your leatherworking skill doesn't seem to have improved much." Jira grins. "I don't know if it is a lot or a little, but I hope it serves you well."

Once again, their generosity astounds me. I find it funny, that for the majority of my time here, currency was never an issue. The trolls have a village that is built on community. For my first thirty days, gold never crossed my mind. Not until I entered a human city.

I have a feeling ten gold will go quite a long way in these smaller towns. "Thank you. Both of you."

They both embrace me before I leave, and I'm certain it will not be the last time we meet.

When I step out into the courtyard, everyone is gone. Even Kea has left her stew unattended. The children that normally train to the other side of Jira's hut are nowhere to be found.

"Where is everyone?" I ask the chief, but she doesn't answer. Instead, she says, "Follow me."

I follow her out of the village center and into the forest. We walk in silence, dead leaves crunching under our feet. We come to the spot where we battled Glenn's army, the broken trees the only reminder of the chaos. It's then that I see the translucent figures of the entire village as they sit stone silent in two rows facing one another.

A loud crack echoes as each of them claps their hands and rises to their feet. They all take a step back, making a path for me to walk.

At the end of the line, closest to me, Malak and Jojin face one another. They stomp their feet, then beat their chests. As they finish, the two trolls closest to them repeat the action. Then all four of them stomp their feet and beat their chests. The next two repeat the action. The thunder of their movements grows with each new addition. Then all six continue the cycle, with two more joining in. The cycle continues until the entire line of trolls has joined and their movements rumble the very ground.

Chief Rizza nudges me forward, and they all fall silent. As I step in front of Malak and Jojin, they all let out a roar so loud that the birds in the trees take flight. They begin another beautiful tribal dance, filled with stomps and thunderous chest-beats, thigh-slaps, and roars that clear the forest of animals for miles. I let the sounds and vibrations wash over me.

At the very end of the line, Gord and Tormara face one another. Gord's nose ring flicks with each movement, and Tormara's braid whips like a viper. I step past them, and they all fall silent once more.

Far behind me, a song erupts. It's a song without words, but a guttural cry as Chief Rizza wails into the sky. It's a song of power and melancholy. A song of farewell.

Suddenly, my body erupts in electricity. For a moment, shockwaves course through my veins, threatening to explode out like lightning. Then just as quickly, it fades away.

You have been blessed by the forest trolls.

CHAPTER THIRTEEN

MYTHOS' MOST WANTED

The farewell dance will be burned into my mind for as long as I live. Much like the dance I witnessed my first night in the village, the power and might in those movements resonates in my bones. Maybe the dance called to something primal in me, to my very troll nature.

Aside from the notification telling me I had been blessed by the forest trolls, none of my stats have changed. Not like when Hawkin hit me with his Aura of Vigor. Still, there was something powerful about the blessing. Something happened, I'm sure of it. How else do I explain the electricity that seemed to course through my veins?

"Did you feel it?" I ask Limery. He sits perched on my shoulder watching colorful birds as they jump from limb to limb.

"Feels what?" His eyes are locked on the birds. He conjures a fireball, and I know exactly what is about to happen. A moment later, a bird is engulfed in flame and falls to the ground. Limery hops from my shoulder to claim his prize.

I guess it was just me who was affected by the chant. I wish I could have stayed to ask, but after such a mighty performance, I didn't feel like I should hang around and ask questions. When a moment like that comes around, I think it's best not to ruin it.

Even if there was no buff, the gesture itself was momentous. The entire tribe sending me off like that, it really shows the impact I made in my short time there. Not to mention the impact they had on me. I may not ever understand what it's truly like to be a troll or have the history they have, but I know that I will always be a forest troll, even if I go back to the real world.

Now that I have no obligations, I feel both free and lost at the same time. It's a strange feeling, not having anything to do. Since I first came into *Isle of Mythos*, I've had one quest right after another. And not just "help me clear these wolves that keep killing my livestock" quests, but big, world-spanning quests. Now, I finally get to experience the game without an entire race depending on me. It's nice. I'm a free troll with nothing but time to kill until Taryn shows up.

Speaking of Taryn, he has to be getting close by now.

My first order of business: travel to Lynchton. I'd like to get the lay of the land and remind everyone there what I am capable of, so that they are on their best behavior when the first envoy of trolls arrives. There will definitely be a transition period, but if Lillith comes back with enough translators, things will go a lot smoother. The least I can do is give the village some warning of what to expect when the trolls arrive.

I pull Petrified Staff from my satchel and cast a Horror of Finesse. The blue, imp-like creature falls in line behind me. Since I've got some time to kill, I might as well do a little leveling.

Most of the creatures in this forest are far below my level now, but every little bit helps. Once Taryn levels up more I'd like to find some higher level areas, wherever they may be.

The first unlucky creature to cross my path is a deer. The young buck squares off with me, antlers lowered, and begins his charge. When it's several yards out, I cast Horror of Vitality, and the bonus effect of the summoning slows the charge. The Horror of Finesse bites and claws at the creature, while the furry Horror of Vitality lowers its own horns and collides with the deer's antlers. The collision disorients the deer and breaks off one of his antlers. With a few swings of my scepter, my XP bar moves a small amount. I loot the corpse of its hide and antlers.

Limery returns from bird killing just as I finish removing the hide.

I'm contemplating whether I should save the meat or cook it now when I hear a loud crash from beyond a thicket of trees. Branches crunch and something grunts in disapproval.

We follow the source of the noise and find an ogre pulling trees from the ground and breaking them in half. The small-headed, lumbering fool grunts to itself as it carries on its meaningless work. I focus on the monster and view its stats.

Ogre. *Level 6. Big, strong, and ugly. Ogres are quick-tempered, powerful brawlers.*

It turns at our approach, revealing a set of crooked brown teeth. The top row is dull, but the bottom row is jagged and sharp. It's draped in an assortment of furs, and a bone necklace dangles across its pasty yellow chest.

I've seen that necklace before. That's when I realize that this isn't just any ogre; this is the asshole that killed me!

His bloodshot eyes cut at me. "You!" he roars. Thanks to my communication stone, I can actually understand him this time.

"Hey there. Long time, no see, big fella. I love what you've done with your hair. How do I get it to come out of my nostrils like that?" I taunt him. If we're going to fight, I might as well get him angry beforehand.

He lifts a tree trunk and charges, his ogreboobs flopping with each step.

"Limery, stay back. He's mine." Limery lands on a tree limb to watch the carnage unfold.

I cast three more horrors in rapid succession, bringing my total to five.

"Bad troll!" the ogre shouts, spittle flying from his mouth. Each fat roll jiggles as the monster rushes towards me. He's taller than I am, and definitely weighs more, but he's about to get payback from our first encounter.

I use Sacrifice, and all five horrors vanish, a portion of their energy flowing into me. I gain +1 Dexterity for each Horror of Finesse, +1 Strength for the Horror of Power, and +1 Constitution for each Horror of Vitality. My muscles bulge and heart pounds with the sudden increase of stats.

"Bad troll," he says again, displaying his extensive vocabulary.

He swings the club, and I dodge it with ease. The force of the attack knocks the ogre off balance. I rake my claws along his side as he stumbles, and he cries out in pain as thick black blood flows down his side.

He regains his balance and swings again, but my high Dexterity is too much for the level-six cretin. I duck under the blow and land a right hook to the side of his pea-brained head. He staggers back and forth from the punch.

"You might want to get a colonoscopy after all this butthurt." I taunt him again, but the effort is lost on him.

"Get him, Chods!" Limery cheers me on.

The two attacks have dropped the ogre's HP to fifty percent. Even though he's a significantly lower level than me, he still has a high Constitution. I really was an idiot to try and fight him when I was only level one.

The follies of youth.

When the ogre's head quits spinning, he tilts it head back and roars. His HP slowly begins to regenerate.

"That's a nice trick."

I put away my Petrified Staff and pick up a wooden club off the ground. We're going to finish this the old-fashioned way. With blunt force.

He pulls back his club to swing, and I do the same thing. Our clubs collide with a violent crash, exploding into debris and sawdust. The ogre mumbles something unintelligible as he scrambles for another weapon. He leans down to pick up a tree trunk, and I plant my foot against his ass, sending him sprawling to the forest floor.

I find a nearby boulder and lift it above my head. "Sorry, dude. It's not business, it's personal." I drop the boulder and score a critical hit.

In the aftermath of the fight, I realize the ogre shit himself. The realism of this game never ceases to amaze me. Even though the ogre could speak, I don't feel bad about killing him. Not after the story Gord told me about his father. The fewer murdering nitwits we have roaming the forest, the better.

"Good job, Chods. Yous kicked his butt!" Good to know I'll always have one cheerleader everywhere I go.

The bonus stats from Sacrifice wear off and I feel like my normal self again. I try to imagine what it would feel like if I had a full army of horrors when I used the ability. +20 Strength, Dexterity, and Constitution. Could Warwick or Kassidy stop me if I were that powerful? Too bad the buff only lasts as long as the remaining time on each horror. Would it make more sense to keep my strength spread out among my horrors since they don't decay in battle rather than have it all on me?

Questions for another time. For now, I'm going to enjoy the sweet taste of revenge.

There's not much to loot from the ogre's corpse. The furs he wears are mangy, and I couldn't be paid enough to eat that meat.

Limery and I follow a deer trail through the forest, making idle chat about what happens next.

"In a few days, there's someone I want you to meet." I duck below a low branch. "He's an old friend of mine."

"Really?" His bulbous eyes go even wider. "Chods's old friend?"

"Yeah, he comes from where I do. Once we meet up, we can all go adventuring together."

"Oh yes, Limmy loves adventures." He grins.

"Now that we don't have any quests, is there anything that you want to do?" Since I met the little guy, he's followed me practically everywhere. I'd like to do something he wants for a change.

"Limmy just wants to adventure with Chods."

We camp for the night near the edge of the forest. Even with the newfound peace, I don't want to show up to Lynchton's gate at night in case I frighten them. Limery tucks himself under my arm, and the sounds of howling wolves lull us to sleep.

The next morning, sun beams through the boundary of the forest, bringing the day to life. All around us, the forest erupts with sound. Birds chirp, bees buzz along the forest's edge, and critters scurry along the underbrush.

Something tickles my arm, and I look down to see a bright red lizard licking at my skin. Smoke plumes out of its nostrils. A flick of my wrist sends the creature soaring into a bush.

Limery wakes with groggy eyes and stretches his small arms overhead. I have the strong urge to rub his tummy, but I refrain.

"Ready to explore?" I ask.

"Oh yes! But first, Limmy needs to eats." He rubs his stomach and takes flight. Fire crackles as he sets out in search of breakfast.

After devouring some roasted fowl, we step out of the shadows and into the open stretch between the woods and Lynchton. Several wagons are already entering the city, loaded with the day's produce.

I walk confidently towards the town, as if entering the city is the most normal thing in the world. We catch several glances, but my reputation precedes me, and no one says a thing.

A familiar face greets me at the gate to Lynchton. Jameson, the soldier who awoke to a hundred trolls demanding entry the night we spawn-camped Glenn, stands guard at the gate along with another young soldier. Their armor isn't as polished and pristine as the soldiers in Vanaria. This is armor that is used both for training and battle, armor that is mended when dented and passed down from father to son.

"Morning." I nod, gauging their response.

"Come to humiliate me again, have you?" He cocks an eyebrow but offers no resistance as we enter.

Several pieces of parchment nailed to the gate catch my eyes. They're wanted posters, and I recognize the men pictured.

Jude Duggan: *wanted for attempted murder and breaking out a prisoner.*

Glenn Orickson: *wanted for escaping the town dungeon.*

Their faces stare at me from the yellowed parchment. This is not good. This is so not good.

"What happened? What does it mean that Glenn escaped?"

Jameson lets out a long sigh. He waves a wide-eyed man driving a wagon through the gate after his partner inspects its contents.

"A couple of days ago, this fellow in black shows up at the dungeon, demanding that he be let in. The guard on duty immediately recognized the wanted mark on his head, but before he could sound the alarm, the man stabbed him and took the cell keys. He and Glenn disappeared into the night."

"And what about the guard? Did he survive?"

"Barely. He's lucky that their shifts changed only minutes after the attack or else he would have bled to death all alone." Jameson shakes his head at the thought. "Truth be told, I don't care that they're gone as long as they stay the hell away from here."

Fat chance of that. Seems like Jude is recruiting for his troll-hating army. "Was there a paladin with them? Big guy, golden hair, silver and blue armor?"

"Not that I've heard. As far as I know, he was alone. Why? Should we be expecting more?" Jameson jabs the butt of his spear into the ground.

"No. He got what he came for." For now, at least.

I struggle with what to do with the news. At level one, it'll be some time before Glenn is strong enough to form any sort of attack on the village, but I still need to let the chief know. A warning could be the difference between life and death.

If Jude is running the show, then I'll be the one they're after. But that doesn't mean they won't go through the village to get to me. They know how much I care about the other trolls. There's not a bone in my body that believes they wouldn't hurt them.

At least they won't be able to buy anything from towns or villages. That'll slow them down some. Without access to a blacksmith or tailor, they'll probably resort to killing travelers for items. Anyone who meets them will know they are wanted by the crown. I'm sure they'll either head for the wilderness, or somewhere the king's justice doesn't reach.

North, perhaps. The wanted mark might not even work outside of the king's borders.

I turn away from the wanted posters, back to Jameson. "There will be more trolls coming in a few days to trade with the village. Make sure that you let them know about these two so that they can prepare."

Jameson flashes me a fake smile. "More trolls. Great."

I don't blame his reticence towards the trolls. He had to have gotten a pretty strong talkin- to after letting us all into the town that night. Not that he had a choice.

"Good seeing you, Jameson." I leave him to brood by the gate as we enter the town.

The last time I was here, the moon shone overhead. The town is even more quaint by daylight, igniting my desire for adventure. The blacksmith, tailor, and apothecary are to my left. To my right are the stables, The Dancing Donkey Inn, and a market. The market is filled with people at this hour, and the smell of roasted meat wafts through the air, causing me to salivate. Farther down, there are several buildings that sell everything from pottery to spices. The steeple from the town church rises high into the sky from the center of town, and farther back are the houses with their thatched roofs.

"Excuse me." I try to get the attention of a woman walking by with a basket of fruit. She jumps at the sound of my voice before running off.

Several people stare at me, covering their mouths as they whisper between themselves.

I walk over to one of the stable boys and try again. The young man with curly brown hair struggles with a horse as he attempts to saddle it.

"Excuse me, but do you know where I might find the mayor? I'd like to have a word with him."

The man looks up from his work and does a doubletake. He lets the saddle drop to the ground, abandoning the attempt for a moment. "Uhm. Probably at the Spice Emporium. Everybody knows he fancies Ms. McGee." He shuffles back and forth. "Say, you're that troll, aren't you? The one who did that to Glenn?"

"Yeah, about that—"

"I, for one, am glad you did it. He deserved it for what he did to my brother." A fire burns behind his brown eyes. "Tucker never was a fighter. He fancied himself a poet, and yet, somehow, that bastard convinced him to go off and fight your lot. My brother wasn't the only one either. Lots of folks who normally wouldn't do such a thing followed him to their deaths." He takes off his gloves and extends a hand. "If you ever need anything in Lynchton, come to me and I'll do my best to get you sorted. Name's Luka."

"Nice to meet you, Luka. I'm Chod. This is Limery." He shakes Limery's small hand. "We need to see the mayor, but thank you for your kindness."

The staring townspeople don't bother me as we walk to the spice shop. I can't stop thinking about what Luka said about his brother. How is it that Glenn was able to convince so many people to join his cause? People that normally wouldn't. And not just once, but multiple times.

"Chods, we's here." Limery snaps me from my thoughts.

I open the door and a little bell rings, announcing our arrival. There's a sharp intake of breath that I suppose I should be getting used to, and a woman wearing a pink frilled dress clasps a hand over her mouth. The wrinkled old sot I remember yelling at me just before I executed Glenn leans against the counter.

"Can I help you?" the woman squeaks.

"Actually, I'm here to see him." The tension visibly leaves her body.

"Ah, yes." The mayor stands away from the counter. "I assumed I would be seeing some of your ilk around here eventually. Congrats on your peace. I hope your days of mischief are over."

"It would seem you have enough mischief without me. I see Glenn managed to escape."

"I've alerted the king. As long as he stays away from Lynchton, he's no longer our concern." He hands the woman behind the counter a few coins and takes a jar of orange spice. "If you'd follow me, we can speak in private. I was actually looking forward to our first contact with trolls. I'm the only one in the village with a communication stone." He lifts his head a little higher, like a strutting peacock. "Perks of being the mayor. No one here speaks troll either. It's a very harsh language, wouldn't you say?"

I ignore his rude comment and carry on with business as we walk down the street. "I actually may have a solution for that."

"Is that so?" He leads us into a stone cottage next to the church. Inside, it's well kept. Several pieces of parchment litter a table. There's a leather couch and a fireplace. A bottle of amber liquid sits on a smaller table in front of the couch, and a fire fizzles in the fireplace. "Please, have a seat. Can I offer you a refreshment?"

I decline, but Limery eagerly accepts.

The mayor fills a pot with water and stokes the flame of the fireplace. After a moment, it roars to life and he hangs the pot from an attachment over the fire. Once it comes to a boil, he adds a sprinkle of the orange spice and pours himself and Limery a cup. "What is it you have in mind?"

I tell him my plans for the Imp Messaging Service and the propositions that the forest trolls have for the forests. "I wanted to give you a warning so that perhaps the other trolls are not greeted in such a manner as I was."

"Not much I can do about that, I'm afraid. Living so close to the forest, our people have had more than their fair share of run-ins with trolls over the years. I don't think I have to tell you that they haven't been the most pleasant. And the whole debacle with Glenn. Right or wrong, a lot of our men lost their lives. It will take time."

I can't really argue with the logic of that.

"But I have a plan," he continues. "As a gesture of good faith, I have a quest for some of the trolls who will take it. Monsters have been harassing some of our farmers. They've destroyed acres of crops, killed livestock. If something isn't done about them, soon it'll begin to affect the local economy. We don't have the manpower to spare, and there haven't been many heroes in this area recently. Seems like the perfect opportunity to build trust between our communities."

"That's actually a really good idea."

"You're more than welcome to participate yourself. Here." The quest displays in the corner of my vision.

Quest Alert. *You have been offered the quest "Save the Farms." Monsters have been destroying crops and killing livestock around Lynchton. Find and kill the monsters before the economy begins to suffer. Bring the head of the slain monster to the town mayor to claim reward.*

Reward: 1 silver per monster.

"If you don't mind me asking, what is the currency here? We haven't had much need for money in the forest."

The mayor laughs at my comment. "Ah, to be a troll. You'll find that out here, money rules everything. Bronze is the most common, with one hundred bronze coins for every silver, ten silver for every gold, and 10 gold for every platinum. Platinum is the currency of royalty, so I wouldn't set your eyes on acquiring that any time soon. There is a branch of the Royal Bank in every town, where you and other trolls can safely store coins if you desire. It is all regulated and insured by the master banker in Vanaria."

One silver for slaying a monster sounds like a pretty fair price for the dangers involved. If he only knew how many gold coins Limery and I had between us.

"If I had to guess, I think your monster problem will be handled in short order. Limery, what do you say we go track down some of these troublemakers?"

"Oh, yes! Limmy wants more monies." He drains the rest of his beverage in one chug.

I accept the quest and several markers appear on my map, displaying areas where the monsters have attacked.

Before we leave, I want to take some time to check out some of the shops. I have all of this gold; it'd be a shame not to use it.

"Want to do a little shopping before we hit the road?"

Limery's eyes light up with excitement. I'm sure he's aching to spend his stolen coins.

Staying true to his nature, the first thing he spends his money on are various smoked meats. We have to exchange some of our gold coins for smaller denominations at the bank in order to pay for it.

After sampling some of the meats, I'll give it to the humans, they know their way around a spice rack. They really play off the different flavors in ways that roasting meat over a fire simply doesn't.

We're in and out of the tailor in a flash. Aside from a pretty cool cloak, there's not much that tempts me away from the freedom of my loincloth. The blacksmith offers some sturdy weapons, but nothing that outclasses my Petrified Staff or

Forlorn Scepter. Limery picks up a small silver dagger for a couple of silver, but with his fire magic, I'm sure it's more for show.

If we want the good stuff, I think we'll need to go to a larger city or hit up some dungeons.

We pass a small jewelry shop next to the Dancing Donkey, and Limery refuses to let me pass by without entering. Inside, it's full of rings, necklaces, and bracelets. Some with quality enchantments, but most of them not. I wonder if NPCs can analyze the items like I do.

Limery presses his fingers against the glass display case, eyeing a pendant in the shape of a blue flame. The owner's face contorts at the smudged surface, when the door behind us opens and a shimmering knight clanks through.

Pressley Allen
Level 23
Knight
Human

With each step, the knight's armor clanks and jingles. Each piece of silver plate mail is pristinely polished and in far better shape than any of the guards' in Lynchton. Beneath it, vibrant chainmail protects any weak spots. My reflection stares back at me from his helmet as he passes, unconcerned with my presence.

He lifts his hand and a purple amulet falls out, dangling from a golden chain. "How much?" he asks the shopkeeper, cutting right to the chase.

The shopkeeper inspects the amulet, pulling out some sort of magnifying glass with a green lens. She mumbles to herself as she turns it over, examining every inch of the jewelry. "Two gold."

"Done." The knight doesn't even try to haggle for a better price.

"Wait," I interrupt. "What is it?"

The knight takes the amulet back and shows it to me. "An amulet of protection. I looted it from a dungeon two days ago."

Tiny yellow bolts run through the amulet's center, like a tropical thunderstorm. I focus on the item and its stats appear.

Item. Amulet of Grounding. *Protects wearer from the elemental effects of lightning-based abilities. Does not block damage, but does negate stuns, chains, and explosions associated with electric attacks.*

The memory of the wisps from the faerie dungeon comes to mind. The cluster of shocking puffs of energy would have killed me if not for Limery. This amulet would have allowed me to walk straight through the first level unimpeded.

"You don't want it?" I ask. It seems like a pretty valuable item to me.

"It's not a matter of wanting it. I want gold. Lots of gold. I'm not going to stop to rest until I have enough." He lifts the visor of his helm and brown eyes flecked with gold look at me with authority. His dark complexion is pronounced against the silver of his armor. "I don't care about the trolls. I don't care about the squabbles of the other heroes. I care about gold. So, unless you want to pay me more than two gold for this amulet, I don't care about you either."

"I think I'll pass." Three gold is a lot to spend on something I don't really need. "What are you saving up for anyways?"

He stares at me before answering. "This is a do-over. Most of these clowns don't see that. They want to kill and backstab and plot. Prison didn't teach them a damn thing. Me? I want an empire and ain't nobody on this island gonna stop me from getting mine." He hands the amulet to the shopkeeper, and she gives him two gold coins. "You understand, though." He looks me up and down, as if surveying me. "Yeah, you know what's up."

I stand in stunned silence. An empire, huh? I just want to have a little fun.

"That's enough chit-chat for today." He shuts his visor with a clank. "I've got to restock and get back on my grind. I'll see you around, troll."

As quick as he entered, the knight is gone. Off to whatever adventure awaits him next. I'm glad to know that there are other players in here for things besides vengeance. Players who actually want to play the game. Maybe some of them actually want to be rehabilitated. I wonder what Pressley is in prison for anyways. He's not short on ambition, and he's got the levels and mindset to make the most of this world.

"He come in here a lot?" I ask the shopkeeper.

"Oh, yes. Sir Allen is one of my greatest suppliers. Quite the adventurer, that one."

Limery points to a small silver ring with a red stone. "That one."

"Five silver."

He hands the shopkeeper a gold coin, and she gives him the ring and his change. "What'd you get?"

He slips the ring on his finger and it magically adjusts to his size. "Something to makes Limmy stronger." He snaps his finger and flame erupts in his palm. It seems denser and more vibrant than before.

"Get out!" the shopkeeper yells. "Get out before you burn the whole place to the ground!"

Outside the shop, I pull up my map, searching for the nearest location of the mayor's quest.

CHAPTER FOURTEEN
COMMUNITY SERVICE

The locations of the quests are marked on my map with red exclamation marks. There are over a dozen areas that have been ravaged by monsters. The closest farms are only a few miles away.

Far off in the distance, something gleams on the horizon, reflecting the bright sunny day. I wonder if it might be Pressley the knight heading off to his next adventure.

At level twenty-three, he's the strongest player I've met so far. He must have really been grinding to get that high. If he really does want an empire, then he's going to be grinding for a while. With each new level, it becomes increasingly more difficult to get to the next.

I can't even imagine how much gold it will take to start a town, much less advance it to a kingdom. It sounds like a lifetime of work.

Ping!

My message icon flashes, and I pull up my new message.

Incoming Message (Taryn): *Yo Chode! Just kidding, bro. I'm getting close to the forest. Where should we meet?*

Message (Chod): *Call me that again and I'll spawn-camp your little noob self all the way back to level one. We're at a group of farms outside of Lynchton. I think we're going to complete a few quests for the mayor. If you make it here in time, you can help out. That is, if you're strong enough.*

. . .

Taryn doesn't respond, so I assume he is on his way. There's no point in just standing around and waiting for him to show, especially when there is a silver to be earned for every monster we kill. We should head to one of the farms and find out what's causing all the damage.

The first farm we come upon is a small hut with a thatched roof, surrounded by acres of crops. A wooden fence to the rear separates horses and a few goats. A trail of upturned soil snakes through several rows of cabbage. Nearby, some sort of coop or building lies in shambles, with pieces of wood scattered everywhere.

The farmer trudges behind a plow being pulled by a donkey as it re-plows his mangled garden.

"Excuse me!" I shout, giving him plenty of time to prepare before we are face to face. "The Mayor of Lynchton sent us. He said you were having problems with monsters destroying your crops."

The farmer lifts his straw hat and raises an eyebrow. "The mayor sent you? Now ain't that something. Us countryfolk are usually left to fend for ourselves." He wipes sweat off his brow with a dirty sleeve. "We can't pay heroes, and the townsfolk never seem to have enough men to part with. If you're looking for money, we don't have any to spare, not with the attacks."

"No need to worry about payment. The mayor thinks it is in the best interest for all parties if we eliminate this threat as quick as possible. We're at your service. And before long, there should be several other trolls to help put this problem to rest. I'm Chod. This is my companion, Limery."

"I've never been one to turn down good help. Especially if it's free. You can call me Dewitt." He takes off his hat and places it over his chest.

"So, Dewitt. What is it we're dealing with here?" It looks to have been a pretty big creature, judging by the tracks left behind.

"Moulhaugs. I've never seen them down this far in the grasslands before. Normally, they call the foot of the mountains home, but recently, more and more have been showing up." He leads us over to the upturned earth and points at giant hoofprints sunk into the ground. "You see, they love eggs. Normally, they ram their giant horns against trees to knock them from the nests of large birds. Out here, they can seem to smell our chickens from a mile away. I rebuilt the damn coop twice, and twice, it got destroyed. I'm not even bothering with it again. If I don't have chickens, then the moulhaugs won't be destroying my crops."

If he doesn't have chickens, then the townspeople don't have eggs. "Leave it to us and the moulhaugs won't be troubling you again. Now, how do we go about finding them?"

The farmer laughs at my question. "I don't think that'll be a problem. Follow the trail of destruction and you'll come on them eventually. Just be careful when they're sleeping. Their mossy backside looks like a giant boulder when they're not moving. Their horns are powerful, even for someone as big as you."

"Good to know. Thanks." Sounds an awful lot like my Camouflage ability.

"I wish I could help you more, but I have seeds that need sowing. Or else the townsfolk might start eating one another." He chuckles before returning to his crops, leaving Limery and I standing over the giant hoofprints.

"Pretty big, huh?" The hoofprint engulfs my own as I step inside it.

"Very bigs. Very, very bigs." Limery hovers from one footprint to the next.

"It's not like we haven't faced bigger. We did kill a giant wyrm." Plus, they can't be that high of level if they are around here.

We follow the trail of the moulhaug from one farm to the next. Each farmer has the same story, with a promise to forego eggs as long as it saves their livelihoods. I don't blame them.

At the fourth farm, we come to another destroyed chicken coop. This one sits right next to a massive boulder covered in green moss. A soft snoring noise comes from the giant rock.

Moulhaug. *Level 18. A hulking, moss-covered quadruped with a single horn in the center of its snout. Generally peaceful creatures, moulhaugs scavenge for eggs from high in the treetops by swinging their massive horns like a battering ram. When provoked, they will lock onto a target until it is no longer visible or dies.*

"How in the hell is this thing level eighteen and hanging out around Lynchton?" No wonder the townspeople can't do anything to help. They'd be massacred.

"Theys comes from the mountains." Limery points to the range in the distance, its snowcapped peaks rising high. "Monsters is toughs up there."

Remembering the wyrm, I'd have to agree. Everything is coming together. If the moulhaugs are typically found near the mountain, then of course they are a higher level. They aren't in their natural habitat. Which means that whatever caused them to leave is even stronger than they are.

We'll deal with that later. For now, we have a beastie to kill.

"I'm going to summon a bunch of horrors while he's sleeping," I tell Limery, and three horrors appear in a puff of smoke. "Go and scout the surrounding areas for more moulhaugs while I prepare." We don't want to accidentally attract more of them while fighting. One, we can take. More and it starts to get tricky.

"Limmy's on it!" The imp disappears as I continue to summon new horrors as soon as the cooldown allows.

With a one-minute cooldown on each horror and a ten percent life decay every minute they are out of combat, I'll be able to summon thirty horrors just as the first set begin to die. Once the battle starts, there's no limit to how many I can have active at once.

At level eighteen, I'm sure the moulhaug has a substantial amount of health. Could exploding all thirty horrors be enough to kill it? It'll cost me three thousand mana just to summon all of them. If there is more than one moulhaug nearby, more than half my mana will be gone along with my horrors. My mana regen is pretty fast, but it's still a risk.

Once the horrors are all summoned, I equip my Petrified Staff for the added attack range on my physical attacks and wait for Limery to return. As each of the old horrors fades away, I summon a new one in its place. They grumble and snarl, my own personal army. Some of the Horrors of Vitality ram their horns against one another in boredom, and the Horrors of Finesse ride the Horrors of Power like a mount.

Limery zooms around the farmhouse like a bat out of hell. "Two monsties in the next field. Both is sleeping."

That's good. They're far enough away that our fight likely won't disturb them. That makes this the perfect opportunity for a test run.

"Ready?" I ask.

Limery nods, and two fireballs erupt in his palms.

"Alright, light 'em up!"

I use Petrified Staff's ranged attack at the same time as Limery tosses his fireballs. They connect with the mammoth bulldozer of a creature and it stumbles to its feet, eyes red with rage. The damage is barely noticeable against the moulhaug's thick hide. It lets out a vicious snarl, displaying teeth that, while not sharp, could probably crush whatever it bites like a trash compactor.

This is going to take the big guns. "Limery, start working on a mega fireball. When I give the word, I want you to throw it with all you've got."

The moulhaug paws at the earth, leaving craters where its hooves smash.

Limery hovers next to me, his hands overhead as a vortex of fire swirls into a sphere.

The rhino-like creature charges, each step a miniature earthquake. It swings its head side to side as it tramples across the field, destroying what's left of the crops. I run out of the way as it comes pummeling through and order my horrors to do the same, but several of the furry Horrors of Vitality are not quick enough in the thick soil of the garden and explode as the moulhaug's horn snuffs them out of existence.

I quickly summon more as the moulhaug turns for another charge. I forego my ranged attacks, since they seem to have little effect against the tough monster.

The beast charges again, and I lose several more horrors that are not quick enough to escape. Right now, I'm wishing I had an actual weapon that could stab and slice as it goes by instead of a glorified walking stick. That's what I need to spend my gold on.

"Ready!" Limmy shouts, and I send my horrors toward the moulhaug just as it turns again.

The few Horrors of Vitality left manage to slow the creature somewhat as they wrap their furry little arms around its tree-trunk legs.

"Now!" I order, and Limery lets the fireball fly. It soars across the field, torching the plantlife beneath its path and distorting the surrounding air.

When the fireball is several feet away, I cast Kamikaze, exploding all but my Horrors of Power. Half of the beast's HP vanishes in an instant, and the fireball collides in an explosion of heat and fire. The backdraft of the explosion singes the hair on my arms and causes my eyes to water.

Smoke clears and the moulhaug still stands with a quarter HP remaining. One tough motherfucker. Its mossy backside is burnt away, revealing tough, gray, rock-like skin.

My Horrors of Power attack, goring their tusks into the creature's legs while it thrashes its horn about like a giant wrecking ball.

Limery erects two flame walls along both sides of the monster and its HP drops slowly. He sets my horrors ablaze in the process, but they continue their savage attack until their life disappears.

Favoring one leg, the moulhaug crashes to the ground. With a great amount of effort, it rises again, its skin blistered and legs in tatters. Ropes of flesh hang from where the horrors gored it. It lets out a cry. A bellow of pain that reverberates out across the plains.

A moment later, a resounding call answers.

Shit.

CHAPTER FIFTEEN

GET RICH OR DIE TRYING

Limery blasts the moulhaug with fireballs, slowly whittling away at its health, but not nearly fast enough to kill the creature before its friends show up to ruin our party. I summon horrors as quickly as I can, all the while slinging ranged attacks from my Petrified Staff, but it just doesn't seem to be enough.

If I don't do something more than what we've been doing, we'll lose the kill and we might not get another chance with a moulhaug alone. I feel bad for the townspeople if that's the case.

Screw it. There's no way I'm letting this kill escape. If I'm going to be the baddest player on the island, then I need the XP. I need to find ways to defeat enemies when the going gets tough.

I sprint toward the moulhaug, switching to Forlorn Scepter as I do so. The obsidian shaft is cool to the touch. Its added range for summoning allows me to drop the horrors right on top of the beast as I run. One by one, I summon and explode them, taking out small chunks of health. Just not nearly enough.

The creature is slow with its injured legs, no longer capable of charging, but its horn still has the power to kill. One wrong move and I'll be respawning in the forest.

Using the built-up rage from all my previous attacks, I activate Bite and Claw and leap for the moulhaug.

Its powerful horn slams into my side like a battering ram, cracking several of my ribs and knocking the breath completely out of me. Limery flies down to me, concern radiating from his face.

"Chods, is you okay?" His bulbous eyes are full of worry.

"I'm fine," I get out between painful breaths. "Just...keep attacking."

Pain shoots through my ribs as I stand. Is this what being hit by a truck feels like?

The other moulhaugs will be showing up any minute now, and this one still has five percent health.

Five percent. That's all that stands between us and victory.

Time to go all in.

I activate Berserker Rage and my vision goes red. Increased Strength bulges my muscles and raw power flows through my veins. The pain in my side vanishes as my health rapidly recovers from the attack and my bones begin to mend themselves. I ready Bite and Claw, this time approaching the beast from the rear.

With a running start, I leap onto its back and bury my claws into its side. They rake along the moulhaug's burnt skin, tearing flesh and spilling blood. The beast thrashes about, trying with everything it has to throw me off. Its horn swings with enough ferocity to bludgeon me to death if I'm unlucky enough to land in its path. I dig my claws in deeper until they scrape against bone. Hot blood coats my hands and runs down the moulhaug's side.

I sink my tusks into its back and the silky, hot taste of iron fills my mouth. Fireballs connect all around me, damaging both of us. The Phoenix Feather I wear in my braid and increased healing from Berserker Rage mitigates most of the damage.

The moulhaug sways, blood loss causing the creature to move slower. Its thrashing grows less erratic as its HP trickles down. A trumpeting cry sounds nearby at the same moment as the moulhaug collapses to the ground.

"Run!" I tell Limery. "We can come back for the body later, but right now, we need to get the hell out of here."

The mourning cries of the other two moulhaugs can be heard over a mile from where we left the body. Their long resounding wails sprout goosebumps down my spine.

Once I feel we are far enough away, I stop to catch my breath. Even though forest trolls have more speed than other troll races, we weren't built for sprinting long distances. We're predators, built for the attack. My heartbeat pounds in my ears with each breath. Limery lands on a fence post and doesn't even seem winded.

How fast is he truly capable of going? Or any imp for that matter. They're like gazelles of the air, never running out of energy. It makes sense that they would be great messengers.

"Good job, Chods. We beats the monsty." He curls his tiny hand into a fist.

"Yeah, now we just need to find a way to take its head off without the others finding us." I don't relish the idea of carrying that giant horn all the way back to Lynchton, but silver is silver.

"Theys will go to sleeps soon. Theys mostly come out at night."

"Alright, we'll give them some time and then head back over." I focus on my messaging tool and compose a quick message for Taryn. Maybe we can finally meet up in the downtime.

. . .

Message (Chod): *Dude, you are slower than my grandmother. Where the hell are you?*

A minute later, I receive a reply.

Incoming Message (Taryn): *And you're about as impatient as mine. Heaven forbid a new player actually try to explore the game instead of rushing to meet you. Suck on a butterscotch, and I'll see you when I get there.*

Sarcastic asshole. I love it. He's only ever that outspoken and crude with me. For a big guy, he's awfully quiet and reserved. It takes time for Taryn to open up to new people. Put him in a room with strangers, and it's like he lost his voice. Even when we would play together, he'd talk so much shit, but as soon as the stream went live, he'd go silent.

Incoming Message (Taryn): *I just passed the first farm. Where are you?*
   Message (Chod): *Stay away from the farms! We had a bit of a SNAFU. It is not safe right now, especially for you. Meet me here.*

I send him my location on the map and hope the other moulhaugs don't accuse him of killing their brother.

Several minutes pass by with no response, so I take a moment to clear my mind and reorient myself. After a fight, I'm always on edge until I have a chance to calm down and breathe a little. Even when I just played online, a good fight would send my pulse racing.

I sit down and lean back against a post, letting the gentle breeze wash over me. The air smells so clean, not like New York where it was all smog, car exhaust, and street vendors. Not to mention the occasional homeless person that took a shit on the sidewalk.

Today is beautiful and sunny. Fluffy, white clouds float by overhead and I lose myself in their shapes. My muscles relax and the tension I've been holding begins to disappear.

I'm admiring a cloud in the shape of an axe when a small red bird flies down and perches on a post near Limery. Little does it know the danger it has just placed itself in.

The bird watches me intently, cocking its head and fixing one yellow eye on me. Limery licks his lips when he notices the bird. He has such an affinity for birds that I wonder if he has ever eaten fried chicken. If not, I bet it would blow his little imp mind. My mouth waters at the memory of that deep-fried goodness.

The air around his hands shimmers and a flame bursts to life in his palm. A quick flick of his wrist sends the fireball hurtling at the poor bird.

The fireball hits the bird, and there's an explosion of feathers as the bird transforms into a short, stout man. He falls off the fence with a thud.

"Ouch! Ouch!" he screams, patting his smoking body. "What the hell did you do that for?"

Limery already has two fireballs ready for the follow-up when the man puts his hands up in surrender.

"Chod! Call him off! Call him off!" he squeals.

"Taryn? What the hell? Is that you?" He scoots away from Limery's wrath. This makes absolutely zero sense. How was he a bird? "Limery, it's okay. This is my friend I was telling you about."

I take a moment to analyze him, just to make sure.

Taryn Jones
  Level 9
  Druid
  Ebony Dwarf

A dwarf and a druid? Quite the change from his normal support or tank role. Looking at the pint-sized dwarf before me, aside from the color of his skin, he's about as different from the real Taryn as possible. His normally giant afro has been replaced with thick dreadlocks. Outside the game, Taryn is built like a linebacker, tall with broad shoulders. The dwarf lying before me can't be over four feet tall. He has the typical bushy dwarven beard, and it's segmented with golden clasps that are engraved with runes. He lays on a dark green cloak and next to him lies a gnarled staff tipped with a boar's tusk.

Limery's eyes dart between Taryn and me. "Yous sure? This is yous friend?" I can't blame him for being untrusting of a bird that just transformed into a dwarf.

"I'm sure. Limery, meet Taryn. Taryn, this is my partner, Limery."

The imp extinguishes his flames and offers Taryn a demonic smile. I'm not sure if it's welcoming or terrifying.

Taryn slowly stands. "Thanks for the warm welcome." He brushes dirt off his arms and shoulders.

"How were we supposed to know you were a bird? You didn't tell me anything about you, so I think you had it coming." I wrap him in a massive bear hug. "Congrats on being the first dwarven hero."

He smiles at that, revealing a set of pearly whites that contrast with his dark complexion. "Oh man, they love me up there. Honest to goodness, they treated me like royalty. Though they were a little disappointed I wasn't a battle mage or a cleric. Still, I got some nice items to start out with for free."

"Why druid, anyway? It's never really been your style. And why were you a bird?"

He laughs. "If you're impressed by that, you've got another thing coming. That's a level-one druid ability. I can transform into animals. Mostly basic stuff, but I can upgrade it later on." He bends down to pick up his staff. "Why did I choose druid? I don't know. I guess because I've spent my entire life living in a city." He kicks the bottom of his staff and it swings forward like a pendulum. "You know, I've never even been to upstate New York. The only experience I have with nature is Central Park, and you're just as likely to see a man's dong as an animal. This seemed like a good time to see what it's all about. Nature, not the dongs."

I burst out laughing at his explanation. "You're always so chill about everything. I think you'll be a great druid. What other abilities are you packing?"

"Let's see. Right now, I have six abilities. I have another point to spend, but I'm saving it for a special ability that unlocks at level ten." His eyes have a far-off look to them, like he's looking at something we can't see. I wonder if I look like that when I check my stats. "I started out with Transform, Lightning Bolt, and Strong Wind. Transform lets me transform into any creature my level or under that I've seen in the past twenty-four hours. I get one animal that I can always turn into. For me, it's a red bird. I don't get any special abilities they may have, but I look and sound just like them. It's really good for traveling without being noticed. Lightning Bolt is just what it sounds like. I call a nasty bolt of electricity from the sky. Strong Wind increases my movement speed and that of anyone around me."

Taryn pauses to adjust his cloak and satchel. Limery eyes him cautiously, as if debating whether or not to trust the dwarf.

"I've since unlocked Restoration, which heals me while I am communing with nature, Nature's Aegis, which makes me immune to elemental effects like stuns and slows; and then Nature's Bulwark, which means animals will only attack me if I provoke them. What about you?"

I take a few moments to describe my abilities to him, how I am a double-class barbarian and summoner and my chosen summoner class plays well off my race.

"That's pretty cool. I'm guessing that dead monster back there is your handiwork?"

"Yeah, we're working on a quest for the Mayor of Lynchton. Each one of those moulhaugs is worth a silver."

"Only a silver?" He arches an eyebrow. "Those things are a much higher level than anything else in this area. You're being robbed."

I scoff at him. "This isn't the dwarven capital where people wipe their butts with golden coins. Money is hard to come by around here. Plus, we think they wandered down from a higher-level zone. Once we get you leveled up, I'd like to go and see what could have driven them off. But first, we need to get that thing's head and take it back. Maybe let the mayor know that people should be doing this quest in groups."

"I hope you don't expect me to help you lug that thing around." In a flash, he transforms in a small red bird again and lands on my shoulder.

. . .

Incoming Message (Taryn): *Carry me on, noble steed!*

CHAPTER SIXTEEN

EBONY AND IVORY

The moulhaug head is cumbersome as I drag it by the horn down the dirt road. It leaves a trail of dark red ichor in our wake. If I would have known how big they were, I might have purchased a wagon before leaving Lynchton. I feel like ten gold would definitely be enough for a wagon and some horses.

I offered the rest of the moulhaug body to the farmer who lived there. He said the meat could be used for jerky, but otherwise wasn't really palatable to humans. He seemed grateful that we eliminated one of the threats to his crops and wished us a speedy return. I only wish we could have taken care of the other two, but it won't be long before more trolls show up. If they manage to clear the area and win the farmers' favor, that will do a lot of good for our reputation.

As I carry the giant head, Limery perches on one shoulder while Taryn sits on the other, still in bird form. We've been communicating through the messaging system about Mythos Games and the outside world. Things that Limery doesn't need to know about.

Message (Chod): So how long are they letting you in for?

Incoming Message (Taryn): A month to start with. My parents will get an automatic deposit each week, so I don't have to worry about that, though I can request to be pulled at any time if I want. I still think it's strange how the system malfunctioned when you were pulled out. I mean, that's weird, right? I wonder if it's had the same effect when others have been pulled?

Message (Chod): I don't know about the others, but it's definitely weird. It makes you wonder if our minds are anything more than just points of data if the system can just lock onto them like that. The whole concept makes my head hurt just thinking about it. Like how we are even here at all, feeling, tasting, and smelling while our bodies are being fed and cleaned by tiny robots.

> ***Incoming Message (Taryn):*** *No kidding. It's easier not to think about it.*
> ***Incoming Message (Taryn):*** *Can I ask you a question?*
> ***Message (Chod):*** *Yeah, what's up?*
> ***Incoming Message (Taryn):*** *With as real as this game seems, do you feel pressure to stay and play? I mean, I know it's awesome. Everything about it feels more real than outside. I'm a tiny dwarf, but I actually feel like a dwarf, you know? Every person I met at Seascape, they felt as real as you and me. Each one had their own quirks. I did a quest for an old lady who couldn't find her cat. And I haven't been here as long as you. You and Limery, I can tell you have a connection. And not a 'pet in a video game' connection. It's real. Don't you worry about what would happen to him if you let the system fail?*
> ***Message (Chod):*** *Yeah, that's easier not to think about, too.*

Taryn transforms back into his dwarven form and slides off my shoulder. "I could get used to that. I see why you keep him around, Limery."

"Limmy likes Chods. Chods is Limmy's best friend." He pats me on the shoulder.

"We've got that in common then. Do a lot of imps go adventuring?" Taryn asks.

"No. Mommy says we used to be great messengers. We's used to travels all over, but not Limmy. Limmy wasn't a baby yet."

"But here you are now, leveled up and kicking ass." Taryn winks at Limery, and I have a feeling these two are going to get along just fine.

A few hours later, we arrive at Lynchton.

Shocked faces stare at us as I drag the moulhaug head through the gate and drop it in the town center. Twilight is nearing and the market has shut down for the day, but there are still people about the town. Several men sit on the porch of The Dancing Donkey drinking ale and having a laugh.

Luka, the stable worker, comes over and greets me. He holds a brush in one hand and a small pick in the other. "Now that is a mighty beast. You kill that thing all by yourself?"

"I had a lot of help from Limery here."

"You're doing the gods' work, I tell you. It will not be a pleasant day in my house if we don't have eggs. It's not my fault, but the wife'll take it out on me all the same." He shuffles his feet. "Well, these horses ain't gonna groom themselves. Take care."

No sooner has Luka left than I see a red-faced mayor marching in our direction. "Get. That. Out. of here!" I'm afraid for a minute his head is going to explode as he spits out the words.

"What? How else am I supposed to prove that I killed the beast?" I grab the moulhaug head by the horn and show it to him. "I thought you'd be grateful."

"I— I am," he stutters. "You didn't have to bring it inside. It's going to rot and stink up the whole town. Here, take your silver and get that blasted thing out of here!"

I do as I'm told and deposit the head outside of the gate, not that I think it will do much for the stench when it begins to decompose. The mayor really should have thought of a better way to confirm completion of the quest. It would save a lot of time and traveling for those who are completing it if they don't have to bring the head all the way back to town after every kill.

Jameson, the guard, stands slack-jawed as I leave the head and return to the town. "What am I supposed to do with that?" he asks.

"Take it up with the mayor." I turn to Taryn. "What do you say we get a room at The Dancing Donkey tonight and head out in the morning?"

"Works for me. I have some gold I need to deposit anyway."

We catch several glares as we enter the inn, but everyone moves out of our way and lets us pass. Someone in the group of drinkers makes a comment about a troll, a dwarf, and an imp walking into the bar, but we don't stay to hear the punchline. We pay for our rooms for the night, which also includes dinner, and take a seat at one of the tables on the bottom floor.

A serving maid makes her rounds, and a bartender pours drinks at the bar.

We're able to see the entire room from our table in the corner. Its dark wood is stained from years of use and tiny gashes are permanent reminders of the many men who have stabbed their blades in drunken revelry. The smells of roasted meat and smoking tobacco intertwine to form a savory and spicy aroma. In one corner, a man sits smoking a pipe, the fog around him so dense his face is barely visible. At another table, a group of travelers watch us out of the corners of their eyes and steal brief glances when they think we aren't looking.

"First round's on me," offers Taryn. He sets his staff down and returns a moment later with three mugs full of amber liquid. Limery's is a quarter of the size of the other two, but he holds it with pride.

"Cheers." We all tap our mugs together.

"I haven't seen many dwarves south of the mountains." I take a sip of my drink and it bubbles down my throat, malty and delicious. "Only one, actually, and that was at Vanaria. He was working as part of some trade agreement with the dwarven kingdom."

"Makes sense. They—I mean we—have a beautiful kingdom. The ivory dwarves are masterful stoneworkers. Plus, I kind of get the feeling that they like to keep to themselves." The golden clasps in his beard catch the light of the sconces on the nearby wall.

"Ivory? What's that all about? I noticed that you are an ebony dwarf." The first dwarf I've ever seen rocking dreadlocks.

Limery lets out a loud belch, causing the other guests to turn and look. He looks shocked that the noise escaped him. "Excuse Limmy."

"Nice one." Taryn fist-bumps the imp. "They're different sub-races. Like the forest and mountain trolls. The ivory dwarves are what most people think of when they imagine dwarves. White skin, thick beards, work in the mountains. Really good craftsmen that make weapons and build things. The ebony dwarves are the lowland dwarves. We originated in the desert between the mountains and Seascape. We're more the hunter-gatherer type, but amazing craftsmen as well. We make some of the finest jewelry on the island. Our towns are so well hidden that you might pass them by if you didn't know where to look. And then there are the blood dwarves. Known for their dark red skin, they used to mine obsidian in the heart of the volcano when it was still active. They say the fire and lava permanently turned their skin red and that lava runs through their veins. They are the rarest of the bunch."

"Wait, there's another volcano on the island?" I remember Kassidy saying that the stone for the walls and towers in Vanaria were raised from a dormant volcano. This is the first I've heard about one in Seascape.

"It's dormant. The entire city of Seascape is built on its remains." He takes another long draw of his ale, draining half the mug. "It's kind of crazy how there are so many ecosystems on one island."

"Ecosystems," I laugh. "When did you become such a nerd?"

"Since I knew the only way I was making it out of the block was with an education. Well, until I had this opportunity." His face goes serious for a moment. "Do you think I did the right thing? Skipping out in the middle of the semester to come play this—" He lowers his voice to a whisper. "—game?"

"You can always go back." I pat him on the shoulder. "The money you'll make while you're here, that'll really help your family. Stay here long enough and you might not even have to work at the burger joint when you go back."

His smile returns. "Yeah, you're right. I didn't even think of it like that. Want another round?"

Limery sways back and forth, his bulbous eyes glazed over.

"Sure, why not? I think Limery can sit this one out. He's tanked."

Not long into our second drink, Limery passes out at the table. He curls into a ball and a tiny balloon of snot bubbles from his nose with each snore.

"Lightweight," jokes Taryn.

"Maybe so, but he could kick your ass." I give him a playful shove and accidentally push a little too hard, nearly knocking him off the bench. "He's been with me in almost every fight and is only a couple of levels below me now."

Taryn returns with another round, noticeably more intoxicated.

"I never knew you liked to drink," I say, taking the mug.

He flashes me a goofy smile. "I didn't. I tried one of Pop's beers once. Tasted like piss. I don't know if it's because I'm a dwarf or what, but it goes down so easy now. Not to mention the feeling. It's like my whole head is vibrating, like a gentle buzz." His eyes light up like he just had a realization. "Wait! No way! Is that why they called it being buzzed?"

My deep laugh startles the nearby table, causing one man to knock over his drink. "I guess so. You know, I can't eat fruit since becoming a troll. My palate has completely changed. I can eat raw meat, but I can't eat fruit."

"That's wild, bro."

Several hours pass as we drink and chat. It feels so good to have Taryn here, to let my guard down and just chill out like before. Eventually, we both stumble to our rooms.

When I close the door, I'm greeted with a notification

Welcome to *The Dancing Donkey!* *You may set your respawn point in your room for as long as you are staying here. Once your stay is over, your respawn point will be reset to its previous location. Would you like to bind here?*

I decide not to, since we are only staying for the night. It's a useful feature if you are paying for an extended stay.

Limery grumbles as I carefully place him down on the bed, but he doesn't wake. The little guy is out cold.

Feeling completely content, I drift off to sleep.

CHAPTER SEVENTEEN
THE BEAR NECESSITIES

Sun spills through the window of my second-story room at The Dancing Donkey. The daylight assaults my sensitive eyes, so I bury my head beneath the blanket. My head pounds, like a tiny gnome has crept into my brain with a sledgehammer. Not to mention my parched mouth. I stumble from the bed in search of the pitcher of water and accidentally knock Limery to the floor. He falls on his head with a thunk, letting out a confused groan. When he stands up, he looks every bit as hungover as I feel. His bulbous eyes are bloodshot and squint at the burning light as he sways back and forth searching for his balance.

"Some night, huh?" I ask.

He responds with incoherent babbling.

We gather our belongings and I head to Taryn's room to check the damage he inflicted on himself. He opens the door with a smile.

"You look like hell." He laughs. "Both of you." He's already packed and stands there, staff in hand, with his satchel tossed over his shoulder.

"Why aren't you hungover?" I ask.

He shrugs. "Dwarven immunity?"

Limery clings tight to my shoulder. "Chods, more quiet, please," he whispers.

"You two need some breakfast," suggests Taryn, grinning. "It'll fix you right up."

True to his word, breakfast does wonders for our hangovers. After devouring loads of eggs and sausages, we leave The Dancing Donkey.

We slept through most of the morning and the sun sits high overhead. When we step out into the market, Taryn grabs me by the arms and points to the square.

"Aren't those your people?" he asks.

There are several groups of trolls spread around the market in pairs.

"Yeah, but they shouldn't be here yet. Not without Lillith and the imps."

Malak and Jojin stand in front of a table laden with knives. So many types of knives that I don't even know the uses for them all. Some are short, others long. Most are plain, but a few are embellished with jewels or engraved with runes. I don't remember seeing this table here when I left yesterday. It must be new.

The two guardian trolls carry some of the looted armor from the village. They must be here to trade. Malak sets the weapons down on the table and picks up a knife, examining it with great interest. With such sharp claws, trolls don't really need knives, but trading the weapons away will bring the two sides together.

I want to say hi, but something tells me to stand back and watch the interaction. There are no imps here yet, so they can't communicate other than by pointing at the items they wish to trade. Why would Chief Rizza send out the trolls without translators? It doesn't make any sense.

The man behind the table eyes them suspiciously. He wears a royal blue tunic, much finer than most others in the market. My guess is that he travels from village to village selling his items. His acquaintance seems to be his muscle, clad in all black with broad shoulders and a sword by his side. His bald head is scarred in several places.

We step up behind the two trolls, quiet so that they don't notice. The man selling knives must not recognize who I am because he talks freely to his companion. "They kill these people's men, then they bring their weapons back to trade. Isn't that messed up?"

The other man nods. "That's why you don't negotiate with savages. They can't be trusted."

Taryn makes to say something, but I put out my arm to stop him. I send him a message, telling him to let this play out.

Malak holds the knife in front of him in one hand and the weapons in the other, offering the exchange.

"No," says the man. "For you, coin." He reaches into his pocket and pulls out a silver coin. "Coin," he says again.

"Coin," Malak repeats.

The man in black questions the other. "You really think they have coin?"

"Does a troll shit in the woods?" He snickers. "You think all those poor souls who died in the forest never had coin on them? You think that hero that kept dying kept all his money in the bank? No, they have gold. I'm sure."

Jojin reaches into his pocket and pulls out a gold coin. "Coin," he says to the man.

The man's eyes light up. "Stupid trolls," he tells his partner. "That knife can't be worth more than five copper." He reaches for the gold coin.

"Enough!" I shout, pushing Malak aside. "How dare you take advantage of them because they can't speak your language. Malak, Jojin, leave us be. I will explain in a moment."

The two trolls move out of the way, and I'm leaning across their table before I know what I'm doing. The man in black draws his sword and points it at my throat.

His partner gives me a sniveling smirk and raises his eyebrows. "This is why we don't trade with savages. They only know violence."

"You were about to rip them off simply because they don't know any better," I roar. I'm the only reason he didn't.

"It's a free market. And they are free not to purchase. They can learn their lessons just like the rest of us."

Taryn pulls on my arm. "Hey, Chod. I think we should leave them be. We're drawing a crowd."

Fire courses through my veins. I turn around to see the entire market has gone silent.

Screw them. I'll tell them where they can all go. "All of you ca—"

Incoming Message (Taryn): *Bro, take a deep breath. You can't let one bad seed ruin it all.*

He's right. I don't need to be causing problems before I leave

I heed Taryn's advice and take a breath, trying to rein in my temper that has so often gotten me in trouble. If anything, I should be educating the trolls so that they don't become victims.

"What's going on here?" The mayor steps out of Ms. Mcgee's spice shop.

"Nothing," I say. "Just a misunderstanding. Trolls, would you come with me outside the gate? We need to talk."

I want to thank Taryn for keeping me in check, but when I look for him, he's disappeared. I glare at the shady knife salesman as we leave. He's smirking at me when something splats on his shoulder. He lets out a yell of surprise. "Are you kidding me? I've been shit on by a bird."

Up above him on the palisade, a red bird sits on the fence. It winks at me as we leave.

Outside the gate, all of the trolls look confused.

"Chod, what is the meaning of this?" asks Malak.

"That man was going to take advantage of you. That coin you were going to give him, you could have bought half that table."

"So? The trolls have no need of gold. What does it matter as long as it gets me what I want?"

I bury my head in my hand. "It's the principle of the matter. If you let him take advantage of you, then pretty soon they all will. And then the trolls will have nothing left to trade. Why are you here anyway? I thought you were waiting on the imps?"

Malak hangs his head. "I did not want to wait. I am ready to see the world."

I grab him by the shoulder. "The world will still be waiting when the imps return, I promise you. It can't be much longer."

"Fine," he grumbles. "Let's return to the forest."

Is this what it is like to have children? Constantly needing to watch out for them so that they don't hurt themselves or get taken advantage of. Or if you're my parents, hiring a nanny.

"You did good back there." Taryn pops up behind us. His brilliant smile pokes through his beard. "I'm glad you didn't murder that guy."

"Me too. It just made me so angry to see them taken advantage of like that." I clench my fist at the memory. His bodyguard has no idea how lucky he is.

"Some things they'll have to learn for themselves. You can fight their battles, but you can't run their lives."

"Yeah, you're right. It's hard not to feel responsible for them, though. Thanks for taking care of that prick for me."

"Anything for you." He laughs. "Now, what do you say we get me leveled up?"

Several miles from Lynchton, I'm only half paying attention when Taryn casts Lightning Bolt and a giant flash of raw energy cracks into an unsuspecting deer, giving him the XP he needs to hit level ten. Daydreams of cleaving the knife merchant in two keep popping into my mind. The way he looked at us, so smug, so superior. I should have rearranged his face.

"Chod, are you listening?" Taryn glares at me. "I said I can finally unlock Tame."

"Tame, what's that?" I hope he hasn't already told me, or he's going to be pissed. If I could only get out of my own head.

"It allows me to tame any beast that's less than five levels above me. All I have to do is get it down to five percent health." His eyes glaze over as he unlocks the ability.

"That's pretty cool. Is there a limit to what you can tame?"

"Yeah, I can't wait to try it out. It only works on beasts, though—nothing capable of talking. No unique monsters, and for every new pet I tame, I lose five percent influence over all pets I have. So if I have ten pets, they may not listen to me half the time. And I can only tame something new every six hours."

"That's probably for the best. I can imagine some people getting into bad situations with an ability that lets them tame their peers." Glenn comes to mind. "Is there a limit to how many creatures you can have tamed at once?"

"I don't think so, but the more I have, the less they will listen to me. They'll just be pets, so I don't have to monitor them, not like your horrors that you are capable of controlling. I can give them orders, but I can't actually enforce them."

"Well, let's go test it out." I try to push the thoughts that are bothering me to the back of my mind. I'm here with my best friend, playing the most awesome game on the planet. *Enjoy it*, I tell myself.

I cast a few horrors, and we move further north. The mayor's quest can wait for the other trolls. "What type of pet do you want first? There's a pretty good variety around here."

"I don't know." He shrugs, then runs his fingers through his beard. "I always thought it would be cool to have a pet bear."

I laugh. "At your size, you could probably ride it."

Taryn's eyes light up at the thought, and I think I just gave him an idea.

For the next few hours, we see dozens of animals, but not a single bear. Deer, warthogs, coyotes, even a few kobolds and gnolls. But of course, the moment we're looking for a bear, it's like they went extinct.

"Come on, T. Can't you just settle for a warthog or something? If you grind a little, we can probably even get you a moulhaug."

"Dude, a little patience." He cuts his eyes at me. "What are you in such a hurry for? I'm going to take to the skies. Maybe I can spot one from higher up. Limery, want to join me and leave this crybaby alone?"

Limery sticks his tongue out at me and takes to the air. A moment later, Taryn transforms into a bird and flutters away. I take the time to rest against a tree while they scour the area.

It doesn't take long before I receive a message from Taryn telling me he's spotted a mother and her cubs. He shares his location with me, and I set off to join him.

I find Taryn and Limery hiding behind a tree, watching the mother bear and her cubs as they play around an old tree stump. The three young cubs fight for supremacy, knocking each other to the ground. The mother bear is level eight, but the cubs are level one.

"What's the plan?" I ask. I don't think he wants a bear cub, but it also seems downright cruel to take the mother from her spawn.

"We wait for them to leave and follow them. Hopefully, they'll lead us to their den," he says without looking away.

I roll my eyes at him. "Great, more waiting."

Taryn whacks me on the side of the head with his staff, and Limery bursts out laughing, startling the bears and sending them running. I guess that's one way to get them moving.

We have to run to keep up with the surprisingly agile creatures. Even the cubs are faster than I would have expected. They lead us across a field and up a hill into a thick copse of trees.

We're following them into the trees when a massive brown bear appears out of nowhere. It rises up on its hind legs, easily taller than Taryn.

Umber Bear. *Level 12.*

The reddish-brown bear roars at us, arms outstretched, warning us to stay away from its family. Its dark muzzle reveals powerful teeth capable of snapping bones in half. There's a beauty in its power and brutality.

Without warning, Taryn casts Lightning Bolt, hammering the unsuspecting bear with a stream of raw energy. The bear charges him, and Taryn casts Strong Wind, giving himself added speed as he runs away.

"You gonna help me or not?" he yells.

I forgot he only has the one offensive ability, and he's unlikely to smack the bear to death with his staff. How did he manage to get to level nine only using Lightning Bolt?

"Limery, let's help him out. No matter what, do not kill the bear." I cast a Horror of Vitality, slowing the bear's charge, and then follow up with Horror of Power and Finesse.

The three horrors attack the bear, drawing its attention and filling my rage meter. I activate Claw, and along with the attack bonus from Horror of Power, my next attack drops its health by forty percent.

A couple of fireballs from Limery drop it further. The bear sinks its teeth into the Horror of Finesse, crushing the poor thing with its powerful bite. Horror of Power gores the bear with its tusks just before a mighty strike sends it to a sliver of HP.

Another bolt of lighting zaps the bear, dropping its HP into the required area for Tame to work.

The bear stands there, stunned, as Taryn moves into position. A green aura surrounds him, and his hands glow a vibrant yellow. The bear looks almost hypnotized as Taryn steps into its attack radius. It places all four feet on the ground and huddles into itself, allowing Taryn to place his hands on the bear.

When he touches the creature, the yellow glow from his hands transfers to the animal. The bleeding wounds stop flowing and begin to mend themselves. Slowly, the bear's health recovers until it's like the fight never happened.

The bear uncurls and looks around, the menace gone from its eyes.

CHAPTER EIGHTEEN
MARSHLANDS

Leaving the rest of the bears in peace, Taryn, Limery, and I set off in search of our next battle. We need to level up Taryn so that he can actually be useful in a tough fight. It won't take long if we can find the right monsters.

"Tell me, how is it you managed to get to level nine with one offensive spell?" After witnessing Taryn's battle with the umber bear, it's clear he'd have a tough go at fighting creatures without my help. The cooldown on Lightning Bolt isn't quick enough for him to spam it, and the staff he carries isn't made for bludgeoning. His abilities are nice, but he's better off as part of a team early on. Once he's tamed enough beasts, they can do his dirty work for him. Just like my horrors.

"Very carefully," he says. He rides on the back of the umber bear as it traipses across the meadow. We're heading back east, away from the moulhaugs and the mountains for now, to an area that should be more suitable for leveling. After using Tame on the creature, it seems to obey Taryn's commands, all of the fire gone from its eyes. "I'm sure it's easy for you, using brute strength to plow through monster after monster. For those of us who didn't go melee, and aren't the equivalent of a walking fridge, it's an actual grind to level up. You can kill a bear by yourself. For me, I have to slay a hundred bunnies. I got lucky and completed several quests in the capital, but most of it has been a real grind. But now that I have Berry, here, we'll be a formidable force in battle."

"Berry? Seriously?" I shake my head. "You cannot name your pet bear, Berry."

Taryn turns to me, his face scrunched. "And why not? You don't think he looks like a Berry?"

"Unless they're a fat old man with an alcohol problem, nobody looks like a Berry. You're riding him into battle, the least you could do is give him a proper name. He's a beast, not a fruit."

Taryn shrugs me off, petting the bear behind the ear. "Don't listen to him, Berry."

Limery snickers on my shoulder.

"You think this is funny?" I scowl at him.

He flashes me his sharp teeth. "Oh, yes. Limmy likes Berry."

Taryn slows the bear's pace, mirroring my own. "Now that I've got a pet, why don't we try to find some tougher competition. The sooner I level up, the sooner we can find out what it is that's driving the moulhaugs south."

"What'd you have in mind?"

"I was thinking maybe we could try to find a dungeon. I heard there might be one in this area. Normally, we'd need to hire a guide or buy a map, but if I take to the air, maybe I can spot the entrance."

"There's an easier way." My map practically shows me where every dungeon is just based on the location of the ley lines.

"What do you mean?" Berry comes to a halt and Taryn stares me down, his dreadlocks dancing in the breeze beneath his antler helmet.

"When I agreed to complete the first quest for Chief Rizza, she gave me access to a map that only the trolls have. It shows the ley lines that run across the entire island. If I look at the concentrated areas of magical energy, that usually means there is a dungeon nearby."

"You've got to be kidding me." He turns his head up to the heavens. "Could you be any luckier?"

"Hey, it was a hard road getting to where I am right now. I didn't have a tutorial. I got dropped in the forest and had to find my way. Yeah, maybe I got a little lucky here and there, but everyone who wasn't a troll would have killed me on sight a month ago. Everything I have now, I worked for." If he thinks this has been easy for me, he's clearly misinformed. Fighting the mana-infused wyrm wasn't easy. Nor was the faerie dungeon. Hell, I plotted the entire battle that defeated Glenn and his army.

"Yeah, yeah, yeah. Poor baby. Poor six-hundred pound, seven-foot-tall, double-class, hero of your people, and friend to King Favian, baby. Cry me a river. But first, how about you point me in the direction of the closest dungeon?"

I should make him beg me for my information, but it's more important to level him up than stoke my pride, so I pull up the map and locate the nearest ley line. Several miles from our location, there's a small cluster of magical veins. Nothing big, but hopefully something that'll give Taryn a level or two.

I share the location with Taryn. "Lead the way, your bearness."

He just strokes his beard and carries on. A half-hour later, the meadow grows soggy, transforming into a marsh.

My feet sink into the muddy earth. The water line is just barely below the surface. Reeds and other tall grasses blow in the wind. Occasionally, we startle a flock of birds, and they take to the air, but not before Limery torches a few for himself.

There are no trees or large bushes, just miles and miles of wetlands. Frogs croak and splash into the surrounding pools as we navigate toward the cluster of magical veins. Brightly-colored fish dart between the reeds, stirring up mud and silt.

"Is this it?" asks Taryn. His bear struggles to move through the muddy earth the same as I do. Each step is twice as hard as normal with the mud suctioning to our feet.

"Almost. Looks like it's about a half a mile that way." I point in the direction of the ley line.

Sick of sinking into the mud, I equip my Aquatic Boots. My prize from completing the faerie dungeon, they allow me to walk on water. Their magical properties prevent me from sinking into the mud.

"Hey, no fair," quips Taryn as his bear struggles with the new terrain. Beasts like that were not made for these environments.

"It's going to be tough to fight here. Maybe we should find another area that's more forgiving."

"We're already here. Let's just see what it has to offer. I'm going to scout ahead. This should help you and Berry keep up." The boar tusk on the tip of his staff glows blue and a strong gust seems to push me from behind.

You have been targeted with Strong Wind. Your movement speed has been increased.

Suddenly, Berry's feet move a little quicker through the mud. It's still tough for him, but it doesn't slow us as much.

Taryn transforms into a red bird and disappears into the sky.

I wonder where this dungeon will be. There are no trees or rock formations for as far as I can see, and it's unlikely to be underground with all the surrounding water. As if to answer my question, I receive a message from Taryn.

Incoming Message (Taryn): Dude, this is wild. There's some kind of design formed by the water that runs through the marsh. It looks like a giant symbol.

Message (Chod): Any idea what it means?

Incoming Message (Taryn): Not sure, but I'm guessing it has something to do with the dungeon. On my way back.

Up ahead, Taryn waits for us, perched on a swaying reed. When we're close enough, he returns to his dwarf form and his feet sink into the marshy earth.

"This is the edge of the symbol." He points to the water just before where we are standing. "It runs in a circle several hundred yards that way."

I pull up the map again. We're definitely in the right place. "Ready to see what it's all about?"

He nods, and we step forward. As soon as my feet touch the water, I'm greeted with a notification.

Marshlands. *Would you like to enter?*

I confirm and take another step forward. Taryn follows my lead, legs wrapped around Berry as he floats alongside me. A second later, there is a flash of light that runs through the water, not just in front of me but throughout the entire circle Taryn pointed out. A translucent barrier appears around the circle's edge, keeping others out but also keeping us in.

"Looks like we found our dungeon," I say.

Limery flies from my shoulder and touches a finger to the barrier. It clinks when his nail taps against it. I follow him and do the same. The barrier feels like glass, but it's made entirely of magical energy. He throws a fireball at the barrier, but it does nothing to the forcefield.

I've never seen a dungeon like this. No rooms, no levels, just wide-open space.

"What now?" asks Taryn.

"Now, we explore." I walk atop the water like some biblical prophet. It's strange, expecting to sink but walking on firm ground.

With Taryn riding him, Berry's nose is only a few inches above the water. Limery flutters in the air not far behind us.

The water gently splashes as we follow nature's path through the marsh. Berry disturbs the waterbed, making it impossible to see anything below the surface. The sun has only just begun to descend, so we still have a few hours before darkness. Not that it matters much to me or Limery with our night vision.

"Do dwarves have night vision?" I ask. With all the mining they do, it is certainly possible.

"Not quite." The water deepens and Berry's front legs wade through. "We have dark vision. It allows us to see better in dimly-lit areas, but not in complete darkness."

"Better than nothing."

All around us, insects rattle, birds chirp, and frogs croak. Where are the monsters?

Taryn stops moving and points a short dark finger to the marsh ahead. I don't immediately notice what he's showing me, but then I spot two orange eyes just above the water's surface and about a foot away, two nostrils.

I try to focus on it to reveal its stats, but there's not enough of the creature visible. Taryn lifts his staff and motions towards the monster.

I nod. A second later, there's a thunderous crack overhead and a bolt of lightning rips into the creature. It roars in pain before emerging from the muddy depths.

Mutated Crocodile. *Level 14. Mutated by the ancient rune magic of the Marshlands, this reptile walks on powerful hind legs capable of jumping long distances. They are fierce brawlers with unnatural strength.*

The crocodile that emerges looks more like a dinosaur than anything I've ever seen on the Discovery Channel. Burnt orange scales tipped with black match its fiery eyes. When it stands, the beast is easily seven feet tall. I hope Taryn is ready to party.

He dismounts and sends his bear on the attack, but in the water, it doesn't have the same attack speed it does on land. Even when he rises on his hind legs, the bear is still waist deep in muddy water. The crocodile lunges at Berry, sinking its teeth into the Berry's front leg. With a powerful strike, the bear smashes the crocodile in the side of the head, releasing its hold.

We need to get in there and help. "Limery, hit it with fireballs."

I summon my horrors while Limery pelts the reptile with fire. The flames sizzle against its orange scales but do little damage. My horrors float through the water like children at a pool party, unable to gather enough speed for an attack.

"Dammit, we need to get out of the water and onto the bank. It's muddy, but it's better than this." The water is the crocodile's element.

As soon as the cooldown allows, Taryn casts another Lightning Bolt. It stuns the creature in place, allowing Berry to land a few blows before retreating to the high ground. I gather my floating horrors and toss them onto land. Taryn casts Strong Wind, helping him and Berry make land.

"Got any bright ideas?" I ask.

Taryn's eyes are focused on the croc. "If you tank the damage, Limery and I can take him down with ranged attacks."

I summon a Horror of Vitality on the monster, slowing the crocodile's movement as it crawls out of the water. A wall of fire blocks its path, forcing it to go around just in time for Taryn to hit it with another bolt, dropping its health to sixty percent.

With a powerful leap, the bipedal crocodile covers the distance between it and me in a single jump. It crashes into me, and I fall onto my back in the sandy mud. The Aquatic Boots only keep my feet from sinking, not my whole body. We scrape, claw, and bite at one another as we roll through the muddy marsh. The crocodile grips me with his arms and kicks out with its legs, shredding my own legs with its talons. Berry tackles the creature, pulling it off me. I activate Claw, and jump back into the fight, piercing its scales and drawing blood. My own legs are streaked with blue. I manage to stand, and a powerful kick sends me stumbling away.

My legs sting like I just walked through a thorn bush naked, so I take a moment before rushing in. Summoning more horrors does no good. Each new one is so slow in the muddy terrain that the crocodile punts them away like soccer balls, so I resort to exploding them as soon as they summon, taking out chunks of health in droves.

When a bolt of lightning finally stuns the monster again. I sink my tusks into its neck and score a critical hit.

"Finish him off!" I tell Taryn so that he will get the kill bonus.

"Lightning Bolt is on cooldown." He lifts his arms as if not knowing what else to do.

"Use your brain."

A moment later, he transforms into an exact copy of Berry and the two maul the crocodile for its last bit of health.

"Woohoo!" yells Taryn after transforming back. "Now, that's how you get experience. A couple more of those and I'll be level eleven." He comes over to where I'm sitting and treating my wounds. "Ooh, that's nasty." He grimaces.

I down one of the health potions I crafted, and my wounds slowly begin to heal. "Here, give this to Berry." I hand him one of the potions.

"Thanks, but we don't need it." He tosses me the potion. "Check this out." He calls Berry over and has the bear sit beside him. His fur is matted with blood, and gashes from the crocodile cover his body. Taryn closes his eyes and begins chanting, both hands on Berry. As he does, a green aura surrounds their bodies. The gashes that run along the bear's sides quit bleeding and soon close. A moment later, he's completely healed.

"What was that?" I toss my empty clay vial back into my satchel, feeling better already.

"Didn't you listen when I was explaining my abilities? It's called Restoration. I can recover HP for me and my pets while communing with nature. The only downside is that I'm immobile while I do it, so I need someone to watch my back to make sure I'm not attacked." He climbs on the back of the freshly-healed bear. "Now, how about we see what else this dungeon has to offer?"

CHAPTER NINETEEN

PEST CONTROL

The Marshlands. Or as I like to call it, The Suckity Swamp, also known as a great way to use all your health potions while helping your scrub friend level up in the worst terrain possible.

For the next few hours, we slay mutated crocodiles the size of a small truck, go half-deaf fighting bats that do sonic damage, and fend off a nasty school of barracuda. Taryn uses his level eleven stat point to learn Imbue, an ability that increases the size of a summoned monster or pet. I stay back as much as possible, so I'm still a ways off from hitting level twenty.

Imbue is actually a pretty cool ability. He can even cast it on my horrors, effectively doubling their size. The long cooldown means Taryn can usually only imbue one pet at a time unless it's a super long fight. Berry is the chosen target more often than not, and when imbued, he even towers above me. He tanks the monsters and when the fight is over, Taryn heals him back to full health. The crocodiles fall a lot easier when he's tanking the brunt of the damage. Once we put a little armor on him, he'll be a force of nature.

There's not a lot of good loot from the monsters we've killed, so I'm holding out hope that whatever boss we stumble upon has all the spoils.

"That's my last potion." After another battle with a crocodile, I toss the vial into my satchel. "I'll need to search for ingredients to craft more once we're done with this place."

"You think we'll finish by dark?" Taryn gazes towards the horizon. We can't have more than an hour of daylight left.

"Doubtful. And I don't think that barrier is going down until we beat the boss." In the twilight, the barrier is even more pronounced. It seems to have its own ethereal glow.

As the day comes to a close, the rattle of insects grows louder. Limery and I will be fine to fight at night, but Taryn doesn't have our night vision. And this is definitely not a suitable place to camp, when creatures are lurking just below the surface.

Berry comes to a stop, pawing at something buried in the mud.

"What's this?" Taryn dismounts to get a better look.

Berry continues digging around the object. It's some sort of shell, dark brown and about the size of a trashcan. It looks almost like a cocoon with its layered ridges.

"I don't know, but I'd rather not find out. Go ahead and smash it. Maybe you'll get some free XP."

Taryn takes the end of his staff and jabs it against the shell. The shell doesn't break, but a small crack forms. Then, the shell shakes, something moving inside.

"Limery, burn it before it hatches," I order.

He tosses a fireball, but it doesn't explode the shell. Instead, the shell absorbs the heat, turning a vibrant red. A claw breaks through the crack where Taryn stabbed it, and the shell begins to crumble from the inside.

Without warning, the shell explodes, raining bits of debris all over us as a giant winged creature emerges. It flaps its wings, taking flight, and a deep rattle resonates from its chest.

Glouwseeker. *Level 15. While fragile and harmless in their larva state, once evolved, these winged insects are deadly warriors. Their stingers are coated with a paralyzing venom, capable of immobilizing even the liveliest of enemies. Like most insectoids, they have a fascination with lights.*

Great. Giant bugs.

Fully unraveled, the bug is monstrous. A good five feet with double the wingspan. A dangerous proboscis, capable of stabbing or drawing blood, protrudes between giant, bubble eyes. Six long, spike-covered legs attach to its thorax, and a nasty-looking stinger extends from the bottom of its abdomen, coated in a slimy substance. Two translucent wings flap rapidly, keeping it afloat.

This bug was made for battle.

Taryn draws first blood, hitting the giant bug with a lightning bolt. The energy runs through its exoskeleton, briefly revealing its hollow insides.

The bug dives for Taryn, ripping the dwarf from his mount with its serrated legs and flying off. I quickly cast a Horror of Vitality and sling it by its horn at the glouwseeker, exploding it at the same time as Limery's fireballs burn through one of its wings.

Our attacks cause the insect to drop Taryn, and he lands in the mud with a splat.

With only one wing, the bug falls to the ground on top of him. Once he's downed, it's pretty easy to finish him off.

"That wasn't so ba—"

Something wet plops against my back. A second later, my back burns like hell and I turn to see three more of the bugs hovering in the air. One of them spits a green ooze from its proboscis that goes sailing by my head.

"Watch out for the ooze! It burns like hell." The stinging pain doesn't fade as I get into position. "Limery, take out their wings."

A lightning bolt crashes into one of the insects, while another dives for Taryn. They must really have a thing for dwarves.

Limery zooms through the air, slinging fireballs and lighting up the sky with his personal brand of fireworks. He takes out the wings of one of the bugs, and I turn my attention to the other two. The wingless one can wait.

Berry stands at his full height, protecting Taryn as one of the bugs harasses them. It changes course at the last second, extending its stinger and injecting the bear right in the chest before zipping away.

Paralyzed, Berry falls to the ground. Taryn rushes to aid his downed mount.

"Leave him," I order. "You can heal him after the battle. Right now, I need your help."

In response, he calls another bolt of lightning. This time, it lets off a chain reaction, jumping from one bug to the other. Their exoskeletons glow as electricity courses through them. I try to swat at them with my staff, but they flutter just out of reach. Limery zooms through the air, but the bugs seem determined to avoid his fireballs.

The one downed bug crawls across the marsh toward Berry, its long legs refusing to sink in the mud.

I take off toward the insect and tackle it into the water. Its chitinous shell cuts against my body like barbed wire. Even with my thick skin, it stings pretty bad. I wrap my hands around one of its barbed legs, using my strength to crack it in two. A dark yellow substance drains out like rotten crab legs. Activating Claw, I rip a hole in its abdomen, spilling its innards. It sinks to the bottom of the marsh.

One down, two to go.

Back on land, Limery has downed another bug. Without wings, it moves in a grotesque manner, bending several sets of knees like something out of a horror movie.

Taryn calls forth another lightning bolt, and this time, it's lucky enough to stun. He then transforms into a replica of Berry and rips two of the bug's legs off one side before the stun wears off. Imbalanced, the bug stumbles in the mud and Taryn moves in for the finishing blow, ripping its head off and spilling yellow ichor into the marsh.

Limery and the final glowseeker play a game of dodgeball in the air. Limery tosses his fireballs and the creature shoots its acidic projectiles, each one missing by only inches.

I summon two horrors and toss them at the insect, exploding them just before impact. The bug turns towards the distraction, which is all Limery needs to damage one of its wings.

"Thanks, Chods!" he shouts.

By the time we kill it, Taryn is already healing Berry.

"Good job, guys. That was some quick adaptation."

Taryn is oblivious to my comments as he communes with nature to heal himself and his bear. Limery flies over to the decapitated glowseeker and dips his finger in the yellow goo that spills out of its neck. He licks it and then spits it out.

"Yuck, Limmy no like." He scrunches his nose and continues spitting like a cat that just licked a lemon.

I use my empty vials to milk some of the venom from the glowseekers's stingers.

Item. Glowseeker Venom. *When injected into the bloodstream, glowseeker venom immobilizes target. Length of stun dependent on size of target, resistances, and amount injected.*

"Pretty neat," I say as I describe the effects to Taryn.

"Berry caught the full stinger to the chest, no wonder he froze. Almost to level twelve, though," says Taryn. He pats Berry on the head and the bear grunts softly, no traces of its previous wounds. "It's getting dark. What should we do now?"

"I've got an idea that might bring a few more glowseekers to us now that it's dark." And hopefully some easy XP.

With the remaining daylight, we gather reeds, dead bushes, anything that seems the least bit flammable, and the bodies of the fallen glowseekers. We pile them together on the densest plot of mud we can find, until we have a pyre that is five feet tall.

"You think this is going to work?" Taryn looks skeptically at the pile of debris and body parts.

I shrug. "If not, I think we are mightily fucked." Truthfully, I've got a very good feeling about this.

"That's reassuring." He turns to Berry. "If we die, it was nice knowing you." Berry gives him a sad groan.

"Alright, I'm going to step away now. All of this experience is for you and Limery. Don't screw this up and maybe we can get the hell out of here." I give them a wide berth and wait for Camouflage to take effect, saying a silent prayer that just because we're in a fantasy game, some things never change.

When I'm far enough away, lightning shoots from the sky, hitting the pyre and starting a small fire. Two orange balls of flame erupt in Limery's palms. He tosses them into the pyre and it rages even higher, sending flames shooting into the night sky.

The call of insects roars across the open expanse as the fire crackles.

Dark shapes begin moving across my night vision. Suddenly, a giant fireball explodes as one of the glowseekers barrels into the flames. A bolt of lightning zaps the pyre, sending a thousand tiny embers drifting through the air.

The air around me fills with buzzing as dozens of glowseekers and other insects are enraptured by the giant beacon. One by one, they burst into flames, drawn to death's beautiful and fiery embrace.

For half an hour, I sit back and watch as they add their bodies to the pyre, growing it higher and higher. Eventually, the winged meteors become less and less frequent as the population dies off, until finally minutes pass between deaths.

"You genius!" Taryn pushes me when I return. "That was bloody brilliant! I got three levels off of that. Three levels!" He grins from ear to ear. "I went ahead and upgraded Lightning Bolt to level two so that it deals more damage and cuts down on the cooldown."

"'Bloody brilliant?' You want some tea and crumpets with that?" I roll my eyes. "What about you, Limery?"

Limery gives me a devilish grin and then explodes into flames. Not just his hands, but his entire body. Even from several feet away, I can feel the heat radiating from him. I have to put my hand up to shield my eyes.

"Limmy doesn't just makes fire. Limmy is fire," he laughs at his own joke.

With the experience from all those kills, Taryn is now level fourteen. Limery is not far behind me at level seventeen. All in all, our squad is pretty strong. I wonder if anyone else thought to power-level this way. I don't imagine too many people choosing to tackle this dungeon at night.

The marsh is eerily quiet with the glouwseekers gone. There's the occasional splash and slither in the depths, but the slosh of Berry's footsteps is the loudest thing around.

"Could you be any louder?" I ask Taryn.

The torch he carries made from a glouwseeker leg leaves nothing to the imagination when he flashes me a rude gesture. "Oh, I'm sorry that I don't have a pair of magical boots for me and my bear."

"Three levels and he thinks he's the king of the world. I'm just trying to help you out. Making that much noise, you'll be the first target if—"

A shrill hiss cuts me off.

CHAPTER TWENTY

DRAGOMANDER

Water sprays us as a large, dragon-like creature emerges from the marshy waters. It's at least ten feet long from nose to tail, shaped like a salamander, and perfectly fitted to conceal its massive body beneath the shallow depths of the marsh. From an orange and black speckled head, two large, glossy black eyes stare at us, reflecting the flame from Taryn's torch. Its slick, scale-less skin shimmers against the dancing light.

We're going to need more than a single torch for Taryn to see well enough to fight.

The creature's mouth is wide and curved, unlike the pointed snout of most dragons. It hisses menacingly before a forked tongue extends and tastes the air. Two small wings that look more for show than flying adorn the shoulders of the long, winding creature.

Dragomander. *Level 17. This amphibious, fire-breathing dragon is equally dangerous whether on land or water.*

With each predatory step, webbed feet keep it from sinking as they splat against the mud. It takes a few more steps before hissing again, making a show of dominance.

"You think this is the boss?" asks Taryn. He plants the torch in the mud and grips the fur of Berry's neck with one hand while holding his staff in the other, ready for a fight.

"I don't know. Usually, bosses are a little more unique." It looks tough, but one single monster for all of this seems a little too easy.

"It's a dragon-salamander. How does it get more unique than that?" He gives me a bug-eyed look and shrugs.

"I guess we'll—"

Another splash cuts me off as a second dragomander appears from the water. This one is twice as large, with two heads.

Twin-headed Dragomander. *Unique Monster. Level 20. Mutated by the ancient rune magic of the marshlands, both heads are capable of emitting elemental magic.*

Awesome. If fire-breathing wasn't enough, this one gets elemental magic, too. The twin-headed dragomander steps beside the lesser beast. As it stands there, the coloring of its skin changes from orange to yellow to blue, like a rotating advertisement in Times Square. It doesn't just reflect the firelight, the coloring of its skin seems to come from within, much like my own mana-infused skin.

Both heads let out a hiss, and the other dragomander joins in. A moment later, a third dragomander, this one level seventeen, crawls from the water.

"I don't know how many more there are, but I suggest we get to fighting before they call in any more friends." I grip Forlorn Scepter tight, readying my mana for a brawl. This is going to be a tough fight, seeing as how they already out-level us and I don't have any horrors at the ready.

Poor foresight on my part.

A lightning bolt smashes into the boss monster, starting the battle. The flash of lightning ignites the sky for a moment, and the twin-headed dragomander launches at Taryn with ridiculous speed, knocking Berry aside with its massive body and sending Taryn flying through the air. It lunges at his floundering body as Taryn is tossed skyward. At the last moment, Taryn transforms into a red bird and zips out of the way, leaving the monster snapping at air.

I don't waste any time watching the battle unfold before jumping into the action and summoning three quick horrors. Limery pummels the dragomander closest to him with fireballs, drawing its attention and leaving the final monster to me. A jet of flame pours from its mouth, setting the three horrors ablaze. I quickly use Kamikaze to explode them, taking out a chunk of health and dealing as much damage as I can before my horrors perish.

Fire. "Why is it always fire?"

"Limmy likes fire!" the imp shouts from over my shoulder.

I turn to see him, body aflame, riding the other dragomander like a cowboy as it tries to buck him off. His tiny hands hold onto the dragomander's small wings while the rest of him bounces with each thrashing movement. The beast's health slowly fades from Limery's radiating heat.

Pain flares through one entire side of my body as fire engulfs me. Flames sear my flesh, and the heat distorts my vision. My health drops by ten percent from a single attack, and the lingering burn damage takes slivers of HP each second. Half my body burns, but I try to fight through the pain as I attempt to locate the monster, but before I can, another wall of flame scorches my backside. A quarter of my health is gone in an instant.

Abandoning all thoughts of fighting, I run toward the water. Toward safety. When I jump, my Aquatic Boots keep me from its cool embrace. Without thinking, I take off the boots and toss them aside, sinking into the muddy water. The burning slowly fades, and I suddenly realize what a big mistake I've made just as something slimy and cold coils around my midsection, pinning my arms to my sides.

I'm only a few feet below the surface, but the clenching tightness around my body weighs me down as the dragomander attempts to crush my ribs and drown me. I fight the coiling dragon, but this is what it was made for. I'm in its element now. Its grip is ironclad against my body. The more I struggle, the tighter it becomes. As my lungs beg for air, stars dance at my vision in the blurry water.

I hope Taryn and Limery are having better luck than I am, because I'm about to be dead.

Not knowing what else to do, I activate Berserker Rage. The ability that has saved my life more times than I can count. My body grows stronger from the increased stats, putting even more stress on my bones as they fight against the mounting pressure. My health regenerates rapidly, healing my burned body and mending my tired muscles, but it does nothing for the fact that I am a sinking weight in the muddy marsh water. I try to walk, to grip anything, but the silty bottom only sucks me deeper.

I feel a rush of water around me, and claws dig into my shoulders. My body slowly moves toward the bank.

The claws shred my skin, but I'm grateful for the pain when my head breaks through the surface and air rushes into my lungs. Not enough air to fill my lungs, but enough to put the stars in my vision at bay.

Berry unleashes a monstrous roar as he tries to peel the dragomander from around me. His teeth sink into the dragon's neck, but the creature only grips tighter. It would rather die than release me.

Thank God for that bear. If I make it out of this, I'll never make fun of his stupid name again.

Limery zips through the edge of my vision, and I turn just in time to see a bolt of lightning shooting into the air, missing him by inches.

Why in the hell is Taryn shooting lightning at Limery?

Berserker Rage ends and my muscles reduce to their normal size. The momentary slack in the dragon's coil gives me enough leeway to squeeze my arms free. With a full rage bar, I activate Claw and rip through the dragomander's flesh. It lets out a shrill hiss and squeezes tighter around my midsection. It hurts like hell, but at least now I can fight back.

The dragomander's body goes hot as it erupts a stream of flame, but the fire shoots into the sky, burning no one. Berry still has his teeth sunk like a vice into the monster's neck, able to aim the blast like a firehose. My body jerks with each massive heave as Berry pulls at the dragomander's neck like a dog playing tug-of-war.

I quickly burn through all my rage, clawing the dragomander until its ribs are exposed and my sharp claws can puncture its insides.

I bury my hand inside its body, my sharp nails ripping through organs until finally, the tension releases and I can take my first full breath since the fight began. I barely enjoy my first unencumbered breath before a cannonball of ice knocks me on my ass.

"Chods!" Limery's voice rings out from somewhere nearby as I suck at air. "Chods, is yous okay?" That should be his catchphrase at this point. His warm hands grip my shoulder as I stumble to my feet. He grabs me by the tusk and forces my head towards him, his giant yellow eyes examining me.

"I'm fine. What the hell just happened?" The huge ball of ice that nearly killed me sits in the mud, slowly melting.

With my dragomander dead, Berry has already joined another fight. He charges the two-headed beast, his muscles rippling beneath thick fur with each step.

I look around, but Taryn is nowhere to be seen, though I do spot the corpse of the other one-headed dragomander.

There's no time to search out Taryn. Berry and Limery's safety depend on me finding a way to defeat this monster. If Taryn is dead, he will respawn. They won't be so lucky.

Berry is a few steps from the twin-headed dragomander when its skin changes from light blue to yellow. It rears back one of its heads and a stream of lightning explodes from its mouth, setting Berry's hair on end and stunning him in place. The second head changes color, turning back to light blue and unleashing a stream of ice that freezes Berry for even longer. The bear's fur is covered in a thick layer of ice as he stands there, unable to move. The two attacks drop his health by half.

Now, I understand. Each color that the dragomander changes to affects the elemental attacks it uses.

Rather than let the bear die while I stand by watching like a jackass, I jump into action, summoning three horrors and tossing them at the dragomander. I explode them when they are in range. Without my Aquatic Boots, I sink into the mud with each step, making it hard to gather any speed for a physical assault.

Whatever Taryn and Limery did to fight the beast worked, because its HP is over halfway gone. It's not very tanky; the damage it deals is our main source of concern. Getting close enough to deal damage to it is the problem.

There's a rustle in the nearby bushes and Taryn appears from a thicket with nearly three-quarters health.

"Thanks for holding it off while I healed, Limmy." He lifts his staff and a bolt of lightning strikes the monster. "Chod, glad you could finally join us."

The dragomander shoots flame in his direction, but he swiftly transforms into a bird and dodges the attack. A moment later, he returns to his dwarven form, unleashing another bolt of lightning. He's mastered the ability to use Transform as a defensive maneuver.

He casts Imbue on Berry, and the bear nearly doubles in size. The spell also grants him a small boost of health.

Limery summons a flame wall between the dragomander and Berry, protecting the bear from being trampled while he's stunned. The imp follows up with a barrage of fireballs.

Both dragomander heads turn dark blue and spit out a blast of water, turning Limery's fireballs into puffs of steam.

I continue throwing horror bombs as quickly as they become available. Each explosion takes out a fraction of the monster's health.

Fire, ice, water, and electricity cycle through the dragomander's attacks. We dodge what we can, but the twin heads act of their own accord, seemingly attacking at random. The lightning attacks are the worst, as there is no rhyme or reason to their path of madness. They explode out of the dragomander's mouth, zig-zagging until finding a target.

Poor Berry takes a massive beating. He and I are the only ones willing to get within the monster's range and he lacks my mobility, even with Taryn's Strong Wind buff increasing our movement speed.

He and I spread out, taking opposite sides and keeping the dragomander from focusing on either one of us for too long. When the monster charges, Taryn and Limery attack it from the rear, drawing its attention to the other side. When it charges again, they repeat the process.

Limery, Taryn, and I slice down the monster's health from afar with fire, lightning, and exploding horrors until it eventually collapses.

When the dragomander falls, the barrier around the Marshlands vanishes. Several notifications clutter my vision, but I focus them away for now. My muscles bulge slightly, letting me know without checking that I just hit level twenty.

A glowing stone falls from the dragomander just as tiny bubbles form in the marsh's waters. They grow bigger, until they are the size of my head. For a moment, I'm afraid the battle isn't over. Then I notice several chests have floated to the surface. Each one has a faint aura around it. Runes run along their weathered lids.

"Sweet! We've got loot." I slosh through the marsh and gather two of the wooden chests, piling them on land. Each one is waterlogged and slimy. Who knows how long they have sat at the bottom of this marsh. The metal clasps are rusted, and the wooden corners have been weathered to a smooth surface.

Limery sways through the air, his eyes full of greed as he carries a chest nearly as large as he is. Nearby, Taryn focuses on healing Berry. The fiery surroundings offer him enough light to see by.

By the time Taryn finishes communing with nature, Limery has already cracked the ancient lock. He flips the lid and buries his head inside.

His lips pout when he lifts a water-filled jar from the chest. Flashes of white clink against the jar, barely visible in the muddy water. He opens the lid and pours out its contents, letting them fall through his fingers.

Item. Jar of Teeth. *Nothing special, just a jar of teeth.*

"Limmy no likes." His frown grows larger.

The teeth fall to the ground and disappear into the mud.

"Maybe if you weren't so greedy," I offer, but Limery has already buried his head back in the chest, riffling through its contents.

Taryn takes a chest for himself and sets it down beside me. "Let's hope I fare a little better." He strikes the lock with his staff and it comes undone.

"Wait." I stop him. "First, I want to know how both of you killed the first drago-mander." I'm a higher level and almost died to one. They killed the first and put a dent in the boss monster, too. It doesn't make any sense.

Taryn waits to open the chest. "You can thank Limery for that. He basically boiled the dragomander alive. I guess they mimic their temperature to their surroundings like most reptiles and amphibians, because he did his little flame thing and pretty soon, its chest exploded. We were able to tag-team the big one, until I noticed you were getting your ass kicked and sent Berry to help you."

"And a good thing, too." I pat him on the shoulder. "I owe you one for that."

"How about we loot this treasure and call it even?" He flashes me a toothy grin.

"Deal."

Taryn lifts the lid and reaches in. After a few seconds, he pulls out a gnarled and waterlogged staff. It looks like trash, much like the chest, with a cloudy stone set in the tip. I focus on the staff and analyze its stats.

Item. Staff of the Marshes. *+1 Intelligence. An enchanted staff, capable of muddying any water source.*

"Dude, this is so lame. When would anyone ever have a need for this?" Taryn jabs the end of the staff into the mud and searches for more items. "What a crappy dungeon."

Limery continues to take items out of his own chest. So far, he has a soggy boot, a couple of empty jars, and a sack of bronze coins. Hardly a treasure.

After pulling out the other matching soggy boot, he kicks the chest away and crosses his arms. "Hmmph." He pouts.

Berry sits on his butt watching the show unfold. The next item Taryn pulls out is a bow. The string is made of some kind of marsh weed, and the wood looks like it might snap with the least bit of pressure.

"Oh, wow..." Taryn's sudden change of tone has me interested.

Item. Bog Bow. *Capable of firing arrows underwater as if on land. Arrows will fly as true as the archer's aim.*

Wow, indeed. "That's actually a damn good weapon."

"Yeah," echoes Taryn. "But realistically, when would we ever use it? Neither one of us can breathe underwater. How often are we going to be battling sea creatures?" He lays the bow aside.

The seaside trolls would have a use for it. "I bet it'll fetch a high price at an auction."

Next, he pulls out a brown orb. It looks like a coconut, but with a green weed dangling out of it.

Item. Bog Bomb. *An explosive with a waterproof fuse.*

"Pretty cool. There's two of them." Taryn's smiles as he looks them over. "Okay, these we can definitely use. There's one more chest. Do you want to do the honors?"

I twist the lock and the wood creaks as the latch gives way. I lift the lid in antici-pation of the crappy loot that awaits.

The first item is a vial of dark purple liquid.

__Item. Infernal Darkness Potion.__ Covers opponent in a veil of darkness, making them unable to see or smell their surroundings for one minute.

Not bad. I pull out another vial. This one is a deep pink color with a layer of black silt on the bottom.

__Legendary Item. Angel of Death Brandy.__ When drinker falls below 1HP, a metaphysical event will occur, rewinding time for the user to two seconds prior to death.

Taryn and I both just stare at each other. Essentially, we just found an extra life. One with no penalties, no levels lost, and no respawns.

"Holy shit, this is huge." I carefully place the vial aside.

"No shit. Is there anything else?"

I rake my fingers against the bottom of the chest and touch something metal. It's heavy as I lift it, one end weighing far more than the other.

The chest must be enchanted, because what I pull out couldn't possibly fit inside.

When I take the item out, the trident shimmers with the reflection of the surrounding flames. Runes run all along its golden shaft, and there is an indentation beneath the barbed spears for attaching an enchanted stone.

__Item. Sea Scorpion.__ An enchanted trident capable of taking on the property of 1 enchanted stone. Bonus: deals splash damage. +3 Strength.

The only other weapon I've seen capable of taking on enchanted stones was Peacemaker. They must be pretty rare.

I equip the trident and feel its weight in my hand. The six-foot-long spear gives me plenty of reach. I know I have my staffs, but this just feels so much more natural. I'm not meant to stand back and cast spells. I'm meant to be in the action, fighting side by side with my horrors as we overwhelm opponents with brute force and violence. With Taryn leveling up, I can get back to my more natural role.

What's the point of having this strong body if I'm just going to play it safe? I practice a few thrusts. I could skewer several enemies at once on its pointed tips.

"What makes you think you get the trident?" asks Taryn. He stands beside me, arms crossed in expectation.

"Because I can actually lift it without falling over."

He stares at me for a moment before bursting into laughter. "You got me there." The metal clasps in his beard jingle against one another as his chest rumbles. "What do you say we get the hell out of this shithole and make camp?"

After retrieving my Aquatic Boots, we divide the rest of our loot, setting aside what we will keep and what we will trade. In the end, Taryn takes the Bog Bombs and the Infernal Darkness Potion. We elect to auction or sell the Bog Bow and the Staff of the Marshes. Not sure of how to handle the Angel of Death Brandy, I hold on to it for now. I'm sure it could fetch a small fortune. It's probably something even kings would fight over. For now, we'll keep it hidden. Limery's items are all returned safely to the chest he pulled them out of, minus the teeth that have by now settled into the mud.

"Wait a sec!" I suddenly remember the stone that fell from the dragomander and rush to the monster's corpse. The glowing stone has submerged into the mud, but it still casts a faint glow from beneath.

I dig my hand in and pull out the stone. It cycles through the same colors as the host it came from.

Item. Elemental Stone. *10% bonus to elemental attacks.*

The stone would be great for Limery or Taryn, seeing as how they both use elemental damage, but I have the feeling that Taryn could use the boost more than the imp right now.

I hand him the stone and he uses it to replace the boar tusk that was attached to his staff. I didn't realize his staff was capable of taking enchanted stones.

"We'll get you something next time, buddy." I try to comfort Limery, but his inner greedy pig refuses to be placated for the moment.

He sits on my shoulder, stewing as we make our way back to solid ground.

Now that we are in the boring part, I pull up the notifications I discarded earlier.

You have defeated a unique monster: Twin-headed Dragomander.

Item. Elemental Stone. *10% bonus to elemental attacks.*

Congratulations! You have reached level 20. +1 stat point to distribute. +1 Strength and Constitution racial bonus.

New ability unlocked.

Sweet, it's been a while since I've gotten a new ability. Too bad I don't get another ability point until level twenty-one. I pull up my abilities, focusing on the ones that haven't been unlocked. They are separated by the class or trait that unlocked them.

Barbarian:

Iron Will. *Immune to slows and stuns for 30 seconds. Cost: 50 rage. 180 second cooldown.*

I'm Always Angry (Passive). *Once rage meter is at 50%, it will not deteriorate below 50% when out of combat.*

Both of these seem like a waste of an ability point now that I have better abilities.

Melee:

Cleave. *Your next attack causes bleed damage, dealing 1% of opponent's health per second for 5 seconds. Cost: 10 rage.*

Battle Cry. *You let out a ferocious roar, increasing rage by 20. No Cost. 60 second cooldown.*

Cleave could be useful. I wonder if it stacks with Claw or Bite?

• • •

Wisdom:

Perception. *For 10 minutes, gain increased awareness of your surroundings. Spot hidden objects, as well as unusual sounds, odors, and tastes. Cooldown: 6 hours.*

This is nice, but not much better than what I can already craft with a perception potion.

***New* Summoner:**

***New* Champion.** *Summon a copy of the most recent enemy you have defeated. Decays 10% every minute out of combat. Cost: 50% of mana pool. Cooldown: 6 hours.*

Holy smokes! The ability to summon whatever I have killed recently. Imagine summoning a dragomander or a mana-infused wyrm. They could turn a fight instantly. The mana cost is pretty high, as well as the cooldown, but that ability will be a game-changer once I unlock it.

I briefly glance over the rest of my unlocked abilities. None of them are a priority and half of them are easily covered by abilities I already have. Aside from Perception, I doubt I will be using a hard-earned ability point on any of them.

When I analyze Taryn, it looks like he has gained another level, too.

All in all, not a bad day.

CHAPTER TWENTY-ONE
SMALLTOWN

As soon as we are out of the Marshlands, we make camp for the night underneath a towering oak. Its leaves rustle together in a gentle lullaby. After so much fighting, Taryn and I are both pretty wiped out.

The ebony dwarf uses his cloak as a blanket as he lays against the soft fur of his bear. Limery takes his normal sleeping position in my arms.

The last of my horrors pops out of existence nearby. They are steadfast guardians until their health fades to nothing. Since finding myself unprepared in the marsh, I try to keep a constant supply at the ready when we are traveling. Unless I know for a fact we are safe, it pays to be prepared.

"I know that we got some pretty good items." Taryn pulls his cloak up like a blanket, obscuring everything but his bearded head. "But that place really was a shithole. I'll be happy if we never go back. I say we stick to solid ground from now on."

"I respect that. Perhaps tomorrow we can go see what scared away the moulhaugs. Now that you've leveled up a little, I don't feel so worried about you dying at the drop of a hat."

Taryn mumbles something about saving my ass before drifting off to sleep. Limery snores softly, blowing warm breath against my bicep.

His bulbous eyes shift underneath his closed lids. I wonder what he is dreaming about. Killing birds or stealing coins, probably. He doesn't look it, but Limery has grown into a powerful imp. The day I met him might be one of the luckiest moments I've had in my life. At level eighteen, he could rival almost any of the other heroes in a duel. And his power, it's raw, elemental magic, never seeming to fade. That, combined with his blinding speed and small target zone, makes him a force to be reckoned with. Not to mention his never-ending desire to make sure I don't die.

Better than all of that, he's a great friend. Sure, he's wild at times, but he's still young. In time, I have no doubt that he will outgrow his less endearing qualities.

Closing my eyes, I let the sounds of the night lull me to sleep.

The next thing I know, the smell of roasting meat wakes me. I open my eyes to find Limery turning a spit loaded with four birds over an open flame.

"You're up early." I wipe the sleep from my eyes.

Berry sits next to Limery, drooling in anticipation of a delicious treat. After yesterday, I'd say he's earned it.

"Limmy was hungry. Didn't wants to wake Chods." He takes one of the birds off the spit, grabbing it with his open palm, and hands it to Berry without so much as a wince.

I guess all the fire he handles makes him pretty much immune to burns. Berry devours the bird in only a few bites and hungrily waits for more.

"Where is Taryn?" I ask. He's nowhere to be found, but his bags are still next to the tree. It seems like I was the last one to wake.

"He goes flying. Saids he wants to look ahead." Limery pulls off another bird and tosses it to me, then takes one for himself. His razor-sharp teeth rip the meat apart.

Truth be told, transforming into a small bird might not be the smartest option for Taryn.

I take my time with breakfast, electing to actually savor what I eat. As I'm gathering our belongings, Taryn appears on a branch above my head, his short stubby legs dangling just above my eyesight.

"Morning," he says with a smile.

"What has you so chipper?" I toss my satchel over my shoulder and grab Sea Scorpion. The trident feels more natural almost every time I hold it.

"Have you ever watched the sun rise from a thousand feet in the air? Without a building in sight to block the view?" His smile grows a little wider, reaching all the way to his dark brown eyes. "I'll never get used to it. Birds might not be the toughest of creatures, but damn, do they get a view."

I've never watched the sun rise from a thousand feet, but I get what he means. The little things about this game are what make it so unique. What will make it a hit if it ever goes mainstream. It's not always about fighting and weapons, but those small experiences that actually make you feel like you are here, that you are a part of something bigger. Here, the fantasy is real.

"See anything good while you were up there?" I gaze out to the mountains looming in the distance.

"More moulhaugs moving south. Whatever is happening at the base of the mountain, they want no part in it." He slides from the branch and lands with a soft thud.

"Let's check it out then."

The journey to the mountain is boring and uneventful. We make our way back to the Mythroad and pass a few travelers as we head north. Most of them are clad in dull rags. I'm sure the sight of a troll, an imp, a dwarf, and a bear is quite alarming, because many of the other travelers clear the road altogether, stepping aside or hiding behind trees or bushes.

This is all still new to them and will be for some time, so I try not to take offense. We're so far away from Vanaria and its protections that I'm sure these people are used to fending for themselves.

"If you weren't so ugly, they probably wouldn't be so scared," Taryn teases. "The rest of us are pretty lovable." He winks.

Limery snorts on my shoulder and I conveniently stretch, raising my arms overhead and knocking him to the ground. He frowns at me and crosses his arms, before sticking out his tongue and flying ahead.

There are not many houses or farms this far from Lynchton. According to my map, the closest settlement is a small trading post at the base of the mountain.

With the Greystone Mountains looming ever larger, they appear almost insurmountable. Their snow-covered peaks reach above the clouds in places and stretch from one side of the isle to the other. The only way to travel from the southern half of the island to the north is by climbing over. No wonder the two kingdoms don't trade more.

Fast-travel could change all that. The ability to get from Vanaria to Seascape in a matter of minutes instead of weeks. Too bad the portals are closed. Perhaps forever. Hiding whatever dark secrets loom on the other side.

No, they wouldn't be there if they were going to remain closed forever. There are other continents out there. Other races. More quests and objectives. If the portals are still there, then there has to be a quest to unlock them. The next time we are in a capital city, I need to spend some time investigating.

When I first logged into *Isle of Mythos*, I saw the world. It was large and sprawling. This small island is but a blip on the map. There's—

"Snap out of it." Taryn whacks me on the shoulder with his staff. "You see that?" He points to a giant boulder in the distance.

It sits off to the side of the road next to a lone oak. Now that I think about it, I haven't seen any boulders for miles. Kind of a random place for a rock so large.

The wind changes direction and I'm hit with a whiff of rotting flesh. Then I realize that it's no boulder. "Moulhaug?"

Taryn nods, covering his nose with his cloak.

When we arrive, the moulhaug is rotten to the core. Exposed ribs frame a rancid cavity filled with squirming maggots. My stomach turns at the sight, and Limery casts a fireball, holding it close to his nose. Even Berry lets out a dissatisfied groan.

"Something big had to have caused this. Something, really, really big. You see that?" He points to the moulhaug's face. Several gashes run along the side of its head. Big, seeping gashes. "Those are claw marks."

Remembering our own encounter with a moulhaug, it was like fighting a bulldozer. It would take something truly powerful to inflict that kind of damage.

"Limery, can you burn the body? Let's try to do everyone within a mile radius a favor and end this smell?"

Limery plugs his nose and erects two fire walls on both sides of the carcass. He then hits it with several fireballs until it begins to cook. Cooked meat, even if it's rotten, will smell a hundred times better than the current situation.

Over the next few hours, we burn two more moulhaugs before arriving at the small settlement at the base of the mountain.

The settlement is just that, not nearly big enough to be called a town or a village. It has a small inn, a shop, and a stable. There are no houses or huts, so I can only imagine that the workers all live at the inn.

A small sign in front of the inn reads, "Welcome to Smalltown."

How original.

First, we step into the shop. Berry waits outside with my horrors. I'm sure a troll, a bear, and several dozen demonic looking creatures would be a little much for whoever waits inside.

The inside of the shop is filled with basic necessities for traversing a mountain. Spikes, pickaxes, ropes, satchels, and blankets adorn one wall. Another has potions and pots filled with herbs and powders. A bin in the center has an array of basic weapons. A rack of dull black tunics and cloaks sits beside it.

"All of this is way overpriced." Taryn holds one of the potions in his hand. "Kind of like running out of gas in the desert."

I don't have much experience with potion prices, but I'll take his word for it.

An old, balding man with a fluffy gray beard sits behind the counter with his eyes closed. I tap a bell sitting in front of him and it rings, startling him awake.

"Uhnn." He looks lost for a moment. "Uh, sorry. How can I help you?" He sits forward and adjusts his tunic. The ends of the fabric are tattered, and several holes adorn one shoulder.

"We're just passing through. We saw the moulhaug carcasses on the way in. I was wondering if you had any information on what was killing them?"

"Not in the slightest." He shrugs. "Not many people come through these parts nowadays. Most of our staff have left to safer areas. Those of us that remain, we don't get out much. Too many dangers to risk one's life."

"What do you mean, 'too many dangers'?" I ask.

He sighs, and then scratches his beard, making it look even fluffier. "Monsters killing moulhaugs. Bandits robbing and killing travelers. No offense to you, I'm aware of the king's peace with the forest trolls, but the mountain trolls and goblins are always a problem to anyone passing through the mountain. They say that the heroes are supposed to set the world right, but it seems they bring more problems with them."

"Have bandits always been a problem?"

"Never before. But with half a dozen attacks this week, people are afraid to venture north. The western passages may be safer. I've sent a raven to the king, but this far north, I doubt we'll receive help."

Taryn and I make eye contact. "This has the smell of Glenn and Jude all over it.

They know they can't set foot in a shop, so they are killing people and taking their belongings."

Taryn steps forward. "If we find these bandits, we'll make sure they pay for all the trouble they've caused."

"Heh." He looks Taryn square in the eye. "What's a life worth to someone who never dies?" An awkward silence hangs in the air. "If there's nothing I can help you with, there's plenty of room in the inn."

Outside of the shop, Taryn finally speaks. "Damn, he really has something against heroes. And you're a troll hero. That makes you a double whammy."

"Don't worry, Chods. Limmy likes yous." He puts his hand on my neck.

"Thanks, buddy."

We have no intention of staying the night in the inn, so we set out along the base of the mountain. Since we are low on potions, I use the time to level up my herbalism skill and make more health potions. I still have a fair amount of blood-fennel, but I need more horned thimbleberry and powdered crow's feet to complete the potion.

"Limery, do you think you can track me down some crows' feet?"

He gives me a wicked grin and then disappears into the trees.

I activate my herbalism skill, and the outlines of all the plants I have identified glow in the distance. It makes it easy to locate exactly what I'm looking for, since I can filter out specific plants to locate. I wish I had spent more time with Yashi to learn more. Perhaps, when we return. Actually...

"You're a druid, right?" I ask Taryn.

He cocks an eyebrow. "What gave it away?"

"I mean, that means you have a strong knowledge of plants and wildlife, right?"

"Yeah, so?"

"Then you can help me increase my herbalism skill by showing me new plants. Right now, I'm looking for horned thimbleberry. But once I have enough, I'd love to learn some more. What level is your skill anyway?"

His eyes glaze over for a moment. "Right now, I'm a journeyman. You?"

"Still a novice, so I'm sure there is a lot to learn."

I find some horned thimbleberry in a thicket of bushes. The thick, brambled stems run through the bushes, making the fuzzy leaves and large pink berries diffi-cult to reach for predators.

I take the stem and berries and mash them together in my mortar with the bloodfennel and a drop of my own blood. While I wait for Limery to return with the final ingredient, Taryn introduces me to a few new varieties of plant.

"These are called golden buttons." He points to a tiny plant that grows at the base of the tree. A patch of small green leaves hugs the bark. "The flowers come out at night. They are poisonous to humans, but other races seem just fine around them. It's said that long ago, the dwarven king Voluck Lighthorn served ale brewed with golden buttons at a feast and all of the humans died. That was the beginning of what was later known as the Button War."

"How do you know all this?" That's an awful lot of detail for one plant. It's almost like he's reading from a book.

"Comes with the territory." He gives me a devious grin. "Seriously, though, my passive ability for being a druid allows me to identify certain plants and animals. My knowledge base increases as I level up." He pats me on the lower back. "Brains over brawn, my friend."

"You know you're not a dwarf in real life, right?"

"True. I've got the best of both worlds."

I roll my eyes at his stupidity. "Just show me some more plants."

Next, he shows me echo hedge, a plant that absorbs sound; spiky poppy, a beautiful yet dangerous flower; jester broadleaf, used to make laughing potions; and oboil, whose secretion causes anyone unlucky enough to brush against it to erupt into violent boils.

All the new knowledge increases my herbalism skill another level.

Congratulations! You have leveled up the skill 'Herbalism.' You are now a level 6 Herbalist (Apprentice). Increase your skill and learn advanced techniques for herbalism by finding an advanced herbalist (journeyman or above). Ranks: Novice, Apprentice, Journeyman, Expert, Artisan, Master, Grandmaster.

"Sweet! I'm an apprentice now." That makes herbalism my highest ranked skill. Close behind is my apothecary skill, used for potion-making.

Limery returns carrying a handful of crows' feet. Their bodies are nowhere to be found, but his stomach does seem to be protruding a little more than usual.

I take the feet and grind them to a paste in the mortar, then I add in the rest of the ingredients. They mix together, forming a deep red liquid that I pour into several vials. With all of this, I'm able to make a half-dozen health potions.

I offer several to Taryn, but he scrunches his nose. "Not sure I want to drink anything that has your blood in it. I think I'll stick to my natural remedies."

"You are turning into a hippy." I laugh. "Want me to gather you some flowers so you can put them in your hair and beard?"

"Save some for yourself and maybe people won't be so scared of you." He crosses his arms, waiting for my comeback.

"Whatever. At least I can reach the top shelf." That shuts him up for a minute.

We search our surroundings for clues on the giant beast, but there's no evidence of the creature that has been killing the moulhaugs. No giant footprints. Nothing. Whatever it is, it seems to be pretty selective of moulhaugs, because the trees are still full of birds. Deer and other animals roam the forest. Even wolves skulk in the shadows.

What could be singling out the moulhaugs? And why?

Hours pass as we continue our search. I'm afraid that night may come, and we'll be forced to wait until tomorrow to continue. Limery and I could search in the dark, but giving Taryn a torch to see by would draw all kinds of predators to our direction.

Taryn comes to a halt, extending his staff to block my path. "Do you hear that?"

"What?" I try to use my advanced hearing to sense anything out of the ordinary. There are animals scurrying along the forest, insects rattling, newborn birds loudly squawking somewhere nearby on the ground. I listen for the thunderous footsteps of an apex predator, but there's nothing out of the ordinary.

"What am I listening for?" I ask again.

"Babies." His face is stone cold as his eyes scan our surroundings.

"The mighty Taryn, afraid of a few baby birds?"

"Those aren't birds," he whispers. "We need to leave and come back with a plan. Before the mother retur—"

A shrill caw flares through my eardrums, and echoes across the forest. I call my horrors to my side, and we slowly back away. What is it that has Taryn so spooked? I have a full army of horrors. I'm sure we can take whatever it is.

Something silver and gray moves between the trees. It paws at the earth as it approaches, releasing threatening high-pitched screeches with each step. All other signs of wildlife have fled the scene.

A golden beak huffs in agitation as the half-eagle/half-lion walks towards us. I've seen this monster before. In Vanaria.

Griffin. *Unique monster. Level: 30. Known as the 'King of Beasts,' the griffin is one of the oldest and wisest monsters. Both proud and intelligent, they will only fight with their masters, not for them.*

Something about this one is different than the one the king rode. Something is out of place. One of its wings hangs lopsided, almost like it's broken.

"We need to go," says Taryn. Urgency coats his voice.

"It's injured." I'm sure we can take it if it can't even fly.

"How do you know?"

"I've seen one before. This one's wing is broken. Look how it hangs to the side."

"You've seen a griffin? How? Nope, not the time." He shakes his head. "We still need to go. Griffins are smart. I don't care if it is injured. You've seen what it did to those moulhaugs."

The griffin marches towards us, head held high. Even injured, it stands its ground with pride.

"We need to help it." This isn't just an animal. This is an intelligent creature, as smart as any one of us. We can't just leave it like this.

"We most certainly do not. You and I might come back if it kills us, but I don't want to risk Limery or Berry's lives on something this stupid. There's a reason they call griffins the king of beasts. Their claws are sharper than most metals. They're fast. And they attack with foresight."

We continue to backpedal as we talk, trying not to make any sudden movements. I still don't get what Taryn is so afraid of.

"We have to. It's killing the moulhaugs because they eat eggs. The moulhaugs would have killed its babies. It did the only thing it knew would drive them away. If you heal it, it will go back to the mountains."

He doesn't say anything for a moment, then lets out a resounding sigh. "Dammit. How in the hell do you propose we subdue this thing long enough for me to heal it?"

That is a very good question.

CHAPTER TWENTY-TWO

A MURDER MOST FOWL

Even in its injured state, the griffin is a beauty to behold. It carries itself with pride. A creature with the head, wings, and front-quarters of an eagle, the hindquarters of a lion, and the regality of both. King of land and air all rolled into one. Its left wing flutters in agitation, but the right wing just hangs limp.

It screeches again, and I can't help but wince at the cutting sound. Limery cups his hands over his massive ears. He must be in awe of the creature, because he hasn't said a word since we spotted it.

It's safe to say this is one bird he won't be eating.

"You're gonna have to subdue it." Taryn's golden clasps jingle as we continue our backpedal.

The griffin hasn't charged us yet, but it keeps our pace, making it undeniably evident that we are not welcome here.

"Why me? Can't you lull it to sleep with some of your druid magic?"

"First, this is your stupid idea. And second, I'm not sending Berry within a hundred feet of that griffin. It's twice his level and will rip him to shreds." He pats Berry on the head. "Dwarves have a healthy respect for griffins. Working high in the mountains, we've seen what they are capable of. There are ancient stories of dwarves being carried off by griffins, never to be heard from again."

I wonder if that is why King Favian has taken the griffin as his sigil?

Berry makes a sad groan, letting us know that he has no desire to die today.

My horrors grumble as I force them to retreat. Several puff out of existence and I summon three more to replace them. With sixty active, I have an additional 2,736 health, bringing my total to over seven thousand as long as they stay alive. My attacks hit for an additional sixty percent as well. Both will rise and fall like the tide once a battle starts. If only there was a way to keep them out of harm's way during a fight so I could have a permanent health boost.

The griffin paws at the ground again, its sharp talons ripping through the earth. What the hell are we supposed to do? Attacking it will only make it angry. Plus, we're trying to help the creature, not hurt it. Neither Taryn nor Limery have any crowd-control abilities. All I have are my Horrors of Vitality with their slows.

So here I am, a level twenty troll forced to subdue one of the island's most dangerous creatures, and it's ten levels ahead of me.

Fuck.

It's not like I haven't been in this position before, though. The mana-infused wyrm that blocked the ley lines was out of my level. But that was different—I had to kill it, not restrain it. A massive amount of critical hits saved my ass that day. That won't work here.

"Alright. Stand back. I'm going to try and subdue it. Don't move in until I give the okay."

Taryn says something to Limery, and the imp and bear move back even further. Taryn has his staff at the ready. He just shakes his head.

This really is a stupid idea.

I urge my horrors to move forward. "Come on, man. We've got this. We're heroes. Let's do something stupid and heroic." The griffin bows its head and unleashes another warning caw.

"It's your funeral," says Taryn.

"Yours too, if I fail."

Taryn buffs us with Strong Wind, but we move forward slowly. Cautiously. I need to play this smart. The griffin shuffles its wing in agitation once more. It must sense that something has changed. I summon another round of horrors to the rear of the line. The weakest ones are stationed at the front. They'll be the first to die.

I hold Sea Scorpion tight. I don't want to injure the beast, but it might help me keep it at bay. Maybe I could use the prongs to pin one of its legs to the ground.

Hoping for the element of surprise, I lift one of my Horrors of Vitality and sling it by the horn at the griffin. I'm hoping its passive slow will give me a slight advantage.

As the orange and blue fluffball flies through the air, the rest of my demonic army charges.

The griffin plucks the horror out of the air like a trained seal eating fish. With blazing speed, it pounces forward, the powerful feline hind legs closing the distance between us in a single leap.

Before I even have my trident raised, the griffin decapitates half a dozen horrors, snapping its beak in a blur. I summon three more horrors, but the griffin rips through my line quicker than I can replace them.

I dive for its neck, hoping I can tackle it to the ground, but a sharp talon wraps around my arm and slings me to the side. The wound hurts like hell, blue blood spilling down my arm.

Up close, the griffin is even larger than I imagined, standing several feet taller than me. It pecks at my horrors like a chicken eating bugs. The force of its snap severs them in half. They don't even have time to pile on the creature before it ends their short lives.

I attempt to subdue it from behind. Maybe if I can wrangle it from the rear, then I can pull it to the ground and pin it. With a running jump, I soar toward its backside.

I land on its back and wrap my trident around its throat, pulling with everything I have in an attempt to make the catbird pass out. It cocks its head back, smashing the back of its skull into my face. My nose crunches at the impact and blood pours from it like a fountain, but I don't let go.

With a massive leap, the griffin carries me through the air. It lowers its head when we land, tossing me from its back.

I duck and roll, avoiding damage, but my satchel catches on a bush and snaps, spilling its contents across the forest floor. Jira warned me I needed to work on my leatherworking, but I didn't listen. I dive for a health potion, chugging it quickly as I cast a few more horrors. At this point, they are nothing more than a distraction. The slow of Horror of Vitality seems to have little effect. Either it's not working, or the griffin is even faster than I thought.

If only there was a way to stun the creature. Taryn's Lightning Bolt has a random chance of a stun, but if the griffin turns on him, he's toast.

Then it hits me. A vial of bright yellow liquid litters the ground with the other contents of my satchel. Glouwseeker venom.

Item. Glouwseeker Venom. *When injected into the bloodstream, glouwseeker venom immobilizes target. Length of stun dependent on size of target, resistances, and amount injected.*

The glouwseeker sting froze Berry completely, even when he was imbued. If I can somehow inject the griffin with the venom, it might paralyze the creature long enough for Taryn to heal it.

The griffin pounces for me, and I barely dodge the attack. The talons smash into the earth, destroying several health potions.

"Taryn! A distraction please," I beg for anything to give me a second to breathe and form a plan.

A moment later, an arc of lightning rips through the canopy, setting limbs ablaze as it crashes into the griffin. The creature turns towards the source of the attack, but Taryn has already transformed into a red bird and zips through the trees. It pounces after Taryn as he swerves amongst limbs.

I use the time to open a vial of glouwseeker venom and pour it on the barbs of my trident. I use two whole vials for good measure, and by the time I'm done, the prongs glisten with a vibrant yellow sheen.

Casting another horror, I toss it at the griffin, regaining its attention. I send Taryn a quick message.

Message (Chod): *As soon as it comes for me, hit it again. I need the element of surprise.*

. . .

The griffin lunges through the air toward me, clearing twenty yards in a single bound. Mid-stride, a bolt of lightning strikes the majestic creature, setting its hair on end. The blow barely does any damage as it crashes to the ground in front of me.

I dive behind a tree just in time for it to turn again, searching for the dwarf. I use the opportunity to plant my trident in its rear haunch. I bury it as deep as I can. The griffin lets out a cry of pain. It turns, talon raised to swipe at me, when suddenly it freezes in place.

"Get over here quick! I don't know how much time we have."

There's no witty banter as Taryn takes his position. He falls to his knees and begins casting Restoration, a faint green glow enveloping him and the griffin.

Sooner than I would like, the griffin begins shuffling its paws. Taryn isn't even close to healing the wing yet, so I uncork another vial of venom and make a cut along the griffin's back with my own claw. I pour the entire vial into the open wound, and the griffin grows statuesque once again.

I watch as the wounds heal, and the broken wing retakes its normal shape. Once it is mended, I pull the trident from its hindquarters. The final piece of the puzzle is the glouwseeker venom being expelled and the punctures closing.

The griffin rises to its feet like a newborn horse, knocking Taryn aside in the process. I step in front of him, trident extended. A handful of horrors remain at my side.

We are locked in a stare-down, neither of us blinking.

A powerful screech sets my hair on end. The griffin shuffles its wings. When it realizes they are no longer broken, it extends them fully. The wingspan is angelic, nearly twenty yards when fully unfurled.

No wonder King Favian likes to ride above the clouds. He could fly forever on wings that broad.

The griffin retracts its wings, then steps forward. It clicks its beak together several times before bowing its head. Taryn and I return the gesture. A sound resembling a purr comes from its throat, and then it turns and saunters away.

Taryn collapses to the ground next to me. "Bro, I almost shit my pants."

"I'm thankful for both of us that you didn't." I extend my hand and help him to his feet. "Good work. We helped a lot of people today."

"Yeah, I guess we did the right thing after all." He bends down and picks up the last vial of glouwseeker venom. "What do you say we get a room at the inn tonight and you can work on your leatherworking skills?"

Gathering my belongings and stuffing them in a makeshift pouch made out of the scraps of leather, I'm surprised it lasted as long as it did.

CHAPTER TWENTY-THREE

THE MOUNTAINS ARE CALLING

Congratulations! You have leveled up the skill 'Leatherworking.' You are now a level 3 Leatherworker (Novice). Increase your skill and learn advanced techniques for working leather by finding an advanced leatherworker (Apprentice or above). Crafting Ranks: Novice, Apprentice, Journeyman, Expert, Artisan, Master, Grandmaster.

I set my satchel down on the table at the Smalltown inn and admire my handiwork. The stitches are a little more uniform, the thread a decent quality.

The materials cost me a pretty penny, due to the exorbitant prices this far out, but my leather satchel is patched and repaired. It's amazing what a difference a needle and quality thread can make in holding the seams together.

Miss Velma, one of the owners of the inn at Smalltown, is a pretty talented seamstress. She seemed happy to teach me a few new techniques once she heard we had removed the threat to the moulhaugs.

"Much better." I fit the last of my belongings back into the satchel. Once again, I find myself out of health potions due to the griffin smashing them all.

"Congrats, you've advanced from kindergarten to first grade." Taryn laughs from the table beside mine where he enjoys a frothy ale. "Honestly, I'm surprised your giant fingers could hold a needle." He smirks. "You could just buy a quality satchel. For a few gold, you can even buy one with an expandable inside."

"What? Do you mean like a Bag of Holding?" I examine my bag again. It might not look the best, but it gets the job done.

"Pretty much. How do you think I managed to fit the Bog Bow, Staff of the Marshes, and everything else we've looted in a bag the length of my arm?"

I hadn't really thought about it, but now it makes perfect sense. Undoubtedly, his magic bag is another benefit of starting out in an actual city. It's not like I really need one, though. I'm a big troll. I can carry a lot.

"Here's your dinner." Miss Velma sets down a piping hot bowl of chowder in front of all of us. She has a warm, motherly demeanor about her, but living this far out, I'm sure she's tougher than she looks. "I'll be feeding the scraps to that bear of yours. I'm sorry he has to stay in the stables, but rules are rules."

"We understand." I take the bowl from her. "If you make an exception for us, then you have to make one for everyone."

She gives me a warm smile. I wouldn't have expected such a motherly woman to be this far out near the mountains. Maybe her gentle exterior is just a front.

"Yum!" Limery pours the steaming chowder into his mouth without waiting for it to cool.

I rip off a chunk of bread and dip it in my bowl. The chowder is savory and delicious, with chunks of meat and hearty vegetables. I wash it down with a dark brown ale.

My vision goes hazy around the edges by the time I'm finished. Alcohol really does take the edge off.

When the sun sets, the door to the inn opens and the bearded man running the shop steps through. His heavy boots clank against the floor as he approaches us.

"Velma told me what you did." He places his hand on the back of a chair at my table. "We're grateful. It's not often outsiders come through these parts willing to help. Most are just looking to pass through. Mind if I sit?"

"Be my guest." I motion to the chair in front of me. I'm probably better company than Taryn, at least until he gets a few more beers in him and comes out of his shell.

Velma brings over another bowl of chowder and a mug of ale for the man. She kisses him on the forehead before going back to her work.

"Name's Keaton. Me and Velma have been running Smalltown for many years now. Our children help out when they can, but our boys are usually in the mountains. They guide those unfamiliar with the area from one side to the other." He blows on his chowder before taking a bite.

"Is it a difficult journey?" I ask.

Limery laps at the last drops of his chowder, already finished.

"There's a lot of dangers in the mountains. Dangers most lowlanders have no knowledge of. Usually, my boys aren't gone more than a week." He sets the spoon down before continuing. "My boys are tough. They're warriors. Had more than their fair share of run-ins with goblins, beasts, and even a few mountain trolls. But it's been ten days and I haven't heard nothing." He takes a swig of ale. "Maybe it's nothing, but maybe it's not. An old man like me isn't fit for hiking the mountains. If you'd be willing to check in on them, I'll outfit you with whatever supplies you need for the journey."

I turn to Taryn. He sets down his mug, froth coating his burly mustache. "We'll be happy to help, but if the mountains are as treacherous as you say, I'm taking another pet."

Quest Alert. *You have been offered the quest 'Find my sons.' Ten days have passed since Keaton and Velma last heard from their sons. They expect trouble. Travel into the mountains and search for signs of the men.*

Reward: None.

Bonus: By accepting this quest, you will be given items for your journey.

We walk through the forest at the base of the mountain. The area where the griffin had nested is now empty. Cracked eggs and white feathers that drift aimlessly are the only memory of the powerful creature and its young. I suspect they are now tucked away somewhere high in the mountains.

"You want a moulhaug?" I ask Taryn again. That's a mighty big creature to tame.

"Why not?" Taryn gazes out into the forest depths atop Berry, searching for a sign of the large beast. "They're big, they're strong, and they can tank for us. What's not to like?"

He has a point. They are powerful beasts. And one more layer of protection for whatever comes next. "You're right. And if this whole adventuring thing doesn't work out, you can always join the circus."

"Haha, make fun of the little guy." He rolls his eyes. "You should really get some new jokes. I'm going to take to the air and see if I can spot any. With the griffin gone, they should be coming back soon."

In a flash, Taryn transforms into a red bird and disappears into the trees. Out of all the creatures he could transform into, I still don't get why he chooses a small red bird.

"You don't want to join him?" I ask Limery.

The imp quits flapping his wings and lands on my shoulder. "Limmy wants to stay with Chods." He puts a small hand on the back of my neck.

"Everything okay?"

"Limmy like Chods, but sometimes he misses Mommy and Leo. And Daddy, too." He sighs.

He's homesick. "I'm sure they miss you too. You can always go back home if you need to. I would understand." I never once thought that he might miss his family. Just because I'm better off without mine doesn't mean that everyone thinks that way. Some people have families that love them. That show them love.

The closest thing I have to a brother is Taryn, and he's here with me. I'm sure Limery misses his own brother, even if Leo does pick on him. And his dad, Limery hasn't seen him since he sold himself into slavery in an attempt to save Leo's life.

"Limmy will stay with Chods. Chods needs his help." He gives me a half-smile. A smile that would scare anyone who didn't know him. "Mommy says it's okay to be sad. She says it's okay to miss Daddy. It means we loves him."

I don't know why, but I feel a hollowness in my chest. It feels both empty and full at the same time, like a giant ball of nothingness is threatening to explode from within. Or swallow me whole. I can't imagine ever having a talk that real with my mother.

She was the queen of hiding her emotions. She and father both.

"Your mother is a smart woman." I try to smile but it's only skin deep.

Luckily, a message from Taryn pulls me from my sobering thoughts.

. . .

Incoming Message (Taryn): I've got one. Level eighteen. The quicker you get over here, the quicker we can get back to the mountain.

He sends me his location. It's about a mile away.

When we arrive, I find Taryn, still in bird-form, sitting on the horn of the moulhaug as it basks in the sun.

Message (Chod): What are you doing?
  Incoming Message (Taryn): Chilling.
  Message (Chod): I can see that. Do you want to die before we get to you?
  Incoming Message (Taryn): Did you forget about my passive? Nature's Bulwark. Animals will only attack me if they are provoked.
  Message (Chod): Well, if you sat on my nose, I'd definitely say it was provocation.

With a flap of his wings, he takes to the air, flying towards Limery and I.

Message (Chod): Don't even think about it.

With an explosion of feathers, he returns to his dwarven form.

"You're no fun." He looks at me and his face softens, the mischief vanishing from his eyes. "Everything okay?"

"Just having an off day." I don't really know how to put it better than that.

He nods. It's not the first time Taryn has seen me affected by my relationship with my parents. More often than not, I can hide it, but sometimes, I just wish I had what others do.

"Come on." He pats me on the lower back. "It's nothing fighting a giant monster won't cure."

He raises his staff, calling a bolt of lightning into the slumbering creature. The moulhaug jerks to life, a scorch mark smoking from its backside.

With four of us, we are able to bring the moulhaug down to five percent without taking any damage. Berry and I hold the creature down while Taryn uses Tame to bond with his new pet.

True to his word, by the time the battle is over, Limery and I both have smiles on our faces. Berry, on the other hand, seems a little jealous as he walks beside the moulhaug. Every time the moulhaug's head swings Berry's way, the bear's lip curls up in a snarl.

The moulhaug even seems rather content, considering we just beat the snot out of it. I wonder if Tame makes them forget about the battle that just took place, or if they just don't care anymore?

Atop the moulhaug's back, Taryn towers above us all. "Now this is what I'm talking about." The only thing he is missing is a howdah, the resplendent Asian carriages that used to sit atop elephants and carry the wealthy over long distances.

He looks natural on his new mount. The level eighteen creature is the size of a large van. It sways its head from side to side as it walks. I still remember the force of the moulhaug horn that smashed me near Lynchton. The creature's mossy gray skin blends nicely with Taryn's dull green cloak. Traveling through the mountains, they might not even be noticed at a distance.

With the newest member of our party, we make one last stop in Smalltown to gather supplies before we leave. Keaton offered anything we needed for the journey at no cost. Aside from a few potions, I think we have everything we need to make do. However, Taryn really wants to load up on free supplies.

I guess it has something to do with his life back home. He's never really had excess. Free goods don't have the same luster to me.

In the shop, Taryn carries a wicker basket, filling it to the brim with potions and other supplies. "I've never been on a shopping spree before." His eyes light up as he tosses in several strips of jerky.

I leave him to his shopping and find Keaton in the backroom, bringing out more stock to replace what he is giving away. "Thanks again for the supplies."

He sets the wooden crate down on the floor. "No, thank you. I just pray it isn't too late."

"From what you've told us, your sons are tough. Whatever they've gotten themselves into, they will be fine. Here, let me help you with this." I pick up the crate and set it out in the main shop. "While I've got you here, I was wondering if you could send a raven to Lynchton. I want to let them know that the moulhaugs will be returning north and that there is no reason for them to be killed any longer."

"I can take care of that for you." He scribbles the message on a piece of parchment and ties it with a string.

Taryn pushes a large satchel into my hands. "I know you worked really hard on the other one, but this will really serve you a lot better on the road. I mean, look at that stitching. Miss Velma has a gift."

I can't argue that the bag doesn't look a million times better than the one I made, but I made mine. It's something I can be proud of. "I think we've taken enough of their supplies. I'll make do with what I have." I give a final nod to Keaton. "Time to hit the road."

CHAPTER TWENTY-FOUR
SHOOT THE BIRD

The moulhaug trudges up the mountain. For all its power, it is as slow as molasses. Taryn has loaded it up with a satchel on each side. They are cinched around its massive frame with rope from the shop in Smalltown. Limery clings to the moulhaug's horn, enjoying the rhythmic bobbing as it marches along. He reminds me of a pirate searching for landfall from the crow's nest. Berry pulls up the rear, a kid's teddy bear compared to the moulhaug.

I know from experience that moulhaugs can charge with surprising speed, so I have no idea why it walks like an elderly snail when out of combat.

"Can't you speed this thing up?" I ask Taryn.

He looks down from the moulhaug's back, finally taller than me. "And what? Cause a rockslide?" He pats the moulhaug's spine. "I'd rather not kill us all because you can't slow down and enjoy the moment."

"You think Keaton's sons are enjoying the moment?" I counter. "We have no idea what has happened to them."

"You can go ahead if you want, but there is nothing I can do about Stompy here." His mustache curls up at the edges when he reveals his new pet's name.

"Stompy? Really?" I guess I should consider myself lucky he didn't name it Horny.

The pass that goes through the mountains is a bit daunting. It clings along the edge of the mountain, curving and winding. At times, it's steep, then levels out for miles. We go up and down, traversing from one mountain to the other.

The thing about climbing mountains is that we can't just go straight up and over. It's too steep, so instead, we journey for hours and hours in a roundabout way.

"We'll need to camp soon," says Taryn. The sun has already dipped below the mountains, engulfing the entire side in shadow. "The path is too dangerous for us to travel at night."

For now, our mornings will be bright and our evenings dull, until we cross the other side and it will reverse.

We find a shallow cave to settle in for the night. Limery kills a mountain goat for dinner, and we roast it over a small fire near the back of the cave. Smoke gathers overhead, choking us in the enclosed space, until Taryn has the genius idea to cast Strong Wind. Even though we aren't moving, the breeze that accompanies the spell clears the smoke.

Stompy lies at the front of the cave, concealing most of the entrance. His hide is a similar color to the surrounding stone, so nothing passing by will have any idea we are inside.

"What do you think happened to them?" Taryn asks me as he cuts off a piece of goat meat with one of the knives he took from the shop.

"Could be anything. Goblins, monsters...trolls. They could have gotten lost or had an injury." I take a piece of goat for myself, slicing it off with my sharp claw. "Sounds like a dangerous place by the way Keaton told it."

"Hopefully, we find them soon and then get on the way north. I really think you'll like the dwarven kingdom." He finishes eating and snuggles up next to Berry in the warmth of the fire.

I curl up against the cool cave wall with Limery tucked between my arms.

Day two in the mountains is much the same as day one. A lot of slow walking, narrow passes, and echoes. A single rock bouncing down the canyon walls seems to carry for miles. Unlike in New York City, where the city seems to swallow every noise and spit it back all at once.

A strong gust of wind shakes the trees, so even this desolate location feels alive with trouble. Even though we seem so isolated and alone, I can't help but feel like there are threats lurking around every bend or inside every cave we pass.

Not knowing what to expect has me constantly alert, so I keep my horrors at the ready. They grumble and bump against one another in the narrower passes, and several times, I lose a horror to the depths below.

As the day drives on, we avoid fighting monsters when we can to prevent drawing attention to ourselves. The few times we are forced to fight, we destroy our opponents with no restraint in an explosion of horrors, lightning, and fire.

When a small host of spear-carrying lizard men ambush us from a cave, I block their retreat by throwing my horrors against the mountain and exploding them to create a rockslide. Then Stompy takes the lead along the narrow pass and shovels them aside like a plow on a snowy day.

The mountainsides are filled with so many caves that the threat of danger waits around every corner, but so far, we have been lucky. We make camp for the night and as the temperatures drop, we huddle a little closer to the fire.

On day three, Taryn decides to take to the skies.

"The mountain range is too wide for us to find anything following a single path.

We don't even know if this is the trail they followed." He stares up at the mountain peak, where a hawk circles high overhead. "From up high, I'll be able to get a better view."

"Alright, just be careful."

He pats Stompy on the head before transforming into a red bird and disappearing into the sky. The rest of us carry on with our march, climbing ever higher like some twisted version of *The Fellowship of the Ring*. Judging by the map, we are about halfway through the mountain pass.

Taryn is right. This is like finding a needle in a haystack. There's no way to know which path Keaton's sons took. Neither one of us are rangers or have very good tracking skills. Hopefully, Taryn can find a sign of their whereabouts from up above.

After a few hours, I check in with him.

Message (Chod): *Any luck?*

Incoming Message (Taryn): *Not yet. There are lots of paths up this high. The tree-cover makes it hard to see much of anything happening on the ground. I did see a few goblins, though. They disappeared into a cave carrying pickaxes. Mining, I suppose.*

Taryn returns and we stop for lunch. As he transforms from bird to dwarf, I'm hit with a fascinating question.

"Do you ever eat worms when you're in bird form?"

He just cocks an eyebrow and stares at me.

"I mean, I just wonder if they taste different when you're a bird? I ate a raw rabbit when I first got here."

He rips off a piece of jerky and stuffs it in his mouth. "No, I haven't eaten worms," he says in a deadpan tone.

"What about bugs?" I fight the grin that hides at the edge of my mouth. I toss the bone from a deer leg I'm eating to one of my Horrors of Power as a distraction, and it crushes it in its strong jaws.

"Limmy eats worms sometimes." He flashes a toothy grin. "Limmy likes birds and worms."

"I think Limmy just likes to eat," I tease, poking him in the belly.

He erupts into laughter. "Stop, Chods."

"If we don't find his sons, what then?" Taryn is stoic. Maybe that's why he didn't laugh at my jokes. "Do we just abandon the quest? It seems wrong, don't you think?"

He's starting to feel the same way I do about this game. There are no random NPCs here. Abandoning a quest means they face the consequences. "I don't know. We'll make that decision when the time comes. For now, we keep our eyes peeled."

He returns to the sky, and another hour passes before I hear from Taryn again.

. . .

Incoming Message (Taryn): *I think I found something. There's smoke coming from a cluster of trees. I'm sending you the location.*

It pops up on my map. The location is only a mile or two from where we are. I'm checking our route when I receive a second message.

Incoming Message (Taryn): *Chod, get here quick! I've been shot. I don't think I can make it back.*

"Shit!" I say aloud. How the hell did he get shot as a small bird? I send Taryn a quick message telling him I'm on the way, but there's no reply.

Limery turns to me, his bulbous eyes full of alarm.

"We need to get moving. Taryn is hurt." I don't know how serious the injury is, or if he's still stuck in bird form. All I know is we need to get there ASAP.

"Limmy will fly ahead. Makes sure Taryns is okay."

Before I can stop him, the imp has left. I pray he doesn't get shot, too. Is this what happened to Keaton's boys?

"Dammit! Why does everything have to always fall to shit?" I yell. Berry lets out a huff of agitation.

I jump on the back of the moulhaug and use the rope that keeps the satchels in check for balance. "I know Taryn told you to go slow, but we need to get moving. Berry, lead the way."

The bear trots ahead of us, and the moulhaug starts moving. Trudging at first, it seems like it's going to keep its slow pace, but then its movement increases. Rocks fall from the mountainside with each thunderous step, and pretty soon we're moving like an avalanche, leaving a dust cloud in our wake. My horrors rush to keep up as we barrel down the mountainside in search of my friend.

Taryn's location grows steadily closer until we turn a bend and I see smoke wafting up from a recess in the mountain. The crevice goes back pretty far, like someone hit the mountain with a giant axe, leaving an enormous gash in its rocky exterior. A small forest has grown in the crevice, concealing what lies within its depths.

Limery stands guard over a green lump of clothing on the ground, squaring off with a handful of goblins. He holds two fireballs, and even though he's half their size, the goblins look hesitant to attack. Some hold spears, others pickaxes or small bronze swords.

The goblins stand there, weapons pointed at Limery. They exchange glances, none of them wanting to attack first. Limery has an almost feral rage in his eyes as he stands his ground. The goblins have dull green skin, lanky arms, and pointed ears. Their eyes are a dark shade of orange, and tiny noses hook over a wide mouth full of sharp, triangular teeth. They are all dressed in rags or scraps of leather, and each one has a thick metal collar around their neck.

They jump with surprise at the sight of a charging moulhaug with a troll on its back, before screaming and retreating deeper into the recess.

Taryn stirs beneath his cloak, and I'm thankful that he is still alive. I jump from the moulhaug and rush to his aid.

"Ungh." He grimaces. When he emerges beneath the cloak, an arrow protrudes all the way through his bicep. "The little bastards shot me right through the wing." He touches the arrow and flinches in pain. "If you can get it out, I'll be able to heal myself."

The arrow is tipped with a stone arrowhead on one end and feather fletchings on the other.

"I'm going to have to break it in half. It might hurt a little."

He nods and closes his eyes, extending his arm to me. As quick as I can, I snap off the end of the arrow and pull it through his arm. It slides out with ease, leaving a hole that trickles blood down Taryn's bicep and drips to the dusty ground.

He runs to a nearby tree and takes a knee, letting the green aura of Restoration envelope him.

When he returns, he looks much healthier. The color has returned to his face. He looks past me, eyes wide, toward the area where the goblins were and points.

When I turn, my stomach drops. Several muscle-bound mountain trolls emerge from the trees carrying stone clubs. The small goblins snicker at their feet.

CHAPTER TWENTY-FIVE
KRONAN THE BARBARIAN

The center troll smacks his club ominously against his palm like some sort of street thug in an eighties movie. His muscles flex with each motion. Two other trolls flank his side, and the goblins we scared off flit between their legs. Each one of these trolls is built like a bodybuilder, and they range from level fifteen to twenty-two.

I remember the character creation screen saying that the mountain trolls were the strongest of all trolls. Looking at these three, I believe it. I'm no chump, but these dudes are ripped. Thick, corded muscle covers every inch of their bodies. Their arms are like braided steel, veins pulsing with every movement.

The center troll is the biggest of the three. His plum-colored skin is scarred in many places, with a pronounced lilac scar running diagonally down his chest. His shoulders and arms are dotted with speckles of gray, allowing him to blend in with the surrounding mountains. A long hawk nose nearly touches his lips, and two short, girthy tusks jut upwards from the corners of his mouth. His hair is braided into a long mohawk that runs down his back.

The trolls beside him look in a similar fashion, but with shorter mohawks. They all stare at us, furious, their muscles twitching.

"I hope you have a good reason for setting foot on mountain troll lands?" the deep voice of the center troll rumbles. "Outsiders stick to the gaps or they pay the price."

"We're looking for two travelers. Two humans." I stand my ground. "Have you seen them?"

The center troll looks to his comrades and they all burst into laughter, even the goblins laugh in a shrill, high-pitched tone.

What's so funny? Considering I'm not cracking jokes right now, their laughter sets me on edge.

Taryn steps up beside me. "I have a bad feeling about this," he whispers.

So do I.

A few of my horrors pop out of existence, but I wait to cast more. It feels like we're in a volatile situation and I'd hate to accidentally set it off.

"You travel with a dwarf and search for two humans. Who are you?" He lets his club fall by his side.

"I am Chod, hero of the forest trolls." I say it with all the authority I can muster. These guys look tough, and we don't know how many of them there are beyond those trees. Perhaps my confidence will make me seem higher than the level twenty that I am. At least I have Conceal to hide my true level.

"A hero, you say? You don't look like any forest troll I have ever seen." One of the goblins bumps against his leg, and he swats it on the head. The goblin falls to the ground and then scurries to safety, cowering behind a different troll. I wonder what type of relationship the two races have, because they definitely seem to be on the same side.

"I would like to speak with your leader. If she will see me, then I can explain everything."

"She?" The three trolls roar with laughter. "Okay, you truly are a forest troll." A laughing goblin steps too close, and he smacks it away. "Follow us, and I will take you to the chief. You may keep your weapons, but know if you raise them against us, we will have your heads, Chod, hero of the forest trolls."

So this isn't the same female-led society as the forest and seaside trolls. What else do they do differently?

He turns and kicks another goblin, sending it sprawling to the ground. The goblin squeals before running ahead and vanishing into the trees.

The sun dips below the mountain, leaving the sky bright but casting the mountains in shadow. We walk among the pines, passing dozens of goblins that sit around small fires. Some roast birds, others squirrels or some mystery meat. They all look up warily at the passing trolls.

Eventually, we exit the trees and enter a clearing that extends into the mountain. A half-dozen caves line the sides. A massive fire rages in the center of the clearing, and next to it, in a wooden cage, a group of men press their faces against the bars.

Behind the fire, a plum-colored troll, much larger than the other three, sits on a stone throne. A fur shawl covers his broad shoulders. One of his tusks is cracked at the tip. He wears his hair in a braided mohawk with the braid hanging over his shoulder. When I analyze him, I see he is level twenty-five. On a smaller throne to his left sits a female, and several other females sit on the ground next to her. She holds a small troll in her lap, feeding him strips of meat from a stone platter held by a goblin. The females are built more like the female forest trolls, slender but still muscular. They have the same white or gray hair as the males, but their mohawks are much wider.

Goblins run about, some carrying flanks of roasted meat to the trolls, others bowls of water. One stands on a platform behind the chief, waving a fan made of a strip of leather tied between two branches.

Each goblin wears the same metal collar around its neck. Are they slaves?

The troll on the larger throne looks in our direction as we approach, then leans towards the troll to his left and whispers something in her ear.

"Chief Kronan," the most muscled of the three trolls addresses the chief. "It seems a forest troll and his companions have wandered onto our lands."

"He doesn't look like any forest troll I've ever seen." The chief stares me down.

"He claims to be a hero." The muscle-bound troll laughs.

It's a condescending, mocking, assholish laugh that makes me want to smack the sneering grin off his face.

The king smirks. "I suppose we can test that easily enough."

The last of my horrors vanish. Even though I am surrounded by potential enemies, their health continues to decay unless I am actually engaged in battle. I pull my mana to my fingertips so that it is ready to cast at a moments notice. My anger simmers beneath the surface as these goons mock me. If I didn't think that summoning a horror would set them off, I would have summoned more already.

Looking at the mountain trolls, there is no doubt they are strong, but we have magic. The great equalizer.

Limery grows warm against my shoulder, and I know he must be thinking the same thing.

If things go to shit, Taryn and I don't risk a lot by dying other than losing our items and a level, but Limery and the others are not so lucky. I don't even trust that Limery could fly out of here unharmed after what happened to Taryn.

"Speak, troll," the chief bellows. "What business does a forest troll and his companions have with the mountain trolls? Speak wisely, hero, or we may just put that claim to the test."

This is so not the welcome I received with the forest or seaside trolls. This guy puts Gord to shame on the dick-o-meter. I clench my fist, fighting back my rising anger. That innate desire to pop off. I need to choose my words carefully. Our lives depend on it.

I take a deep breath and try to remain calm. "I am on a quest to find two men that have gone missing on their journey. I also have an offer of peace from King Favian of Vanaria. He wishes to make peace with all of the troll races, to build a better future together."

A goblin approaches the chief to fill his cup, but the chief smacks him away, spilling the liquid and knocking the goblin to the ground. The female trolls murmur behind him.

"Silence!" he roars, and the crag goes quiet. Clearly, I said the wrong thing. "The forest trolls were once a mighty race. They took what was theirs and they ruled our people with pride. Even the mountain trolls followed their lead. And now, here they are, ruled by their females, doing the bidding of humans, and taking offers of peace. How the mighty have fallen." He spits at the ground. "In the mountains, we take what is ours." He points to the men in the cages. "These men wandered onto our lands and they will pay the price. We will dine on their bones tonight." He looks down into the fire before making eye contact with me. "You will not come onto my lands and disrespect me with demands and offers of peace. The only peace we will have is the peace we take by force." The three trolls behind me beat their chest at his words. "Brutus, kill the troll, and throw the others in the cages. Dwarf sounds especially delicious tonight. Forest troll, if you are a hero, then tell your king what I think of his peace."

Before Brutus can lift his club, I have my trident pointed at his throat. "Attempt to harm me or my companions and I will kill you before you lift a finger."

His eyes radiate hatred, but he doesn't move.

Limery's fireballs crackle next to my ear, and behind me, the moulhaug snorts in agitation.

The three trolls stare at me, none of them willing to make the first move.

I call to the men in the cages. "Are you Keaton's boys?"

"We are. What is going on? Can you get us out of here?" one of them shouts back.

I ignore his questions. Right now, I need to figure out how to get us out of here without dying. I don't want to let Keaton's sons die, but if it is them or Limery, I will save my friend.

"You will die for this." Brutus leans his neck against my trident as he says it, letting the blade prick his skin as he snarls. "And I will pick my teeth with the bones of your friends."

Incoming Message (Taryn): *What's the plan here?*
Message (Chod): *Follow my lead, and try not to die.*

We are fucked. So, so fucked. I do the only thing that I think might give us a chance at getting out of here alive.

"Chief Kronan, I challenge you to a duel."

The clearing goes quiet. The only sounds are the crackling of the fire and the breathing of the animals.

"A duel?" There's amusement in his eyes. "Is that how you southerners do things? What do I have to gain from dueling you that I wouldn't take already by letting my trolls kill you?"

"For one, I don't kill Brutus right here and now." I press my trident a little harder into Brutus's throat until a trickle of blood runs down his chest.

Brutus doesn't flinch. He's the type of warrior that would run to death and call it glory. I'm sure Kronan is the same way. People don't get that kind of bravado by running from fights. I'm just hoping that as leader of the mountain trolls, maybe Kronan has at least a little brains.

"Go on." He runs a clawed finger down his jawline. The amusement is gone, replaced by something else. Curiosity.

The time has come to see if I can bluff my way out of this. "You may talk big, but I know the truth. Alone up here in the mountains, your people are slowly dying.

Losing more trolls will cripple you further. You may pretend that the goblins serve you because of your power, but the truth is that you don't have the power to take care of everything without them. You are slaves to them just as much as they are slaves to you. You hide away in your mountain caves, capturing those who walk through your lands, and call it power. But tell me, what is the real reason you don't set foot off of these mountains?"

The chief's lip curls up, and he stares daggers at me. He says something to one of the goblins, and it runs toward a giant gong near the fire, smashing it twice with a large bone. The gong reverberates throughout the crag, echoing over itself several times.

A moment later, goblins descend from the mountainsides, and a patter of footsteps comes from the caves that line the mountains. Torches glow from within their depths, and soon, dancing shadows begin to appear. Goblins and trolls emerge from the caves and gather around the chief. A trail of goblins from one cave all carry pickaxes. Some of the ones that descend the mountain carry spears or bows. They all chatter amongst themselves, no doubt wondering what has happened to leave Brutus with a trident pointed at his throat.

By the time the caves empty, there are over one hundred goblins and maybe thirty trolls. Only a handful of troll children are among them. Unless there are other tribes, there are even fewer mountain trolls than I thought. Perhaps I hit way too close to home with what I said.

"Everyone, gather around." The chief stands from his throne. At full height, he is even taller than I thought. "Tonight, I show this forest troll how we do things in the mountains." He removes his shawl and tosses it to the female troll sitting next to him.

When he steps forward, two giant scars that cross his chest in an X shimmer in the firelight. Several more scars cover his arms and shoulders. It's evident that he has fought many battles. He's stronger than me and has at least a foot height advantage.

The chief orders his people to form a circle in the back of the crevice near the caves, and they pack in tightly. The goblins we passed on the way here have joined the spectacle as well.

"Release Brutus and choose your weapon."

My heart pounds in my chest. What have I gotten myself into? I have no reason to trust that they won't attack us once I remove my trident from Brutus's throat other than the fact that I believe the chief values his strength above all else. A gamble that I'm betting all our lives on.

I pull back Sea Scorpion, and Brutus grunts at me.

His lips curl up in a devilish smile. "Let's see what you're made of, hero."

Taryn rushes to my side. "Chod, are you sure about this?"

"This is our only way out. You heard what they said they were going to do to you. At least this way, we have a shot at survival. If it looks like I am going to die, use the distraction to take Limery and flee."

He gives me a grave nod, before patting me on the backside. "Good luck, friend."

"Chods will win. Limmy knows it." Limery jumps from my shoulder and hovers beside Taryn.

"Lock the others away," orders Kronan.

Brutus and another troll take Taryn by the shoulders and lead him and Limery to a cage next to the men.

As I approach the ring of trolls and goblins, one of the men in the cages shouts at me, "What's going on?"

I ignore him. Right now, I have bigger problems than calming this fool who managed to get himself caught.

Kronan cracks his knuckles and paces as he waits for me. "Choose your weapon, hero." The way he says 'hero' is like it's the most disgusting word he's ever heard.

"I'll use my trident." I display the golden weapon for him to see.

He smirks. "We are a long way from the sea. Rholi, bring me Crusher."

One of the other trolls who brought us here disappears into a cave. A minute later, he returns carrying a giant silver warhammer that glitters in the dull light. It reflects the flames onto the ground like a speckling of fireflies.

Kronan turns to his own people. "For anyone who attempts to interfere, I will kill you myself." He faces me. "Brutus, if his companions attempt to escape or interfere, kill them. And when I slay this so-called hero, we'll prove once and for all that the mountain trolls have no equals."

The other trolls beat their chests, and the goblins squeal with delight.

Kronan twists the warhammer in his hands, feeling its weight. The massive weapon looks like it was meant to hammer trees into the ground. It must weigh at least a hundred pounds. He gives it a few practice swings, and the metal sings as it swipes through the air. A few hits from that, and I'll be respawning far, far away.

That just means I better not get hit. Forest trolls are known for their agility, after all. At least compared to the other troll races.

I summon a round of horrors and they pop to life on the battlefield. Gasps hiss all around me. Clearly, they didn't believe that the group of horrors that came in with us were my summons. That must mean they don't have any magic users in the mountains. The horrors follow me around as Kronan and I circle one another.

To the outsider, which one of us looks like the predator?

Kronan makes the first move, swinging his warhammer at me, and I dive to the side. It crashes into the ground, sending a spray of rock and debris into the air, literally ripping the ground open.

I quickly summon three more horrors and send them to the ring's edge. I back away from Kronan as he readies his hammer for another attack. Until I get an idea of how he fights, I need my horrors to stay out of the way, and most importantly, stay alive.

We circle each other, and every time the cooldowns are up, I summon more horrors. When Kronan charges me, I keep as much distance between us as possible. He swings with a mighty force, but once he has selected his target, there is no adjusting the blow. The warhammer carries him like an anchor to his chosen target.

His weapon crashes into the stone, leaving gashes that will remain long after our battle is over, tattooing our fight on the mountain he calls home.

"Are you so afraid to meet your doom?" He lifts his hammer from the newly-formed crater and holds it over his chiseled shoulder.

For all the force he puts into his swings, he doesn't seem to be tiring. Not yet, at least.

Without warning, he leaps through the air, the warhammer raised above his head. I dive between his legs and roll out of the way as his hammer connects to stone with an ear-aching crash.

I could attack him as he lifts his weapon, but I'm playing the long game. There's no room for error. Before I attack, I need to make sure I can win.

He grunts as he lifts Crusher. "No wonder the forest trolls are ruled by females. Even their heroes are cowards."

The crowd laughs at his comment.

For any other forest troll, that comment might have baited them into attacking. For Gord, I know it would have. Not so long ago, it might have baited me.

I smile at him. It was a good effort, I'll give him that, but this isn't my first rodeo. I've been baiting innocent players into attacking me for years. One of my greatest strengths as a streamer was taunting other players into attacking before they were ready.

I focus on my breathing, making sure to keep enough distance between us. I grip my trident tight. Sea Scorpion is light to my adrenaline-fueled muscles.

I cast three more horrors in rapid succession, bringing my total to twenty-one. As I circle around our makeshift arena, it's beginning to look more like a warzone than a clearing. Chunks of rock litter the area next to hammer-sized holes.

Kronan lunges for me again, and this time, I barely dodge the attack when my foot slips on the rubble.

He laughs at my near fall. "Time is running out, hero." He lifts the warhammer again, readying his swing.

"You're right." I summon three more horrors and instantly use Sacrifice on all twenty-four of them. Their bodies vanish in a puff of smoke, and the crowd erupts into a dull roar of murmurs. My Strength, Constitution, and Dexterity increase by eight points each. My muscles bulge with the influx of stats, and in only a matter of seconds, my size rivals Kronan's.

I flex my newly-invigorated muscles, feeling their promise of power. Hell yes!

His eyes go wide for a moment, before returning to their angry slits.

He swings his warhammer at me, and I parry it with my trident. They clink against one another, and the hammer explodes the earth. I kick Kronan in the side, and he tumbles to the ground, taking his warhammer with him.

I leap towards his downed body, trident pointed at his neck, but he lifts his warhammer, pressing its shaft between the spears of my weapon. With a swing of his hips, he kicks my legs out from underneath me, sending me sprawling to my back.

Heat emanates from Kronan's body as he crawls to his feet, his rage building.

He brings the warhammer across his body in a sweeping strike, and I jump in the air. The weapon hums as it passes underneath me.

Mid-air, I jab Sea Scorpion into his shoulder, drawing first blood. Kronan grimaces at the wound, and in the same motion of his first swing, brings his warhammer overhead and smashes it into the ground beside me. The force of the blast sends rubble spraying into me like a shotgun blast.

He lifts the hammer, and takes a step back. His chest heaves with each breath, and sweat steams off his skin.

I use the moment to summon three more horrors, sacrificing them and increasing my stats again.

I take the offensive and lunge at Kronan several times with my trident. He parries each of my jabs, using the massive head of his warhammer as a shield. Sparks fly, and the ding of metal on metal echoes against the walls of the crag.

He grunts with each swing of the warhammer as he presses again. His attacks still move with amazing speed, but I watch my footing, dodging each blow as he pounds the mountain to gravel beneath us.

"Fight me!" he shouts after I dodge another attack. "Fight me, you coward." He beats his free hand against his chest, and the trolls in the crowd do the same.

It sounds like a stampede as they beat their chests like drums of war. The goblins join in with shrill yodels that cut through the bass.

A wicked grin crosses Kronan's face, and my vision goes fuzzy.

Warning! You have been targeted with Goblin Battle Cry. Effects: Confusion.

What the hell? That's cheating. I try to say the words, but they get stuck in my throat. All I see are fuzzy silhouettes all around me. I can't pinpoint Kronan to save my life.

Something collides with my side, cracking several ribs and knocking me off my feet. The impact sends my trident flying through the air, and it drops my health by ten percent.

I try to scurry away from the looming silhouette that follows me around, but it's like there is a water tank on my head, sloshing with each step I take. If this confusion doesn't wear off soon, I'm done for.

Another sharp pain flares through my other side as I try to stand, knocking me on my back. Everything around me sounds like muffled buzzing. The beating chests, squealing goblins, and Kronan's taunts all muffle together.

Every breath I take sends pain down my sides. There's no telling how many broken ribs I have.

Taryn sends me a message, but the words come through as squiggles. This confusion, it effects everything but the thoughts in my own head.

Another hit drops me down to fifty-percent health. I must be bleeding internally, because my health continues to drop as I writhe on the ground.

Kronan is toying with me, otherwise he would have caved my head in with the warhammer. This is bad. I can't even focus on my Tiger's Eye Pendant long enough to activate its ability. There's only one way that is going to get rid of this confusion.

I activate Berserker Rage, and the world comes spinning back together, like I just traveled through a wormhole.

Kronan stands over my body, arms outstretched, basking in the glory of his people.

My blood pumps as Berserker Rage takes effect, allowing me to see everything clearly and rapidly replenishing my health. Kronan still hasn't noticed I'm no longer confused, so I lie on the ground, waiting for my moment.

Kronan lifts his warhammer over his head. "This is what happens to anyone who would challenge the mighty Kronan."

He swings for my head, and I kick out, sweeping Kronan off his feet. He falls with a thud, but I'm already halfway across the ring searching for my trident. I find it sticking out from the rubble just as Kronan stands, and I pick it up.

"Still has a bit of fight left in him." Steam continues to rise off his muscled body. "Not for long." He tilts his head back and lets out a monstrous roar, silencing the crowd. In that moment, the air around his body distorts as he goes into a rage.

We charge at one another. My vision is red, and all I see is Kronan. I level my trident at his throat, ready to end this here and now.

He rears back his warhammer. When he swings, our two weapons collide with a crash of metal on metal that sets my ears ringing. Both weapons fly from our hands, disappearing high into the sky.

Kronan lunges for me, and we lock our hands together in a show of strength. We push one another with all of our rage-fueled might, but neither of us budge.

With a full rage-meter, I activate Bite. I extend my arms, pressing them out wide, and sink my tusks into Kronan's shoulder. He brings his knee up to my stomach, the impact forcing me to release my grip.

"Fine." He smiles. "We will finish this like our ancestors." He swipes at me, and the tips of his claws rake across my chest.

I jump toward him, tackling the mountain troll to the ground. We claw, bite, and kick one another in a primal brawl.

My Berserker Rage is the first to end. I kick Kronan away and retreat to temporary safety. He chases after me, and I cast a Horror of Vitality in an attempt to slow him down, but due to his Berserker Rage, it has no effect. He does stop for a moment to attack the furry horror, killing it in one strike and granting me a brief reprieve.

Picking up a giant rock, I hurl it at Kronan like a major league pitcher. The rock goes wide to the right and crumples in the face of an unlucky goblin.

I search for my trident, but it's nowhere to be found. However, I do catch the gleaming face of Kronan's warhammer.

His rage wears off, and he spots the warhammer at the same time I do.

We both take off toward the weapon, hand-checking one another the entire way. Our claws shred each other's skin as we race across the battlefield, covering us both in a thick layer of blood. I'm thankful for the Dexterity bonus from my horrors. It grants me just enough to keep up with a troll five levels higher than me. I summon another Horror of Finesse and use Sacrifice. The additional bonus point in

Dexterity allows me to pull ahead by a few inches. I dive for the warhammer and feel the cold metal against my palms.

With the warhammer in my hand, I roll over, keeping it out of reach of Kronan. He grasps for it in a panic, but I manage to kick free. Rising to my feet, I swing the hammer as he tries to grab it, connecting with his ribs.

He picks up a boulder and tosses it at me, but the warhammer easily smashes through it. He slowly backs away from me, knowing I have the upper hand. Without a weapon, he's finished.

I cast Horror of Vitality, and the furry ram-demon charges ahead of me. Kronan stomps the horror into the ground, but not before its crowd-control slow takes effect.

The warhammer connects with Kronan's knees, shattering his left kneecap and knocking him off his feet. He grimaces at me as I stand above him.

"Go ahead. Finish me." His eyes are full of hatred. Self-hatred.

I unleash a guttural roar as I raise the warhammer in the air. It looms above him. Heavy. One motion and it would all be over. I hold the fate of his people in my hands.

I could kill him. Kill him, gain a load of experience, and probably take his ancient warhammer as my prize. But then where would the mountain trolls be? They need leadership to avoid extinction. Perhaps Brutus would take over. But he has already proven to be much the same as Kronan.

I drop the warhammer beside his head. "Save your people, before there are none left to save."

The crowd stands in shocked silence. They part before me without a word as I leave Kronan lying on the ground. On my way to the cages, I spot Sea Scorpion's gleaming shaft among the rubble and retrieve it. Brutus looks on in disbelief as I release the prisoners from their cages.

"Don't talk. Just go," I tell them.

CHAPTER TWENTY-SIX

GREAT, MORE WALKING

My horrors hiss and grumble as we travel down the mountain with great speed in an attempt to put as much distance between us and the mountain trolls as possible. Occasionally, a Horror of Vitality will lose its footing and be trampled underneath Stompy's massive hooves.

The mountain trolls were so shocked by the turn of events that they let us leave without a problem, but that doesn't mean they won't change their mind once they take stock of the situation.

I may have defeated the chief, but if a hundred goblins come chasing after us, we're gonna have a serious problem.

"Thank you so much," one of Keaton's sons says for the tenth time. His curly brown hair hangs against his broad shoulders. His forearms are brawny from years of wielding a sword. He wears tattered clothing, and his face is covered in dirt and soot, remnants of his time in captivity. His only possession is a stick for walking. All their belongings must have been stored in one of the caves, because there was nothing near the cages. "They were going to eat us. They were actually going to eat us." He shakes his head at the thought. His face is pasty white beneath the layers of dirt.

"What were you doing on their lands to begin with?" I cast three more horrors to pull up the rear. "Your father said you were warriors."

When I analyze them, I see that they are indeed warriors—level five, in fact. Which makes it all the more stupid that they would be on troll lands.

"It wasn't us," his brother answers for him. He looks much the same as the other one, aside from having short black hair. He also seems more composed and less shell-shocked. "We've been through these mountains a thousand times. We know better than to stray too high." He cuts his eyes at the other two men we rescued. The ones who have yet to say a word. "These two had the bright idea that there would be hidden treasures in the high caves. Said that we wouldn't be paid unless we took them to investigate. We'd have been within our right to let them die."

"What did you think you would find in the caves?" I ask the two men.

They just stare at me with wide eyes. Their clothes are of a finer quality than Keaton's sons. Even in their ripped and tattered state, the stitch quality is noticeable. The tan lines on their fingers tell the story even further. The trolls probably brought in quite the spoils from these two, not counting whatever goods they were traveling with.

"Good luck getting them to talk," the black-haired son says. "Neither one of them has said a word in three days. It's like talking to a wall. They were traders of some sort, that's all I know. They brought treasures from the south to trade with the dwarves. This was their first time using the pass at Smalltown. I expect it will be their last."

Up ahead, Taryn leads the way on Stompy, while Limery rides beside him on Berry. I'm glad I'm not the imp's personal mount for a change.

We reach far enough down the mountain that the trail forks in two directions. One leads back towards Smalltown. Keaton's sons and the merchants will be on their own from here. There are still several mountains to traverse, but each step will take them farther away from the trolls and goblins.

The other trail leads to the north, but at a much lower elevation.

I empty my pack and give the humans enough of our supplies to get them home. Taryn reluctantly parts with a dagger he took from Keaton's shop. The black-haired son gives us directions for the quickest and safest route through the mountains.

"Be safe out there." I watch them as they go, the two traders following Keaton's sons like dogs on a string.

"You think they'll make it back in one piece?" Taryn watches them leave.

Stompy snorts and paws his feet, ready to be on the way again.

"The two sons seem like they know what they're doing. The other two might need some serious counseling when they return." I slap Stompy on the backside and he starts moving. This time, we take the lower route.

"We haven't had a chance to talk about it yet, but damn, where did you learn to fight like that?" Taryn cast Strong Wind on us, increasing our speed. Since we aren't on such an incline, we can quicken our pace without worry. "Back there, that was on another level than what I've seen you do. It was brutal. And I know your scrawny ass can't fight like that in real life, so what gives?"

"I don't know, man. When my rage takes over, it's like I'm running on autopilot." I kick a rock and it goes tumbling off the trail. "My body sets out to destroy anything that's in my way. It's like when you learn a new ability and you just instantly know how to use it." I try to find the words to accurately explain what it feels like, but I can't. "It's hard to explain. Like with herbalism, once you learn a new plant, you can see its outline without even having to search for it. Fighting is just like that; my body just knows what to do. I think my mind and years of gaming are what give me an edge."

Taryn runs his fingers through his beard, thinking. "Hmmm. I guess it's the

same with me. I don't know how to actually pull lightning from the sky, I just do it."
His eyes light up when he has a thought. "Wait, do you think you'll know how to
fight when you log—when you go back?" He turns to Limery, to see if the imp
caught his slip-up, but the imp is fixated on my horrors that pop in and out of
existence.

I laugh at the absurdity of his question. "Do you think you'll be able to call lightning from the sky?"

"If so, they'll be calling me Black Lightning." He grins. "And you can be my
sidekick, White Thunder." He leans back and cackles, nearly falling from the
moulhaug.

Following the directions from Keaton's son, we make it through the mountains
in two days with no problems. At one point, we pass an area that has a pretty
sizable number of ley lines, perhaps some hidden mountain dungeon, but Taryn is
so excited to show me the dwarven side of the island that we don't stop to
investigate.

When the mountains finally end, and we find ourselves in the valley beneath
them, a beautiful meadow stretches for miles. Flowers are in full bloom, and the
wind sweeps across it in waves, like a turbulent rainbow sea.

Stompy goes to the side of the trail and gathers a mouthful of flowers. Taryn
tries to lead him back to the trail, but the moulhaug will have none of it.

"All of that power and he eats flowers and eggs." Taryn shakes his head as
Stompy rips another massive bouquet and chews it up.

"You survived on soda and fast food, so you aren't that different." Those were
good times. I can remember so many nights when that was all we ate. Soda, chips,
Chinese delivery or pizza.

"What's fast foods?" asks Limery. "Limmy is fast. He can catch all the foods."

"I'm sure you can," says Taryn, grinning. "Fast food is when I take a piece of
meat and throw it at you really fast. You have to catch it out of the air."

"Ooh!" Limery claps his hand together. "Can we plays fast foods?"

"Yeah, we need some food first." Taryn laughs. "You want to catch us
something?"

"Limmy's on it!" He zooms away among the flowers.

"You know he is going to want to play fast foods about twenty times a day now,
right?" I watch Limery as he zips above the flowers, hurling fireballs at birds and
other creatures hiding in the underbrush. Limery's fascination with food knows no
bounds.

He returns with several dead birds and a nest full of turquoise eggs. Standing
proudly, he presents his spoils to Taryn. We stop for lunch, and they roast the food
over an open fire.

I lean against the moulhaug's side, eating a bird wing and watching Taryn
throw pieces of meat at Limery, who flies to catch them. No matter how fast or how
far Taryn tosses it, Limery zooms through the air, never missing a piece.

I can't help but smile at their antics. At home, on the rare occasion we had
dinner as a family, we ate our meals in silence. The sounds of slurping water and

mastication were enough to drive anyone mad. Mom and Dad would talk business; I would sit quietly.

This wouldn't fly there.

The few times I had dinner with Taryn and his family, it was the complete opposite of my home life. His family laughed and joked. They talked about their day. They even asked me questions. It felt so different, so welcoming.

Taryn might not have grown up with money, but he had something far more valuable. Family.

"Go long." I load an egg in my palm and point far into the meadow.

Limery takes off, and I launch the egg. It soars through the air, so high that I can't even see it against the blue sky. Farther than any baseball player could possibly throw a ball.

The imp soars into the sky and a moment later, I hear his cheer as he catches the egg.

Once we cycle through the remainder of the eggs, we're back on the road.

As we journey away from the mountain, the flowery meadow begins to thin out. We walk beside a stream as the terrain transforms into grassland, and then gradually, the grass grows sparse and becomes nothing but sand. When the stream of water disappears underground, we come to a stop.

Ahead, there is nothing but desert for as far as I can see. When I pull up my map, I see it stretches even farther.

"We should stock up on water now." Taryn dips his leather canteen in the stream. "We'll need to reconnect with the Mythroad, and we might not find another water source along the way." He puts the cork in his canteen. "Once we reconnect with the Mythroad, that'll lead us straight into Sandholde."

"Sandholde?" I've never heard of it, but to be fair, the only dwarven city I know is Seascape, and that's because it's the capital.

"Yes, it's the second largest dwarven city on *Isle of Mythos*. It also happens to be the home of the largest ebony dwarf population on the island, located in the center of the desert."

Judging by my map, we are at least a day's journey from the Mythroad, the massive road that runs from Vanaria to Seascape, connecting the two kingdoms. We never reconnected with it after the Marshlands, instead following smaller roads that led us to Smalltown. I wonder if the Mythroad passage through the mountains is a safer journey.

Looking closer at the map, the Mythroad is the only major road that goes through the desert. There's only one city in all of the sand-colored landscape, so I assume that is Sandholde. The Mythroad is the shortest and most direct route to Seascape, and it passes straight through Sandholde.

Roads and towns surround the desert on both sides, but the desert is short and wide, shaped like a saucer, so it appears that it would double our travel time to bypass it. Plus, I wouldn't get to see the native home of Taryn's people.

As we travel, Taryn tells me all he knows about Sandholde. "It's an oasis among the desert. Truly remarkable. If I hadn't been on my way to meet you, I could have spent days there." His eyes light up with excitement as he talks about the architecture and fashion. "It's said that in ancient times, Sandholde refused passage to outsiders for various reasons. Without enough water to make it back to safety, many men were laid to waste outside their gates begging for entrance."

"That's harsh." I wipe sweat from my brow. The desert sun is already beating down upon us. "What would cause them to close their gates?"

Taryn shrugs, his dreadlocks swaying back and forth. "Who knows? War or politics would be my guess."

He pulls his cloak over his head. Since entering the desert, he has exposed very little of his body to the sun, keeping his cloak around him like a tent. To me, it seems like that would cook him like an oven, but he doesn't complain.

Limery, whose body is a natural furnace, doesn't seem affected at all. He zooms ahead at times, occasionally returning with some slithering creature he's managed to catch.

Berry moves sluggishly behind us. The fur-covered bear wasn't meant for these conditions.

Taryn orders the moulhaug to stop. Climbing down from Stompy, Taryn gives the bear some water from his leather flask and pats him on the head. "You can do it, buddy. I promise it'll be worth it."

The bear weakly grunts. His beautiful umber coat has grown a lighter color from all the sand.

The day drags on, and the blistering heat of the desert sun beats down from overhead. There's nothing but sand for as far as I can see. Why would anyone want to live in such a desolate and angry place? The plants are covered in spikes or needles, and the monsters are all venomous. The entire area is hellbent on killing one another.

We come across a dune and something shifts beneath. Sand ripples like crystallized water as the monster beneath rises up. Grains of sand fall off its body, concealing its true form beneath the facade of a sandy ghost. It thrashes forward, revealing a worm-like monster with dozens of sharp teeth that spiral down into its throat. It has a hardened exterior with rows of spiked barbs that run down its body.

I would expect nothing less from such hellacious terrain.

Sandworm. *Level 18. These eyeless predators attack from below ground. Without eyes, they track their prey by feeling movement in the sand. The sandworm's circular mouth is capable of ingesting enemies whole.*

The sandworm rockets from the sand, mouth open, and dives for my horrors. It devours several of them in one bite before disappearing beneath the sand.

I wipe the sweat from my brow and get into position. It's too damned hot for this.

Following the ripples in the sand as the sandworm moves below, I ready Sea Scorpion for attack when the sandworm breaks the surface.

My weapon clinks against its hardened exterior, doing no damage as it passes by, and the worm ingests several more of my horrors.

"Its shell is too hard to damage with melee weapons," I tell the others.

Taryn cast Lightning Bolt from Stompy's back, but the electricity only runs along the sandworm's exterior, doing very little damage.

Stompy unleashes a powerful war cry and paws at the sand.

When the creature rises again, displaying its open mouth, it reminds me of our battle with the mana-infused wyrm. I see an opening. "Limery, dive down its throat!"

Without a moment's hesitation, the imp burst into flame and darts at the sandworm's open mouth. Its teeth chomp down as Limery enters, but it's too late. He's is already barreling down its throat.

Heat radiates from the sandworm's body as Limery crawls along its insides. It rears up, unleashing a demonic cry before collapsing to the ground.

A moment later, Limery burns a hole through the creature's side and emerges, covered in mucus. He shakes off his arms and the slimy substance splats in the sand.

"That's one way to do it." Taryn walks over to examine the body for loot. "Nothing worth taking. It's mostly shell."

Not long after, we come across another dune and a sandworm rises to attack. We're all grouchy from the heat, so before it can even attack, Limery turns into a scorching ball of flame and flies straight into the creature's throat, cooking it from the inside. Taryn and I stand back, watching the imp roast it alive. His molten temperature burns through the creature's stomach as it curls up in agony. We leave it to bake in the sun.

***

Night comes, and we finally connect with the Mythroad. Sand covers the road, but its even elevation and worn path leaves no doubt that it's what we are looking for. Looking around, there's not a soul in sight in either direction. I don't know why I thought there would be. The two kingdoms don't really trade. They send ambassadors and workers to go to the other kingdom and show them their ways.

We're only a few hours from Sandholde, so we decide to push through instead of camping in the desert, where predators are more likely to attack at night. Once we're there, we can find a nice inn and wash some of this sand away. It's in my toes, in my braid, and I'm pretty sure I could build a sandcastle with what has found its way into my ass-crack. For the first time since coming here, a hot shower sounds amazing.

Limery perches on my shoulder, and soon soft snores ring in my ear.

We make better time now that we are on a main road. The buff from Strong Wind has us all moving at a fast pace.

The desert is a strange place. Eerily quiet most of the time. Occasionally, a creature howls or something slithers in the sand, but for the most part, the only sounds we hear are our muffled steps on the sand-covered Mythroad, and the grumbling of my horrors.

I tilt my head back and look to the stars. Millions of them twinkle overhead, and they are like nothing I have ever seen. Millions of stars, but not a single recognizable constellation. It makes me appreciate the detail that went into this game even more. It's not a copy of Earth. It's something brand new. A world with its own history, its own future. The choices that I and these other heroes make will decide that future.

That's pretty wild.

To my left, Taryn hunches atop Stompy. In the darkness, with his cloak covering his features, he looks like some shadowy villain.

Up ahead, something twinkles in the distance, catching my eye. The longer I look at it, the more I see until it's an entire line of twinkles.

I'm pondering what type of monster we're about to fight when I notice the outline running beneath the twinkling. It's a wall. And those twinkles are fires.

We've made it to Sandholde. The outline becomes clearer the closer we get, until I can see the entirety of the wall as it towers above the sand. It's massive, stretching for many hundreds of yards. A citadel in a wasteland of nothingness. A faint glow escapes from inside, projecting on the humongous palm trees that tower above the walls. With so many, it looks like a tropical paradise is waiting on the other side.

A large crowd surrounds the gate, waiting for entrance. I hear laughter before I ever see their faces. There are several wagons covered in canvas. A few of the people are extremely tall and lanky, and I wonder if they are some race I haven't heard of.

Then one of them rears its head back and blows out a stream of fire, igniting the emblem on the side of one of the wagons.

A red lion. The same red lion I saw before on the door of the Underground Circus.

CHAPTER TWENTY-SEVEN
WHERE'S WALDUR?

A man with a painted face approaches us from the circus crowded at the gate. He wears a multi-colored striped tunic, billowing pants, and fanciful shoes that curl up at the end.

"Hawkin?" I recognize the bard from the Underground Circus as he gets closer. His face is painted white, with a green clover painted over one eye and a black diamond over the other. The colors match the rest of his outfit. "What are you doing up all the way up here?"

"I should be asking you the same thing." He flashes me a smile. "I took your advice. We've brought the Underground Circus on the road." He walks closer to Taryn, examining the moulhaug. His eyes follow it from its horn all the way down its massive body. "Now, this is a fascinating creature. You don't happen to be in need of employment, do you, Mr. Dwarf?"

"I'm afraid not. We're just passing through." Taryn removes his hood, and his dreadlocks fall beside his face.

I take a moment to introduce the two. "And you haven't formally met Limery." I point to the imp, still asleep on my shoulder.

"You travel in rare company, Mr. Troll." He flips a golden coin with his thumb. It's similar to the one he gave me the first day we met.

"How has it been on the road?"

"Life outside the capital has been absolutely marvelous. Most of the townsfolk have never seen our brand of entertainment. And the dwarves, they love us. They view us as performers, not just freaks." He beams. "If things hold up, we may never return to Vanaria again."

"Wow, that good?" I look over at the wagons. They are loaded to the brim with crates and bags. How is it possible that they left after me but still managed to make it to Sandholde ahead of us? "How did you manage to get your caravan through the mountain in one piece?" Most of the wagons look like they could topple over at any moment.

He looks at me with confusion. "What do you mean?"

"It took us five days to cross the mountains. I can't imagine navigating some of those passes with all that cargo."

"You didn't take the Mythroad through the mountain?" He cocks his head in bewilderment.

"No, why?" No one gave us a road-map with directions.

"It's the safest route. There's a tunnel that goes straight through the mountain, carved by magic long ago. You have to pass through dwarven customs. They are very particular about what they let into their country, but the time it saves makes up for the hassle. The only ones who travel through the mountains are adventurers, criminals, or those with something to hide."

No wonder Smalltown is so small. Keaton and his sons are smuggling items from one kingdom to the other.

And what about Glenn and Jude? Does that mean they had to cross through the mountains to avoid being detected?

"Hawkin, we're through!" someone yells from the front of the caravan, and they begin filtering in through the gate.

"I must take my leave now, but we will be having a show tomorrow. I hope to see you there." He leaves to rejoin his people.

When Hawkin is out of earshot, I turn to Taryn. "Why didn't you tell me the Mythroad went straight through the mountain?" It would have been some nice information to have. That way, we would have at least had the option.

"I didn't know. I flew through the mountains to save time." He shrugs nonchalantly. "Who would have thought that sweet, old couple from Smalltown were part of a smuggling ring?"

"Tell me about it. They seemed so nice."

Limery stirs on my shoulder as we approach the gate, grunting and looking around in confusion.

Several dwarven guards block our entry as soon as the circus passes through. They range from level fifteen to twenty, and stand side by side, holding obsidian spears tipped with gold. They each wear silk loincloths and sandals, with a golden sash wrapped around their waists. The white fabric stands out prominently against their dark skin. Golden necklaces shimmer as they hang across their bare chests. Each dwarf has a thick, black beard similar to Taryns, but they all wear their hair fairly short.

Taking them all in, they look more for show than actual battle. With no armor, all their weak points are exposed. Kind of like me, I guess. Maybe I shouldn't be so quick to rush to judgment.

"What is your business in Sandholde?" one of them asks in a deep baritone voice. He wears his hair in a mohawk and has a brilliant sapphire ring on one hand.

"We're just passing through." Taryn steps forward. "I wanted to show Chod here one of the greatest cities in the world on our way to the capital."

The dwarves stand a little taller at the compliment, puffing out their chests.

"Keep a wary eye," says the dwarf to his right. "Several dwarves have been reported missing. If it keeps up, I expect our gates will be closed to outsiders soon."

Taryn and I exchange glances. Missing people? This has Glenn and Jude written all over it. If he's started gathering another army...

The guards step aside, allowing us entry into the city.

A sprawling road leads down the center of the city for several hundred yards to a giant pyramid that rises high into the sky. The center road is pristine with thousands of neatly-laid bricks. The mortar between each brick is visible, without a grain of sand caught between. Numerous fountains gurgle along the side of the road, with lush gardens surrounding them. Brightly-colored tropical flowers blossom in the moonlight.

Taryn was right, this place is an oasis. You'd never know it from the outside, but I haven't seen this much life since the meadow at the base of the mountains. This feels like paradise.

Farther out from the road, there are lines of beautiful buildings made from sandstone. Eclectic patterns are carved into them, almost like Egyptian hieroglyphics, except the images are all dwarves and monsters.

"You might want to lift your jaw up off the ground or you're going to trip over it." Taryn gives me a smug grin.

"This place is beautiful." It's almost too much to take in. I can't imagine what it will look like in the daylight. "I don't know what I was expecting, but it wasn't this."

"We can explore tomorrow. I think we're all pretty beat. Let's find us an inn." He hops down from Stompy and leads us down a side street.

Taryn scratches Berry behind the ears and the bear nuzzles against his arm, glad to finally have some attention.

The manicured streets are eerily quiet at this hour. That's until we turn a corner and hear drunken revelry on the steps in front of a sandstone building.

White columns surround a porch filled with dwarves. Above the entrance, there's an engraving of several enormous mugs of ale.

As we approach, the raucous noise becomes more distinguishable. Many of the dwarves are singing a song about a maiden in the mountains. They clink their tankards together, and their drinks splosh on the ground.

Candlelight flickers from inside the open door.

Taryn instructs Berry and Stompy to wait outside while we make arrangements for the night. Many of the dwarves shout "Welcome, brother!" to Taryn as we pass. They're all clad in similar forms of canvas robes or silken loincloths. Many of them wear gaudy rings, gold bracelets, or necklaces. I notice that a few of the dwarves don't have beards, and I can't help but wonder if they are the females. If that's the case, there is very little to distinguish them. They stumble along merrily. Some eye me cautiously as we pass, but I don't hear any of the rude comments I heard in the southern towns.

A beardless dwarf stands behind a marble counter as we enter. The dwarf wears a long silken robe, with a gold sash tied around the waist. "Welcome to The Sand

Dune Inn." The voice has a softer tone than Taryn's or the other male dwarves I've met, so I assume my hypothesis is correct. Still, I don't trust it enough to test it and allow Taryn to do the talking.

"I'd like two rooms for me and my friends. And a place for my pets in the oasis." He slides a gold coin across the counter.

The hostess rings a bell, and a dwarf appears from a back room. She whispers something in his ear, and he hurries past us.

"Right this way, please." She motions towards an immaculate staircase. It's engraved and set with jewels along the balusters. A hammer is carved into the knob at the end of the handrail.

Limery's eyes linger on the jewels as we pass.

"Don't even think about it," I warn, and he blows out of his nostrils.

Taryn falls in step beside me. "So, what do you think? Pretty nice, huh?"

"This place is amazing. You didn't have to spring for something so fancy." Honestly, we're just sleeping here. All we need is a bath and some food.

"I didn't. This is actually on the cheaper side." He laughs. "Believe it or not, there's not a lot to do in the desert, and dwarves are master craftsmen. Mix boredom and sandstone and you get inns that look like royalty stays here."

The hostess shows us to our rooms. "Food is available downstairs, and the hot spring is located in the rear." She smiles, revealing a set of pearly white teeth. "Enjoy your stay."

"Did she say hot spring?" I toss my bags on the bed and race downstairs.

In the courtyard outdoors, a stone-walled tub steams in the moonlight. There are several torches burning nearby, and a shirtless dwarf sits in the pool, drinking a frothy liquid and relaxing.

"Hop on in," says Taryn. "I'll grab us some drinks."

We should be resting, but how can I pass this up? It may be hot, but clean skin is worth the price.

I stand on the ledge, wondering if I should leave my loincloth on or let my troll-berries swim in all their glory when the dwarf looks up at me.

"I promise not to bite if you don't." He chuckles and takes another swig of his beverage.

I climb down into the hot spring. It's definitely dwarf-sized, because when I sit my butt flat against the bottom, the water barely comes past my stomach. Still, it feels amazing and I'm beyond grateful for a chance to wash away the dirt and sand.

"You're a big lad." The dwarf looks on with amusement.

"That's what they keep telling me." Dirt cakes off my skin as I rub at my forearms.

Limery dips his toes in the water, then scrunches his face. "Limmy goes to bed. Goodnights, Chods."

"Good night, buddy. I'll see you in a few." I splash water against my face and taste the saltiness as it washes away days worth of sweat.

Taryn returns with two mugs, passing Limery as he leaves. "Who knew you were actually blue under all that dust?" He laughs as he hands me my mug. The liquid inside is creamy and white.

"What is this?" I take a sip and it's a mixture of sweet and bitter.

"Fermented goat milk. It's an ebony dwarf specialty." He sets his mug on the edge and climbs in.

"Cheers to that!" says the other dwarf. "Name's Krenshaw Glassbreaker. What brings a troll to the finest city in all of the dwarven kingdom?"

"We're visiting the capital," answers Taryn. For being such a quiet and shy person around new people, he seems awfully chatty with the dwarves. "But I didn't think a visit to the north would be complete without a stop at Sandholde."

"Aye, I'm actually on the way to the capital myself." He drains the rest of his mug. "They say the king is planning a great announcement in the coming days. I'm hoping for a tournament myself. It's been a good while since we've had a dwarven tournament. There's word that a hero has finally been blessed to the dwarves. It'd be a sight to behold if he showed up."

Taryn and I exchange glances.

"We may just have to check it out." The edge of Taryn's mustache twitches. I guess the dwarves really do love their heroes.

———

I wake up the next morning ready to explore the city. My first dwarven city! If it's anything like what I saw on the way to the inn, I'm in for a real treat. After relaxing in the hot spring last night with Taryn and Krenshaw, I feel as rejuvenated as ever. Maybe it was something in the fermented goat's milk.

Limery sits on the end of the bed, watching me. I don't know how long he's been up, but he looks like he's been expecting me. His bulbous yellow eyes stare intently. He grins, showcasing his both frightening and endearing smile. "Good mornings!"

When I open the door to the hallway, a dwarven guard waits outside. "You have been summoned by Lady Brollen to the great pyramid." He is dressed in the same garb as the dwarves from the entrance, but instead of a spear, he carries a short-sword that hangs by his side.

"Is Taryn awake yet?" I ask. We're not under arrest, so I can only assume that this is a cordial visit. She must have somehow found out that two heroes were in her city.

To answer my question, the door across the hall opens, and Taryn looks out in surprise.

"We've been summoned," I say.

He raises his eyebrows. "Do we at least get breakfast first?"

"Food will be provided," says the dwarf. His fingers rap against the hilt of his sword. "If you'll follow me." He takes off down the stairs.

We hurry to follow him, leaving our belongings in the room for later. He's surprisingly swift for such a stocky fellow. Taryn's stubby legs practically run to keep up.

Downstairs, the inn is crowded with dwarves, and the smell of roasting coffee wafts across the room. I try to take a gander at some of the platters, but the dwarven soldier is out of the door in a flash, forcing us to catch up.

Bright light blinds me for a moment as we step into the street. In a matter of seconds, I'm already sweating. Forest trolls were not made for this type of environment.

In the daylight, the city is even more resplendent than I imagined. To our left, a pyramid towers over the rest of the city. I don't know how I didn't notice it last night. We pass fountains of dwarves that spout water out of hammers, axes, horns, and shields. The beautiful engravings almost pop off the buildings. Tropical birds flutter through the city streets, flying from one fruit tree to another.

One fountain is drained, and a group of dwarves unload a cube of marble from a wagon. Another dwarf looks on, holding a hammer and chisel.

Several dwarves sweep the city streets. That explains why everything looks so clean.

"Why do you think they want to see us?" I ask Taryn. "Did they ask to see you last time you were here?"

Taryn runs beside me. Without his mount, he forced to keep up on his own. He shakes his head. "I have no idea. I didn't tell anyone we were heroes, so I don't know what they could possibly want."

Two guards wait outside the entrance to the pyramid, guarding a gleaming golden door that depicts a fight between a dwarf and a sandworm. Our guide says something to them, and they move aside.

Inside, we're hit with a rush of cool air. The cold air jolts my sweat-covered body, sending chills down my spine. Limery shivers on my shoulder for a moment before his feet grow warm.

There's a low ceiling and a path that meanders between several pools of water covered with flowering lily pads. Brightly colored fish swim just beneath the surface. The pools themselves are cubical, and the entire room looks like a giant game of Minesweeper with the way the path leads through the pools.

A dozen different doors surround the perimeter of the room. They must lead into the rest of the pyramid. At the far end of the room, a dark-skinned, beardless dwarf with long, curly, black hair, and wearing a silken white robe, sits on a throne of glass. The throne has glass spikes that stick up from the back of it, and they shimmer with the light of the surrounding torches. Several guards stand off to each side.

I focus on the dwarf on the throne and her stats appear.

Lady Brollen. *Level: ???*

Of course, she has her stats concealed. I wonder how powerful she truly is.

"It's not every day that we have the great honor of housing two heroes in our fine city." When she smiles, her face lights up. I'll never get over how beautiful ebony dwarf teeth look against their dark complexion.

"How do you know we are heroes?" asks Taryn.

"No one can hide their identity from city officials." She looks at me and winks. "But you have no need to worry. It is a great honor to host you. Please, come and join me for breakfast." She rises from the throne. "We shall dine in my chambers."

Limery licks his lips at the prospect of food, and I have the strong urge to toss him in the fish pond.

When Lady Brollen stands, her robe clings to her body. She's built very differently from the female dwarves I saw at the inn. Less stocky, more curvy. There is no confusion that she is a female.

Taryn stares on in wonder.

She leads us through a door at the rear of the room and up several flights of stairs. Inside of her room, the slanted walls are lined with floor-to-ceiling windows. They must be painted or enchanted on the outside, because I don't recall being able to see into the pyramid from the street.

We must be near the top of the pyramid, because the windows offer a complete three-hundred-and sixty-degree view of the city. The center street is visible, along with the homes and inns in one corner of the city. In another, I spot a lake as blue as sapphire surrounded by trees and vegetation. There are fields full of crops and from this high up, dwarves move among them like tiny ants.

Two dwarven soldiers take their post by the entrance.

"Please, have a seat." She gestures to two sofas surrounding a golden table loaded with grapes, figs, bread, roasted fowl, and fish.

Limery reaches for a piece of fish before we even sit down.

"Thank you." I take a seat, admiring the rest of the room. Marble floors with a swirled pattern of tan and aqua blue feel cool against my feet. Several miniature sculptures adorn a desk littered with papers, scrolls, and heavy tomes.

"What do you think of our fair city, Chod?" Lady Brollen asks.

"It's lovely. How do you manage to keep it so lush in the middle of the desert? And how is the pyramid so cool?" Air conditioning is a luxury of my past, yet, here we are.

She picks up a grape, grasping it between her fingers. Tiny veins of ice spread out from where she touches it, covering the grape until it has a layer of frost surrounding it. She places the grape on the table and it clinks against the gold.

An ice mage!

"One thing my people are known for is making sure that those with power find themselves in the right places." One side of her mouth curls up in a mischievous grin.

"You're an ice mage?" asks Taryn, his mouth wide open. "That's awesome."

"Indeed, I am. Controlling the temperature of the air around me is one of my specialties." She picks up another grape and seductively bites on it while staring at Taryn.

Even his dark skin can't hide the blushing as blood rushes to his cheeks.

She eats the other half of the grape and returns her gaze to me. "The water gardens, the lake, the forest, and the plants, all that is the work of our druids and water mages. They are the reason Sandholde is the most beautiful city on the island."

I can't argue with her about that. I have yet to see a single part of the city that couldn't appear on the cover of a travel magazine in the real world.

Limery picks up an entire fowl and sinks his teeth into it. Lady Brollen watches him with fascination. We really do need to work on his manners.

"I hear you are on your way to Seascape." She leans back against the sofa, waiting for our response.

I wonder how many spies she has placed throughout the city. Maybe even the dwarf in the hot spring is in her employ.

"That's right," Taryn says between bites. He gives her a goofy grin, and I'm not sure if he's playing it cool or trying to be sexy.

I settle back and enjoy some of the food while Taryn does whatever it is that Taryn does. The roasted fowl and fish are delicious. They have a certain spicy flavor to them that I haven't tasted before. Probably some ethnic herbs and spices.

Lady Brollen watches us for a moment before speaking. "I can't wait to see what crazy idea the king has this time. If he knows you'll be in attendance, I'm sure it'll be extra special." She sighs. "But truth be told, I've called you here for more than simple chat. Over the past week, several of our people have gone missing. There have been no signs of foul play. No blood or anything that would suggest a struggle. Not so much as a note explaining why they left. But the sheer number of vanishings point to something more at play. Even my own brother, Waldur, has disappeared without a trace." She leans forward, her icy blue eyes piercing my own. "You may be headed north, but I don't believe it is blind chance that brought you upon our fair city. Keep your eyes open, and if you notice anything suspicious, here or on your travels, I implore you to investigate. Find out what has happened to our people, and you will be greatly rewarded."

Quest Alert. *You have been offered the quest "Where's Waldur?" Discover where the missing dwarves have gone and to what end. Return to Lady Brollen with information to claim your reward.*

Reward: Unknown.

Bonus: Return with Waldur.

Not the greatest quest, but if these missing people have anything to do with Jude and Glenn, then we're already on the trail.

"We will do our best." Taryn nods.

"I cannot ask for more than that." Her gaze lingers on Taryn. "Now if you will excuse me, I have important matters to attend."

When she doesn't move, it becomes clear that we are the ones expected to leave. Apparently, I am the only one who notices, because I have to jab Taryn in the side before he takes his eyes off Lady Brollen.

He scowls at me before rising. "Ugh, thank you, my lady." He bows, the clasps in his beard clinking.

When we are outside of the pyramid, I burst out laughing. "Somebody has a crush."

Limery echoes my enthusiasm, pointing a skinny red finger at Taryn. "Somebodys has a crush," he chants.

"Oh, knock it off. I was just being polite." He tries to play it off, but his red cheeks give it away. Even though he was the tall, dark, and handsome type in real life, his shyness kept him from being a hit with the girls at school.

"Don't you mean 'knock it off, my lady'?" I let out a deep and boisterous laugh. "Tell me, do you even know what color her eyes were?"

"Dude, shut up. She was pretty." He shoves me in the side. "What do you want to do now?"

"The circus performance isn't until this evening. We can explore the city until then and head out tomorrow?" I suggest. A bead of sweat runs down my brow. "I'd love to check out that lake."

"Sounds good. I think it might be time for me to upgrade my outfit too." He looks over the tunic and cloak he's wearing. "I picked these up in Seascape. It'd be nice to get something more climate appropriate."

Our first stop is a tailor for Taryn to buy some new clothes. He ends up purchasing a tan cloak, light brown pants, and a white cotton shirt that laces up the front.

I settle for a patterned white and green shawl that wraps around my head and shoulders. The tailor said it will help to cool me off in the heat. I've grown accustomed to wearing nothing but a loincloth, and I don't plan to stop now that I have money.

After trying it on, I ask Limery if he would like one.

"Limmy doesn't need it. The hots is fine."

Imps. They don't get tired. They don't get hot. The little guy doesn't know how good he's got it.

With our new clothing, the heat does seem a bit more bearable. I guess the lightweight fabric has a way of reflecting the heat back or something.

We follow a narrow stone path through dense vegetation that leads us to the lake. Several dwarf children splash about in the water, and on the far side, I spot Berry and Stompy relaxing beneath the shade of a palm tree. When Berry sees us, he takes off running toward Taryn.

"What are they doing out here?" I ask. I figured they would be in the stables.

"Perks of the inn. They take great care of pets and mounts here. They can pretty much roam free in the park as long as they behave."

Berry leaps on Taryn, tackling the dwarf into the sand. Meanwhile, Stompy sits basking in the shade, barely acknowledging us.

A strange-looking camel catches the corner of my eye. When I focus on it, I notice it has a large silver protuberance sticking out of its head.

Unicamel. *Level 5.*

That's just too weird. A camel-unicorn hybrid. I point it out to Taryn and his face lights up for a moment. It's quickly replaced by a frown.

"I wish I could have one. Stompy would take offense if I got another horned creature." He gazes at the unicamel longingly.

"Sounds like Stompy is running your life now." I watch the camel as it leans down to take a drink from the lake. With its long, skinny legs, it wouldn't be much use in a battle, not unless that horn has some special powers, but I'm sure it's an excellent mount, especially in this climate. It probably couldn't carry me, though.

"Admiring The Gore Queen, are you?" a husky voice calls from behind us. When I look at him with confusion, he elaborates. "That's what I call me mount. She's a right beaut."

I stare at him for a moment. Not because of anything he's said, but because I'm shocked to see an ivory dwarf in Sandholde. He wears a light blue tunic with a white undershirt, keeping most of his skin from exposure to the sun. Thick leather boots cover his feet, a battle helm protects his head, and a vibrant red beard hangs across his chest. It matches the color of his sunburned nose. His tunic has a patch of a golden hammer sewn on one sleeve. In one hand, he holds an iron scepter that trickles water out of the end. In the other, a flask.

He looks more out of place than I do.

"She is quite gorgeous," says Taryn. "I didn't think the mountainfolk visited Sandholde often?"

"Eh, we don't. Wee bit of bad luck on my end." He pokes the end of his staff into the ground and takes a swig of his mystery beverage. When he unstops it, a faint whiff of alcohol hits me. "It's been quite a time since a water mage has been born in Sandholde. Until they can supply their own, water mages from the capital are sent on rotation to keep the city alive. It's a beautiful city, but damn if she isn't a pain in me arse."

"Wait, do you mean that Sandholde isn't actually an oasis? All of this is dwar-ven-made?" Taryn's mouth hangs open in shock.

I smack him on the back of the head. "Lady Brollen told us this not even an hour ago, but I guess you were focused on other things."

The water mage bypasses my snide remark. "That be the truth of it. In the next life, if I ever find the dwarf who thought this would be a good idea, I'll kick him in the balls meself." He lifts his helm and wipes at his perspiring forehead. Bright red hair is matted with sweat. "That's enough chatting for me. I need to top off the lake, and then water the crops." He gives us a two-finger salute and takes off toward the lake.

I imagine it's quite the change from living in the cool mountains to spending his entire day in the desert sun.

"Do you mind if we tag along?" asks Taryn. "I'd like to see how it's done."

"Be me guest."

A flock of brightly-colored birds lands in a palm tree overhead. Limery hops from my shoulder and takes off after them.

"Limery!" I shout after him. "We are guests. Do not go killing any of their wildlife."

He gives me such a pitiful frown that I think he might cry. I just shake my head at him. It's not going to kill him to learn a little restraint.

Berry galumphs along behind Taryn as we head down to the bank of the lake. Several of the children have gathered around the water mage. They must know what is about to happen.

On the far side of the lake, dwarves are fishing. A few canoes paddle in the open water.

The water mage lifts his scepter into the air and a stream of water shoots out of it into the lake. At first, it trickles like a faucet, and I can't help but wonder how he will ever fill the lake with that weak of a stream. Then, the water flow sputters, like it's backed up. The water shoots outs in jolts, a little at a time, then suddenly a geyser erupts from the end of the scepter, like someone popped the lid off a fire hydrant. The water shoots out for twenty or thirty yards, creating a rainbow as the sun is refracted through the mist.

Children rush into the lake, standing under the torrent of water, laughing and playing. Their parents watch from the bank, soaking in the sun.

For the next thirty minutes, water continues to pour from his scepter. Taryn stands beside the mage, watching with amazement.

I try to focus on the mage, but his stats are unreadable. For him to have that much continuous power, he must be pretty strong.

The water flow stops to wails of disappointment from the children.

"I come here every day, and every day, they cry when I leave. It's off to the crops for me."

"Take care." Taryn waves at the mage before turning back to me. "Can you imagine? Having the responsibility of keeping an entire city with water. I know he hates it down here. I mean, he must be roasting alive."

"Yeah, but the good thing is that the king is keeping the city alive. The unhappiness of one to save thousands. Not to mention the Mythroad would be useless without Sandholde."

We take a seat in the sand next to Stompy. The moulhaug raises his head for a moment before plopping it back in the sand. Of course, Taryn had to make a pet out of one of the laziest and most stubborn creatures in this game.

"We haven't talked about this new quest yet." He pulls out his flask, takes a drink of water, and passes it to me. "What do you make of it?"

"It sounds like the work of Glenn. Probably Jude too, if they are working together." I hope we can find the missing dwarves before they suffer the same fate as those in the forest. So many villagers lost their lives attacking the trolls because he convinced them to fight for him.

"How does he do it?" Taryn stares off in the distance, watching the dwarf families as they play in the lake. "How does he just convince them to follow him, no questions asked?"

I can tell by the way he is watching them that he no longer views them as NPCs. How could he? Spending five minutes alone with any of them and it's impossible to believe they are just numbers in a system.

"I don't know. Valery said he was a psychopath. Maybe that has something to do with it. Maybe he has some special abilities because of it." If so, that seems like a seriously fucked up thing to do. Or could it be like what happened with me? Is it possible that the game adjusted to him based off the way his brain works?

"If what you say is true, then we're better off finding them before they find us."

CHAPTER TWENTY-EIGHT

THE GREATEST SHOW ON MYTHOS

The striped tent of the Underground Circus stands tall in the center of the main thoroughfare. Against the backdrop of the city, it looks out of place, like something from another era altogether. Bright colors against a sandy landscape.

A large man with a black beard stands by the entrance. He wears a black tunic emblazoned with a red lion's head. I recall him as the man who took my coin when I first visited the Underground Circus all the way back in Vanaria. His mismatched eyes are hard to forget. One brown, the other a brilliant sky blue.

He takes coins from each dwarf as they enter.

"Welcome back." He winks, refusing our coin and ushering us through.

Limery sits on my shoulder, and Taryn walks beside me.

"I went to a circus once," he says. "Mom took me and my sister when we were younger. At the time, I thought it was pretty awesome."

"I'm sure this will be on a whole other level." If my underground encounter was any indication, they have quite a few tricks up their sleeves.

We walk down a tented corridor into a giant auditorium. Hundreds of seats fill one side, with a stage at the bottom. There's no way that all of this should fit inside the tent we saw outside.

"It has to be enchanted, right?" I ask.

Taryn nods. "I don't see any other way." He looks around, taking it all in. "I've heard of enchanted bags, but not an enchanted tent. The cost to make something so large, how could they afford it?"

"Maybe they didn't have to buy it." Considering Hawkin is a bard, it's very possible that they have an enchanter in their midst. Probably others who are magically inclined as well.

"Mr. Troll!" a childish voice calls out to me and I look over to see Brock, the young black-haired boy who snuck into my chamber at the castle. He carries a platform around his neck filled with popcorn. No longer dressed in tattered clothing, he wears a well-made red tunic similar to the man at the entrance. "Hawkin told us you might be coming. It's a surprise to see you all the way up here."

"I'm sure it is. Are we in for a good show tonight?" I honestly don't know what to expect. When I went to the Underground Circus, it was more of a party than a performance.

"It's gonna be great, I tell ya." He smiles. "Enjoy the show."

I attempt to buy a bag of popcorn from him, but he refuses my money. "I insist. Keep it for yourself." I press the gold coin into his palm, and he smiles.

Many of the seats are already filled, so we take a spot near the top. Being that I'm about twice the size of everyone else here, I don't want to be the dickhead that blocks their view from the show.

After we take our seats, I spot a man wearing a cat mask walking through the crowd. He wears the emblem of the circus and carries brightly-colored drinks that fizzle and smoke. The dwarves are going crazy over them, and he sells out in a matter of seconds. The circus doesn't disappoint, however, and as soon as he is gone, another man steps up with a new batch.

If these are anything like the drinks I had, then the dwarves are going to be ecstatic.

Taryn waves the man down and tries to buy a round for the three of us.

The man pushes away his coin. "On the house."

I take the cup of fizzing blue liquid. Tiny bubbles jump out at me, tickling my chin as they pop. I sip at the drink and it fizzes all the way down my throat.

Limery chugs his beverage, downing nearly half of it in one gulp. He hands me the cup, and his face contorts. He places his small hand over his stomach. "Limmy don't feels so good."

I laugh at him as dozens of bubbles fly out of my mouth. They billow in the sky.

Forgetting his pain, Limery reaches out and pops one with his finger. He laughs and bubbles spout from his mouth. Every time we laugh, more bubbles fill the air.

Below us, many of the dwarves' drinks have the same effect. Some blow steam out of their ears, others smoke from their nostrils. The show hasn't even started yet and the circus has already won them over.

As we wait for the crowd to filter in, the stands are alive with a maelstrom of bubbles, smoke, and steam.

Taryn points down to the front row. "Look, it's Lady Brollen." Bubbles float from his mouth with each word.

"Yeah, are you wanting to go sit in her lap?" I joke, but Taryn just rolls his eyes.

Eventually, every seat is filled and the candlelight dims to almost complete darkness.

A single spotlight falls upon the center of the stage. It doesn't flicker like candle-light, but burns steadily.

A woman steps before the light, her golden hair shimmering. I recognize her face and her lion-like hair that falls down her shoulders. Leona.

She opens her mouth and a mighty roar carries across the tent. The roar of a powerful beast. She bows, then disappears into the darkness. A moment later, Hawkin steps into the light.

He wears his juggler's attire, but this time, the pattern is all black and red, matching the circus.

"Welcome to the Underground Circus." He holds his hands together like he is praying as he talks. "Tonight, you will enter a land of whimsy, where anything is possible if you only believe. Tonight, you will see things that shouldn't be possible, things that are not possible, but for tonight, they will be."

He claps his hands together and an explosion of smoke obscures the spotlight. The light goes out, and for a moment, we are enraptured in total darkness. Then, the candles reignite, and light slowly returns as their flames grow. The stage is now filled with many silhouettes. They become more visible with each passing second.

Music surrounds us. The slow strum of a violin, then horned instruments, and drums. Only it appears to be coming from around us, from overhead, from behind.

Braziers erupt on the stage, igniting the performers in light. A dark-skinned man with fiery red dreadlocks dances across the stage, flipping and spinning. He somersaults through the air and his dreadlocks burst into flame.

Above him, a man and woman with splotched skin swing on a trapeze. The woman lets go of the trapeze, and for a moment, she flies through the air unencumbered before grasping hands with the man. He rockets her through the air, and she catches the next trapeze with the back of her knees.

The crowd erupts into applause.

Giant men on stilts step on the stage, juggling as they walk amid the flying acrobats. More dancers join them, and it descends into organized chaos. Every person has a place, a job, and they intertwine perfectly.

The music slows and the dancers file away into the darkness. There's a whistle, and a red lion with a black mane steps out into the spotlight. It roars as it paces. Several men appear, holding burning hoops. The lion roars and then jumps through. As it passes through the hoop, its mane erupts into flame. The lion stalks to and fro, huffing when it comes too close to the crowd, before running and jumping through another flaming hoop.

Next, flame-spitters and sword-swallowers take the stage. The crowd oohs and ahhs at their performances. The flame-spitters spit out cones of flame that turn into birds and dragons and fly around the tent. When one flies up to where we are sitting, the heat emanating from it is reminiscent of Limery's fiery form.

With so many fire elements, I can't help but wonder if there is a fire mage in their midst.

Hours pass as show after show mesmerizes the crowd. One oddity after another does a performance, each receiving grand applause. Drinks flow freely and one thing is certain: dwarves appreciate quality entertainment.

Limery sits enraptured on the edge of his seat, clapping and laughing with delight. I'm sure he's never seen anything so grand.

After a performance where a woman balances two swords tip to tip on her forehead while riding a unicycle, the tent goes dark and the spotlight reappears. Hawkin steps forward holding his fiddle.

He pulls the bow and visible neon soundwaves shoot out across the room. The soundwaves seep into the bodies of the crowd, turning their clothes the color of the soundwave that hit them. As his rhythm speeds up, the waves grow short, and when he slows down, they grow thick and seem to waft through the air.

I receive a notification, but I push it away for now, not ready to break my immersion.

The light of the candles changes to pastel before sending up plumes of glowing smoke that billow above our heads. The clouds absorb the soundwaves, pulling them in as tiny sparks of lightning form inside.

Thunder rolls across the tent. Then, with a final pull of his bow, the candles extinguish, and rain falls on our heads. It patters against everyone, and I imagine Limery and I alone are the only ones who can see in the darkness. There's a final crash of thunder, the rain stops, and the candles reignite. On the stage, there is no trace of the performers. The entire audience is covered in splotches of pastel, like a watercolor painting vomited all over us.

One by one, the performers retake the stage. When they are all there, they bow, and the crowd goes wild. Dwarves clap and yell and beg for more.

"Dude, that was awesome!" says Taryn. His beard looks like cotton candy from all the pastel raindrops.

Limery looks like he was dumped in a bucket of chalk.

While the crowd filters out, I check my notifications. There's actually two of them.

You have been targeted with Aura of Vigor. +1 Constitution for 2 hours. All debuffs have been cleared.

You have been targeted with Rains of Contentment. You will feel an overwhelming joy for the next hour.

A show and a buff. Not a bad way to spend an evening.

CHAPTER TWENTY-NINE

DESERT STROLLS

We rise early the next morning and stock up on provisions before leaving. With a satchel full of food and water, we won't have to stop to hunt. The quicker we are out of the desert, the better.

Our stay in Sandholde was brief, but it has been memorable. We have a new quest, and I have an overwhelming curiosity for what the king may be announcing. Maybe it's another regional event. And Taryn, well, he has hearts for eyes right now.

He looks around as we exit the city gates. I guess he was expecting Lady Brollen to see him off.

"You'll see her again. Especially if we find her brother." I try to console him, but he seems lost in his own head. If I didn't know any better, I'd say he was under some kind of charm.

With my shawl covering my head and shoulders, we set out into the miles and miles of desert before us. Strong Wind increases our pace, but we still have several days before we reach Seascape.

After spending two nights resting in an oasis, Stompy is in a bit of a mood, huffing and puffing as we travel. He and Taryn are perfect companions for one another right now.

I keep to myself as we walk. The monotonous sandy tones are all I see. It reminds me of the lab at Mythos Games, all white and pristine. Boring. I think about sending Valery a message, but I don't really have anything to say. I'm not ready to log out, and if she had news from my parents then I'm sure she would have reached out to me. Over a month and a half that I have been in this game, and I've heard nothing from them.

I notice I'm clenching my fist and try to push the thoughts away. Nothing good will come of thinking about them. I've made my own family in this world. Honestly, if Taryn wants to stay, I may never go back.

"—Chod?" Taryn calls my name, and I realize I've been on autopilot, putting one foot in front of the other like a mindless drone. "I said I'm going to fly overhead and get a view of our surroundings."

I give him a thumbs-up, and he transforms into a red bird. With a quick flap of his wings, he's off.

Watching him flutter through the air, it makes me wonder why he didn't pick something more capable of traversing long distances, like a hawk or a falcon. No one has ever been scared of a red bird.

I focus on the road ahead. It's nothing but sand for as far as the eye can see. Hills and mounds of sand. My new shawl makes it more bearable, but my ass cheeks still drip sweat like a snow cone in July.

Eventually, Taryn returns.

"See anything good?"

"Not really." He scratches Stompy behind the ears. "Some interesting-looking rock formations to the east, but nothing we'd want to waste our time with. Full steam ahead to Seascape."

"Can I ask you something?"

"Yeah, what's up?"

"Why a red bird? You can change into pretty much any creature you see. Why pick something so small?"

He smiles before answering. "It's my mom's favorite animal. It's my little way of keeping her with me."

"Do you miss them?" It's a stupid question, but I ask it anyway. Why wouldn't he miss them? He has an amazing family.

His smile fades, and he stares off into the distance. "Yeah. This is great and all, and I'd be lying if I said there weren't times when I was so caught up in it all that I didn't think about them, but they're my family. Even with school and work, there were always a few minutes each day where we just sat down and talked. I think I miss that most."

I don't respond. How can I? I have no idea what that is like. One thing is clear, and that's that no matter how much Taryn loves this game, he'd never come here for good. How could I blame him for that?

He's here now, though, and that's all that matters. It's not like I'm stuck here permanently. Any time I want to leave, I can. I just have to accept the fact that if I do choose to stay, he won't be here with me.

That's enough being emo for one day. I can deal with all of that when the time comes. For now, we need to get to Seascape, find out what the king has planned, and shut down Jude and Glenn before something bad happens.

As we travel, we eat jerky and bread. Without a need to cook anything, we can eat without needing to stop. Limery sits on Berry's back, and my horrors pop in and out of existence.

The new ability that I haven't had a chance to unlock crosses my mind.

Champion. *Summon a copy of the most recent enemy you have defeated. Decays 10% every minute out of combat. Cost: 50% of mana pool. Cooldown: 6 hours.*

I can't wait to try it out, but I still need to hit level twenty-one for a new ability point. The spell itself seems highly volatile. The fact that I could only summon the most recent being I've defeated means I would have to be super selective about what I kill. Summoning a twin-headed dragomander would be awesome. Summoning a rabbit would not.

Using the ability in a dungeon would mean I'd have almost no control over what the creature would be. Unless I find myself in the perfect situation, my horrors will always be my bread and butter.

Something moves across the road up ahead. At first, I think my eyes are playing tricks on me, but the closer we get, the bigger it becomes. It crosses the road and trudges slowly through the sand, carrying something behind it.

It can't be.

Desert Troll. *Level 15.*

The desert troll is a dull tan with dark patches of toffee-colored skin on his shoulders and neck, allowing him to blend in with the sandy terrain almost seamlessly. His hair is a vivid orange, pulled into a ponytail, and his tusks are short and thick surrounding his stumpy, bulbous nose. His body looks far less muscular than the forest or mountain trolls. A thick layer of fat covers whatever strength he may be hiding underneath, but even from far away, I can tell he is several feet taller than me and much wider.

He carries a massive bone club in one hand, and wears bone armor lashed with strips of leather around his forearms. A tattered loincloth drapes over his upper legs. Long arms hang down to his knees as he lumbers through the sand. In his other hand, he drags a dead scorpion twice his size by the tail.

"Hey!" I cup my hands around my mouth like a megaphone.

The troll looks over his shoulder, but then carries on with his slow pace.

"Wait up! I just want to talk." I increase my speed and the others fall in behind me.

"Chod, are you sure you want to do this?" Taryn urges Stompy to keep up with me as I jog toward the troll. "Don't you remember our encounter with the mountain trolls?"

"It's the first desert troll I've seen. I can't just not say something." I might not have another opportunity.

"Alright, but if this blows up in our faces, it's on you."

When I'm about fifty yards away from him, the troll stops moving, freezing in place.

"Hey, I'm Chod, the, uh, hero of the forest trolls. I just wanted to say...Hi. I've never met a desert troll before." I step forward, making sure to keep my horrors far behind me. For a lone troll in the desert, I'm sure we can be quite intimidating.

"Leave me be." His voice is a deep baritone. The words come out slow, dripping from his mouth like molasses.

"We mean you no harm."

"Leave me be," he says again. His head turns slightly, and his orange eyes lock with mine.

"I'm sorry. We just wa—"

He turns and unleashes a mighty roar. Tilting his head forward in an act of dominance, spittle flies out from his mouth and his cheeks flap like sails in the wind. The roar carries on for seconds and when it's finished, the desert troll's chest heaves. He clenches giant fists that look like sledgehammers.

"I think we should give him his space." Taryn has his staff lifted, ready to attack the moment he feels threatened. "Not everyone wants to be your friend."

"Alright." I put my hands up and slowly back away. "We'll leave you be."

The troll doesn't move a muscle as we leave. Even after we have rejoined the Mythroad and are half a mile away, when I look back, he's still frozen.

"What the hell was that?" I cast a few more horrors, replenishing the ones I lost while trying to be nice.

"He's was not a nice trolls." Limery floats over and lands on my shoulder. "It's okays, Chods."

"A troll who didn't want you in his business." Taryn takes a final look over his shoulder. "If I had to guess, that scorpion was food for his tribe. He probably thought you were out to steal it."

"Well, that's ridiculous." I pull up my map and sure enough, there is a cluster of magical veins a few miles from where we spotted the troll. That could be where they live.

"Is it?" He casts Strong Wind, and my legs move faster. "Put yourself in his position. You live in a harsh climate where finding food is already a struggle. You have people depending on you, and then one day, a group consisting of an ugly-ass forest troll, an imp, a devilishly handsome dwarf, and an army of tiny little monsters approaches you, wanting to talk, while you're alone on a sand dune. What do you do?" He doesn't wait for me to answer before continuing. "You run, and you lose your dinner. You fight, and you might die. Your best bet is to try and intimidate them into leaving you alone. I say good for him. Not everyone has to like you, you know?"

"What's that supposed to mean?" I stop in my tracks. That's the most ridiculous thing I've ever heard. "I don't need everyone to like me."

Taryn cocks an eyebrow at me. "Really? Come on, man. If you want to be real, let's be real. You used to stream because you wanted followers. You were shy in real life, just like me, but online attention, you thrived off that. When you first started, people liked you for you. Because you were genuine. When you screwed up, you laughed about it. You did crazy things that others wouldn't try, and most of the time you failed but occasionally, you'd win and it'd all be worth it. You got addicted to the comments and the views, and you wanted more. So you tried to be funny. The worse things got at home, the meaner your jokes became. When we played together, things were fine, but when you played alone... Man, you could be a savage. Over a game. Over nothing. I think it has a lot to do with how your family treated you, and that's on them, but it doesn't change the fact that you have always been searching for something you never felt at home. Appreciation."

We stand in silence for a moment. The tension is like an invisible wall. Limery has no idea what just happened, but the way his eyes dart between both of us, he knows something is up.

"You're a dick." I say it, and I mean it. My face grows hot, and I know that if I don't leave, I'm going to snap. What does Taryn know about my home life? About not being loved. His family had everything. How in the hell could he possibly know what I feel?

"Bro, come on."

"Nah, you're a dick. Leave me alone."

He cuts his eyes at me, and I know I've hurt his feelings, but I don't really care. He pats Stompy on the side of the head and they take off down the road.

"Chods—" Limery starts, but I cut him off.

"Go with Taryn. I need to be alone."

His bulbous eyes well up with tears, but he doesn't argue. He doesn't understand what's going on, but I don't have the time or energy to comfort him right now. He flies away and lands on Berry's back. I hear sniffles before I turn away.

I sit down in the sand. Not thinking, just fuming. If there was anything around me besides miles of fucking sand, I'd break it. My horrors slowly pop out of existence, and I don't care enough to replace them. One by one they vanish until I am completely alone.

I let out a deep breath, trying to let go of some of my anger with it. The sun's warm rays blaze against my back. I don't need people to like me. Taryn is full of shit. I want people to like me, but I don't need it.

Do I?

My heartrate slows and the anger that threatened to boil over has almost receded entirely. Our argument replays in my mind. There's probably some truth to what he said. Why else would I have freaked out on Taryn like that? He's my best friend, and he's never said a bad thing about me. I just didn't want to hear it.

God, I'm an asshole.

I turn around to find them, to apologize, but they're gone. I wonder how long I have been sitting there stewing, because I can't see them at all. Long enough for my horrors to die and then some. Jumping to my feet, I scan the area. There's no trace of Berry or Stompy's giant moulhaug butt on the horizon. Did I piss off Taryn enough that he used Strong Wind and left me behind?

Limery would never let that happen. I just need to catch up to them, to make things right.

I could send Taryn a message, but it needs to be in person.

I take off at a near sprint to find my friends. Sweat pours down my back as I push my body to its limits in the raging heat. I continuously summon horrors, and they struggle to keep up.

After twenty minutes of running, I feel like I am going to die. My head pounds, my heart races, and cramps run through both legs and my side. Forest trolls were most definitely not meant for desert sprinting.

I bend over, hands placed on my knees, when I hear a crack of thunder in the distance. I look up to see a multitude of dark blotches on a distant dune.

Fuck. They're in trouble.

With my stamina depleted, there's no way I'm going to make it there in time to help, so I do the only thing I know how. I activate Berserker Rage, replenishing my stamina, and take off toward the battle.

While Berserker Rage is active, I feel like I could run a marathon in the desert, but it ends far too quickly, and my stamina begins to deplete once again.

The battle grows clearer with each step, and eventually, I can make out what is happening. Taryn and Limery are squared off against a group of giant scorpions. They look identical to the one the desert troll was pulling—golden, with a black stripe running down their backs. There's at least five of them, and each one is the size of a small car. They scurry around, clicking their pincers and striking with their stingers.

Limery tosses fireballs and occasionally, a lightning strike rips into one of the creatures, scorching its shell.

"I'm coming!" I yell, but they can't hear me above all the chaos.

A stinger stabs into Stompy's rear leg, and he bellows in pain. Berry launches himself at one of the scorpions and rips off one of its legs with his teeth. It walks lopsided in the sand, but it manages to grab him with one of its giant pincers.

Berry roars as the pincer rips through his fur. He tries to push it away, but the creature's grip is strong. While he is subdued, the scorpion stings him in the neck and the bear goes limp. Venom drips from the tip of the stinger.

He's going to die if I don't get there in time.

I sacrifice all the Horrors of Finesse I have summoned, taking their speed boost and sprinting with everything I have. I arrive just in time to tackle the scorpion's tail as it prepares to sting Berry again.

For being so large, the scorpion is surprisingly lightweight. It tumbles with me and we go rolling down the dune. I wrap my legs around its tail and pull with all my might. Something cracks, and the tail breaks free, spraying me in a squirt of bodily fluids. The tailless scorpion turns on me, but I take my trident and stab it through the center of its body until its legs curl up in death.

Berry whimpers as he crawls through the sand, leaving a trail of blood behind him. He's on his last bit of health.

"Taryn, save Berry! I'll hold the others off."

He leaps from Stompy, transforming into a red bird and fluttering over to Berry.

"Taryn, I'm—"

"Not now," he says as he returns to dwarven form. He leans over Berry, casting them both in a green glow.

My horrors battle against the other four scorpions. Several of them are chopped in half by pincers, and more fall to strikes from stingers. A few Horrors of Vitality are able to slow one scorpion enough for Limery to erupt a fire wall underneath it, cooking the monster alive.

That leaves three level sixteen scorpions against me, Limery, a limping Stompy, and about a dozen remaining horrors.

Piece of cake.

One scorpion sees Taryn hunched over Berry and makes an attempt at an easy kill.

"Limery, wall!" I order.

A flaming wall ignites beside Taryn, stopping the scorpion's advance. I grab the creature by the tail, and with one good spin, I toss it as far away as I can like a hammer thrower at the Olympics. Limery pelts it with fireballs as it soars through the air.

The two other scorpions surround Stompy. He thrashes his head from side to side, warning them to back off. One of the scorpions strikes, but Stompy parries the blow with his horn. The action leaves his other side exposed and the second scorpion jabs its stinger in his side. A string of yellow slime stretches from the wound to the stinger. Stompy bellows in pain and swings his horn to the other side, but the scorpion has already retreated out of range. His health trickles down as the venom takes effect.

Over my shoulder, Limery bursts into flame and darts for the lone scorpion, leaving me and Stompy with the other two. Taryn is taking longer than usual to heal Berry, and I don't know if it is the lack of plant life in the desert or something else entirely.

Whatever the reason, it means I'm essentially on my own to finish these two off. I use Intimidation, unleashing a roar that momentarily confuses the two scorpions. Their eyes glaze over, and I realize each one has several sets. Two up top and another pair on each side of its mouth.

As they sway back and forth, I quickly use my trident to stab out all three sets of eyes on the scorpion nearest me, completely blinding it. When Intimidation wears off, the blinded scorpion lashes out at no one, striking with its tail and lunging with its pincers. It'd be comical if my friends weren't dying all around me. I leave him for later and focus on the other.

I try to stab out its eyes, but it blocks the blow with one of its pincers. Stompy lets out an angry bellow beside me, but his wounded leg makes it impossible for him to charge.

These scorpions are dangerous, but at the end of the day, they're just giant bugs. Bugs with hard shells and very little muscle.

I stand in front of the scorpion and wait for it to strike. When it does, the strike is too quick for me to stop, so I take a stinger straight to the chest. Before it can retract the stinger, I wrap my hands around it and pull with all my might. The scorpion tries to pull it back, but I refuse to let go. The venom burns like hell as it creeps through my veins.

The scorpion's pincers reach for me, but I jump over them. I twist the stinger until it snaps off and then slam the pointed barb down hard through the creature's head. Venom to the brain is super effective! My health continues to tick down and my racing heartbeat thumps in my eardrums.

I use my Tiger's Eye Pendant to cleanse the venom from my body and bask in the sweet relief.

It doesn't last long, though. A sharp pain plunges into my backside, and a fresh influx of venom enters my veins. My luck must be pretty fucking shitty today for me to be the victim of a blind scorpion.

There's a flash of lightning, and suddenly, I can't move. When the stun wears off, the blind scorpion retracts its stinger. The creature's body smokes from the lightning attack. I just happened to be unlucky enough to be attached to the end of it.

The scorpion lunges at nothing in particular. Then, a fully healed Berry sinks his teeth into the creature's pincer arm and bites it clean off. The scorpion strikes at Berry, but without sight, the stinger hits nothing. When Berry rips off the second pincer, the weight of the scorpion's tail topples the body over, revealing its soft underbelly, which the bear has no trouble tearing open.

With the threats gone, I collapse to the ground, exhausted.

"Here, take this." Taryn's face gives very little away, but his voice is soft. He hands me a health potion he purchased in Sandholde.

"Hey, man. I'm sorry—"

"I know." He smiles and the corners of his mustache twitch up. It's not a smile born of laughter, but of love.

"No, I need you to hear this." I hold the health potion in my hand, not ready to take it until I've made peace. My back burns and the venom creeps through my shoulders and arms, but I need to say this. "You were right. About all of it. I was a dick a lot of times just to be a dick. I hated my home life, and it gave me a sense of power to tear others down, a sense of control. But mostly, I did it for the attention. My parents wouldn't notice me, so it felt good when others did. They noticed me, but they didn't like me. How could they like someone like that?" I wince as a fresh bolt of pain goes through my shoulder. "This has been a chance at a do-over. The friends I've made here, it's been because of who I am, and because of the choices I have made. I'm sorry I took what you said so personally." He's one of the few people who have always been there for me. I hope my apology is enough.

"Hey, I know you're a good guy. That's why we're friends. I just want you to know that you don't need the entire world to like you in order to be important. You're important to us." Taryn wraps his arm around me. "Now, will you take the damn potion?"

I uncork it and pour the red liquid into my mouth. Immediately, the potion soothes my aching veins and my health slowly restores.

"And Limery..." I turn to find the imp standing sheepishly behind me. "I'm sorry I yelled at you. You've been my best friend since coming here. You've looked after me, had my back time and time again. You deserve better than to be dismissed."

He flies over to me and wraps his tiny arms around my neck. "Oh, Chods. Limmy is yous best friend."

I hug him back, thankful for his wonderful, crazy self.

We gather up the stingers and pincers and stuff them in my bag. The venom will probably sell well in Seascape, and the pincers could make for decent weapons.

As I put them away, I notice I have a new notification. I must have missed it due to half my body being ablaze with venom.

Congratulations! You have reached level 21. +1 stat point to distribute. +1 Strength and Constitution racial bonus. +1 ability point to distribute.

I use my new ability point to unlock Champion. It's kind of cool knowing that I can summon a giant scorpion any time I need one. I have two skill points, but I'm not sure where to allocate them at the moment. Dexterity or Intelligence seem like safe bets, since Strength and Constitution are through the roof due to my racial bonus. However, with Champion depleting my mana pool by half, it might be smarter to invest in mana regeneration, so maybe Wisdom.

I leave it be for now. If nothing else, I can debate the pros and cons on the fifty miles of desert we still have left.

With our emotional meltdowns behind us, we set off for Seascape.

CHAPTER THIRTY
SEASCAPE

My heart jumps when I see the first signs of plant life returning. Beautiful green plant life. It doesn't happen all at once, but slowly, the desert fades and we walk next to green grass and towering oaks.

No longer surrounded by sand and dust, I remove my shawl and stuff it in my pack. Limery zooms through the trees, chasing the birds he has missed for many days. There's a certain weight that's lifted just by the change in environment, which is fine for me. I'm happy to put what happened in the desert behind us.

As the day goes on, we eventually come to a crossing where the roads that bypassed the desert on both sides reconnect with the Mythroad. According to my map, we will arrive at Seascape within a day.

Lots of dwarves are on the road, coming and going from both sides. Most take the road north to Seascape, some go east or west, but no one seems interested in taking the Mythroad to Sandholde.

There's a mixture of ebony and ivory dwarves in the crowd. The ebony dwarves that live outside the desert dress more like the ivory dwarves, wearing tunics and pants. Some even wear armor.

Taryn makes chit-chat with other dwarves as we walk, and they speculate on what the king could be announcing. Apparently, he sent out a regional alert before we crossed the mountains, because almost everyone in the kingdom knows about it.

"Haven't seen this many dwarves on the road since the king's seventy-fifth birthday feast," says an ivory dwarf pulling a cart loaded with burlap sacks.

"He's that old?" Taryn asks.

The dwarf burst out laughing. "Old? I expect he's still got a few hundred years in him."

Taryn's eyes go wide. "Do dwarves really live that long?"

"Blood dwarves do."

Taryn turns to me. "I had no idea that the king was a blood dwarf. I mean, I knew they were rare, but why did no one tell me our king was one? It's kind of a big fact to leave out." Whenever it comes to dwarven knowledge, he just can't get enough.

"Maybe they thought everyone knew," I offer.

"Yeah, maybe." He turns back to the other dwarf. "What else do you know about blood dwarves?"

I listen in on their conversation as we walk. I don't really care that much about blood dwarves, but it beats staring at the trees. Limery sits on Stompy's horn, bobbing along as the moulhaug and the bear take up the majority of the road, blocking anyone from passing us. Strong Wind moves us along, even as we make our way uphill.

"Blood dwarves are very rare," the dwarf continues. "And they are dying out. It's said that whenever they have children with one of the other dwarf races, their red skin doesn't come through. So most blood dwarves only marry other blood dwarf families. They can recognize one another by their skin color, but if you take away that, they're no different than you or me. You only really see them in the capital these days. The families have grown smaller over time. They say that magic is strongest in the veins of blood dwarves, and that they have produced more paladins, clerics, and mages than the other races combined."

Taryn hangs on every word, absorbing the knowledge of his people.

By the time Seascape comes into view, I know more about dwarven culture than I ever cared to.

For being a city by the sea, Seascape appears more like a mountain that rises from the ocean. We cross a bridge that goes over a ravine, separating Seascape from the mainland. The smell of saltwater comes up in gusts from the violent tides below. Seascape itself juts high into the sky, steep cliffs on all sides protecting it from interlopers. The only way on or off Seascape is the bridge we are crossing.

At the end of the bridge, there's a drawbridge guarded by a dozen well-armed sentries. They all wear resplendent plate mail, engraved with images of warhammers and axes. I find it strange that the dwarves are so defined by the things they make and the tools they use. The sentries' beards are braided, and beautiful red cloaks embroidered with golden thread adorn their shoulders. The bridge remains down, and they stand aside as the crowd filters through. With the king's announcement, I'm sure that the influx of dwarves has been nonstop.

Since they aren't checking those entering, Glenn and Jude might have made their way inside the city. If they were on dwarven soil when the king's announcement went out, then they are aware that something big is happening. I doubt they would miss it. And since King Favian's laws have no merit here, Jude and Glenn are free to travel without worry.

I suddenly feel uneasy, like I could be attacked at any moment. My towering blue body is hardly inconspicuous among all these dwarves.

Once we pass the bridge and return to solid ground, the road zigs and zags, ascending toward a masterpiece of dwarven architecture.

The castle reminds me of something out of history books. Dozens of towers, spires, and flying buttresses reach for the heavens. It dominates everything in sight. Sculptures of dwarves adorn each of the hundreds of stained-glass windows that depict imagery from their long history. There are gargoyles and intricate carvings along almost every inch of the castle.

It's a beauty to behold, simultaneously fragile and imposing. A mixture of fine lines and details on a behemoth of a structure.

When my eyes are finally able to look away, I take in the rest of the city. It's just as magnificent as the castle. Every building is made from brick or stone. Even the outermost shops and homes, where the poor would normally live, are far beyond anything I saw in Vanaria, save the castle. We pass jewelers, armorers, more black-smiths than I can count, pubs, and dozens of inns. Everything is so tightly packed together that they had no choice but to build vertically.

As much as I try to look away, my eyes are drawn to the city's beauty. One detail leads into the next, drawing me into a maze of architecture. "I thought Sandholde was beautiful, but this is something else. It's like a gothic New York."

"I know. It's crazy that something like this could be made without machines." He looks on with lust at the surrounding structures.

We pass a rowdy tavern named The Slobbering Ogre, where dwarves sing loudly inside; and an inn called The Merry Kobold, where several dwarves who traveled with us stop to leash their ponies. As we journey deeper into the city, it seems like there is a tavern on every corner.

"Want to stop for a drink?" Taryn stares up at a sign with a dog standing on two legs. The Dancing Hound.

"Maybe we should find an inn first. With so many people coming into town, I'd like to make sure we have rooms for tonight, and somewhere for Berry and Stompy to stay."

Dwarves filter around the beasts' massive bodies while we are stopped in the street. Limery is focused on an imp gargoyle on the side of a nearby building.

"Yeah, that's a good idea." Taryn licks his lips one last time before turning away from the tavern. "I know of a nice inn near the castle. I stayed there when I first came here."

As the sun sets, the windows of the castle come to life, the stained-glass glowing from the light of hundreds of torches. Even though it is made of stone, the castle feels alive. No matter where we go in the city, its towers are always visible. Always watching.

The streets become less crowded the closer we come to the castle. At the top of the hill, we enter an open courtyard in front of the castle gates. It is beautifully designed, arranged so that the different colored bricks depict images of warham-mers and axes. In the center of the courtyard, there's a tall and elegant archway, almost identical to the one in Vanaria. Dozens of plainly-clad dwarves surround it, looking on with awe. Runes and symbols run along the sides of the arch. It's slightly elevated from the surrounding area, with a mosaic of stones circling outward from its base. The entrance to the arch is sealed with stone, but a dark purple energy radiates from between the stones

"That's different." The portal in Vanaria didn't have any sort of energy around it.

Taryn turns from the rows of buildings. "Yeah." He scrunches his brows at the arch. "That's...odd."

"What's odd?"

"That energy. It wasn't doing that last time. It was sealed, but you could walk right up and touch it."

"You think this has something to do with the king's announcement?"

"I wouldn't doubt it." He stares intently at the portal.

Limery jumps from Stompy's horn and flutters to my shoulder. "Limmy doesn't like. There's is evils coming from thats." He points a long skinny finger at the arch.

I feel it too. There's something off about the portal. Something unsettling.

On the other side of the courtyard, near the castle gates, dozens of guards stand at attention, covered in heavy battle armor. Their helmets sit low upon their brows and the nose guards conceal all but their eyes and beard from view.

"That's a lot of guards." I analyze them. Each one is a member of the kingsguard, all level twenty-five.

"They take protecting the king very seriously," says Taryn.

One of the dwarves near the portal reaches out to touch it. When he does so, the dark energy strikes out like lightning. There's a loud scream, and the dwarf falls to the ground. He doesn't move.

A female dwarf rushes to his side, screaming. "Help! Someone help! Someone help my husband!"

The guards don't move. No one comes to the man's aid, so I sprint over, parting the crowd.

One look at the body, and I know he's dead. His eyes are open, yet unseeing. Why does no one else seem to care?

"Why would he do that?" I ask the woman, but she just weeps loudly over her fallen husband. I put my hand on her shoulder, but it does nothing to ease her pain. The rest of the crowd doesn't even seem to notice the dead dwarf in front of them. They all just stare at the portal with longing.

Another dwarf reaches out, and I pull him away. It takes a moment before his eyes register what's happening. He shakes his head, as if coming out of some fog.

"Uhn, what happened." He looks down and sees the dead dwarf. "Oh, no. Did I—"

"You almost touched the portal. Whatever that energy is, it's deadly. I suggest you go home." I step in front of the portal, blocking his view.

"Th-thank you, sir. I don't know what happened. I remember looking at it. It was so beautiful, and then...and then, you pulled me away." The dwarf blinks rapidly. "I must be going."

When I turn around, Taryn and Limery are ushering the other dwarves away. They all have the same realization as the dwarf I stopped. It's like they were transfixed by the energy. No longer enraptured in the portal's spell, some of the dwarves help to carry the dead husband away. To where, I have no idea.

After the crowd leaves, the energy that radiates through the portal dims. Is it possible that the power grew as more dwarves looked on it?

"That was weird." Taryn strokes his beard as he looks at the portal. His eyes droop a little and his words begin to slur. "Why did no one else help them?"

I grab him by the shoulder and make him face me. Whatever affected those dwarves, it seems to be having a similar effect on him.

The guards stand as still as ever. Berry and Stompy remain where we started, almost as if they are wary to come any closer to the portal.

"Let's get the hell out of here." I shake his shoulder. "Where's that inn you were talking about?"

"It's right around the corner." He rubs his head like he's fighting a headache. "Closest inn to the castle. It'll cost a gold a night, but we'll be right in the action."

I take one last glance at the arch. "Honestly, I'd prefer to stay a little away from the action."

We enter the front door of The Golden Hammer, and the place goes quiet.

The tavern has thick stone walls. Black banners with a golden hammer sigil hang from the ceiling. Mounted heads of various beasts adorn the walls with torches blazing in between. A mighty fire roars in the fireplace against the far wall. There's a bar on one side and plenty of tables on the other. A handful of dwarves are scattered around the room. The barkeep leans forward, whispering to a lone patron at the bar.

"You've got some balls on you," says a dwarf at the closest table. An ivory dwarf with a jet-black beard. He wears golden chainmail under red leather armor. "I saw what you did. I've seen many a dwarf lured to their death in front of that portal. There's no helping them once they've fixed themselves on it. The priests and paladins are the only ones who can go near it without feeling its pull. You're lucky to be alive."

Then why the hell was no one blocking it off?

"How many people have died to the portal? And why wasn't anyone there to warn us?" Taryn scowls at the dwarf.

"More than I can count. Most of us natives know to stay away. Only the outsiders venture through the castle square these days." He takes a swig of his drink. "Shoulda been someone telling you to turn away, but my guess is they either felt the pull and left, or they were one of the ones that got caught in its snare."

"The pull?" I ask. I didn't feel a pull, but it certainly looked like Taryn did.

"Whatever ancient power has awakened in that portal, it calls to the dwarves like a siren song." He shakes his head. "The only ones who don't seem to be affected are the blood dwarves and those with holy magic. Still, not a dwarf that has touched the energy has lived to tell the tale." He lifts his mug. "Have a seat, grab a drink, celebrate the fact that you didn't die."

I don't think either one of us feel like celebrating right now after watching an innocent dwarf die. And his poor wife... I just want to lie down.

Taryn walks over to the barkeep and orders us two rooms.

"Our large beast stables are farther down the street. Does that work for you?" the barkeep asks.

"As long as they are safe, that'll be fine."

The barkeep snaps his fingers, and a dwarf who was sitting in the back of the tavern rushes out the door.

Taryn leans against the bar. "After all that, I think I need a drink." He looks over to me. "You in?"

We take a seat at the table, and the barkeep brings over two of the biggest mugs I have ever laid eyes on. Big enough that they actually fit my troll hands.

"And one for the little one." He places a smaller mug in front of Limery.

Taryn lifts his glass. "To the king."

"To the king." We clink our glasses.

The dwarven ale is delicious. A deep dark brown, it's nutty and smooth and goes down like water.

True to his nature, after a few sips, Limery's head begins to bobble back and forth.

More dwarves filter in as the night goes on, and after a few more mugs, we forget all about the troubles with the portal.

"I love you, bro." Taryn places his hand on my arm. "I'm sorry I hurt your feelings."

"Don't worry about it. I needed a wakeup call. You're a good friend." I slap him on the back, making his dreadlocks dance and causing him to spill a little ale as he tries to take a drink.

A red-haired dwarf with a matching beard takes a seat on the bench beside Taryn. He gazes at me with a drunken stare. "You're a big fella. I bet you're strong. What do you say we put it to the test?"

I laugh at him and scoot back a little from the table. I guess you haven't really lived until you've been in a dwarven bar fight.

He slams his elbow down on the table. He flexes his hand a few times before extending it to me. "Loser buys the winner a beer?"

Arm wrestling. He wants to arm wrestle me. A drunken smile crosses my face, and I put my own elbow on the table. "You're on."

The other dwarves take note of our challenge and gather around the table. Taryn takes bets on who they think will win.

When we grip each other's hands, the red-haired dwarf speaks. "You're about to find out why they call me Uluf Steelgrip."

Another dwarf pipes in over my shoulder. "We call you Uluf Steelgrip because that's what yer mother named ye."

The entire bar erupts into raucous laughter. They countdown from three, and then we square off.

The dwarf is pretty strong for his size. His forearms are built like a baseball player, all thick, corded muscle and bulging veins. His face goes red as he flexes, pushing against my arm with all he has. At level sixteen, he's a strong dwarf. He could probably beat Taryn. Unfortunately for him, he just happens to be going against a level twenty-one forest troll.

I slam his wrist against the table. "I'll be taking that beer now."

He scowls at me before heading to the bar.

One by one, the other dwarves line up, each of them eager for the opportunity to test their strength against a troll. Pretty soon, our table is filled with empty mugs, and the world dances in and out of focus. Taryn and Limery cheer me on.

The rest of the night passes in a blur, but I have visions of daggers stabbed into tables, dice games, and an endless flow of beer.

And most of all, laughter.

CHAPTER THIRTY-ONE

BATTLE ROYALE

Regional Alert! *King Orso Brightgaze will be making an announcement at noon in the castle square.*

My head throbs, which has become a common occurrence on the days following an evening of drinking with Taryn. I focus the notification away and pull the feather-stuffed pillow over my face.

"Uhn," I moan. I'm a giant blue monster, why is it that Taryn can drink me under the table?

"Uhn," Limery echoes my sentiments from the floor.

I have no idea why or how he happened to end up on the floor. Blurry visions of daggers, drinking, and arm-wrestling flutter through my mind.

There's a knock on the door and by the time I sit up, Taryn enters. He has returned to the clothing he wore the first time I saw him in-game. A dark green cloak and a tan tunic. He hits me in the foot with his staff.

"Get up, you bums. We want to get a good spot for the announcement. It's not every day you get to see a king in person." He pulls the covers off the bed. "Up! I've already ordered breakfast for you lightweights."

I crawl out of bed and my head threatens to roll off my shoulders. Limery stands up and runs straight into the bedpost. I've never second-guessed letting the imp drink. Honestly, I don't know how old he is. Young for an imp, but he could be older than me for all I know. Besides, what's the drinking age on the island? No one has ever refused him service.

Taryn leads us downstairs to the tavern. Raucous applause greets us, resounding in my head like thunder.

"There's our champion!" Uluf Steelgrip slaps me on the back. "Strongest troll I ever did see."

I nod, not quite ready to engage in conversation.

Uluf is bright-eyed and full of cheer. The room is nearly packed with dwarves, and not one of them is nursing a hangover.

"Eat up." He laughs. "It'll take the edge off."

A platter of sausages, eggs, ribs, and potatoes waits for us. Next to it, a mug of frothy ale.

My stomach lurches at the thought of more ale.

Taryn notices my hesitance. "Hair of the dog." He motions for us to sit. "It'll set you right."

By the end of the meal, I'm feeling better and can finally focus enough to listen in on other conversations.

"Could be he wants someone to encase the portal in stone," says one dwarf.

"Maybe he knows what's causing it," says another.

"Could be a blood dwarf cursed it. How else do you explain that it doesn't affect them?"

"Maybe the volcano is alive again. You know that the castle is built on its ruins."

They shout out speculations, one after the other. Some plausible, some down-right ludicrous.

"You ready?" Taryn asks the moment I take my last bite. He stands from the table.

I'm not going to be the one to kill his enthusiasm. "Let's go."

When we step out the door, the streets are packed. The sun shines high over-head. It must be almost time.

Limery sits on my shoulder, and I bulldoze my way through the crowd. There are a few angry faces, but once they look at me, they part with ease. Taryn follows closely in my wake.

There are only a few yards between the door of The Golden Hammer and the castle square. Most of the square is empty. Nearly a hundred armed guards keep the crowd pressed back, creating a barrier between us and the portal. Where were these guards yesterday?

A dozen or so red-skinned dwarves stand back against the stairs that lead up to the castle entrance. Blood dwarves. Some wear robes, others wear armor. There are a few females in the mix. Holy energy surrounds them as they stand at attention, but their black eyes give them a sinister look.

Once we make our way close enough to the front of the crowd, I lift Taryn into the windowsill of one of the shops. The ledge is deep enough for him to stand on without falling.

"What's going on?" I ask.

"No idea." He scans the square and then looks out behind us into the crowd. "This is all kinds of weird."

I'm watching the blood dwarves, when a bright glare catches my eye. Across the courtyard, standing in one of the streets that empties into the square, a large knight towers above the surrounding dwarves. Pristinely polished plate armor gleams in the sun.

. . .

Pressley Allen
  Level 24
  Knight
  Human

The last time we saw him was in Lynchton, when he sold that amulet to the shopkeeper. What the hell is he doing here? He's gained a level since we last saw him, and at his level, that takes some work.

I wonder how he found out about the king's announcement. Maybe he thinks there will be gold. If there is gold to be had, then he is the one hero I would expect to be here. I still remember his words, "I only care about gold."

Pressley leans over, whispering something to a smaller man in a red cloak. It takes me a moment, but I realize I've seen him before as well. A thick, black chain hangs from his neck.

Richard Hummel
  Level 18
  Cleric
  Human

The cleric who serves the God of Chaos. He wears the same red robes and black chain as when I met him in Vanaria. He's a long way from The Green Giant Inn. What is he doing here, and why is he with Pressley?

I've got a very strange feeling about this. If those two are here, I'm sure Jude and Glenn are here somewhere, too. And who knows who else.

I should have an army of horrors on hand, but with so many people here, there's no way to summon them without causing a scene. As if I don't have enough eyes on me just for being a giant blue troll.

"There are other heroes here," I whisper to Taryn.

"Where?" He scans the crowd.

"Across the courtyard. Giant knight and cleric with the red hood."

"They could just be curious." He stares in their direction.

"For them, maybe, but it means Jude and Glenn might be here, too. Keep an eye out for any more humans. If they tried to attack the king, it could start a war."

"I'll see what I can do." He transforms into a bird and flies over to the roof of a nearby building. He hops along the edge of the roof, surveying the crowd beneath.

Bells ring from inside the castle. Several of them. They echo through the streets, and everyone falls silent.

The large metal doors of the castle open, and a small crowd of dwarves step through. A half-dozen kingsguards in their silver armor and red capes. A priest stands to one side, clad in a white robe that only draws more attention to his red skin. In the center stands the king.

He is at least a foot taller than the other dwarves. His skin is the dull red of cooling magma. He has bushy black hair that falls to his shoulders, and a black beard intricately braided and adorned with silver clasps. He wears a black tunic and black cloak, each embroidered with silver thread. A red breastplate engraved with a silver warhammer protects his chest, and a glowing red crown sits atop his head. The tines of the crown have alternating battleaxes and warhammers.

When I focus on him, his level is unreadable.

King Orso Brightgaze. Level: *???*

At the edge of the stairs, the kingsguards move aside and the king steps forward. I can only imagine what it must look like for him up there. Standing on that precipice and seeing his kingdom before him. Lands that stretch for miles. Thousands of dwarves packed in the streets of his city, all watching him.

He holds his hand in the air and there is absolute silence. When he speaks, his voice carries over the crowd like a loudspeaker, as if magically amplified.

"Thank you all for joining me here today. For many years now, the Kingdom of Seascape has lived in peace. It has been many ages since we were last at war. Longer still since our people battled the dark one before he retreated, sealing all the portals with him. With the closing of the portals, we lost contact with the other continents. As great monsters patrolled the seas, sea travel vanished.

"In the time that has passed since the day the portals closed, most of the island has forgotten the atrocities we witnessed, that our forebears faced." He pauses, looking across the crowd. "Some of us are not so lucky. Ever since I was a young dwarf, I have been reminded of the last great war. Of what it may mean if the dark wizard should turn his gaze upon us once again. For years, I have been reminded, but for years, we have lived in peace. That peace may be coming to an end."

The crowd stirs. Whispers begin snaking in waves, causing the guards to adjust their stances.

The king lifts his hand, bringing quiet with it. "I do not say that to frighten you. I tell you so that you may prepare. The Seascape portal has been reactivated. The enchantments put on it by the dark wizard still hold, but dark energy swirls within it. The energy calls to most, luring them to their doom, but it does not seem to affect the dark races. Blood dwarves, imps..." His gaze finds me and lingers. "Perhaps others. You may be asking yourself, 'What does this have to do with me?' A valid question. Most of you are aware of the curse of the blood dwarves. That whenever we mate with those outside our race, our most defining feature is lost. Many of you may have the blood of my ancestors running through your veins, and you don't even know it.

"We did not build our empire by sitting idly by while kingdoms rose and fell all around us. Nor do I want to sit idle while our enemies gather on the other side of our portal. I want to break through the enchantment and discover what is lurking on the other side before they are ready for us. Our clerics and paladins of the castle have tried to break the enchantment to no avail. Maybe one of you have the ancient power within you. Maybe one of the so-called heroes from the south have that power. All I know is that the portal must be opened. Therefore, I am offering a keep, and all of its attended lands, to anyone who can break through the wall that blocks our portal. Who will answer the call of your king?

"You're more than welcome to participate yourself. Here." The quest displays in the corner of my vision.

Quest Alert. *You have been offered the quest "Open the Portal." Dark magic has arisen in the Seascape portal and the king wants to take action. Find a way to open the portal so that he may discover what is on the other side.*

Reward: Dwarven keep and all attended lands.

The crowd murmurs like a pot about to boil. Several dwarves around me speak in hushed voices, wondering if it is possible that they are descended from blood dwarves.

Message (Chod): *See anything?*

Incoming Message (Taryn): *I've spotted a few humans in the crowd, but none of them are heroes. There's so many people. It's impossible to see everyone.*

"I will answer the call!" a deep voice booms from the street behind me.

The crowd parts, and a stocky ivory dwarf with a scraggly brown beard steps forward. His tunic is tattered in places, and his pants are ripped at the knees. The warhammer he carries shimmers, but the leather bindings along its shaft are old and flaky in spots.

The guards allow him to pass. He approaches the portal, and the eyes of the clerics and paladins follow his every movement.

"Who are you?" asks the king.

"I be Tramond Volcanobreaker, Yer Highness." He bends down to one knee. "I am but a farmer from the small village of Oakside. My great-great-grandfather was a blood dwarf. This warhammer belonged to him and has been passed down through me family fer generations."

The king nods at the dwarf.

He approaches the portal cautiously, as if worried the energy will lash out at him. No doubt the stories of the portal's power have circulated throughout the city.

He lifts the warhammer over his shoulder. With a heave, he swings it against the enchanted stones that block the entrance.

The warhammer connects with the stone, and an explosion of energy catapults the dwarf and his warhammer into the crowd.

Shit! The portal blasted him like a cannon.

"Next," says the king.

"I will try!" someone yells from several streets over.

He makes his way to the guards, armored from head to toe in brilliant plate mail. A flowing yellow cloak trails behind him. When he steps past the guards, someone tries to pull him back, grabbing his cloak.

"You know yer not a damned blood dwarf!"

"Quiet, you!" the ivory dwarf curses at the dwarf who tried to stop him. "I am Brimgurd Proudsword, Your Highness."

The king nods and the dwarf approaches the arch, head held high. He carries a double-headed battleaxe. As he walks closer, his gait changes. His head begins to droop and the swagger he carried himself with before all but vanishes. The axe falls from his hand, clinking against the stone. He reaches toward the portal and a bolt of dark energy strikes his hand. The dwarf falls to the ground, his platemail clanks against the square and the gasp of the crowd sounds like all the air has been sucked from the world.

Limery's claws dig into my shoulder.

I can't help but wonder if this is all for nothing. Those with blood dwarf ancestry might be lucky enough to fight another day. But for the rest, is a keep worth risking their lives? Not to mention what might be on the other side of the portal.

Several clerics rush to the body and carry it away.

I guess he wasn't a blood dwarf after all. What a prideful idiot.

"I will open your portal!" a crisp, clear voice that couldn't possibly belong to a dwarf shouts.

"Step forward and reveal yourself," says the king.

A moment later, a tall, blond man wearing massive blue and silver armor steps forward. A billowing blue cape trails behind him. I'd recognize that heavenly glow anywhere. He was Jude's partner back in Vanaria. Have the two teamed up again or is he here of his own accord?

Michael Didato
   Level 19
   Paladin
   Human

The armor swallows him whole and might actually fit me if I were to put it on. He's replaced his warhammer with a new broadsword at least four feet long. His enormous shield is emblazoned with a white raven on a blue background. Either he finally found the one we took from him outside the dungeon or got it replaced. Everywhere he steps, golden light shines down upon him.

He bypasses the guards and stands before the king.

"I am Michael, paladin and hero to the people of Vanaria, but I have come to answer your call."

"What makes you think you can unlock this portal?"

"Only light can repel darkness. Your blood dwarf paladins and clerics may not be affected by the pull of dark energy, but neither can they combat it. I will open your portal, and then I will take a keep by the sea."

"Very well."

Michael the Paladin steps toward the portal. For a moment, his stoic pose falters, but then he lifts his sword and a ray of light showers him. His entire body takes on an ethereal glow. He swings his sword, gathering momentum, and brings it down upon the enchanted stone.

Black lightning explodes from the portal, instantly defusing the paladin's holy glow. He screams in agony before collapsing to the ground. His body shakes violently, rattling his armor. Then, in a flash, his body vanishes, leaving only his armor behind.

A dwarven paladin moves forward to pick up Michael's armor and weapons when someone yells at him to stop.

"Wait!" Pressley the Knight moves through the crowd. "Wait!" Richard the Cleric skulks close behind.

"Yes?" asks the king.

"I will open the portal, but when I succeed, I will take the paladin's armor as well." He brushes through the guards and their armors scrape against one another.

The king laughs. "So be it."

Pressley unsheathes his sword and gives it a few practice swings. The cleric tries to move past the guards, but they block his passage, apparently under orders to only let one person in at a time.

"He's with me," says the knight.

They allow the cleric to pass, and he brushes off his robes once he is through, as if rubbing against the guards made him dirty. He takes position behind Pressley and begins chanting. I can't quite make out the words, but as he does so, a purple aura envelopes the knight. It seeps into him, turning his armor from silver to a dark plum.

Sparks of lightning run along Pressley's sword as he stalks toward the portal. He raises his weapon and brings it down with a slash across the enchanted stones. Black energy jumps out from the portal and runs along the knight's blade. It sticks to the blade like goo, slowly trudging toward his body. He attempts to relinquish his weapon, but the dark substance crawls through his gauntlets and into his suit of armor.

He screams, his wails of pain setting my hair on end, as he crumples to his knees. His head falls forward, his helm resting against his breastplate.

We all stare on, waiting for his body to vanish and his armor to crash to the ground.

It never happens.

Instead, his head rises.

"Oh, noes." Limery grips me tight on the shoulder.

I don't know what's going on, but if Limery is worried, I think I should be too.

The knight stands. The purple aura that surrounded him is now black. Something buzzes from inside his armor. Pressley lifts his visor and all I can see is blackness.

The guards all turn from their positions, swords and spears pointed at Pressley.

"What the hell is going on?" I ask no one in particular.

"Fall back," a guard orders. "Protect the king."

Something about Pressley has changed, but nothing that would warrant that kind of reaction. Then I analyze him and see why they are so afraid.

Pressley Allen
   Level 24
   Death Knight
   Human

A death knight. The townspeople try to run away in the crowded streets, but those far away have no idea what is happening. Pandemonium takes over as hundreds of dwarves push against one another.

Suddenly, the pieces all fit together. The tower in Vanaria blessed by a cleric. The tapestry of men fighting skeletons. The dark wizard. The dark energy that transformed Pressley into a death knight.

The dark wizard was a necromancer. One who brought death on *Isle of Mythos* before. A fear that both humans and dwarves share.

Pressley raises his sword and points it at Richard. "You said this would work! You said it would allow me to open the portal."

The cleric laughs. "What can I say? God works in mysterious ways."

Pressley stabs the cleric through the chest. There's half a scream before empty robes fall to the ground. The crowd fights to escape him. He hasn't done anything, and yet his very presence is enough to cause a panic. The death knight picks up the fallen paladin's armor and disappears into the escaping crowd.

As most of the dwarves shove to get past me and down the hill, a rather large group marches toward the portal from the other side. Among them, two humans are giving orders.

A force of at least thirty or forty dwarves moves across the square. To one side, stands Jude. His beard is shaggier than ever. He walks shoulders first, hunching like a predator. He carries two shortswords, and several daggers hang from his belt.

Glenn marches on the other side. He walks with a deadly swagger. The only armor he wears is a bit of chainmail beneath his tunic.

"Taryn!" I call out. Shit is about to get real ugly.

"I see." He appears in his dwarven form right beside me. "What's the plan?"

"I don't know, but if they want to get near that portal, then I'm pretty sure we don't want to let that happen."

We move past the escaping dwarves and into the castle square. The king's guards line the stairs, but they hold their position for now. They must be letting this play out.

Why? I don't have a fucking clue.

I pull up Glenn's stats to try and gain an idea of what we are dealing with.

Glenn Orickson
    Level 12
    Warrior
    Human

Only level twelve. He must not have been power-leveling like Taryn has. I guess he had more important things on his mind. He'll be easy enough to handle.

As he marches forward, I can't help but think that I've never seen a plainer looking man in my life. He has such a forgettable face, like someone you could pass on the street and forget about as soon as they are out of vision. And yet, he commands followers so easy.

Is it his Charisma? When I increased mine, it was like a drug. I felt I could do anything, convince anyone of anything. Could his psychotic tendencies be the reason he has such an effect on others?

Fire crackles as Limery prepares for battle on my shoulder. I summon a quick array of horrors and wait.

Glenn, Jude, and their followers march with purpose.

"What are you doing?" I ask Jude. Of the two, he's the only one I have a chance of reasoning with. "Why would you follow a man like Glenn? He's nothing but trouble."

Jude laughs. It's a cruel laugh, absent of joy. "He's the only one who sees you for what you are. Trouble. You kill other heroes for no reason. You make threats and demands to the king. And then...and then, you are rewarded for it." He spits at the ground. "What kind of justice is that? King Favian is not around to protect you now."

I had a reason for every one I killed. My people were dying. The humans treated us like dirt, and I had to send a message that it wasn't okay. Remembering the way he talked about the trolls, like we were nothing, it has my blood boiling.

I analyze his stats as we square off. Despite losing a level at King Favian's feast, Jude has managed to level up to nineteen. Most of the other dwarves range from level five to ten. Whatever happens, Jude is the top priority.

"So what, you're going to kill me?" I shrug. "I'll just come back and find you. You already saw what I did to Glenn. We can put this behind us right now, and no one else has to die."

"Once we open the portal, we'll be under the king's protection. If you attack us, we'll wipe the forest trolls off the map." He snarls. "Hell, we might do it just for fun."

I have to hold back the anger that wells up in me. No one threatens my people. "And how do you expect to do that? You saw the others fail."

He flashes a devious grin. "There's strength in numbers. Attack!"

Their march turns into an all-out sprint as the dwarves raise their weapons in attack.

I don't want to hurt these dwarves, but I can't let Jude and Glenn accomplish whatever sick and twisted goal it is they have in mind.

"Limery, fire wall!"

He flies into the air and erupts a wall of flame in front of the charging dwarves. The dwarves don't stop. They run straight through the flames, their clothes and hair catching fire.

The guards on the step look to the king for orders, but he stays silent.

With fifteen horrors summoned, I send them out with instructions to wound but not kill. I don't want the blood of innocent dwarves on my hands if I can help it. If we can kill Glenn, then whatever influence he has over them will end. It happened in the forest the first time I ever saw him.

My horrors collide with the flaming dwarves, momentarily slowing them. The Horrors of Power sink their tusks into the legs of the dwarves, knocking a few to the ground. The overwhelming number of armed dwarves quickly ends them.

"We need to kill Glenn," I tell Taryn and Limery. "Kill him, and they'll stop."

Glenn is at the back of the fracas, avoiding combat. He wears a demented grin, watching the chaos unfold. This isn't like the forest, when he was on the front lines, enjoying the pain and suffering he brought on the trolls. He has something planned.

We all three take off towards him, when a glowing dagger from Jude stabs me in the ribs. "I don't think so. You're mine." He readies another dagger.

"You two deal with Glenn. I've got this asshole." At level twelve, Glenn should be easy work for the two of them.

Poison from Jude's dagger enters my veins, burning me from the inside. I elect to save my Tiger's Eye Pendant for now, in case I'm attacked again. I have more than enough health to handle a few minutes of poison.

I cast more horrors and send them at the dwarves. Jude marches toward me, spinning a glowing dagger around his finger. The dwarves have stopped their march and now surround Glenn, ready to defend him as he squares off with Taryn and Limery.

Several dwarves lie in the square with either broken or bleeding legs.

Jude throws another dagger at me, but this time, I swipe Sea Scorpion and send the blade ricocheting down the street.

Dammit! I'm torn between fighting Jude and helping my friends. I was hoping to save Champion, but unless I use it now, I'll lose the ability to summon a giant scorpion and be stuck with a level five dwarf instead.

Casting Champion, half of my mana drops in an instant and the giant demon of an insect appears in a cloud of smoke. It's the same as the scorpion I killed, only its color has changed. It's now gray, with a black streak running down its back. It clicks its pincers, and the stinger on its tail pulses a violent red.

I send it to help Taryn and Limery, and it scurries away, armed with three horrors on its back.

Jude unsheathes his swords and charges at me. His outline blurs with each step.

When he's several feet away, I stab my trident at him, but he dodges to the left, leaving a distorted blur in his wake. Before I retract my weapon, he stabs me in the side.

He's gotten faster since the last time we fought.

I swing my trident in an arc, but he jumps back, leaving a shadowy version of himself in his place. The shadow disperses into smoke as my trident cuts through it.

"You might be big and strong, but good luck catching me." He crosses his swords in an X and then his body splits in two. Two mirrored versions of himself laugh at me.

He's like a ninja with a doppelganger, and I can't tell which one is real.

Thunder cracks and lightning flashes nearby, but I don't have time to take in the action. Jude might be two levels under me, but I've proven before that levels aren't everything. He wants to see me hurt, and he has the speed to do it.

The two Judes spread out, splitting to both sides of me. With his speed, if I sit still, he is going to pick me apart. But if I go on the offensive, he might do the same. My only hope is that he makes a mistake. One mistake is all I need to crush his shaggy little head.

I jab my trident at the Jude to my right. He dodges the blow, leaving a blur behind, and before I've even fully extended my arm, another sharp pain flares in my side.

My health continues to trickle down from the poison. I lash out at the other Jude, and am rewarded with a sword to my blind side.

We continue our game of cat and mouse until I'm down to fifty percent health.

I'm fast for my size, but I'm not that fast. I summon a Horror of Vitality near the Jude on my left. Its passive effect slows him, and I stab with all my might. If the blow lands, it will pierce him completely.

Sea Scorpion stabs through Jude's heart and he explodes into gray smoke just as another attack cuts against my ribs.

Taryn's cry of pain causes me to lose all focus, and I turn to see my friend lying on the ground. My blood runs cold. For a moment, I forget that we are in a game, because to me, this isn't a game anymore. I let out a breath of relief. I have no idea what happened, but Limery stands over his body, flaming walls erupted on three sides of them. He pummels fireballs at the dwarves that try to push through, and a mound of bodies pile up at the edge of his fire walls. My scorpion is nowhere to be found.

A sharp pain in my shoulder is the price I pay for my lack of awareness.

Forget Jude, I need to help Taryn. I need to help my friend.

Abandoning all thoughts of Jude, I take off for Taryn, but something stabs through my calf, causing me to fall to the ground. My trident bounces off the stonework just out of my reach.

I'm crawling toward the fight when a trumpet blares from down the street. It carries on for a moment, like a declaration of war. Then, there's a loud crash and the sound of wood splintering, followed by thundering footsteps.

The blade in my calf twists, just as Stompy barrels around the corner, eyes red with rage as he plows through the escaping crowd. Berry follows close behind, both pets drawn to the battle by their psychic bond with their master.

The moulhaug smashes into the group of dwarves, head swinging like a wrecking ball and tossing their bodies like bowling pins.

I let out a sigh of relief. Taryn is going to be okay.

"Where do you think you're going?" Jude asks. He grabs me by the foot and pulls me. The stone floor grates against my open wounds.

That's when I realize that during our game of cat and mouse, he has lured me right beside the portal. Its dark energy moves in waves around the arch.

Jude pulls a vial of yellow liquid from a pouch on his belt and splashes it on my body. The liquid stings against my open wounds, and suddenly, I can't move. I can't reach my Tiger's Eye Pendant to activate its debuff. I'm helpless.

My only choice left is Berserker Rage.

I activate the ability just as Jude rolls me against the portal.

CHAPTER THIRTY-TWO
BLESSINGS

I roll against the enchanted stone and tendrils of dark energy surround me. Everything goes black.

I'm no longer stunned, but I also can't move. There's nothing but darkness. I try to remember where I last set my spawn point, but I can't. I could end up in the forest for all I know.

Words appear in my vision. Blurry at first, but slowly, they come into focus.

Blessing of the Forest Trolls Activated.

A massive force explodes against my back, and the blackness peels away from my eyes as I'm launched into the castle courtyard. My senses overload as I land back in a world of color and smell. Everything smells of sulfur. Stone and rubble fall all around me. Berserker Rage continues to cleanse my body of poison and stitch my cuts back together.

A notification pops up, but I push it away. I try to gain my bearings.

To my left, dozens of dead or injured dwarves litter the courtyard. Stompy and Berry sit beside Taryn's slumping body. He's not dead, or his body wouldn't be there.

What the hell just happened?

Limery's ferocious scream catches my attention and I look over by the portal to see him with his tiny hands wrapped around Jude's throat. Limery's body burns a vibrant red, flames licking at the air all around him. Jude's skin melts from his neck and face before he suddenly vanishes.

Behind Limery, the stone wall that blocked the inside of the arch is gone. The black energy has vanished as well, replaced by a peaceful white swirl. Several of the runes around the arch's edge glow a dull red. Others don't glow at all. They're just empty carvings now.

There's movement on the stairs as the king makes his way down.

"Limery," I try to get the imp's attention.

He turns to me, his eyes bloodshot and filled with tears. "Chods?" In a flash, he's by my side. "Limmy thoughts yous was dead."

"I'm okay, buddy. What happened?"

He wipes his eyes. "The bad mans, he throws you in the portals."

I remember Jude pouring something on me. Something that paralyzed me. Was it glouwseeker venom?

Out of the corner of my eye, I see two bodies enter the courtyard at a full sprint from one of the side streets.

"Get them!" the king shouts, and his guards race from the stairs.

Glenn and Jude run across the courtyard toward the portal. They must have set their respawn points nearby. The two men have a head start, and before the guards are even halfway there, both men leap through the swirling arch. As they disappear, the runes flare for a second and then return to a dull glow.

"Dammit!" the king shouts. "Form a perimeter! I want this portal secured at all times. Detain anyone or anything that comes through." He turns to one of his kings-guard. "Yorn, gather enough men for an envoy. I want to know what is on the other side of these portals by nightfall."

Escorted by several clerics and paladins, the king approaches me. At full height, he's barely taller than I am sitting. "How did you destroy the dark energy?" His tone is urgent as his black eyes bore into me.

"I—I honestly don't know. I think it was the troll blessing."

"Troll blessing?" He looks to one of the clerics. "What do you know of this?"

The cleric strokes his beard for a moment. "If I recall, the trolls were one of the few races unaffected by the dark wizard's temptations. Perhaps it is a form of protection."

The king kneels next to me. "This blessing, can it be replicated?"

Thinking back on the dance and the chants that the forest trolls did before I left, I would imagine it could be. "I think so."

"Good. Kurzol, I want a raven sent to King Favian and one to the forest trolls. Let them know what has happened. Let them know how to unlock the portal." He looks back at the arch. "Tell King Favian that once the portal in Vanaria is open, I request an audience with him."

I struggle to my feet, only half-healed by Berserker Rage. "Do you know where they went?" Wherever it is, it's far away from here. Whoever is on the other side has no idea how dangerous those two can be.

"It's impossible to tell. Each of the red runes are portals that are open on other continents. The empty runes are portals that remain closed. This one..." He points to an empty rune in the shape of an R. "That is the lair of the dark wizard. Our portal hasn't been opened in my lifetime, but I have prepared for this all the same. I did not see which rune activated when they stepped through. They could be on any one of them." He pauses, looking at the devastation all around him. "My council advised me not to interfere in the battles of heroes. They warned me that you all had your part to play. I should have known that there are bad seeds in every bunch.

My inaction has caused much needless death here today. Gather your companions and wait for me in the castle. There is more to discuss, but first, I must address my people."

A cleric leans over Taryn's body, healing him with holy light. When the light fades, Taryn stands up groggily. "What the hell happened?"

"Jude and Glenn escaped through the portal."

His eyes go wide when he sees the swirling white vortex. "How did they manage to open it?"

"They didn't. It was me. On accident."

He scrunches his face.

"I'll tell you all about it inside."

We're led into an intricately decorated throne room. Columns carved with Celtic-looking knots ascend into a vaulted ceiling. The walls are engraved with mighty battle scenes. Even the ceiling is painted with brightly colored images of days past. Statues of great dwarven kings stand on pedestals against the walls. But for all of the decoration in the throne room, the throne itself is simple. One large chunk of obsidian carved with clean edges. No ornamentation.

As the king addresses his people outside, his voice carries through the castle. He speaks of the opening of the portal, the threat of days to come, but also of the hope that we may unite with the other continents to put a stop to the darkness once and for all.

I tell Taryn everything that happened to me, explaining the blessing and the explosion. "It protected me from the dark energy somehow. It's like I overloaded whatever spell was holding it in place."

Limery holds tight against my shoulder as I recount the events. Ever since I came back from the portal, he hasn't let go. That's twice now that I've scared him into thinking I was dead.

Taryn shakes his head. "What happens now?"

The door to the throne room opens and King Orso enters, escorted by his kings-guards. Taryn drops to one knee as the king passes and takes the throne.

"These two men that entered the portal. They are enemies of Vanaria, yes?" The king's red skin is prominent against the black throne.

"How do you know that?" I thought their wanted marks would vanish once they entered the north.

"Others may not see, but a king sees all. Especially on my lands." He leans forward. "If they are enemies of Vanaria, then henceforth, they are enemies of Seascape as well. The world as we know it is on the verge of change. Once the portal to Vanaria is open, I intend to make plans for what comes next. Make no mistake, a war is coming. The dark energy that has sealed these portals is old, and it is strong. A day will come when the dark wizard opens his own portal once more, and on that day, we will need the heroes of this world on our side. You must use this time wisely. Strengthen your bodies, your minds, your very bonds with one another. For when that dreaded day comes, we will need all the help we can get."

A long silence passes as we take in the king's words. Several dwarves have gathered around the throne, waiting for their orders.

The king is right. For the people of *Isle of Mythos*, their world is about to change. I trust that King Orso and King Favian will prepare their people for what comes. No one knows what waits on the other side of that portal, but if war is coming, I need to make sure I am strong enough to answer the call. And with a little luck, maybe I can rally more heroes to our cause.

SENTENCED TO TROLL 3

PROLOGUE

"Boss, you need to come see this." Thompson stared at the monitor above Chad Johnson's pod.

Valery cursed under her breath, wondering what could be happening this time. It had been weeks, but they'd made no progress in determining the connection between Chad and the AI going haywire. Tomorrow, they would be pulling him out again.

"What is it?" Valery hovered over Thompson like a hawk.

He pointed at the screen monitoring Chad's vitals. Everything looked normal.

Valery wasn't in the mood for games. She would be giving a presentation to the board in only a few short days, and while there was progress to report on the subjects' brain functions, the fact that one of the subjects was unable to log out without the system crashing would not be well-received.

Valery narrowed her eyes. "Are you going to tell me what I'm looking at, or should I find someone else who can?"

Thompson swallowed hard. "Look at this number." He pointed to the display for Chad's body mass. "And then look at this." He handed her a tablet with Chad's initial vital statistics.

The numbers were different, which should have been impossible. The nanites were designed to keep the body in perfect stasis. They prevented muscle loss and fed the subjects with the precise amount of nutrients so that they didn't lose or gain weight.

"What does this mean? Are the nanites feeding him too much?" She compared the stats once again. It wasn't a major difference, but it was noticeable.

"I don't think so. The weight he's gained isn't fat. Look at this." He pointed to a second reading. "His muscle mass has increased."

Valery froze in place. If this were true, if the nanites were actually improving

Chad's body based on what he did in the game, then this changed everything. The ability to rewire a mind was one thing—meditation had been shown to accomplish a similar feat for years—but going into a pod and coming out with a stronger body? That could change the world.

But was this an artifact of the strange connection between Chad and the game, or was it happening to everyone? Valery darted over to the next pod. Her hands shook as she called up the stats on the occupant.

CURRENT STATS

Chod, Level 21 Barbarian/Summoner Forest Troll
  HP: 4485/4485
  Mana: 5000/5000
  Rage: 0/100
  XP: 403,625/415,000

Strength: 38
  Dexterity: 24
  Constitution: 39
  Intelligence: 10
  Wisdom: 15
  Charisma: 6

+1 Strength and Constitution racial bonus per level.

2 stat points available.

0 ability points available.

Abilities:

. . .

Bite. *Using your massive tusks and powerful jaw, you take a bite out of an opponent, dealing immense damage. Cost: 10 rage Level 2.*

Claw. *You attack with sharp claws, swiping at an opponent and dealing extra damage. Cost: 5 rage. Level 2.*

Intimidation. *You stare down your opponent, confusing them so that they are unable to attack for two seconds. Cost 10 rage.*

Berserker Rage. *(Ultimate) Attacks and physical damage build your rage meter. 5 rage per attack. Rage meter deteriorates over time when out of combat at a rate of 5 rage per second. Activating Berserker Rage fills rage meter. For 30 seconds, rage meter does not decrease, deal increased damage, health regenerates at 5x the normal rate, cannot be stunned, slowed or otherwise affected. Cooldown: 10 minutes.*

I'm Always Angry *(Passive. Available at level 10). Once rage meter is at 50%, it will not deteriorate below 50% when out of combat.*

Increased Regeneration. *(Passive) Regenerate health at a faster rate. Level 2.* **Rapid Regeneration.** *(Passive) When below 10% health, regeneration is doubled.*

Nightvision. *(Passive) Increased vision in darkness and low light.*

Thick Skin. *(Passive) Take 10% less damage from physical attacks.*

Camouflage. *(Passive) When out of combat and not moving for 20 seconds, trolls blend in with their surroundings.*

Sweeping Slash. *Form a sweeping arc in front of you, dealing damage and knocking your opponent off balance. Cost: 5 rage.*

Conceal (Passive). *Hides level from anyone who is not a guard on city grounds.*

Summon horror (Passive). *Ability to summon a horror. Each horror grants a unique ability. For every horror active, gain 1% increased damage and health points. Horrors decay 10% for every minute outside of combat.*

Horror of Power. *Summon a horror with 20% of your strength. Cost: 100 mana. Cooldown: 30 seconds. Bonus: Your next attack deals double damage.*

Horror of Vitality. *Summon a horror with 20% of your health points. Cost: 100 mana. Cooldown: 30 seconds. Bonus: Opponents near Horror of Vitality are slowed by 20%.*

Horror of Finesse. *Summon a horror with 20% of your attack speed. Cost: 100 mana. Cooldown: 30 seconds. Bonus: Your next attack heals you for damage dealt.*

Sacrifice. *Sacrifice X amount of horrors to receive a temporary buff. Horror of Power: +1 Strength. Horror of Vitality: +1 Constitution. Horror of Finesse: +1 Dexterity*

Kamikaze. *Sacrifice a horror to deal a burst of damage.*

Champion. *Summon a copy of the most recent enemy you have defeated. Decays 10% every minute out of combat. Cost: 50% of mana pool. Cooldown: 6 hours.*

Available Abilities *(1 ability point to unlock):*

. . .

Massive Bite. *Deals double damage. Cost: 20 rage*

Claws. *Swipe at opponent with both hands, dealing extra damage. Cost: 10 rage*

Multi Attack. *Bite and Claw at the same time. Cost: 20 rage*

Iron Will. *Immune to slows and stuns for 30 seconds. Cost: 50 rage 180 second cooldown.*

Perception. *For 10 minutes, gain increased awareness of your surroundings. Spot hidden objects, as well as unusual sounds, odors, and tastes. Cooldown: 6 hours.*

Cleave. *Your next attack causes bleed damage, dealing 1% of opponent's health per second for 5 seconds. Cost: 10 rage.*

Battle Cry. *You let out a ferocious roar, increasing rage by 20. No Cost. 60 second cooldown.*

Current Items:

Item. Phoenix Feather. 10% resistance to fire-based attacks. *A very rare item, phoenix feathers can only be gathered if they are willingly given by the host. Feathers plucked from unwilling birds turn to ash.*

Item. Tiger's Eye Pendant. Removes one debuff. Cooldown: 10 minutes. *A rare stone believed to ward off evil and bring balance to life.*

Item. Petrified Staff. An enchanted staff capable of taking on the properties of up to 3 attached stones. +3 Intelligence. +3 Wisdom. Bonus: *While holding Petrified Staff, the user can cast ranged physical attacks once every 10 seconds.*

Item. Forlorn Scepter. +5 Intelligence. *Increases the range of summoned creatures by 50%.*

Item. Glouwseeker Venom. *When injected into the bloodstream, glouwseeker venom immobilizes target. Length of stun dependent on size of target, resistances, and amount injected.*

Item. Sea Scorpion. +3 Strength. *An enchanted trident capable of taking on the property of 1 enchanted stone. Bonus: deals splash damage.*

Legendary Item. Angel of Death Brandy. *When drinker falls below 1HP, a metaphysical event will occur, rewinding time for the user to two seconds prior to death.*

CHAPTER ONE
GOLDSPIRE

I roll my shoulders, trying to relieve some of the tension. I'm not the only one on edge, though. Dozens of guards surround the fast-travel portal located in the city square of Seascape.

They stand like statues, rigid and immovable.

Waiting.

King Orso Brightgaze looks down upon us from above the long set of stairs between the square and the castle. His kingsguard stands at the ready, their resplendent silver platemail shimmering in the midday sun.

Fast-travel has returned to *Isle of Mythos*. This should be a time for celebration, but the blood of fallen dwarves still lines the cobblestone streets.

The dwarven king towers over the dwarves surrounding him, at least a foot taller. His dull, red skin is the color of cooling magma, announcing to the world that he is one of the few blood dwarves that still exist. Bushy black hair falls to his shoulders. His black beard is intricately braided and adorned with silver clasps. He wears a black tunic and black cloak, each embroidered with silver thread. A red breastplate engraved with a silver warhammer protects his chest, and a glowing red crown rests on his head. The tines of the crown have alternating battleaxes and warhammers, emblems of his people's lineage. His face is set in stone as he watches us.

Four hours have passed since Jude and Glenn started a battle in the square that led to the deaths of many innocent dwarves. Even though both men were slain in combat, they had set their respawn points near enough that they were able to slip through the portal amid the chaos. Through a portal that had not been opened in centuries.

I worry about the havoc they may cause on the other side, wherever that may be. No one saw which rune flashed as they jumped through the portal, so the king has organized scouting parties to travel to each one, to warn the locals and search for answers and allies for what is yet to come. With a four-hour head start, even if we manage to find the correct portal, they've had plenty of time to disappear.

I still don't know if it was dumb luck or something else that caused me to open the portal. Jude tossed me against the archway, and it swallowed me in a vortex of dark energy. Somehow, the blessing that the forest trolls had bestowed upon me broke whatever dark magic had kept the portal sealed for so long.

Truthfully, I think Jude tried to kill me. Had I died, I have no doubt that he and Glenn would have killed their entire army of mind-controlled dwarf minions to try and break the seal. There was no way for him to know that I had been blessed. That portal had claimed the lives of countless men and dwarves alike who'd attempted to pass through. Only the blood dwarves were immune to the deadly effects of the dark energy, but even they received a horrible backlash from its sinister power.

I take a deep breath, trying to mentally prepare myself for what's on the other side. The king gave us notes combed from Seascape's libraries, but so much time has passed since they were written that they may no longer be accurate. A betting man would say they aren't.

Even though dozens of us surround the portal, nobody moves. I'm sure they are all just as nervous as I am. The guards may be stoic, but the rest of us are not. An ebony dwarf constantly shuffles the butt of his spear, repositioning it with each breath. The blood dwarf paladin beside him rubs his stubby fingers against the back of his neck. None of us know what lies in wait, and if I had to guess, no one on the other side knows our portal is open either. Four hours and no one has come through. I don't know if that's good or bad.

White energy swirls inside the rune-covered archway. Hints of silver flash within the ethereal whirlpool. Half of the runes that run along the arch have a faint red glow, indicating the portal has access to a counterpart on the other side. The rest are empty engravings, their portals still blocked by dark magic, including the lands where the dark wizard vanished to centuries before.

Vanaria's portal is also among the inactive.

For now.

Isle of Mythos is about to change. For the better, I hope. Both ends of the island could use a little diversity.

While we all prepare to venture into unknown lands, Limery speeds south. First, to the forest trolls, and then to the human capital with news of how to open the portal.

King Orso was prepared to send ravens south, but I thought it would be smarter to send Limery. The imp can fly far faster than even the speediest raven, and both Chief Rizza and King Favian will trust his word.

Every second we waste is more time for Glenn and Jude to gather forces on the other side.

"Ready?" I ask Taryn.

"Not one bit." He looks at the polished marble courtyard, his dreadlocks covering his eyes. Caked blood fills in the cracks. He taps the butt of his gnarled staff against the marble tile a few times before making eye contact. His pet bear nuzzles against the druid's leg.

Taryn is still shaken up from the battle. I don't blame him. This was his first battle where he wasn't just killing monsters. When he cast Lightning Bolt, the smell of burning dwarven flesh filled the air. This may be a game, but it sure doesn't feel like it. When those dwarves died, they screamed and bled like real people. Some cried out the names of those they wished to see in their final moments. Others shit and pissed themselves with their last breaths. No, I don't blame him one bit.

White energy swirls inside the stone archway as the first group moves forward. Two blood dwarf paladins, an ivory dwarf warrior, and an ebony dwarf dressed in fine linens step up to the platform surrounding the archway.

As they approach, the active runes along the arch burst to life, glowing a fiery red that matches the skin of the blood dwarves. They look to their king for approval.

He nods before speaking. "Focus on the rune you wish to travel to." His deep voice carries like a megaphone, somehow magically amplified. "When it is the only one left glowing, step through. You will emerge in new lands. Make contact with the locals, hand them the parchment with my message, and then return home at once. If trouble arises, return to safety. Our guards will be waiting on the other side." The king raises his warhammer into the air, and the four dwarves slam a fist against their chests. The runes all fade except for one that looks like a triangle with a V passing through its center.

One by one, the dwarves step through the portal, vanishing from sight. As soon as they are through, the next scouting party takes their place. The crowd surrounding the portal grows smaller and smaller until our group is all that remains within the circle of soldiers surrounding the perimeter.

I pull up the quest King Orso gave us.

Quest Alert. *You have been offered the quest 'First Contact: Goldspire.' Travel into the lands of Goldspire and deliver King Orso Brightgaze's message to its leaders.*

Bonus: *If Jude or Glenn have traveled to Goldspire, apprehend them and return to Seascape so that they may face justice.*

Reward: *Increased favor with Seascape, potential allies in Goldspire.*

Taryn and I approach the portal, his two pets following close at our heels. Berry, the umber bear with a beautiful golden coat, keeps close to Taryn. The bear guards him like a loyal dog, always obedient. Stompy brings up the rear. The mighty moulhaug with a broad, moss-covered backside and a single horn that protrudes from the center of its snout behaves more like a common housecat, if that housecat was capable of wrecking an entire building. The horn on its snout can swing with such force that it acts as a battering ram. Stompy snorts, voicing his displeasure. Despite his moodiness, Stompy has saved our asses on more than one occasion.

Further back, my small army of horrors begin to puff out of existence as their cooldowns expire. The demonic creatures won't be joining our journey through the portal for fear of what those on the other side might think. The last thing I want is to show up with a small army and start a war unintentionally. But at least they will give me an added stat boost for a few minutes before they fade away.

I hope I don't need it.

When we step on the platform surrounding the arch, I focus on the rune for Goldspire, two vertical lines with a caret symbol over the top. The rune resembles a house, or an arrow with two shafts instead of one.

The other runes dim, leaving the one for Goldspire burning a vibrant red.

As we step through, white energy surrounds our bodies, and for a moment, everything is silent. Then, just as quickly as we entered, we step into a world of chaos.

CHAPTER TWO

YOU CAN'T MILK THOSE

The white swirl of the portal fades, and we step into a sandy arena. A rustic stone coliseum towers around us, obscuring the landscape except for blue skies overhead. The sun beams down from above, hot and dry. Clashing metal draws my attention, followed by roars, screams, and blaring trumpets that echo across the pit.

What is this place?

Wherever it is, it's far from *Isle of Mythos*. The sun was overhead when we left, but now it is closer to the horizon.

Stompy paws at the ground and releases an agitated snort. Several spots of rust-colored sand surround his hoofprint. Blood. Berry sniffs at the blood-soaked sand and curls his lips in a snarl, revealing teeth capable of snapping bones like twigs.

I feel you, buddy. How many happy endings start with a blood-covered entrance?

A packed crowd fills the stands, spectating as a half-dozen battles rage around the arena. In the blazing sun, only their outlines are visible. A dark silhouette falls to the arena floor and the crowd erupts in applause. I have no idea what we stumbled into, but I don't want to stick around to find out. I search the perimeter of the arena for an exit, but all of the tunnels are barred.

The only way out is back through the portal.

"What the hell is this place? Some kind of gladiatorial arena?" I ask.

"I don't know, but there is a giant fucking cow walking right towards us!" Taryn climbs onto Stompy's back and readies his gnarled staff to attack.

I turn to see a minotaur that's every bit as tall as I am and a little bit wider stalking in our direction. Its powerful muscles ripple with each aggressive step, and a trail of dust follows in its wake. The minotaur's broad shoulders are covered in radiant golden fur. Obsidian horns stretch the width of its body, their tips dangerous weapons capable of goring anyone unlucky enough to step within their range. A silver nose-ring dangles from its nostrils, nearly twice the size of the one Gord has. The only clothing the minotaur wears is a black leather loincloth, and the only armor, two vambraces that shield its forearms. A thick chain hangs from its waist like a belt, the end tipped with a sickle that holds the weapon in place. The minotaur's clenched fists remind me of giant sledgehammers. Sand plumes into the air with each step it takes before it comes to a stop a few yards away. Steam shoots out of its nostrils, and I take a moment to analyze it.

Dakota
  Level 33

Level thirty-three. That's one badass bovine. I wish I had my horrors with me right about now. I grow weaker by the minute as they puff out of existence on the other side of the portal.

"You wish to enter the lands of Goldspire?" His voice rumbles.

"We are on a quest from King Orso to deliv—"

"Yes or no," the minotaur cuts me off.

Another silhouette falls in the distance to the cheers of the crowd.

"Yes." I force my voice to stay even, clenching my fist while sharp claws dig into my palm.

I hate being cut off mid-sentence. There are few things as disrespectful as disregarding what someone else has to say. I take a deep breath, remembering why we are here.

"Very well. Goldspire is no place for the weak. If you wish to enter our lands, then you must prove your worth on the fields of battle."

Taryn and I exchange nervous glances. This guy could probably kill Taryn in two or three hits. Hell, he could probably kill us both.

Looking around the arena, I don't see any way Jude or Glenn could have made it out of here. Then again, I wouldn't put anything past those two. This is about more than finding two murderous heroes. It's about making allies for the war to come. Something caused the portal in Seascape to come to life, and we need to prepare for the worst.

King Orso was right. We are going to need allies for what comes next, badass minotaurs included.

If our only way out of this arena is through a giant fucking cow, then so be it.

I lower my body, pointing Sea Scorpion at the minotaur. The golden trident shimmers in my hand. "Let's get this over with."

Stompy unleashes a warning call and the sound echoes across the coliseum.

"Try not to get hit." I lean in close to Taryn so Dakota can't hear me. "And if it looks like we can't win, you take Berry and Stompy and return through the portal. I have my spawn point set in the Seascape square, so that is where we will meet."

Taryn nods. His normally cheerful disposition is gone, his eyes focused on the hulking threat before us. His entire demeanor has changed since the battle at the square.

Dakota cracks his knuckles and steps forward, flexing his golden muscles.

I quickly summon three horrors and they burst to life in front of me. All pretense of peace is over. Now, all that matters is surviving so that we can deliver the king's message.

Dakota raises an eyebrow as the horrors appear.

Yeah, I'm full of surprises. I give him my best attempt at an arrogant smirk.

I step down from the platform surrounding the portal. "Spread out so that we can keep him distracted."

Taryn and his two pets go to the right and I take the left with my horrors. In response, the minotaur backs up to keep us both in his vision. He looks tough as nails, and I'm pretty sure we're going to need more than skill to get past him.

I force away the sounds of the crowd and the other battles, focusing all my attention on the threat before us. Right now, he is all that stands between us and exiting this arena.

I summon another round of horrors, but Taryn is the first to attack. He casts Lightning Bolt, and there's a crack of thunder as lightning rips through the air. Dakota is faster than he looks, sidestepping the attack just as it hits, leaving a jagged glass sculpture in the sand.

I use the distraction to lunge with my trident, putting my full weight behind the blow. The horrors follow my lead, going for the minotaur's legs. In a blur, Dakota smashes his vambrace-covered forearm against my weapon, parrying the attack. Sea Scorpion slides off the vambrace with a screech, and I stumble to my knees. There's a sickening crunch, and I feel my horrors' presence vanish behind me.

As I rise to my feet, the crack of breaking bones and a loud yelp draws my attention. Berry lies on the ground with Dakota standing over him. The bear has his teeth bared, but he doesn't move.

Dakota kneels over Berry.

"Nooo!" yells Taryn. He raises his staff and a lightning bolt plunges toward Dakota.

Dakota dodges the attack with ease, faster than I have ever seen anyone move. But Taryn doesn't give up, he's already charging, Stompy's horn swinging back and forth with each step.

I press on from the other side, summoning more horrors as I do. Maybe we can pinch him between us.

The golden minotaur raises both arms above his head, fists clenched. When we are several feet away, he slams his fists into the earth. The ground explodes, debris and rubble from the sandy floor rocketing us into the air with concussive force and taking out a chunk of health. Taryn falls from Stompy's back but uses Transform to turn into a red bird mid-flight. The small bird weaves through the chaos, narrowly dodging the raining rocks. The moulhaug falls to the ground with a thud.

Sea Scorpion flies from my hand when I hit the ground, lost somewhere among the dust and scattered earth. And just like that, three more horrors are gone. I can't summon them fast enough before they die.

I can't help but feel like I am out of my element here. He's running circles around us. But why? It's four against one. Or was Limery the linchpin that held our little band together, a small force of raw power?

When the smoke clears, Dakota stands among the rubble, a deep laugh rumbling in his gut.

"Is that all you've got?" he goads us. "I didn't expect much from the half-man, but you looked formidable." Steam shoots out of his nostrils. "I guess looks can be deceiving." He unhooks the sickle that holds the chain belt in place around his waist. "Time to send you back to whatever hole you came from. You aren't strong enough for Goldspire."

Nearby, Taryn has returned to his dwarven form and leans over Berry. Both emanate healing light as Taryn casts Restoration on his downed pet, slowly repairing his cracked bones and gored flesh.

Dakota tosses the sickled end of the chain over his head and spins it like a helicopter. The curved blade whistles in the wind as it gains momentum, eventually becoming a blur.

I have to do something, because Taryn is helpless while he tries to heal Berry. As strong as Dakota is, that weapon could rip right through him. Every second that passes feels more and more like we aren't making it out of here alive.

Three horrors appear in front of me in a puff of smoke. Before they even have a chance to move, Dakota swipes his chain with so much force that it severs all three of them in half with one motion.

I charge at him and when he swings his weapon again, I jump. It passes underneath my legs with enough power to break bone.

I'm halfway to him when the sickle whizzes back in my direction, this time a little higher. He's trying to catch me mid-jump, so instead, I duck, barely dodging the blow as it grazes my back.

Readying Claw, I launch myself at him, sinking my claws into his chest and pushing him to the ground. The chain loses its momentum, coiling like a snake through the air. I land on top of the minotaur, but he uses my momentum against me and rockets me off his knees like an acrobat.

I twist through the air and land on my feet, stirring up dust. Dakota crawls to his feet, blood streaking from the gashes on his chest, the first blood we've drawn against him.

"Ha ha," he rumbles. "You can't milk those!"

He flicks the chain and the sickle flies back into his hand.

My attack bought Taryn enough time to finish his spell. Berry scrambles up from the bloody splotch of sand, wounds healed and ready to fight once more.

For a moment, Dakota just stares at us, an amused grin on his face. His Constitution must be through the roof, because my attack barely touched his HP.

I summon three more horrors, even though I know they'll be dead in an instant. I spread them out, trying to flank Dakota, but he retreats, keeping them in view.

"We could run," I tell Taryn. We're risking a lot by staying here, and I'm almost positive Jude and Glenn aren't here.

He climbs atop Stompy once again. "A few hits and you're ready to call it a day. I thought you were a troll?" His beard twitches at the edges.

Finally, some of the Taryn I remember. Not his best joke, but I'll take it for now.

"You know, hamburgers do sound nice. Say, Dakota, are you grass-fed by chance?"

Taryn bursts into laughter. Dakota has no idea what I mean by the joke, but he can obviously sense it's at his expense because the grin fades and steam shoots out of his nostrils when he snorts.

With blazing speed, he whips his chain in my direction. The distance between us is the only reason I'm able to dodge the attack, and even then, I can hear the whir of the blade as it flies past my ear.

Before the chain retracts, my horrors are already on the offensive. Horror of Finesse is the first one on Dakota. It quickly dies, a massive hoof flattening the gangly blue creature into the sand. The Horror of Power stabs its tusks into the minotaur's calf. Blood spurts out, covering the muscled horror in dark red ichor.

Dakota flicks his wrist, recalling the sickle-tipped chain again. It recoils with blinding speed, and he catches the blade in his free hand, using it to stab my horror through the skull.

The Horror of Power puffs out of existence just as Horror of Vitality slams against a thick golden leg. The fluffy blue-and-orange horror does no damage, but a confused look on Dakota's face lets me know he's been slowed.

"Now!" I shout.

Lightning rips through the sky, followed immediately by a crash of thunder. Dakota makes to dive out of the way, but this time, he's not so fast. The Horror of Vitality's passive slows him just enough for Taryn's bolt to hit home. The attack fries my horror, but it also manages to stun Dakota in place.

Taryn casts Strong Wind, increasing my movement speed as I race toward the stunned minotaur. His eyes are red with rage. I summon more horrors as I run, tossing them ahead of me and exploding them against the stupefied cow.

Taryn casts Imbue on Stompy, making the moulhaug larger than ever. His hooves shake the ground as he charges with Taryn on his back. Berry's grunts let me know he is on the other side of the moulhaug.

We're all in. This is our chance.

Stompy collides into Dakota just as the stun wears off. Using his horn like a wrecking ball, he knocks the minotaur into the air with amazing force. I ready Bite and Claw, imbuing my next attacks with extra damage, and as soon as the minotaur hits the ground, Berry and I descend on him, dealing damage by any means available.

We kick, bite, and claw until dark red blood fills my mouth and covers my body. It's warm and satisfying.

"Enough!" shouts Dakota as he retaliates.

A powerful fist smashes into my jaw, sending stars streaming across my vision.

The next thing I know, I'm flying through the air in another explosion of earth and debris.

My horrors are all dead, so I summon another round as I stagger to my feet. By the time the stars vanish from my vision, Dakota has regained his weapon. I still have no idea where Sea Scorpion is.

There's a flash of lightning, but Dakota dodges it with ease, leaving another glass sculpture buried in the sand.

Our momentary reign of terror managed to shave ten percent off Dakota's HP, but I've lost a quarter myself. Taryn still has sixty percent, but one wrong move can end him in an instant.

To my left, Berry breathes heavily. To my right, Stompy paws at the earth, readying for another charge, Taryn on his back.

I use Intimidation at the same time Dakota whips the sickle in my direction, unleashing a mighty roar and hoping it confuses Dakota long enough for Stompy to knock him down.

Taryn charges, but my ability has no effect. Is it because Dakota is a higher level than me or something else entirely?

The sickle stabs me in the chest, piercing deep and lodging in one of my bones. Sharp, hot pain flares through my body as blood spills down my midsection.

Dakota jerks the chain, but it doesn't come loose, instead pulling me forward onto my face. I fight through the pain, grabbing the chain and ripping the sickle from my chest. It leaves a gash deep enough to store items in.

Explosions and thunder echo around me, and by the time I'm on my feet, a cloud of dust fills the air. I summon my horrors, and my health continues to trickle down from the continuous blood loss. My rapid healing isn't able to keep up with such a deep wound.

Lost in the smoke, I can't spot Taryn or his pets anywhere. The grunts of battle let me know they are in there somewhere.

I roll the dice and cast Champion, my ability to summon a copy of the last enemy I defeated, but just as I suspected, a lowly ivory dwarf, probably a farmer, emerges on the battlefield. One of my horrors must have killed him during our battle with Glenn and Jude.

He rushes into the chaos and a moment later, his presence vanishes among the dust cloud.

There's a loud smash from within the dust, and Stompy soars through the air. He crashes to the ground with a thud, his body covered in bruises, cuts, and gore marks. Half his HP is gone. Slowly, he stands, ready for more.

A red bird zips out from the cloud of dust and Taryn returns to his dwarven form near the safety of the moulhaug. He places his hands on Stompy's side, casting Restoration and basking both in a splendid aura. Berry is nowhere to be found.

I summon three more horrors and send them into the chaos. The dust fades just as their presence vanishes, revealing Dakota, covered in blood, but with far more health than I would like. He's probably covered in more of our blood than his own.

Without warning, he whips his chain in Taryn's direction. I try to warn him, but the weapon is too fast. It strikes Taryn in the side, plunging the blade deep into his ribs. Taryn collapses to the ground, ninety percent of his HP gone after the attack.

The sickle is still lodged in his body, so I rush toward him, leaping for and grabbing the chain just as Dakota tries to pull it back.

I anchor my feet to the ground and activate Berserker Rage. Rage pumps into my muscles, fueling me with barbarian energy. My vision goes red as my Strength and health regeneration increase. Dakota pulls on the chain again, but I don't budge. We're finally on equal footing. My feet sink deeper into the sand as we lock in a battle of tug-of-war.

The chain groans as we both pull with all our might. Behind me, Taryn squirms and groans.

"You have to remove the blade. I've got about thirty-seconds before he overpowers me." If he doesn't get the blade out, he's toast.

Taryn places his hands around the sickle and grimaces in pain. "I don't think I can," he pants. "It's too deep."

Careful not to let go of the chain, I summon a set of horrors and instruct them help Taryn.

Stompy places a hoof on the chain behind me, holding it in place in case I'm overpowered.

Taryn screams for a few agonizing seconds of what I can only assume are my horrors removing the sickle.

"Okay, it's out." He sounds weak, but at least he is alive.

"Alright, find Berry and then go for the portal. We'll live to fight another day."

Dakota pulls again, but my grip holds. Steam radiates from my skin as sweat evaporates from my overheating body.

Out of the corner of my eye, Taryn comes to a stop over a giant pile of sand. He bends down for a minute, and then the sand shifts and Berry shuffles to his feet. The poor bear has taken a hell of a beating today.

"Let's go!" Taryn runs past me.

"No, you take the others. I'll follow once you're through."

He cuts his eyes at me just as Dakota pulls again. Berserker Rage is almost up. "I'm not leaving you behind." He reaches into his satchel and pulls out a vial of dark purple liquid. "Infernal Darkness Potion. When I throw this, let go of the chain."

He tosses the glass vial at Dakota, and I release my grip just as Berserker Rage expires. The minotaur falls backward from the sudden slack. The vial clatters against the ground and black smoke rapidly fills the air around Dakota. A deep, dark smoke that seems to absorb the light around it.

"I forgot you had that," I say.

No matter where Dakota moves, the darkness follows.

Taryn smirks. "We've got a whole minute before it wears off."

Now that we are finally no longer in imminent danger, I take in the rest of the arena. Several bodies lay scattered on the other side. Some are still engaged in combat. Others bask in the cheers of the crowd as they toss items into the arena. The closer I look, I realize that many of the other combatants are beast-people. Like the minotaur, but with different animals. One has an elephant's head, another a tiger's. They all have stout, humanoid bodies, with furs or thick hides.

I'm more intrigued than ever, but it's time to go back to *Isle of Mythos.*

"This is one hell of a place." Taryn climbs on Stompy's back. Both of his pets look pretty ragged. "We'll have to come back some time." He winks.

The portal swirls peacefully before us. I focus on the rune for Seascape, two horizontal squiggly lines that look like waves, and it flares a bright red.

"After you." I motion for Taryn and Stompy to pass.

He's a few feet from entering the portal when I hear a grunt from behind us. I turn just in time to see Dakota, no longer covered in darkness, whipping his chain in our direction. He holds the sickle in one hand, this time tossing the weighted end of the chain. It sails through the air, passing inches from my face and wrapping around Taryn's neck. It coils down his body several times, pinning his arms to his sides. Dakota pulls, unseating Taryn from Stompy and launching him back onto the battlefield.

Stompy and Berry pass through the portal, unaware of what just happened.

Taryn soars through the air, constricted and unable to transform into his bird form, at the same time as Dakota charges. When his fist collides with Taryn, the druid's HP drops to zero. His body vanishes and his items fall into the sand.

"Ha-ha." Dakota laughs at the carnage. "If you mess with the bull, you get the horns."

Anger takes over. "You're going to pay for that!" I roar, spittle flying from my mouth as I leap from the platform.

Summoning three more horrors, I charge the arrogant minotaur. I ready Claw and Bite, not caring that he out-levels me. I know I should be grabbing Taryn's items and making a run for it, but he killed my friend, and he is going to pay. I'll mount his head on the walls of Seascape before this is over.

I bare my teeth and unleash a guttural roar. Blood pounds in my ears as my pulse races.

"Feisty. I like it." Steam shoots out of his nostrils, and he charges in my direction.

I pull Petrified Staff from my satchel and equip it, using its passive ability to fire a ranged attack at Dakota. Unsurprisingly, he dodges the attack.

Without skipping a beat, he slings the weighted end of his chain at me. It arcs in a semi-circle, decapitating both the Horror of Finesse and Horror of Vitality before wrapping around my calves. The chain pulls my legs together like a zip-tie and I fall face-first into the sand. Horror of Power's presence vanishes, and a hulking shadow stands over me.

"Anger is the enemy of strategy," Dakota huffs.

Those are the last words I hear before his giant hoof stomps my head into the ground.

CHAPTER THREE

SHOP TIL YOU DROP

The darkness fades and I come to my senses lying against the cool stone of the Seascape square. I'm on my knees wearing nothing but my loincloth.

My satchel. My items. My weapons. They're all gone. I punch the stone floor in frustration and a surge of pain runs through my knuckles.

"Dammit! Stupid, stupid, stupid!" I shout. Not only did I lose all my items, I lost Taryn's as well. We went through so much to get those items. Some were gifts from the chief. Not to mention the legendary Angel of Death Brandy we looted after defeating the dragomanders. "I'm such a fucking idiot." I let out a defeated sigh.

A small hand grabs my shoulder. "What happened?" asks Taryn.

I turn to see him wearing nothing but a simple gray tunic that falls to his knees. He doesn't look angry, though. Probably because he doesn't know what I did yet.

Give it time.

"Bro, I screwed up." I hang my head in shame.

"I think we both made some mistakes." He smiles. "We were outgunned, after all."

"No, I mean I screwed the pooch. I could have grabbed your items and ran. Instead, I got pissed and rushed into battle. Then I got my head stomped into the sand." I wait for his wrath. For him to tell me what a moron I am and how typical it is of me to lose my temper. It's what I deserve.

Instead, he cocks his head back and lets out a boisterous laugh, dreads swaying back and forth. Hand over belly, it pours out of him. Not at all what I expected.

"What's so funny? Why aren't you upset?"

He wipes tears from his eyes. "They're just items. I'm sure we'll find more. Berry and Stompy made it out alive, I consider that pretty lucky. You losing your cool, on the other hand, is hilarious." He chuckles again before patting me on the back.

"Man, you've gone off the deep end."

The portal flashes beside us and a group of three ivory dwarves and one blood dwarf step through. They make straight for the castle, at a brisk pace. The guards move out of the way, allowing them passage up the stairs.

"That looks important." I watch as the group moves with purpose, taking two steps at a time with their short dwarf legs. "What do you say we follow?"

Taryn instructs his pets to wait near the portal and we set off in pursuit of the dwarves.

As we walk, I pull up my most recent notification.

Alert! You have died. All items on your person have been lost. Items can be retrieved at the site of death in the event they have not been looted. One level and any stat points associated with it have been removed.

Fuck.

Back to level twenty. Plus I lose my newest ability, Champion.

How in the hell are we supposed to retrieve our stuff without any weapons? I can say with confidence that Dakota is now the proud owner of all our items.

"What do you think happened?" asks Taryn.

"No idea. Maybe they have news of Glenn and Jude. Whatever it is, they aren't wasting any time."

We practically run up the stairs to catch up, cardio kicking my ass by the time we reach the top. I envy Kassidy's ability to teleport up and down the castle in Vanaria right now, and wonder if the pot-bellied wizard will be joining King Favian when they meet for council.

When we arrive at the throne room, one of the ivory dwarves is already addressing the king.

"—possible that they came through. There is a land of snow and ice, where several mountain tribes still rule that do not follow the laws of the kingdom."

Sitting on his obsidian throne, the king scrunches his nose. "And what of my proclamation? My request for allies and peace?"

"They would like to meet with you in person, Your Highness." The dwarf bows his head.

"Very well. Make the arrangements. Perhaps I can convene a round table with King Favian and all of the great leaders." King Orso looks over in our direction, raising an eyebrow. "What news of Goldspire?"

Taryn steps forward and bends a knee. I do the same.

"Unfortunately, we were not able to make it out of the arena," Taryn begins. He goes on to tell King Orso of our battle and everything we saw before dying.

The king sits in silence for a moment, running his fingers through his beard. "It is as I feared. Goldspire is an advanced zone and only those powerful enough will be allowed access to the continent. The beast-people are said to value Strength above all else. I do not wish to risk the lives of my people with times being as they are, but it is clear that Goldspire will be an asset in the wars to come should we convince them to join our cause." The dwarves surrounding the king nod in agreement. "Chod, Taryn, I know I have asked much of you already, but I would ask one more thing."

"Whatever we can do to help, Your Highness." Taryn speaks to the king with reverence.

Is that how I sound when talking to Chief Rizza?

King Orso smiles for a second. "Gather forces and return to Goldspire. We need them as allies." He leans forward, eyes boring into Taryn. "Not all allies are formed through peace. Some, like Goldspire, will be created by force. They will respond to power, because they do not want to risk their lives for those who cannot hold their own. Take the time you need to level, to make sure you will not fail again. When the time comes, show them the worth of the *Isle of Mythos*. Kurzol will show you to our troves for items and weapons. Take what you will, but before all is said and done, win Goldspire to our cause."

Quest Alert: *You have been offered the quest "Win strength with Strength." Return to Goldspire and gain access to the continent.*

Reward: *An alliance with Goldspire and increased favor with King Orso.*

Taryn bows again. "Yes, Your Highness."

I bow as well. "We will do our best, but what of Glenn and Jude?"

"For now, they will remain as outlaws on all of Mythos. Once I meet with the other leaders, I aim to make them wanted men from Pruxford to Wandermere and everywhere in between." He lifts his warhammer and points it in our direction. "Now go, there is still much to be discussed."

Kurzol takes his leave, the blood dwarf cleric ushering us into the hallway. "Follow me." He doesn't wait to see if we are coming before setting off deeper into the castle, his red robe swishing as he walks.

He takes us through several doors, down flights of stairs, and through more doors until I'm not sure I could find my way out if I tried. I don't relish the idea of returning to Goldspire, but with a few more levels and a solid team, we might be able to give them a run for their money. Having Limery around would raise the odds in our favor considerably.

Would we fight Dakota again? Or one of the other champions?

We enter a tightly-packed hallway clearly not designed with trolls in mind. I duck my head to avoid scraping it against the ancient stone. Just like the rest of the castle, the walls are adorned with engravings and ornamentation. Flickering torches hang from sconces, casting us in an eerie light and making the scenes along the wall come to life. At the end of the hallway, we stop in front of a dark and ancient wooden door crossed with iron latches. A shiny silver padlock keeps whatever secrets lie in wait on the other side hidden. It's out of place against the weathered stone and wood.

Kurzol places his hands on the padlock, and that's when I notice that it doesn't have a keyhole. He mutters something under his breath, and the lock flashes for a second. The locking mechanism unhooks with a clank and he removes it from the latch.

"That's cool," whispers Taryn. He leans around me to get a better view. "A magical lock."

With a groan, the door opens. Kurzol steps aside and ushers us in.

"Holy shit." Taryn's mouth hangs open in astonishment.

Holy shit is right. I walk past Kurzol and step into a room filled with more gold, items, and loot than we could possibly carry, even if we loaded up Stompy and Berry with saddlebags. There are enough items here to outfit every troll in the forest and then some. Everything glitters from the burning torches, reflecting sparkles along the walls and ceiling.

"What is this place?" I pick up nearby items, examining them.

"This is the king's personal treasure trove. All items have been passed through the Brightgaze family over the years. Some are gifts from foreign rulers or great families, others were won on the fields of battle, some are special items looted from dungeons or dropped from magical creatures. There is no greater vault within the kingdom." Kurzol puffs out his chest, following us inside.

"And we can take anything?" asks Taryn, picking up a golden helm with a plumed feather sticking out of the top and placing it on his head.

"By the king's orders. May I assist you in your search? I had the pleasure of conducting the most recent audit."

"Yeah, that sounds good." I place a silver chalice that transforms whatever is poured inside into mead back on a table. "Do you mind if we look around for a bit first?"

Kurzol nods and steps back against the door, giving us the freedom to explore.

"We sure hit the jackpot." Taryn lets a handful of golden coins pass through his fingers and clank against the floor.

I leave him to his wonder and step deeper into the room. Tables, cabinets, and shelves packed with items stretch forever. This is truly the hoard of generations of kings and queens. It goes beyond wealth. A dynasty, perhaps.

Picking up a golden tankard engraved with a warhammer, I examine it.

Item. Brimming Tankard. *A magical tankard that, once filled, will never go empty. Warning: Once filled, contents cannot be changed. Only works on beverages.*

Interesting. A never-ending mug of ale sounds nice, but even more practical would be to fill it with water. Whether it be a desert, cave, or wherever, we'd never need to find a water source again as long as we had this.

I press the lever that opens the lid and look inside. It's empty.

Perfect.

"Kurzol, are there any of those expandable satchels in here?" I need something to store items in before I forget.

"Ah, yes. The cupboard to your right. Next to the green suit of armor."

I locate the suit of armor, which is quite beautiful. It has leaves etched into the breastplate and the stats are actually pretty amazing. Each individual piece has its own stats, but since the armor is equipped on a wooden manikin, I can view it as a whole.

Item. Verdure Armor. *Complete set. +25 Constitution. 50% reduction to earth-based attacks. Ability to blend in with surrounding trees or shrubbery when all pieces are equipped.*

The armor is the perfect size for a dwarf, but I assume it magically fits to the wearer. The stats are nice. Still, I don't think I'm ready to give up my mobility. Especially considering I have the ability to camouflage already. Any armor I choose can't affect my mobility or weigh me down. I'm going for power and speed.

The cupboard to the right of the suit of armor has clawed feet and is ornately engraved with knotted squares and triangles. Inside, dozens of leather goods line the shelves. Everything from simple knapsacks to duffels to backpacks. I rifle through them until I find a satchel that looks approximately my size.

Item. Expandable Satchel. *A bag capable of holding enormous content and only burdening the wearer with ten percent of its weight. Simply focus on the item inside and it will appear in your hand.*

Testing it out, I toss the tankard inside. It disappears in the vastness of the bag and when I focus on the item, its cool porcelain handle appears against my palm.

"Sweet! Taryn, take one." I grab a smaller bag that looks about his size and toss it across the room.

Taryn snatches it out of the air and looks inside. "Oh, wow! This is far better than anything I've seen in the shops."

Kurzol lets out a slight chuckle. "These are the items of royalty, made by great enchanters of days past, not your common artisan. You won't find items of this quality on the streets."

For the next few minutes, we search through the array of treasures. Some items are beyond my level, giving me no description when I focus on them.

Item. Silver Raven. *???*

It's only a metal sculpture, but it must have some secret ability. The same goes for the Voodoo Doll and bright green Mysterious Egg.

There are more trinkets than I could possibly look through in the time we have. Rings, amulets, bracelets galore. Vials full of unidentifiable liquids. A bell without a clapper, which I assume isn't broken because it's in here and not in the trash somewhere.

There's not enough time for us to ask questions about every item, so I return to Kurzol. "What weapons would you recommend for us?"

A wide smile spreads across his red face. "I thought you would never ask." Clearly, he takes pride in knowing the contents of the vault. "Tell me, what is it you are looking for. What are your needs?"

"For me, Strength and Constitution are a top priority, as well as Dexterity. I want to move quick and smash hard. My horrors benefit from those stats, so there is not much need to invest in Intelligence or Wisdom." I look down and spot a red mask with a bird beak that conceals the identity of whoever wears it. "Oh, and nothing with Charisma," I quickly add at the end, noticing the plus-three Charisma associated with the mask. I'm still not ready to go down that road again.

He nods. "And what about you?" He turns toward Taryn, who is still looting items.

"Uh, I'm a druid. So, uh, things that would make me a better druid. Do you have any cool staffs?"

I raise my hand to interrupt. "If we're being honest, he could do with some better melee damage." Remembering the cooldown on Lightning Bolt, his only offensive ability. "That's one of his weaker areas."

Taryn rolls his eyes. "And you could do with some deodorant," he mumbles.

I ignore his jab, but I notice Kurzol's lip twitch as he attempts to hide a smile.

Kurzol strokes his beard. "Okay, you first." He points at me. "Follow me."

He leads me through a maze of artifacts I can't identify until we come to a corner of the room filled with weapons. So many weapons. They adorn the walls and tables, and some are littered on the floor. There are barrels filled with arrows, axes, pikes, and swords. Some are ornately designed; others are rather plain looking. One has a blue blade that pulses with energy.

How did we get so lucky?

Oh, right. I was an idiot who got his brains stomped out. If anyone asks, this was all part of the plan.

"I'll pick a few for you to choose from." Kurzol walks over to the wall and takes down several pieces. He stares at the table before grabbing another. He sets them down in front of me. "Ah, one more." He goes to one of the barrels and after a moment of clanking, comes back with a flail. "Each of these weapons are capable of taking on stones and further increasing their power. They will serve you well, whichever you choose."

Each of the weapons is truly amazing in its own right. I take my time, carefully examining them, imagining their use in battle, their strengths and weaknesses. In my short time here, I've had some truly remarkable weapons already, but I have a feeling that what I choose today will be my life and death for the foreseeable future.

The first weapon I lift is the flail Kurzol just set down. The lightweight metal staff is wrapped in dark leather, except for two settings for placing magical stones. A spiked ball dangles from the end, connected by a chain. It feels deadly in my hand, the head amplifying whatever force I swing with.

Item. Thunder's Roar. An enchanted flail capable of taking on the properties of up to 2 attached stones. +4 Strength, -1 Dexterity. *Named for the thunderous crash the weapon makes when colliding with armor.*

Pretty cool. The spiked ball attached to the end of the chain definitely has the ability for some powerful hits, but the lack of precision could be the difference between winning and losing. Dakota could probably wield this with impunity, but not me.

Next up is a long silver spear with an axe head on the end. The flat side of the axe head is etched with an array of tiny clouds.

Item. Whistler. An enchanted pike capable of taking on the properties of up to 3 enchanted stones. +4 Dexterity. *A ranged weapon capable of keeping opponents at a* *distance.* ***Bonus Ability: Wind Sweep.*** *Slashing attacks deal bonus air damage. Cost: 5 mana per attack.*

This would actually be a great weapon in the arena, but in a cave or dungeon, there's no guarantee I would have the freedom to swing it. I pick it up. It's lightweight and I could still stab with the spear, but it feels unwieldy in the tight quarters.

Beside the pike are two small warhammers. They look identical and when I examine them, it turns out they are a set.

Item. Twin Turbo (Set). Two one-handed warhammers, each capable of taking on the property of an enchanted stone. +2 Strength, +2 Dexterity per weapon. A set of warhammers created for the dwarven warrior Dorfid Speedrunner, famed for his Dexterity and blurred attacks. Bonus Ability: Whirlwind. With one weapon in each hand, spin in a circle, unleashing random gusts of wind capable of dealing magical damage. Cost: 50 mana per second.

Those could be useful, but they aren't really my style. I'm not a rogue or a quick-handed fighter. I'm a barbarian. I smash and look good doing it.

The final two weapons on the table are an axe and a two-handed warhammer. Right up my alley.

The axe is massive. Not a double-edged axe like Peacemaker, it has a single blade capable of splitting man or beast in two. Crafted from a dark gray metal that flirts with being black. Tiny flakes of red sparkle throughout and black leather criss-crosses down the shaft.

When I lift the weapon, it's lighter than I would have thought.

Item. Dark Fiend. An enchanted axe capable of taking on the properties of up to three stones. +3 Strength, +2 Constitution. This ancient axe was forged in the heart of a volcano. Bonus Ability: Burn. Attacks deal bonus burn damage. Cost: 5 mana per attack.

Burn damage. That sounds both painful and highly efficient. I've been burnt myself a few times, and the memories are still fresh. Lingering, excruciating pain that flared all over. Maybe it's worse because I'm a troll, but it's definitely something I would wish on my worst enemies. I almost don't even pick up the warhammer. Remembering Peacemaker and the way it felt in my hands has me ready to swing an axe all over again. The staffs were nice and added a little bit to my summoning, but truth be told, being up close and personal has always been more fun.

My horrors should be alongside me in battle, helping me to rip my enemies to shreds, not leading the front lines while I sit back and watch, wasting my Strength and Constitution. I'm a wrecking crew, not a mage. If I want to cast a horror further away, I'll pick it up and throw it. Why do I have this big strong body if I'm not going to use it?

I run my thumb along the blade of the axe. With the slightest pressure, it cuts through my thick skin and a tiny drop of blue blood trickles down.

My thoughts drift back to Peacemaker, to the trolls. It feels like a lifetime ago when I was a noob being escorted to the chief. They took me in; they believed in me. Gave me one of their most prized possessions for a shot at survival. That was one of the few rare weapons they had, and they'd entrusted it to me. Looking at the literal treasure trove before me, it paints an even greater picture of the difference between the trolls and the other races. They have nothing except for each other.

And me, their one and only hero.

I need to see them soon. With the portals reopening, everything has changed.

There's a real possibility for the trolls to make a place for themselves in the world. Maybe I can help with that.

I set Dark Fiend down on the table and pick up the warhammer. As comfortable as the axe felt in my hand, comfort alone is no reason to settle.

The warhammer is similar to the axe, and despite its massive size, feels light in my hand. The two weapons must be made of the same material; red speckles gleam from within the dark metal. It could be the material or something to do with the volcanic heat that makes them so lightweight. The shaft is thick and easily four feet long, with runes and etchings running down the sides. Dark red runes run along the top half of the shaft. At the head of the weapon, there is the hammer for bludgeoning on one end, and a spike for piercing on the other. There's another spike on the tip for stabbing in close quarters. The sockets for setting stones are on the left, right, and top of the hammerhead. It's a beauty to behold. I pull up the weapon's stats.

Item. Destroyer. An enchanted warhammer capable of taking on the properties of up to three stones. +2 Strength, +3 Constitution. *This ancient warhammer was forged in the heart of a volcano.* **Bonus Ability: Inferno.** *With each consecutive hit, Destroyer grows hotter, allowing it to warp or pierce through even the hardest metals. Multiplier works when hits are less than five seconds apart. Cost: 10 mana per attack. Cooldown: 10 sec.*

I place the weapon back on the table, admiring it next to its twin.

Wow, I didn't expect this to be such a tough choice. Dark Fiend is amazing. With its burn damage and slashing attacks, it's just what I'm used to. But then there's Destroyer, a true brawler's weapon. With a war coming, we may be facing more armored foes. Something that could crush through skulls and armor might be just what we need.

I select Destroyer and place it in my bag.

"How is it that all of these weapons have bonus abilities? I haven't seen many weapons like this." Actually, I haven't seen many rare weapons at all outside of loot and the few that Chief Rizza gave me.

"These weapons aren't just forged; they are crafted by enchanters. Seascape had some of the finest enchanters in years past. We still have very good metal-workers, but enchanters are hard to come by these days. They make a marriage of metal and mana. A weapon of this power could take a year to create."

An entire year to make one weapon? I go back over to the table, running my fingers along the intricately-engraved runes and symbols. So beautiful. No wonder they hide them down here.

"Now, go select your armor while I help out our dwarven hero."

Kurzol disappears among the maze of treasures, leaving me to my own devices.

There are lots of chainmail, plate mail, and other bulky items lying around, but while beautiful and undoubtedly tough, none of them fit what I'm going for. Even the lightweight armor is cumbersome. Not just in weight, but the way it fits.

That is until I spot a simple piece of shoulder armor. It reminds me of something out of ancient Rome. Something a gladiator might wear.

Item. Spaulder of Swiftness. +1 Constitution, +1 Dexterity. *Lightweight, durable leather mail designed to protect the off-hand shoulder during battle.*

It checks all the boxes for what I want, and even though it has no bonus abilities, the bonus attributes are nice. I equip it and set off to find Taryn. The leather armor covers my shoulder and arm down to the elbow, perfect for absorbing a blow with my off-hand.

Along the way, I pass a basin filled with magical stones. Some are enchanted, while others are the cores of mighty beasts. I end up taking two that modify my Dexterity, and one that allows me to walk almost silently.

Barbarian Assassin Summoner, here I fucking come!

I don't want to be greedy, so I go to find Taryn. Along the way, I toss the Mysterious Green Egg into my satchel. A loud crash of metal gives away his location no problem.

He stands holding two daggers, both blades broken off near the hilt. A pile of armor lays scattered on the floor beside him.

"Don't tell me you managed to break a pair of ancient daggers in the time I left you alone," I tease.

"Hardly. Check this out."

He grips the daggers a little tighter and what I can only describe as shadow blades appear where the metal is broken. Dark, shadowy energy pulses, distorting the light around them.

"What the hell?"

"Shadow daggers," says Kurzol. "Capable of bypassing armor and draining the victim's mana and life force. Very rare, indeed."

Taryn swipes at a helm on a nearby table. The shadowy blades pass directly through, but a moment after, it's like a magnetic energy pushes the helm off the table, clanking against the floor.

"You wanted me to be able to do more damage. I think this will do the trick. I won't have to worry about armor, just stabby-stab-stab." Taryn waves the blades through the air like a crazed lunatic. "Plus, each attack actually drains mana. Perfect for fighting other heroes."

"And there's nothing that can stop it?" I step back, not wanting to accidentally get stabbed. That could be one of the most dangerous weapons I've ever seen.

"Holy armor. They're basically useless against paladins." Kurzol moves closer to me. "But aside from that, they are very powerful items."

"What about clerics?" I remember Richard, the cleric I met in Vanaria who serves the god of chaos.

"It depends on their alignment. Most clerics don't wear armor, and shadow energy will still pierce through unarmored flesh."

"Sounds like a winner. What else did you get?"

A broad smile crosses Taryn's face. "Check this out." He puts on a gray cloak that falls to his knees and a pair of brown boots. Neither one looks spectacular by any means—in fact, they kind of look grungy—but I'm sure there has to be something special about them.

Taryn walks over to a table filled with vials and picks several up, pouring their contents onto the floor. Kurzol places his hand over his face at the wasted potion.

"Oh, it's fine," murmurs Taryn. "It's just a souped-up health potion."

The red liquid spreads across the stone floor, creating puddles in the cracks. Then, Taryn walks through them.

Red liquid splashes up with each step, but it doesn't make a sound. And when he steps out of the puddle, there are no tracks.

"How?" I ask, jaw hanging wide open.

Taryn raises both eyebrows at me. "Sexy, right? The boots hide my tracks, and the cloak conceals the sound of my movements. I figured when the time finally comes to track down those two goons, we might need the element of surprise. And there is no way in hell you are sneaking up on anyone."

"Actually." I pull out my warhammer and show him one of the enchanted stones I equipped. "This one lets me move silently."

"No shit?"

"Shit," I confirm.

Taryn tucks the daggers in his belt. "Now, all I need is a staff and I'm golden. Anything you'd recommend, Kurzol?"

"I have one that I think would be especially fitting for a druid. One moment."

Kurzol returns carrying a green branch. It still looks to be alive and covered in leaves, despite being locked in an underground vault.

Item. Sapling Staff. +3 Intelligence, +3 Wisdom. *A living staff capable of sending out whip-like vines.*

Kurzol hands the staff to Taryn and the tiny vines reach down his arm, embracing him like some toxic goo out of a superhero movie. There's a moment's hesitation where I see a slight panic in Taryn's eyes, but it quickly passes and he accepts the vines as they wrap around his forearm.

"Wow." He lifts the staff, pointing it at a nearby table. Tiny vines unravel and shoot out, entwining around a small cup and lifting it into the air. "This is so cool!" A second later, the cup falls to the ground and shatters.

Kurzol crosses him arms. "I trust that you have enough items to get you started on your journey."

Point taken. It's time to get the hell out of here.

CHAPTER FOUR

TREEHADEN

After gathering Berry and Stompy, we pick up provisions for the road and set foot out of Seascape. Our destination is the troll forest, but with no set timeline on when we need to reach them, we're free to go at our own pace and level up along the way. It'll be nice to see some of the smaller dwarven cities and villages.

I hope Limery will be waiting for us when we make it to the forest. Though, I have a feeling he'll be able to find us wherever we are. Imps are full of surprises. In fact, I'm interested to see if Lillith was able to gather more imps as translators for the forest trolls.

With no idea where Glenn and Jude truly are, our only goal is to grow stronger so that when we do find them, we will be ready. Not to mention the host of other threats that may be waiting on the other side of the portals. One day, we will return to Goldspire and retake what we lost.

Maybe I can convince a few heroes to join us along the way.

The roads are less crowded than when we first entered the city. Now that the portal has opened, the excitement of the king's challenge has worn off. Dwarves are returning to their homes. For most of them, they'll probably never set foot through a portal, content to live their entire lives farming, crafting, mining, or whatever their profession might be.

Even so, I'm sure they dream of it. Finding new worlds, becoming heroes, and living a life of adventure. They may be lines of code, but in every way that matters, these are real people. Artificial intelligence but intelligent, nonetheless.

With every day that passes, this feels more and more like my real world. Now that Taryn is here, it's been days since I last thought about New York, about my family. I'm not sure if that's good or bad.

My life is consumed with excitement now. Leveling, exploring, making a name for myself in this world. Or at least in this section of the world.

We haven't heard from Valery since Taryn logged in, so I'm assuming they've made no headway with the system error that's preventing me from logging out. That's fine by me. This is my home now.

For a moment, I think back to when I logged out. Back when I thought my sentence was over and I'd be going home. I remember the new pods that were lined up along the far wall. Whatever happened to that? Are they bringing in more players? Certainly not until they've solved the issue with the AI. They let Taryn in, but that was a special circumstance.

"Oh, great," mumbles Taryn. "Get out of the way, grandmas."

A wagon full of ebony dwarves takes up most of the narrow bridge that connects Seascape to the rest of the island. We follow behind them at a slow pace as they stare at Taryn and I with wide eyes. As if a dwarf riding a moulhaug wasn't strange enough, it's not every day they run into heroes, let alone a dwarven and troll hero together.

We're quite the oddball family. Even more so when Limery is around.

The bridge ends and we nod to the ebony dwarves as we pass.

"Which way do you want to go?" I ask Taryn.

The Mythroad leads straight through the desert, past Sandholde and directly through the Greystone Mountains, but there are other roads that bypass the desert, going around the edge of the island through many of the small towns.

Taryn strokes his beard, lost in thought, when a panicked ivory dwarf comes running up the road. The dwarf's eyes are set on the castle until he sees us and comes to an abrupt halt, boots skidding across the dirt road and sending a plume of dust into the air.

Sweat beads down his brow as he bends over, gasping for air. A deep gash runs along the side of his flushed face, caked with blood.

Taryn climbs down from Stompy, rushing to his countryman's aid. "What's wrong? Are you okay?"

"The village," he gasps. "It's under attack. All of our guards were in the castle for the king's event and there was no one left to protect our stores. Now the kobolds are running off with our livestock. Please help!"

Quest Alert. *You have been offered the quest 'Protect the Village.' The village of Treehaden has fallen victim to an attack of angry kobolds. Their livestock are being stolen, and their very lives threatened. Save the village before their livelihoods are destroyed.*

Reward: *Increased alliance with Treehaden.*

"Let's go!" Taryn grabs the dwarf by the arm. "Here, you ride Stompy and I'll take Berry."

The villager is nervous at first, but Taryn helps him climb onto Stompy's saddle. Stompy snorts at the unfamiliar rider, but accepts him anyway.

I pull up my map and look at the towns marked across the northern half of the island. Aside from Sandholde and Seascape, they all remain nameless.

"How far away is your town?" I ask.

"About half a day. I would have gotten here faster, but the bastards snuck our horses out in the middle of the night. Dirty monsters!" He waves his fist in the air. "They attacked when we were left unguarded like the cowards they are."

I look over the map, searching for the closest town. There's one near the road, a little south from the coast. That must be Treehaden. Taryn casts Strong Wind, increasing our movement speed, and we barrel down the road toward our next adventure while the villager fills us in on the details.

"What's your name?" Taryn glances at our new companion.

Berry and Stompy keep in stride with one another as I jog slightly behind.

"My name is Drury Hornstone. My family has been farming these lands for ages." He fumbles with Stompy's reins, clearly uncertain about riding such a massive beast, unlike Taryn who could probably sleep while riding. "Kobolds have always been a problem, but usually they skulk about in the night, stealing what they can without being caught. I've never seen them so bold before."

I think back on the few times I've faced kobolds in *Isle of Mythos*. They were always skittish creatures, behaving a lot like hyenas and roaming in small packs. The ugly, goblin-esque lizard creatures were annoying, but I could never see them attacking a village, not unless there was something greater at play.

"How many attacked you?" I increase my speed until I'm right beside Drury.

"Enough to overwhelm us." He sighs. "We tried to fight at first, but there were just too many of them. I took a claw to the face fighting them off. Once we backed off, they seemed more concerned with the animals than with us. I did my best to get everyone hidden in the cellar beneath the village temple." A pained expression crosses his face. "I hope they are okay."

Taryn and I exchange glances.

"You don't think—" He lets the words fade in the wind, scrunching his eyebrows as he puts the pieces together the same as me.

This has Glenn written all over it. A normally passive species attacking a village without fear of repercussion. Except it shouldn't be possible. We watched him go through that portal. Did he somehow manage to sneak back through?

There were dozens of guards waiting around the portal in Seascape. There's no way he made it back without being noticed.

"It can't be," I say finally. "There has to be another explanation."

We travel in silence after that, the only sounds are the pattering of feet, hoof, and paw against the dirt road. With Destroyer safely put away in my satchel, it doesn't give me the silent movement bonus until I equip it. Not that I need it right now.

Eventually, we make it to the outskirts of Treehaden. The village is small, smaller than Lynchton, and eerily quiet for the middle of the day. The farms surrounding the village remain empty, almost like a ghost town.

I equip my warhammer and the enchanted stone immediately muffles my movement.

"Psst," I call Taryn towards me. "Leave Stompy and Berry here with Drury. You and I can sneak around quietly and see what's going on."

Taryn nods before returning to the others and instructing them. The last of my horrors vanishes and I don't summon any more. Right now, I want the element of surprise, not strength in numbers.

We step through the wooden palisade that surrounds the village. The gate hangs askew from the earlier attack. Inside, it's mostly quiet except for some grunting coming from behind one of the buildings. Stray chickens run through the streets, clucking as they zig and zag. The stables to the right are empty.

A scratching noise comes from the end of a row of small houses with thatched roofs. Taryn and I run toward it—no need to move carefully since our movement is muted. At the end of the row, I peek through an open window. The place is simple and rustic. A single pot and pan hang from the ceiling and a cauldron burns over dying embers. A kobold wearing old leather rags rifles through a cupboard. A rusty shiv hangs from its belt. Everything about the creature is primitive except for a glittering ring it wears on one finger. Probably stolen. It's much too high-quality to be kobold-made.

The kobold empties the cupboard, tossing items across the floor with no regard. When it finds something it likes, a hiss that sounds almost like laughter carries out the window.

"Yes, yes." The mumbling kobold stuffs a silver goblet in its leather satchel.

Having found something of value, the kobold makes to leave.

Not if I have anything to do with it.

As soon as the creature steps out of the door, I bring Destroyer down upon its head. The force of the blow crumples the lizard like paper, smashing its frail frame into the ground. A flash of red streaks down my weapon as Inferno engages, readying the heat multiplier for my next attack.

"What the fuck!" Taryn stares at the carnage with wide eyes.

"What? No one heard anything."

Except that's not completely true because another three kobolds turn around the corner, hissing in alarm.

They are all level ten, which shouldn't be a problem unless we're overwhelmed.

"Hel—" one of the kobolds screams, but before I have a chance to move, Taryn slams the butt of his staff against the ground and three vines shoot out from the weapon, entangling the kobolds and pulling them together. Vines cinch around the three reptilian throats, quelling their cries for help. Taryn drops the staff and takes out his shadow daggers.

The kobolds struggle against their entanglements as Taryn swoops in, running the dark energy of his blades through each of their chests until their lifeforce drains completely. At level sixteen, Taryn has the clear advantage over the kobolds.

There's no blood, no wounds, but the kobolds die nonetheless. The shadowy blades fade away before he picks up his staff and the vines retreat.

"Giant oaf." He cuts his eyes at me. "I can't take you anywhere."

"Okay, fearless leader." I give him a mock salute. "What do we do now?"

He looks down at the four bodies. "We track down the rest. Try to find out where they are going, and who they are working for."

"Wait." Taryn is already leaving the scene when I spot something out of the ordinary. "Look at this. They all three have this same ring." I bend down and lift one of the slain kobold's hands. A glittering ring sparkles in the daylight. "The kobold I killed had on one, too."

With a little effort, the ring comes off and I'm able to examine it.

Item. Ring of Bliss. +1 Charisma.

I hand it to Taryn before removing the rings from the other kobolds. They are all the same.

"Why in the hell would a bunch of kobolds have Charisma rings?" He stares at the ring as if it will give him the answer.

"Here, let me see your hand."

I take his hand in mine and slide one of the rings onto his finger. It's only one Charisma, but his eyes gloss over the moment I put it on.

"Mmhm." He smiles. "This is nice." He places a second ring on, and his shoulders visibly loosen. "Man, why are we wasting time doing errands for the king? We should be running this island. Hell, we should be—"

"Alright, that's enough of that." I reach out to take the ring off and Taryn pulls away. Luckily, I'm about ten times as strong as him so I remove it no problem.

With the rings removed, Taryn returns to normal. His face is a little paler than usual.

"Holy..." His words trail off. "That was something else. I felt like a king."

"Yeah, this is a one-way ticket to bad decisions." I place the rings in my satchel, out of Taryn's sight, and he visibly relaxes. "Now, how and why would a group of kobolds end up with rings like this?"

"Someone had to give them the rings." Taryn rubs his brow.

"My thoughts exactly."

We search the rest of the town, but there are no more kobolds to be found. All the livestock are gone, minus a few stray chickens, and several of the houses have been looted.

Once we're sure that the town is safe, we find Drury. He leads us to the temple and unlocks the cellar door.

There's a gasp and several screams as I open the cellar.

"Don't worry," Drury holds his hands up as he tries to calm them. "They are here to help."

"Drury—"

"What happened?"

"Are they go—"

Dozens of voices vie for attention all at once.

"One at a time," Drury orders. "Everyone out, and I will fill you in."

The dwarves exit to the village center. Many look worried or apprehensive, their eyes darting between Drury, myself, and Taryn. Several children cling tightly to their parents' legs, their chubby, round faces unsure of what is happening as they stare openly at us newcomers.

"Our livestock is gone. Some of us may have lost items, but it doesn't seem their intent was to rob our homes, but to take our way of life." He buries his head in his hands. "It doesn't make any sense."

"What are we going to do?" a freckled-faced female dwarf asks. "We used our animals for everything. They plowed our fields, fed us, clothed us. How can we possibly replace all of that?"

"Don't worry." Taryn pats her on the shoulder. "We'll track down the kobolds and return your property. And we'll make sure that whoever is responsible pays for what they've done."

It's a great sentiment, but I have no idea how we're going to track down the kobolds. We have no way of knowing where they came from or where they went.

Drury must agree with my suspicion, because he pulls Taryn and me aside. "Do you truly believe you can return our livestock?"

Taryn puffs out his chest. "If we can't return your animals, then Chod and I will plow your fields until you can afford to buy new ones."

Seriously, what the actual fuck? My cheeks suddenly feel hot. The last thing I want to do is pull a plow from sun-up to sun-down. Taryn better have a plan, or I might punt him into the ocean.

"Then you must hurry." Drury takes Taryn by the shoulder, pointing him toward the gate. "Kobolds are fast and tricky. No doubt they will try to confuse anyone following."

Taryn flashes him a stupid grin that I want to smack away. "I don't think that'll be a problem."

We leave the villagers to repairing their broken gate and destroyed property. Once we are outside of earshot, I let go of the anger I've been holding in.

"Dude? What the hell? We're on a mission to level up. How in the hell do you think volunteering us to work on a farm is going to help that at all?"

"Bro, calm down. Finding the kobolds will be the easy part." He's still grinning like a fool. Almost like he knows he's getting under my skin.

"And how exactly is that?" I cross my arms, waiting for his response.

"Because a bear's sense of smell is about two thousand times greater than a human's." He reaches into his pouch and pulls out a piece of crude leather armor. The kobold's. "And I also have this."

CHAPTER FIVE

HELLA ENCHANTED

Nose to the ground, Berry follows the scent with ease. The kobolds must not have been worried about being tracked, because we follow their trail in a straight line for several miles. Truth be told, I never thought about all the uses Taryn's pets would have outside of combat. They are so much more than just battle companions. Stompy can pull and carry anything we need. He'll complain and groan the entire time, but the moulhaug would follow Taryn into the depths of Hell, grumbling all the way. And Taryn can still tame a few more pets before they start to get unruly. From what he told me, the more he tames, the less control he has over their actions. I don't know if that means they won't behave, or if there is a chance they won't listen to him at all.

Time will tell, but I have a hard time believing Berry would ever disobey a command.

The bear leads us through a copse of trees and across a small creek. We pass through the water without missing a beat, and we're on their trail again. Every so often, Berry will turn around to make sure we are still following before bounding ahead.

"I'm sorry I got angry," I apologize to Taryn. The worst part about losing my temper is the apologizing, because there's never really an excuse for my behavior. It's just something stupid I do when things aren't going the way I want. I'm trying to get better, but old habits die hard. "I should have known you would have a plan."

Taryn winks at me. "Don't worry about it. We'll kick some kobold butt and return their livestock in no time. Then, we'll be back on the road. I'm sure there will be some awesome places to visit around the island."

That's one of the things I love most about Taryn. He never holds a grudge. I've done enough asshole things in my day to turn him away, but he never holds it against me. He sees me for who I truly am: an asshole, but one with his heart in the right place.

"You feel a connection to them, don't you?" I ask.

"Who?" He raises an eyebrow.

"The dwarves." We pass an area of upturned soil filled with reptilian footprints and hoofprints. Not that I doubted Berry, but it confirms we are going in the right direction. "I can tell. I feel the same thing when I'm around the forest trolls. It's hard to explain, but it's kind of like this sense of kinship. Like I would do anything to protect them. I know I'm not really a troll, but it doesn't stop me from feeling like I am, you know?"

"Yeah, I totally know what you mean. It's hard to believe this is a game sometimes." He holds up his hand and looks at it, staring at the back of his palm. "Most of the time, actually. Knowing what I look like in real life, it doesn't make sense that I would feel so comfortable in this skin. But I do. I feel like I've been a dwarf my entire life. I don't expect to be three feet taller or have a longer reach. This feels like who I am. Everything is so...natural. Do you think it's our minds, or do you think the AI somehow influences our perception?"

I shrug. I hope it's the first, but the second seems just as possible. How else can I explain the way Charisma affects our mental state? The nanites that keep us alive in here could be rearranging the way our bodies work, altering their chemical composition for all I know.

The hair on my neck stands on end. It's better not to think too much on those things.

Berry comes to an abrupt halt and Stompy almost runs into him, sliding to a stop so fast that Taryn nearly falls from the saddle. The umber bear stares intently at a group of boulders nearly a hundred yards away.

"What is it?" asks Taryn. I'm not sure if he's talking to Berry or me.

The more I look at the boulders, I sense that something is off about them. There's a shimmer to the air, like the horizon on a scorching hot day, only it's not hot at all. The coastal breeze is cool against my skin.

"Something's not right." I watch the fluctuating air, not quite sure what it is. "Those aren't boulders."

"Trolls?" ask Taryn.

"I don't think so. I've always been able to see other trolls when they are camouflaged." Those were forest trolls, though. Maybe these are desert or mountain trolls. Maybe it's some sort of magical area, where the mana is flowing aboveground.

I pull up my map, but there doesn't seem to be any ley lines running through the area.

"Well, this is where the trail ends." Taryn stuffs his items into his satchel. "Let's investigate."

At a hundred yards away, if it's more than just a boulder, then whoever or whatever it is has already seen us.

"Taryn, meet me behind Stompy. Out of view of the boulders."

He climbs down from the saddle and we meet behind Stompy's massive body.

"What's up?" Taryn looks up at me with questioning eyes.

"If they've already seen us, then we need you to sneak in. Turn into your bird form. If it is a troll or some other sort of monster, then they'll have no idea you left."

He smacks me on the arm. "Sneaky. I like it."

In a flash, Taryn turns into his animal form, a bright red bird, and flutters into the sky. I peek around Stompy, watching the shimmering boulders as he flies over them, landing in a nearby tree. It doesn't take long before he sends me a message.

Incoming Message (Taryn): *Chody boy, you are not going to believe this. It's some kind of an illusion.*

Message (Chod): *What do you mean? I need more details than that.*

Incoming Message (Taryn): *It could be some sort of enchantment that's cloaking the area. Whatever it is, it's not as strong when being viewed from above. I can see movement underneath, but it's kind of grainy. I'm pretty sure there are wagons, and kobolds. I definitely saw a few sheep. No idea if there is more to it than that.*

Message (Chod): *Alright, keep an eye on it and let me know. If you can get closer, go for it, just be safe. No need to be rash until we know what we're dealing with.*

Something is definitely up. The kobolds didn't just randomly walk into an enchanted area. I've never seen a kobold that could cast magic, either. Someone has to be pulling the strings.

But who?

And wagons? Are they loading them with animals, and if so, to what end? This all makes no sense.

I peek around Stompy, trying to find anything that might give me a clue as to what is going on, but all I see are the boulders. They look real enough. If I hadn't noticed the shifting air around them, I probably wouldn't have thought twice. Good thing we had Berry.

If it is an illusion, then there has to be some sort of caster nearby, probably within. With a full army of horrors, I could charge in there like a mad-man, but I'd like to plan this out for once. I've had my head stomped in the sand one time too many as it is.

As I stare at the boulders, something changes. A small green elbow protrudes from one of the rocks. Just as soon as it appears, it retracts back into the safety of the illusion. If the kobolds can move in and out of it at will, then that proves it's not an actual barrier.

There's a flash of red as Taryn swoops down from the tree and disappears behind the illusion. I wait in anticipation as a long minute passes before I hear anything from him.

Incoming Message (Taryn): *There's a guy in here. Another player. He's hiding his level and class, but his name is Jon Bailey. He looks like a dweeb. I'd put all my money that he's casting the illusion.*

Another player? That's interesting. What could he possibly want with Treehaden's livestock? My mind races with possibilities as I wait for more information alongside Berry and Stompy.

The good news, at least, is that this Jon Bailey doesn't seem bent on hurting NPCs. Not that taking their things isn't wrong, but he doesn't seem to be another Glenn.

Incoming Message (Taryn): *All of the kobolds have the same rings. It's like this guy has made a little crackhead army. They're loading the animals into the wagons. I think they're planning to leave soon.*

Not if we have anything to say about it.

There's so much opportunity for heroes in *Isle of Mythos,* why would he resort to stealing from poor farmers? I wouldn't be surprised if this guy was in prison for robbery.

Message (Chod): *How many kobolds are there? Do they seem concerned with our presence?*

Incoming Message (Taryn): *About thirty, give or take. There are a few watching, but I think they assume you're just resting. No one seems alarmed.*

Message (Chod): *Do you think you can distract them long enough for me and the gang to make an appearance? Let's take these clowns out and get Treehaden their property back.*

Incoming Message (Taryn): *When I give the signal, full speed ahead.*

. . .

Message (Chod): *What signal?*

I wait for his response, but it doesn't come. Instead, there's a crash of lightning that rips through the illusion.

"Goddammit, Taryn! I thought we were being smart this time."

I let out a stream of curses as I follow Berry and Stompy into battle. For all the talk of me losing my temper, Taryn is the one to go rogue. I summon a quick burst of three horrors as I run and equip Destroyer.

Stepping through the edge of the illusion, I'm greeted with scattered chaos. I search for Taryn, but he is nowhere to be found. A wagon sits broken and smoldering, pieces of debris littering the ground around it. Kobolds try to gather the startled livestock until they see me and Taryn's pets. They freeze in place at our sudden appearance, and I immediately sic my horrors on the closest kobolds while continuing to look for Taryn.

A man wearing a dull blue robe, and glasses with two different colored lenses, snarls at me, lifting his diamond-tipped staff into the air. It flashes white for a second and the man splits into two identical versions of himself. Each one tan and lean with shaggy brown hair, built like a runner.

Are they clones or illusions? And more importantly, are they capable of dealing damage? I focus on them, but all I see is the man's name: Jon Bailey.

Berry and Stompy stand by my side, waiting for orders. My horrors fall, but not before taking out a couple of kobolds with them. We all stand in a moment of shocked silence, waiting for someone to make the next move.

"I've heard about you." Both versions of the man speak at the same time. The words slither out of his mouth in an uneasy echo; greasy, like a used car salesman. "The troll who can't seem to mind his own business."

"Let us take the livestock and no one has to get hurt." I'm offering him a way out. More than he deserves.

"I think not. I plan to make a hefty profit selling them at the market." He smiles for a second, a cocky, devilish smile. "Minions, I'll craft a plus-two ring for whoever lands the killing blow on this one." He extends a slender finger in my direction.

The kobolds hiss in unison, making my hair stand on end. Suddenly, it all makes sense. This guy is an enchanter, capable of crafting items. Has he addicted them to Charisma? Is that why they're following him?

A bolt of lightning crashes into the left version of the man. He vanishes in a wisp of smoke, and the bolt explodes against the earth. The man steps back, raising his staff into the air once more and creating another doppelgänger.

Both versions repeat the movement and another copy appears. They raise their staffs over and over until there are at least ten of the man. He must have a hefty mana pool to cast so much so quickly.

"Kill them!" they shout in unison.

A bright glow catches my eye from under one of the wagons. Taryn hides beneath, casting Imbue on Berry and doubling his size just as a group of kobolds leap onto the bear's back. They stab and claw as Berry thrashes, eventually tossing the kobolds to the ground.

He'll be able to hold his own. Right now, it's time for me to fuck shit up.

I swing Destroyer at the closest kobold, connecting with its head and sending the lizard creature soaring across the field like a golf ball. Red flashes through my warhammer as Inferno takes effect.

Kobolds surround me, the belle of the ball, their eyes orange with greed and the promise of more Charisma.

"Sorry to disappoint, but I don't think you're going to like the outcome of this fight." I twist Destroyer against my palms, letting the head of the warhammer spin.

The first kobold leaps at me and I smash him into the ground with enough force to displace the earth. For the next thirty seconds, I play whack-a-kobold as they try to get close enough to damage me. By the time the last one falls, Destroyer is glowing molten red.

Stompy lets out a trumpet call as he smashes into a wagon, destroying Jon the Enchanter's only method of transporting his stolen goods. Berry finishes off another few kobolds while Stompy smashes the last of the wagons.

All the kobolds are gone, but there's no sign of Taryn or Jon anywhere.

Until I hear the crash of thunder in the distance and turn to see eight men in blue robes with identical movements running from a dwarf.

Taryn runs full speed, using Strong Wind to keep up with the enchanter, staff in one hand and shadow dagger in the other. Strong Wind boosts his speed long enough for him to stab one of the men. The man vanishes in a puff of smoke.

The buff from Strong Wind only works when out of combat, so as soon as he attacks, he falls behind.

As soon as the cooldown is up, he casts Strong Wind again, catching up and stabbing another clone. Down to six.

I leave the livestock and set off in pursuit. Jon has been here a lot longer than Taryn, so there is a high probability that he out-levels the dwarf. We've yet to see him cast any offensive spells, but that doesn't mean he doesn't have any. I'd rather be there to back up my friend just in case.

Sprinting at full speed, I slowly make up lost ground. Blood pounds behind my ears as my muscles fatigue, but I don't slow down. Berry is several strides ahead of me, and Stompy is a little behind. The umber bear's muscles ripple beneath his thick fur with each powerful step.

Taryn has managed to cut the illusions down to four, and I've almost caught up with him. He raises his staff to cast Strong Wind again, but nothing happens.

"Dammit!" he yells. "I'm out of mana!"

I could possibly catch the enchanter, but my own stamina is beginning to wane. If only there was a way to slow the speedy little fucker down.

An idea pops into my mind and I want to punch myself for not thinking of it sooner. I summon a Horror of Vitality in front of me and grab the chubby little furball by the horn as I run by. Planting my foot in the grass, I sling the horror with as much force as I can muster straight ahead.

It looks at me with a face of absolute betrayal as it soars through the air like an astronaut adrift in space, landing right in the middle of the group of enchanters. Their movement speed slows by twenty percent, which is more than enough for what comes next.

I explode the horror, and the three other clones disintegrate.

Berry rushes toward the lone enchanter. Jon raises his staff to cast a spell, but the bear tackles him. Using his massive paws, he pins the frail man to the ground.

"Please don't let him eat me!" Jon begs, squirming but unable to move. "Please! I'll do anything."

Berry's snout is inches from Jon's face, teeth bared and drool dripping from his exposed gums. Jon winces, as if closing his eyes will make the threat go away.

Taryn finally catches up to us, his face flushed and sweat beading down his fore-head. "You mother fu—" He has his dagger drawn, but I grab him by the arm, stopping his attack on an unarmed man.

"Easy there, killer." I loosen my grip, and when Taryn doesn't immediately attack, I release. "How about we question him before you get all stabby-stabby?"

"Fine." He stares daggers at Jon. "But if you try anything sneaky, I'll gut you like a fish."

"What do you know about gutting fish?" I tease, trying to diffuse some of his anger. "You grew up in Brooklyn."

"Screw you! I know how to gut a fish."

"You're a nerd. When have you ever been in a position to gut a fish?"

"I know how to gut a fish." He crosses his arms.

"How? How could you possibly know anything about gutting fish? Worms, now, I bet you know a thing or two about worms."

Taryn makes a rude gesture at me before returning his attention to Jon. Stompy has joined us as well and has taken up a hulking position just above the enchanter's head.

"Talk." Taryn kneels next to Jon, doing a damn good job at being an intimi-dating mobster.

I guess that makes me the good cop.

"W-what do you want to know?" There's real fear in this guy. It probably has something to do with the fact that having one's face eaten off by a giant bear would be, at the very least, unpleasant and more than likely very painful.

"Well, for starters, why you attacked Treehaden? And then maybe we'll get around to your little army of kobolds and the illusions."

"Can—" He gasps for air. "Can you maybe let me breathe a little?"

"Berry, off," Taryn orders. No sooner has Berry lifted his paws before Taryn has Jon fully bound using the vines from his new staff. "I don't trust you. Now, talk."

"Ugh. I'm just trying to make some gold, man. Nobody got hurt."

"You don't think that people will be hurt when they can't provide for their fami-lies, when they can't eat?" Taryn's anger is rising all over again.

Jon scrunches his face. "They aren't real, man. It's all a game."

The words hang in the air for a long moment. He's right. They aren't real, not truly. Maybe not to him. But to Taryn and I, they are. Can we really fault him for treating this as a game even if every sensation tells us that it's not?

"Have you ever sat down and talked to one of them?" The anger has vanished from Taryn's voice. "Have you spent a minute with any of them that wasn't at a shop or inn?"

"No."

"Maybe you should. Then tell me how this is just a game. Now, why steal from these people? Why not go dungeon-diving like the rest of the heroes?"

Jon sighs. "Because I fucked up. I thought it would be cool to be an enchanter. I thought I could make awesome items, sell them, and get rich. Turns out crafting is hard. You have to level that shit up. There are textbooks that are expensive if you want to learn the good stuff. I can only do the most basic enchantments right now. Nobody is willing to pay much for a plus-one Charisma ring. I don't even have a single offensive ability. Crafting and illusions. Being an enchanter is not all it's cracked up to be."

"Why the kobolds then?" asks Taryn.

"Dumb luck." Jon flashes a half-smile. "I was searching for materials in the forest and three of them ambushed me. Probably would have killed me had I not tried to bribe them. I tossed out everything I had. One of them picked up the ring and that was all it took. Their whole clan wanted some."

"Then why not take the kobolds to a dungeon to fight for you?"

Jon's eyes light up. "You know that's not a bad idea. Why did I never think of that?"

I step a little closer. "How'd you end up in prison anyways, Jon?"

"Burglary." He lets out a dry laugh. "One of the few things I was ever good at."

Taryn stands up and retracts the vines to his staff. "You couldn't have been that good."

Jon sits up, watching us with skepticism. "What's going on?"

Taryn extends a hand to Jon. "We're gonna give you a chance to make things right and maybe do some good for once."

CHAPTER SIX

WALK THE WALK, TALK THE TALK

Taryn and I stand about twenty feet away from Jon the Enchanter, huddled in conversation. Jon brushes off his arms and back, trying to wipe away the dirt from his tumble in the grass.

"You want to bring this weaseling little snake with us?" I don't know what druid herbs Taryn is smoking, but this seems like a bad idea. He's a criminal. "What makes you think he won't rob us in our sleep? Or worse?"

"You're a criminal. Are you going to rob me in my sleep?" Taryn stares at me while I process the information. Technically, I am a criminal.

"It's different." I'm not a real criminal. Not like these guys.

"Is it? Look, if he wanted to run away, he could right now." He points at Jon. "No one is holding him hostage, but he's standing there. Waiting."

I can think of at least one reason he's not running away. Jon reaches out to pet Berry, but the bear snarls, flashing his dangerous canines. Jon takes a couple of steps back, holding up his hands in surrender.

"I don't know, man. It seems like a bad idea." I've had too many bad experiences with other players to want to trust one. Glenn, Jude, Richard the Cleric. Even Pressley the Death Knight and Michael the Paladin haven't been the most pleasant experiences. Everyone in this world is looking out for themselves. Now, Taryn is wanting us to sleep beside a guy who just robbed a village.

"King Orso told us to make allies. Jon can be the first. If we're not willing to take a chance on anyone, how are we going to build alliances? Don't you remember when no one would take a chance on the trolls?"

He's got me there, damn logic. I run my fingernail through the tip of my braid, trying to think of a valid argument.

"Fine. If this blows up in our faces, it's on you." I'll go along with his stupid plan, but I'm not going to be happy about it.

I sling my satchel over my shoulder. We return to Jon and prepare to get moving.

Taryn dishes out orders. "First thing on the agenda is to gather up the rest of the livestock and return them to Treehaden. We can get to know one another along the way." He climbs onto Stompy and motions for Jon to lead the way.

Surprisingly, Berry is very adept at herding animals, running to and fro and rounding up the stragglers. Maybe he's a dog trapped in a bear's body.

Jon looks uncertain at first, turning back every few seconds to see what we are doing, but eventually, his shoulders relax, and he walks more leisurely.

I walk in silence for a while, content to let Taryn mastermind this foolishness, but as they continue to talk about pointless topics, I'm forced to intervene.

"So, Jon. What level are you?" His Wisdom is obviously high enough for him to know Conceal, but that doesn't say much considering he's an enchanter. He probably had more Wisdom at level one than I do now.

"Ugh." He hangs his head before looking up with a grimace. "Level ten."

"Ten?" My mouth drops. "How in the hell have you been in here longer than both of us and you are only level ten?"

He brushes shaggy brown hair from his eyes, frowning. "I told you I don't have any offensive abilities. I've died a lot. That's part of the reason I wanted to sell the animals, so I could pay someone in the city to train me."

I can understand the toll that might take on someone, entering this world and then realizing you screwed up your character creation. Still, it's no reason for him to be a dick. "Well, what can you do?"

"I can enchant small items, and I can cast illusions. That's about it."

"Give us a little more detail than that," I snarl. "If you're level ten, you should have access to seven abilities. What are they?"

"Fine." He sighs. "I can enchant a small item with plus-one Charisma. I could have chosen any of the basic stats, but I went with the most useless one. The first time I used a Charisma item, I thought it was so cool, the way it changed how you felt, but it turns out no one is looking for them. Well, no one with coin to spend. I can also enchant a gemstone to provide light." He taps his staff on the ground and the diamond tip glows brightly. "When I managed to level up, I was stuck in a dungeon and my torch was on its last legs. Another wasted point. I can also enchant my voice so that it sounds like it's coming from several directions. It's great for misdirection but hasn't helped me kill anything. The rest of my points were put into my doppelgänger ability and Conceal Area." He stares out in the distance. "I'm a glorified distraction. That's about it."

"Hey, man." Taryn pulls Stompy up beside Jon. "Don't be so hard on yourself. I'm sure you're more powerful than that."

"Thanks." Jon gives him a half-smile before averting his eyes.

"So what if you're a distraction?" I know I've been a dick to this guy, but seeing how defeated he is in this world where I'm having the most fun in my life puts things in perspective. Not everyone is a natural at games. "If you put those abilities to use in the right circumstances, they could turn the tide of a fight. Every team needs support. You could be an invaluable part of the right team."

Jon's eyes light up. "You really think so?"

I nod. "Let's get these animals returned, and I'll show you."

I catch Taryn grinning out of the corner of my eye.

For the most part, the journey back to Treehaden is easy. Berry wrangles the livestock, with some help from my horrors to keep the wanderers in check. Only once do we lose an animal, but Taryn is able to track it down in his bird form before it truly escapes.

Jon becomes more friendly as the day goes along. The more I'm around him, the less I think he's a bad guy. Really, he just got caught in some unfortunate situations.

"How'd you end up in prison anyways? I know you said burglary, but why?" I've never had the inclination to steal something that didn't belong to me. Maybe because I've never really wanted for material goods, but even if I did, I don't think I'd have it in me.

"I don't know, man." He shrugs. It's clear that this is something he doesn't enjoy talking about. "Desperation. I was so tired of living paycheck to paycheck, you know? The never-ending grind." He rubs his forehead, as if choosing his next words carefully. "I met this girl. That's how most of the bad decisions in my life begin. Fucking women, you know? That's the real drug—a woman's love. Shit'll make you do anything. Anyways, I was in love. I wanted to buy her something nice for our anniversary, but I wasn't making shit. It's hard to show your love when you're making minimum wage."

"So what happened?" Taryn has guided Stompy right beside Jon to listen to the story.

"I thought if I couldn't buy her something nice, maybe I could take it from somebody who wouldn't miss it. I worked at a body shop, fixing cars. I've always been pretty good with my hands. One of our clients left his car with us, said he was going to be out of town for a week. It was a nice car, so I figured the house was probably even nicer. Turns out it was. I picked the lock, broke in, and the police were waiting for me by the time I was done. I tried to run and accidentally bulldozed a cop on the back steps. The pig charged me with assaulting an officer on top of it all. It wasn't my first strike, so here I am."

"Do you regret it?" I ask.

Jon laughs. "I regret getting caught. Those guys wouldn't have missed anything I took. I didn't even go for the whole stash, just a necklace and some earrings."

"You're a regular Robin Hood." The sarcasm must go over Jon's head because he smiles back at me. "Do you know much about the other players here?"

"A little bit." His smile fades. "We spent some time together during our physicals and what-not. And we all started out in the capital once we got in the game. Once they found out I was useless, nobody wanted to partner up. Been going at it alone ever since."

Damn. That's rough. I feel bad that a few hours ago, I was ready to cast this guy out. He's no saint, but he's not a murderer either.

"What do you know about the other guys?" This could be our chance to gain an upper hand on those that we are playing with. Maybe understand how they think or at the very least, have some leverage to use against them.

"Uhm, well, some of those guys I never went around. They had a real nasty vibe about them. Three or four of them gravitated to one another and they just watched everyone. Real creepy like. You can just tell with some guys, you know. Like, it's better to just leave them alone. The docs made sure not to tell us what people were in for. So it's hard to know who was telling the truth. I heard some things, though. Most of the guys are innocent." He winks.

"What about Glenn? Do you know what he was in for?"

"Oh man, he was a strange bird. They kept him in isolation, so we only ever saw him when we were logging in. I heard he came from a crazy house. Must have been something bad. The weird thing is that he was such a nice guy the few times I met him. You'd never know there was anything wrong with him."

All in all, Jon really doesn't know shit about the other players, aside from their names and classes. Once I've milked him for all I can, I fall back, leaving him and Taryn to talk about the weather.

When we arrive at Treehaden, the villagers are more welcoming to Jon than I would have imagined. But seeing as how they have never actually seen him, only his army of kobolds, they have no reason to suspect his involvement in their recent troubles.

Taryn is treated as royalty, and once the animals are safely locked in the stables, dinner is prepared in our honor. By the time we finish eating, it's almost nightfall, so we decide to stay the night at the inn.

The Rowdy Rooster is nothing special as far as inns go, but it's a roof over our heads and ale in our bellies. With full bellies and a decent buzz, we retire for the night with a promise of adventure tomorrow.

The next morning, I wake and gather my belongings. Taryn is already waiting in the first floor of the inn, gorging on eggs and bacon. The smell of fried meat has my mouth watering.

"Morning," he gets out between bites. Speckles of egg coats his dark beard. He reminds me of Limery the way he shovels food in his mouth.

"Where's Jon?" I expected him to be down here with Taryn, but he's nowhere to be found.

"Sleeping?" Taryn shrugs.

Something feels off. I turn to the bartender, a weathered, gray-haired dwarf. "Did our companion, the human, pass through here?"

He sets the mug he was polishing on the hardwood counter. "Ah, yes. He was up with the roosters. Seemed in an awful hurry."

"Dammit!" I slam my fist on the table, causing Taryn's plate to jump. "I told you he couldn't be trusted."

Taryn picks up a piece of bacon, crunching it in his mouth.

"Why are you not upset?" I roar. "Get up, let's get Berry and track him down."

"Why?" Taryn raises an eyebrow. "If he's gone, he's gone. What do we have to gain by chasing him?"

I let out a low growl. I hate feeling like a chump. Taryn and his stupid ideas. This is the last time I let him make the decisions. "Whatever. We never should have brought him with us in the first place. I'm going to get some fresh air."

I slam the door behind me as I step out into the courtyard. I love Taryn's chill attitude most of the time, but sometimes, I just wish he would get upset about the same things I do.

To my left, I notice a crowd has gathered around one of the shops. Curious, I walk over to investigate. Nearly a dozen dwarves are huddled around the entrance. A faint glow pulses from within.

Once I'm close enough, I notice that Jon is sitting on the steps of the shop. He holds a gemstone in his hand, carving something into it. He's focused as he works and doesn't notice my approach. Once the inscription is finished, the lines glow bright for a moment before fading away. A pile of gems sit at his feet, and several dwarves hold others in their hands. They tap the stones with fascination, each touch causing the gem to burst to life with light.

I stand back and watch for a moment as Jon works. He's clearly not trying to escape, but what is he up to? Trying to swindle more dwarves out of their money?

"What's going on here?" I ask.

Jon looks up from his work and flashes me a smile. "I'm putting my skills to use. The item shop had some low-grade gemstones lying around, so I'm enchanting them for the townsfolk. So they can travel at night without needing a torch. Or, you know, read or whatever."

I guess I misjudged Jon after all. Him and Taryn. Jon's kind of like that barking dog at the pound. The one with fur on edge that's unwilling to come to the gate, but once you get him home, he's as cuddly as can be. Not that Jon and I cuddled.

Drury turns around, holding a glowing yellow stone. "He calls them flashlights." He taps the stone over and over, turning the light on and off like a kid with a new toy. "Pretty amazing."

"How long has he been at this?" The amount of enchanted stones floating about leads me to believe it's been a while.

"Since daybreak. These flashlights will do wonders for our town. We no longer have to force our schedules to the sun."

I return Jon's smile. "Meet us in the inn when you're finished here. It's time to level you up."

CHAPTER SEVEN
SALT IN AN OPEN WOUND

We find the dungeon tucked away along the coast, almost invisible from the mainland. If not for the map that Chief Rizza gave me detailing all the ley lines around the island, I doubt I would have found it at all. Yet another reason why I am better off than Jon. I've had help from the trolls since the beginning.

"That was real cool of you back there, Jon." Taryn rides atop Stompy, his dreadlocks blowing in the coastal breeze. "Bringing modern technology to a fantasy world using magic. I love it! I wonder what else we could create."

"I felt bad about what I did." Jon places his hand over his heart. "I know it doesn't make us even, but maybe it helps."

"I'd say your debt has been paid. To Treehaden, at least. They got all of their livestock back, and now they can farm late. With the lights, there's so much potential for them." I slap him on the back. "Now let's go kill some things."

Before we begin, I invite Jon to officially join our party. His location appears on my map, and we can now send one another private messages.

A hidden stairwell leads us down to the dungeon's entrance. The stairwell is made from flaky stones, unlike most dwarven architecture, which is cleanly carved. Once Stompy puts one hoof on the ancient stone, it begins to crack and dislodge, forcing him to wait at the top of the stairs. Whoever made it didn't have beasts the size of barns in mind. Or maybe they didn't want them inside the dungeon.

The stairwell itself overlooks the sea, and as we descend, salty spray from the crashing waves below gathers in droplets on my skin. The roar of waves blasts up the cliff. My horrors grumble and bump into one another on the narrow path. Stompy blows a sad trumpet once we are out of his vision. Berry, on the other hand, seems excited for some one-on-one time with Taryn. He nuzzles his nose against his master every chance he gets.

At the bottom of the stairs, a dark crevice disappears into the cliffside. It's not big enough for any of us to crawl through. Limery might fit inside, but he's not around to test it out. I'm greeted with a notification.

Salt Caves. *Would you like to enter?*

A string of runes runs along one side of the entrance, the only part that gives away that this isn't a natural formation. As soon as I accept, the runes flash and the crack widens with a groan of grating rock. I barely fit through the entrance, but once inside, I can see in the almost complete darkness. Taryn, Berry, and Jon aren't so lucky, so Jon leads the way, his staff casting light for them to see by.

The cavern is a dull white. Its jagged and abrasive formations cause Taryn's cape to snag several times on protruding salt rocks before he eventually rolls up the end and carries it in one hand. After about twenty feet, we come to a stop as the cavern empties into a polished room. Someone put a lot of time and effort into carving this cave into an actual room, making the floor and walls gleam like marble in the reflection of Jon's light. On the far side, two identical wooden doors await.

Jon eyes the doors with suspicion. Clearly, he's had a few bad experiences with dungeons. He turns around to us. "What's the plan?"

"We'll pick a door, and then we'll see this through. The three of us should be able to handle this no problem."

Taryn runs his finger across the polished salt. The residue turns his black hands a milky white before he licks it. "Salty."

Berry follows his master, pressing his tongue against the wall before recoiling and licking his lips repeatedly.

"Two peas in a very strange and misshapen pod." I shake my head at their child-like behavior and turn to Jon. "Alright, Jon. Once we go through this door, I have no idea what is on the other side. You're a part of this team, and we need you to play support. My horrors, Berry, and I will deal damage and take the brunt of the attacks. You and Taryn focus on ways to help out. Stay out of range of whatever we end up facing."

"Hey, I can deal damage!" Taryn flashes his two shadow daggers in front of my face, their illusory blades coming to life as he grips them.

"Alright, lead the way then, champ." I equip my warhammer and spin its weight against my palm. Several horrors expire and I summon new ones to replace them.

Taryn approaches the two doors and examines them. They look practically identical, both old wood with metal clasps bolted to the walls. A latch and padlock bar our entry. A gash in the wood of the door on the right is the only detail that sets them apart.

"You think that means someone tried to get into this one after exploring the other?" Taryn runs his fingers over the damaged wood. "It was definitely made by an axe."

I join him and inspect the damage. The gash is just as faded as the rest of the door. It's most likely a remnant from a very old adventurer.

Aside from the two doors, the room is entirely barren. "That's the only clue we've got. Do you think we need some kind of key to open them?"

Taryn grabs the handle of the door on the right. As soon as he touches the metal, the padlock unlocks and falls to the side. When he tries the same thing on the other door, nothing happens.

"That answers that." Taryn pulls the door and it opens. He steps behind the door, motioning for me to go. "After you."

Our fearless leader isn't so fearless after all.

There's a small passageway and then stairs that descend deeper into the cliff. Tiny claw marks run along the walls of the stairwell, carved into the salt blocks. The size of the marks doesn't alarm me, but the amount of them does. I grip Destroyer a little tighter as I follow my horrors down into the abyss.

My horrors wait for me in an empty room at the bottom of the stairs. There's a door on both sides, but nothing else aside from a single pillar in the middle of the room. Why is everything so empty? Whatever happened to having a dungeon with a few goblins here and there that we smash and move on from? Empty rooms make everything feel more dangerous.

The pillar has some weird etchings along it, but they don't look like runes or any type of language I've ever seen.

Berry sniffs at the air behind me. I wonder if the salt is having any effect on his sense of smell.

"Time to pick another door." Taryn pushes his way through my horrors and goes for the door on the right.

As he passes the pillar, it begins to crack. The rest of the room stays still while tiny pieces of salt flake off and fall to the floor. Hairline fractures creep up the pillar from floor to ceiling, making the pillar appear like it is writhing and alive.

A piece of rock breaks off, and an eye stares in my direction. With an audible crack, a six-inch piece of salt rock detaches and a small impish creature pries itself from the pillar, raining down rubble as it flexes its body for the first time in however long. It leaps from the pillar, and translucent wings emerge, lifting the ugly monster into the air.

Cracks continue to echo throughout the chamber as more and more of the tiny creatures emerge from the pillar until it is nothing more than a small pole.

Salt Fairy. *Level 17. Made of a harder substance than most fairies, salt fairies have no problem pouring salt in an open wound.*

The bone-white fairies are translucent, their organs visible beneath their brittle exterior. Their fingertips are pointy and sharp, and bat-like wings keep them aloft while menacing tails with spiked tips thrash about. They hover in the air, clicking their tongues in our direction. This is not going to be fun.

Taryn has returned to the safety of my horrors, and Jon lets out a stream of curses behind me.

I send my horrors out into the room, giving me more space to swing my warhammer. "Jon, stay behind me." I move in front of him, blocking him from view of the fairies as best I can.

The fairies dive for my horrors, stabbing and clawing at them with incredible speed. Tufts of orange and blue hair float across the floor as the Horrors of Vitality are ripped to shreds. Their passive slows seems to have no effect on the airborne creatures. One Horror of Power leaps into the air, jaws snapping on one of the fairy's tails. It pulls the fairy to the ground and paws it to dust.

One down, only about thirty more to go.

The spiked tails function like needles, stabbing my horrors in vital areas. Many of my horrors run around blind, eyes gouged out and attacking wildly, sometimes damaging other horrors.

The fairies are so quick that they dip in and out, dealing damage before the horrors have a chance to react.

I step forward, and one dives for my head. I swing my warhammer, but the creature is too quick, darting past my weapon and raking its claws across my face.

Instantly, my vision goes blurry as tears well up in my eyes. My face burns hot as salty claws rip into my skin, setting off pain receptors left and right. Even with my thick skin, it stings like a thousand papercuts.

"I can't do anything without killing your horrors!" Taryn yells as he swipes his dagger at a diving fairy. He misses and catches a spiked tail to the shoulder before the fairy buggers off.

It'd be really nice to have Limery here right about now. He'd give these fairies a run for their money.

Another fairy dives for me and this time, I lift my shoulder to cover my face. The spiked tail stabs into my spaulder, lodging inside of the leather armor. The fairy tries to pull away, but its tail is stuck. I hit it with a hard thump, and the fairy's head detaches and soars across the room, leaving a trail of pink blood.

Jon gags at the sight behind me.

I cast a few more horrors to replace the ones I've lost. They're being picked off without doing much damage, and Taryn is about as useful as nipples on a breastplate. He can't cast Lightning Bolt in such an enclosed space without killing my horrors and potentially the rest of us. He's imbued Berry, making him a mammoth bear, but the fairies are attacking his blindsides. Blood has matted his golden fur on his back and hindquarters.

All in all, this is not going well.

"How the hell are we going to get out of this!" I yell as another fairy claws my back before scurrying away.

"They're too fast!" Taryn swings at another with his shadow dagger but misses.

"Wait." Jon steps up beside me. "Everyone lie down, and quit moving."

"What? That's stupid." I turn to face him, and he stares at me with such intensity that I'm sure he has a plan.

"Just do it! Trust me." He points at the floor. "All of you, down."

I give Taryn an apprehensive glare, but I listen to Jon and instruct my horrors to quit moving and huddle against the floor. The fairies attack with free rein, tiny claws ripping horror flesh. I crouch down myself just as Jon lifts his staff. With a flourish, the diamond tip flashes blue.

The fairies quit attacking and hover in the air, looking around like they are lost.

. . .

Incoming Message (Jon): *Stay quiet. I cast Conceal Area. They can't see anything below three feet unless they go beneath the illusion.*

Incoming Message (Taryn): *That's brilliant! Now what?*

Incoming Message (Jon): *Now you kill them? I don't know. This was all I've got.*

No longer sensing a threat, the fairies begin to gather around the pillar in the center of the room. They hook their claws to the salt column and cling tight, fitting perfectly against one another. Before long, all of them have gathered on the pillar once again.

As soon as we step out of the illusion, they'll attack again. We have to find a way to defeat them before they recognize we are here.

Message (Chod): *I think I have a plan that might work, but there is no guarantee.*

Incoming Message (Taryn): *If it doesn't include hiding under an illusion and waiting for the fairies to die of old age then I say it's a lot better than what we are currently doing.*

I summon another round of horrors. If this is going to work, I'm going to need as many as I can get. Since the fairies are no longer attacking us, that means thirty is my max.

Message (Chod): *I need you guys to get away from the pillar. Up the stairs if you can manage it. Just stay under the illusion.*

Taryn crawls on all fours past me. Berry does the same, his large frame barely fitting below the illusion. His wet, matted fur brushes against my shoulder, streaking me with blood. For all the shit I give him, that is one tough and loyal companion.

As quick as I'm able, I continue to summon horrors until I have a full army. Very carefully, I send all thirty of them to gather around the pillar. Horrors of Vitality go closest to the pillar, followed by Horrors of Power, and finally Horrors of Finesse.

Once they are in position, I stand. The fairies immediately begin to stir, but before they have time to unfurl, the Horrors of Vitality move in close together, forming the base of my plan. Next, the Horrors of Power leap onto their backs.

Horrors of Finesse climb their way up until they are forming a horror pyramid around the pillar.

Just as the first salt fairy detaches, I cast Kamikaze, exploding all the horrors at once.

The force of the blast is enough to shatter the column, along with the bottom-most fairies.

With the column destroyed, the ceiling begins to sag. It groans loudly now that the floor above has no support.

"Get back!" I shout, rushing toward the stairs right as the ceiling collapses, killing the rest of the fairies underneath a mountain of rubble. Dust and smoke fill the room, making it hard to see even with my night vision.

"Did it work?" asks Jon.

"I think so. It's kind of hard to s—"

"Nnggghhh." A loud, deep grunt cuts me off, followed by several more.

As the dust fades, several squat shambling bodies emerge from the rubble. They look like dwarves, but with glowing blue eyes and white, leathery skin. Their beards are coated with dust and clothing hangs in tatters around their bodies, revealing a deathly form underneath. They look like zombies, but less smelly and decaying.

Salt Draugr. *Level 19. Normally decayed, these undead dwarves were preserved by the salt of the mines, making them stronger and more powerful than their aboveground counterparts.*

I grip the handle of Destroyer a little tighter. "Preserved zombies. Great."

CHAPTER EIGHT
FASTBALL SPECIAL

One of the undead dwarves opens its mouth and a white puff of dust spews out. The noise that follows is like nails on a chalkboard, grating against my senses. As the draugrs crawl out of the rubble, their heinous cries echo through the dilapidated room.

Milky white eyes lock on our location.

They wear tattered garments and distressed leather armor. Clothing of the common class. Alabaster skin shows through in places, their skin white as chalk. The salt of the mines has halted their decomposition, leaving the draugrs' skin and muscle intact, albeit very dehydrated. Their skin clings to muscle and bone like spandex, making the normally full-framed dwarves ghastly to look upon.

"Hey man, I didn't sign up for zombies!" Jon steps even further up the stairs. With the ceiling collapsing, his illusion has been dispersed. "I don't want to be a zombie. I might be a shitty enchanter, but at least I'm alive."

He rushes to the top of the stairs, but the door has already closed, blocking our escape. Jon beats on the door. To what end, I'm not sure. There's no one on the other side to let him out.

"Help! Somebody help!" he shouts, fist pounding frantically.

"Easy, man," Taryn tries to coax him down. "If we work together, we'll get out of this fine."

The dwarven draugrs climb across the rubble in our direction. I summon three more horrors and send them out to buy us time while we get Jon under control. The passive slow of Horror of Vitality impedes them slightly, gaining us a few more precious seconds.

"Jon!" I roar with everything I can muster, and it momentarily stops his antics. "We're in this together. If you don't want to die, then it's high time you start helping us out."

He stands at the top of the stairs breathing heavily with his shoulders slouched. He hangs his head for a moment before turning around. "Okay." He sighs. "Let's do this." It's not inspiring, but at least it's something.

The draugrs rip through my horrors with their superhuman strength. One of them steps close enough for me to attack, and I hit it with a mighty swing from Destroyer. The blow sends it stumbling backward into two other draugrs, knocking them down like bowling pins. The metal flashes red as the hammer grows hotter.

The attack doesn't do much damage. The draugrs might look brittle, but they are still dwarves with decent Constitution.

I count six draugrs amongst the debris. Six level-nineteen draugrs against a level-twenty troll, a level-ten enchanter, a level-sixteen druid, and a level-twelve umber bear. Hardly a fair fight.

The good news is that they don't appear to be reanimated warriors. Judging by their clothing and lack of chainmail or plate armor, these were worker dwarves before they turned.

Taryn casts Lightning Bolt and the resulting thunder shakes the walls, sending even more dust and rubble raining down from above. Lightning crashes into one of the draugrs, taking out a chunk of its health and setting its clothing on fire. The draugr is unphased by the flames erupting across its body as its health trickles down. With no fluids in their bodies, the dwarves are walking tinder. Very strong walking tinder.

Despite their brittle appearance and vulnerability to fire, these monsters are still strong and tough to kill. My blow with Destroyer only took out ten percent of the draugr's health. Jon does practically no damage and Taryn does very little unless it's with his lightning. So this battle falls square on the backs of Berry and me.

Three draugrs step into my range and I use Intimidation, unleashing a roar and confusing them for two seconds. They stumble back and forth, unsure of where to go or what to do. I knock one of them to the side with Destroyer, where Berry pins it to the ground and mauls it. In the same motion, I spin around and connect my weapon with a second draugr. It flies back into the pile of rubble where the pillar once stood. Red flashes down my warhammer as Inferno gains power.

My next attack connects with the draugr's chest. I hear the crunch of breaking ribs as I send it flying into the others. Finally, a critical hit! When it stands, charred flesh and fabric still sizzle from the attack. Each hit does more damage than the last as Inferno grows hotter.

I search for my next victim, but no one is in range. Destroyer goes cold again as its timer expires.

Berry yelps as one of the two draugrs he is fighting lands a blow to the bear's ribs. Both draugrs dig their hands into Berry's fur, refusing to let go and continually kneeing and kicking as they ride him like drunks on a mechanical bull. Berry tries to claw at them over his shoulder and thrashes about in an attempt to throw them off, but it does nothing to deter their attacks. Taryn rushes to his pet's aid, stabbing a draugr with his shadow blades. It doesn't do much, but it does enough for the undead dwarf to release his grip on Berry.

With a hard swing, I send the other one sprawling into the corner.

I move away from the group in an attempt to spread out our opponents. Instead of drawing one or two my way, five of them lock on to me. Before I realize it, I'm trapped in a corner with five draugrs pressing in on me. They rush toward me with surprising speed.

I set my feet and prepare for their onslaught.

Lightning rips across the room, hitting one of the draugrs and knocking the rest of them into me. I try to toss them aside, but they weigh far more than I imagined, knocking me off balance. They claw and bite me, and I drop Destroyer as they tackle me to the floor. I summon horrors as I fall, and they attack the undead dwarves. Pain runs through my body as their hardened nails rip into my skin. The salt that coats most of their bodies only intensifies the pain, setting my flesh on fire. I hope the others are okay, because I can't hear anything over the screaming that surrounds me.

I try to fight to my feet, but the five of them have me trapped on my back. Panic flares within me as my HP continues to drop. For all my strength, I'm helpless. Trapped. It's like waking up from a nightmare only to be trapped in a blanket.

Not knowing what else to do, I activate Berserker Rage.

Bonus Strength pumps within my muscles, giving me the power I need to roll over to my side and crawl free. I kick one of the draugrs in the face and its teeth spill to the floor like marbles.

Destroyer is lying somewhere, but I don't have time to look for it. Instead, I summon more horrors, activate Bite and Claw, and rip into the throat of the closest draugr. As I tear into its throat, dust pours out. I punch the next closest one and kick out at a third, retreating toward my group just in time for Taryn to cast another lightning bolt.

It rips into the group, setting several more on fire.

"Everyone, on the stairs!" Jon orders.

Berserker Rage expires, and I do as he commands. A moment later, a half dozen of Jon's doppelgängers run past me and into the room. They spread out to all four corners. Jon cups his hands over his mouth and whispers something. Seconds later, his voice booms from every corner of the room. "Hey, dickweeds!" The draugrs that were staring into our direction begin turning rapidly, not sure which way to attack. They spread out, none of them going for the same target.

Several of the draugrs are pretty low on health. One only has a tenth of its HP, and two others are below fifty percent. A single attack is all it takes for them to dissipate one of his illusions, but as soon as they do, Jon sends out another one. His voice continues to bounce off the walls, calling them names my followers would have been proud of. Insults come from every direction, taunting our opponents.

"Douche canoe."

"Lint licker."

"Captain skinny-dick."

"Fuckass."

Thanks to Berserker Rage, I'm back to full HP myself.

"How long can you keep this up?" I ask Jon.

"I've got about five more clones left."

"Alright, keep it up as long as you can. I'm going to try to finish this. Taryn, I want you casting lightning on the opposite side of wherever I am. Have Berry stand guard in case this goes wrong and I end up dying. You'll need him to protect you."

Taryn nods gravely, taking position behind Berry.

I search the room for Destroyer and spot the glittering metal shaft protruding from the rubble across the room. There are two draugrs between me and my weapon.

I rush out to grab it with one of Jon's duplicates following alongside me into battle. We split at the last minute, drawing one of the draugrs away. Grabbing the weapon right as the other one gets to me, I swing up without looking. Destroyer connects with a crunch and explosion of dust. The one with the lowest health falls to the ground without a head.

"Come on over, you walking wounds! I've got your bag of dicks right here." Jon's voice shouts from the wall behind me.

Two draugrs turn to face me, but Taryn casts Lightning Bolt on the other side of the room, momentarily distracting them. I use the opportunity to knock them both to the ground, sweeping their legs with my warhammer. Inferno engages and I dash to the other side, where two more draugrs are chasing one of Jon's clones. The heated warhammer connects with ribs, leaving a warhammer-sized scorched indentation as the draugr flies through the air. With four stacks of Inferno, I swing the hammer for the head of the next closest, turning it to dust with one hit.

Not wasting any time, I bolt back to the other side and pummel the draugrs once again. By the time Jon sends out his last clone, all the draugrs are defeated.

I sit on the steps, letting out an exhausted breath. "I...was not prepared for that."

"A collapsing ceiling? How could we be?" Taryn takes a seat beside me, patting me on the back. A battered Berry lies on the ground in front of him. "It's just not the same without the little guy, is it?"

Limery's bulbous eyes flash in the front of my mind. I can't wait for him to be a part of the team again. "You're right about that."

"Hah! I got a level and a new ability point." Jon beams with pride.

"What are you going to use it on?" Taryn asks after healing Berry.

"I could make my current illusions stronger, or I could add a new stat to my enchantment abilities. Or there is an illusion that summons a copy of a nearby creature. What do you guys think?"

"Your doppelgängers came in pretty handy. What's the upgrade do?" Taryn stands, stretching his arms overhead.

"It makes them corporeal, whatever that means."

Taryn laughs. "It means it gives them actual bodies. They won't be just smoke and mirrors anymore. Do that one!"

"Sweet! They won't be able to do much damage, but if they can take a beating, then it'll make it harder for our opponents to pick me out."

"Exactly!" Taryn high-fives Jon.

Jon steps past and goes to loot the bodies.

"Anything good?" I ask, not ready to get up.

"Lots of salt crystals." Jon tosses a chunk of white rock to me. "Might be worth something at the market."

"Not sure I want to be seasoning my food with the remains of zombie dwarves. It's all yours." I toss it back.

Once we rest and heal up, we examine the two doors on each side of the room. It's impossible to tell which one to pick. They're similar to the ones in the first room, but both of these doors have been damaged by our recent fight.

"Do you think it matters?" asks Taryn. He's careful not to touch the door and unlock the enchantment.

"Honestly, I have no clue. I'm sure they are all connected in some way. Let's just pick one and keep moving." It's probably just a matter of the easiest route to the boss room and if we want to do a complete clear or take our levels and run.

I summon more horrors, determined to go into the next room with a full army.

While Taryn contemplates over which door to choose, Jon focuses on the collapsed ceiling.

"Maybe we should check up there?" He points to the room above us.

It's a good fifteen feet from the floor and crumbling around the edges.

"And how exactly do you propose we get up there?"

"Can you toss one of these guys up there?" He pats a Horror of Vitality on the horn and it swats him away.

"I mean I could have them look around, but I have no way of knowing what it is they are seeing in order to tell them what to do. They could accidentally trip a trap or something worse." Not a bad plan, just not very effective.

"What about Taryn?" Jon looks away as soon as he says it.

"Excuse me?" Taryn raises his eyebrows and leans forward. "I don't think I heard what I think I heard."

I fight to conceal the smile spreading across my face. "Come on, man. Let me toss you."

"No way!" He shakes his head, and the clasps in his hair jingle with the motion. "Nope. I'm a dwarf. I have my pride. Besides, I could just fly up there if I wanted."

"Come on, let me toss you. Just this once, and I'll owe you one. There could be a clue to help us navigate this maze we've gotten ourselves into." I give him my best puppy dog face, which I'm sure doesn't have nearly as an endearing effect as I hope.

"Yeah, Taryn." Jon winks at me. "Let him toss you."

Taryn stares at me for a long moment before rolling his eyes. "Fine, but you owe me big time. And no one else hears about this ever."

I nod, keeping my jokes to myself and not pushing my luck.

Taryn is heavy, but not too heavy for me to hold him like a small child with my palm placed squarely under his bum. With a heave, I shout, "Fastball special" and toss him to the room above us.

The ceiling groans for a moment, but then everything is silent.

"Nothing up here but two doors," he says. Dust rains down as he walks around the perimeter. His footsteps are silent due to the noise-canceling properties of his boots.

"Alright, come on down then. I'll catch you." I can't hide the laughter in my voice as I say the last words.

"Wait, I've got an idea. Do you think we can open a door up here and down there?"

"I doubt it. Remember what happened in the first room? You could only open one door."

"Yeah, but maybe you can only open one door in each room. What if we can open one down there and one up here?"

"How is that going to help us?" It's not like Berry and I have any shot at getting on the second floor.

"I could lure whatever is in this next room into here, make it fall through the floor, then we don't have to fight it on the way out if we want to clear both sides."

I'll be damned. That's actually a pretty good idea. "So how are we doing this?"

"Touch one of the doors to disable the lock, but don't open it. Once you do that, I'll try the door up here."

There's no way of knowing which door is better, so I just pick one. Jon stands closely at my heels as I touch the handle and the lock falls open.

"Done," I shout.

"Okay, get ready to catch me."

There's a clank of a door opening and then dust falls from the ceiling as Taryn runs across the floor. He jumps from the room above without looking, and I catch him midair, holding him like a baby. I rock him a few times before he pinches my nipple, forcing me to let him go.

"Alright, let's get out of here." I rub my twisted nipple with a face of mock pain.

"Oh, give it a re—"

Taryn's words are cut off by a crash from above like a bowling ball on concrete. As we listen harder, the noise grows louder as it approaches our direction, like someone knocked over an entire rack of bowling balls and they are spilling down the street.

"What the hell?" asks Jon, backing up even closer behind me.

The noise grows until it is right on top of us. The ceiling shakes right before a torrent of white spheres crash through the open ceiling and smash against the floor. They crack open, shards exploding everywhere.

I'm able to focus on one right before it collides with the floor.

Salt Golem. Level 18. These monsters can curl into a ball and travel with blazing speed, bludgeoning opponents to death.

One by one, the golems shatter against the stone floor. They might be tough, but a fifteen-foot fall at full speed is all it takes to crack their shells. I get a nice chunk of experience for doing absolutely nothing other than being part of the team.

"Dude, that was genius." I extend my fist to Taryn and he returns the fist-bump.

"Yeah, baby." He flashes me a toothy grin. "That's what I'm talking about!"

"That's awesome!" Jon pumps his fist in the air. "I'm already halfway to level twelve."

I walk over to inspect the remains of the salt golems. Lots more salt crystals. I'm less wary about taking these and shove a few in my satchel.

Summoning another round of horrors puts me at full capacity, so I suggest that we enter the next room. Once everyone is ready, I open the door.

The polished walls and floors that made up the last two rooms are no more. This room is reminiscent of the crevice we walked through at the entrance. Hundreds of salt stalagmites and stalactites adorn the walls, floor, and ceiling. A narrow path winds to a single door on the other side.

We wait and listen, but the only sound is the water dripping from the stalactites overhead. That doesn't mean much though, considering the pillar and the fairies that emerged once Taryn walked past. This could be exactly like that.

None of us want to take the lead, so I send my horrors in first to make sure it's safe. No sooner have they passed through the door than the nearest stalagmite explodes, sending razor-sharp shards flying like shrapnel. My oldest horrors die from the blast, but the newer ones have enough health to absorb the blow, though they lose a good amount of HP. Before they can return to me, however, another stalagmite explodes, then several more in a chain reaction that wipes out a quarter of my horrors on the spot.

"What was that?" Jon asks, wide-eyed.

"No idea. I didn't see a trap or anything." I search the path for anything that my horrors might have tripped, but there's nothing out of the ordinary.

I send another horror forward, and the next stalagmite explodes, shredding through the closest of my minions. The two stalagmites adjacent to it shatter a moment later. At this rate, if we push forward, all of my horrors will be dead before we make it halfway.

"There has to be a way through that doesn't set them off, right?" Not knowing what is causing the explosions means we're going to be doing some trial and error.

"You would think so." Taryn strokes his beard. "Maybe the rocks are sensitive to movement or the floor responds to a certain weight limit? Try calling them back and send one in by itself."

I call my horrors back, though I don't see how Berry or I are making it across if the floor has a weight limit. I send out a single Horror of Finesse, the lightest of all my horrors. The gangly blue monster walks forward and the moment it is next to a stalagmite, the rock explodes.

"Wait a second." Jon grabs me by the arm. "Let me try something. I haven't used my ability point, so my clones are still just illusions. Let's see what happens when I send one out."

Jon lifts his staff and a duplicate of him jumps out of his body. It walks down the path silently, and when it reaches the nearest stalagmite, nothing happens. His clone walks further, past dozens more stalagmites, but it doesn't set them off.

"I don't get it. Do we have to destroy literally every single one of these things in order to cross this room?" Taryn lets out an exasperated sigh.

"Now, let's see what happens when..." Jon's voice trails off.

I look to see his eyes glaze over when, I assume, he opens a stat menu.

I'm looking across the room when another explosion rocks the cavern. Jon's clone falls to the ground, blood seeping out of hundreds of small wounds.

My heart thuds in my chest. "What the fuck was that?" I shout.

"Uh, I made him corporal," says Jon with a grimace.

"Corporeal," corrects Taryn.

"As soon as he took a step, they exploded," adds Jon.

"Wait, so it didn't set them off as soon as it changed? Only after he moved?"

Jon scrunches his eyebrows. "I-I think so."

"Hmmm." I reach in my satchel and pull out one of the salt crystals. It's light. Way too light to set off any weight enchantment.

I toss it across the room. It clatters as it lands, setting off another chain reaction.

"I think I know what's setting them off." I equip Destroyer and step out into the room. If I'm wrong, this is going to be very painful.

Cautiously, I press forward until I'm at the spot where Jon's clone died. One of the enchanted stones that I have equipped to Destroyer muffles my movements. I take one more step into the radius of the next stalagmite and close my eyes. I'm certain I could survive a single explosion, but the prospect of shrapnel ripping through my flesh makes me wince all the same.

I wait, but nothing happens. Opening my eyes, I let out a sigh of relief. The room is so quiet that I could hear a pin drop, which is a good sign. It means I'm not being sliced by a thousand tiny salt fragments.

A cold sweat erupts on my neck when I hear a soft crunch back near the entrance. New stalagmites form from the ruins of the exploded ones, trapping me in the middle of the cavern.

Still focused on my plan, I start walking back as they repopulate. With each step, nothing happens. It's just as I thought. It's not weight or movement setting off the explosions.

"It's sound," I tell my companions, but before I finish my sentence, searing pain shoots up my legs and midsection as I'm assaulted by thousands of glass-like shards. They tear through my skin, setting my body on fire and dropping my health by a third as a chain reaction of exploding stalagmites rips through me.

I fight against every urge in my body not to scream, embracing and focusing on the pain, and eventually the explosions stop. I huddle against the floor, blood seeping into a pool around my feet and knees. Every part of my lower half burns and aches. Skin hangs off my palms in tatters as blood drips to the floor.

How could I be so stupid?

Eventually, the pain fades as my increased healing takes effect, and I'm able to look up. Jon and Taryn both stare at me with concerned expressions, neither one brave enough to come to me. I crawl to my feet and return to where they are standing.

"It's sound," I finally get out. "That's what sets off the explosions."

"You couldn't have waited to tell us that?" Taryn grimaces as he looks at my wounds. "Here, take this." He reaches in his bag and pulls out a vial of red liquid.

I kneel so he can pour it in my mouth. As soon as the cinnamon-flavored liquid touches my tongue, I begin to feel better. The health potion kicks my healing into overdrive and the hundreds of cuts begin to mend themselves.

"Thanks."

"Don't mention it. So if the rocks respond to sound, how are we getting everyone through here?" He looks into the cavern. "Berry and Jon don't have sound distorting items. Not unless you can magically craft something?" He turns to Jon, but the enchanter just shakes his head.

I stand in silence for a moment, mulling over ideas in my head. I can't summon horrors quick enough for us to send them across the room. We could try throwing items ahead of us to make a path, but there's no telling if the respawn on the stalagmites are universally timed or random. One explosion is likely enough to send Jon back to wherever he set his spawn.

Brute force isn't getting us through this one, but maybe Strength will.

"We carry them. You carry Jon. I'll take Berry."

Taryn blinks at me. "He weighs like eight hundred pounds."

"Leave that to me." I flash Taryn a smile. "Saddle up, noble steed."

Jon climbs onto Taryn's shoulders like a kid trying to get a better view in a crowded room. I can't resist poking a little fun at them.

"Put on a trench coat and you might be able to get into the R-rated movies."

Taryn cuts his eyes at me. "I think you should worry more about how you plan on carrying Berry across the tunnel and less about how awesome Jon and I look."

"Awesome, right." I chuckle.

I step back into the entryway as the last of the stalagmites reform. I really hope my plan works, otherwise we are all going to be in a lot of pain.

"I need Berry to be completely silent while I carry him across. A single grunt or groan could be all it takes to set off an explosion."

Taryn nods. "I'll do my best." He sets Jon down and whispers a few words into Berry's ear. "Alright, let's do this."

Jon climbs onto Taryn's shoulders once again. Berry stands in front of me, waiting for orders.

"Alright, buddy. I need you to climb on my back. Wrap your arms around my shoulders and I'm going to hold your back legs."

I bend my knees and lower myself to make it easier for him to climb on. He wraps his massive paws around my neck and I grab his back legs, hefting him onto my back like a child. A thousand-pound child.

Immediately, my muscles burn from such a heavy weight. I take the first step and my legs shake with the movement. If not for having Destroyer tied around my waist, each step would be thunderous. As it is, the only sounds are my heavy breathing.

Taryn takes the lead, following the narrow path that winds between the stalagmites. I follow close behind with shaky steps. Sweat beads down my forehead and my grip starts to loosen on Berry's legs.

We're nearly a quarter of the way there, but there is no way I'm going to make it at the current rate. Luckily, I thought all of this through. I send Taryn a quick message.

Message (Chod): *Time to pick up the pace.*

Taryn doesn't respond, but his speed quickens. I'm sure he could carry Jon for an hour if he needed to. The man is like a twig.

My grip falters and I know I can't wait any longer. I activate Berserker Rage and suddenly carrying Berry becomes exponentially easier. I readjust him and set off down the path.

The bear's hot breath pants against my neck, but so far, he hasn't made a sound. We pass the halfway mark and I still have twenty seconds left on my ultimate. The path is narrow, and I freeze when Berry's leg hits one of the stalagmites. Luckily, his fur muffles the sound and nothing happens. I let out a sigh and continue.

Up ahead, Taryn and Jon have finished, and pound their fists in the air in silent victory. I'm a quarter of the way when I notice the countdown on Berserker Rage is at ten seconds.

I heft Berry up higher on my back and lean forward, sprinting the rest of the way. Destroyer jostles against my waist and I'm afraid for a moment it might come loose.

I'm only a few steps from safety when my buffs expire and the full weight of Berry comes crashing back down against my body. I stumble forward, losing my footing and tumbling to the ground.

Explosions crash all around me as my face collides with the cold hard floor, and sharp pain shoots through my legs. I wait for the concussive force of an exploding stalagmite to the face, but it doesn't come. Instead there is nothing but darkness as Berry's massive body covers my upper half and absorbs all the shrapnel.

He roars in pain, crawling off my body toward Taryn. I raise my head and see Taryn rushing to his pet and casting Restoration, basking them both in a golden aura. Berry's snout is bloody, and he's covered in rubble.

Two small arms grab my shoulder and attempt to pull me forward, but I'm too heavy. I climb to my feet and very gingerly walk to the open space where I promptly collapse. My legs are tattered and bloody, but at least we made it. Berry's fur absorbed most of the damage and once Taryn is finished healing him, he looks as good as new.

Jon hands me a health potion that soothes my stinging legs. After a moment, the pain is gone entirely.

"It wasn't a bad idea." Taryn extends a hand and helps me to my feet. "Making it through there with a few cuts is about the best we could have hoped for."

"Yeah, I guess they can't always be pretty." At least we made it through.

At the end of the cavern, there is only one door waiting.

"Looks like this is our next challenge."

Jon, Taryn, and Berry stand behind me as I press my hand to the enchanted door.

TEAMWORK MAKES THE DREAM WORK

The door groans as it swings open, revealing a long hallway. It's narrow and straight with polished walls and floors, no different from a passageway in most castles. The light from Jon's staff shines on an assortment of white and gray tiles that line the floor, covered in a thick layer of dust. Clearly, no one has set foot in this area of the dungeon for quite some time. From where I'm standing, I can see another door at the far end. Jon and Taryn stand behind me, waiting for me to enter.

"Seems way too easy. Jon, can you send a clone down the hallway?" I have a healthy distrust for empty hallways.

"No problem." Jon raises his staff and a duplicate of himself steps out from his body.

Five steps in, the floor shakes and stone grates together just before a scythe swings down from the ceiling, cutting the now corporeal clone in half. Blood and guts splatter the hallway as Jon watches himself die and crumple to the floor. The scythe swings back and forth a few times before coming to a stop.

Jon grimaces. "Does it really need to be that graphic?"

Taryn pats him on the back. "At least you know you have guts. Now we know what you're made of."

I imagine this hallway is full of traps. This is the exact situation where unlocking Perception over Conceal would have paid great dividends. Avoiding traps are not my favorite type of challenge. I'd much rather battle monsters with brute force than have to puzzle my way across this.

"I hope you have a strong stomach, Jon, because we are going to have to test this out a few more times." I summon three horrors and send them forward a few seconds apart from one another.

They bypass the scythe and I hear a click as one of them trips a trap. The Horror of Finesse makes it through but the other two are crushed by a massive salt block that plummets from the ceiling. The salt block is the width of the hallway, blocking our vision of the other side. A moment later, I feel the last horror's presence descend deep into the cliff before it vanishes.

My immediate thought is a vanishing tile or some kind of trap-door.

"I guess we move forward." I shrug. "Watch your step and keep an eye out for anything out of the ordinary."

I take the lead as we move down the hallway, pushing the giant scythe aside so that I can pass by. When I climb on top of the salt block, I notice a missing tile in the floor, revealing a hole that descends into complete darkness.

Jon points his staff at the hole, but the light doesn't go very far. "I do not want to find out what's down there." He takes a step back.

We're halfway down the tunnel, but who knows what traps are still waiting?

"Your turn." I nudge Jon in the arm.

He casts his clone and it barely makes it past the hole before a second scythe emerges from the wall and slashes with enough force to completely decapitate it. The head rolls along the floor before falling into the dark hole.

"You've got to be kidding me." Jon places his head in his hands. "I'm starting to regret making my illusions this realistic."

"It's for the good of the party." I climb down from the salt block and send out another horror. "Better one of your clones meets a grisly end than one of us, right? Besides, if you plan on leveling up the old-fashioned way, you're going to be seeing plenty of blood and guts."

The Horror of Vitality waddles across the marble floor, mumbling to itself when a second stone block falls from the ceiling and crushes it. If I had a drink, I'd pour it out in honor of all the horrors that have died so that we may live. Horror of Power goes next, using its powerful legs to jump up the salt block and onto the other side. It doesn't go far before I feel its presence come to a stop.

"I think that might be it." I climb the salt block and find the horror waiting at the door.

This wasn't the most difficult hallway I've experienced, but who knows how we would have fared without Jon's clones and my horrors. Not every hero comes with a set of test-dummies.

The door at the end of the hall is different from the others. There's no lock, but instead, it has a large rune carved into the wood.

"Any idea what it means?" I ask.

Taryn shakes his head.

Jon scrunches his nose. "Doesn't look like any of the runes I've encountered."

"Let me stock up on my horrors before we enter. If there is a special rune on this door, then I want to be prepared."

After taking time to summon a full army of horrors, I press my hand to the door. The rune flares a bright white and a crash rumbles from the other side. The door creaks open, revealing a circular room with a massive white turtle standing in the center. Torches line the wall, filled with blue flames that cast the room in an eerie glow.

Halite Tortoise. *Unique Monster. Level 25. Known as the Salt Turtle to the Ivory Dwarves, the Halite Tortoise is a symbol of luck and prosperity for miners.*

The turtle's skin and shell are milky white and translucent, almost like it was carved out of salt, with icy blue eyes that follow us as we enter. Its thick legs and shell are covered in murky gemstones, providing it with natural armor. My horrors spread around the room, surrounding the turtle on all sides.

I take a step back when the turtle opens its mouth and speaks.

"It has been many years since someone has trespassed into my mines. Many years since I have had a worthy opponent." The words that trickle out are raspy and deep.

The door behind us closes with a slam. The turtle clicks his beak a few times before speaking again.

"Perhaps we should make this a fair fight."

The tortoise lowers its shell to the floor and retracts its legs. Once they are inside the shell, white smoke spills out of the holes. It's thick and heavy, lingering on the ground. My horrors cough as it overwhelms them, and I feel their HP draining by the second. The horrors with the lowest HP vanish from existence.

"What is this?" Taryn asks as he backs closer to the wall.

The smoke touches my skin, but it doesn't burn or otherwise affect me. The smoke continues to pour out until a thick layer coats the bottom two feet of the room. My horrors continue to cough and die.

"I don't know, but it looks like it only affects you if you breathe it in."

Half of my horrors have died and the rest will join them soon if I don't do something. Instead of letting them go to waste, I cast Sacrifice and gain a buff for each horror as it explodes into the ether. My muscles bulge as I'm filled with bonus Strength and Constitution for the next few minutes. I even feel quicker on my feet from the influx of Dexterity.

As soon as the horrors are gone, the smoke that has coated the floor vacuums back into the turtle's shell.

"Ah." Its legs extend and lift the enormous body off the ground. "Much better." It clicks its beak a few more times.

Taryn and I exchange glances. So it looks like my horrors are a no-go this round.

"What's happening?" asks Jon.

"It seems the turtle isn't a fan of my minions. Everyone spread out. Taryn, how about you get this party started?"

We move to four separate areas around the room. The turtle doesn't move, but its eyes follow me. Does it view me as the primary threat?

Taryn raises his staff and a bolt of lightning arcs toward the turtle. At the moment before impact, the turtle retracts into its shell. A single tile on the shell opens and swallows the lightning bolt inside. The shell shakes, rumbling against the stone floor before several tiles along the edge of the shell open and four bolts of lightning shoot out.

The action is so surprising that none of us dodge the attack. The lightning bursts out with as much force as it entered with. A bolt hits me in the chest, dropping five percent of my HP and setting my hair on end.

"Ouch, ouch, ouch!" Jon screams as he jumps around, shaking as if he is having a seizure.

Berry groans, his frizzy hair making him look more like a teddy bear than the ferocious beast he is.

Taryn taps the butt of his staff against the floor. The passive from Nature's Aegis gives him immunity to elemental effects, but he still lost fifteen percent of his health. "I'm not gonna lie, that was pretty awesome. Any idea how we are supposed to beat this thing?"

I give Destroyer a few spins against my palm. "Anybody in the mood for turtle stew?"

The turtle is back standing, and I take off running toward it with my warhammer raised over my shoulder. I bring it down on the turtle's shell with as much force as I can muster. The turtle retracts its body into the shell, and when I hit it, the turtle shoots off like a rocket, ricocheting off the wall and colliding with Berry. The shell hits Berry with enough force to knock him off his feet, plowing straight through him and hitting the wall again before zooming toward Jon.

The spindly man barely moves out of the way before the shell bounces off the wall. The turtle extends its legs, flipping itself into the air and landing with a thunk near the center of the room.

Well played, turtle. Well played indeed.

It stares at me with its piercing blue eyes, and I'm almost certain it smiles.

"What the hell? This thing is unkillable!" I fight back the urge to smash my warhammer into the floor.

Taryn's lightning doesn't work. The turtle destroyed my horrors, and my own attacks turn it into a cannonball. How are we supposed to defeat this thing?

"Maybe if we flip it over, the underside will be softer," offers Taryn.

That's actually a brilliant idea. "Alright, get ready. I'm going in!"

I rush toward the turtle, intent on flipping it upside down. When I'm a few steps away, it retracts into its shell. Perfect! I can flip it over without worrying about having my hand bitten off.

I reach out to grab the bottom of the shell, but it starts spinning. In a matter of seconds, the turtle shell spins in a blur. I try to stop it, but the rough edges of the shell rip into my palm, tearing at my flesh. I recoil at the pain, and blood streaks down my arm.

Before I have a chance to complain, the turtle barrels into me like a bumper car, knocking me to the floor. It zooms toward Jon, hovering inches off the ground.

Jon tries to escape, but the shell runs him down, smashing him into the wall and dropping half of his HP in a single hit. Berry and Taryn both rush to his aid as the shell continues bouncing around the circular room.

Jon hobbles delicately, supported on one side by Taryn.

I run over to them just as the shell stops spinning and the turtle emerges once again.

"I've got a plan, but it's going to take all three of you out of the fight."

"Dude, no way." Taryn shakes his head. "That thing will kill you."

"One more hit and it's going to kill Jon." I grab Taryn by the shoulder. "Trust me on this."

He nods.

"I need you to use Transform and turn into a duplicate of Berry. Jon, I want you on Berry's back. Then I want you to make as many clones as you can. One of them is going to ride Taryn. Scatter the others around the room."

"And what are you going to be doing?" asks Jon.

"I'm getting us the hell out of this dungeon."

I stalk toward the turtle with my hammer raised, and just as I predict, the turtle retracts into its shell. Destroyer smashes into the hard exterior, sending it off like a rocket once again. The reptilian projectile crushes into the knees of one of Jon's clones, hyperextending them and launching him like a rag-doll.

I watch as the shell hits the wall and ricochets. I follow the pattern as it hits another wall and another, waiting for the perfect moment to implement my plan.

The shell soars between both versions of Berry and Jon, and I'm not quite sure which one is which. The turtle hits the wall again and comes straight in my direction.

I stand my ground as it comes barreling toward me. When it is half a dozen feet away, I summon three horrors and explode them right as the shell makes impact. The force from the explosion flips the shell end over end, and it comes to a grating halt right beside me.

Turtle legs extend and grasp at the air as it tries to flip itself over. The underbelly of the beast is slick and shiny. The first hit with Destroyer does little damage, but as Inferno builds with each hit, growing hotter, the shell eventually cracks and the turtle's struggles cease.

Notifications flash across my vision, but I ignore them for now.

The blue flames on the wall change to orange, and the door into the room clicks open. A chest made of driftwood appears next to the turtle's corpse, right beside a portal that will take us to the entrance.

"How is everyone feeling?" I ask. I'm sure this is more action than Jon has seen in a while.

Taryn returns to his dwarven form and casts Restoration on Berry.

Jon chugs a health potion as he hobbles over. "Who cares about how I'm feeling. Let's see what's in the chest."

He shuffles past me and hovers over the weathered treasure.

"Go ahead; do the honors." I point at the chest. He's earned it.

He lifts the lid and a soft white glow emanates from within. A wide smile creeps across his face. "Nice!"

"What is it?" Asks Taryn.

"Man, this is so cool! Way better than any of the items I've found on my own." He grins from ear to ear.

"Alright, let's have a look." I reach down in the chest and find an assortment of items and take a moment to inspect each one.

Item. Halite Shield. A lightweight translucent shield capable of taking damage without reducing visibility.

The shield looks like a replica of the tortoise's shell. Salt crystals cover the edge and center, but the majority of the shield is completely see-through. The wearer could block an attack without losing any visibility of the attacker, or hide behind it as a battering ram. Not a bad item at all.

Item. Vial of Salt Gas. Covers an area with gas that reduces visibility and deals damage-per-second to anything that breathes it in.

The gas wiped out my horrors in short order. I wonder if this one has the same low-hanging density, or if it will work on larger foes?

Item. Greater Salt Crystal. A powerful mineral that can be used as a conduit to increase the range of spells.

I could attach the salt crystal to Destroyer, but that would mean giving up one of the stones I already have. I don't think the trade-off would be worth it. It'd probably be better for Jon or Taryn.

Item. Lucky Tortoise Foot. Increased chance of rare items and quests.

The dried-out tortoise foot is kind of gnarly, but I can't really argue with its effects. Better loot is always welcome.

I turn to Jon. "You saved our asses back in the first room. You should take the first pick."

"Really?" His eyes are wide with surprise.

"Absolutely. Welcome to the team."

He reaches in the chest and pulls out the tortoise foot. "I think this will be worth it down the road."

"Taryn, which item do you want?"

He puts his hands up. "Nah, man. You're next. We all would have been smashed to a pulp if it wasn't for you."

I take the Halite Shield because neither of them could use it. I'll probably end up trading or selling it at the next town. Maybe I'll donate it to the forest trolls. Taryn takes the Vial of Salt Gas and then gives the salt crystal to Jon. The enchanter is practically giddy with excitement.

All in all, Jon was a pretty valuable member to the team. Once we get Limery back, I think we'll be a hell of a squad.

We all take a moment to look over our notifications.

You have defeated a unique monster: Halite Tortoise.

You have defeated Salt Caves. Claim dungeon prize.

Congratulations! You have reached level 21. +1 stat point to distribute. +1 Strength and Constitution racial bonus. +1 ability point to distribute.

I use the ability point to unlock Champion once again. I still have two stat points, but I'm not quite sure where I want to allocate them just yet.

Jon and Berry both gain two levels from the fight, while Taryn gains one.

"Well, do you want to go back and clear the rest of the dungeon?" I ask. There's still the entire upper level we haven't checked.

Jon shakes his head. "I don't know about you guys, but I'd rather count my blessings and stop for lunch."

Taryn laughs. "Alright, man, but you're cooking."

CHAPTER TEN

CHAOS RISING

We're all in good spirits after clearing our first dungeon as a team. Night creeps in, and we sit around a small fire beneath a copse of trees eating roasted rabbit. Taryn leans against Berry, eyes closed, and Stompy snores softly behind us.

"What are you spending your new ability point on?" I ask Jon as I take a swig of water from the Brimming Tankard I picked up in Seascape.

Jon rips into a rabbit leg. "I haven't decided. I could upgrade one of the spells I already have, or I could learn to enchant something new."

"Like what?" I ask. Enchantment and illusion abilities are fascinating to me. To think that, with enough practice, Jon could craft a warhammer like Destroyer is mind-blowing. It would take years for him to grow that powerful, but that doesn't mean it can't be done. With dwarves having such long lifespans, no wonder they have been able to craft such wondrous items.

"Well, I could make my illusions more powerful. Either making Conceal Area harder to detect for smaller areas or making it capable of concealing larger areas to the same degree it does now. Or I could make illusions of living creatures instead of just doppelgängers." He tosses the leg bone to Berry. "If I had access to the right books, I could learn all kinds of enchantments for physical objects."

"Maybe you should save it for now. By the time we get to a city, you might have enough loot to trade for one of those books."

Jon scratches his chin. "That's not a bad idea." He reaches into his satchel and pulls out a salt crystal and a feather quill.

"What are you doing?" I ask.

"Figured I might make a few more flashlights before bed so that I can sell them at the next town we go to." He holds the baseball-sized rock in his hand and presses the quill to it. "Clear crystals provide the best light."

I move over and sit beside him. "How does it work?"

He displays the salt crystal in one hand and the quill in the other. "I etch the rune for light into the crystal with my pen, then I push some of my mana into it to seal the spell." He presses the tip of the quill to the crystal and it cuts a mark into the stone.

"How is the quill able to carve into the crystal?"

He smiles. "The tip is enchanted. It makes the process faster, otherwise it would take me hours to do a single simple enchantment."

I watch as he carves the rune into the translucent crystal. When the rune is complete, he presses his fingers to it and the rune glows bright white for a moment before fading away. Then the rock emits a gentle glow like a lantern.

Jon tosses the flashlight to me. "Tap the rune to turn it on and off."

I play with it for a few minutes, watching the rock flick on and off. "Does it ever run out of light?"

"Eventually. It doesn't drain a lot of mana to make them, but it should work for a few months before it needs recharging. There are enchantments for stronger lights, self-charging lights, or even ones that can cast a stream of light in a certain direction. I haven't learned any of those yet."

"Still, it's pretty cool. I bet you'll sell out." I hand it back to him.

A droning rattle grabs my attention and I look over to see drool trickling down Taryn's beard. So much for just resting his eyes.

Jon stares at me intently, opening his mouth a few times like a fish out of water. "Hey, man, can I ask you a question?"

"What's up?"

He taps the rock repeatedly, the light flashing on and off. "You weren't in the initial group with us. What did you do to end up here?"

I sit in silence for a moment, not sure what to say. No one but Taryn knows why I'm really here. The smart thing would be to keep my secrets to myself. There's no telling how the other heroes will view me after learning I'm in here because I yelled at someone online. These are hardened criminals. Well, maybe not Jon. He accidentally ran into a cop.

"Come on, it can't be that bad."

"It's not."

"Well, then lay it on me. I told you about my stupid mistake. What's yours?"

What harm could it do? Jon is a part of our party, so I decide to trust him.

"I got in trouble for cyberbullying." I wait for laughter, but instead, he just looks confused. I can only imagine how someone who has spent time in prison would think of me being there for calling someone names.

"Cyberbullying? Never heard of it."

"I told someone on my team to go kill themselves in a broadcast. Instead of giving me jail-time, I got sent here."

His brow furrows. "Broadcast? You some kind of celebrity or something?"

"Nah, nothing like that. I played video games online, and people watched me."

"Wait, you're just a kid?"

"I'm in college. Well, was in college."

He shakes his head in disbelief. "You're kidding me? You've got to be kidding me. They were going to send you to jail for something you said on the internet?"

"Technically, this is my sentence."

"Damn. The world ain't what it used to be. We used to call each other names just for fun when I was growing up. Seems like they are policing everything these days. You can't even fart without the government sniffing it."

I laugh at his joke. He may be right, but here we are in a game, where literally every move we make is recorded and broadcast on a feed above our pods. The only privacy we have are the thoughts in our heads, and I'm not even one hundred percent sure about that.

We retire for the night and take turns keeping watch. When it's my turn, I lean against Stompy's massive backside and listen to the sounds around me. The last embers of the fire crackle away, bugs rattle, and in the distance, an owl hoots in a melody with the howls of some untamed beast.

The sky overhead is full of millions of twinkling stars. As I watch them, I can't help but wonder how this could be a game. The work it must have taken for this much depth. It feels more real than anything I've ever experienced in the real world.

I don't care if I ever go back. My parents will be fine without me. In here, there are people relying on me, and for once in my life, it feels like I have a part to play in the fate of the world around me. It's like—

Something stirs behind me, interrupting my thoughts. I grab Destroyer and turn to find Taryn wiping the sleep from his eyes.

"Is it your turn already?" I ask.

He comes and sits behind me. "Not sure. I was having this terrible nightmare about the draugrs from the salt mines. I was trapped underneath a mountain of them while they ripped me apart." He shudders.

"Those things were pretty creepy." I laugh. "You were right, though. About Jon. He saved our asses in there. And I think he might view this game a lot differently going forward."

Taryn smiles, and his teeth catch the glow of the moon. "You brought it out of him. I know you don't see it, but when you really invest in someone, you have a way of getting the best out of them."

I'm surprised by his statement. I might have helped open Jon's eyes, but it was Taryn who believed in him, who wanted to give him a chance.

"He's only one guy, though." I pick up a twig and toss it into the fire. "We're going to need a lot more for what's coming. Hell, we're going to need a lot more just to get into Goldspire."

Taryn strokes his beard, the golden clasps jingling as they touch. "It will all work out. Now, go get some sleep. I can take it from here."

I wake to the smell of fried eggs and find Taryn cooking with a small iron pan over the fire. Jon sits beside him, enchanting more flashlights.

"I hope those aren't *your* eggs." I squint an eyelid at Taryn. There's no way I'm ready to eat something that came out of him while he was in bird form.

He shakes his head as he flips the eggs over. "First off, I transform into a male bird. Secondly, even if I could lay an egg, it would hardly be enough to eat." He places an egg on a small metal plate and shoves it toward me. "How about you be thankful that I scoured the trees for our breakfast while you were still snoring your life away."

He gives me a rude gesture as I take the plate. Point taken.

"Where'd you get all the cooking supplies?" I devour the egg in one bite.

"I picked them up before we left Treehaden. Thought it might be nice to try cooking something besides roasted meat for a change."

"Thanks for breakfast. Are you all about ready to get on the road?"

"I'm excited." Jon places his newest enchanted object in his bag and stands up. "Where are we going first? More dungeons?"

I pull up my map. There's a town between where we are and the next cluster of ley lines. "There's a town we can hit up to resupply. It might be a good spot to sell off some of your items as well."

We gather our things and set off for the next town. We make good time, thanks to Taryn casting Strong Wind while we travel. It doesn't allow for me to level my herbalism or other skills, but those aren't a priority right now. We stop in front of a wooden sign that displays the town's name, Narthensted, outside of the palisade.

Even though it is still daylight when we arrive, the entry is barred. I rap my fist against the wooden gate a few times before someone answers.

"What's yer business in Narthensted?" a gruff voice asks from the other side.

"We were hoping to buy and sell, maybe stay at your inn for the night." I spot a brown eye peeking through a slit in the wood. Something is definitely up with this place.

There's movement and shuffling as a board is removed from the other side of the gate. A bushy-bearded ivory dwarf pushes the door open a few feet and motions for us to come in. He wears a plain gray tunic and weathered boots, and his eyes look past us suspiciously as he ushers us in. He breathes heavily as he opens the door further for Berry and Stompy to enter.

"Hurry up, hurry up," he mumbles. Once we are all inside, he boards the gate again.

"Everything okay here?" I ask.

"These be dangerous times. All of our guards have not returned from Seascape, and there is word of undead roaming the Glossop Forest."

"Oh, great," moans Jon. "More zombies."

"So, it is true?" the dwarf asks with wide eyes.

"Calm down, brother." Taryn places a hand on the dwarf's shoulder. "We were in a dungeon. I can't speak for your forest, but if you would like, we can check it out for you."

"You'd do that? I know a lot of the women and children would sleep a lot more soundly if they knew we had heroes dealing with the threat."

The women and children, sure. "We'd be happy to help once we've finished our business here."

"Speak for yourself," says Jon.

"Come on, Jon. You're part of the team." I slap him on the back, and he stumbles forward.

Taryn takes Berry and Stompy to the stables, and we split up to handle our business.

Narthensted is a small town, but it has a few shops where we are able to sell our loot and resupply on food and health potions. Most of the buildings are either stone or wood, with thatched roofs. Their supply is limited after the massive influx of people to Seascape for the king's announcement, but we're able to grab the basics. I hold off on selling any of the more valuable items for when we come to a larger city.

While digging through my bag, I come across the Mysterious Green Egg I found in the castle. I'm still not sure what it does and when I try to analyze it further, all I see is a series of question marks. I drop it back in and go search for the others.

I find them both waiting outside of the Stedfast Inn

Jon jingles a bag of coins. "Not a bad haul. I should have been selling flashlights from the start instead of tricking kobolds into doing my dirty work."

"You don't say," mumbles Taryn before turning to me. "Want to grab a drink and see what we can find out about this haunted forest?"

We bypass the inn for now and go to a tavern called The Spotless Toad. After stepping inside, I think it should be called The Grimy Toad. The floors and tables are stained with a layer of dirt and grease. A thick fog of smoke coats the ceiling thanks to an ebony dwarf intensely smoking a hookah pipe. An ivory dwarf with a patchy beard and a boil on his nose stands behind the counter. He smiles, revealing a mouth full of yellow, crooked teeth.

"How can I help yous?" he asks.

"Three ales, please. We'll take a table in the corner." I drop a few coins on the bar, and we head to the back.

A group of dwarves sit at one table with dirt-stained clothing. They look like farmers. Taryn nods to them as we pass.

"This reminds me of some of the places I used to hang out back in the day." Jon winks.

I come to an abrupt halt when I spot a cloaked figure sitting in the corner, hood drawn over his eyes.

Jon runs into my back, splashing some of his ale on the floor. "Chod, what the heck?"

The cloaked figure wears red robes with a giant gash in the middle. A black chain hangs from his neck. I've seen this man before.

Richard Hummel
  Level 17
  Cleric

Human

He's a level lower than the last time I saw him, when he was partied up with Pressley the Knight as they attempted to open the portal in Seascape. When their plan backfired, it created the chaos that allowed Jude and Glenn to march on the portal.

They are the reason Jude and Glenn escaped *Isle of Mythos.*

My heart pounds, and I grip Destroyer tight against my palm.

"There's no need for that." Richard sits forward and points to his chest. The spot where Pressley stabbed him. "I've paid my dues."

I step forward until I'm towering over his table. The other dwarves have stopped talking and I'm sure they are watching every move I make.

"Maybe you paid your dues to Pressley, but what about all of the innocent dwarves that died because of your actions?"

I'm surprised when he lifts his hood and two vibrant blue eyes stare back at me. The man has a chiseled jawline and short blond hair. "My actions? Did I brainwash them and force them to march into a heavily-guarded regional event? Did I summon the monsters or cast the spells that sent them to their graves?" He leans back against his chair. "I'd watch where I were throwing stones if I were you, Mr. Troll."

I lift Destroyer, ready to bring it down on his weaseling little head.

"Chod," Taryn calls to me.

"What?" I whip my head around, spitting out the word with more ferocity than I mean to, and Taryn takes a step back.

He cuts his eyes at me. "It's not his fault. Jude and Glenn are the enemy."

I lower my weapon.

Richard points to the chair next to him. "Have a seat."

I take a deep breath, knowing that if I don't, I'll smash my hammer through the table. My heartbeat lowers and I try to rationally view the situation. Whatever Richard and Pressley had planned, it was separate from Jude and Glenn.

I take a seat at the table. "So what happened?"

He lets out a low chuckle. "Chaos happened."

That's right; he serves the god of chaos. "What exactly does that mean?"

"Buy a down-on-his-luck cleric a drink and I'll give you all the details."

I wave over the bartender and order another ale. A moment later, he sets it on the table and Richard takes a long swig.

He sets his mug on the table. "You don't know much about clerics, do you?"

"No, not really." I don't know much outside of what I was offered to play as a troll. I'm aware that there are multitudes of classes and races still waiting to be unlocked.

"What about you two?" He glances between Jon and Taryn and they both shake their heads. "Figures. Why choose the path of religion in a game like this?"

He twists from side to side, cracking his back, before continuing. "Allow me to enlighten you. Different classes have various ways of leveling up and gaining experience. For most classes, it's raiding dungeons and killing monsters. Clerics are primarily a quest-based class. We can level the other way, but we very rarely have offensive abilities for ourselves. We do make great supports, however. Each cleric has a primary deity that they serve, and when an opportunity presents itself to please the deity, a quest appears. Experience is given upon completion of the quest."

He takes another long draw of his ale and snaps his fingers for another.

"And that's why you were with Pressley?" I tilt up my glass, finishing my own drink. My mood has lightened, and my head has started to buzz around the edges.

"More or less. We were in the same town when the regional event occurred. I received a quest to help him and I took it."

"Did you know your spell would backfire when he attacked the portal?" asks Taryn.

"I had no idea, but I've learned to expect the unexpected."

"Any idea where he is?" I ask.

"Pressley? Your guess is as good as mine. I've heard the rumors of undead in the forest, but I don't really have a desire to get stabbed in the chest again." His fingers run across the slit of exposed flesh in his torn robe.

If he's not looking to party up with Pressley again, maybe I can at least convince him to join our cause. We're going to need all the heroes we can get. I don't trust him one hundred percent, especially considering who he serves, but I didn't trust Jon in the beginning either.

"You know the portal in Seascape was reopened?"

His mouth curls at the edge. "I received the notification."

"Jude and Glenn escaped into one. We're not sure which, but I'm gathering forces to go through and warn the other leaders. King Orso believes that the dark wizard is still alive after all these years, hiding behind a closed portal somewhere. He fears an attack is imminent and we need to be prepared. Will you join us?"

Richard drains the rest of his ale in one gulp. "Oh, I wish I could, but unfortunately, I have prior commitments." He gets up and heads to the door. Hand on the door, he turns back in our direction. "Thanks for the drinks."

The door slams behind him as he leaves.

I have no idea where he's heading, but I'm certain trouble won't be far behind.

CHAPTER ELEVEN

GLOSSOP FOREST

Jon looks me in the eye, arms crossed. "Let me get this straight. You want us to go into a haunted forest at sunset?"

"What's the big deal? Taryn and I can both see at night, and you have your light. We'll be fine. Plus, there's no proof it's haunted. It could have been Pressley that scared them." If there's a chance I can find the death knight before he moves on, I want to try. It's very rare to run into another hero, so if he's here, I can't squander the opportunity.

"I'm leaning with Jon on this one." Taryn stands beside the enchanter. "Who knows what kind of monsters and creepy crawlies come out at night in there?"

"Bro, you're a druid. You're supposed to be one with the forest. Don't think of them as monsters. Think of them as potential pets."

A devious grin spreads across his face. "You know, that's not a half-bad—"

"Oh, come on!" Jon puts his fists over his eyes, and for a moment, I think he's going to scream. "Not you, too."

"Two against one, let's go." I give him my best smile.

Jon crouches down, covers his face, and groans. "Fine, both of you owe me one."

We stop by the stables for Berry and Stompy and set off toward Glossop Forest. It's rife with ley lines, so either there is a dungeon or it's full of magical activity like the troll village. Either way, I'm excited to see what happens. If Pressley is there, then it has to be worth it. All he cares about is gold.

Thanks to Strong Wind, we travel the few miles to the forest quick enough. The road bypasses the forest entirely, so we are forced to make our own path once we enter the woods.

The sun dips closer to the horizon, casting the world in shades of lilac and tangerine, but as soon as we step into the trees, it's all grays and blacks.

With my night vision, I can see in complete darkness. Dwarves have darkvision, allowing them to see in dimly-lit areas like the forest, but not complete blackness like a cave or tunnel. With Jon around, there's no need for either. He activates his staff, the diamond tip glowing like a lantern and reflecting off the eyes of silent watchers in the trees.

Jon keeps close to me. So close that he steps on the back of my heel several times before I tell him to back off. My horrors lead the way, grumbly little minions that will take the brunt of any surprise attacks.

The forest is creepy at night, I'll give them that. Branches snap in the distance and animals scurry in the trees. Weird noises echo from the forest's depths, and due to Jon's light, I have a hard time seeing past twenty yards.

I've spent time in the forest ever since arriving on the island, so I know the biggest fears are the ones that linger inside the mind.

"How do you suppose we find this guy anyhow?" Jon pushes a low branch out of the way.

I shrug. "Follow the sounds of chaos and destruction?"

"I'll have Berry keep his nose alert for any unusual smells." Taryn rides on the back of his beloved bear.

Stompy tramples through the forest, making enough noise to alert anything nearby.

I come to a stop when I see a pair of glowing eyes in the distance. The green dots focus on me for a moment before disappearing.

"What is it?" Jon steps a little closer.

"Some wild animal. I think we scared it off." I pull up my map. Ley lines run throughout the forest, one right beneath us.

I freeze in place as several of my horrors vanish instantly. I'm not sure why since they had more health than some of the others that remain.

"Guys, something just killed three of my horrors." I search the vicinity for signs of a threat but see nothing.

Stompy unleashes a bellowing trumpet, and I turn to see his back leg vanishing into a pool of complete darkness beneath the earth. He struggles to pull himself free as tendrils of dark energy wrap around his leg.

Lightning crashes into the darkness and it recoils back into the earth. Several more of my horrors vanish.

"Run!" shouts Taryn. "It's darksand. Get moving or it will devour us whole."

I don't waste any time, running deeper into the forest. Something cold wraps around my leg, stopping me in my tracks. I fall forward and my tusks smash into the ground.

A dark black substance creeps up my leg. I smash it with Destroyer, but it does nothing. My mana and health both begin to drain, and I struggle for my freedom. I focus on the darksand, hoping for any knowledge that might help me escape.

Darksand. *Level 18. This sentient, carnivorous sand thrives in darkness, absorbing the life force and mana of anything unlucky enough to be caught in its grasp.*

Jon rushes to my aid, pointing the tip of his staff at the black goo. It recoils from the light, releasing me.

"Get up!" he yells.

We stampede through the forest like a herd of buffalo until we empty into a small clearing.

"Holy shit! What was that?" I gasp.

Jon has his hands on his knees as he pants for air. "That's why you don't go into the forest at night."

Taryn examines Stompy's leg, making sure he's okay. "It's called darksand. It's like quicksand, except it's sentient and eats you alive, draining your life force. This place must be crawling with magical energy for it to be here."

"Weird. I've never heard mention of it in the troll forest."

"It's pretty rare, from what I've read. And it needs a mana source to survive, so it's likely any that was in the troll forest died off when the ley lines were blocked." Taryn pets Stompy on the shoulder, trying to calm the startled beast.

I know how he's feeling. "We'll need to keep an eye out going forward. How do we kill it?"

Taryn scratches his head. "I'm not sure how to kill it completely. I think they only die when their mana and health are completely depleted. For something that can separate like sand, that's easier said than done. I know it recoils from light and heat."

"It'd be nice to have Limery right about now." I wonder where the little guy is.

Jon stands up, finally breathing normally again. "What the hell is a Limery? You keep saying that word, but I have no idea what it means."

Taryn and I both burst out laughing.

"Limery is an imp. He's small and red and powerful as hell. He's one of my best friends, and he's gotten us out of some sticky situations." I smile. I really do miss the little guy.

Jon cocks an eyebrow. "One of your best friends is an NPC?"

I know it sounds crazy to say that one of the beings I am closest to in the entire world is a string of code I've known for a couple of months, but it's true. Is it really any different than someone bonding with a plant or pet? Just because he was artificially created doesn't mean he doesn't have thoughts and a personality.

Instead of telling Jon all of this, I just say, "Wait until you meet him."

I summon more horrors, and we go deeper into the forest. Jon leads the way this time, using his light to make sure we don't step into any darksand again. My horrors flank him on both sides.

He comes to a stop underneath a massive oak tree and steps back a few paces. "Guys, the trees are moving." He points above to branches that bend and move like appendages.

"It's okay. They're infused with mana. As long as you don't try to harm them, we should be fi—"

A limb smacks me on the side of the head and stars dance across my vision. I stumble forward and hear Taryn grunt behind me.

"The forest is trying to kill us!" yells Jon.

Another limb swings at me, its branches curled into a fist. I duck at the last second, leaving it swiping at air. A group of horrors get smashed into the ground by another limb. Something has to be causing the trees to behave so violently, but what?

"Let's get out of here!" I turn to find Taryn dangling in the air, held around the midsection by a large branch.

The branch lifts him higher, and then thrusts him toward the ground. His dreadlocks whip as he's rocketed toward the forest floor. I equip Destroyer and jump in the air, smashing my warhammer into the branch. It connects, breaking the branch in half and raining down splintered wood as Taryn falls to the ground with a thud.

I pick him up and toss him onto Stompy's back. "Get out of here!" I yell, smacking the moulhaug on the backside.

Jon has used his ultimate ability, and a half-dozen versions of him lay scattered on the ground broken and bleeding. They all grimace and clutch at wounded body parts. I have no idea which one is the real Jon.

Next to me, branches continue to smash into my horrors. A group of horrors band together and pin one branch to the ground.

"Jon!" I call out, trying to find the real enchanter.

"Over here," a weak voice replies.

Jon is pinned to the ground by a collection of smaller branches. I rush to his aid, narrowly dodging swinging limbs like a blue-skinned acrobat. Destroyer smashes the limbs that pin him to the ground, and I toss Jon over my shoulder, running in the direction of Taryn and Stompy.

I find them in another clearing. Stompy is covered in scrapes and gashes. Taryn has a knot on his forehead seeping blood. I sit Jon down beside them and search my bag for health potions to hand out.

"Where's Berry?" Taryn clutches his forehead.

"I thought he was with you." I look around, but there is no sign of the bear. He must be back at the trees. "Stay here and heal. I'll go find him."

My head still throbs from the blow to the back of the head. I bound through the forest, scanning every tree I pass for signs of movement. I can't help but think I may have made a mistake coming here at night. Jon isn't prepared for this. I keep thinking we can do things like we did with Limery around, but the truth is that we can't. His value can't just be replaced. Without his quick speed and fire magic, things are a hell of a lot more difficult.

I come to the spot where we were attacked. There are broken branches and upturned soil everywhere. It looks like a warzone. Several of the branches clench in my direction, daring me to come near. All my horrors are gone, and there is no sign of Berry anywhere.

There's so much debris from the fight that it's hard to make any sense of the situation. The upturned soil makes it impossible to search for tracks.

I stand back, careful to not get too close to the swinging limbs. It appears that only the trees within a small circle are mana-infused. Their roots must go directly into the ley line.

I'm about to go back to Taryn and the others when I hear a roar nearby, a roar I've heard hundreds of times.

Bolting through the trees, I cast more horrors and ready Destroyer for what might be waiting. The roars grow louder and more vicious, and I can't help but wonder what foul creature Berry is fighting. I come upon a ravine, and the roars echo around me louder than ever, but there is no sign of the bear anywhere.

The roars fade and a shrill laugh cuts through the silence. Atop the ravine, a shriveled old lady looks down on me with dirty yellow eyes. She has green skin, long gray hair, and a hooked nose. Her robes are tattered and covered in dirt and moss. Her laugh reveals a set of crooked brown teeth.

I focus on her and realize what a mistake I've made.

Green Hag. *Level 21. Although appearing as frail and weak, hags are anything but. They have ravenous appetites and use their powers of mimicry and illusions to lure unsuspecting adventurers to their doom. Three or more hags in one location becomes a covey, unlocking spells a single hag cannot perform alone.*

I should never have split the party.

CHAPTER TWELVE
NEVER SPLIT THE PARTY

The hag leaps from the top of the ravine with amazing finesse for such a withered old lady. She lands right in front of me, grabbing me around the biceps with her gnarled fingers. I'm surprised by how much it hurts. I try to sling her off, but her grip is powerful. Blackened nails dig into my skin, drawing blood, and rancid breath assaults me as she cackles madly.

"It was foolish to enter the forest at night. Something might try to eat you." She licks her lips, and there's malevolence in her black eyes.

"I'm not afraid of monsters," I snarl. "I am one."

I activate Bite and sink my tusks into her shoulder. The hag cries out, releasing me from her grip. Sour blood fills my mouth and I fight back the urge to gag. When I spit it out, it's as black as her soulless eyes.

I use Intimidation, staring her down and momentarily confusing her. I need to get away and back to the others. At level twenty-one, she's just as deadly as I am. I turn to run, and her shrill voice cuts through the air.

"Spirits of the earth, I summon thee. Capture the interloper!"

Come on, lady, I'm just trying to find a missing bear. No need to bring in backup.

The ground shakes on both sides of the ravine. Dirt breaks away from the embankment, crumbling to the ground and revealing two stone golems buried within. The golems pry themselves free, and more dirt collapses into the imprints they leave behind.

Rock Golem. *Level 18. Unintelligent elemental power, golems tend to the wishes of those who control them.*

Great, just what I needed—a hag and her minions. I summon a few minions of my own.

The golem to my right swings at me with its boulder of a fist, but I'm fast enough to dodge the attack. It stumbles forward and I smash Destroyer into its backside. A chunk of rock flakes off from the blow.

Good to know that I can break them down—another reason I'm glad I took the warhammer over the axe.

I look for the hag, but she is nowhere to be seen. The second golem charges me, and I attempt to climb out of the ravine. My feet slip in the soil, and I slide back down just as it tackles me to the ground.

The monster is solid rock, and I struggle to free myself underneath its weight. There's a crash, and then I sink deeper into the earth as the other golem dogpiles on top of me.

Their combined weight is too much for me to lift. They crush my ribs, making it hard for me to breathe.

I summon three horrors to my right and explode them, creating a crater beside me. When the cooldown is up, I repeat the process, making the hole deeper and deeper.

After the third round of explosions, I activate Berserker Rage. The added stats give me just enough strength to roll the golems off me. With a heaving push, they fall into the crater I created. They try to climb out, but they weigh too much. The soil crumbles around them as they attempt to scale the embankment.

The hag cackles behind me, and I turn just as a blast of green energy hits me in the chest, taking out fifteen percent of my health. Destroyer falls from my grip, and I tumble into the crater with the trapped golems.

The golems clobber me with their powerful arms, dropping my HP with each hit. I do my best to fight back, but it's a losing battle. Claw scrapes against their tough bodies, barely doing any damage. Using Bite means risking a broken tusk, and Berserker Rage is on cooldown.

I summon horrors and explode them against the golems. They do damage, but the cooldown is too long for me to destroy the golems with my horrors alone. That's when I remember I have Champion.

Champion. *Summon a copy of the most recent enemy you have defeated. Decays 10% every minute out of combat. Cost: 50% of mana pool. Cooldown: 6 hours.*

It will deplete half my mana pool, but I have enough mana that it shouldn't be a problem. The bigger issue is the six-hour cooldown, but it won't matter if I die in this hole.

I cast Champion and a copy of the Halite Tortoise appears in front of me along with a list of notifications. I don't have time to check them in the chaos, so I push them aside.

The tortoise is indistinguishable from the real thing, all the way down to its piercing blue eyes.

The golems switch their focus to the turtle. One of the golems smashes his fist into the translucent shell just as the turtle retracts into the safety of its carapace. The golem's fist connects with the jagged exterior and a crack shoots up the golem's arm. If Destroyer couldn't crack the shell, what luck would stone have? That's when I remember my new shield that I looted from the salt mines.

I equip the Halite Shield from my expandable bag, and the see-through shell allows me to keep complete view of the golems while remaining behind its safety.

The golem punches the turtle again and its fist splits in two. The second golem charges me, and I use the shield to deflect its attack. As it punches my shield, flakes of rock explode into the air. The golems continue to clobber my shield and the turtle's shell until their arms crumble up to the elbow.

"Imbeciles!" the hag screeches. "Must I do everything myself?"

She lifts her hand and a green aura surrounds it. She thrusts her hand forward, sending out a beam of energy. It heads straight for me. I cower behind my shield when I hear a click from the turtle behind me.

My mana drops suddenly. One of the tiles on the turtle's shell opens and draws the green energy toward it, suctioning it inside. The tile closes and the shell shakes for a moment, glowing a bright green, then three tiles around the base open, shooting three beams at my opponents.

A beam blasts into each of the golems, and their stone bodies return to the earth. A third beam hits the hag, stunning her in place.

I take the opportunity to use the golems' bodies as a ladder to climb out of the hole. I don't waste time searching for Destroyer, instead jumping on the downed hag. I activate Claw and Bite, ripping into her rotten flesh. By the time the stun wears off, she's already dead.

I fall to my knees, visibly shaking as adrenaline pumps through my veins.

Holy shit, that was close.

The Halite Tortoise attempts to climb out of the crater with no luck. I have no choice but to leave it there as its health decays by the minute.

"You saved my life. Too bad I'll never be able to summon you again." Now that I defeated the hag, she's next up once the cooldown for Champion resets.

Something whimpers not too far from where I am, and I go to inspect. I find Berry pinned to the ground by a massive network of vines. He looks at me with panicked eyes, unable to move.

"Don't worry, buddy. I'll set you free."

I use my claws to cut through the vines. They've dug so deep into his skin that he is bleeding in several places. Once I've removed enough vines, he's able to break free. Half his health is gone, but he seems to be okay as he licks my knuckles.

"Did the mean old hag trap you in these vines?" I ask him, scratching behind his ears, but he just licks at his wounds. "Taryn will get you fixed up once we find him."

Berry's ears perk up at the sound of his master's name.

I take a moment to look over the notifications from during and after the fight.

*You have summoned **Halite Tortoise**. You have summoned a copy of a unique monster.*

The following abilities will drain directly from your mana pool.

__Salt Fog.__ Halite Tortoise releases a dense, unbreathable gas that deals damage per second to its victims.

__Consume and Destroy.__ The shell of the Halite Tortoise will open, consuming magical energy and dispersing it back at enemies.

Spiral. *The Halite Tortoise retracts into its shell, spinning in a circle and making it impossible to grab.*

I receive a fair amount of experience from my encounter with the hag. Not enough for a new level, but it moves me much closer than if I had tackled it with the others. Surprisingly, there's not a single item to loot aside from her tattered clothing, so I track down Destroyer and head to find the others.

———

Berry and I hobble into the clearing where Jon, Taryn, and Stompy are still recovering from the first encounter.

"What the hell happened to you two?" Taryn jumps to his feet and rushes over. He immediately begins casting Restoration on Berry.

"I ran into a hag. She'd trapped Berry, and I think she was planning on eating him." I go on to tell the rest of the story about the golems and how I was able to defeat them.

"I told you it was a bad idea coming here at night." Jon throws his hands up in the air. "But what do I know?"

"Alright, alright. You were right. Happy?" I walk over to a tree stump and take a seat. "We're here now, though, so we might as well see it out. Pressley has got to be around here somewhere."

Jon picks at a rip in his robe. "Is this guy really worth it? Is having him on our side worth possibly dying?" He shakes his head and sits beside me. "I mean, I just started leveling up. I don't want to lose all my progress."

I understand his frustration. Jon has spent the majority of his time here being an under-leveled loner. At least I had Limery around even when everyone was trying to kill me.

"Listen, I don't want to die. I don't want any of you to die either, but this is the path we are going down if you choose to stay with our party. I've made promises that I intend to keep. Something big is coming to Mythos. Something we need to be prepared for. I know you haven't had a chance to see these people like we do, but if we don't gather forces for when the time comes, they could all die. And they won't respawn." I sit there for a moment, letting the words hang in the air. "Do you really want to be stuck in a game where all hope is lost, where darkness wins? If so, is this place any better than prison?"

No one speaks for a long moment, and the only sound is the voice of the forest.

Jon nods. "Alright, we'll do it your way."

Time to go find us a death knight.

CHAPTER THIRTEEN

THE DEATH KNIGHT RISES

After healing up, we prepare to journey deeper into the forest. Everyone is on edge after our first battle, and every shadow looms as a potential threat. We walk cautiously, inspecting the forest before moving along. We're here to find Pressley, not to level up or engage in battles with the local flora and fauna.

Truth be told, I'll be happy if I never see another hag again.

The deeper we go, the more difficult it becomes to avoid the forest's monsters. We're forced to fight a group of spiders that refuse to leave us be, and we almost run into a minefield of darksand trying to escape the ravenous pincers of the spiders.

We're following a well-worn path when suddenly a streak of green light ignites the sky. A gust of wind hits us head-on like a tidal wave before the forest sits in a stunned silence.

"What the hell was that?" Taryn gazes at the streak of light high above the trees.

"No idea, but it can't be good." I grip Destroyer and strengthen my resolve. "So, naturally, that's where we need to go."

Jon sighs audibly beside me, but he doesn't complain.

We follow the glowing green beam like a guiding light. The closer we get, the more the aura seeps out into the forest, casting everything in its eerie glow. Grunts and explosions grow louder until we come upon the source of the chaos.

Three hags stand near one another, and the giant green aura makes perfect sense. I remember part of the description for the hag I defeated. *Three or more hags in one location become a covey, unlocking spells a single hag cannot perform alone.* This can't be good.

A forcefield of energy surrounds the covey as they cackle madly. Pressley the Death Knight stands across from them in all his glory.

. . .

Pressley Allen
   Level 25
   Death Knight
   Human

He's a far cry from the gallant knight I saw at the jewelry shop in Lynchton, but he is stronger than ever and looks like a total badass. He's already gained another level since Seascape, making him the highest-level hero I've seen. His silver armor is now a dark gray, with chainmail as black as night underneath. Dark energy radiates from his body, and the slits in his helm are full of darkness. Deep purple sparks trail up and down his glimmering obsidian sword.

He's surrounded by a group of skeleton warriors. One of them runs at the hags, but when it hits the green barrier, its bones disassemble and fall to the ground in a clatter. Pressley grunts, raising his hand as another skeleton charges. This one carries a rusty dagger. It swipes at the shield, and a blast of green energy explodes, sending more bones rattling to the ground.

As I look around, I realize what a dire situation we've stumbled upon. Two massive ogres stand inside the shielded area with the hags. They wear armor made from bones, and each one has a glowing medallion around its neck. The bones look like they belonged to dwarves or humans. There are also several huts in the area, constructed from a mixture of mud and bones. The entire area looks like a graveyard.

Pressley lifts his left hand and a black aura surrounds it. The aura grows larger as his health ticks down. He must be powering the spell with blood magic! The ball of infernal energy swirls in his palm like a fireball composed of pure darkness. His health drops to ninety percent and he unleashes the blast of energy. It hurls at the shield, exploding like thunder against its surface. A tiny crack forms at the site of impact.

"Holy shit!" gasps Jon.

I couldn't have said it better myself. He's even stronger than I thought.

The hags inside the shield raise their arms in unison. The forcefield pulses for a moment, and another gust of air rips through the forest.

Dozens of angry eyes appear in the darkness surrounding us, reflecting the green light. They grow bigger as their hosts approach.

"He's going to die." Taryn steps beside me. "There's no way he can handle all of them."

Taryn is right. The three hags are each level twenty-one. The two ogres are level eighteen. Not to mention whatever they just called in as reinforcement. I don't care how strong Pressley is, he can't defeat them all. And there's no telling where he set his spawn point. If he dies, it's possible I'll never see him again.

A mangy wolf steps into the light of the forcefield and lunges at Pressley. The death knight spins like a dancer, with speed no one that size should have, and slashes his sword at the beast. There's a brief yelp before the wolf's head falls to the forest floor.

The ogres step through the forcefield wielding clubs made from the bones of some great beast. The skeleton warriors charge the ogres, bones rattling as they run. Wolves, warthogs, and giant spiders leap from the darkness, their glowing eyes set on Pressley.

"We need to help him!" I shout as I run into battle.

"What the hell am I supposed to do?" yells Jon.

"Be useful!" I don't have time to hold his hand. Not for this. We're already massively out-leveled, even with Pressley, and Jon needs to figure this out by himself. The time for coddling is over.

The hags hide behind the safety of their forcefield while the minions of the forest do their dirty work. Well, two can play at that game. My horrors rush into battle by my side while I unleash devastation. A giant snake slithers along the ground and I smash it into the earth. Its skull crushes beneath my warhammer. Horrors swarm the lower-level monsters that emerge from the forest, and I summon more as quickly as I am able.

Pressley turns in my direction as a Horror of Power gores a spider's abdomen with its tusk. Green ichor drips from the open wound.

"What are you doing?" His voice is deep and distorted, like he's calling from the end of a cave.

"We're here to help. We can talk later, but first, what is it you're after?"

A bolt of lightning rips through the trees, stunning a wolf and setting a bush on fire. The forest is pure chaos as skeletons, horrors, and wild beasts fight it out.

"I'm here for the hags. They use a magical gem called a hag eye to control the ogres and other creatures. Help me retrieve it, and I will hear you out." He stabs a spider between the pincers and a streak of green goo spurts into the air.

"How do we get through the forcefield?" Destroyer hits a warthog in the ribs, sending it tumbling across the battlefield.

"I'm not sure." His sword glows purple, and when he stabs a wolf, his health shoots up a few ticks.

One of the ogres grunts as it swings its bone club. The strike rips through my horrors, sending many of them soaring through the trees.

Berry's muzzle is coated with blood as he fights with a pack of wolves. They have him surrounded, but Taryn charges in riding Stompy, and the moulhaug uses his massive horn like a sledgehammer, knocking them aside.

This gives me an idea. "Taryn, try to charge the forcefield with Stompy!"

Pressley looks over in my direction, a spider speared on the end of his sword. "Stompy?" His sinister voice is full of disbelief.

"Don't ask."

Jon's clones run around like headless chickens, while his voice echoes from every corner of the battlefield. I have no idea where the real Jon is, but he's causing a lot of chaos.

Stompy paws at the earth, and his massive horn swings from side to side. He lets out an angry snort, and Taryn lifts his staff in the air. Stompy builds up speed as he runs, until the trees are shaking with each step. He lowers his horn and collides with the hag's forcefield.

The shield bounces Stompy straight back and Taryn flies from his saddle, smashing headfirst into the forcefield. He looks shaken up as he crawls to his feet.

A spider descends from a tree above him, dangling by its thread. Its pincers click as it reaches for the dwarf. Taryn has no idea he's about to become arachnid food.

I lift a Horror of Vitality by the horn and prepare to toss it, but a streak of purple energy shoots across the forest, hitting the spider and draining its HP. It falls to the ground and its legs curl up in its final embrace.

"Are you going to watch or are you going to fight?" Pressley's voice draws me back to task at hand.

His health is down to seventy-five percent. Did he just blow a quarter of his HP to save Taryn?

The ogre unleashes a mighty roar, and the bone armor it wears rattles. I ready my warhammer to fight, when Pressley steps up beside me.

"I'll handle him. You focus on the others." He lifts his sword above his shoulder, ready to attack.

This is his show, so I leave him to it. I jump in the fray with my horrors, crushing skulls and taking names. As the battle rages on, I start to have fun. It all becomes a beautiful dance of devastation.

I summon a Horror of Power, and it doubles the damage of my next attack. I swing, crushing warthog ribs and adding a stack of Inferno to Destroyer. Then I summon Horror of Vitality on my nearest enemy. The passive slow buys me time to get in position before summoning Horror of Finesse. The bonus from summoning it grants me healing on my next attack, repairing any glancing damage I may have taken in the fracas.

I repeat this process until Destroyer is glowing a vibrant red. Every swing I take cooks flesh and singes hair. Berry and I fight back to back, bringing pain and suffering on everything around us. I lose myself in the glory of battle and for the first time in a while, I let go of the thoughts of protecting Jon and Taryn. They are perfectly capable of taking care of themselves. I let the barbarian in me take control.

A guttural cry captures my attention. I turn around to find Pressley standing over the ogre as he drives his sword through its chest. The second ogre has retreated behind the safety of the forcefield.

Taryn sits atop Stompy, using his staff's special ability like a whip and cutting the thread of any spiders that try to sneak down on the battlefield. When the spiders fall, my horrors and Pressley's skeletons swarm them like ants on a fallen ice cream cone.

The last of the green-eyed monsters falls and the forest is quiet. The only sound is the buzzing of the forcefield. The hags are no longer laughing. Instead, they look upon us with hatred in their black, soulless eyes.

Not only are the hags quiet, but so is Jon. His bodies lay strewn across the ground. Some are missing limbs, others are gored or covered in bite marks. One has his head completely caved in.

I search for the real Jon. I expect him to step out from behind a tree, complaining about how scary and dangerous this all was, but he's nowhere to be found.

"What are you looking for?" asks Pressley.

"The enchanter, Jon, I don't see him."

Taryn jumps down from Stompy and starts checking the bodies. "I don't know how to tell if one of them is really him."

"You don't think he..." I don't finish the sentence, letting the words trail off into the ether.

I promised Jon I would take care of him. I told him that he was part of the team, then I left him alone in the fight. I thought he could take care of himself, but I was wrong. He'd only just learned to fight as a team. This was too soon.

"I'm sorry," I whisper.

I should have done better. If he never joins up with us again, I won't blame him. Some kind of leader I turned out to be.

"Guys." Jon's voice echoes around us. "Can one of you help me get down from here?"

I look around, but there's still no sign of him. "Where are you?"

"Oh, sorry. Look up."

I do as he says, but there are only trees. I search the branches for signs of him, but there's nothing. Am I imagining his voice?

Suddenly, there's a shimmer in the trees and Jon appears on one of the branches, clinging to the trunk. "I cast Conceal so that none of the monsters could see me, but I'm kind of afraid of heights."

Laughter runs through me. Deep from in my belly, it pours out, echoing off the trees. Taryn joins in, and I'm sure Pressley thinks we're insane.

I was right after all. My instincts were right. The little thief can take care of himself.

I climb up the tree, and he wraps his arms around my neck. A moment later, we land safely on the ground.

Pressley grunts. "Now, if you all are done, I'd like to return to the objective at hand."

He sheaths his sword and lifts both hands slowly into the air. A black aura surrounds his hands; it pulses as tendrils of dark energy whip at the air. The tendrils grasp for one another.

Pressley's health trickles down as the energy grows. The tendrils coil together, forming a ball of darkness between the death knight's hands. It continues to grow until it takes up the majority of his chest.

With a flourish, Pressley sends the energy hurling at the dead ogre lying on the ground. It penetrates the ogre's body and the energy disperses within.

What in the hell did I just watch?

A moment later, the dead ogre stirs. It opens its eyes, and they are void of all recognition. Pressley bends over and rips the medallion that hangs from its neck, and the ogre rises to its feet.

Pressley's health has fallen to fifty percent after summoning the monster.

"Are you okay to fight?" I ask.

"I'll be fine." He clenches his fist. "Let's finish this."

I nod. The sooner we settle this, the better.

CHAPTER FOURTEEN
AN EYE FOR AN AYE

My hands tingle as I hold my warhammer. The green forcefield shimmers in front of me, while on the other side, three hags and an ogre stare at us with hatred.

These hags are less talkative than the one I met earlier. I don't know if it is because they are focused on maintaining the forcefield, or if there is more at play. From where I'm standing, it looks like they are in some sort of demented Halloween snow-globe. The ogre smacks his bone club against his hand, as if telling us to come get some.

All in due time. We have our own ogre, freshly resurrected by the death knight to my side. Pressley used half of his health to summon the creature, so I hope it was worth it. If Champion wasn't on cooldown, I could have landed the killing blow and summoned a second ogre, but we're not that lucky. Pressley still has a handful of skeleton warriors, and I have a half dozen horrors. With Jon, Taryn, Stompy, and Berry, we have the numbers advantage, but I have no idea what these hags have up their sleeves. Three of them makes it a covey, unlocking special powers, like the forcefield that's keeping us from going in there right now and ending this.

Pressley unsheathes his sword and steps in front of the glowing green shield. "Let's tear this bitch down."

One of the hags turns her head toward Pressley. "Leave now and we will grant you safe passage. No one need die."

Hmmm, that's odd. Taryn must agree because he furrows his brow. I've never seen a monster offer to let someone go before. Do they have a sense of self-preservation? In a game like this, why wouldn't they?

"You know I can't do that." Pressley's demonic voice sends a shiver down my spine. He raises his sword overhead.

I've got a feeling his endgame here is bigger than just loot and glory.

I ready Destroyer. There's a brief moment where no one is breathing or talking, where my horrors aren't grumbling, and the buzz from the forcefield is like sitting too close to an old television. Then our weapons fall.

I summon a Horror of Power and my attack hits for double. The warhammer crashes against the forcefield and recoils hard against my hand. I quickly swing again, gaining stack after stack of Inferno until the hammerhead is glowing a vibrant red.

Lightning crashes into the forcefield from the other side. The zombie ogre's bone club rattles with each hit. We attack the barrier with everything we've got, but still it holds.

Destroyer glows bright red as I hammer repeatedly. I summon horrors when I'm able, and each one claws and rams against the forcefield. I hit the dome again and a crack shoots out like a spider vein.

The hags raise their hands and a fresh gust of wind rips into us. My horrors and some of the skeletons are blown away. The crack spreads as I continue to bludgeon the forcefield.

"Not much longer!" Pressley's sword hits with an explosion and a crack shoots from the point of impact and connects with my own.

"Everyone, get back!" I order.

They step back and I send all my horrors to the forcefield. They climb upon one another, forming a horror wall from Pressley's crack to mine.

"You want to fire up one of those black balls of doom?" I ask Pressley. I've got a plan but could use some added insurance.

He grunts and sheathes his sword, placing his hands together as a ball of dark energy forms between them. His health trickles down as the orb gains power. Once it is big enough, he launches it at the forcefield.

I activate Kamikaze seconds before his attack hits, detonating my horrors. Dozens of cracks spread across the forcefield and when Pressley's attack hits, the dome shatters into the ether.

Their ogre lifts his club and charges out.

The hags chant faster than ever, and my communication stone allows me to decipher what they are saying.

"Spirits of the forest, I summon thee. Spirits of the forest, I summon thee. Return to your vessels and protect us."

The earth shakes and the dead monsters groan all around us. The broken bodies of the slain rise to their feet, fueled by magical power.

"You have got to be kidding me." Jon backs closer to Stompy with his staff raised. "What is it with you people and zombies?"

"Maybe you should climb back in that tree." I point overhead. "I have a feeling things are about to get real uncomfortable."

Before the undead minions are fully on their feet, I start playing whack-a-mole with Destroyer, crushing anything and everything I can. If I can limit our opponents before they've done any damage, all the better.

The hags' ogre crosses the threshold where the barrier once stood. He raises his club and swings. Pressley's undead ogre answers the call. The two clubs connect with a crash, and both bone weapons shatter. The two monsters maul at one another, clawing and biting. It's primal. Blood and spittle fly from their mouths as they go at it with everything they've got. No magic, no spells, just raw nitwit power.

A bolt of lightning zips across the forest, electrifying a group of reanimated wolves. Jon's voice echoes around us, adding to the chaos as he calls the hags a slew of inappropriate names.

A second lightning bolt rips through the canopy, crashing into my three recently-summoned horrors.

"Easy there, Taryn. Watch the friendly fire."

"That wasn't me," he shouts as he uses his staff's special ability to wrangle a warthog within its vines. He jumps on the tangled beast and stabs it in the head with his shadow dagger.

A third bolt of lightning arcs straight for me, and I barely dodge it at the last second. Thunder rumbles overhead and then the heavens pour out. Thick drops of rain rattle in the trees above.

The strings of energy that connect the three hags have changed to yellow. They must have called in a lightning storm. What have I gotten us into?

Lightning strikes through the trees again and again, sometimes hitting our minions, sometimes our opponent's. Pure chaos. Other times, it crashes into the trees, sending scorched and burning limbs raining from above.

"Ouch! Hot, hot, hot!" Jon's voice echoes around us, but when I look up, there's no sign of him.

"We must get to the hags!" Pressley slices a zombie spider in two, spraying black ichor across a group of nearby horrors. "If we kill one, this madness will stop."

Just ahead of us, the two ogres are covered in blood and open wounds. Both of their HP are nearly depleted. The zombie ogre has a broken leg and has fallen to one knee. The living ogre picks up a boulder and lifts it overhead.

Pressley shoots a beam of black energy at the ogre, and its health drops to zero. The ogre collapses to the ground, and the boulder falls on top of its pea-brained head. Pressley's own health jumps up by a tick. He reaches down and snatches the medallion from the ogre's neck.

The attack reminds me of some of the blood magic champions I used to play while streaming. I would bait low-health opponents into thinking I was weak and then drain their life force, turning the battle in my favor.

"Charge!" Pressley points his sword toward the hags.

Lightning crashes behind him, spraying dirt and cooking the flesh of dead monsters. Rain continues to pour through the trees, creating puddles and slippery mud.

Taryn jumps on Stompy's back, and we press forward with what few horrors and skeleton warriors remain. A skeleton wielding a bow sits on Berry's back, firing arrows at the hags. The arrows pass through the hag like she's some kind of apparition.

"They're illusions." Jon's voice echoes over my shoulder. "The real hags must be somewhere near."

Have they been illusions the entire time, or did they disappear when we weren't looking?

Pressley rushes into the clearing where the hags stand. He stabs one in the face, but the apparition doesn't flinch.

Rain patters off his armor. "Dammit!" he shouts as he stabs the other two. "Where did they go?"

A cacophony of mad cackling answers.

"Jon, do you see anything?" I ask.

"No," his voice echoes.

"Taryn, what about Berry? Can he track them down?"

Taryn shakes his head. "Their stench is all over this place. Unless they took off running, he won't be able to fin—"

A streak of bright green light shoots out from the darkness and hits Taryn in the face. His lips fuse together, sewn shut. He mumbles, but nothing is audible.

"They've got us surround—"

Another flash of green hits Pressley and his words fall short. Thunder continues to roll in the sky above.

I search for the source of the magic, but see nothing. Nothing but empty forest that surrounds us. I send my horrors out into the depths of the forest to inspect. Before they've even made it a few feet away, I'm hit with a blinding green light and my mouth locks in place.

Alert! *You have been hit with a silencing curse. You will be unable to talk until the spell wears off or the caster is defeated. Timer: 2 hours.*

You've got to be kidding me! How many tricks do these hags have up their sleeves? How are we supposed to fight them without being able to communicate?

"Guys? What's going on down there? You're awfully quiet." Jon's voice echoes all around us.

At least they don't know where he is. Maybe I can use that to our advantage. I send him a quick message.

Message (Chod): *We've been cursed. This is the only way we can communicate. And since Pressley isn't a part of our party, you need to talk to him for us. And whatever you do, don't let the hags find you.*

Incoming Message (Jon): *I'm on it.*

"Hey, Pressley. I'm sure you know this, but you're cursed. So are the other guys. They can't chat with you since you're not in our party. Do you want to join us?"

Pressley shakes his head as he stalks the perimeter searching for the hags. Water splashes around his massive boots. What possible reason could he have for not joining us?

"You had your chance to leave," a shrill voice calls from the depths, but when I turn, nothing is there.

"We will very much enjoy our new playthings," a second voice echoes.

"Very much, indeed," a third voice joins in. "They should stay for a while. I'd love to have them for dinner."

The ground shakes and roots reach up from the earth. They swirl around my legs, locking me in place. I rip at them with my claws, but for every root I cut, another takes its place.

All around me, the others are suffering a similar fate. Many of my horrors die from the roots that strangle them, and Pressley's skeleton warriors have their bones pulled apart. Stompy unleashes a bellowing trumpet as he struggles to free his hooves.

A long tendril of a root reaches for Taryn, attempting to pull him from the moul-haug's back, but he transforms into his bird form and disappears into the trees.

At least one of us got away.

"Oh, yes. You are a special one. You and your friend here," a voice whispers in my ear, and I almost jump out of my skin.

I reach out behind me, attempting to grab whoever is there, but I'm left grasping at air.

"Yes, indeed. These will do very nicely."

I can feel the hag's icy breath on my skin. Goosebumps erupt all over my body. She's there, she has to be.

I close my eyes and listen.

"This one is full of more mana than any troll I've ever seen. Quite the specimen, indeed."

I listen as rain pours down all around us. Thunder rolls. Berry and Stompy struggle for their freedom. A twig crunches beside me, and I hear the soft suction of a footstep.

"And this one. It has been quite some time since we have seen such dark energy."

The footsteps move from my right to left, closer to Pressley. I open my eyes and see the smallest of indentations in the muddy soil.

They're invisible! I try to shout, but the words lodge inside my mouth. The hag is just out of my reach. I wave for Pressley's attention, but he's focused on something else. I send Taryn and Jon a message instead.

Message (Chod): *The hags are invisible. I'm not sure how it works, but I can hear their footsteps and see their footprints once I locate them.*

A red bird lands on the tree limb next to me. It winks at me, and I know it's Taryn.

I extend a finger, pointing in the direction of the invisible hag. The bird tilts its beak in affirmation.

The spot of sunken earth moves, and a tiny track trails toward Pressley before the rain washes it away. He thrashes about, swinging at an invisible object. I assume the hag is whispering in his ear the same as she did me.

Mad laughter fills the air. "You can't catch what you can't see."

Taryn's pets continue to grunt as they struggle to free themselves from the roots that hold them in place. The good news is that the roots don't seem to be getting any tighter.

In my brief distraction, I lose the positioning of the hag. Curse it all!

My body erupts with pain as lightning strikes my shoulder. My entire body stiffens from the jolt of electricity and every nerve in my body screams at me. Rain steams off my skin.

I lose a quarter of my health from the strike. We're all sitting ducks. If we don't do something soon, we're done for.

Another lightning strike hits Pressley and for a brief moment, the man beneath the darkness glows inside of his helm. His face contorts in anguish and his body seizes.

"Don't cook them too much," one of the hags laughs. "I like mine on the rare side."

Taryn flies down from his branch. Mid-flight, he transforms back into his dwarven form and extends the vines from his staff. They wrap around the hag a few yards in front of me, disrupting her invisibility spell. Taryn hits the ground and slides through the mud, toppling the hag. The vines continue to pour out from the staff, wrapping around her until she is entombed in foliage.

She screams, "Release me!"

Taryn pulls his shadow blade and buries it into her skull. The rain suddenly stops, and the roots that bind us in place release.

Hell yeah! Way to go, Taryn. Swinging in like an acrobatic dwarf!

Even though Taryn freed us, the curse that binds our lips is still in effect. It must have been a product of an individual hag and not the covey.

I search for signs of the other two hags.

"Behind you!" Jon's voice bounces off the forest.

I turn around to see two glowing green hands pointed in our direction. The limb above me shakes and Jon jumps down from the tree, tackling one of the hags to the ground. Both hags become visible, and the second hag blasts Pressley in the chest with a bolt of green energy.

The death knight stumbles back, rights himself, then charges.

The first hag grabs Jon by the robe and tosses him across the forest like a ragdoll. He slams into a tree and falls to the ground.

Noooo! I scream inside my head.

Anger floods my veins and I activate Berserker Rage without thinking. The silencing spell disappears, and my vision goes red as I leap on the hag. Her spindly fingers and long nails dig into my arm, but it doesn't deter me. She's absurdly strong to be so small.

Right now, all I can think about is revenge. Jon risked himself to save us, and this bitch is going to pay for hurting a member of my party. I activate Claw and drag my nails across her shriveled old chest. Black blood oozes from the wounds.

Screams and explosions echo behind me, but my focus is lasered in. The hag's hands begin to glow again, and I smash my forehead into her nose. The attack does enough to cancel her spell. She pushes me off with barbaric strength.

I roll to my feet and equip Destroyer. She turns to run, and I swipe at her legs. She falls down and looks up at me with a snarl. I swing Destroyer with all my might, but she rolls out of the way at the last second and it smashes into the ground.

Vines zip past me and grab the hag by the legs. She trips and falls, finally trapped. I bring down Destroyer on her head, ending her torment.

A notification flashes across my vision, and there's a sharp intake of breath beside me as her silencing spell lifts on the others. I push the notifications away for now.

With her out of the way, only one hag remains. I turn to find Pressley kneeling over the downed hag, his gauntlet is wrapped around her neck. Black energy radiates from his hand. Her health depletes and what color she has drains from her face. Pressley's own health recovers bit by bit.

She tries to speak, but Pressley presses harder, cutting off her words. Her body convulses a few times before she falls limp against the forest floor.

Pressley pulls out a dagger and sticks it into the hag's eye socket. He rocks the dagger back and forth before there's a pop and a jewel comes loose.

Taryn gags at the sight. I'm taken aback myself. What the hell just happened?

Pressley moves to the hag I killed and rifles through her brain matter before pulling out another jewel. He then walks over to the body of the third hag without saying a word.

I'll get answers later, for now, I need to check on Jon.

I roll him over and he stirs.

"Ugh. What happened? Did we win?" His head sways back and forth.

"Yeah, man, you came in pretty clutch." I help him sit up, then search through my bag for a health potion. "Here, take this."

He downs the potion and I return to the others. Taryn is using Restoration to bring Berry and Stompy back to full health. Pressley searches the remaining corpses for loot.

He kneels next to a dead spider and breaks off one of its pincers, stuffing it in his bag.

"Find everything you needed?" I ask.

He grunts in affirmation. I guess he's not offering up information unless I probe him for it.

"What's the deal? Clearly this wasn't a dungeon, or we wouldn't have been able to gain access." I look over the corpses of the fallen monsters, but don't see anything worth taking. I wouldn't trust any of the meat, not after it has been reanimated.

"There were certain...items I needed." He reaches in his pouch and tosses me a plum-colored gem.

Item. Hag's Eye. *The jewel from the eye of a hag. This enchanted jewel is created* *when a hag joins a covey. It replaces one of their eyeballs. The original eyeball is then worn by a minion, sealing the pact between them. The minion then functions as a summon, controllable by the hag.*

Interesting. "What do you plan on doing with these?" I toss the gem back to him.

"My new class allows me to use them for certain spells. This is one of the few forests on the island where hags still dwell." He goes back to searching the bodies.

Pressley is being incredibly vague and mysterious. If I'd been sabotaged and turned into an undead warrior, I'm sure I would be hesitant to give out too many details, too. For now, he can keep his secrets.

"Whoa!" Jon kneels over the hag I killed. "You missed something."

He displays a vial of glowing pink liquid.

"What is it?" I ask.

He walks over to me and carefully hands me the vial.

Legendary Item. Potion of Reincarnation. (Only usable by heroes.) *User gains increased size and doubles all stats for the duration of the potion. Health drains with each step. When user's health reaches zero, their character is randomly re-rolled to level 1.*

"Wow," I whisper as I reread the description for the fourth time. "It's a do-over."

"Yeah, but you lose all progress and have no choice over the character you get." Jon shakes his head. "You'd have to be in one hell of a bind to use something like that. I'd rather be a shitty enchanter than a shitty halfling farmer. Who knows, there could be something worse."

He's got a point. I can't imagine anyone willing to risk the rest of their in-game existence being stuck as something they hate. Especially after spending months leveling. Remembering all the options I wasn't able to pick in character creation, the likelihood of getting a race and class that I would want is slim. Still, it is a legendary item. My pulse quickens when I remember my own legendary item that I lost in Goldspire.

"Let me see." Pressley extends his hand.

I hand it to him, and he looks over the potion. He turns it in his hand, watching the thick liquid run down the sides of the vial. "Interesting."

"Take it. It's yours," I offer. "We don't want any of the loot. This was your battle, and we helped in good faith. All that I ask is that you hear us out."

He stuffs the vial in his bag and takes a seat. "Alright, let's hear it."

Jon mumbles something about loot, but I pay him no mind.

I take a deep breath and sit across from Pressley on the ground. If I weren't so scared of what might happen, this would be a great opportunity to use a few of Jon's Charisma rings.

I look deep into Pressley's helm, searching for eyes, but all I see is swirling darkness. He looks downright sinister. But if anyone should know that looks don't determine the worth of the individual, it's me. I sit up straight. "Pressley, we need your help."

CHAPTER FIFTEEN

SOMETHING DOESN'T FEEL RIGHT

"So what do you say?" I ask Pressley. I've filled him in on everything I know about the new portals, Goldspire, and the potential to travel to other locations.

He places both armored hands together and they clink softly. "You saw how they looked at me in Seascape. After I turned into this—this monster. They'll try to kill me before I ever set foot in the city."

"They were frightened," Taryn interjects. "This entire island has a fear of the undead because of what happened long ago. If you join our cause, then we can make sure you have safe passage through the city."

Remembering the tower and walls in Vanaria that were designed to keep out the undead, Pressley would likely not even be able to set foot on city ground. "He's right. The king himself has sent us to gather forces. You're the strongest hero I've seen. We need you." I stand up and pace. I need to convince him that teaming up with us is better for him than going at it alone. "Besides, you need tougher opponents. You won't be able to grind here forever without wasting your time. You want power, right? Gold and power? Then this is how you get it. We don't know what's on the other side of the closed portals, but if you wait around to find out, then there's a chance you'll lose everything."

He grunts in response. It's difficult to get a read on the man since we can't see his eyes or facial features. That's part of the reason people wearing masks always creep me out. It's hard to gauge a person when you can't see their eyes.

Pressley stands up, his armor clanking as he does so. "I will help you, but I have certain conditions."

My heart jumps with joy, but I try to conceal my excitement and keep from smiling. "What are the conditions?"

"I want no part in your dealings with other heroes. My business with the Cleric is mine, and your business with Glenn and the others is your problem. I don't need any more targets on my back."

I nod. "That seems reasonable. What else?"

"I will not be joining your party. I still have business to attend to, and I don't wish for my whereabouts to be known. I will see you to the edge of the forest, but then we will be going our separate ways. When the time comes to move on Goldspire, I will reconvene with you in Seascape."

"How will we find you when the time comes?"

"I'll be in the city before you return. You can find me at the Brown Boar Inn."

It's not an ideal situation, but if it means having him on our side, then I'll take it. I extend my hand.

"Deal."

He grasps my forearm and I feel a tingly sensation. I wonder if it's the dark energy that turned him into a death knight.

Jon claps his hands together. "Alright, great. We're all friends. Now, can we get out of the creepy forest?"

I pat him on the shoulder. "Sorry, man. We need to rest before exhaustion kicks in. The worst is behind us, though."

He rolls his eyes. "Pfft. I'll believe that when I see it."

Taryn takes first watch, and we all settle down for the night. The forest is surprisingly quiet without the hags. The only noise is the gentle hoot of an owl. After everything that happened today, my body is exhausted. I fall asleep as soon as I close my eyes.

I wake to the sound of something breaking. It's morning, and streaks of sunlight filter through the canopy overhead. Another crash comes from inside one of the hag's huts.

Pressley and Taryn both sit up. Taryn's beard is matted from how he slept on it.

"Whasgoinon?" he mumbles.

I grab Destroyer and stealthily walk to the hut. Through the window, I see Jon inside smashing clay pots with his staff.

"What in the hell are you doing?" I ask.

He jumps, and a squeak escapes his lips. He turns around, startled. "I was looking for loot."

"By breaking pots?"

He shrugs. "You never know."

I shake my head. "You couldn't have just turned it upside-down?"

He looks back at the wreckage he has caused. "You know, I'll be honest, that did not occur to me until just now."

I sigh. "Come on, let's get going."

Jon walks across the broken mess, shards of clay cracking with every step. "Wasn't anything worth taking anyways."

We gather our belongings and set off toward the edge of the forest. In the daylight, everything is less haunting. We're able to spot mana-infused trees and darksand long before they are a threat. It might have been a mistake entering the forest at night, but it all worked out in the end.

Pressley and Jon lead the way, followed by me. Taryn pulls up the rear riding Stompy, and Berry trails right beside him. I feel like we have enough of us that I don't bother summoning any horrors. We don't plan on engaging in any battles until we're out of the forest anyway.

I suddenly remember that I never checked my notifications from the fight with the hags. I was so caught up with talking to Pressley that it slipped my mind. I quickly pull them up.

You have defeated Glossop Forest Covey. *Due to the death of a member, this covey has been disbanded. All related skills and abilities have been lost. To form a new covey, a new member must be recruited and rites performed.*

Congratulations! You have reached level 22. +1 stat point to distribute. +1 Strength and Constitution racial bonus.

Nice! One more level and I'll get another ability point. I've still got three stat points to distribute, but I'm not entirely sure where to allocate them. I could go with Dexterity, and build on my barbarian fighting style. Or I could put them in Intelligence or Wisdom and maybe help with my summoning skills. The one thing I know is that I have zero desire to add them to Charisma. My low Charisma has had zero effect on people liking me, which makes me believe that it truly only affects how the individual perceives the world, not the other way around.

I focus on the others. Both Taryn and Jon managed to gain a level, making them levels fourteen and eighteen respectively. Both are even levels like me, so they won't have any new abilities.

Jon leans in toward Pressley. "So, big guy. What are you in for? I remember seeing you at the physicals, but you always kept to yourself."

For the longest time, Pressley doesn't respond, then he lets out a deep breath that sounds more malevolent than any sigh I've ever heard. "I made some bad decisions. Got caught up with the wrong people, and I paid for it."

Jon laughs. "Oh, come on, Mr. Secretive. Give us more than that."

Pressley grunts, and I wonder if it's a side effect of his new class.

"I used to be a bouncer at a club. A damn good one, too. One night, this guy comes in, real rich type. Thousand-dollar suit, Bentley, the whole nine yards. He asks me if I want to make a little money on the side. I'm young and I'm hungry, plus I've got a daughter to provide for, so I say, 'Why not?'" He clenches his fist, as if he's reliving the memory. "They wanted me to be an enforcer, to go around and collect outstanding debts. I figure maybe I scare a few guys, rough up someone every now and then. You know, not much different from a night at the club. Turns out it wasn't that simple."

"It never is." Jon shakes his head. "So what happened?"

"For the first few months, it was easy money. Then they said that they needed to send a message. That I needed to round up this guy and meet them at the docks. I figure it's just some extra scary shit to get the guy to pay, but when I get there, they hand me a gun. I tell them there's no way I'm killing anybody. They say to do it or I'll never work for them again. I refuse, and they kill the guy anyway. When the police find the gun, it has my prints on it and no one else's."

Damn. I glance at Taryn, and he has the same wide eyes that I'm sure I do. I wonder how much of that is true. Jon did say that everyone in prison was innocent. Is it possible Pressley really killed a man? He has such a calm demeanor and is always strictly business. He doesn't seem like a murderer. Not that I would be a good judge of who seems like a murderer.

Regardless of what he did in the past, he's on our side now.

I speed up until I'm right behind them. "So, how'd you end up working with Richard?"

He balls his hand into a fist. Clearly, he still has some issues with the cleric. "We were staying at the same inn when the announcement went out about the king's challenge. He told me that his god had a plan for me. That he had a spell that could grant me holy energy and allow me to open the portal." He clears his throat. "He didn't mention that his god was a trickster, that I would be turned into this." He extends his arms, displaying his dark armor.

"What's it like?" Taryn shouts from behind us.

"What is what like?" asks Pressley.

"Being a death knight."

Pressley stops walking, and we all gather around him.

"It's...different. I feel different. More...hollow might be the right word, but it doesn't fully describe it." He lifts his hand in front of his face, as if he can see right down to the bones. "Everything changed when I hit the portal. All of my abilities, my appearance. For a moment, all I felt was overwhelming anger and sadness. Is that grief? I ran away as fast as I could until I could make sense of it all."

"Have you?" asks Taryn.

"It's a process. But I'm on the path to understanding."

Listening to his story has the hairs on my neck standing on end. I've personally experienced the way this game can change how someone feels. If he's feeling all of that constantly because of a decision he made in the game, I wonder if there is more at play. Could it be part of the rehabilitation or is it as simple as an effect of switching classes?

We're all in the same pods being fed and cleaned by the nanites. There's really no telling what other chemicals they might be putting in our bodies. I push the thoughts away. I'm just being paranoid.

Time passes quickly and before I know it, we reach the edge of the forest. We say our good-byes and Pressley heads back toward Narthensted while we take off for the Greystone Mountains.

CHAPTER SIXTEEN
NEVER HAVE I EVER

"That was pretty weird, right?" I ask Taryn as we travel down the desolate dirt road.

He shrugs. "What, Pressley? Not much different than anything else we've experienced in here."

I suppose he's right. I'm a troll; he's a dwarf. We've done things we could never possibly do in real life, and it all seems so natural. He's a regular Snow White when it comes to pets, and I can go into a barbaric rage and not end up in jail for it. Why wouldn't a supposed death knight have emotional problems and mood swings? Maybe that's why it's such a rare class.

We pass the last of the major towns surrounding Seascape, and for the next two days, we only encounter small villages. More often than not, village is overstating it, and they're just a couple of farmhouses that offer a room to weary travelers.

Not many people take the eastern road to the mountains. The Mythroad is the safer and more populous route that cuts straight across the island. I'm sure once the portal is opened in Vanaria, it will be used less and less.

It's unfortunate for those that depend on travelers and tourism, but such is the price of progress.

We're about a day's ride from the base of the mountain, even with Taryn using Strong Wind to speed up our travels. The journey is long and boring. What I wouldn't give for some in-game music to help pass the time.

I check every tab of my user interface, but there's no such luck. Instead, we're forced to rely our own devices, playing "I Spy" and "Never Have I Ever."

Jon taps his finger against his chin. "Never have I ever...flown on an airplane."

I put down one of my fingers, leaving two up. Taryn still has all three of his.

"No shit?" Jon tilts his head. "I thought I was one of the few people to have never flown. I've got a terrible fear of heights. Can't even imagine looking down from the inside of a plane."

I'm surprised I'm the only one who has flown in a plane. "It's not so bad. When you're up that high, it doesn't even look real. It's like staring down at some kid's playset. The trees, the cars, they all look like models. Taryn, have you really never flown?"

He gives me an incredulous look. "To where? My family never had money for vacations. My vacation was a long walk through Central Park." He laughs. "Or a weekend at your place."

I smile. "We had a lot of those."

Thinking back on all the times I flew in a plane, there were too many to count. There was a time when we would take vacations as a family. I remember playing on the beach in Mexico with Maria, my first nanny. Dad was on the phone practically all day. Maria took me down to the beach and we built sandcastles.

Or the time we flew to Colorado to ski. I ended up building a snowman outside of our cabin with Rosa because Mom had a meeting and couldn't go to our skiing lessons.

So many trips spent with people who weren't my family. By the time I was a teenager, I didn't even bother going anymore. They were nothing more than glorified business trips. Staying home and playing games was more fun. At least there I had people I could count on. People who noticed me.

"Your turn, Chod." Taryn's voice pulls me from my own head.

"Hmm. Let me think." I search my brain for something that I think both of them have done that I haven't. "Never have I ever..." I pause. "Had a girlfriend."

Jon laughs before he realizes I'm serious. He and Taryn both put a finger down.

Jon's mouth hangs open. "You're a rich streamer guy and you've never had a girlfriend?"

"No, it just never happened. All the girls I liked never liked me."

"Don't give me that." Taryn mocks shoving me away. "You never tried. You don't get to be a popular streamer without a few girls throwing themselves at you. Be honest. You just weren't interested."

Jon stops in his tracks and puts both hands up. "No offense, but are you..." He whispers the word, "gay? Not that there is anything wrong with that."

I can't help but laugh. "No, not at all. I like girls. I guess I've just never had that desire that most guys have. I like girls, but they don't consume my thoughts. Maybe I'm just waiting on the right one."

"Maybe you're just afraid of rejection." Taryn crosses his arms.

Maybe he's right. I went on a date once. I was so nervous that I spilled my water across the table. I had spent so much time babbling about myself to try and fill the awkward silence. I got a hug at the end of the meal, the kind of hug where their crotch is far away from you and they just pat you on the back a lot. It was not my best moment, not by a long shot.

That's enough time delving into my personal life. "How about a new game?"

"What'd you have in mind?" asks Taryn. He sits atop Stompy, his dreads swaying in the gentle breeze. He looks very regal on top of the moulhaug. Give him a crown and some brightly-colored fabric to drape down Stompy's side and he'd pass for royalty.

"Give me a few minutes." I close my eyes to see what I can come up with. Anything to avoid more personal conversations.

I take the next few minutes to summon a few Horrors of Finesse. The blue gangly creatures are perfect for what I have in mind.

"Alright, each of you pick a horror and adorn it with something so that we can tell them apart."

Jon gives his horror a Ring of Bliss. I'm actually surprised when I see the +1 Charisma take effect on the small horror. Its body loosens and it walks with a new swagger, smoothly wrapping an arm around one of the other horrors.

Taryn takes a piece of leather and ties it around his horror's neck like a necklace.

"Good, mine will be the one with no items." I stop walking for a moment to explain the rules for the game I've created. "We're going to have a race. We'll leave the horrors here." I draw a line in the dirt. "Once we are far enough away, the horrors will take off. Whoever's horror reaches us first will be the winner."

"Can we try to slow them down?" asks Taryn.

I nod. "Yes, but only using abilities. We all have to stay put."

Once we are about a quarter of a mile away, I lift my hand in the air. "On three. One. Two. Three!"

I instruct the horrors to run to our location and wait to see what happens.

Jon makes the first move, sending out two doppelgängers. They leap out of his body and charge toward the horrors.

"Hey, not fair!" shouts Taryn.

"What?" Jon raises his hands up as he shrugs. "It's an ability."

"Not cool." Taryn lifts his staff and a bolt of lightning crashes into one of the doppelgängers.

"Oh, come on." Jon frowns, then he sends out a third clone.

The three horrors are neck-and-neck. I wait on taking any action, biding my time. Jon's horror waves at us as it runs, its Charisma in full effect. They are halfway to us when Jon's doppelgänger tackles my horror to the ground.

My horror quickly disengages but is now way behind the other two. I summon a Horror of Vitality and grab it by the horn. Taryn and Jon are bickering as I toss the horror as far as I can. It lands with a thud, losing a chunk of health from the impact, before running toward the other two.

The two Horrors of Finesse run past the Horror of Vitality without slowing down at all. That's when I realize my mistake. Its passive slow doesn't work on my own summons. I instruct the Horror of Vitality to chase the others, but they are too fast.

Since that failed, I summon a Horror of Power and send it out.

Taryn casts Strong Wind on his horror, but since it effects any party members surrounding the spell, both his and Jon's horrors speed up. My own horror falls even further behind.

Horror of Power launches itself into Taryn's horror, tackling it to the ground.

They tumble in the dirt for a moment, giving just enough time for my Horror of Vitality to catch up. Together, the two horrors pin Taryn's to the ground and my own Horror of Finesse passes it by.

Jon's horror is in the lead by a good margin, when a lightning bolt crashes into it. The horror loses all but ten percent of its health. A moment later, the passive health loss due to being out of combat vanishes it into thin air, leaving only mine and Taryn's horrors remaining.

"Suck it, Jon." Taryn laughs.

My own horror is about to cross the finish line when Stompy steps forward and crushes it underneath his massive hoof.

"Last one standing. I win!" Taryn tosses his arms up in victory.

"Not if you don't cross the finish line." I cast Kamikaze on the two horrors pinning Taryn's to the ground, and they all three explode. The game is a draw.

Jon bursts out laughing. "No, you suck it, Taryn." He howls with laughter, clutching his stomach.

And that is how we pass the next five hours.

CHAPTER SEVENTEEN

RUBIES ARE RED

The Greystone Mountains tower above us, a watchful boundary that separates the kingdoms of Seascape and Vanaria. Home to goblins, mountain trolls, and who knows what else.

Clouds cover the highest peaks, hiding the mountains' best-kept secrets. Before we pass through, I intend to uncover some of those secrets. My map shows various locations with ley lines. The only problem is that the map is two-dimensional, while the mountains are not. A cluster of ley lines under a single mountain could mean a lot of searching. Who knows how many crevices and cave entrances we might need to check?

Still, we need to continue to level up. What good is it if we gather more heroes, but none of us are strong enough when the time comes? Finding a dungeon seems a lot smarter than aimlessly leveling as we travel.

There has to be a dungeon here somewhere. I can feel it in my bones.

As we ascend the mountain, I spot a cluster of snowy moss that glitters in the fading light. It's been a while since I have invested in my herbalism or potion-making skills, but I remember that snowy moss is one of the ingredients in perception potions. If I could make one, then it would help us notice anything out of the ordinary.

I think back to my training with Yashi, the potions master of the forest trolls, trying to recall the other ingredient. It mixed with the snowy moss and turned it pink. Jackal's blood!

Climbing up a few branches on the tree, I cut away the snowy moss with my claw.

"What are you doing?" asks Taryn.

"I'm going to make us some perception potions, but I'm going to need your help."

Jon walks over and examines the snowy moss. "What's it do?"

I open my hand, showing him the bright white moss. "By itself, nothing. But when you mix it with jackal's blood, it heightens your senses. Kind of like the Perception ability. This isn't as strong as Perception, but it lasts for two hours instead of ten minutes."

Taryn climbs down from Stompy. "Let me guess, you want me to fly around and see if I can find a jackal?"

I flash him a smile. "You don't even need the potion to be perceptive."

He rolls his eyes. "Did you come up with that all by yourself? What is it I'm looking for?"

"They're like a cross between a fox and a wolf. I saw a lot of them in the troll forest, but I'm hoping they might roam here too. They usually travel in packs, but one should be enough. We just need enough blood to grind the snowy moss into a drinkable liquid."

"Alright, I'll see what I can do." He turns to his pets. "Berry, Stompy, behave until I get back."

Berry shakes his stump of a tail, but Stompy just snorts. Typical.

Taryn transforms into a red bird and disappears amongst the trees.

We continue with our journey up the mountain. There's no point in lounging about while Taryn searches for a jackal. In his bird form, he'll be able to find us wherever we are. Stompy's massive frame takes up most of the path. Hopefully, we don't run into any other travelers.

After an hour passes, I send Taryn a message.

Message (Chod): *You've been gone a while. Any luck?*

Incoming Message (Taryn): *I've found a pack of them. I've got an idea. Let me handle this on my own.*

Message (Chod): *Try not to get yourself killed.*

Not that I don't think he can survive a run-in with a pack of jackals, but he doesn't have Stompy or Berry to protect him. I have no idea what he's up to, but Taryn is smart, so I don't argue.

A few minutes later, I hear thunder on the other side of the mountain. I'm not sure if it's Taryn or an actual storm we're heading into. I fight the urge to check in on him again. If he's in trouble, he'll let us know.

Jon hurries up beside me, his blue robe swishing as he walks. "Hey, man. I just wanted to say thanks. It means a lot that you took me under your wing. I've done more in the past few days than I did in the first two months of being here. Whatever happens, I won't forget that."

Wow. His words catch me by surprise. I'm not really sure how to respond, but I do my best. "You're a good guy, Jon. No matter what you did to get you here, I think your heart is in the right place. You're not a villain." I slap him on the shoulder. "You're a valuable member of our team now."

I must have said something right, because I've never seen Jon smile so wide. We continue up the mountain until Berry stops. He sniffs at the air, then takes off at a full sprint.

Jon and I exchange glances. What the hell is going on?

"Stay with Stompy!" I order and take off after Berry.

Jon protests, but I leave him anyways. Berry has a connection to Taryn, so if he is running, then something is up.

Running at full speed, I turn the corner and plow into the backside of the umber bear. After narrowly avoiding tumbling off the side of the mountain, I notice the reason why Berry stopped.

Taryn scratches the bear on the chin with one hand and pets a jackal with the other.

He winks at me. "What do you think?"

"Another pet?" I ask.

He flashes me a brilliant smile. "Yep, meet Ruby."

Ruby looks up at me and yawns. She has a slender snout and wide-set golden eyes. Her fur is a beautiful straw color, with a streak of black that goes down her back. She's smaller than the jackals I saw in the troll forest. Her ears are long and pointy, like a fox, and her big bushy tail curls around her left leg as she sits.

I extend my hand and let her sniff the back of it. "She's beautiful. I know I'm going to regret this, but why the name Ruby?"

Taryn's lip curls up at the edge like he's holding back laughter. "Rubies are red. So is blood. And since she is going to be donating her blood to help us..."

I shouldn't have asked. I don't even acknowledge Taryn's comment. "Welcome to the team, Ruby."

The small jackal walks over and licks at my fingers.

"She's a great judge of character it seems." Taryn runs his fingers down her back. "Plus, she comes with some nice perks."

"What do you mean?"

"Having pets is different than having something you summon. Your horrors have abilities that you are able to control when you cast them. Pets have their own skills, but I can't control them. Take Berry, for instance. He's a great tracker with an excellent sense of smell, but I can't tell him to follow a smell and automatically know where he's leading us. It's up to him to decide if he wants to listen to me. Stompy can pull a barn down, but he will only do it if he's in the mood. Ruby here, she has an excellent sense of perception on her own. She's able to see, smell, and hear things you and I never will, but it's up to her to let me know what she finds." He scratches her ear. "She's a good girl, though. Aren't you, girl?"

Ruby nuzzles her head against his hand. Berry steps in between them and licks the jackal on the head.

"Someone is jealous." I laugh. "Now that you have three pets, what does that mean for your ability to control them?"

"It drops to eighty-five percent. If I had to guess, I imagine Stompy will be the rebellious one. It doesn't mean that they will actively betray me, more so that they won't do things exactly to the letter each time. Maybe I'll tell them to attack one enemy, and they go after the one next to him. Things like that."

Or maybe you'll tell Stompy to go and he'll sit down instead.

I pet Berry a few times so he doesn't feel left out. "Well, now that you're keeping her as a pet, how are we supposed to get her blood?" It feels kind of wrong bleeding a living animal, let alone a pet.

"She'll be fine. We'll make a little cut and then once we have enough blood, I'll use Restoration and heal her." Taryn climbs on Berry and Ruby jumps in his lap.

She's really taken to Taryn quite quickly.

"If you say so—"

"Hey, what's going on over here?" Jon turns the corner, followed by Stompy.

Taryn waves at the enchanter. "Hey, Jon. Just introducing Chod to my new pet. Meet Ruby."

Jon's mouth drops open. "Wow. She's pretty. Can I pet her?"

While Jon is enamored with Ruby, Stompy turns his head away from us and snorts.

"Oh, don't be like that," Taryn scolds. "I love you all the same."

Stompy paws at the earth and huffs again.

"Meh, he'll get over it. You guys ready to get moving?" Taryn maneuvers Berry until they are facing up the mountain.

"Aren't you forgetting something?" I ask.

Taryn stares at me blankly.

"The potion?"

"Ah, yes." He climbs down from Berry and strokes Ruby on the head a few times. "I'm sorry about this, girl, but it's for the good of the party."

He rummages through his pack before pulling out a small knife and an empty vial.

"You sure this is okay?" I ask. I'm hesitant to draw blood if it's going to hurt Ruby. She seems so sweet and innocent as she rubs her head against Taryn.

"It'll be fine. A quick cut and it's all over. It's not like we're going to torture her. I don't think it's much different than a veterinarian drawing blood." He takes the knife in one hand and the vial in the other. "Now, I need you to hold her."

I feel slightly queasy as I hold the small jackal in my arms. She nuzzles against my chest, unaware of what is about to happen.

Quicker than I expect, Taryn makes a small incision in her foot. She flinches for a moment, but she remains calm. Taryn places the vial underneath, catching the blood as it drips.

Taryn gently caresses Ruby's leg. "I'm going to fill this vial up. I'd rather make extra than have to do this constantly."

When the vial is full, Taryn hands it to me and takes Ruby. He casts Restoration, and a few moments later, she is as good as new.

I pull my mortar and pestle from my satchel and take a seat against the mountain. Remembering what Yashi taught me, I place the snowy moss in the mortar and grind it with the pestle. Next, I add a small amount of the jackal's blood until it forms into a light pink paste. I add a little more until the mixture swirls around in the mortar.

Item. Perception Potion. *+2 Wisdom. This potion heightens awareness of details and that which might normally go unnoticed. Duration: 2 hours.*

I take a sip and pass it to Taryn and Jon. Immediately, my senses feel sharper. I can hear better, see better, and even smell better. I pack away the remaining potion and extra ingredients, and we continue on our journey.

As we walk, I scan everything we come across. I'm able to notice things that would normally pass me by, such as bird nests, animal burrows, and areas where the stone is loose on the mountainside. Plants that I know appear from farther away. It's like the world is a puzzle and I'm able to see all the pieces.

Taryn rides atop Stompy in an attempt to calm the grumpy moulhaug. Berry follows behind his master while Ruby prances along at the front of the group. Due to the narrow path, I have no horrors summoned currently.

We travel for hours, until the sun begins to dip behind the peaks. A notification pops up, telling me that the potion has expired.

"Dammit. I really hoped we might find something useful from all that." I pick up a rock and toss it off the side of the mountain in frustration.

Taryn brings Stompy to a halt. "Give it time. There's a lot of mountain here. Who knows what we might come upon?"

We travel a little further, searching for a place to make camp for the night. Suddenly, Ruby lets out a low bark and runs ahead. When we don't immediately follow, she turns around and howls.

Taryn and I look at each other.

"What's that all about?" I ask.

He scrunches his nose. "No idea. I think she might have found something."

He climbs down from Stompy and we follow Ruby on foot. She's stopped in the middle of the trail, staring at the mountainside.

"What is it, girl?" Taryn kneels beside her. "What do you see?"

She takes a few steps closer to the mountain, until her nose is an inch from the stone surface. She barks again and paws at the mountainside.

I'm shocked when her paw passes through and the surface ripples.

I'll be damned. A hidden entrance!

CHAPTER EIGHTEEN

BURNING HEART OF THE MOUNTAIN

I reach for the mountainside and my fingers pass through the illusion. I feel my way around until I touch solid rock. After careful examination, I determine the hidden entrance is big enough to walk through.

Jon moves his fingers in and out of the illusion. "Whoever made this has some real skill. It looks like a permanent enchantment. You can't even tell that it's here. If you look at mine long enough, you can see a sort of shimmer in the air. This is high quality, and I bet it has been here for a while."

Taryn scratches Ruby behind the ears. "Look at you, Ruby. You're so smart and perceptive." He turns to me and Jon. "We gonna stand around all day, or are we gonna check this thing out?"

"Lead the way." I step aside and gesture for him to enter.

Taryn puts his hands out in front of him and slowly steps through the hidden entrance. After a few seconds, I follow.

We enter a massive cave that grows larger the farther in we go. It's big enough that even Stompy can fit inside. The air is hot and stifling, like a sauna between two hairy men. Several lit torches hang along the cave walls. Their fires burn, but they emit no heat. When I reach out and touch one, my fingers pass through them no differently than the entrance to the cave.

"More enchantments." Jon picks up a torch and examines it.

A notification pops up across my vision.

Burning Heart of the Mountain. *Would you like to enter?*

I pause for a moment before continuing. The hot temperature and name of this dungeon are giving me second thoughts. Trolls are especially susceptible to fire, and I no longer have my phoenix feather to help mitigate the damage.

Jon and Taryn are already making their way down the corridor, so I summon a few horrors and follow along. We walk for a ways until we come across a massive door with three latches keeping it shut. I try to open them, but they don't budge.

"Wait." Taryn pushes me aside. "There are words engraved into the metal."

They're hard to see, but eventually, I make out the words on the first latch. *What can bring back the dead; make us cry; make us laugh; make us young; born in an instant; yet lasts a lifetime.* They sound like nonsense to me. "Are they riddles?"

Taryn traces underneath the words with his finger. "Looks like it. Maybe you have to answer them to open the door?"

"What's it say?" asks Jon.

Taryn clears his throat and reads the first riddle.

Jon raises his hands and takes a step back. "I swear, if there are zombies involved, then I'm out."

I grab his shoulder. "It's not zombies. You answer the question and then the door opens. Well, there might be zombies if you get it wrong." I turn to Taryn. "What do the other ones say?"

"The second riddle says, 'Mountains will crumble to it, temples will fall, and no man can survive its endless call.'"

Oh boy. We are in for a long night. "And the last one?"

"I was carried into a dark room and set on fire. I wept, and then my head was cut off. What am I?"

I scratch my chin. "I don't know, a burn victim?"

The cavern shakes and then one of the torches extinguishes, casting the tunnel behind us in shadow.

Stompy snorts, and Jon clutches his staff to his chest. "Chod, what the hell? Now is not the time for jokes!"

"Sorry, guys. I didn't know it would take me seriously. I've never been in a dungeon like this."

Taryn takes a step back. "Okay, so we know that it has the ability to understand our answers. So it's probably best to discuss in our party chat before we try again. Losing the torches won't cripple us, but we have no idea what else might happen if we get it wrong."

"Sounds good to me." I move close to the engravings and read them again. "So, either of you have any ideas about these? Puzzles aren't my strong suit."

I read the first riddle out loud again. We stand in silence as our brains try to decipher its hidden meaning.

Incoming Message (Taryn): *This is tough.*

Message (Chod): *No kidding. I hate riddles. The answer is always so simple, too.*

Jon taps his fingers against his lips, and then suddenly, his eyes light up.

. . .

Incoming Message (Jon): *I think I know what it is. A photograph!*

Taryn claps his hands together. "Holy shit! I think that's it. Chod, do you agree?"

I read over the riddle again. It all fits, but something tells me it's not right. "Something is off. This is a fantasy world. They don't have photographs here. They have paintings and tapestries, but those aren't born in an instant. And if it lasts a lifetime, it has to be something that can't be destroyed."

The excitement fades from Jon's eyes. "Damn, I thought that was it."

"It was a good guess," I reassure him. "I think you're on the right track. What is similar to a photograph but can't be destroyed?"

"A memory." Jon covers his mouth with his hand. "Shit, I'm sorry guys."

The cavern shakes, and I raise Destroyer, ready for whatever is about to happen. There's a loud groan as the latch slides open. I release a sigh of relief.

"Ha! Nice work, Jon." I raise my hand, and he gives me a high five.

"Yeah, man. Good thinking." Taryn gives him a fist-bump.

Jon beams with pride. "You can thank my mom for that. When I was little, a house fire destroyed everything we owned. One of mom's favorite things were her photo albums. They had pictures of me and my brothers from when we were babies. She was so sad to have lost them. I remember her wiping away the tears, and she said, 'It's going to be okay. At least we have the memories.'"

I give him a smile. "It was your memories that solved the riddle. I'm sure your mom would appreciate that. Let's see if we can solve the second riddle."

I read the second riddle over and over. "Mountains will crumble to it, temples will fall, and no man can survive its endless call."

Earthquake is the first thing that comes to mind, but I've never felt called to by an earthquake. Erosion could crumble a mountain, but that would take so much time. Time, that's it. No man can survive time!

"Guys, I got it! The answer is time."

Another loud groan and the second latch slides open.

We hoot and holler in celebration. Even Berry and Ruby get excited.

"Only one more." I read it aloud for the others. "'I was carried into a dark room and set on fire. I wept, and then my head was cut off.' Any ideas?"

Incoming Message (Jon): *I was thinking torch, but that doesn't make any sense for the second part.*

Message (Chod): *What about a match? It has a head. But what does weep mean?*

. . .

Taryn jumps up and down, and the clasps in his beard clink together. "I know it! It's a candle."

The third latch slides open, and the torch that had burnt out behind us rekindles.

"How did you know that?" I ask.

He grins. "My mom loves candles. She would trim the wicks every so often so that the flames would burn evenly. She always had a joke about taking a little bit off the top."

I find it interesting how both of their personal relationships with their mothers led them to solving the riddles. But now is not the time for an internal debate on our various upbringings. I'm sure the grass is always greener on the other side. I'd rather focus on the dungeon we're trying to defeat.

With the third latch unlocked, I grab the handle and heave the massive door open. It's wide enough for Stompy to fit through.

On the other side is another long cavern. At the end of the cavern, there's a mirror the same size as the door we just entered. There's no door handle, no locks or latches, just our reflections in the giant mirror.

"That's weird." Taryn presses his hand against the mirrored surface. When his hand touches his reflection, he jerks back and shivers.

"What is it?" I ask.

"Touch the mirror."

I cast him an untrusting glance.

"It's not going to hurt you. Just touch it."

What could possibly have Taryn so shaken up? I do as he instructs, reaching out for the mirror. I expect to feel the cool sensation of glass, but when I touch my reflection, I feel the warm rough calluses that coat my fingers and palms. I immediately retract my hand.

"Whoa, that is weird. What do you think it means?" It's clearly not just a reflection. It's like we're staring into a mirror universe.

Taryn stares at the reflection as it mimics his every movement perfectly. "I think it means we have to get past our reflections to move to the next room."

Jon steps between us and places his hand to the mirror, immediately jerking it back. "Yep, that's creepy as hell."

He takes a step back and casts a doppelgänger. The cloned enchanter walks straight into the mirror, continuously bouncing off the reflection. Their foreheads redden from running into one another until Jon calls it off.

"Any better ideas?" he asks.

I have a sneaking suspicion it won't work, but I try anyways. I equip Destroyer and swing at the mirrored surface. My warhammer collides with the reflection and the recoil reverberates all the way up my arms. The pain rattles in my bones so much that I have to sit the weapon on the floor and shake my hands out.

We spend the next half-hour trying various ways of getting past the door. My horrors bounce off one another. When I stack them and create a wall in order to cast

Kamikaze, it has no effect. Taryn's lightning bolts smash into one another and we nearly go deaf from the explosion.

"There's got to be something we are missing." Taryn slouches against the wall in exasperation.

I don't know why I didn't think of it before, but I grab the perception potion and take a swig.

I pass it to the others. "If we can't get past it with brute force, then it has to be some kind of puzzle like in the other room."

Sitting next to Taryn, I wait for the potion to kick in. When it does, I scour the room, looking for hidden coves, cracks in the wall, anything that might give us some sort of clue as to what is happening.

No luck. We're in an empty cavern. There's nothing special about it aside from the mirror barrier.

Jon sighs. "Maybe this one is out of our league."

It might be, but I refuse to give up. I walk over to the mirror and stare at my reflection. As I stand there, I'm reminded of the character creation screen when I first logged in—the only time I've been able to observe myself in the third person.

I've grown accustomed to this body, so much so that it feels as natural to me as my actual body ever did. I take a moment to appreciate what I am, what I've become. My once forest green skin has a soft blue glow to it thanks to the mana I absorbed. A flat face with two gigantic tusks stares back at me. Deep blue freckles accent my wide nose. Pointy ears jut upward from both sides of my head, where two long, black braids dangle and drape over my powerful shoulders. Each shoulder has patches of rough walnut skin, almost rock-like in appearance. My muscles bulge as I hold onto Destroyer.

I am a complete and total badass, and I refuse to be defeated by a mirror. I've faced a lot worse than my own reflection.

As I stare into the mirror, I notice something out of the ordinary. There are torches hanging from the walls in the reflection, but not on our side. They have a faint aura about them from the perception potion.

"Did you guys notice this?" I point to the torches in our reflection. "They are only on the other side."

Taryn strokes his beard. "Hmmm, that is strange. Maybe we have to use them somehow."

This dungeon just about has me at my wits' end. "How could we possibly use them? We can't get past our reflections to do anything."

Jon scrunches his eyes, as if he's deep in thought. "What if our reflections can pick them up? Maybe that's the key."

Taryn nods in agreement. "That's not a half-bad idea."

Taryn takes a few steps back until his reflection is at the same depth as one of the torches. He moves closer to the wall and reaches out his hand. It takes a few tries, but the druid in the reflection eventually wraps his hand around the torch. Taryn squeezes his fingers and raises his arm higher.

The torch in the reflection comes loose of its sconce.

"Nice!" shouts Jon.

Holding his hand out in front of him, Taryn attempts to pass through the mirror while his reflection holds the torch. When he reaches the barrier, his fist bumps against his reflection.

"Dammit!" Taryn flings his hands down to his side, and his reflection drops the torch.

The flame extinguishes when it hits the ground and the cavern grows a little dimmer. It gives me an inkling of an idea.

There are still three more torches burning in the mirror. I wonder if we extinguished them, would our reflections remain? I'd be able to see in the complete darkness, but the others wouldn't.

I move with my reflection until I am standing next to a torch. With some trial and error, I'm able to remove it from the wall. I immediately toss it to the floor and watch the flame go out.

"Chod, what are you doing?" asks Jon.

"I had an idea. What if the torches are the reason we can't pass through?"

Taryn's expression changes from one of frustration to curiosity. "What do you mean?"

"If a tree falls in the forest and no one is around to hear it, does it make a sound?" I quote the age-old question of existence.

Taryn cuts his eyes at me. "Chod, I love you, but if I have to answer another riddle, I'm going to break something."

I chuckle before continuing. "It's the same principle. If no one can see the mirror, does it have a reflection?"

Their eyes light up with realization.

"You think that if we remove the light source, then we can just walk through?" Taryn asks.

"It's worth a shot. But since none of you can see in complete darkness, I'll need to lead you through if it works. So group up and hold hands or something."

I extinguish another torch while they gather themselves in the middle of the cavern. Jon takes the lead. Taryn stands behind him and uses the vines on his staff to make temporary leashes for his pets. I bet that Ruby has night vision, but I'm not so sure about the other two.

I take my position by the final torch. "Ready?"

Taryn places his hand on Jon's hip. "Ready."

Reaching out, I wrap my hand around where the final torch would be. My reflection mimics my every movement. I lift the torch and drop it to the ground. The cavern goes dark and my night vision quickly adjusts.

Just as I expected, our reflections vanish from the mirror. I move in front of the others and take Jon by the hand.

As soon as we step through where the mirror once was, I'm hit with a gust of stifling heat. It's like we walked into a sauna. There's a bright flash of light that temporarily blinds me, and when my eyes adjust, I take a step back.

A magnificent phoenix hovers in the air over a pit of bubbling lava. In the center, an imp sits on a narrow platform.

What in the hell did we just stumble upon?

CHAPTER NINETEEN
BREAKER OF CHAINS

Flames shoot out from imp's small hands directly into the moat of molten lava.

"Holy..." Jon's words trail off as he stares at the magnificent creature hovering above us.

Phoenix. *Unique monster. Level ??? One of the rarest creatures in all of Mythos. A feather willingly given from a phoenix can guard against fire. Tears of the phoenix heal better than any potion. The lifecycle of the phoenix stretches beyond the lifetimes of many mortal races. When a phoenix fully matures, it will burst into flames, rising from the ashes to start the process anew. Only the most blazing of locations can temper the phoenix's maturation. Many phoenixes will retreat to volcanoes to prolong their matured forms.*

I'm just as awestruck myself, but the fact that we can't see its level is a little daunting. The phoenix flaps its wings, sending a fresh gust of hot air across the room. Its orange and red feathers shimmer like dancing flames.

There's a clink of metal, and I notice a chain that stretches from the phoenix's leg to the floor. A gigantic spike holds the chain in place. Good to know we will have a range where it can't reach.

The phoenix is nothing less than living fire. Dark crimson feathers cover its underside and the topmost feathers on its wings. They gradually fade to tangerine and marigold, with streaks of bronze mixed in. Amber eyes look down at us, but it doesn't attack.

I take a moment to inspect our surroundings. The room we're in is a massive dome with jagged walls cut from the mountain. A moat of lava sits in the center, surrounding the imp on the small platform. The imp must be a full-grown male, because he's about twice the size of Limery. He has the same large yellow eyes, long spindly limbs, and forked tail. His dull, reddish skin matches the lava surrounding him, and his wings remain tucked behind his back.

Something feels off about this. I wait for the phoenix to engage or taunt us, anything that initiates a boss fight, but it never comes. It just hovers in the air, a watchful guardian, occasionally flapping its vibrant wings.

The imp finally notices us, and he appears shocked as he looks at us with blood-shot yellow eyes. "How did you get in here?"

I step forward and answer. "We solved the riddles and opened the doors. What is this place?"

The imp shakes his head, scowling at us. "You should not be here."

This got real ominous, real quick. "What do you mean? Why shouldn't we be here?"

He looks at me, but it feels like he's looking past me. "If Thyrim returns, you may find yourself trapped in here the same as us."

Wait, what? "Did you say trapped? Who is Thyrim, and why does he have you trapped here? Can't you just fly away?"

A fresh burst of fire shoots out from the imp's hands into the lava. "I have been here many years, locked away against my will and forced to keep the lava hot enough so that the phoenix doesn't age."

Jon moves closer. "You're a prisoner?"

The imp nods. "I am."

"We know how that goes." Jon straightens his back. "Can we help you escape?"

The imp goes silent for a moment. "I wish it were so. I am the only reason that the lava does not cool. The mountain is full of enchantments designed to keep me here and keep others out. If the lava cools, then the ceiling will cave in. If I move off of my island, then the lava will rise up and devour me. I am trapped for eternity."

Jon looks between me and Taryn. "There has to be something we can do to help him."

I understand Jon's desire to help the imp, but the last thing I want to do is end up an enemy of some powerful mage. If Thyrim is the one who enchanted this cave, then he's definitely out of our league. He has a pet phoenix for crying out loud.

But what if it were Limery in this situation? Wouldn't I do everything in my power to get that little guy home safely?

The imp's bulbous yellow eyes lock with my own. Fuck.

"What's your name?" I ask.

His face softens. "You can call me Bazel."

"That's a nice name, Bazel. What can you tell us about Thyrim?"

Bazel's eyes narrow. "He is powerful and cunning, capable of changing his appearance at will."

"So, he's an enchanter." Jon taps the butt of his staff against the floor. "How long before he returns?"

"There is no way of knowing." Bazel shrugs. "He comes and goes as he wishes. It has been many moons since I last saw him."

Taryn walks to the edge of the moat and looks down. I join him, watching the molten lava as it bubbles and splashes.

"Have you ever tried to let it cool?" I ask.

"I have not." Bazel sighs. "I do not wish to die just yet. I hold out hope that one day, Thyrim will return and call the phoenix into battle. Only then will I be free."

I strengthen my resolve. We'll find a way for him to escape; we just need time. "And what happens if you leave your platform?"

In answer to my question, Bazel unfurls his wings and takes flight a few feet off the ground. Instantly, the lava shoots up from the moat like a geyser, barring his exit and nearly melting my face off. Jon and Taryn jump back, and Taryn's pets scatter toward the door.

Bazel lands on the platform and the lava returns to its normal state. He hits it with a fresh burst of fire.

"What happens to the phoenix if we are able to get you out of here?" asks Taryn.

Of course the druid is concerned with the safety of the magical beast.

"It will age normally. Eventually, it will burn out and be reborn from the ashes as a chick, continuing its cycle."

Taryn nods. "That's not so bad."

"Were you really questioning if it was worth it for Bazel to be trapped in here?" I shoot Taryn a questioning look.

"I just want to know all the facts before we take action." He gestures toward the lava and the phoenix. "If you hadn't noticed, this is sort of a delicate situation, and the last thing we need is an angry guardian phoenix trying to kill us. We don't even know what level this thing is, but I'm pretty sure it could probably wipe us all off the map."

Point taken. I hadn't even thought about the possibility of the phoenix attacking us. "What if we could replace Bazel's weight on the platform?"

Jon laughs. "The old bait and switch."

Taryn kneels and inspects the moat. "I don't know how we could do that. It would have to be fast, and there's at least ten yards of lava between us and him."

That is the main problem, getting something out there quickly that weighs the same as Bazel. With the risks involved, we'll only get one shot at this. Failure means Taryn, Jon, and I respawn. Everyone else doesn't come back.

"Do you think you could fly up there and see if there's something we're missing?"

Taryn transforms into his bird form and flutters high into the cavern. The phoenix's eye follows Taryn as he flies. It gives me an idea.

Message (Chod): *Hey, you can talk to animals, right?*

Incoming Message (Taryn): *In a manner of speaking. I can communicate with them, but it's not like I can understand what they are saying.*

. . .

Message (Chod): *You could try talking to the phoenix. They're supposed to be noble birds. Maybe it knows something we don't.*

Taryn flutters down until he is right in front of the phoenix. In his bird form, Taryn is barely bigger than the phoenix's eye. He chirps several times and erratically zooms left and right.

An ear-splitting shrill answers him as the phoenix caws. It flaps its wings a few times, and hot air beats down upon us. The chain bound to the creature's leg clanks against the stone floor.

A moment later, Taryn returns to his dwarven form beside me.

"Well?" I ask.

"I think she wants out."

"She?"

"Yep, she's a female phoenix. She's not a pet, either. Well, not a willing pet, at least."

I walk around the edge of the room until I find the chain that is holding the phoenix in place. It's thick. Each of the links are thicker than my fingers. The phoenix must be incredibly strong to stay aloft with something that heavy weighing her down.

I give it a hard tug, but it doesn't budge.

The beginning of an idea starts to form for how to free the phoenix, but I'm still not any closer to freeing Bazel.

"I think a Horror of Finesse could take his place on the pedestal, but I don't know how to get it there." I summon one and compare it to Bazel. They look about the same size.

"Could you throw it? Like you did with Taryn?" asks Jon.

Taryn rolls his eyes at the memory.

"Too bad you can't make a bridge with your vines out to the platform." That would make things so much easier.

Taryn raises an eyebrow. "Why couldn't I?"

"If the enchantment is calibrated to Bazel's weight, then anything using it as a bridge would set it off."

"But what if I didn't attach the vines to the center? What if they went all the way across?" Taryn equips his staff and steps to the edge of the moat.

The vines on his staff begin to extend. Taryn grips the staff and slightly squats as the vines grow longer, reaching across the moat. They bypass the center island and extend until they grip the other side. The tiny leaves and flowers that grow on the vines wilt in the blazing heat. The vines themselves begin to harden as the lava dries them out.

Taryn quickly retracts them back into his staff. "Okay, good to know it works. We'll have the horror walk across. He can step onto the platform the second Bazel takes off."

I really hope this works. If it doesn't, we're all in trouble.

"Do you think the phoenix can understand me?" I ask Taryn.

He nods. "They are one of the most intelligent creatures in all of Mythos."

I walk around until I am directly in front of the phoenix. It flaps its wings and a fresh burst of hot air consumes me.

"Hey!" I yell.

The phoenix tilts its head in my direction.

"We want to get you and Bazel both out of here. I'm going to try to break the chain bound to your leg. Please don't attack me."

The phoenix doesn't acknowledge that I spoke, so I just have to take it on faith that she won't burn me alive. I equip Destroyer and take my position at the base of the chain. Taryn stands near the moat, staff in hand. Jon waits near the exit with Taryn's pets.

Taryn turns to Jon. "If this looks like it's going downhill, you take them and you get the hell out of here. We'll meet up with you later."

Jon shakes his head. "Don't talk like that. This is going to work out."

"Alright, everyone. Get ready. Bazel, you know what to do, right?"

Bazel blasts fresh fire into the moat. "I do."

I lift Destroyer overhead and bring it down with a smash on the chain. The clash of metal on metal rings throughout the cavern, and the tip of the warhammer flashes red as the first stack of Inferno takes effect.

I swing again and again, until my ears are constantly ringing. My arms grow fatigued from the effort, and Destroyer's head glows a vibrant red, matching the chain links. The chain is blazing, but the metal refuses to give.

Why the hell isn't this working?

My swings grow more labored and my speed slows as my stamina wanes. I activate Berserker Rage to keep from tiring out. Fresh adrenaline pumps into my muscles and I swing faster and harder than ever, but the chain still doesn't give. Maybe it's enchanted too.

I glance at Taryn, and he knows something is wrong. He says something, but I can't hear over the ringing in my ears.

He lifts his staff, proceeding with the plan. I hammer even harder. When I look back over my shoulder, the vines are nearly across the moat, forming a bridge.

I summon a Horror of Finesse and send it toward Taryn. I don't stop hammering. The heat from Inferno has traveled up the chain, and now several links glow red.

The horror walks across the bridge of vines and steps onto the platform. Bazel flies upward.

Lava erupts from the moat, shooting straight into the sky, and my horror dies immediately from the heat. Taryn takes off running for the door, and I hit the chain one last time before bolting away.

I curse our luck. The platform must not have been monitoring Bazel's weight. And now Bazel is going to die because we fucked this up.

A wall of lava continues to shoot up from the moat, concealing Bazel inside of it. I wish that there was something, anything, that I could do.

A violent caw cuts through the chaos, so loud that I hear it over the ringing in my ears. I look up to see the phoenix diving toward the wall of lava. She opens her wings, and her feathers turn black. She tilts her head back and absorbs the heat from the lava into her body. I can literally see the trail of heat as it escapes the molten lava. Color returns to her feathers and a shimmer surrounds her body. The chain melts away from her leg and coils to the ground.

Where there was once a wall of molten lava, now, there is only hardened rock. I use Destroyer to break a hole and crawl through. Inside, I find Bazel curled into a ball, his small body covered in sweat. He's worse for the wear, but he's alive. I lift him off the ground and carry him to the others.

His body burns against my skin. The hairs on my arms melt away and I do my best to ignore the pain as his body blisters my skin.

Gently, I lay him on the floor. "Someone hand me a potion."

Jon digs through his bag and hands me a vial of red liquid. I pour it in Bazel's mouth. His body begins to cool, and eventually, he stirs. My own burns will heal in time due to my natural regeneration.

His eyes flutter open, and he grabs my arm. "Thank you."

Above us, the phoenix circles the cavern. She flaps her wings, sending gust after gust rushing past.

"We need to get out of here," says Taryn.

"What about the phoenix?" I ask.

"I think she'll be able to take care of herself. We need to get far from here before Thyrim discovers what we have done."

I pick up Bazel and carry him in my arms like a small child. We hurry out through tunnels until we emerge back onto the mountainside. We step into the night, and I relish the cool, fresh air of the mountains.

There's a rumble inside the cavern, right before a gust of dirt and debris explodes from the entrance. The tunnel collapses, and the phoenix bursts from the cavern in a dazzling display of fire and color. Her caws echo through the mountains as she rises high, a brilliant meteor against the night sky.

I can't explain it, but a sense of peace washes over me as I watch her fly. I follow her flight until she disappears among the clouds. *Enjoy your freedom, girl.*

CHAPTER TWENTY

KING OF THE MOUNTAIN

After hiking several miles from the hidden cave, we make camp on the side of the mountain. I hunt down a mountain goat, and we roast it over the campfire. I hand a piece of roasted meat to Bazel and he devours it.

"Feeling better?" I ask.

He looks much better now that the potion has taken full effect. He's less shaky, and no longer sweating. I didn't even think that imps could sweat. I was definitely worried about him for a minute there.

Bazel smiles, showing us his demonic teeth in the firelight. "This is the first time I have breathed fresh air in many years. It feels good."

"How did you end up there anyhow?" I take a bite of goat leg and the delicious juices trickle down my chin. The light char on the skin offers a crisp bite.

Bazel's eyes droop for a moment, like he's reliving some distant memory. "Thyrim is a man of great trickery. He promised to help me in exchange for my services, but once I was in the cave, he trapped me there. He took advantage of my situation and used it to his own ends. I'm sure I'm not the first one to fall prey to his wicked motives. And I don't even know..." His voice trails off before he sits back in silence.

I pat him softly on the knee. He leaves me with more questions than answers, but after what Bazel has been through, I don't want to pressure him to talk about it if he's not ready.

Jon cuts himself a slice of meat and sits on a log beside Bazel. "What do you plan to do now that you're free?"

"I'll return to my home. I'd like a life without adventure for a while." He cracks off a bone with his teeth and sucks at the marrow.

"Spoken like a true prisoner." Jon laughs.

Bazel tilts his head. "You have been a prisoner, too?"

Jon stares at his feet. "Unfortunately, yes."

The imp reaches out and pats Jon on the arm. "Then I am glad you found your freedom, too."

If he only knew the truth behind us being here. I may have served my sentence, but the others are still prisoners, even if it may not feel like it at times.

"You're more than welcome to travel with us," Taryn finally chimes in. "We are heading to the troll forest. They have formed an alliance with many of the imps, so you may find your family there."

"That is most interesting. It seems a great deal has changed since I've been gone. I don't remember a time when the trolls roamed free anywhere, and now I see one with a dwarf and a human." Bazel stands and scratches his belly. "I will accompany you through the mountains for the assistance you have given me, but then I am afraid I must make my own way. If my home is empty, then perhaps I shall venture to the troll forest. But for now, it has been too long since I last slept."

We take turns keeping watch for the rest of the night, nestled in a crevice with Stompy blocking the entrance. Today was an amazing and unbelievable experience that I can't stop thinking about it.

I'm still in awe of the phoenix. The image of her soaring through cave with wings of fire will forever be burned into my mind. She saved Bazel's life. Who knows where she is flying to now? Hopefully somewhere that she can roam freely, to eventually burn out and start over.

A new beginning. Something I know all too well.

As great as it is that the phoenix is free, I still have my worries. My main concern lies with Thyrim. In order to capture a phoenix, he must be pretty powerful. Unless he somehow managed to trick her the same way he did Bazel. I will have to enquire about him with King Orso once we return to Seascape. If anyone will have knowledge of this man, it would be the dwarven king.

I watch Bazel as he sleeps. Little bubbles of snot rise and fall with his breath, reminding me of Limery. I've learned to never be surprised by an imp. I'm not sure any other creature could have survived being trapped in a mountain for so long under those circumstances. I pray that he finds his family and has a very safe life for years to come.

Eventually, Jon taps me on the shoulder, relieving my watch, and I quickly drift off to sleep.

A beautiful clear day awaits us as we journey up the mountain. Bazel sits atop Stompy's horn, swinging back and forth with each step, but the moulhaug doesn't seem to mind. Jon rides Stompy's back, while Taryn rides Berry and Ruby sits in his lap. I'm the unlucky one who has to hoof it.

Most of the day is spent traveling in silence. I try to enjoy the moment as much as I can. Here I am, in a beautiful fantasy world with a view of magnificent mountains, attempting to save the world from some dark force that hides in the shadows. It's almost unbelievable, but it is my life now.

There's so much opportunity here in Mythos. Someone like me can build themselves up from nothing, making friends, going on adventures, and really finding a purpose for their life. I wonder, how many of the other heroes can say that? I want to make this world a better place, for me and for others.

"What do you say we stop by the home of the mountain trolls?" I ask.

Taryn stops in his tracks. "Do you have a death wish? Don't you remember what happened last time you were there? We all nearly died."

"Yes, I remember. But I gave Kronan the option for a better life for his people. Maybe he took it." He might have been a brute, but I think deep down, he cared for his people and their well-being.

"Who's Kronan?" asks Jon.

"He's the leader of the mountain trolls. Big brute of a troll."

Jon shrugs. "I wasn't there, but it sounds like a bad idea to me."

I shrug. Maybe they're right. But what good am I doing if I don't follow up on my actions?

"Screw it, we're going."

I know that if it comes down to it, I can win a fight with Kronan, but I've got a feeling I won't need to.

Everyone looks at me like I'm crazy, except for Ruby, who swishes her tail from side to side.

"We'll be fine. He might need our help," I plead.

Jon glances at me with suspicion. "Well, if I die, you're retrieving my items."

"Deal." I shake his small human hand.

I search for the location of the caves where we encountered the mountain trolls and plot our destination. It'll take at least an extra day to get there but it'll be worth it. King Orso might have tasked me with uniting the heroes, but I have a feeling that when the times comes, we'll need every able-bodied fighter we can get.

At such a high altitude, the air is cool against my skin. Every breath is like inhaling after eating a peppermint and I love it. It's truly refreshing. I'm admiring the beauty around me when a screech cuts through the air above us.

I look up to see a griffin descending below the ring of clouds that hide the peak from view. It flaps its powerful wings and dives straight for us.

"Everyone, get your weapons!" I rally the others and summon a round of horrors. This was the last thing I was expecting to happen today. Griffins are deadly, intelligent beasts.

As soon as I equip Destroyer, I notice there's a rider on the griffin's back. The rider wears boiled leather with a griffin emblem branded on the chest. A pair of large goggles conceal his face, and his short brown hair whips in the wind as they dive.

I lower my guard and laugh. What are the chances?

I raise my hand, signaling the others to stand down. "It's okay. I know this man. It's King Favian from Vanaria."

"What the hell is he doing all the way up here?" asks Taryn.

The griffin comes to a sliding stop several meters ahead of us. Its beak clicks at the air, and Favian climbs from the saddle. He removes his goggles and offers me a warm smile.

"Chod, I didn't expect to run into you here." His blue eyes sparkle with adventure.

"That makes two of us. You're a little far from home." A long ways from home, actually.

"Truth be told, I'm here on business. Searching for a mate for Grimclaw. There are very few griffins on the island, but the ones that are here live high in these mountains." He strokes Grimclaw on the neck. "What brings you here?"

"Have you not heard? The fast-travel portal has opened in Seascape. I sent Limery south to instruct you on how to open yours. King Orso wishes to call a meeting."

The king's eyes go wide. "I'm afraid I've been away for a few days. If what you say is true, I must return at once."

"Wait!" Bazel grabs me by the arm, and his sharp nails dig into my skin. "Did you say Limery?"

I pull away, but the imp doesn't loosen his grip. What's gotten into him? "Yes, he has been my companion for some time. Do you know him?"

Bazel grips me harder. "He's my son! Does that mean... Did Leo—" The words get stuck in his mouth.

It all comes flooding back to me. Limery said that his father had been tricked. That when Leo was sick, a healer promised to help in exchange for his father's service. Is that how he ended up in that cave?

"Leo is fine. I saw him recently. Lillith, too."

Bazel releases me, overcome with emotion. I pat him on the back as his body shakes underneath his heaving sobs.

"I was afraid I lost them." He sighs. "I'm afraid I must go."

I understand completely. Were I in his position, I would do the same thing. "Go to the forest. Lillith is leading the alliance between the imps and the trolls. They will know where to find her."

Bazel moves from one of us to the other, hugging us. "Thank you for freeing me. I will not forget it."

The imp takes to the air, and in a flash, he is gone.

King Favian looks at us in disbelief. "I feel there is a story there, but first, tell me about the portals."

"When King Orso announced the challenge to reward anyone who could unlock the portal, thousands of people flooded the capital, even a few heroes. Many people attempted. Some even lost their lives from the dark energy that surrounded it. Then, Glenn and Jude showed up with a small army of mind-controlled dwarves."

King Favian scowls at the mention of Jude's name.

I continue. "There was a fight, and I was thrown into the portal. The dark energy surrounded me and for a moment, I thought I would die, but then a blessing that had been bestowed on me by the forest trolls saved me. It did something to the energy too, because when I got up, the portal was accessible."

The king places his finger on his lip for a moment before speaking. "And you think this can be replicated?"

"We believe so. We sent Limery to the forest to gather a few trolls to march south."

"That is most interesting." He turns to the griffin. "I'm sorry, Grimclaw, but it looks like your search for love will have to wait."

The griffin huffs in response.

"But before we leave, introduce me to your friends. I'd also love to hear the story behind the imp. It sounds most fascinating." He raises his eyebrows.

I motion to Taryn. "This is Taryn. He's a druid."

Taryn nods his head. "Pleasure to meet you, Your Highness."

"And this is Jon. He's an enchanter."

Jon drops to one knee and lowers his head. "Your Highness."

The king smirks. "An enchanter, you say? We don't see many of those nowadays. How is your training coming along?"

Jon stands. "It has been a slow start, but since meeting Chod, I've seen some real progress."

King Favian winks at me. "There is no doubt that you have. Where this one goes, greatness follows. I may be able to offer you an opportunity to advance your skills far quicker than traveling from dungeon to dungeon."

Jon straightens his back. "I'd love to hear more."

"Vanaria has one of the greatest libraries on the island. We haven't produced as many master enchanters as the dwarves, but we do have great scholars. And I happen to have one enchanter who could help teach you at an extraordinary rate. You'll learn in days at our library what would take weeks on your own. If you would like to return to Vanaria with me, I will make sure you push your limits like no other."

Jon's mouth hangs wide open, practically dragging the floor. His eyes dart between me and Taryn before answering. "Are you serious? That, uh, would be amazing."

"What is your enchanter's name?" I ask. I have a sneaking suspicion that he might be the one who locked Bazel away.

"Her name is Sirina. She has served us faithfully for many years."

A woman. So it wasn't Thyrim. Still, Favian might know of him. "Do you know an enchanter by the name of Thyrim?"

The king furrows his brow. "How do you know that name? Thyrim is Kassidy's brother. He holds a small keep outside of Vanaria."

Ah, Kassidy. The teleportation mage who always has food in his beard. Power must run in their family. "He's the one who trapped Bazel in the mountain."

King Favian places his hands together and brings them to his chin. "Trapped, you say? This grows more curious by the minute. Please enlighten me."

I tell him the story of the hidden entrance, of the puzzles, and then the phoenix and Bazel trapped inside. Then I inform him of how Bazel was tricked in the first place.

The mirth has vanished from the king's face. "I am sorry for the imp's troubles. I will make sure to have a talk with Thyrim the next time I see him. While I cannot justify his actions, I can understand them to a degree. Phoenixes have a natural predisposition toward darkness and the undead. They are very rare, but exceptionally powerful. There is a long history of fear of all things of a dark nature on the island, especially the undead. If what you say is true and the dark wizard is afoot, then a phoenix would have been a great weapon in the wars to come." He gazes off into the direction of Seascape. "I don't agree with his methods, but what is one imp in exchange for one of the most powerful creatures on our side when that day comes?"

I'm surprised when Taryn answers. His face is set, and I don't know if I have ever seen him so serious. "It's the difference between us and them. We don't sacrifice our own without their permission. We don't take the lives of those we should protect just because it might give us an advantage or make things easier. Every life matters, and Bazel deserves the chance to live his own life and make his own decisions just as much as any of us."

Chills run down my spine. I couldn't agree more.

Favian lifts his hands, palms up. "I can't argue with your reasoning. Many a king has kept himself up at night pondering over this very question. For you, it is simple. You live for yourself and use your abilities to protect others. For me, I have an entire kingdom to rule over. Thousands of lives that I need to value. Do I tend to the needs of a hero like yourself, who could possibly turn the tide of a battle, over an infantryman when the time comes? Or do I make the tough decision when the time comes, losing one man but saving thousands. Nothing is black and white, not even good and evil."

Taryn sits speechless atop Berry. I understand the feeling. I couldn't possibly imagine having to look out for so many people. One thing I'm certain of is that Favian is a good king. Many leaders only look after themselves and expect their subjects to fall into place. He cares about his people and wants what is best for them.

"Perhaps one day we can discuss this in more depth, but for now, I must return to see what new adventures await my kingdom." He turns to Jon. "Will you be joining me?"

Jon turns to me like a small child waiting for their parent's permission to go play at the park.

I smile. In the small time we've been together, I've watched Jon grow from someone who was selfish and just looking for a way to get by to an actual caring teammate, and dare I say, maybe even a friend. "Go ahead. You'll be a great enchanter. I'm sure we will see each other again."

I extend my hand, but he bypasses it and wraps his arms around me. "Thank you, for everything." When he releases me, there's a glisten to his eyes. "And you were right. After talking to Bazel and hearing his story, I know what you mean now. This place is the real deal."

I slap him on the back a little too hard, knocking his glasses askew. "And that is exactly why we need to protect it."

CHAPTER TWENTY-ONE

GIANT PROBLEMS

"Looks like it's just you and me again." I duck under a low branch from a tree that grows on the side of the mountain.

We're traveling toward the mountain troll caves, and I have no idea what to expect. After our last encounter, there's no telling if they are friend or foe.

Stompy refuses to duck and powers through the branch with his horn until it snaps. Debris falls on Taryn as they pass.

He picks pieces of broken bark from his beard and flicks them away. "I know. We were just starting to be a formidable group, and now I only have you to watch my back."

"I'm sure we'll see them again. I can't wait for Limery to see his father. I bet he'll be so happy." I still can't believe he was trapped in a cave for years on end. I get bored sitting alone with my own thoughts for more than five minutes. I can't imagine spending years with no one to talk to.

"You know, I have missed his antics." Taryn grins. "And what about Jon? His luck turned around pretty fast."

One of my horrors slips and falls off the mountain. I feel its presence as it tumbles down the mountainside, losing bits of HP with every hit until it disappears altogether.

Now, that it's just me and Taryn, I keep as many horrors on hand as I can. I want to be prepared in the event we come upon anything dangerous.

"Yeah, good for him, though. It's an amazing opportunity." Jon's a good guy, and it's about time he caught a break.

By early afternoon, we near the mountain troll lands. Around the next corner is where I first found them tucked away in a massive crag. I keep an eye out for goblin scouts, but so far, all is quiet. I equip Destroyer, both for the added protection and its ability to muffle my movements. Unfortunately for Taryn, his boots' abilities don't transfer to his pets. Berry and Ruby walk quietly, but there is no mistaking Stompy's footsteps.

The crag is filled with many full-grown trees in its opening. A well-trodden path winds between them until we find ourselves in a clearing surrounded by mountain on three sides. There are remnants of the fire pit and chairs carved out of stone, but there's no sign of the trolls or the goblins. Where could they have possibly gone?

Taryn and I search the premises. There's nothing to give the impression of a struggle or fight, so they must have willingly moved.

"Maybe he did take your advice." Taryn stands in front of the entrance to the largest cave. "Want to check it out?"

I shake my head. I've had enough cave adventures for the time being. "It's a little too soon for me."

He laughs. "I feel you on that. I guess it's back to the trail then. Were you wanting to take the route to Smalltown or go a different way this time?"

Ah, Smalltown, the best place to have your items smuggled from one kingdom to the other. I wonder how their business will be affected once the portals between Seascape and Vanaria are both open?

I don't imagine many people will be venturing through the mountain unless they have something to hide. And if there is one thing I know, it's that if you deal with unsavory characters, you'll get unsavory results.

Pulling up my map, I see that there is a more direct route to the forest. Our last time through, we strayed into the marshes to level Taryn up, and it took us a bit out of the way.

"Let's take a new route. There's no use exploring the same old places when there are plenty of opportunities for new adventure. Lead the way."

As soon as Stompy turns away from the cave, a loud rumble echoes from within. I've had enough experience in this world to know that's not a good sign.

Taryn and I exchange glances, and I can tell he's thinking the same thing as me. Fight or flight?

The rumble fades, replaced by a light patter reminiscent of a heavy rain on a roof.

"What the hell?" Taryn stares at the cave. "Is that rain?"

While I wouldn't say it's impossible for there to be rain inside the mountain, I highly doubt it.

I've seen enough movies to know what's coming. "No, that's a bunch of small creatures running down the cave toward us."

Just as I say it, a speckling of tiny orange dots appears in the depths of the cave. They grow bigger as the sound increases. I grip Destroyer tight, ready for whatever comes next.

Fifty or sixty goblins emerge from the tunnel. Green-skinned, with lanky arms and pointy ears, some carry torches, others wield spears and beat them against their crude wooden shields. They're clad in rags and scraps of leather. Their orange eyes stare at us with intrigue. There's no sign of any mountain trolls among their ranks, and the metal collars they wore around their necks are gone.

I take a step forward. "Where is Kronan?"

One of the taller goblins shoves his way through the crowd on the back of a mangy looking wolf. His bright orange eyes stare at us with menace. "Kronan go. Now you go." His voice is high pitched and shrill.

"Where did he go?" I ask. Would the mountain trolls really leave the goblins behind?

The goblin points past us, repeating himself. "Kronan go. Now, you go."

Whispers snake through the group, growing louder until the entire group is chanting "go, go, go," and pointing their fingers or weapons at us.

"I think we might should go." Taryn slowly backs Stompy away.

I think he has a point. Maybe we could take the entire group at once, but I don't like the odds. Even if they aren't as strong as us, there is strength in numbers.

I raise my hands. "Okay, we're going."

Another thunderous rumble echoes from the cave, and the hair on my neck stands on end. There's still something inside.

The goblins move aside and fall silent, creating a path down the center.

"Chod, I've got a bad feeling about this." Taryn backs Stompy away a few more steps.

I know we should run, but there's also that part of me that wonders what might be coming. What new challenge awaits?

I stand my ground. A loud groan escapes the cave, and the goblins all gasp. Two massive gray legs appear from the darkness. Each step thunders as more of the creature becomes visible. Each leg is as big as I am. When it fully emerges, the monster is twice as tall as me, and it carries a stone club that could potentially end me with one hit.

Giant. *Level 22. As tough as the mountains from which they spring, giants' bodies regenerate at such a rapid rate that the only way to kill them is to remove the head.*

Oh, fuck.

I thought all the giants had left the island with the dark wizard. This one must have taken up residence in the cave after Kronan left.

I take in the grotesque creature. Skin as gray as the mountain itself. Two bulging eyes the color of pus and teeth that look like wood. Stringy gray hair mixed among the bald patches stick to its sickly face. Boils cover its hawk-like nose. By far, this is the ugliest creature I have ever come upon. It's so ugly that I can't help but stare. But underneath the flaky skin and disgusting appearance is the body of a warrior. Muscles bulge and contract with every movement until it stops between the two groups of goblins.

The only reason I can imagine as to why the giant and goblins are living in the cave together is because the goblins flock to creatures with power. They take a bit of abuse for the solace of protection.

To each their own, but I can already smell the garbage bin that resides in its mouth and can only imagine the smell inside that cave.

I slowly back away. "Sorry to disturb you. We mean you no harm, so we're just gonna turn around and be on our way."

The giant shakes his head. "No," his voice rumbles.

"Look, I can see your time is precious. And you're a man of few words, which I can appreciate, so just let us be on our way and no one has to get hurt." I turn to leave when something warm and squishy hits me in the back.

I look over my shoulder to find a goblin laying dazed and confused on the ground.

"No way. You did not just—"

Before I even finish my sentence, the giant picks up another goblin and throws it at me. I step out of the way and it goes sailing into the trees, screaming the whole way.

"So, that's how it's going to be? Two can play at that game." I grab a Horror of Vitality by the horn.

"Chod, don't—" Taryn tries to stop me, but I've already committed.

I hurl the horror at the giant with all my might. The fluffy horror looks at me with betrayal as it soars through the air and bounces off the giant's chest without doing so much as a trickle of damage. The giant grunts and smashes the horror with its rock-like foot before lifting his club overhead and unleashing a mighty roar. Spittle and drool fly past his rotting teeth.

I roll my shoulders and answer his call, roaring with all the defiance I can muster.

"Bro, this is not going to end well." Taryn's face is full of worry.

"Dude, he threw a goblin at me." I toss my hands in the air. "I can't let that stand."

The giant charges, and for the briefest moment, I think about running. Then I remember I'm a goddamn troll and I take off to meet him head-on. Taryn jumps off Stompy, but I don't wait around to see what he does.

"Keep the goblins off me, and I'll handle the giant."

Me and Mr. Giant are the same level. Time to find out what happens when an unstoppable force meets an immovable object.

Time seems to slow down as we approach one another. He swings his club and I duck, sliding through the giant's legs and feeling the displaced air as it barely misses rearranging my face. As I'm sliding, I summon a horror and explode it right on his nut-sack.

The giant howls in pain. Even though it didn't do more than a sliver of damage, there's no way that didn't hurt.

He yells at the goblins to attack, and Taryn finally makes his move. I send all my horrors with Taryn and his pets to handle the goblin horde. Lightning crashes into the group of goblins, and all hell breaks loose.

While I'm still on the ground, the giant swings his club at me like a sledgehammer. I roll to the side, and the club caves in the stone ground, exploding rubble into the side of my face. I quickly scamper to my feet and back away.

He's actually pretty fast to be so big. I may not be as strong, but I know I'm faster, so I'll need to use that to my advantage.

The next time he swings, I meet the blow with Destroyer. A chunk of stone breaks off from the giant's club, but I take the brunt of the attack as its recoil reverberates through my forearms. The giant laughs at me and kicks out, planting his foot into the center of my chest and knocking me back several feet before I land on my back.

I gasp for air like an asthmatic. Damn, that hurt. Luckily, I don't think he broke anything. The giant stalks over me with the slow pride of someone who thinks they have won the fight. Bad news for you, buddy, because I don't fold that easily.

I summon another horror and toss it at the giant. A half second later, I do it again. He swings his club like a baseball bat at the first horror and it dissipates in a puff of smoke. The second horror strikes home on the giant's family jewels before he has time to react.

The giant falls to his knees, grabbing his groin. Two for two.

"Hey, man. You started it. Play dirty, you get the dirt."

His booger-colored eyes look at me with disgust, but I don't care. I jump to my feet and smash Destroyer into his side. The giant grimaces in pain before stumbling to his feet.

"Troll not nice!" he roars.

I check on Taryn, and he's managed to back all the goblins into the mouth of the cave. The horrors and his pets have formed a barrier, blocking the goblins from getting out.

Alright, so it's just me and the big guy. No problem.

The giant rushes me again, club raised over his head. I'll give him this, he really goes all out. The club crashes into the earth as I sidestep out of the way. While he's still lifting his weapon, I hit him in the side of the kneecap with my warhammer. Something crunches, and he falls to one knee.

The giant grunts as he attempts to stand, eventually using his club as a crutch.

"Bad troll," he grunts.

I feel the presence of most of my horrors behind me and call them to my aid. The giant reaches down, attempting to grab me, and I barely escape his reach.

I send my horrors after the giant, and they rush him, biting and clawing at his legs. He steps on several horrors, and I summon more. Their attacks do almost no damage to his hardened skin. Every time I hurt him, his regeneration kicks into gear. Currently, he still has ninety-five percent of his health.

There's no way I'm going to be able to whittle him down at this rate. I'll need a killing blow—something he can't recover from.

I keep a healthy distance from the giant while I try to formulate a plan. He crushes my horrors with ease, but at least they are keeping him distracted.

"Taryn, I need your help."

A moment later, he's beside me. "What's up?"

"If I create a distraction, do you think you can tie his feet together with your staff?"

He frowns. "I don't want to get anywhere near that thing."

"Come on, dude," I plead. "It's the only way I see us beating him."

He raises his eyebrows. "Maybe you should have thought of that before you got us into this situation." He sighs. "Fine. I'll do it."

"Alright, get ready." I really hope this works. The giant is strong, but he's not the brightest. If I overwhelm him with too many things at once, I think we've got a real chance.

I summon another round of horrors. The Horror of Power and Horror of Finesse rush in to join the others. I take the Horror of Vitality by the horn and chuck him at the giant's face.

As the horror flies, I wind up Destroyer and let it fly. The giant grabs the horror out of the air, and I explode it against his hands. At the same time, I cast Kamikaze on the rest of the horrors attacking his feet and legs.

It distracts him enough that he doesn't see my warhammer coming straight for his face. It hits him in the chin, and he stumbles backwards. His eyes cross for a minute as he regains his senses.

"Special delivery, air mail." I chuckle at my own joke.

Taryn is already on the move, vines extending from his staff and wrapping around the giant's legs. They keep pouring out until they cover him completely from ankle to calf.

Now is the time for the finishing touch. I run for my warhammer, and the giant focuses on me. He tries to step in front of me, but his legs are tied. He wobbles back and forth, trying to regain his balance, but it's too late. He tumbles to the ground just as I grab Destroyer.

He reaches for me, but I smash his hand into the ground. When he recoils, I land a blow to his rock-hard head. His eyes droop from the blow. The tip of Destroyer flashes red with each hit. The giant's head bobbles like a fighter about to fall. It takes several hits before the skin breaks, several more before bones crack, but eventually, the giant lies lifeless on the floor.

I sit down on the remnants of Kronan's throne, thoroughly exhausted. The goblins stare at us from the cave, but they take no action.

"Nice going. Couldn't have done it without you." I reach out and fist-bump Taryn.

I check my stats. After the fight, I'm not too far off from level twenty-three.

"Sweet, new level!" Taryn pumps his fist.

When I focus on him, I see he is now level nineteen. We've bridged the gap pretty nicely and now he is only three levels below me.

"Nice! Any new abilities?" I ask.

His eyes glaze over. "Let me take a look."

He goes quiet for a moment.

"Dude, I've got three new options! One is Barkskin. It allows me to buff anyone in my party with tougher skin, as if they were wearing wooden armor. The second is Summon Fungus. It summons mushrooms that release poisonous gases, but they are poisonous to us as well. The third is Stonewall. It summons a stone barrier wherever I want."

All of those seem pretty handy. "Which one are you going to choose?"

He strokes his beard. "I'm not sure. I could also further buff my current abilities. A level-three Lightning Bolt would be nice, too."

"Your call." I set Destroyer on the ground and stretch my arms over my head.

Taryn paces, tapping his staff on the ground. "I think a new ability would serve us better, especially since it's just the two of us for now. You've already got pretty tough skin, and I'm not much of a brawler, so I think Barkskin is out for now. Summon Fungus and Stonewall both seem pretty good options. It'd be nice to summon a wall if we're retreating or need to keep someone out, but I think Summon Fungus could accomplish the same thing, but it could also be used offensively as well. What do you think?" He looks at me for approval.

"Sounds good to me. It'd be nice to have some more crowd control abilities aside from Horror of Vitality's passive slow." I go back over to the giant's body to look for loot, but aside from the giant club, there's not really anything there.

It makes me wonder even more how he and the goblins found themselves together.

"Ready to get out of here?" I ask.

Taryn glances at me out of the corner of his eye. "Sure you don't want to start another fight beforehand?"

I laugh off his comment. "I know, I know. I let my temper get the best of me again. What can I say? I just don't like being disrespected."

Taryn calls his pets back from the cave entrance. The goblins just stand there, watching us. They truly are strange creatures.

"Enjoy having the place to yourself." I give them a two-finger salute and turn toward our next destination.

We've still got a few more hours before sunset, so we should be able to make some good progress. I imagine we have at least a couple of days before we're out of the mountains, even with Taryn using Strong Wind to increase our speed.

As we make our way down the mountain, I hear something behind us. I turn around with Destroyer at the ready.

An army of green descends the mountain, stirring up dust and gravel as they come. Taryn steps up beside me, his staff raised.

"These guys don't learn, do they?" His staff glows brown for a moment, and a cluster of mushrooms spring up across the path. Light brown mushrooms with purple spots and bulbous caps. There's no way anyone is passing through them without taking some damage.

The goblins come to a halt, sending a dust cloud wafting in our direction.

"Are you looking to die?" I raise my hammer. "Go back home."

The larger goblin comes forward, still riding his mangy wolf. "You strong. We follow."

Taryn and I look at each other, confused.

"You have got to be shitting me."

CHAPTER TWENTY-TWO
BRIDGE OVER TROUBLED WATER

Taryn bursts out laughing. "You killed their new leader, now they're all looking to you. It's like they're lost ducklings and you're the first thing they saw." He wipes a tear from his eye.

After I used my horrors to disable the mushroom traps, the goblins have been following us ever since. They hunt for themselves. They don't bother us, but they won't take no for an answer. Sometimes, I look over my shoulder and they are just staring at me. It's so creepy.

"Let this be a lesson to you. You don't have to fight everyone who wants to fight you." Taryn holds his stomach as a deep belly laugh takes over.

I roll my eyes. As if my grumbling horrors weren't enough of a responsibility, now I have fifty goblins following my every move.

As we journey through a narrow pass of the mountain, the line of goblins and horrors stretch behind us for a great distance. It's like we're some banished group on a pilgrimage to a new land. With such a large troop, at least we don't have to worry about being attacked unaware. However, we'll have a harder time being inconspicuous, and I'm sure enemies will spot us from further away.

Unfortunately, Strong Wind doesn't work on a group this large, so we are forced to travel at a more moderate pace. We could just cast it on ourselves and leave the goblins in our dust, but Taryn is having so much fun watching them follow me around that he won't use it.

Who knows, maybe I can pawn them off on the forest trolls once we finally arrive at the forest.

As we make camp for the night, howls fill the air in the direction of the grasslands below the mountains. Usually, we hear one or two creatures howling at the moon, but this is different. Dozens, maybe more, howl in unison. The sound sends a chill down my spine.

Ruby sits up, ears pointed and head cocked, as she stares in the direction of the howling.

I turn to Taryn. "That's odd. I've never heard anything quite like that. Any idea what it is?"

He closes his eyes, attempting to listen. When he opens them, a frown paints his face. "No idea. They aren't wolves, coyotes, or jackals. Whatever it is, it sounds like a bunch of them."

The next night, the howls sound even closer, and I can't help but wonder what we might be walking into.

The mountain path widens the lower we descend, allowing us to spread out as we walk. When we make camp, the goblins form a circle around myself, Taryn, and his pets.

The largest goblin approaches me. "You sleep. We watch." His orange eyes are piercing as he stares at me over his hooked nose.

I nod. For whatever reason, I'm strangely comforted by the gesture. In an alternating order, half the goblins sleep, while every other goblin faces away from the group, watching for threats. For the first time since staying at the inn, Taryn and I both sleep through the entire night.

When I wake up, I feel refreshed and ready to take on the world. A new notification flashes in the top of my vision.

Regional Alert! *The portal to Vanaria has been reopened. Fast-travel is now permitted to Vanaria.*

Awesome! It looks like the troll blessing worked after all. And at this rate, we'll probably arrive at the forest around the same time as the others return.

Taryn wipes the sleep from his eyes. "Things are changing fast. I can't imagine what the island will be like now that both portals are open."

I know what he means. The world just got a whole lot more interesting.

I summon horrors as we descend the final stretch of mountain and empty into the lush grasslands below.

Berry stuffs his nose in the grass, sniffing as we go along. Stompy rips a bunch of wildflowers from the ground and eats them. I think he and Stompy are both glad to be back on flat ground.

A few hours in, we come upon a river blocking our path. As far as I can see, there are no bridges or methods of crossing. I wade in a few steps, but the bottom quickly falls out. There's no way we're crossing with the goblins, and it's too far for me to throw them across.

"Let me take to the air. I'll see where the closest crossing is." Taryn doesn't wait for a response before transforming into his bird form and disappearing into the sky.

I soak my feet in the cool water while I wait for him to return. Several goblins use their spears to fish in the shallow parts of the river. They offer me food, but I decline. I watch them roast fish over a small fire when a red bird lands on my shoulder.

I jump, startled by the sudden appearance.

Taryn transforms back into his dwarven form. He looks at me with a devious smirk. "Got you."

"Ha-ha." I scowl at him. "Very funny. Did you find anything?"

"It looks like we have two options. There is a ferry several miles east. I imagine it would be pretty costly to get all of us across."

I nod. "And what's the other option?"

"A few miles west, there's an abandoned bridge. It looks a little worse for the wear, but if Stompy can swim across, then I think the rest of us could take the bridge."

I pull my feet from the water and return to the goblins. "Alright, troops, time to get moving."

The goblins rush to action, extinguishing the fire and gathering their belongings. They are truly devoted to me and follow every command I give. Stompy could take a few notes.

When we arrive at the bridge, "worse for the wear" is an understatement. The thing looks like it could fall apart at any moment. Several planks are missing and many more look rotten and dilapidated. The first step creaks as I put my weight on it, and there's a section in the middle with a three-foot gap we'll need to cross.

I'm sure the goblins are lightweight enough to cross, but for Berry and me, we might want to take our chances in the water.

"You think this will hold up? It doesn't look like it's been used in ages." I place my hand on the railing and it wiggles back and forth.

"It probably hasn't been. We're quite a ways from the main roads. This thing looks like a relic from the past, but I don't see many other options. I can fly further downstream and see if there's another crossing."

I shake my head. There's no point in wasting more time. I'm anxious to get back to the troll forest and see what's happening.

To make matters worse, the current is a lot rougher here than in other spots. Rapids bubble on both sides of the bridge. If anyone falls in, they'll be taking a long ride downstream.

Standing around all day staring at the bridge isn't going to get us anywhere, so I call everyone to action.

"Goblins, you're up first. One at a time, please." I step aside so that they can cross.

The head goblin steps up first, riding on the back of his mangy wolf. "I go." He flashes me his teeth in what I assume is a smile.

Before he leaves, I stop him. "What is your name?"

He tilts his head to the side before answering. "This one is called Cheevus."

"Okay, Cheevus, show them how it's done."

Carefully, the wolf steps onto the rickety bridge. Since he's the heaviest of the goblins, this will be a good test. The wolf meticulously chooses its steps, placing each paw delicately on the aged timber before moving forward. A few times, it changes its foot placement mid-step.

When they arrive at the section where all the boards are gone, the wolf lowers itself, and I can see the muscles rippling just before it launches across the divide. They land and the bridge wobbles for a moment. Cheevus tenses up, gripping the wolf's fur. A minute later, they step off the bridge onto the other side.

"Awesome!" I turn to the rest of the goblins. "Form a line and cross one at a time."

It's a lengthy process, waiting for each goblin as they slowly make their way across. A few of them struggle to jump the gap in the center. One almost misses the leap entirely and dangles precariously with his feet dipping in the water before a second goblin comes out and helps him up.

Eventually, they all wait on the other side. Ruby crosses with no problem, and then it's just me, Taryn, Stompy, and Berry left.

"How are you planning to get Stompy across? I'm pretty sure the water is deeper than he is tall, and the current is moving pretty fast." Not to mention he has to weigh a couple of tons. Honestly, I'm not even sure if he can swim.

Taryn winks. "I've got it covered."

He climbs on the moulhaug's back and Stompy steps toward the riverbank. Taryn raises his staff. It glows for a moment and then Stompy trumpets as his body suddenly doubles in size.

After casting Imbue, Stompy is larger than an elephant. I'm still not sure if he's big enough to withstand the current, but it'll be close.

Stompy steps on the edge of the riverbank and the earth collapses into the river. Taryn holds steady as they slowly enter the tumultuous water. Stompy leans into the current, battling nature with his massive frame.

On the other side, Ruby paces on the river's edge.

"I guess it's time for you and me to get moving." I scratch Berry behind the ear and step onto the bridge. "I'll go first."

As I move across, I have the uneasy feeling that the entire thing could collapse at any time. I'm halfway across when I hear Taryn curse to my right. I turn just in time to see Stompy sliding closer to the bridge in the raging current. He tries to push forward, but each step drags him closer to me.

His head is only inches above the water, and Taryn is holding on for dear life as the river covers him up to his waist. He could easily transform and fly away, but there's no way he's leaving Stompy to fight through this alone.

"Easy, boy." Taryn tries to comfort the struggling moulhaug. "It's going to be okay. Just one step at a time."

Stompy slips, and both he and Taryn disappear beneath the surface. The bridge shakes and I think they've smashed into it, but a second later, both Stompy and Taryn break the surface gasping for air. I can't do anything but watch in horror.

I think about retreating until they make it across, but when I turn around, Berry is already halfway to me.

"Berry, go back!" I shout. "The bridge can't support both of us."

The umber bear's eyes are focused on Taryn. He grunts and groans as he watches his master struggle.

"Berry! Go back."

I'm so focused on getting Berry off the bridge that I don't notice when Stompy loses his footing and collides into the bridge. Wood splinters and the bridge cracks in half from the weight of the moulhaug.

The impact knocks me into the water, and I sink underneath the rapids. I fight to swim to the surface, but the current pulls me under. My back hits the silty bottom of the riverbed, and I tumble in the river's violent grip before it releases its hold on my body.

My head breaks water and I gasp for air. Up ahead, Berry and Stompy are both bobbing in the current, but Taryn is nowhere to be seen. The goblins run along the riverbank, following us as the current carries us away.

I fight to keep my head above water. In the raging river, that's all I can do. Any attempt to move to the shore is useless. We're forced to take the whims of the river until it decides to release us.

Suddenly, a tight pressure cinches around my wrist. A vine trails from my wrist to the side of the river, where Taryn stands with his staff pointed at me.

"Grab the others!" he yells.

I fight against the current, and my muscles burn until I reach Berry. The vine extends and wraps around his paw. I grab Berry's other paw and swim toward Stompy as best I can. He bobbles up and down as his hind quarters flirt with riverbed. I grab hold of his saddle and yell for Taryn to pull us over.

Water rushes into my open mouth. With one hand on Berry and the other on Stompy, I'm like a buoy at sea. There's a slight pressure as we begin moving toward the eastern side of the river.

My head bobs above water and I see Taryn surrounded by fifty goblins as they all pull on the staff like a giant game of tug-o-war. Inch by inch, we move closer until the current releases us and I feel muddy earth beneath my feet.

I crawl to the bank and collapse in the grass. Closing my eyes, I let the sweet relief of fresh air fill my lungs.

When I open my eyes, dozens of orange eyes look down on me.

"Chod okay?" asks Cheevus.

"Yeah, I'm good." I cough a few more times before finally sitting up.

Beside me, Berry shakes the water from his coat, drenching us in a heavy mist. Stompy sulks a few feet away as Taryn tries to calm him.

I take a deep breath and try to calm my racing heart. At least we made it across.

CHAPTER TWENTY-THREE

OH GNOLL YOU DIDN'T

I find myself looking at the goblins in a new light. Without being asked, they rushed to Taryn's aid, not only saving me but Berry and Stompy as well. I'd always viewed them as unintelligent monsters, nothing more than lackeys for the trolls or giants or whoever they were following at the time, but they are much more than that.

They might not follow those that appear weak, but they are blindly devoted to those they do follow. They respect power above all else. So I decide that going forward, I'll treat them with more respect.

Something I doubt they have ever experienced.

We're about a day's march from the edge of the forest. That still leaves us with another day of travel through the woods before we make it to the troll village.

Looking at my map, I don't foresee any major obstacles on the way.

When we camp for the night, the goblins take their positions around me and Taryn, forming a protective circle. I nod to Cheevus before lying down and letting the sound of chirping crickets pull me into slumber.

A loud howl wakes me. As I wipe the sleep from my eyes, I notice the goblins are on their feet with their spears, pickaxes, and rusty swords pointed into the darkness. I nudge Taryn and get to my feet.

Something is up, but I'm not sure what.

Another howl pierces the night, followed in quick succession by several more. Whatever creatures we heard howling when we were in the mountains, we've stumbled right on top of them.

"What's going on?" I ask Cheevus.

The leader of the goblins turns to me. "Gnolls coming."

I search the perimeter, but see nothing. My night vision only allows me to see for so far. After that, it's up to the moonlight, which is currently hiding behind the clouds.

I equip Destroyer, not sure what to expect but wanting to be prepared. Quickly, I summon three horrors.

Berry lets out a low growl, and Stompy paws at the earth. Clearly, they can sense something is amiss. Ruby stares out in one direction, rigid as a statue.

"She sees something." Taryn squints, though if I can't see it, then he definitely won't be able to.

Something howls behind us. All I hear is a loud swish as we all turn at once. A second howl echoes from my left, and then another from my right. They pour out of the darkness until we don't know which way to face.

"Everyone, stay calm and hold your positions." I do my best to keep an air of authority. "If you see anything, call it out."

The howling continues to the point where I can't tell where one howl ends and the other begins.

I continuously summon horrors since there is not much else I can do.

One of the goblins screams and points into the darkness. I'm able to make out the shape of some bipedal dog-like creature. A second later, another becomes visible.

As they get closer, I begin to make out their features. They look like hyenas, with stubby snouts, spotted fur, and short dumpy ears. Taller than most humans, their bodies are lean and muscular with thick necks. Their eyes are solid black and devoid of emotion, and their lips curl up in a permanent sneer. They wear leather armor and wield rustic spears. Some appear to have damaged armor or dented metal weapons. All in all, they look like scavengers.

More and more approach from the darkness, until we're surrounded by a pack of at least twenty. Finally, they get close enough that I'm able to focus on their stats.

Gnoll. *Level 15. Nomadic scavengers, gnolls wander the countryside looking for victims to rob and towns to pillage. Gnolls often travel in packs, submitting to the will of the pack lord.*

Before I even have time to question what a pack lord is, he appears before me. Similar to the other gnolls but bigger and wielding a massive sword he no doubt stole.

Gnoll Pack Lord. *Level 20. Leader of the gnoll tribe, the pack lord is able to bind the lesser gnolls to a common cause. A pack lord can also rally his pack with Rampage.*

Great. Us and a bunch of goblins against a pack of hungry killers. We outnumber them two to one, but I don't see the goblins offering much help in this situation.

"What do you want to do?" asks Taryn.

The gnolls continue to stalk toward us, like predators preparing for the hunt. After saving my life, I don't want to put the goblins at risk, but I don't see any way out of this besides fighting.

"We're gonna have to fight. Or at least scare them enough that they run off." I've summoned twelve horrors since the gnolls appeared, putting the numbers slightly more in our favor. "Maybe if we swarm them, they'll run."

"Honestly, I don't have a better plan. Let's do it." Taryn climbs atop Stompy.

"Goblins, group up. I want at least four goblins to a group. Run out to the closest gnoll and hit it with everything you've got. It's time to raise hell!" I lift my warhammer into the air.

Cheevus does the same with his spear, and the goblins join in. Their high-pitched yelling fills the air, causing the gnolls to stop in their tracks.

"Attack!" I roar.

Like an explosion, we disperse on our attackers. Several of the gnolls exchange glances, uncertain of what is happening. I rush toward the pack lord, and several goblins and horrors follow me.

He slashes his sword at the same time I swing Destroyer. The two weapons clash, and it rings through the night. The sword flies from his grip and sticks point-down in the nearby grass.

The pack lord roars, and two gnolls rush to his aid. Goblins jump on them, biting, clawing, and stabbing at any exposed areas. Lightning crashes somewhere behind me as Taryn joins the fight.

I catch a glimpse of Stompy bulldozing one of the gnolls into the ground. His hoof caves in the creature's chest as he runs him over.

Everywhere I look, goblins and horrors overwhelm the gnolls. They cling to them like spiderwebs in a dark attic. Clearly, gnolls aren't the smartest creatures.

Destroyer crushes the ribs of the nearest gnoll and the tip flashes red. A second gnoll stabs a spear at me, but I parry the wooden weapon with ease. The pack lord retrieves his sword and comes back for more. He charges at me, but stumbles forward as Cheevus's wolf pounces on him from behind, sending him stumbling to the ground.

I step on his sword as he tries to stand. He jerks at the weapon, but I weigh too much for him to pull it free.

"You picked the wrong group." I smash my warhammer into his ribs and he flies several feet.

He snarls at me as he crawls to his feet. All around him, his men are bruised and bleeding. Some have already turned and ran, freeing up the goblins to overwhelm the others.

Cheevus lifts his spear and points it at the gnoll. "You go!"

For a moment, I think the gnolls might actually retreat, but they all group together around the pack lord.

The pack lord tilts his head back and howls. The others follow his lead. A red aura forms around them, then I notice that their black eyes are now bright yellow. Their bodies twitch as muscles grow and expand. Claws lengthen and teeth extend, and suddenly, their health bars replenish completely.

The pack lord smirks at me. "I think we'll stay." His voice drips with venom.

They charge at us. With those teeth and claws, they don't even need weapons.

Taryn casts Lightning Bolt, but the gnolls move aside. Lightning explodes into the earth like a grenade.

I step in front of the goblins and take a deep breath. I'll do my best to protect them. I call my remaining horrors and summon a few more. Then I remember I have an ace up my sleeve.

I cast Champion, and a fifteen-foot giant appears out of thin air. He bends down and picks up the pack lord's sword. The mighty weapon looks like a dagger in the giant's hand.

The giant meets the gnolls head on. He swings the sword with raw power, severing two gnolls in half with a single blow.

The goblins cheer at the devastation.

Taryn casts another bolt and we all rush into battle. The giant has turned the odds heavily in our favor. Stompy charges through the group of gnolls, head swinging like a battering ram. They fly to the side, and horrors and goblins swarm them like ants on candy.

For the second time today, I watch the pack lord lose his cool as the giant lifts a gnoll with his free hand and crushes its skull like a rotten apple.

He slings the body aside, and it collapses like a ragdoll.

The gnolls turn to retreat, and we chase them for a few hundred meters before they disappear into the night.

When I return to our camp, many of the goblins stand in a circle. I push my way through to see what's going on.

Cheevus kneels next to a small green goblin with a wooden spear sticking out from his throat. The goblin's lifeless orange eyes gaze up at the heavens. Cheevus reaches down and closes them.

He died protecting us.

"What was his name?" I ask.

Cheevus strokes the goblin's cheek. "This one is called Doren. Very brave."

"Very brave, indeed. We will give him a proper funeral." The goblins should be given the opportunity to mourn their fallen.

Cheevus stares at me for a long moment. I can't tell what he's thinking.

"Thank you." He kneels beside Doren, removing the spear and crossing Doren's arms over his chest.

I use the spiked end of Destroyer to break apart the ground, then dig the upturned soil with my hands. Doren is so small that I don't have to dig far to make a suitable grave.

No one talks as I work. Even Taryn stands stoic next to the goblins. When the hole is big enough, I pick up Doren. He feels like a small doll in my hands, and memories of holding Limery come flooding back. I find myself fighting back tears as I place the small goblin in the grave.

I stand there, looking at his frail body, wondering how a game could ever feel this real. Not just the sensations and experiences, but the emotions that come with it.

The goblins gather around the grave, silently watching their fallen brother. I take a step back to give them the opportunity to mourn however they see fit.

Cheevus reaches down and picks up a handful of dirt. He squeezes it in his fist, closing his eyes. When he opens them, his grip loosens and the dirt falls into the grave grain by grain, like sand through an hourglass.

"Good-bye, Doren." Cheevus tilts his head, and once the dirt has emptied from his hand, he steps back.

The words are simple, as is the gesture, but it pays respect to the fallen in a way only the goblins know how. Each goblin takes their turn, saying good-bye and placing a handful of dirt in the grave. When they are finished, Cheevus drops to his knees and begins shoveling the rest of the dirt while the others return to their duties.

I kneel beside him and help. We don't talk; we just shovel. And when the grave is filled, Cheevus places Doren's sword point down at the head of the gravesite.

Wherever you are, I hope you rest easy.

CHAPTER TWENTY-FOUR

NEW FRIENDS IN OLD PLACES

The journey to the edge of the forest is somber and uneventful, which is good. After losing Doren to the gnolls, I'd feel sorry for anyone or anything unlucky enough to come across us right now. There's a lot of hurt and anger flowing through the group.

"That was really nice of you back there." Taryn strolls up beside me, riding Berry. "I'm sure it meant a lot to them."

I give him a half-smile. "Thanks. I just did what I thought was right. It's a delicate balance, the urge to play this like a game, but also taking into account that everyone here has the ability to react like real living creatures. It's a mindfuck, sometimes."

"I totally get it. We kill to level up, but at the same time, seeing a group of goblins mourn their fallen is a sobering experience." He takes a deep breath. "It's a fine line, indeed."

A familiar comfort washes over me as we step into the forest. Is this what returning home feels like? The magnificent trees that tower overhead, the lush vegetation, birds and bugs that fill the forest with their orchestra. My shoulders relax and the tension I've been carrying lessens.

"So this is it?" Taryn looks around, taking it all in.

I forgot that he has never been here before. I ran into him while on the quest for the mayor in Lynchton. He never got the chance to see the troll village.

I shake my head. "This is the forest. Once upon a time, the forest trolls ruled over all of it, but now, their numbers are so small that they all reside in a single village."

"Well, maybe now that they aren't being hunted, their population can grow and expand."

Wouldn't that be nice.

Stompy comes to a stop and rubs his backside on a massive tree, scratching some unknown itch. The tree shakes with the movement, sending nuts raining down from above. The goblins scatter out of the way to avoid being hit.

Taryn just laughs at the moulhaug's antics.

We prepare to make camp for the night. By this time tomorrow, we should arrive at the village. We find a clearing where all of us can sleep safely, when something catches my eye. A few hundred meters away, I spot the translucent outline of a forest troll.

I do a double-take to make sure I'm not imagining it. Why would a guardian troll be this far out? He's way outside of the tribal boundaries.

"Taryn, do you see that?" I point in the direction of the troll.

When he shakes his head, I realize my mistake. Only other trolls or creatures with high perception can see the outline of a troll using camouflage.

"There's a guardian troll over there. He's awfully far from the village. Stay here while I go check it out."

"You sure?" He raises an eyebrow.

I nod. The trolls all know me.

"Be careful. Scream like a little girl if you need us." He pretends to punch me in the arm, pulling back at the last second.

I equip Destroyer and use its ability to muffle my movements to my advantage. If it's Malak or Jojin, maybe I can give them a good scare. As I get closer, I realize that this is a troll I don't recognize. He must have been gone last time I was at the forest.

When I realize why I don't recognize him, I freeze in place. It's because he's not a forest troll, he's a mountain troll. What in the hell is he doing all the way out here? And alone, at that?

The mountain troll has some stark differences from the forest trolls. His skin is a light plum-color, dotted with speckles of gray. His hair grows in a short gray mohawk. He has a long hawk nose that nearly touches his lips, and his tusks are shorter but more girthy than mine. Mountain trolls are stockier than forest trolls, built for strength and not speed. And they're really great at tossing boulders down the mountain.

I put away Destroyer, so that I don't alarm him when I reveal myself.

"Hey, you're a long way from the mountains." I put my hands up so that he knows I mean him no harm.

The translucent sheen fades and his color returns as the mountain troll stands, ending his camouflage.

He eyes me warily before speaking. "Ah, you. Our devoted hero."

I can't tell if he is mocking me or not. My experiences with the mountain trolls have been far from pleasant.

"I passed through the mountains. There were no other trolls there. What happened?"

He steps closer. His body language is tense, but not hostile. "I'm afraid that is not my story to tell. Kronan will fill you in."

"Kronan is here, too? Are all of the mountain trolls in the forest?"

He sighs. "You do ask a lot of questions, even for a forest troll."

"Fair enough. What's your name?"

He stands up straight, puffing out his chiseled chest. "I am Ekon."

Time to extend a little hospitality. "Welcome to the forest, Ekon. I'm traveling with a group of goblins and a dwarf. Would you like to join us for dinner?"

I can see the internal debate raging behind his eyes. Eventually, he nods.

Good, at least he doesn't completely hate me.

Several goblins have already started a fire by the time I return, and a few others set out to hunt.

Ekon looks at the goblins with suspicion. "The goblins follow you now?"

"Yeah, after I defeated the giant, they wouldn't take no for an answer."

His eyes squint even further. "You defeated a giant?"

I laugh. "Look who's the one with all the questions now."

Ekon grunts but remains quiet.

"This is my friend, Taryn. We're on our way to the troll village."

"Nice to meet you." Taryn extends his hand and smiles.

Ekon nods in return but doesn't move his hand. Maybe I got in his head with my comment.

It doesn't take long before the goblins come back carrying a wild boar over their heads. The beast greatly outweighs the small goblins, but eight of them manage to keep it from dragging the ground. They skin it and remove the entrails, and soon enough, it is roasting over a spit. The savory aroma drifts to my nostrils, and I have to wipe away a bit of drool.

We all sit around the fire, and I take another crack at getting some information out of Ekon.

"So, you can't tell me why you left the mountains. What can you tell me?"

He scowls at me. "Why must you know everything?"

Taryn burst out laughing. "I like this guy."

Ruby crawls into Taryn's lap and curls up.

I feel myself getting angry, so I take a deep breath. "Fine. Let's just eat."

The goblins slice up the boar and give both Ekon and I an entire leg. Ekon rips into the meat, and the juices stream down his face.

"Mmhm. Good." He manages between bites.

I pass my brimming tankard around and we wash down our boar with a never-ending supply of fresh cool water. Whatever the enchantment is that allows it to replenish itself is fascinating. It only refills when the tankard is in an upright position. When turned upside down, the water stays inside. I imagine this is to keep people from accidentally flooding areas by knocking the tankard over.

The goblins pick the boar to the bone, leaving nothing for the scavengers that may come after we're gone.

Once he's finished, Ekon stands. "Thank you for the food. Now, I must return to my post."

"Anytime." I wave at him as he leaves.

He starts walking, then turns around. "We are here to make the trolls great again. We are tired of hiding."

Before I have a chance to respond, he leaves.

Taryn nudges my shoulder. "You did it, man. You really did it."

It feels good to know I had some part in it, but I can't take all the credit. "Whatever it is they are doing, Kronan made the decision. I may have helped open his eyes, but that's it."

Taryn rolls his eyes. "Whatever you say. Time for me to get some sleep, I'm looking forward to meeting all of the trolls you've been blabbing about."

Truth be told, so am I.

A soft tickle moves up my arm, and I reach down to scratch it. Sharp pain flares through my finger, pulling me from sleep, and I wake up to find a small red lizard with its mouth wrapped around my knuckle. A hard shake sends the creature flying into the bushes.

I curse loudly, waking the others. They all look at me like I'm crazy.

"A lizard bit me." I hold up my finger to show them, but the wound has already healed.

We pack up everything and set off for the village. I instruct the goblins to stay behind me. If there are more guardian trolls this far out, then I want me to be the first thing that they see. It's more likely to be peaceful that way. The forest trolls will welcome me with open arms, but if there are more mountain trolls, I'm not sure how privy they are to my relationship with the forest trolls.

As we travel through the forest, the effects of the ley lines become gradually clearer. Trees and vines that move of their own accord, flowers that bloom as we pass or curl up in defense. One plant mimics the look of a tropical bird almost perfectly, going so far as fluttering its leaves so that they look like wings moving. I smile fondly at the memory of the glowing flowers that would light a path through the village at night.

Taryn's mouth hangs open. "Dude, this is amazing."

We pass another mountain troll, cloaked in camouflage. He watches me, but he doesn't move as we walk by. Ruby is the only one aside from me who notices him.

I see a few more trolls in the distance as we continue onward. When we're only an hour from the village, I spot a familiar face.

"Malak! What are you doing up here? I thought you guarded the southern border?"

Malak runs to me and embraces his hand around my forearm. Several goblins are startled by his sudden appearance as he decloaks.

"Chod! It is good to see you! Much has changed since you left. We are trading with Lynchton, the mountain trolls now help us protect the forest, and the chief has left for Vanaria to help the human king." The words spill out of his mouth.

Good to see he is as easily excitable as ever.

"Easy there." I pat him on the shoulder. "One thing at a time."

He smiles wide. "Now is a good time to be a troll. For the first time in a long time, we feel like we are a part of the world." He claps me on the shoulder in return, his green eyes gazing intently into mine. "And it is all thanks to you."

I introduce Malak to Taryn and the two shake hands.

"Any friend of Chod's is a friend of the forest trolls." He smiles.

"Likewise." Taryn grips the troll's massive hand with both of his own.

I move right into business. "Are any of the council members around? There are things I would like to discuss."

"Tormara is still in Vanaria as part of the alliance. Chief Rizza, Gord, and Jira left to help the king, along with a few other trolls. Kronan is holding a seat on the council in their absence."

Kronan has a seat on the council. That is very interesting. I can't wait to find out how that came to happen.

Malak decides to accompany us as we head to the village. As we go, he fills us in on what has changed since I left. Lynchton has become a bustling town, where humans and trolls trade. People travel from all over to buy troll potions. Humans are now allowed to hunt in the forest as long as they stay away from the village, and now that the mountain trolls have moved to the forest, they are able to send scouts to farther areas.

We bypass several more trolls along the way. Some wave from the distance. The ones that do not I assume are mountain trolls.

I'm so caught up in conversation that I'm startled when we pass the barrier into the village. The illusion that keeps the village hidden from outsiders is fueled by the rich flow of mana beneath the soil. No doubt Jon would be amazed to see it. One minute, we're looking at an expanse of lush forest, and the next, I'm walking down a path with the village visible in the distance.

The thorns and vines that form a wall around the perimeter unravel and create an opening for us to pass through. As soon as we are inside, the hole closes, forming a barrier once more.

My mouth waters as Kea's famous stew wafts in our direction. A giant pot is always boiling, providing nourishment to anyone who is hungry.

My heart warms as I spot the young trolls running between the huts, swinging clubs carved out of wood. Like all the architecture in the village, the huts are formed from living trees.

"Chod!" A familiar voice calls my name, and I turn to see Ismora carrying a small troll on her hip.

She sets the troll down and sends him off with the others. I'm surprised when she wraps me in a hug. I return the gesture, giving her a hearty squeeze. It's so nice to be around familiar faces.

"Everyone, this is Ismora. Weapons master and a great fighter." Her face is covered in scars from her many battles over the years. Nowadays, she trains the children in the ways of troll weaponry and fighting. Limery's handprint is seared into the side of her neck from our first adventure together, one where she almost lost her life.

"Yashi will be thrilled to see you! Right now, she is out gathering herbs for potions. We've been selling them to the humans at the market." She beams with pride.

"That's great to hear. Are any of the imps around? I'd love to speak to Lillith. I hear she might have found out some exciting news."

Ismora shakes her head. "No, they are all at the market. Their help with translating has been invaluable. Come, have a rest. I'm sure you are tired from your travels. We can have accommodations for all of your party by nightfall."

"By nightfall? We don't mind sleeping on the ground. How are you going to have something ready in such a short amount of time?" asks Taryn.

Ismora winks. "The forest provides. If you want to show your friends the village, we'll get started right away."

"That would be great." I embrace Ismora again, and she disappears into the village.

Taryn gives me a questioning look.

"Mana infusion. Trolls can infuse mana directly into living objects. Our skin is tough enough that raw mana doesn't burn us. You see how the huts are formed out of living trees? The roofs are made from the leaves. Mana infusion allows the plants to understand our will, and they do as we say."

He looks confused. "So all of this, the moving plants, the blossoming flowers, it's all because of mana?"

I nod. "Yep. Trolls are one with the forest."

The village hasn't changed much since my last visit. Leather boils under a giant pergola while one of the female trolls stirs it with a long stick. A wide assortment of hides lay draped across a section of vines. Under another, the many weapons the trolls have looted over the years are organized by type. I know from experience that they keep the best weapons in Jira's hut, but I'm sure these are great for trading with the townspeople.

Just as always, the village is home to mostly females. The male trolls take turns guarding the boundaries. I'm honestly surprised that the mountain trolls had no problem with it. Almost all village business is handled by the women. I would imagine they handle the majority of the trading as well.

A female mountain troll and forest troll are engaged in conversation. They stare at us as me and my goblin troop make our way to the village center. When we arrive, a fire burns in the fire pit. Its embers are low, but it will be blazing come nightfall.

"Chod!" A deep, cavernous voice calls my name.

Kronan. The plum-colored troll, larger than any of the forest trolls, myself included, glares in my direction. A fur shawl covers his broad shoulders, despite no longer being in the mountains. One of his tusks is cracked at the tip, and he wears his hair in a braided mohawk with the braid hanging over his shoulder. At level twenty-five, I'm still surprised I defeated him.

"Kronan. Long time, no see."

He looks past me, observing the goblins. Cheevus steps up to my side, his chin held high.

"I see you've gained some new companions." He clenches his fist, and for a moment, I worry that he wants to fight. It has to be a blow to his pride to see the goblins following the troll who bested him in front of his own tribe.

He reaches in a pouch that hangs from his side and pulls out a vial of frothy yellow liquid. He hands it to me. "I pray they serve you well."

I examine the vial. It's sweetwater, a specialty of the forest trolls. It's deliciously sweet, but burns like hell going down.

Is this a gesture of peace?

I uncork it, take a swig, and pass it to Taryn. The familiar burn trails into the pit of my stomach.

"What made you come here?" I ask.

He stares at me for a moment. "Follow me."

I instruct the goblins to stay in the village center with Taryn's pets while Taryn and I walk with Kronan. We follow him until we come upon the council area. Chief Rizza's throne, along with the chairs for the council, are all empty. They are constructed in the same way as all troll architecture—bent into shape out of living plants. Beautiful white flowers blossom while they remain empty. Kronan takes a seat near the end and the flowers retract everywhere except around his head.

It says a lot that he doesn't take Rizza's seat even though she's not here.

He motions to the chairs across from him. "Go ahead, have a seat."

I do as he says. It wasn't that long ago that I was a member of the council, until I vacated my seat to Gord before setting off to find my own path.

Kronan raps his fingers against the armrests of the chair. He stares at his feet, as if wondering where to begin.

He clears his throat. "After our battle, I was furious. More angry than I had ever been in my life. My hatred for you was so hot that I could feel it sizzling in my very veins. For days, I hid away in the caves, unwilling to show my face to anyone. I lost my purpose. If I wasn't the greatest warrior, then what was I? The goblins abandoned us in defeat, and the mountain trolls were at a point of decision." His claws dig into the bark of the chair. "We could continue down our ways, and eventually, there would be no more mountain trolls. Or we could embrace the ways of our ancestors and take what was ours."

His eyes bore into me. "Through it all, I saw your face. As I slept, as I woke, it was always there, looking down on me, judging me. I would wake in the night and see you with my own warhammer raised above my head. Your words cycled through my mind." He sits back and laughs. "And then one day, I reached up and I took the warhammer back. The visions stopped, and I marched my people here. Chief Rizza was not what I expected. She is no weakling as I had thought. She has a strong mind. We have formed an alliance, and we aim to bring more troll societies to our cause."

He stands up. "I have been to the nearby village. I've seen with my own eyes that men do not attack us like they once did, and I am told that you are to thank for that. I would rather use my weapons on the beasts of the forest than on fighting for survival. My people deserve peace and safety, a chance to raise their families." He walks over and extends a hand. "So, thank you, Chod, hero of the forest and mountain trolls, for showing me the way."

I take his hand in mine, but the words get stuck in my mouth. I'm truly and utterly speechless. My eyes are suddenly wet, and I blink rapidly to fight back the tears.

I'm glad his people have found peace, but the fighting is far from over.

"Uh..." My first attempt at talking is a croak. "That is wonderful to hear, but I'm afraid we may need your warhammer before you find true peace."

His face turns to stone. "What do you mean?"

"Call a council meeting. I will fill in everyone on the details."

It takes a while for Kronan to gather everyone, but eventually, the council takes their seats while Taryn and I stand before them.

Kina sits to my left, one of the few trolls who doesn't wear her hair in a braid. Her bluish-black hair would make even the most confident supermodel green with envy. Next to her sits Guilda, Gord's mother, and one of the elders of the village. A long gray braid drapes over her shoulder and into her lap. On the other side, Kronan is to my right. He stares at me with intrigue. Next to him sits Sonji. There's nothing remarkable about her. She wears her hair in a black braid, and her clothing is the typical leather of the average troll. You'd never know she held a seat of power just by looking at her.

Four members is the smallest council I have seen, but they govern the forest in Chief Rizza's absence, and I must inform them of what is coming.

"What is it you would have us know?" Guilda doesn't look annoyed, but rather ready for me to get to the point.

I take a deep breath, thinking of the best way to put this. "As you know, the fast-travel portal has opened in Seascape. And now, the portal in Vanaria has been opened as well. In many ways, this is great. It will open up trade between the dwarves and humans. Everyone, trolls included, will benefit from the races mixing more openly."

They all watch me intently, and I try to make eye contact with each of them as I continue.

"There are other continents out there, as well. And the portals will have access to many of them. I believe the majority of them will trade with us. Some will probably send their own warriors or adventurers to *Isle of Mythos* in time. For heroes like me and Taryn, there is a whole wide world of opportunity for us to grow and level. But the truth of the matter is that not all of the portals are opened."

The council members exchange glances, and Kronan sits on the edge of his seat.

"The dark energy that kept ours closed for so long still keeps several portals closed and their secrets hidden. We don't have the ability to open portals from our side. They can only be opened from the destination. King Orso believes that the dark wizard who wreaked havoc long ago is still out there, and that one day, he will open his portal again. We don't know if the other closed portals are allies or enemies, and we have no timeline for when they might open, but when they do, we need to be ready."

"What are you proposing?" asks Guilda.

I wait before answering, because I know what I am about to say will not be taken well. The trolls finally have peace. They are finally rebuilding from everything they have lost over the years. Even the mountain trolls have fallen into a better way of thinking. I wish desperately that they could hide away in the forest and that all of this would pass them by. But in my gut, I know that is not the case. Every troll is worth at least five men, and they will be integral in what's to come.

I straighten my back and strengthen my resolve. "It is time for the trolls to prepare for war."

For the first time since I've known her, Kina loses her cool. She stands to her feet, snarling. "This is preposterous! We are finally safe again and you want us to march to war? Do you have so little respect for us?"

Guilda counters. "Easy, Kina. Chod has always been a friend of the forest trolls. He is the reason we have risen to where we are."

Kina shakes her head, and her beautiful hair shimmers in the fading sunlight. "This is not our fight. Let the humans and dwarves go with their massive armies. Let the heroes fight the darkness. I will not see our children become orphans of war."

Sonji nods. "I agree with Kina. We have come too far to lose it all now. Let someone else fight this war, we have fought for long enough."

Kronan makes to speak, but as he opens his mouth, Taryn steps in front of me.

He raises his hand, asking without words for them to listen. To my surprise, they do.

"You're not wrong to fear losing what you have worked so hard to attain. In my own life, I've had to work for everything I have. Some people are given things. They wake up in the morning, and they have what most of us dream of. Things that they take for granted." He shakes his head and the clasps in his beard jingle. "This isn't about losing what you have. It's about standing idle while everything is taken away from you. If the men and dwarves and all the heroes go to face this threat and we lose, what will happen to you then? Who will stand up for the trolls when we have all fallen? Who will protect the little ones that run through the streets of your village? If you sit by while we go into the unknown, you may find yourself standing alone if we fall."

I try not to take his comments personally, but I know he's referencing me and my life outside of the game. I never took Taryn as the jealous type, and maybe he's not, maybe he's just trying to relate to the trolls, but it still stings. I didn't choose the life I had any more than he did.

A smirk spreads across Kronan's face. "The half-man speaks the truth."

Taryn spins on his heel, pointing at Kronan. "I'm a dwarf, asshole!"

Kronan tilts his head back, laughing. "Right you are." He turns to the others. "The dwarf speaks the truth. My people have sat idle for too long, afraid of dying out and in turn slowly fading into nothing. While I cannot determine the fate of the forest trolls, for the mountain trolls, we will relish the opportunity to go to war among allies. For if we fade from this world, it will be with a weapon in our hands and a roar in our throats."

The others sit in contemplation. Sonji twiddles her thumbs, Kina silently shakes her head, and Guilda stares off into the forest.

Finally, Kina speaks. "We will discuss this matter with the chief once she returns. Her guidance has not led us astray yet. I am sorry for my coarseness, Chod. You have always done well by us. Though this news is not welcome, it is not your doing, and I should not have lashed out at you."

I smile. "I won't take it personally. I've lost my temper on occasion."

Guilda shuffles in her seat. "If there is nothing more to discuss, then the council meeting is over."

"Good speech." I have a hard time hiding the disappointment in my voice. Maybe I'm just being sensitive, but I still can't stop thinking about what Taryn said about those born with things that others want.

Taryn steps closer until he's looking up at me. "Hey, man. It wasn't personal, and it wasn't aimed at you. I just know what it's like to want to hold on to what you have."

"What, and you don't think I do? Just because I had more than you doesn't mean I wasn't afraid of losing it. It doesn't make me a bad person because I grew up in a wealthy family. Those are the cards I was dealt. I didn't choose them."

Taryn shakes his head. "You don't get it. I mean, how could you?"

My hands get jittery, and I feel my breathing quicken. "So it's like that? I shared everything with you. Every new game, I bought you a copy. Whenever we hung out, I paid for everything. And not because I felt sorry for you, it was because you were my friend."

Taryn throws his hands up and turns away. "See, you're missing the point. It's not about you! It's not about what you had or didn't have, what you were afraid of losing or not. It's not about how generous you are. It's about me. My experiences! I can never understand what it is like to be wealthy, but you also can't understand what it's like to come from nothing. It's not your fault; it's just the way it is. Every time I mention my situation, it's not a reflection of yours. And as long as you carry a chip on your shoulder because you resent where you came from, you'll never see it any other way."

He storms off and I start to follow.

He turns around, cutting his eyes at me. "Chod, just leave me be for a bit."

I stand there in the empty council area and watch as Taryn disappears into the woods.

When he's gone, I take a seat on one of the empty council chairs. A fresh bout of anger flows through me and I pound my fist into the armrest. The flowers retract into the safety of the vines. How could he be so rude? I've never flaunted my wealth in front of him. I've always tried to make Taryn feel like an equal when around me.

I sit there for a long time lost in my thoughts. As much as I try, I just can't put it behind me. Was Taryn right? Do I resent where I came from?

When I think on it, all the bitterness and anger in my life is aimed at one thing: my parents. That they cared more about money and lifestyle than they ever did about me. And no matter how many presents or new games they got me, it never filled the void that I was missing from them.

I let out a deep sigh. I am ashamed of where I came from. Because everyone looks at me like I have it all, when in reality, I have nothing. Nothing but a best friend who I just yelled at.

I find Taryn sitting on the bank of the village lake. He skips stones across the water. The goblins have joined him and several swim in the crystal blue water. Berry lays sprawled out in the fading sun while Stompy eats leaves from the tree branches. Ruby turns in my direction as I approach.

Taryn tosses another stone. He looks in my direction, but he doesn't say anything.

"Hey, man. I'm sorry. I shouldn't have taken that so personally. I know you didn't mean anything by it. I just get upset sometimes when people think I have this great life just because I have money. It's like that's all they see when they look at me."

He tosses another stone, but it sinks straight into the pond. "I'm sorry, too. I was a little hard on you." He smiles. "That speech got me all kinds of emotional."

"It was a good speech." I laugh. "And when you called Kronan an asshole, that was priceless."

Taryn joins my laughter and his dreadlocks swing back and forth. "If they ever make a movie of my life, that better be in there."

I put my arm around him. "We good?"

His hand pats me on my lower back. "Yeah, we're good."

"Cool, let's get back to the village then."

Back in the village center, several guardian trolls have returned for the evening. I spot Kronan talking to another mountain troll. They both glance in our direction as we enter, and a scowl immediately forms on the second troll's face.

Brutus. The last time we met, I had my trident pointed at his throat. He looks at me with contempt. His plum-colored skin is scarred in many places, with a pronounced lilac scar that runs diagonally down his chest. His shoulders and arms are dotted with speckles of gray, perfect for blending in with the mountains. He has the same long nose and short, thick tusks that are common among mountain trolls. His hair is braided into a long mohawk that runs down his back.

"What is he doing here?" asks Brutus.

Kronan laughs. "Come now, Brutus. Jealousy doesn't look good on you."

I approach the two, and Brutus continues to stare daggers at me.

"Kronan, may I have a word?" I ask.

We step to the side.

"He'll come around in time." Kronan smirks. "Brutus is a great warrior, but he lacks vision. What is it you want?"

I glance over my shoulder. "It's about the goblins."

Kronan raises an eyebrow. "What about them?"

"Taryn and I have a long road ahead of us. We will be traveling to the other continents as we level and gather others to our cause. I'm glad that the goblins have chosen to follow me, but there's no place for them on this journey. You know as well as I do that they are valuable companions, and we will have need of them in the wars to come, but for now, I would have them stay in the forest to train and learn to fight alongside the trolls."

Kronan grunts. "They will not be happy. Goblins are incredibly loyal to those they choose to serve."

I shrug. "Then they should have no problem following my orders."

"We could always go for round two." He winks.

"I'll keep that in mind as a backup plan." I'm not entirely sure that the outcome would be the same if we fought again.

I return to the goblins, who have gathered around the fire pit. "Alright, goblins, I need to talk to you all."

Over a hundred orange eyes stare in my direction.

"I'm glad you all chose to follow me, but unfortunately, we will have to part ways for a while. I want you to stay here and train with the trolls. A battle is coming, and I will need you ready to fight."

Cheevus stands up. "No. We follow Chod. We ready to fight."

Of course, this is going to be difficult. "I know you are, but where I'm going, I can't take all of you with me. Train here, grow stronger, and we will meet up again, I promise."

Taryn looks at me with amusement as the goblins grow visibly agitated.

"Look, this is not open for discussion. I need you to—"

All the goblins gasp in unison and stare over my shoulder.

I turn to see a massive wyrm slithering between the trees. The wingless, legless dragon glows a faint blue from the toxic gel that coats its scales. Bright blue eyes stare at me. Its snout looks like a beak, perfect for burrowing underground, and it has grown even larger since the last time I was here. It rises like a cobra, nearly doubling my height.

Yashi's small hand waves at me from atop its back. Then she jumps down like an acrobat, landing softly on the ground. The diminutive potion master is as agile as I remember.

"Chod!" she squeals as she runs and jumps into my arms, wrapping me in a hug.

"It's good to see you too." I look up at the wyrm. "What have you been feeding these things?"

She flashes me a sneaky smile. "The forest provides."

"So I hear." I laugh and we end our embrace.

"What brings you to the forest?" She looks past me, finally noticing the goblins. "Your party has grown larger since we last saw one another."

The goblins gaze upon the wyrm with greedy eyes.

"I was actually hoping to leave the goblins here to train with you. The council members will fill you in on the details. I was also hoping to see Chief Rizza before I left. Do you have any idea when they will be returning?" I don't have time to just wait around for them to show, but we need to talk.

"It should be any day now."

I sigh. I suppose we could always go to Lynchton to check on the progress they've made with trading while we wait.

Yashi's wyrm lowers itself to our level. Yashi strokes its hardened snout and its eyes close slightly.

"We should have a celebration tonight." She beams. "To celebrate your return and our alliance with the mountain trolls."

"That sounds nice, but first, I need to have a talk with these guys." I motion to the small army of goblins over my shoulder.

They continue to stare at the wyrm, following its every move.

I walk over to Cheevus and kneel beside him. "Cheevus, I need you to understand. It's not that—"

"We stay." He's still fixated on the wyrm.

I can't help but chuckle. "You know, there's actually two more."

His eyes turn to slits and his lips curl up into a devious smile. I have a feeling the goblins will be just fine without me. I can already picture them riding giant wyrms into battle.

The last beams of daylight fall beyond the trees, casting the forest in darkness. The wyrm's glow seems more pronounced in the firelight.

Ismora emerges between a row of huts and embraces Yashi in a massive hug before coming to us. "Your shelter is ready."

"Alright, troops, let's get you settled in and we will all meetup afterward. I'm sure Yashi will tell you all about her pet wyrm." I wink at Yashi.

As we walk to our new accommodations, I receive a message notification. I expect it to be some snarky comment from Taryn, but I stop in my tracks when I notice it's from Valery.

Incoming Message (Admin): *You've made quite the name for yourself since we last spoke. Our developers have been hard at work on the backend, trying to fix the system error that is keeping you logged in. We may have found a solution, but we'll only know once you log out. I recommend finding an inn and setting your spawn point there. The time has also* *come for Taryn's scheduled break, so we will be pulling you both out at the same time. You have until tomorrow evening. -Valery*

Taryn stands still right beside me, but his expression is unreadable. "Did you get a message too?" he asks.

"Yeah, looks like we're heading to Lynchton tomorrow." I can't explain why, but there's a knot in my stomach. If they've found a fix, what happens to me? Will they still want me to log back in?

My chest is suddenly tight. I'm not ready to go back.

CHAPTER TWENTY-FIVE

LIVE AND LET LIVE

After moving the goblins into their freshly-constructed barracks, we all meet up in the village center for a celebration. This is the most crowded I've seen the village as mountain and forest trolls join in the camaraderie. Sweetwater flows all around as trolls let loose with displays of strength and tribal dancing.

Through it all, I can't get Valery's message out of my mind. Part of me secretly hopes that they haven't found the answer. I know it's their job, but too much is riding on me being here. I will do everything in my power to stay in this world for as long as I can.

Taryn comes and sits beside me, his eyes slightly glazed over from the sweetwater. "I thought the dwarves knew how to party, but this is something else."

We watch as Brutus and Malak face one another, surrounded by dozens of trolls. Drums echo through the night, and the two trolls compete in a ceremonial display. They mimic one another's moves, stomping and clapping in the same fashion as their ancestors. They continue the display until one of them misses a movement, then they embrace to the cheers of the crowd.

Nearby, drunken goblins pile on top of Stompy and ride him through the forest. For such a grumpy animal, the moulhaug doesn't seem to mind.

"How are you feeling about everything?" I ask.

Taryn tilts his head, and his dreads cover part of his face. "You mean logging out?"

I nod.

"It'll be nice to call my mom, but truth be told, I'm already excited to get back here." He takes another swig of sweetwater. "Besides, you can't find this stuff out there?"

I take a sip of my own, letting the burn trail down my insides. "Ain't that the truth."

The more that I drink, the less I dwell on Valery's message. Eventually, I get up and actually enjoy the celebration.

A drunk Kronan approaches me. "There's our hero!" He slaps me on the back and some of my drink spills on the ground.

In my buzzed state, I wrap my arm around his shoulders. He's much more affable after a few drinks.

"Kronan. Good to see you enjoying yourself."

"I can't remember the last time we had reason to celebrate." His face goes suddenly serious. "What do you say you join me in a mountain troll tradition?"

Sounds intriguing. "I'm in."

Kronan gathers everyone's attention. "Follow me! We will finally settle who is stronger—me or Chod!"

I follow him past the huts and into the forest. Kronan comes to a stop, and I have no idea what is about to happen. The area looks like a normal section of forest to me.

He points to two different trees. Each one is over a foot in diameter. "Take your pick."

I examine the two trees, not sure what I'm looking for. "Uhm, what exactly am I picking?"

He grins. "First one to uproot the tree is the victor. Normally, we would toss the tree off the mountain when we're done, but since we are running low on firewood, we can use it for that."

I follow the tree from the base to the canopy. It has to be at least fifty or sixty feet tall. How the hell am I supposed to uproot a tree that large?

I glance around at the others. They all watch like this is perfectly normal.

"You seriously think we can pull a tree this big from the ground?" I ask.

Kronan laughs. "Some of us can."

There's that mountain troll bravado.

"Alright, let's do this." I move in front of the tree to the right.

Kronan takes his position in front of the tree to the left and wraps his arms around it in a bearhug. I do the same. Kronan's muscles bulge as he clasps his hands together. I may have beaten him in a fight, but he still has two levels on me. Plus, he's a mountain troll, the naturally stronger sub-race.

Several feet stomp behind us. A moment later, they stomp again, but more join in. It continues until all the trolls are participating and their stomps thunder through the forest. Then, they add a clap at the end. Stomp, stomp, clap. Stomp, stomp, clap.

As their bodies beat like drums, something stirs inside of me, and I feel confident that I can rip the tree from the earth.

"Begin!" Kronan shouts above the noise.

I squeeze my hands together and lift, but the tree doesn't budge. My muscles tense with the effort, and I expect the ground to at least give a little, but nothing. I heave again to the point where I think I might shit my pants. Still nothing.

Beside me, Kronan's tree rocks gently as he pulls. His normally light purple face is flushed like a dark grape.

I pull again, pushing against the earth with my feet. The tree doesn't budge, but my toes sink into the earth.

"Come on, Chod!" Taryn cheers from over my shoulder.

The trolls continue to stomp and clap, the rhythm slowly increasing. Something crunches beside me, and I glance over to see the roots of Kronan's tree starting to break free from the earth.

Oh, come on. I can't let him pull out an entire tree without at least getting mine to move. It's time to use the advantages that come with being a hero. I summon a round of horrors on the other side of the tree. With their passive stat boost, I feel a little stronger, but the tree still isn't budging. When I hear another crack as a piece of root snaps free beside me, I activate Berserker Rage.

Strength floods my body, and the tree creaks slightly as I pull. I cast Sacrifice on the three horrors, granting me a temporary buff to my stats. I lift again, and this time, I feel the roots give against the pressure. I pull with all my might until I'm certain my body is going to rip in half. Steam rises off my skin as sweat evaporates from my overheating body.

I close my eyes and pull with everything I have. Roots snap and the tree comes loose. I lift it from the earth and sway back and forth for a moment before letting it fall to the ground. Trolls and goblins scatter out of the way as the tree breaks branches as it crashes into the ground in an explosion of dirt and leaves.

I turn around, hands raised over my head and ready to celebrate. My excitement quickly vanishes when I see Kronan sitting on his own downed tree and cleaning his fingernails.

Dammit! I thought I beat him. At least now I know who to call if I ever find myself in need of brute strength.

"Nice try, hero." He laughs. "Kronan has never been bested in a tree pull."

I hate losing, but in this case, I think it's well deserved.

I walk over and grip Kronan on the shoulder. "I'm glad you're on our side."

There's still no sign of Chief Rizza or the others when we say our good-byes. I thought that at least Limery would be here by now. We travel alongside those heading to Lynchton to restock potions and other items.

There are four female trolls who I haven't spent much time with. Feylin, Tezzi, Azra, and Nel carry satchels loaded with items. Their satchels are a much higher quality than anything I've been able to construct myself, but now that I have one with an expandable inside, I doubt I'll ever have need of that skill. I offer to help carry the items, but they turn me down.

"Perhaps you have spent too much time with the human women." Feylin laughs. "We have no need of a gallant hero to ease our burdens."

The others join her in laughter. One thing I can say about the female trolls is that they don't take shit from anyone.

"Hey, Chod. You can carry my things if you want." Taryn holds out his bag and satchel as he rides Stompy.

I pretend to reach for his items, and then shove him off Stompy's back. He falls to the ground, and the trolls laugh even harder.

Thanks to Strong Wind, we make it to the edge of the forest much faster than normal, cutting our time in half. When we step past the tree line, I'm amazed by how busy the road is. Lynchton is far busier than I have ever seen, and people wait to get in.

We make our way to the gate and take our place in line as people enter. We get a few looks, but they seem more curious than hateful.

A familiar face inspects travelers as they pass through.

"Jameson!" I wave at the soldier on gate duty. I hope he's not still pissed about the moulhaug head I left outside the gate the last time I was here.

His old dented armor has been replaced with shimmering new plate mail. He looks up in my direction and does a double-take. After saying something to his partner, he comes out to greet me.

"Chod." He extends a hand, and we shake. "I don't know whether to love you or hate you."

I cock an eyebrow, unsure of what he means. "Why's that?"

"Lynchton has been bustling since we partnered up with the trolls. The inn is packed every night. The market is always full. People come from all over to buy and trade. Things have been so good that the mayor bought us new armor." He flaunts his new armor like a peacock.

"Those sound like good things. What's the problem?"

"What's the problem?" He shakes his head. "The problem is I've never been busier in my life. But what's good for the town is good for me, I suppose. Come on, I'll move you to the front of the line. Bring your friends too. We don't want the trolls selling out of items."

Jameson escorts us to the gate, bypassing the other travelers. We catch a few glares, but no one says anything.

Inside, the market is packed. There are more vendors than ever before. The stables are crowded with horses. The inn is bustling. If I didn't know any better, I'd say we were at the market in Vanaria.

"I'm going to check Stompy and Berry into the stables. Want to meet up at the inn afterward?" asks Taryn.

"Actually, I have a friend I want to say hi to." The stable-boy, Luka, was one of the first friendly faces I met in Lynchton. He lost his brother to one of Glenn's battles with the forest trolls.

I tell Feylin and the others that I will be by shortly, and Taryn and I make our way through the crowd. As people bump into me, I no longer feel like the pariah I was before. I'm just another body in a busy town. Stompy barrels his way through the crowd, and Berry and I follow in his wake. Ruby sits in Taryn's lap, enjoying the view from high up.

At the stable, I find Luka handing the reins of a beautiful black stallion to its owner. He smiles when he sees me.

"Chod, good to see you." He runs his fingers through his curly brown hair.

"You too. We were hoping you had room for Taryn's mounts."

Luka looks up at Stompy and then over to Berry. "You want me to put a moulhaug and a bear in with the horses? Is that safe?"

Taryn offers up a sheepish smile. "They're very well-behaved. Well, most of the time."

Luka ponders for a moment before finally agreeing. "Only because it's you." He looks me in the eye as he opens the gate, and Taryn guides his pets inside.

I pull Luka aside. "Glenn and Jude are still at large. They escaped through the portal that opened in Seascape. I know it's not perfect, and it won't bring your brother back, but they're somebody else's problem for now."

Luka sighs. "Not the news I wanted, but at least they are far away from my friends and family."

"I'm sorry. I just wanted to let you know." I place my hand on his shoulder and offer what consolation I can.

After leaving Stompy and Berry, we head back toward the market. Ruby weaves in and out between people's legs. Every time I think she may get stepped on, she moves out of the way at the last second, always seemingly one step ahead.

"What was that about?" asks Taryn.

"He lost his brother in one of Glenn's battles." I clench my fist, still angry when I think about it. "An entire family heartbroken because of one asshole's grudge against the trolls."

Taryn glances back over his shoulder. "I'll drop him a little extra tip when I pick them up."

My heart leaps when we finally arrive at the troll tables. Dozens of people wait in line for a chance to buy potions and other items. A small army of imps hover in the air, translating between the humans and trolls.

Lillith, Limery's mother, takes a coin and hands a potion to a woman. The woman walks away with a smile.

I push my way through the crowd until I reach her. When she spots me, she flies over and gives me a hug.

"I was right about you, Chod. You are a curious troll. One that is destined to be a part of my family's affairs." She sits on my shoulder and crosses one leg over the other. "Bazel told me what you did. I'll never be able to repay you for giving me my partner back."

"Don't mention it. Where is he anyhow?"

"Spending some long overdue quality time with Leo. The two are adventuring through some of the lower-level dungeons. Leo has dreams of being a hero, you know." She gives me a knowing look.

"I didn't know that. Have you heard anything from Limery?" If anyone is to know where he's gotten off to, it's Lillith.

"Not since he first passed through the forest. If I'm being honest, I would have expected them back by now. But he's a smart boy, and he's with some of the strongest trolls around. I wouldn't worry too much. Limmy has always been an adventurous spirit." She smiles in the way only a mother can.

"It looks like you are all doing pretty well. Most popular vendor in the market." Even though it's afternoon, the line shows no signs of slowing down.

"This was a truly great idea, Chod. I never would have expected it to be so popular, but now there's talk of expanding to other towns." She gestures out over the crowd. "If you would have told me a few months ago that trolls, imps, and humans would all be in the same place, I'd have been certain it was on a battlefield. But here we are, trading. I have more imp volunteers by the day, more than I can possibly use, and we can't stock Yashi's potions fast enough. It might be time for her to train a few more potion masters."

The success of this venture has me elated. Three societies working together, and all benefitting. I couldn't have imagined my little idea would transform into this.

"Well, I won't keep you. There are plenty of customers waiting to buy your items." I reach in my satchel and pull out the rest of the perception potions I have on hand. "Here, add these to the cause."

She gives me a final hug and returns to the table. "Oh, Chod, you're too good to us. And I wouldn't worry about Limmy. He'll find you."

I nod. I'm sure he will.

Taryn looks around at the chaos surrounding us. He's like a small child lost at the airport, and everyone towers over him. "Dude, this is insane. It's like a completely different town from the last time I was here."

It truly is. And not only are the trolls benefitting, the shops and taverns are thriving as well. It makes me wonder how Tormara is doing in Vanaria. The hotheaded troll is part of a diplomatic exchange with Vanaria.

I turn back to Taryn. "What do you say we check into the inn? I'm starving and could use a drink."

Taryn's eyes light up. "You beautiful blue monster, you truly know the way to a dwarf's heart."

The porch of The Dancing Donkey is as lively as ever. People sit around drinking and singing. A woman wearing a red tunic plays a guitar and leads the revelers in an ancient song about a griffin that fights against an army of skeletons.

Inside is even busier, and not a single table is empty. The delicious aroma of smoked meat fills the air, and a thick layer of smoke coats the ceiling. We must have arrived just in time for the dinner rush.

I fight my way to the bartender and ask for a room for myself and Taryn.

He frowns. "I'm 'fraid we're nearly full. Only one room left, but if you don't mind sharing a bed, it's all yours."

One of the drunk patrons turns to me. "I bet the little one can sleep between your legs."

Several more people laugh, but I pay them no mind.

Taryn doesn't find it amusing, however. "Actually, I'll reserve it for you since I'll be staying with your wife tonight."

"Why you little—" The man stands up, ready for a drunken brawl, but when I place my massive blue hand on his chest, he thinks twice about it.

"We'll take the room." I slide a few coins across the bar, and he gives me a key.

Inside the room, I'm greeted with a notification.

Welcome to The Dancing Donkey! *You may set your respawn point in your room for as long as you are staying here. Once your stay is over, your respawn point will be reset to its previous location. Would you like to bind here?*

I agree, doing as Valery told me. I'm not entirely sure when we'll be pulled from the game, but I imagine we still have a few hours before it happens.

Ruby curls up in a ball on the bed, making herself at home.

I set my bags down in the corner. "I know you could kick his ass, but do you really want to start a barfight in here of all places?"

Taryn shrugs. "In the words of my father, 'If you don't start none, won't be none.'"

"Yeah, yeah, yeah. Let's go see if we can get a bite to eat among all this madness."

Back downstairs, there's still nowhere to sit. I scan the room, looking for a friendly face that might share their table with us. I'm surprised when I spot two tables with heroes sitting at them. Two of them I recognize from my first days in Mythos. They passed me while I was camouflaged in the fields outside of Lynchton, back when my reputation had me targeted on sight. They've leveled up quite a bit since then.

Randy Billson
> *Level 26*
> *Rogue*
> *Human*

The dark-haired rogue has upgraded his items and clothing as well. He still wears boiled leather, but his chest is emblazoned with a silver wolf. His gauntlets have silver accents as well, and he wears a sword with a red gemstone in the pommel. On his other hip, he wears a dagger with a silver wolf engraved in the pommel. He also has several glimmering rings on his fingers. Next to him sits a gray-haired wizard.

Don Othello
> *Level 27*
> *Mage*
> *Human*

. . .

The mage wears a dark purple robe. A long gray beard falls across his chest, and I can't help but wonder if the man behind the avatar has one as well. His hands glitter from all the jewelry adorning his fingers.

Clearly, these two have been busy.

Three men sit at a table in the back of the room. One of them points in our direction, and the other two laugh. I focus on the man pointing.

Otis Wiggins
Level 27
Barbarian
Human

Another barbarian! That'll be a nice icebreaker. I wonder if his skills are similar to my own.

The man is clothed in a variety of leathers and furs. A thick, bushy brown beard covers most of his face, while his head is shaved bald. He's a stark contrast to the two men sitting next to him.

Ethan French
Level ???
Warlock
Human

Kevin Harris
Level ???
Sorcerer
Human

Both men have their levels concealed, which isn't surprising considering they are magic users. I'd imagine they are around a similar level to the others, making them more powerful than me and Taryn. It's good to see that most of the other heroes are out actually leveling up instead of being murder hobos like Glenn and Jude.

The warlock has dark skin and sports dreadlocks pulled up into a bun. His face is covered in what resembles tribal tattoos, but I imagine they are somehow part of his chosen class. From what I recall, warlocks are given their power from some otherworldly entity. Not a god, but something similar in power. He wears a black robe, but aside from the amulet around his neck, I can't see any other weapons or items. That doesn't mean they aren't concealed beneath the flowing robe.

Next to him, the sorcerer watches us with amusement. He wears a light gray tunic and a blue cloak. A variety of straps with holsters for potions run across his chest. He wears his hair in a short afro that matches the length of his beard.

"Mind if we join you?" I ask no one in particular, hoping that at least one of the groups will offer us a seat.

The warlock stands up. "I suppose you're the one we have to thank for the mobs running the streets around here."

His voice is so even that I have no idea if he's joking or angry. I decide to be straightforward.

"Yeah, I had a part in it." I suddenly realize that the entire tavern is quiet, watching our exchange.

The warlock stares at me, and I notice his eyes are an eerie red. He bangs his fist on the table. "Well, then let me buy you an ale. The perception potions I've bought from the trolls have saved my life on more than one occasion."

His two partners burst into laughter, and the rest of the tavern returns to a dull roar. Ethan waves to the barmaid and orders a round of drinks.

"Mind if we pull our tables together?" asks Randy the Rogue.

"The more, the merrier." Otis the Barbarian removes his fur coat, revealing a sleeveless leather tunic underneath. His arm muscles are hairy and massive, and they bulge as he lifts the solid wooden table and moves it next to his own.

Taryn and I pull up a seat.

I wave at the group. "Nice to meet you all. This is the most heroes I've seen in one place."

Kevin the Sorcerer leans forward with his elbows on the table. "Ah, yes. You were late to the party." He looks me up and down. "Looks like you've done pretty well for yourself, all things considered."

I shrug. "It was a rough start to begin with. Everyone wanted me dead. I actually hid from these two—" I motion to Randy and Don. "—during my first few days. It wasn't that far from here, actually."

Randy punches Don in the arm. "See, you son of a bitch, I told you I saw a troll that day."

Don raises his hands in defense. "So it seems you did."

"What brings you all to Lynchton?" I ask.

Ethan the Warlock answers. "Same reason as you, I suppose. We're doing our scheduled logout tonight."

That's interesting. I didn't expect them to pull everyone all at once. Maybe they are wanting to test the system with everyone out to see what happens.

The barmaid returns with our drinks and sets them on the table.

Otis the Barbarian lifts his glass. "To Mythos, the best damn punishment I've ever had to endure."

"Cheers to that." I clink my glass against each of them in turn. The ale goes down smooth; it's sweet and malty, reminding me of honey and bananas.

Ethan the Warlock takes a hearty gulp, then focuses back on me. "What I really want to know—" He points a finger and moves it between Taryn and me "—is how the two of you got to be different races?"

I find myself staring at the amulet hanging from his neck. It's made of some black metal with flakes of purple. It's hard to make out, but I'm pretty sure there is a skull engraved into it, with pieces of obsidian for the eye sockets.

The silence draws me back, and I realize they are all staring at me. I'm not ready to tell them what it was that landed me here. I don't know these guys, and even though they may seem nice, I don't trust them just yet. Luckily, Taryn answers before I can.

"Must be because we logged in later. I hear there are even more races available on the other continents."

The group gets excited by that, and I welcome the attention going elsewhere.

"Oh, man, I can't wait to explore some new lands." Randy the Rogue licks his lips at the thought.

Don nods in agreement. "Yep, we're heading to the portal first thing in the morning."

Ethan the Warlock laughs. "I hear Jude and Glenn made it through the portal before they could be caught."

Kevin the Sorcerer slaps his knee. "That's an odd pair if I've ever seen one. Didn't Jude hate Glenn's guts?"

Don shrugs. "I thought Jude hated everyone's guts. Well, except for that paladin he was always with."

Ethan locks eyes with me. "You've got a real way of getting under people's skin, don't you?"

Great, the focus is back on me again. "I like to think I'm a pretty nice guy."

Otis shakes his head. "If you were a nice guy, you wouldn't be here."

Another reminder of what led us all to be here. Well, all of us except Taryn.

We order our dinner and make small talk for the rest of the meal.

Before we go our separate ways for the night, I take the opportunity to try and win them to King Orso's cause.

"We think that a war is coming. That eventually, more portals will open, ones that are not so welcoming. The dark wizard that nearly destroyed this world is still out there. When the time comes, we need you on our side."

Otis flexes his muscles. "What's in it for me?"

Of course he'd ask that. I'm sure that "the safety of innocents" is not a compelling enough answer.

"I'd think that an army of darkness controlled by the most powerful wizard this world has ever seen would have a pretty good loot drop."

A devious smile spreads across the barbarian's face. "Not bad at all." He stands and pushes in his chair. "Catch you guys on the other side."

Eventually, they all leave, until it's just me and Taryn. Most of the room has cleared out now that dinner is over.

"Strange bunch, don't you think?" I ask.

"Yeah, the rogue and the mage seem okay, but those other three, I've got a bad feeling about them." He scrunches his eyebrows.

We can't exactly be beggars and choosers when it comes to getting help. "I mean, they aren't Boy Scouts, but if they can help us when the time comes, I'll take it."

He turns around, watching the warlock as he turns the corner to go upstairs. "Just so long as they don't stab us in the back."

I stand up. "Well, you ready to do this?"

Taryn nods. The time has finally come to be me again.

CHAPTER TWENTY-SIX

BACK TO REALITY

I open my eyes to a blue haze. The door to the pod opens above, and the nanite gel level around me decreases. As I sit up, the blue gel drips effortlessly from my body. I don't feel hot or cold, since the nanites are capable of matching the surrounding air perfectly. I cough a few times, expelling the last bit of nanites from my lungs, and then everything feels normal.

I can't explain it, but when I look at my hand as it grips the edge of my pod, it feels different. Maybe I'm expecting to see my massive blue troll arm, or maybe it's because I've been under for so long, but it feels weird. Weak.

"How are you feeling?" Valery's sensual voice calls from beside the pod. She holds a tablet in her hand, tapping it repeatedly. For once, she wears a labcoat over her tight-fitting dress. Several technicians stand behind her, either watching my feed, or with their noses buried in tablets.

"Off," I answer honestly.

She taps the screen again. "That's to be expected. The longer you're in, the more your mind embraces your digital avatar. Everything will feel normal within a few minutes." She looks up from her tablet and her violet eyes pierce into me. "Thanks again. For staying in while we work this out."

"No problem. I'd be lying if I said I haven't grown attached to everyone I've met in there."

She turns to one of the technicians. "Thompson, how is everything looking?"

He swipes at the screen on his tablet. "So far, so good."

"Chad, do you want to get out and stretch your legs?" she asks.

I almost tell her to call me Chod, but then I look down at my body. This isn't the body of a Chod.

I don't really feel like I need to stretch. The nanites have kept my body in great condition, probably better than I'd do on my own. I don't fully understand the science behind it, but they clean and feed, plus they prevent my muscles from atrophying. If I didn't know any better, I'd say I've put on a little muscle mass since I've been under. But that's impossible, right?

Still, I'd like to look around, so I accept her offer. She extends me a hand, helping me out of the pod. I'm wearing nothing but the spandex style underwear, but I've spent so much time wearing a loincloth that it doesn't bother me like it used to.

I look around, expecting to see the other heroes going through the same motions, but they're all in their pods. The room is the same pristine white and gleaming metal that I remember. I bet I could spot a speck of dust if there were any.

"Where is everyone? I thought they were all being pulled tonight?"

"We're doing it in cycles since we don't need as much staff when we do it that way. These are still violent criminals after all." She winks. "Not to mention, you're a special case."

The black pods against the far wall remain empty, all except for one.

"Is that Taryn?" I point at the one black pod filled with nanite gel.

"It is. Want to take a look?"

We walk over to his pod. The feed on the screen shows Taryn sleeping at The Dancing Donkey. I'm lying on the floor next to him. It's weird seeing the digital version of me still in the game. Ruby curls up on the pillow next to Taryn's head.

Looking at Taryn's real body lying in the pod, it's funny to me how the roles are reversed. He's the massive one. Without his shirt on, he could pass for a football player.

"We'll be pulling the rest of them out in batches of two or three, but we wanted to pull you alone after everything that happened last time."

"Do you mind if I look at the others?" I'm curious how some of the players look in real life.

"Be my guest. I'll be over here if you need me. We'll be logging you back in in fifteen." She walks over to the technicians and quickly engages in conversation.

I smile when I look at the pod to my right. Jon the Enchanter lies in a four-poster bed at the castle in Vanaria. He certainly is doing well for himself. He looks remarkably similar to his avatar.

The next two I don't recognize, nor do the rooms look familiar. It makes me wonder how many towns I still have left to explore in *Isle of Mythos*, not to mention all the inns in Vanaria and Seascape. They could be anywhere.

Next, I stop in front of Ethan the Warlock. The tribal tattoos that adorn his avatar are gone, but he does have a small teardrop on one cheek. I always thought that those were just something they added to movies to make characters look tougher. I wonder what he is in for.

Next to him lies Jude. In the pod, Jude is clean shaven and has an athletic body. His chest and arms are covered in a variety of poorly-designed tattoos. Dice on the back of his right hand. A skull on his forearm. There's a woman tattooed over his heart that looks like a child drew it.

On his feed, however, it's a different story. Jude lies on the floor of what looks like a cave, covered in furs. His beard is long and scraggly.

Next to him lies Glenn. They're either still on the run, or they haven't made enough money to afford an inn. They went through the portal in nothing but their starter rags with no weapons and no money.

I'd sympathize with how difficult it must be if not for the fact that they brought it upon themselves.

I call for Valery and she comes over.

"Where are they?" I ask.

She gives me a devious smile. "You know I can't tell you that."

"Isn't it counterproductive to let them go around the game behaving like this? I thought this was all about rehabilitation." It seems to me like they are reinforcing bad behaviors by letting them go free.

"It is. But we aren't the ones who decide what is right or wrong for them. Our psychiatrists come in every day and monitor what is happening, but it is the AI that guides you all. Who am I to say what works and what doesn't? Not every path is straightforward. Sometimes it zigs and zags. Sometimes it goes backward." She looks up at the monitor, focusing on Glenn. "And sometimes it is about the lesser of two evils."

"What about Taryn then? If he's not being rehabilitated, what is the AI doing to him?"

She grins. "That's a good que—"

"Valery, come look at this!" Thompson calls urgently.

I follow her over, eager to know what's going on.

"What is it?" she asks.

"The system, it's acting up again. I don't know why. I thought we had everything in order this time, but it's going haywire. Respawn timers are off again, and it looks like something is going on with the portals."

I almost feel bad that the news offers me relief. This is their job, and yet I'm secretly hoping it fails just so I can stay in the world they created. But it's not just their world anymore. It's mine. It's the other heroes. And more important than anything, it belongs to the people who live there.

"Dammit, Thompson, I thought you had this figured out." Her words have a bite to them that I haven't witnessed before.

"I thought we did, but we need to get him back in there before something irreversible happens."

"Looks like the tour is over, kid." She gestures toward my pod. "We'll pull you again when we've figured this out."

This time, I give her a wink. "Don't rush it. I'm quite enjoying myself."

She laughs. "I'll make sure to put that on the recruitment posters."

I climb into the pod, and she closes the lid. There's a slight whir as the pod fills up with nanites. When the blue gel covers my face, I take a deep breath, and everything goes black.

CHAPTER TWENTY-SEVEN

PLAYERS REVEALED

I'm the first one to wake up the next morning. I wipe the sleep from my eyes and am flooded with relief when I see my blue troll hands.

Ruby looks down at me from atop the bed with her small paws curled over the edge and her snout buried between them. I quickly get up and shake Taryn. I'm eager to know what his experience logging out was like.

He wipes the sleep from his eyes. "Just five more minutes, mom."

I shake him again. "Dude, wake up! Tell me what happened."

His eyes go wide. "Oh, right, we logged out. Everything was normal for me. I called my family, though they weren't happy it was this middle of the night. Since I'm here of my own free will and can leave at any time, I don't think it's the same as if I were in prison. How'd it go for you?"

"It was fine for a few minutes, then the system crashed again. I have no idea why."

He sits up and swings his legs over the side of the bed, but they don't touch the ground. "Man, that's weird. You think it has something to do with why you're blue?"

I shrug. I am the only one who jumped directly into an open mana source. It's possible that the mana that fuels all the magic on the island is also integral to coding. "I don't have the faintest idea. It has to be something I did if it's not happening to anyone else. Did you feel different when you logged out at all? Like your body felt weird?"

Taryn looks down at his hands like he's examining them. "Yeah, for a bit, but Valery said it was normal."

I sit beside him on the bed, and it creaks under my weight. "Something felt off for me too. I kept expecting to be my troll self. And maybe I'm crazy, but it felt like my body was in better shape than when I logged in."

Taryn laughs. "Well, that's probably because it's not being fed soda, chips, and candy bars for three meals a day."

I roll my eyes. "I don't mean like that. It felt like my body had put on muscle. I've never been one to go to the gym, but it felt like I had some definition to my body. Not a lot, but more than I've had before."

Taryn climbs down from the bed and starts getting dressed. "I don't know. I wouldn't put anything past those nanites. If they can make us experience this, why can't they improve our bodies?"

It's a sobering thought. I close my eyes and try to push it from my mind.

"Speaking of bodies..." Taryn rubs his stomach. "I'm hungry. Let's go grab a bite to eat."

We gather our things and head downstairs. The inn is already full, but we take a seat with Don the Mage and Randy the Rogue. We order breakfast from the barmaid and catch up with the others.

"Morning, fellas. Where are you off to today?" I ask.

Randy bites into a sausage and the juices trickle down his chin. It smells delicious as it wafts across the table. "I think we're heading to Vanaria. We're interested in the new portals. It's time to explore what else Mythos has to offer. Besides, we need to level up if we're going to help you with the big bad wizard." He winks.

"What about you?" asks Don.

"Same, but we're taking the portal to Seascape. We need to meet with the king, then we have some unfinished business in Goldspire. Have you seen the others?" I ask, referring to the three heroes we met the night before.

Randy wipes the sausage grease from his face. "They were out of here early. Looked to be in a pretty big hurry." He leans forward. "If I'm being honest, I don't trust those three. They've got a weird way about them. They aren't as reckless as Glenn or Jude, but I'd never turn my back to them if I could help it."

I wonder if there's any truth to his statement, or if it's just paranoia because he knows them outside of the game.

Our breakfast arrives, and the conversation comes to a halt as we stuff our faces. Before Taryn and I are finished eating, Randy and Don get up and leave, wishing us luck on our travels.

We finish our breakfast and head outside. Before leaving Lynchton, I stop by the troll table at the market. Bazel and Leo are there this time, helping Lillith translate for the trolls.

"Chod, fancy seeing you here!" Bazel offers a big smile, displaying all his sharp teeth.

"Glad to see you're doing well. Good to see you again, too, Leo."

The small red imp with a tuft of black hair flies over and wraps his arms around me. "Thank you for freeing my father."

"No thanks needed." I turn to Bazel and Lillith. "Still no word from Limery?"

"That boy always had a will of his own," laughs Bazel. "He'll be around when he's good and ready."

I'm certain I'll see him again, but that does little for the pocket of imp-shaped emptiness I feel when I think about him. "Well, let him know we are heading back to Seascape. We're going to pass through Vanaria, since it's shorter. So who knows, maybe we'll run into him on the way."

I say good-bye to the trolls, and we pick up Stompy and Berry from the stables. And just like that, we're back on the road again.

While I'm sad I didn't get to see Chief Rizza and the others, I can take solace in the fact that Lynchton is thriving. Things are looking up for the trolls. Maybe they'll be lucky and King Orso's prediction will be wrong. Maybe there won't be a war at all.

I wave at Jameson as we pass through the gate.

"Take care, Chod." He waves back.

We travel in silence for the first few miles. Eventually, the thoughts in my head are too much to manage.

"Do you think I should be worried?" I ask.

Taryn looks at me, confused. "About what?"

"Limery. I know he can take care of himself, but after what happened to his father, it makes me nervous."

Taryn nods. "I know you care for him, so it makes sense to worry, but that little guy has more spunk than the rest of his family combined. And from what you've told me about the others, good luck to anyone who tries to take them on."

That makes me feel a little better. With Taryn using Strong Wind, we make fantastic time. We camp for the night underneath a bridge.

As I settle in for the night, Taryn can't stop grinning.

I don't engage with him, because I already know what he's going to say.

"Oh, come on." He shoves me in the shoulder. "You have to see the humor in this. You're a troll sleeping under a bridge, for crying out loud. There have been stories written about this for ages."

I decide to shut him up. "Remember that time I tossed you to the second floor of that dungeon? That was humorous."

As I fall asleep, I hear him muttering something about paying the troll toll.

"Chod!"

Taryn's screams wake me before they are abruptly cut off. I open my eyes to see him bound by a glowing purple chain. It wraps around his body several times, pinning his arms to his sides. Three figures shrouded in a dark aura stand behind him. The aura conceals their features, but the center figure's eyes radiate a fiery crimson.

Berry stands back a few feet, snarling, while Stompy huffs and puffs beside him.

I make to stand, but the center figure moves forward.

"I wouldn't do that if I were you." The voice is distorted, but it sounds vaguely familiar.

It's still night out, so whoever this is must have waited until we made camp. But what do they want? Did they follow us from Lynchton, or just happen to see us on the road? The fact that Taryn is still alive means that they want more than just our items.

I try to focus on the figures, but whatever darkness it is that conceals their identities is also blocking me from analyzing them.

"What do you want?" I stare at them with defiance, refusing to let them rattle me.

Taryn's eyes are wide as he stares at me. The more I look at the chain, the clearer it becomes that it's magical. It's possible that the spell binding him in place is keeping him from communicating as well.

"It's not about what I want. There are bigger pieces in play here." The figure steps closer. "Stop your foolish attempts to unite the heroes. Nothing but death and destruction will come of it, for you and for all those you hold dear. Go and explore. Become rich and powerful and stay in the forest where you belong."

How do they know about my plans?

I can't shake the feeling that I know this person. I focus on them, looking for anything that might reveal their identities. Even with the shrouds, the figures still maintain their body types. The figure on the left is stocky, with broad shoulders and a wide neck. The center figure is taller than the other two. When I gaze into those flaming red eyes, I realize where I've heard that voice before. He's Ethan French, the warlock. That would make the figure to the right Kevin Harris, the sorcerer, and the stocky one is Otis Wiggins, the barbarian.

So Randy was right about these three. I take a deep breath, hoping that this isn't as bad as it looks. I don't know why they have an issue with me uniting the heroes, but I aim to find out.

"You can cut it with the smoke and mirrors. I know who you are." I keep my voice steady. Calm.

The shroud fades, revealing the three heroes I shared dinner with the night before.

Ethan steps toward me. The fire has faded from his red eyes. "Well, you're not as dumb as you look."

I grunt. "Why do you have a problem with me uniting the heroes?"

He turns his back to me, and I have the urge to attack him. That would be bad, though. Taryn is bound, and the three of them greatly out-level me. I have to play along and hope I can talk my way out of this.

"I don't have a problem with it." He turns back around. "Unfortunately, the being that gives me my powers does. So either you can call off this whole charade, or we can do the same thing to you that you did to Glenn. Then we'll see what kind of an army a level-one troll can raise."

Otis tilts his head back and laughs. Stupid barbarian.

Taryn struggles against his chains. Kevin the Sorcerer squeezes his fist, and they cinch tighter. Taryn grimaces, and I have to fight the urge to engage. Okay, so the sorcerer has the binding spell, and the warlock has the shroud. Good to know.

"There's no need to do this. Just let us go, and no one has to know." I'll try bargaining for my first attempt.

He shakes his head. "It's not that easy. If I piss off my patron, I lose my abilities. Without my abilities, what am I doing here?"

The familiar tightness in my forehead right before I lose my cool makes an appearance. "So, what, you're going to ruin the lives of thousands of people just so you can get what you want?"

"Thousands of people?" He laughs darkly. "You act like they are real. If I'm going to be here, then I'm going to have fun while I'm doing it."

"And how exactly do you plan to enforce this demand of yours?" I ask.

He kneels, smirking at me. "That's not my role. I'm here to deliver the message. We're going to kill you, take your items, and make sure you remember the consequences of your actions. If you keep it up, maybe you see us again, maybe you don't, but you'll always be looking over your shoulder."

It takes everything in me not to punch him in the face. "Looks like I don't have much of a choice."

He stands up, smiling. "Now you're getting it."

"So what now?"

"Now, we get out from under this bridge and you take your punishment in the open like a man. I have a new ability I've been dying to try. You and your friend here will both die, and we will all learn a valuable lesson." He motions for me to stand. "Don't try anything stupid."

I glance at Berry and Stompy. Ruby must have found somewhere to hide.

"What about Taryn's pets?"

Ethan shrugs. "Not my call. The boss wants this message to stick."

My vision goes red. It's one thing to harm me or Taryn over this, but to kill his pets. That's over the line. They won't come back.

As quick as I can, I equip Destroyer and swing for his head. Before the warhammer is even halfway to him, he blasts me in the chest with a bolt of black energy. It takes out a chunk of my health and knocks me off my feet.

Otis and Kevin both burst into laughter.

I clench my throbbing chest. Whatever he hit me with burned through my skin.

Ethan stands over me. "You don't have to make this hard. But if you want to, we can make this very difficult for you."

I crawl to my feet. "Bring it on."

I charge at him with my weapon raised. His eyes flare a bright red, and he lifts one hand, shooting another bolt of energy into me. It knocks me back, taking out another huge chunk of health and dropping me to seventy percent HP. I stand again just as a streak of purple energy shoots out from his other hand.

The purple beam hits me, but nothing happens. A second later, pain flares through my entire body as my health drops another fifteen percent. A bulb of energy shoots from my body and trails back to the warlock.

As Ethan absorbs the energy, his face softens for a fraction of a second. He just stole my health!

I summon a horror and toss it at Ethan, exploding it right in front of his face. The warlock's health drops by a fraction.

He looks over his shoulder at Kevin. "Don't let that happen again."

I summon another horror and repeat the action. This time, the sorcerer raises his free hand and a forcefield emerges in front of Ethan, absorbing the explosion.

"Much better." Ethan cracks his knuckles.

Three attacks and I've lost almost half my health. There's no way I'm making it out of this alive. I'm sure Taryn knows it too. If I'm going to die, then I'm going to do my best to make sure Taryn's pets escape.

"Stompy, Berry, I need you to run! We'll find you when this is over." I don't wait to see if they listen. Right now, I need to become the biggest distraction possible.

I cast Champion, and the Gnoll Pack Lord appears in front of me. I also summon a round of horrors. I can't best Ethan with melee, but maybe my summons can do better.

The pack lord equips his bow and fires an arrow at the warlock. It bounces off of Kevin's forcefield.

"Is that the best you've got?" His eyes flare red again.

I notice his hand glow purple right before the energy shoots out, giving me just enough time to equip the Halite Shield. Its translucent material allows me to block the attack without losing visibility. The beam of energy ricochets off the shield and crashes into the embankment.

The warlock curses. "Dammit, the pets are gone. Otis, handle this while I go chase them down."

Suddenly, shadowy wings sprout from the warlock's back, and he takes to the air. Otis walks toward me with a giant shit-eating grin. He swings a massive axe a few times, and the sharp blade whistles in the air.

"This is going to be fun." He kisses the head of his axe and charges me.

The gnoll shoots another arrow, but the sorcerer blocks it again. My horrors charge, and Otis cuts through them without slowing.

I toss the shield away and equip Destroyer. I'll come back for the shield later. We run at each other, and our weapons clash together in an explosion of sparks.

Otis furrows his brow, clearly confused as to why he didn't just demolish me. He might out-level me, but considering my racial bonuses per level, I'd say we're on a pretty even playing field. If I can handle Kronan, I can handle this piece of shit.

He swings again, and again I meet his blow, only this time I have a stack of Inferno on my weapon. A few more and it might actually make a difference.

The pack lord switches to his spear and stabs Otis in the leg. The barbarian falls to one knee, but still manages to parry my attack.

"A little help here," he calls to the sorcerer.

Kevin grunts. "Useless barbarian."

The sorcerer leaves Taryn, but the chain that binds him stays attached to the sorcerer as he walks. He makes a motion with his hands, and then green gas rises from the ground around me. It obstructs my vision, and then my lungs burn and my eyes sting. My health ticks down each second. It must be some sort of poisonous gas.

I turn to run, but something wraps around my feet, and I fall to the ground.

A moment later, a sharp pain flares through my side. When I touch the wound, all I feel is wetness. My health drops even further.

The poison gas fades, and I witness the massive gash that runs along my side from an axe blade. Blood pours freely from the wound.

I've failed again. And this time, everyone pays.

I activate Berserker Rage to stop the blood loss, and the chains release from my feet—I can't be slowed or stunned by spells while it's active. Still, it won't be enough. Otis raises his battle-axe overhead, and I accept my fate.

A ball of fire shoots through the darkness and smashes Otis into the embankment.

"You no hurts Chods!" Limery's skin is molten lava as he wraps his tiny hands around Otis's neck. He bares his teeth, and pure violence emanates from his small frame. The air shimmers around his scorching body.

Even in such dire circumstances, my heart jumps at the sight of the small imp.

The barbarian's health ticks down second by second as Limery burns him alive.

There's a loud roar to my right as a massive wyrm descends into the ravine. Chief Rizza rides on its back, her braid whipping behind her as blue flames pour from the wyrm's mouth. The sorcerer abandons his chains on Taryn and focuses all his energy into a forcefield to block the flames. Fire pours around the forcefield, scorching the earth to both sides.

Otis goes into a rage and rips Limery from his throat. He tosses the imp away, but Limery rights himself mid-air and conjures fireballs in both hands.

"I am so fucking glad to see you! Let's finish this asshole."

Limery smiles at me, and I feel like I can take on the world. "Limmy's on it!" He hurls both fireballs at Otis.

The barbarian absorbs the attack as his rage rapidly heals him, but the fire burns all the hair off his face. Something rattles to my left, and I turn to see Gord as he jumps down with the dwarven axe, Peacemaker, slung over his shoulder. He looks like a being straight out of hell wearing his bone armor that rattles with his every movement.

"Help with the sorcerer. Limery and I have this one," I call.

Gord nods and rushes into battle alongside the chief.

Taryn scrambles past me in a panic. "I need to save my pets."

A second later, the forest troll shaman, Jira, arrives and sets off in pursuit of Taryn.

"We'll be right behind you." I turn to Limery. "Flame wall!"

The imp erupts a wall of flame on both sides of Otis, leaving him no escape. I pick up Destroyer and march towards him. The flames lick at both of us, but I ignore the burn. It's nothing compared to the rage inside of me.

Otis snarls at me and charges. Our weapons clash, and sparks fly. On his next attack, I duck, leaving him swinging at air. The momentum sends him spinning, and I kick him hard in the back. He falls forward and I bring Destroyer down on his head.

He wobbles back and forth, dazed from the blow. A blazing heat presses against my back, and I turn to see Limery with a mega fireball raised above his head. I step out of the way and let him unleash hell.

When the fire dissipates, all that remains are Otis's clothing and items.

I find Gord standing over the sorcerer's body, pulling his axe from his back. A moment later, the body vanishes, but there's no time for a reunion.

"We need to help Taryn! The warlock is trying to kill his pets."

They don't question who Taryn is or why they should help him. Instead, they rush into battle by my side, because that is what family does. When you're desperate for help, they help—no questions asked.

We climb the embankment and sprint down the road. I hear Stompy's trumpet carrying across the night. A bolt of lightning crashes in the distance.

"That's where we need to go!" I point.

Chief Rizza takes off ahead of us on her wyrm.

"Limery, go ahead. We'll catch up."

The imp zooms off like a bat out of hell.

My lungs burn as Gord and I sprint to catch up. We arrive just in time to see Ethan facing off against Taryn, Jira, Limery, and Chief Rizza. Stompy and Berry both lay on the ground, neither one of them moving.

"It's over, Ethan." I step up beside my friends. "Your buddies are dead. Just leave and let us heal his pets."

The warlock's eyes blaze a vibrant red. "I can't do that."

"You can. No one else has to get hurt."

He laughs maniacally. "You don't understand."

Berry groans in pain, and Taryn rushes forward. Ethan shoots a blast of dark energy at the dwarf, stopping him in his tracks.

"I said no!" The warlock hovers in the air on wings of shadow. "They will die, and my message will be delivered."

I take a step closer. "That's not going to happen."

His lips curl up in disgust. "And who's going to stop me?"

"I will." Chief Rizza moves her wyrm closer, and a stream of smoke shoots out of its nostrils.

"And me." Gord lifts his axe in the air.

"As will I." Jira steps forward calmly, his white-tipped dreads swaying.

"Mees, too." A fireball crackles to life in Limery's palms.

"Then so be it." The warlock's eyes blaze brighter than I have ever seen.

He presses his hands together, and two massive balls of shadow form between him and us. They pulse with dark energy. The shadow is so black that it seems to swallow the light around it. A black clawed hand emerges from within the darkness. Then another. They grip at the edge of the shadow until a demonic face pokes through. A demonic being with a head that resembles a horse's skull peeks through. The demon climbs from the shadow and stands on long hoofed feet. It unfurls the same shadowy wings that keep Ethan aloft, and its eye sockets burst to life with blue fire.

An identical creature emerges from the second shadow.

Shadow Demon. *Level ???*

Chief Rizza gasps beside me, and I instinctively take a step back. What the hell are those things? They have no level, and no description, and I'm pretty sure they're not from this plane of existence.

Tears stream down Taryn's face as he looks at his pets, helpless to save them. I know this is tearing him apart.

I need to rally them, but is it worth losing Rizza or Limery for this? What am I even saying? Of course it is. Taryn cares for his pets just as much as I care for the trolls.

"We have to fight, or his pets don't have a chance." I summon a horror and toss it at one of the flying demons. A foot from hitting the one on the right, the horror explodes into smoke, only I didn't cast Kamikaze.

Taryn summons a lightning bolt. It comes crashing from the sky, but it explodes before reaching the demon. It's like they have some kind of shadowy forcefield protecting them.

"It's over," says Ethan.

Chief Rizza's wyrm unleashes a stream of fire, but it never makes contact. The blue flames curl around this invisible barrier, lighting the night sky. Even Limery's fireballs have no effect.

The demons raise their arms, and shadow blades form in their hands. They swipe them, and I feel a chill through my body. The next thing I know, half my health is gone.

"They're shadow blades." Taryn grimaces. "The same as mine."

Weapons that can't be blocked by armor or magic. We're screwed. My instincts tell me to run, but there's no way I could live with myself if I left Taryn's pets to die like this.

I equip Destroyer and prepare to go out in a blaze of glory, but the chanting next to me stays my attack. Jira stands with his eyes closed, repeating the same phrase over and over. I don't know what he's up to, but the shaman's health is almost completely depleted from the attack.

Ethan looks at him and laughs. "Give it up, old man. No one can stand against the shadows."

Jira's eyes open, and he spreads his arms wide. A red aura surrounds them, and he brings his hands together in a clap. As his hands meet, a fiery phoenix explodes from his palms and takes off toward the shadow demons.

I've seen this ability before, back in the forest the first time I fought Glenn. The phoenix absorbed all the flames from the burning forest, growing stronger with each one. But there's no fire here. At least he tried. At least we all tried.

The phoenix soars toward the demons, a fraction of the attack I witnessed before. It opens its beak and caws. I wince as a shrill shriek cuts through the air from above. The demons flinch at the sound, and their focus moves upward. A second later, the air grows stifling, and I'm reminded of the cave where I found Limery's dad.

The demons raise their swords, but not at Jira's phoenix. They point them overhead.

My night vision fades as the area around me is showered in light. I look up to see fire made flesh as a real, live phoenix barrels down from the sky. Her wings are tucked as she dives like a falcon, and streams of red, orange, yellow, and blue fire trail behind her.

She screeches again, and fire consumes the phoenix as she engulfs the shadow demons. The demons howl in distorted tones as the fire consumes them, and Ethan cries out as he is burned alive.

In an instant, it's over, and we're all covered in ash. I don't know what the hell just happened, and right now, I don't care. Taryn rushes to Berry and casts Restoration. I go to Stompy and gently pet him until Taryn is done. He breathes heavily beneath my touch.

Nobody talks until both pets are fully healed. Once they are both back on their feet, Ruby emerges from the darkness and nuzzles against Taryn's leg. She has a real knack for getting out of dangerous situations. Taryn presses his head to Stompy's jaw, and I give them their space. I can't even imagine what he is feeling right now.

I turn to Jira. "Jira, what in the actual hell was that? That was a real phoenix you called into battle."

He looks at me intently, and I remember how unsettling his red pupils are. "The phoenix is my totem. For the longest time, I felt her dwelling in the mountains, but recently, she has been on the move. The phoenix is the enemy of darkness, and when she felt their presence, she was compelled to assist us."

Chief Rizza climbs down from her wyrm. "She did far more than assist. She is likely the only reason we are all still alive. I have never seen such creatures on the island."

Something stirs beneath the ashes, and Gord raises his axe in alarm. A patch the size of a baseball shakes until a tiny, hairless head pokes through. It opens its beak and squawks.

A tiny reborn phoenix. She sacrificed herself to save us.

Limery flies down to the creature and cups it against his chest. "Look, Chods. Its is a baby."

The small phoenix nuzzles into Limery, no doubt feeling the natural heat that radiates from his body.

"What should we do with it?" asks Chief Rizza.

Jira steps forward and takes the phoenix from Limery. "I will see that she is taken care of."

I can't help but notice the trace of a smile on the wizened shaman's face.

Taryn finally joins us. When he speaks, his eyes glisten. "Thank you all. I would have lost them if not for you. That is something that I can never repay, but I will do my best."

Chief Rizza gives him a loving smile. "You owe us nothing. We will always go to battle for our own and the causes that are important to them."

Taryn just nods. I can tell that he's fighting back tears. I don't blame him. Just because the trolls are monstrous doesn't mean they aren't loving, caring, and willing to fight for each other.

I introduce Taryn to everyone, and then I ask the question I've been dying to know. "Where the hell were you all? I went to the forest expecting to see you days ago. There's no way it should have taken you that long to get back from Vanaria."

She laughs, lightening the mood. "I'm sorry to have inconvenienced you. There was a festival in the city. Once Gord opened the portal, we spent time enjoying the celebrations. Now tell me, how did this come to pass?" She gestures to the devastation surrounding us.

I tell them about the meeting with other heroes at the inn, and how we were attacked at night. To give them more context, I tell them about King Orso's prediction, what he believes waits on the other side of the portals, and how Ethan's patron is likely a part of it.

"King Orso wants to call a meeting with Favian and the other leaders from the lands across the opened portals." I look Chief Rizza in the eye. "You should come."

She shakes her head. "I'm no king."

"No, but you're the leader of two tribes of trolls. If you don't speak for them, who will?"

"He is right." Gord nods, and his nose ring catches the moonlight. "It is time to claim our place at the table."

"Spoken like a true councilman." I say it just to tease Gord, and sure enough, his cheeks flush.

Deep down, I know he is proud to have a seat on the council. "Oh, and I almost forgot! Limery, we found your father. He's waiting for you in Lynchton."

The imp's bulbous yellow eyes go even wider. "You dids? You found Daddy?"

I smile. "We did. I underst—"

Limery plows into me, wrapping his arms around my neck. "Oh, Chods!"

"I understand if you need to go see him. I'm sure he will be glad to see you after so long, but Taryn and I have to go to Seascape. You can come find us when you're done."

Limery shakes his head. "No, Limmy goes with Chods. Limmy will see Daddy later."

"Are you sure? I promise I won't mind."

"Limmy is sure. Chods needs Limmy." He takes a seat on my shoulder.

That might be the truest thing I've ever heard.

"It's settled then. We'll leave for Vanaria in the morning."

CHAPTER TWENTY-EIGHT
VALMAR WORREN

We take turns keeping watch for the remainder of the night, and at daybreak, we hit the road. Chief Rizza talks to me about the progress with Lynchton, while her wyrm scouts ahead. The pride is evident in her voice as she details her plans for the future, which include trading with other towns. No wonder Kronan follows her. She's a natural leader in every way.

Jira and Limery take turns feeding the baby phoenix, and it plucks worms as they dangle them from their fingers. Tiny orange feathers have already sprouted on her small bobblehead.

Taryn keeps to himself for most of the journey. I think for the first time, he realizes there is a real chance he could lose his pets. Last night was terrifying for us all, but I think it shocked him to his core. As long as I've known him, I've never seen Taryn panic like that.

We see the towering castle of Vanaria long before the rest of the city. The keep in the center shimmers with a pearlescent sheen—the blessed stone is the one place on the island where the undead cannot set foot. The spires of the castle rise high into the sky and disappear among the clouds. Eventually, we crest a hill and the rest of the city comes into view with its obsidian walls that gleam with a dark fervor, daring anyone to challenge their protective power. Atop them, the city watch patrols in their silver-and-blue armor.

I still remember the first time we came here, back when our only goal was acceptance. Now we strive for something greater. Unity.

The captain of the city watch greets us as we cross the bridge and enter the city. "Back so soon?" he asks Rizza.

"We're traveling to Seascape. It's of great importance."

He nods. "Very well. I'll have some of my men escort you."

Four guards with gleaming plate mail and billowing cloaks usher us through the city streets. Their weapons are pristine, and the spear tips are sharpened to a razor's edge. I wonder how many of them have seen actual combat.

We pass through the dirty cobblestone of Rat Row and into the inner bailey. My thoughts drift briefly to Hawkin and the Underground Circus. Where could they possibly be right now?

The market bustles with activity. Guards surround the portal, questioning everyone before they enter. I watch as a wealthy couple steps into the portal and disappears. A moment later, an ivory dwarf appears out of nowhere and vanishes into the crowd.

Our guard detail speaks to those around the portal and they motion for us to step forward.

"Focus on the rune for Seascape, and then step through one at a time."

Chief Rizza takes the lead. The rune for Seascape glows a bright red, and then she steps into the portal. In the blink of an eye, her body vanishes. One by one, we follow. Taryn rides through on Stompy, leaving me and Limery as the last two.

I step into the swirling white portal with Limery on my shoulder, and the next thing I know, I'm in the Seascape square. Dozens of armed guards patrol the square. The vibe here is vastly different from Vanaria. In Vanaria, the city bustles with opportunity and adventure. Here, the air feels restless. After what happened with Glenn and Jude, I don't blame them for being on alert.

When the guards see me, they offer to take our pets to the stables and allow us access to the stairs leading to the castle. Chief Rizza is reluctant to leave her wyrm, but I assure her it is in good hands. At the top of the stairs, one of the kingsguard waits to escort us inside.

The massive twin doors to the castle open, and Kurzol, the blood dwarf cleric, waits on the other side.

"You're late." He frowns. "Follow me."

Late? I scratch my chin. I didn't know we had a standing appointment.

Kurzol leads us into the throne room, where King Orso is talking to his advisors. He looks in our direction as we enter.

Taryn drops to a knee, and I follow suit in a gesture of respect, but the others remain standing. He's not their king, after all.

"Chod, Taryn, I see you've brought guests." The king's face gives nothing away.

I stand. "This is Chief Rizza, leader of the forest and mountain trolls; Jira, the village shaman; and Gord, a member of the troll council. They have come to aid Seascape, and discuss plans for what is to come."

King Orso's lips curl at the edges. "Very well. You have arrived just in time then. Several other great leaders wait for me in my private council chamber. Kurzol will escort you there, and I will be along shortly."

We follow the cleric down a long hallway and up several sets of stairs until we come upon an old wooden door. Aside from the fact that guards from several different races wait in the hallway, nothing would give away that this is where the king has his most important meetings.

The guards move aside as Kurzol escorts us into the room. Down the hall, I spot

Warwick, the captain of King Favian's kingsguard, with his hand on his sword. Always the watchful guardian.

Inside, there's a round table filled with leaders and their councils. King Favian nods at us from across the table, dressed in his most stately attire. He wears a blue tunic with a silver griffin embroidered into the chest. Next to him sits Kassidy, munching on an apple.

"Don't be shy, take a seat." Kassidy motions to a row of empty chairs next to him. Chief Rizza and Jira take a seat, while Gord, Taryn, and myself stand. Limery sits perched on my shoulder.

As we wait for King Orso, I use the opportunity to take in the other leaders. Their levels are all concealed, and I wonder if King Orso can see them since it is his castle.

Next to King Favian, two gnomes lean in close together, deep in conversation. They look like tiny humans, but with big noses, and a short limb-to-body ratio. They are clad in vibrant greens and wear jeweled rings on every finger.

Beside them, a centaur anxiously paces back and forth, his hooves clopping against the stone floor. The human half of his body wears brilliant golden armor. A second centaur gazes out the far window overlooking the ocean.

Next to them, a group of catfolk wearing fine silk rap their claws against the wooden table.

There are also lizardfolk, merpeople, and halflings, but my observations are cut short when King Orso enters the room followed by two blood dwarves, an ivory dwarf, and Lady Brollen, the ebony dwarf from Sandholde.

The other leaders all stand as he enters. King Orso nods to them and takes a seat next to Chief Rizza. Everyone else follows suit.

"Thank you all for coming. It is good to know that Seascape still has allies after all these years. We may not know one another, but our ancestors fought together in ages past. It is an honor to have you in Seascape."

The centaur's feet clop in agitation. "Get on with it. Why is it you have called us all here?"

King Orso pauses for a second. "Right, it is best to get to the point. After all, much is at stake." He takes a deep breath. "The short of it is that I fear for our safety, not only of my people but for all of Mythos. How long will it be before the other portals open? And what monstrosities wait on the other side? The majority of the portals that remain closed were conquered by the dark wizard when he last sought to bring the world under his rule. The day will come when he attacks again, and we should all be ready."

One of the catfolk leans forward. When she speaks, her voice has a very sensual quality to it. It reminds of Valery, actually.

"While Seascape's portal has only recently opened, the portal in Antadale has been open for many years. We have witnessed the other portals opening and the world expanding. Every time a new portal opens, there are the same fears, the same worries. But the dark wizard is dead. His army was defeated. There is no point in preparing for a war that will never come."

"How do you know he is dead?" asks one of the gnomes in a high-pitched voice. "None of us were there. Most of the histories have been lost to time, and the ones that remain are glorified tales that cannot be trusted as fact. Only the elves have the lifespans to remember those days, and they all hide behind the portal to Mosstar."

The feline cuts her eyes at the gnome. "If he were there, he would not have waited this long to attack. What possible reason would he have to wait?"

King Favian responds. "The last time the dark wizard was seen was in the Age of Heroes. After he was defeated and sealed off all the portals, there were no more heroes within Mythos. But now, here they are again. If he has word that the heroes have returned, he will attack before they grow too strong. Are you willing to bet the lives of your people on your own arrogance?"

The catfolk hisses at Favian, and the entire room goes into an uproar. King Orso beats his fist on the table to regain order.

"Enough! We are here as allies to discuss the future of our kingdoms. The least we can do is treat one another with respect." He motions to Kurzol, and the cleric brings a massive tome, placing it on the table in front of Orso. "Most recountings of the last great battle with the dark wizard have been lost to history, it is true, but after scouring our ancient libraries, I found this."

He flips the book open and turns to a page near the end. "The rise and fall of Valmar Worren, the dark elf necromancer of Mosstar." King Orso clears his throat, reading from the ancient book. "We are not sure when the rise of Valmar first began. The elves always were an isolated people, and by the time that Valmar rose to power, it was already too late to save the elves from one of their own. After conquering Mosstar, Valmar set his sights on Blacktide, home of the seafaring orcs. Whether through magic or brute force, we do not know, but he won the orcs to his cause. Next, he conquered Grimsbay and the werepeople joined his ranks. With those powerful societies on his side, he ventured to the Shadowlands, and that is where he found the demons and shadowpeople that gave him the confidence to invade the mainland.

"Those were the last kingdoms he allied with, but that was not the end of his reign. Word of his conquest spread far and wide, and the dark races flocked to his cause. The giants and ogres rallied on foreign shores, eagerly awaiting Valmar when he arrived. When he tricked the imps into joining his service, all was feared to be lost."

The entire table glances in Limery's direction. I scowl back at them, knowing all too well what it's like to be judged just for your race.

King Orso continues, "As his army grew, so did his power. One by one, he conquered kingdoms and nations, driving race after race from their ancestral homes. He raised the corpses of the defeated, adding them to his own ranks. Before anyone could stop him, he had conquered half of Mythos. And while many of us banded together, Vanaria clung to itself. The most powerful cleric in Mythos resided in Vanaria, and the Vanarian king commissioned him to create a blessed tower where no undead could set foot in its shadow.

"The dwarves left the island to fight, but the humans remained. The Vanarian king wanted to protect his people, and almost cost us everything. Countless lives were lost as the living battled the dark and the dead on the plains of Wandermere. When hope was nearly lost, the Vanarians arrived, and the king flew in on the back of a griffin. The Vanarian army helped to turn the tide. The heroic cleric rained holy light down on the battlefield, destroying the undead and forcing Valmar to retreat to Mosstar. As we set off in pursuit, the portals closed, blocking our chase. Over the coming days, the portals of Isle of Mythos closed, barring our contact with the outside world. Great creatures have risen in the depths of the sea, making sea travel impossible. I cannot begin to speculate on the fates of those across the sea."

King Orso closes the book. "That is the only recounting we have found of the actual events. We almost lost everything to the darkness because the Vanarian king waited behind the safety of his walls."

King Favian shifts uncomfortably in his seat.

"We cannot afford to let that happen again. We must present a united front and destroy this evil once and for all."

The outspoken catfolk shakes her head. "That was hundreds of years ago. It was a terrible time, that much is true, but those days are long gone. We have prospered for many years. What evidence do you have that there is anything out there that wishes us harm?"

King Orso opens his mouth, but I cut him off.

"I've seen it." I gesture toward Chief Rizza and the others. "We have all seen that there is more at play."

"And who are you?" asks the catfolk.

I stand up straight and speak with all the authority I can muster. "I am Chod, hero of the forest trolls. And I have witnessed first-hand the dark powers that you believe no longer exist. I witnessed a warlock, bound to a hidden patron, summon shadow demons on the island. He demanded I stop my attempts to unite the heroes. This Valmar, if he doesn't know already, will know soon that heroes have returned to Mythos. And he will do everything in his power to destroy us before we can destroy him."

One of the lizardfolk raises his hand to speak. "There are heroes again? This is the first I have heard of this."

King Orso nods. "Heroes have returned to Isle of Mythos. One for the dwarves, one for the trolls, and many for the humans."

"Most strange." He hisses the words.

King Favian stands. "Which is all the more reason we must band—"

Regional Alert! *The portal to Blackspire has been reopened. Fast-travel is now permitted to Blackspire.*

An alarm horn blares from outside the castle. Its deep tone resonates through the room, blaring long and loud.

King Orso jumps to his feet, eyes wide. "Seascape is under attack!"

CHAPTER TWENTY-NINE
BEHEMOTH

Kurzol tries to stop him, but King Orso rushes out of the room with his warhammer in hand. Everyone else follows in quick pursuit.

In the hallways, the guards from the other lands are full of questions.

"Follow the king!" I roar above the chaos. "Seascape is under attack."

We rush down the hallways as the horns of war continue to blare. No one talks as we run, and tension practically radiates from the beautiful carved stone walls.

A bestial roar unlike anything I have ever heard echoes above the sirens. Limery groans on my shoulder, and his claws dig into me.

King Orso pushes the castle doors open with such force that they slam against the walls. I'm surprised they don't break off the hinges. As we step out onto the balcony overlooking Seascape, a knot forms in my stomach. A massive beast, nearly two stories tall, wreaks destruction below. Dozens of guards lay dead, and more try to keep the beast at bay. They point their spears at the monster, but it marches forward, unafraid.

Behemoth. *Unique Monster. Level 40. A monster from the Shadowlands with one purpose: destruction.*

The behemoth is the creature of nightmares. Solid black scales cover the majority of its body and thick, sharp spikes run down its back. A spiked tail swings like a torturous wrecking ball, colliding with the shield of a paladin and sending the blood dwarf flying. Two long tusks hang from its jaw, and four dark eyes look at the world with ill intent. Its maw is full of jagged teeth. Each massive paw has four large claws, and I witness it crush a guard like he's nothing. It opens its mouth and an acidic spray shoots out, rapidly depleting the guard's health.

The catfolk curse loudly as we all stand helplessly by.

I try to swallow, but my throat is so tight that I can't. I've never seen a monster this powerful. Is this what waits on the other side of the blocked portals? My heart pounds in my chest. This is so not good.

King Orso lifts his warhammer in the air, and his entire body glows in a golden aura. When he speaks, his amplified words travel across the city. "Warriors of Seascape, your kingdom needs you!"

The guards in the square shimmer for a moment as the king's ability takes effect, boosting them with some unknown power. Orso rushes down the stairs, and Kurzol follows in pursuit.

The cleric grabs the king by the arm. "Your Highness, you can't. What if something happens to you?"

King Orso jerks his arm free. "Then I will die protecting my people."

King Favian puts his fingers to his mouth, and his whistle slices through the air. A moment later, his griffin lands on the balcony. Favian climbs on its back and joins the fray, diving straight for the behemoth.

I turn to the others. "We have to help them."

"That thing is level forty!" protests one of the merpeople.

"Yeah, and there's only one of it. Look at how many of us there are." I take off down the stairs, summoning horrors as I go, and to my surprise, most of the others follow. I turn to Gord and Rizza. "Help get the wounded to safety. Those of us with range will take on the behemoth."

King Orso still has about three flights of stairs left to go when I witness his true power for the first time. He leaps from the stairs and soars through the air like he was shot from a rocket. His warhammer connects with the behemoth's head, and the resounding crack sounds like a cannon firing. The level forty behemoth loses five percent health from the attack.

The monster stumbles from the blow, and when King Orso lands, he stares up at it defiantly. His kingsguard and what soldiers are left rally behind him. I continue to summon horrors as I descend the stairs.

King Orso's warhammer glows a fiery red as he smashes the behemoth's legs. "It's time to send this beast back to Hell."

The behemoth stomps, and the king rolls out of the way. The earth shakes, knocking several guards off their feet. A centaur gallops past me, bow raised, and fires an imbued arrow at the monster. It strikes the behemoth's scales in a display of fireworks.

We finally reach the square and spill out in every direction, surrounding the creature. Limery takes to the air, and launches a barrage of fireballs. King Favian rides his griffin, attacking the behemoth with his sword every time it faces away from him. A lightning bolt crashes into its back.

One of the gnomes raises his staff, and a giant bubble forms around the behemoth's head, obstructing its view. All the warriors run in, hacking and stabbing until the effect wears off. I send my horrors in with them. The behemoth swings its head and its long tusks nearly kill two of the lower-level guards.

The catfolk who refused to believe we were in danger must be some sort of healer; she tends to the wounded behind me. Gord runs with a dwarf tossed over both shoulders, carrying them to safety. He's a great warrior, but he's out of his element here.

Another jet of acidic spray shoots out, but it disappears into a portal before hitting anyone. The acid exits a second portal and burns through the wall of one of the buildings. Thank God for Kassidy, wherever he is.

I continue to summon horrors and send them into battle. Taryn sprouts a colony of poisonous mushrooms underneath the monster. They explode, covering the area in toxic gas. Jira sends a burning phoenix, but it dissipates against the behemoth's scales. The monster takes a beating as arrows and spells assault its body, but even with a host of high-level warriors attacking it, we've only whittled it down to fifty percent. Many more will die before we kill this thing.

The behemoth stomps again, knocking us all back, and follows up with another acid spray. For a second time, the acid is teleported before hitting us.

I search for Kassidy, but the teleportation mage is nowhere to be found.

"Kassidy!" I call out.

A second later, he appears beside me. "I'm a little busy here. What do you need?"

"Can you teleport something that big?" I point at the behemoth.

He frowns. "Yes, but not very far."

"Can you teleport it over that wall?" I point to the wall that runs along the side of the road, separating Seascape from the cliffside towering above the ocean.

"I can try, but I need the monster to stay in one place long enough for the portal to open."

I nod. "Leave that to me. Just be ready when the time comes."

King Orso charges the behemoth, but he takes a hit from the monster's spiked tail. It sends him flying like a ragdoll. He crashes into a wall and immediately stands up, rushing back into battle.

I call to him as he rushes past me. "If we can keep the behemoth in one spot, then Kassidy can teleport it over the wall!"

"Brilliant! Where is Kurzol?" King Orso scans the battlefield for his cleric.

A host of skeleton warriors runs past, and I turn to see Pressley the Death Knight rushing toward us. Several dwarven warriors turn on him, spears raised, but I rush between them

"He's on our side! He's a hero."

The warriors cast me an uncertain glance, but King Orso nods to them, and they return to the behemoth. Pressley joins the ranks of dwarven warriors and shoots a beam of purple energy into the behemoth's side.

Limery and King Favian zoom through the air, constantly distracting the behemoth. I cast Champion, and a shadow demon joins the aerial attack.

"Kurzol!" King Orso's amplified voice rings out above everything. "Bind the creature."

An out-of-breath Kurzol joins us. "On a creature that big, it will only hold for a few seconds at most."

Kassidy claps him on the shoulder. "That is all we need."

"Very well. It shall be done." Kurzol equips a pearlescent staff and raises it into the air. The ground around the behemoth glows in a white circle. Kurzol thrusts his staff forward and ropes of white energy reach up from the ground, entangling the behemoth and rooting it in place.

At the same time, a second circle forms within the first one, this one a brilliant blue. Kassidy's face strains as the circle shimmers like a staticky TV. For a moment, I don't think the portal will take, but the static fades and a swirling vortex engulfs the behemoth. It falls through the portal and we all rush to the wall overlooking the sea.

I make it to the wall just in time to see the behemoth splash into the ocean. There's a dark splotch in the water that slowly fades as the monster sinks into the ocean's depths.

As the chaos of battle fades, all that is left are the groans of the wounded and the silence of the dead. King Orso looks out over the wreckage of Seascape square. The beautiful buildings that line the courtyard are in shambles. The marble tiles that formed a beautiful mosaic are crushed. The only structure undamaged is the portal itself.

I gain just enough XP to level up from the fight, but that is the least of my concerns. A crowd of dwarves has formed around the edges of the square, where the people of Seascape look on in horror.

King Orso shakes his head. "The buildings can be rebuilt, but the lives lost today can never be replaced." He faces the other leaders, many who talk in hushed whispers or wear stricken expressions. "You have seen firsthand the dangers that oppose us. These are not the delusions of a fearful leader. This is just the beginning. The time has come to stand together, or we will lose everything."

The catfolk healer steps forward. "Antadale will stand with Seascape."

The gnomes nod in unison. "As will Pruxford."

"And Wandermere," echoes the centaurs.

"The merfolk of Mistville will join your cause."

One after another, each of the leaders pledges to the cause.

King Orso turns to Kurzol. "Make sure the wounded are tended to, and then bury the dead. For the time being, I want the entirety of my kingsguard at the portal. I will speak to the people of Seascape before the night is over, but for now, we must convene a council."

The leaders climb the stairs, but I don't move. Chief Rizza, Gord, and Jira will speak for the trolls. I'm a hero, not a leader. Taryn starts to follow them, but I grab him on the shoulder.

"Aren't you coming?" asks King Orso.

I shake my head. "I made a promise to win Goldspire to your cause. It's time I make that happen."

He nods before turning around.

Limery sits on my shoulder, his body still warm from the battle.

"Do you have one more fight left in you for today?" I ask.

"Limmy is ready." He smiles.

I find Pressley at the wall, still staring into the ocean. "What was that thing?" he asks.

"Just a taste of what's coming." I look into the depths of dark energy that conceals his features. "Are you ready for new lands, gold, and glory?"

"Point the way."

Taryn retrieves his pets from the stables, and we gather around the portal. I summon a full army of horrors, ten of each, and Pressley summons nearly as many skeleton warriors.

When we step into Goldspire this time, we'll be ready.

CHAPTER THIRTY

ONE MORE LAST TIME

I focus on the rune for Goldspire and step through the swirling portal. A moment later, the sandy arena awaits. It's closer to nightfall this time, and dozens of pyres blaze around the arena.

Hundreds of people sit in the stands, and I can't help but wonder how much free time these people have on their hands.

A few battles are already underway. I spot two lizardfolk fighting a beastman with the head of a lion. A dark-skinned human battles a spotted minotaur.

"Back again?" A familiar deep voice booms nearby, drawing my attention.

Dakota, the level-thirty-three minotaur, stares in our direction. He's every bit as intimidating as I remember with broad shoulders and beautiful golden fur. His wide obsidian horns glimmer in the light of the pyres, and his nose ring glows orange with their reflection. The thick chain that killed Taryn hangs from his waist like a belt. It's weighted on one end with a ball, and the other end is tipped with a sickle that holds the weapon in place.

"Yeah, but this time, I brought a few friends."

My horrors and Pressley's skeletons spill out into the arena. Stompy snorts beside me, and Berry lets out a low growl. Ruby hides between Stompy's legs. Pressley, Taryn, and I stand beside each other, with Limery on my shoulder. If there was a way to take a screenshot of us right now, I know it would make an awesome poster.

Steam shoots out of Dakota's nose. "Then I guess I'll have to even the playing field. Mordrir!"

A level-thirty satyr runs over from the edge of the arena. The humanoid goat walks on two legs with thick hooves. He's like a leaner version of the minotaur. He's not the half-human/half-goat hybrid I'm familiar with from mythology. This one is big, strong, and powerful. His entire body is covered in light brown fur, and he wears a sash that covers his right shoulder and midsection. His left shoulder has a spaulder, similar to my own, that protects his arm down to the elbow. He wields a long spear with a ring of metal on the butt, making the weapon capable of being swung. Two sharp horns stick out of the top of his head, and a wispy goatee hangs from his chin.

You've got to be kidding me. We come here with extra backup and now we have to fight two?

I talk low enough that only Taryn and Pressley can hear me. "It's going to be okay. We're stronger and smarter than the last time we faced Dakota. We've also got Pressley and Limery. We've got this."

Pressley grunts, and Taryn nods. Hardly the confident reaction I was looking for, but it'll do for now.

"We gots this, Chods!" I can always count on Limery to be my biggest cheerleader.

"Let's hit them with everything we've got."

Pressley's skeletons and my horrors take off across the arena. There's a crackle near my ear as Limery takes flight and conjures a fireball.

Dakota and Mordrir take a fighting stance and prepare for our onslaught. As our minion army swarms them, Dakota unhooks his weapon from around his waist and winds it up like a lasso. He lets it fly, and the weighted end soars in an arc, sending bones flying as it dismembers half of Pressley's warriors.

Mordrir holds his spear at the ready, and when my horrors descend on him, he stabs his spear so fast that it moves in a blur. Perfectly-placed jabs pierce the skulls of a third of my horrors, downing them instantly.

While the beastmen are preoccupied, Taryn lands a lightning bolt on Dakota, stunning him in place. Pressley's skeletons attack the stunned minotaur, stabbing with their rusted blades. By the time the stun wears off, they've taken out ten percent of his health.

Dakota smashes his fist in the sand, and the earth explodes, rocketing the skeletons away. Meanwhile, Limery erupts a wall of fire behind Mordrir, stopping his retreat as the rest of my horrors overwhelm him.

I think we have the upper hand, but Mordrir uses his spear to vault over the horrors and create space. He then spins his weapon in an arc, killing several more horrors.

Limery tosses another fireball, but the satyr rolls to the side and it dissipates against the sand.

Pressley looks over at me. "Are we going to fight or watch them all day?"

Point taken. "Let's get in there!"

We charge into the fray as Dakota and Mordrir focus on the last of our minions. Pressley's armor clanks with each step, and his sword emanates dark energy as purple sparks trail up and down the blade.

Stompy's thunderous steps quake the earth around us, and Taryn casts Imbue on Berry, doubling his size. The two beasts run straight for the satyr.

Mordrir stabs my last horror through the eye, and then uses his spear to vault over Taryn, but Taryn is ready. He raises his sapling staff and the vines extend, wrapping around the satyr as he jumps overhead. As Stompy continues to charge, the force of the moulhaug slams Mordrir into the ground. Stompy drags him through the sand for several meters before the satyr frees himself.

As soon as Mordrir is free, Berry pounces on him, sinking his teeth into Mordrir's exposed shoulder. Blood stains the sash covering his chest.

Dakota lowers his head and charges Berry, ramming his horns into the bear's side. Mordrir quickly crawls to his feet, but we have them surrounded. Pressley, Taryn, and I form a triangle, threatening them from all sides while Limery hovers above us.

Dakota snorts. "I see you've got a few new tricks up your sleeve. Well, so do I!"

He stomps hard and the ground quakes, the earth rising like a wave as the arena floor moves like a mudslide. When the rolling sand hits us, the ground explodes, knocking me into the air. I land with a thud, and the impact knocks the air from my lungs. I crawl away on my back, gasping for air.

Limery flies down to check on me. "Is you okay, Chods?" His eyes radiate concern.

"I'm...fine," I get out between gasps.

I stumble to my feet. We've thrown just about everything we have at them, and they don't seem fazed.

Mordrir stabs Stompy in the leg, and the moulhaug bellows in pain. A new group of skeleton warriors rushes into battle and are immediately destroyed. Limery takes to the air and starts hurling fireballs, but Mordrir is too fast and Dakota barely takes any damage. He must have a pretty high fire resistance.

"Do either of you have a better plan?" I ask.

Pressley turns to me. "We need to eliminate one of them. Can you hold off the minotaur while the rest of us take on the goat?"

"I'll do my best. Limery, put a fire wall between them. We need to split them up."

A flaming wall erupts between the two beastmen. I summon a horror and toss it at Dakota, exploding it right in front of him and drawing his attention.

I point at the minotaur. "You and me, let's go."

Dakota laughs. "You think you can handle me?"

I spin Destroyer in my palm. "Try me."

He spins his chain overhead and stalks in my direction. The chain whirs loudly with each swing. When he lets it go, the weighted end flies at me like a rocket. I swing Destroyer with all I've got and hit the weighted ball perfectly. It flies back at Dakota even faster than he threw it, and he barely dodges his own weapon.

He blinks rapidly. I don't think he was expecting that.

Lightning crashes nearby, but my focus is solely on Dakota. I continuously summon horrors and send them to Pressley and Taryn.

Dakota swings his weapon again, and again, I hit it like it's batting practice. We repeat this process several times. For the moment, we're in a stalemate. His weapon's range keeps me from getting close, but I'm blocking every attack he throws at me.

I summon a horror and toss it in his direction, but he demolishes it before it gets close enough to do damage.

As long as I keep him distracted, the others might have a shot.

I chance a glance in their direction, just in time to see Taryn surround Mordrir with a ring of poisonous mushrooms. A lightning bolt comes crashing down, but the satyr vaults over the ring of fungus. The lightning crashes into the sand, releasing the mushroom's poisonous gas.

Pressley runs in, sword raised, as purple sparks trail down its edge. He swings for Mordrir, but the attack is parried. The sparks jump from Pressley's sword and crawl down Mordrir's spear. Mordrir throws his weapon in a panic before they reach him.

Now's our chance.

I'm tackled to the ground with enough force that my vision goes dark around the edges. A sledgehammer of a fist connects with my jaw and stars light the darkness. Fuck me! I should never have let my guard down.

Another fist rocks my world, and I can't see straight. I activate Berserker Rage and my vision clears. Dakota punches again, and this time, I move my head to the side. His fist only grazes my skull. As he pulls back for another punch, I rake my claws across his chest, and blood spurts all over me. Dakota grimaces in pain.

A burning ball of heat smashes into Dakota, knocking him off me, and Limery immediately returns to helping the others. I retrieve Destroyer and return to Dakota. He's already on his feet, with the sickle in one hand and the weighted end of his chain in the other.

He slings the weighted end at me and I raise my weapon to block it, but the chain wraps around Destroyer's handle. While I'm unable to wield my hammer, Dakota seizes the opportunity and stabs at me with the sickle. I'm forced to decide between fighting for my weapon or not being stabbed.

I let Destroyer go and live to fight another day.

Except Dakota has all the advantage now. He has the range and the weapons.

I equip the Halite Shield, my only defense, and wait for him to make the first move.

He laughs. "Are you going to beat me to death with a shield?" He leans his head back, roaring with laughter. "Look at your friends. It's over."

I turn to see Pressley with a spear stabbed through his side. Mordrid stands on top of him while Taryn looks on in horror.

"Taryn, run!" I yell. If we're going to lose, there's no point in him dying too.

Before Taryn has a chance to move, Pressley's hands glow a vibrant purple. He reaches forward and grabs Mordrir around the biceps. Smoke rises from inside of Pressley's armor and his health begins to rise as Mordrir's goes down.

Taryn extends the vines from his staff, preventing Mordrir's escape, and Limery flies down, pressing molten hands around the satyr's neck.

Mordrir's health drops to zero. Pressley tosses the body aside, and it collapses into the sand. He pulls the spear from his side and crawls to his feet with fifty-percent health.

Now, it's my turn to laugh. "You were saying?"

Pressley lifts both hands in front of him. A black aura forms around them, pulsing with tendrils of dark energy that grasp at the air. His health trickles down as the aura grows. The tendrils coil together, forming a ball of darkness between the death knight's hands. When the ball of energy is as large as his chest, he shoots it at Mordrir's corpse. The satyr's body absorbs the energy and his body stirs.

Dakota looks on in horror as Mordrir stands, his golden eyes now a deep purple.

Pressley picks the spear up off the ground and hands it to his new minion. "I think this belongs to you."

Mordrir takes the weapon and charges at Dakota. This is our chance. We can finally end this. I summon three more horrors and send the Horror of Power and Horror of Finesse right behind Mordrir. I grab the Horror of Vitality by the horn and hold on to it.

Mordrir jabs with his spear, but Dakota parries it to the side. Both horrors attack the minotaur's legs. The Horror of Power jabs with its tusks while the Horror of Finesse rakes with its claws. Dakota quickly kills them, but while he's distracted, I toss my third horror at him. He stabs it through the head, but the passive slow keeps him from escaping Limery's fireball and Taryn's lightning bolt.

Through divine luck, Taryn's lightning stuns the minotaur for a second time. Mordrir stabs his spear through the minotaur's throat, and the fight is over.

A horn blares, and the crowd roars with applause. The pyres burn brighter, and a notification flashes across my vision.

Congratulations! *You have defeated a gladiator in the Goldspire Arena. You now have access to the continent.*

After a moment, the bodies of both Dakota and Mordrir fade away. For the time being, the arena is quiet and there are no battles taking place.

That's strange. I thought only heroes' bodies did that.

Pressley chugs a health potion, and Taryn casts Restoration on Stompy.

Limery lands on my shoulder. "We dids it, Chods. We wons!"

I smile. "You're right. We did it. And we couldn't have done it without all of you." I turn to Pressley. "So, what do you say, want to party up and explore what Goldspire has to offer? I need to find the castle or whatever passes for leadership around here first, but after that, nothing but adventure awaits."

Pressley waits a moment before responding. "I will be there for you when the time comes for us to band together, but for now, there are still things I must do on my own. Good luck in your travels." He extends a hand to me. "It was a pleasure to fight by your side."

He picks his sword off the arena floor and sheathes it. At the far end of the arena, one of the gates is now open. Pressley shakes Taryn's hand as he passes.

I walk over to Taryn and clap him on the shoulder. "It's been a hell of a few days, but maybe we can have a little fun before shit hits the fan again."

He smiles for the first time since nearly losing his pets. "You know, that sounds really good."

I pick up Destroyer and we are heading for the exit when a deep voice calls to me.

"You might want these back."

I turn around to see Dakota holding a small chest. His body looks good as new. There's no blood in his fur, and the hole Mordrir put in his neck is but a memory. Stranger yet, he's still level thirty-three.

Taryn looks just as confused as I am.

"How are you not dead?" I ask.

Dakota laughs. "I'm a Goldspire gladiator. We keep the lands of Goldspire free from the weak, but as long as we are on arena grounds, we never truly die. It has been a long time since heroes set foot in Goldspire, but it is tradition that should they perish and win victory on another day, all items shall be returned to them." He hands me the chest.

I open it, and inside are all the items we lost after dying the first time. Sea Scorpion, my Petrified Staff, the phoenix feather, the legendary Angel of Death Brandy, and more. It's all there.

"You are a resourceful warrior. May your adventures in Goldspire be fruitful."

With that, he turns to the portal as a new challenger appears on the platform.

We take our items from the chest, and I put mine in my satchel. Once again, I have more weapons than I know what to do with, which is fine by me. With Taryn and Limery by my side, Goldspire won't know what hit it.

Complete the adventure in Sentenced to Troll Compendium 2: Books 4-6

ACKNOWLEDGMENTS

Congratulations! *You have finished the* Sentenced to Troll Compendium.
 3 of 6 completed.
 +3 stat point to distribute.
 +1 Review to leave.

Thank you for reading *Sentenced to Troll!* I hope you had as much fun reading about Chod and his adventures as I did writing them. This adventure is just getting started. If you enjoyed your time in Mythos, please consider rating, reviewing, and sharing your thoughts on social media. Word of mouth is the best way to support indie authors like myself.

If you're looking for more books similar to my own, check out LitRPG Books.

ABOUT THE AUTHOR

S.L. Rowland is a cozy fantasy and LitRPG author known for crafting immersive worlds filled with adventure, heart, and a touch of humor. A lifelong gamer and fantasy enthusiast, he draws inspiration from tabletop RPGs, video games, and the fantastical. When he's not writing, he enjoys weightlifting, hiking with his Shiba Inu, and enduring the heartbreak of being an Atlanta sports fan.

SLRowland.com

Patreon-For signed paperbacks, advanced chapters, exclusive short stories, art, merch, and more.

Newsletter: For updates on new releases, sales, and behind the scenes content!

Email: slrowlandauthor@gmail.com

Find out more at https://linktr.ee/SLRowland

ALSO BY S.L. ROWLAND

Tales of Aedrea

Cursed Cocktails

Sword & Thistle

The Halfling's Harvest

There Be Dragons Here

Pangea Online

Pangea Online: Death and Axes

Pangea Online 2: Magic and Mayhem

Pangea Online 3: Vials and Tribulations

Sentenced to Troll 1-6

Path to Villainy: An NPC Kobold's Tale

Collected Editions

Pangea Online: The Complete Trilogy

Sentenced to Troll Compendium: Books 1-3

Sentenced to Troll Compendium 2: Books 4-6